P1.20

Deadly Decisions

Fatal Voyage

Kathy Reichs

arrow books

Arrow Books
Random House, 20 Vauxhall Bridge Road,
London SW1V 2SA

www.rbooks.co.uk

Addresses for companies within The Random House Group Limited
can be found at:
www.randomhouse.co.uk/offices.htm

The Random House Group Limited Reg. No. 954009

A CIP catalogue record for this book
is available from the British Library

ISBN 9780099527749

The Random House Group Limited supports The Forest Stewardship
Council (FSC), the leading international forest certification organisation.
All our titles that are printed on Greenpeace approved FSC certified paper
carry the FSC logo. Our paper procurement policy can be found at:
www.rbooks.co.uk/environment

Printed and bound in Great Britain by
CPI Cox & Wyman, Reading, RG1 8EX

deadly décisions

Kathy Reichs is forensic anthropologist at the Laboratoire de Sciences Judiciaires et de Médecine Légale for the province of Quebec. She is one of seventy-five anthropologists certified by the American Board of Forensic Anthropology. Dr Reichs serves as Vice President of the American Academy of Forensic Sciences, and is a member of the National Police Advisory Council (RCMP/GRC) in Canada. A professor of anthropology at the University of North Carolina at Charlotte, she is a native of Chicago, where she received her Ph.D. at Northwestern. She now divides her time between Charlotte and Montreal and is a frequent expert witness at criminal trials.

Kathy Reichs's first novel, *Déjà Dead*, shot straight to number one on the *Sunday Times* bestseller list and won the 1997 Ellis Peters Award for Best First Novel. It became an international bestseller, as did its successors *Death du Jour*, *Deadly Décisions*, *Fatal Voyage*, *Grave Secrets*, *Bare Bones*, *Monday Mourning*, *Cross Bones*, *Break No Bones* and *Bones to Ashes*.

For more about the author, please visit
www.kathyreichs.com

Also by Kathy Reichs

Déjà Dead
Death du Jour
Fatal Voyage
Grave Secrets
Bare Bones
Monday Mourning
Cross Bones
Break No Bones
Bones to Ashes

Acknowledgements

Many people helped me in writing *Deadly Décisions*. Particularly patient were my colleagues in forensic science and law enforcement. I owe heartfelt thanks to Sergeant Guy Ouelette, Division of Organized Crime Unit, Sûreté du Québec, and to Captain Steven Chabot, Sergent Yves Trudel, Caporal Jacques Morin, and Constable Jean Ratté at Opération Carcajou in Montreal.

Among the Communauté Urbaine de Montréal Police, Lieutenant-détective Jean-François Martin, Division des Crimes Majeurs; Sergent-détective Johanne Bérubé, Division Agressions Sexuelles; and Commandant André Bouchard, Moralité, Alcool, et Stupéfiant, Centre Opérational Sud, patiently answered my questions and explained the functioning of police units. Special thanks must go to Sergent-détective Stephen Rudman, Superviseur, Analyse et Liaison, Centre Opérational Sud, who answered many questions, provided maps, and took me through the jail.

Of my colleagues at the Laboratoire de Sciences Judiciaires et de Médecine Légale I must thank Dr Claude Pothel for comments on pathology, and François Julien, Section de Biologie, for his demonstration of blood-spatter patterning. Pat Laturnus,

Bloodstain Pattern Analyst at the Canadian Police College in Ottawa, also helped with this expertise, and provided photos for cover design.

In North Carolina, I would like to thank Captain Terry Sult of the Charlotte-Mecklenburg Police Department Intelligence Unit; Roger Thompson, Director of the Charlotte-Mecklenburg Police Department Crime Laboratory; Pam Stephenson, Senior Analyst, Intelligence and Technical Services, North Carolina State Bureau of Investigation; Gretchen C. F. Shappert, United States Attorney General's Office; and Dr Norman J. Kramer, Mecklenburg Medical Group.

Others who gave of their time and knowledge include Dr G. Clark Davenport, Geophysicist with Necro Search International; Dr Wayne Lord, National Center for the Analysis of Violent Crime, FBI Academy, Quantico, Virginia; and Victor Svoboda, Director of Communication for the Montreal Neurological Institute and the Montreal Neurological Hospital. Dr David Taub was my Harley-Davidson guru.

I am indebted to Yves St. Marie, Directeur Laboratoire de Sciences Judiciaires et de Médecine Légale; Dr André Lauzon, Responsable, Laboratoire de Médecine Légale; and to Dr James Woodward, Chancellor of the University of North Carolina at Charlotte for their continued support.

Special thanks go to Paul Reichs for his valuable comments on the manuscript.

As always I want to thank my extraordinary editors, Susanne Kirk at Scribner, and Lynne Drew at Random House, and my slam-dunk agent, Jennifer Rudolph Walsh.

Though I benefited greatly from the advice of experts, any errors in *Deadly Décisions* are strictly of my making.

deadly décisions

1

Her name was Emily Anne. She was nine years old, with black ringlets, long lashes, and caramel-colored skin. Her ears were pierced with tiny gold loops. Her forehead was pierced by two slugs from a Cobra 9-mm semiautomatic.

It was a Saturday, and I was working by special request of my boss, Pierre LaManche. I'd been at the lab for four hours, sorting badly mangled tissue, when the door to the large autopsy room opened and Sergeant-Detective Luc Claudel came striding in.

Claudel and I had worked together in the past, and though he'd come to tolerate, perhaps even appreciate me, one would not infer that from his brusque manner.

"Where's LaManche?" he demanded, glancing at the gurney in front of me, then quickly away.

I said nothing. When Claudel was in one of his moods, I ignored him.

"Has Dr LaManche arrived?" The detective avoided looking at my greasy gloves.

1

"It's Saturday, Monsieur Claudel. He doesn't wo—"

At that moment Michel Charbonneau stuck his head into the room. Through the opening I could hear the whir and clank of the electric door at the back of the building.

"*Le cadavre est arrivé*," Charbonneau told his partner.

What cadaver? Why were two homicide detectives at the morgue on a Saturday afternoon?

Charbonneau greeted me in English. He was a large man, with spiky hair that resembled a hedgehog's.

"Hey, Doc."

"What's going on?" I asked, pulling off my gloves and lowering my mask.

Claudel answered, his face tense, his eyes cheerless in the harsh fluorescent light.

"Dr LaManche will be here shortly. He can explain."

Already sweat glistened on his forehead, and his mouth was compressed into a thin, tight line. Claudel detested autopsies and avoided the morgue as much as possible. Without another word he pulled the door wide and brushed past his partner. Charbonneau watched him walk down the corridor, then turned back to me.

"This is hard for him. He has kids."

"Kids?" I felt something cold in my chest.

"The Heathens struck this morning. Ever hear of Richard Marcotte?"

The name was vaguely familiar.

"Maybe you know him as *Araignée*. Spider." He curled his fingers like a child doing the waterspout rhyme. "Great guy. And an elected official in the outlaw biker set. Spider is the Vipers sergeant at arms, but he had a real bad day today. When he set out for the gym around eight this morning the Heathens blasted him in

2

a drive-by while his ole lady dove for cover in a lilac bush."

Charbonneau ran a hand backward through his hair, swallowed.

I waited.

"In the process they also killed a child."

"Oh, God." My fingers tightened around the gloves.

"A little girl. They took her to the Montréal Children's Hospital, but she didn't make it. They're bringing her here now. Marcotte was DOA. He's out back."

"LaManche is coming in?"

Charbonneau nodded.

The five pathologists at the lab take turns being on call. Rarely does it happen, but if an off-hours autopsy or visit to a death scene is deemed necessary, someone is always available. Today that was LaManche.

A child. I could feel the familiar surge of emotions and needed to get away.

My watch said twelve-forty. I tore off my plastic apron, balled it together with the mask and latex gloves, and threw everything into a biological waste container. Then I washed my hands and rode the elevator to the twelfth floor.

I don't know how long I sat in my office, staring at the St Lawrence and ignoring my carton of yogurt. At one point I thought I heard LaManche's door, then the swish of the glass security doors that separate portions of our wing.

Being a forensic anthropologist, I've developed some immunity to violent death. Since the medical examiner turns to me to derive information from the bones of the mutilated, burned, or decomposed, I've seen the worst. My workplaces are the morgue and autopsy room, so I

3

know how a corpse looks and smells, how it feels when handled or cut with a scalpel. I'm accustomed to bloody clothing drying on racks, to the sound of a Stryker saw cutting through bone, to the sight of organs floating in numbered specimen jars.

But I have always been unsettled by the sight of dead children. The shaken baby, the battered toddler, the emaciated child of religious zealots, the preteen victim of a violent pedophile. The violation of young innocents has never failed to agitate and distress me.

Not long ago I had worked a case involving infants, twin boys killed and mutilated. It had been one of the most difficult encounters of my career, and I didn't want to reboard that emotional merry-go-round.

Then again that case had been a source of satisfaction. When the fanatic responsible was locked up and could order no more executions, I felt a genuine sense of having accomplished something good.

I peeled back the cover and stirred the yogurt.

Images of those babies hovered in my mind. I remembered my feelings in the morgue that day, the flashbacks to my infant daughter.

Dear God, why such insanity? The mutilated men I had left downstairs had also died as a result of the current biker war.

Don't get despondent, Brennan. Get angry. Get coldly, resolutely angry. Then apply your science to help nail the bastards.

"Yep," I agreed with myself aloud.

I finished the yogurt, drained my drink, and headed downstairs.

Charbonneau was in the anteroom of one of the small autopsy suites, flipping pages in a spiral notebook. His

4

large frame overflowed a vinyl chair opposite the desk. Claudel was nowhere to be seen.

"What's her name?" I asked.

"Emily Anne Toussaint. She was on her way to dance class."

"Where?"

"Verdun." He tipped his head toward the adjoining room. "LaManche has begun the post."

I slipped past the detective into the autopsy room.

A photographer was taking pictures while the pathologist made notes and shot Polaroid backups.

I watched LaManche grasp a camera by its side handles, then raise and lower it above the body. As the lens moved in and out of focus a small dot blurred then condensed over one of the wounds in the child's forehead. When the perimeter of the dot grew sharp, LaManche depressed the shutter release. A white square slid out and he pulled it free and added it to a collection on the side counter.

Emily Anne's body bore evidence of the intensive effort to save her life. Her head was partly bandaged, but I could see a clear tube protruding from her scalp, inserted to monitor intracranial pressure. An endotracheal tube ran down her throat and into her trachea and esophagus, placed in order to oxygenate the lungs and to block regurgitation from the stomach. Catheters for IV infusion remained in her subclavian, inguinal, and femoral vessels, and the circular white patches for EKG electrodes were still pasted to her chest.

Such a frantic intervention, almost like an assault. I closed my eyes and felt tears burn the backs of my lids.

I dragged my eyes back to the small body. Emily Anne wore nothing but a plastic hospital bracelet. Next to her lay a pale green hospital gown, bundled clothing,

5

a pink backpack, and a pair of high-top red sneakers.

The harsh fluorescent light. The shining steel and tile. The cold, sterile surgical instruments. A little girl did not belong here.

When I looked up, LaManche's sad eyes met mine. Though neither of us made reference to what lay on the stainless steel, I knew his thoughts. Another child. Another autopsy in this same room.

Putting a choke hold on my emotions, I described the progress I was making with my own cases, reassembling the corpses of two bikers who'd been blown apart by their own folly, and asked when antemortem medical records would be available. LaManche told me that the files had been requested and should arrive on Monday.

I thanked him and went to resume my own grim task. As I sorted tissue, I remembered my previous day's conversation with LaManche, and wished I were still in the Virginia woods. Was it only yesterday LaManche had called me there? Emily Anne was alive then.

So much can change in twenty-four hours.

2

The day before I had been in Quantico teaching a body recovery workshop at the FBI Academy. My team of evidence recovery technicians was unearthing and mapping its skeleton when I looked up to see a special agent approaching through the trees. He reported that a Dr LaManche urgently wished to speak to me. Feeling uneasy, I left my team and started out of the woods.

As I threaded my way toward the road, I thought about LaManche and the news his call might bring. I began consulting for the Laboratoire de Sciences Judiciaires et de Médecine Légale after going to Montreal in the early nineties as part of a faculty exchange between McGill and my home university in Charlotte. Knowing I was certified by the American Board of Forensic Anthropology, LaManche had been curious as to whether I could be of any use to him.

Quebec Province had a centralized coroner system, with sophisticated crime and medico-legal labs, but no board-certified forensic anthropologist. Then, as now, I served as consultant to the Office of the Chief Medical

Examiner in North Carolina, and LaManche wanted me for the LSJML. The ministry funded an anthropology lab, and I enrolled in an immersion course in French. For more than a decade now, the skeletonized, decomposed, mummified, burned, or mutilated cadavers of Quebec Province have come to me for analysis and identification. When a conventional autopsy is of no use, I tease what I can from the bones.

Rarely had LaManche left me a message marked urgent. When he had, it had never been good.

Within minutes I crossed to a van parked on the side of a gravel road. I released my hair and ran my fingers backward across my scalp.

No ticks.

After reclipping the barrette, I dug my pack from the back of the van and fished out my cell phone. The tiny screen told me I had missed three calls. I punched up the list of numbers. All three had come from the lab.

I tried dialing, but the signal cut in and out. That's why I'd left the phone in the van. Damn. Though my French had become fluent over the past ten years, background noise and bad connections often caused me problems. Between the language exchange and the weak signal, I'd never get the message straight on this phone. I had to hike down to headquarters.

I unzipped my Tyvek jumpsuit and threw it in a box in the back of the van. Slinging my pack over my shoulder, I headed downhill.

High above the trees a hawk circled some falconic target. The sky was a brilliant blue, with randomly spaced cotton puff clouds drifting leisurely. The course is usually held in May, and we'd worried that this year's April scheduling might mean rain or cooler temperatures. No problem. The mercury was in the high seventies.

As I walked, I took in the sounds around me. My boots crunching on gravel. Birdsong. The whumping of helicopter blades low overhead. The pop of distant gunfire. The FBI shares Quantico with other federal police agencies and with the Marine Corps, and the activity is constant and very earnest.

The gravel road met blacktop at Hogan's Alley, just below the simulated town square used by the FBI, DEA, ATF, and others. I skirted far to the left to avoid intruding on a hostage rescue exercise and turned right on Hoover Road downhill to the closest module of a concrete complex of gray and tan with antennae jutting from the highest roofs like new shoots in an old hedge. Crossing a small parking area to the Forensic Science Research and Training Center, I rang a bell at the loading dock.

A side door parted and a man's face appeared in the crack. Though young, he was completely bald, and looked as if he'd been that way for some time.

"Finishing early?"

"No. I need to call my lab."

"You can use my office."

"Thanks, Craig. I'll only be a minute." I hope.

"I'm checking equipment, so take your time."

The academy is often compared to a hamster cage because of the labyrinth of tunnels and corridors connecting its various buildings. But the upper floors are nothing compared with the maze below.

We wound our way through an area stacked with crates and cardboard boxes, old computer screens, and metal equipment trunks, down one corridor, then along two others to an office barely large enough to hold a desk, chair, filing cabinet, and bookshelf. Craig Beacham worked for the National Center for the

Analysis of Violent Crime, NCAVC, one of the major components of the FBI's Critical Incident Response Group, CIRG. For a time the entity had been called the Child Abduction and Serial Killer Unit, CASKU, but had recently reverted to the original name. Since the training of evidence recovery technicians, or ERT's, is one of the functions of NCAVC, it is this unit that organizes the annual course.

When dealing with the FBI, one must be alphabet savvy.

Craig gathered folders from his desk and stacked them on the cabinet.

"At least that will give you some space to take notes. Do you need to close the door?"

"No, thanks. I'm fine."

My host nodded, then disappeared down the hall.

I took a deep breath, made a mental shift to French, and dialed.

"*Bonjour, Temperance.*" Only LaManche and the priest who baptized me have ever used the formal version. The rest of the world calls me Tempe. "*Comment ça va?*"

I told him I was fine.

"Thank you for calling back. I fear we have a grisly situation up here and I am going to need your help."

"*Oui?*" Grisly? LaManche was not prone to overstatement.

"*Les motards.* Two more are dead."

Les motards. Bikers. For more than a decade rival outlaw motorcycle gangs had been battling for control of the drug trade in Quebec. I'd worked on several motard cases, gunshot victims who had also been burned beyond recognition.

"*Oui?*"

10

"So far, this is what the police have reconstructed. Last night three members of the Heathens drove to the Vipers' clubhouse with a powerful homemade bomb. The Viper working the surveillance cameras spotted a pair approaching with a large bundle between them. He took a shot and the bomb exploded." LaManche paused. "The driver is in the hospital in critical condition. For the other two, the largest portion of tissue recovered weighs nine pounds."

Ouch.

"Temperance, I've been trying to get in touch with Constable Martin Quickwater. He's there in Quantico, but he's been in a case-review meeting all day."

"Quickwater?" It was not a typical québécois name.

"He's Native. Cree, I think."

"Is he with Carcajou?"

Opération Carcajou is a multijurisdictional task force created to investigate criminal activities among outlaw motorcycle gangs in the province.

"*Oui.*"

"What would you like me to do?"

"Please tell Constable Quickwater what I have told you, and have him contact me. Then I would like you to come here as quickly as possible. We may have difficulty with these identifications."

"Have they recovered printable digits or dental fragments?"

"No. And it is not likely."

"DNA?"

"There may be problems with that. The situation is complicated and I would rather not discuss it by phone. Is it possible for you to return earlier than you had planned?"

Following my normal pattern, I'd wrapped up the

11

spring term at UNC-Charlotte in time to teach the FBI course. Now I only had to read the final exams. I'd been looking forward to a brief stay with friends in D.C. before flying to Montreal for the summer. The visit would have to wait.

"I'll be there tomorrow."

"*Merci.*"

He continued in his very precise French, either sadness or fatigue deepening the timbre of his rich, bass voice.

"This does not look good, Temperance. The Heathens will undoubtedly retaliate. Then the Vipers will draw more blood." I heard him pull a long breath, then exhale slowly. "I fear the situation is escalating to full-scale war in which innocents may perish."

We hung up and I called US Airways to arrange for a morning flight. As I was replacing the receiver Craig Beacham appeared in the doorway. I explained about Quickwater.

"Constable?"

"He's RCMP. Royal Canadian Mounted Police. Or GRC if you prefer French. Gendarmerie royale du Canada."

"Um. Huh."

Craig punched in a number and asked about the constable's whereabouts. After a pause he jotted something down and hung up.

"Your guy's in a major case management session in one of the conference rooms down here." He offered the number he'd written, then gave me directions. "Just slide in and take a seat. They'll probably break at three."

I thanked him, and wormed my way through the halls until I'd located the room. Muffled voices came through the closed door.

My watch said two-twenty. I turned the knob and slipped in.

The room was dark save for the beam of a projector and the apricot glow of an illuminated slide. I could make out half a dozen figures seated around a central table. Some heads turned in my direction as I eased into a chair against the side wall. Most eyes stayed fixed on the screen.

For the next thirty minutes I saw LaManche's premonition brought to life in horrifying detail. A bombed-out bungalow, tissue spattered on the walls, body parts strewn across the lawn. A female torso, face a red mass, skull bones mushroomed by a shotgun blast. The blackened chassis of a sports utility vehicle, one charred hand dangling from a rear window.

A man seated to the right of the projector commented about biker gang wars in Chicago as he clicked through the presentation. The voice was vaguely familiar, but I couldn't make out the features.

More shootings. Explosions. Stabbings. Now and then I scanned the silhouettes around the table. Only one had hair that was not closely cropped.

Finally, the screen blazed white. The projector hummed and dust motes floated in its beam. Chairs squeaked as their occupants stretched and reoriented toward one another.

The speaker rose and crossed to the wall. When the overhead lights came on I recognized him as Special Agent Frank Tulio, a graduate of the recovery course from years back. He spotted me, and a smile spread across his face.

"Tempe. How's it hanging?"

Everything about Frank was precise, from his razor-cut gray hair, to his compact body, to his immaculate

Italian-made shoes. Unlike the rest of us, throughout the bug and body exercises Frank had remained perpetually well groomed.

"Can't complain. Are you still with the Chicago office?"

"Up until last year. I'm here now, assigned to CIRG."

Every eye was focused on us, and I was suddenly conscious of my current state of cleanliness and coiffure. Frank turned to his colleagues.

"Does everyone know the great bone doctor?"

As Frank made introductions, those around the table smiled and nodded. Some I recognized, others I did not. One or two made jokes about past episodes in which I'd played a role.

Two of those present were not affiliated with the academy. The fuller hair I'd spotted belonged to Kate Brophy, supervisor of the Intelligence Unit of North Carolina's State Bureau of Investigation. Kate had been the SBI's expert on outlaw motorcycle gangs for as long as I could remember. We'd met in the early eighties when the Outlaws and Hells Angels were at war in the Carolinas. I'd identified two of the victims.

At the far end of the table a young woman typed on what looked like a stenotype machine. Next to her Martin Quickwater sat behind a laptop computer. His face was broad, with high cheekbones, and eyebrows that angled up at the ends. His skin was the color of fired brick.

"I'm sure you two foreigners know each other," said Frank.

"Actually, we don't," I said. "But that's why I'm intruding. I need to speak to Constable Quickwater."

Quickwater graced me with approximately five

14

seconds of attention, then his eyes went back to his computer screen.

"Good timing. We're ready for a break." Frank looked at his watch, then crossed back to click off the projector. "Let's get some caffeine and regroup at three-thirty."

As the agents filed past me one of the members of NCAVC made an exaggerated show of squaring his fingers and peering through, as though focusing on me through a viewfinder. We'd been friends a decade and I knew what was coming.

"Nice do, Brennan. Do you get a deal from your lawn man? Hedges and hair trims, one price?"

"Some of us do real work, Agent Stoneham."

He moved on, laughing.

When only Quickwater and I were left, I smiled and began a fuller introduction.

"I know who you are," said Quickwater in softly accented English.

His abruptness surprised me, and I fought back an equally impolite rejoinder. Perhaps being sweaty and uncombed had made me touchy.

When I explained that LaManche had been trying to reach him, Quickwater slipped his pager from his belt, checked the screen, then tapped it hard against his hand. Shaking his head and sighing, he reattached the device to his waistband.

"Batteries," he said.

The constable watched me intently as I repeated what LaManche had said. His eyes were so deeply brown it was impossible to see a boundary between pupil and iris. When I'd finished, he nodded, then turned and left the room.

I stood a moment, wondering at the man's odd

demeanor. Terrific. I not only had two vaporized bikers to piece together, I now had Constable Congenial as an associate.

I picked up my pack and headed back to the woods.

No problem, Mr Quickwater. I've cracked tougher nuts than you.

3

The trip to Montreal was uneventful, except for an overt snub by Martin Quickwater. Though we were on the same flight, he did not speak to me or move to one of the empty seats in my row. We nodded at Washington-Reagan, then again as we waited in the customs line at Montreal's Dorval. His coolness suited me. I really didn't want to deal with the man.

I took a taxi to my condo in Centre-ville, offloaded luggage, and zapped a frozen burrito. My old Mazda turned over after three tries, and I headed to the city's east side.

For years the forensic lab had been located on the fifth floor of a structure known as the SQ building. The provincial police, or Sûreté du Québec, had the rest of the floors, except for my office and a detention center on the twelfth and thirteenth. The morgue and autopsy rooms were in the basement.

The Quebec government had recently spent millions to renovate the building. The jail was relocated, and the medico-legal and crime labs now sprawled throughout the top two floors. It had been months since the move, but I still couldn't believe the change. My new office had a spectacular view of the St Lawrence River, and my lab was first-rate.

At three-thirty on Friday the normal weekday hustle and bustle were beginning to taper off. One by one doors were closing, and the army of lab-coated scientists and technicians was dwindling.

I unlocked my office and hung my jacket on the wooden hall tree. Three white forms lay on my desk. I selected the one with LaManche's signature.

The *"Demande d'Expertise en Anthropologie"* is often my first introduction to a case. Filled out by the requesting pathologist, it provides data critical to tracking a file.

My eyes drifted down the right-hand column. Lab number. Morgue number. Police incident number. Clinical and efficient. The body is tagged and archived until the wheels of justice have run their course.

I shifted to the left column. Pathologist. Coroner. Investigating officer. Violent death is the final intrusion, and those who investigate it are the ultimate voyeurs. Though I participate, I am never comfortable with the indifference with which the system approaches the deceased and the death investigation. Even though a sense of detachment is a must to maintain emotional equilibrium, I always have the feeling that the victim deserves something more passionate, more personal.

I scanned the summary of known facts. It differed from LaManche's telephone account in only one respect. To date, two hundred and fifteen remnants of flesh and bone had been recovered. The largest weighed eleven pounds.

Ignoring the other forms and a stack of phone messages, I went to find the director.

I'd rarely seen Pierre LaManche in anything but lab-coat white or surgical green. I couldn't imagine him laughing or wearing plaid. He was somber and kind, and strictly tweed. And the best forensic pathologist I knew.

I spotted him through the rectangle of glass beside his office door. His rangy form was hunched over a desk heaped with papers, journals, books, and a stack of files in all the primary colors. When I tapped he looked up and gestured me in.

The office, like its occupant, smelled faintly of pipe tobacco. LaManche had a manner of moving silently, and sometimes the scent was my first clue to his presence.

"Temperance." He accented the final syllable and made it rhyme with France. "Thank you so much for returning early. Please, sit down."

Always the perfect French, with never a contraction or word of slang.

We took places at a small table in front of his desk. On it lay a number of large brown envelopes.

"I know it is too late to begin analysis now, but perhaps you are willing to come in tomorrow?"

The face was army mule long with deep, vertical creases. When he raised his brows in a question, the furrows paralleling his eyes elongated and veered toward the midline.

"Yes. Of course."

"You might want to begin with the X rays."

He indicated the envelopes, then swiveled to his desk.

"And here are the scene and autopsy photos." He handed me a stack of smaller brown envelopes and a videocassette.

"The two bikers carrying the bomb to the Vipers' clubhouse were pulverized, their remains scattered over an enormous area. A lot of what the recovery team is finding is stuck to walls and caught in bushes and tree branches. Amazingly, the largest fragments retrieved so far have come from the clubhouse roof. One chunk of thorax has a partial tattoo that will be useful for establishing identity."

"What about the driver?"

"He died in the hospital this morning."

"The shooter?"

"He is in custody, but these people are never helpful. He will go to jail rather than give anything to the police."

"Even information about a rival gang?"

"If he talks, he is probably a dead man."

"Are there still no dentals or prints?"

"Nothing."

LaManche ran a hand over his face, raised and lowered his shoulders, then laced his fingers in his lap.

"I fear we will never get all the tissue sorted out."

"Can't we use DNA?"

"Have you heard the names Ronald and Donald Vaillancourt?"

I shook my head.

"The Vaillancourt brothers, Le Clic and Le Clac. Both are full patch members of the Heathens. One was implicated a few years back in the execution of Claude 'Le Couteau' Dubé. I don't remember which."

"The police think the Vaillancourts are the victims?"

"Yes."

The melancholy eyes looked into mine.

"Clic and Clac are identical twins."

By seven that evening I'd examined everything but the video. Using a magnifier I'd gone over scores of photos showing hundreds of bone fragments and bloody masses of varying shapes and sizes. In shot after shot arrows pointed to red and yellow globs lying in grass, entangled in branches, and flattened against cinder blocks, broken glass, tar-paper roofing, and corrugated metal.

The remains had arrived at the morgue in large black plastic bags, each containing a collection of Ziploc bags. Each bag was numbered and held an assortment of body parts, dirt, fabric, metal, and unidentifiable debris. The autopsy photos moved from the unopened bags, to shots of the small plastic sacks grouped on autopsy tables, to views of the contents sorted by categories.

In the final photos the flesh lay in rows, like meat arranged in a butcher's case. I spotted pieces of skull, a fragment of tibia, a femoral head, and a portion of scalp with a complete right ear. Some close-ups revealed the jagged edges of shattered bone, others showed hairs, fibers, and scraps of fabric adhering to the flesh. The tattoo LaManche had mentioned was clearly visible on a flap of skin. It depicted three skulls, bony hands covering eyes, ears, and mouths. The irony was priceless. This guy would be seeing, hearing, and saying nothing.

After examining the prints and X rays I'd come to agree with LaManche. I could see bone in the photos, and the radiographs revealed the presence of more. That would allow me to determine the anatomical origin of some tissue. But sorting the jumble of flesh into specific brothers was going to be tough.

Separating commingled bodies is always hard, especially if the remains are badly damaged or incomplete. The process is infinitely more difficult when the dead are of the same gender, age, and race. I'd once spent weeks examining the bones and decomposing flesh of seven male prostitutes excavated from a crawl space beneath their killer's home. All were white and in their teens. DNA sequencing had been invaluable in determining who was who.

In this case that might not work. If the victims were monozygous twins they had developed from a single egg. Their DNA would be identical.

LaManche was right. It seemed unlikely I'd be able to divide the fragments into separate bodies and attach a name to each.

A gastric growl suggested it was time to quit. Tired and discouraged, I grabbed my purse, zipped my jacket, and headed out.

Back home, the flashing light told me I had a message. I spread my take-out sushi on the table, popped a Diet Coke, and hit the button.

My nephew Kit was driving from Texas to Vermont with his father. Intent on bonding, they were coming north to fish for whatever it is one hooks in inland waters in the spring. Since my cat prefers the space and comfort of a motor home to the efficiency of air travel, Kit and Howie had promised to pick him up at my home in Charlotte and transport him to Montreal. The message was that they and Birdie would arrive the next day.

I dipped a slice of maki roll and popped it in my mouth. I was going for another when the doorbell sounded. Puzzled, I went to the security screen.

The monitor showed Andrew Ryan leaning against the wall in my hallway. He wore faded blue jeans, running shoes, and a bomber jacket over a black T-shirt. At six foot two, with his blue eyes and angular features, he looked like a cross between Cal Ripkin and Indiana Jones.

I looked like Phyllis Diller before her makeover.

Great.

Sighing, I opened the door.

"Hey, Ryan. What's up?"

"Saw your light and figured you might be back early."
He gave me an appraising look.

"Rough day?"

"I spent today traveling and sorting flesh," I said
defensively, then tucked my hair behind my ears.
"Coming in?"

"Can't stay." I noticed he was wearing his pager and
gun. "Just thought I'd inquire as to your dinner plans for
tomorrow night."

"I'll be sorting bomb victims all day tomorrow, so I
may be a little zonked."

"You will have to eat."

"I will have to eat."

He placed one hand on my shoulder and twirled a
strand of my hair with the other.

"If you're tired we could skip dinner and just relax,"
he said in a low voice.

"Hmm."

"Broaden our horizons?"

He swept back the hair and brushed his lips across my
ear.

Oh yes.

"Sure, Ryan. I'll wear my thong panties."

"I always encourage that."

I gave him my "yeah, right" look.

"Will you spring for Chinese?"

"Chinese is good," he said, drawing my hair upward
and swirling it into a topknot. Then he let it fall and
wrapped both arms around my back. Before I could
object he pulled me close and kissed me, his tongue
teasing the edges of my lips, then gently probing the
inside of my mouth.

His lips felt soft, his chest hard against mine. I started to push away, but knew that was not what I wanted to do. Sighing, I relaxed and my body molded to his. The horrors of the day evaporated, and for that moment I was safe from the madness of bombs and murdered children.

Eventually we needed air.

"You're sure you don't want to come in?" I asked, stepping back and holding the door open. My knees felt like Jell-O salad.

Ryan looked at his watch.

"I'm sure a half hour won't matter."

At that moment his pager sounded. He checked the number.

"Shit."

Shit.

He rehooked the pager to the waist of his jeans.

"Sorry," he said, grinning sheepishly. "You know I'd really rath—"

"Go." Smiling, I placed two palms on his chest and shoved him gently. "I'll see you tomorrow night. Seven-thirty."

"Think about me," he said, as he turned and headed down the hall.

When he'd gone I went back to the sushi, definitely thinking about Andrew Ryan.

Ryan is SQ, a homicide detective, and occasionally we work the same cases. Though he'd been asking for years, only recently had I started seeing him socially. It had taken some self-persuasion, but I'd come around to his point of view. Technically, we didn't work together, so my "no office romance rule" didn't apply unless I wanted it to.

Nevertheless, the arrangement made me edgy. After

24

20 years of marriage, and several as a not-so-swinging single, new relationships just weren't that easy for me. But I enjoyed Ryan's company, so I'd decided to give it a whirl. To "date" him, as my sister would say.

Oh, God. Dating.

I had to admit that I found Ryan sexy as hell. Most women did. Wherever we went, I'd notice female eyes checking him out. Wondering, no doubt.

I was wondering, too. But at the moment that ship was still in port, the engines stoked and ready to go. The Jell-O knees had just reconfirmed that. Dinner out was definitely a better idea.

The phone rang as I was clearing the table.

"*Mon Dieu*, you're back." Deep, throaty English with a heavy French accent.

"Hi, Isabelle. What's up?"

Though I'd known Isabelle Caillé only two years, in that time we'd grown quite close. We'd met during a difficult time in my life. In the space of one bleak summer I was targeted by a violent psychopath, my best friend was murdered, and I was finally forced to face the reality of a failed marriage. In a display of self-indulgence, I had booked a single at a Club Med, and flown off to play tennis and overeat.

I'd met Isabelle on the flight to Nassau, and we were later paired for doubles. We won, discovered we were there for similar reasons, and passed an enjoyable week together. We'd been friends ever since.

"I didn't expect you until next week. I was going to leave a message about getting together, but since you are home, what about dinner tomorrow?"

I told her about Ryan.

"That one's a keeper, Tempe. You get tired of that *chevalier*, you send him over and I'll give him something to think about. Why are you back early?"

I explained about the bombing.

"*Ah, oui.* I read about that in *La Presse*. Is it just terribly gruesome?"

"The victims are not in good shape," I said.

"*Les motards.* If you ask me, these outlaw bikers get what they deserve."

Isabelle never lacked opinions, and was rarely hesitant to share them.

"The police should just let these gangsters blow each other up. Then we wouldn't have to look at their dirty bodies with filthy tattoos anymore."

"Hm."

"I mean, it's not like they're murdering babies."

"No," I agreed. "It's not."

The next morning Emily Anne Toussaint died while walking to her ballet lesson.

4

Howard and Kit had arrived at seven, left Birdie, and continued on their way. Birdie was ignoring me and checking the condo for canine intruders when I left for the lab at eight to resume work on the bomb victims.

Emily Anne had arrived shortly after noon.

Since I needed space, I'd chosen the large autopsy room. I'd rolled the gurneys with the bomb victim remains to the center of the room and was attempting to construct corpses on two tables. Being Saturday, I had the place to myself.

I had identified and sorted all visible bone fragments. Then, using the X rays, I'd pulled the fragments containing bone, and dissected the tissue to search for landmarks. Wherever I found duplicates I divided them between the tables. Two left pubic tubercles, or mastoid processes, or femoral condyles meant two different individuals.

I'd also spotted evidence of a childhood growth problem in some of the long bone fragments. When health is compromised, a child stops growing and skeletal development goes on hold. Such interruptions are usually caused by disease, or by periods of inadequate diet. When things get better, growth resumes, but the stoppages leave permanent markers.

The X rays were showing opaque lines on numerous splinters of arm and leg bones. The narrow bands ran transversely across the shafts and indicated periods of arrested growth. I placed tissue with affected fragments on one table, and tissue with normal bone on the other.

One of the tangles of shattered flesh contained several hand bones. When I teased them out I spotted two metacarpals with irregular shafts. These lumpy areas showed increased density when X-rayed, suggesting one of the victims had broken these fingers at some time in the past. I set that tissue aside.

Tissue without bone was a different matter. With that I studied the adherent fabric, working backward from the sorted tissue, matching threads and fibers from one table or the other to the pieces of tissue remaining on the gurneys. I thought I could make out a woven plaid, khaki of the kind found in work pants, denim, and white cotton. Later, experts from the hair and fiber section would do a full analysis to see if they could corroborate my matches.

Following lunch and my discussion with LaManche, I went back to the bomb victims. By five-fifteen I'd divided approximately two thirds of the tissue. Without DNA I saw no hope of associating the remaining fragments with specific individuals. I'd done what I could do.

I'd also set a goal for myself.

As I'd waded through the Vaillancourt body parts I'd found it hard to empathize with the persons I was reconstructing. In fact, I felt annoyance at having to do it. These men had been blown up while preparing to blow up others. A rough justice had prevailed, and I felt more bafflement than regret.

Not so with little Emily Anne. She was lying on LaManche's autopsy table because she'd been walking to dance class. That reality was not acceptable. The death of an innocent child could not be dismissed as an incidental casualty of maniacal warfare.

Vipers could kill Heathens, and Outlaws murder Bandidos. Or Pagans. Or Hells Angels. But they must not kill the innocent. I pledged to myself that I would apply every forensic skill I could muster, and however many hours I was able, to develop evidence to identify and convict these homicidal sociopaths. Children had a right to walk the streets of the city without being cut down by bullets.

I transferred the sorted remains back to the gurneys, rolled them to refrigerated compartments, scrubbed, and changed to street clothes. Then I rode the elevator to search out my boss.

"I want to work this," I said, my voice calm and steady. "I want to nail these bastard child killers."

The tired old eyes stared at me for what seemed a very long time. We'd been discussing Emily Anne Toussaint. And the other youngster. A boy.

Olivier Fontaine had been on his way to hockey practice when he pedaled too close to a Jeep Cherokee just as the driver turned the key. The bomb exploded with enough force to blast shrapnel into Olivier's body, killing him instantly. It happened on his twelfth birthday.

Until seeing Emily Anne I'd forgotten about the Fontaine murder. That incident had taken place in December of 1995 on the West Island, and involved the

Hells Angels and the Rock Machine. Olivier's death had raised a cry of public outrage, which led to the creation of Opération Carcajou, the multiagency task force devoted to the investigation of biker crime.

"Temperance, I can't—"

"I'll do whatever is needed. I'll work on my own time, between cases. If Carcajou is like everyone else they're probably short-handed. I could do data entry or historic case searches. I could liaison among agencies, maybe work links to intelligence units in the U.S. I cou—"

"Temperance, slow down." He held up a hand. "This is not something I am in a position to do. I will speak with Monsieur Patineau."

Stefan Patineau was director of the LSJML. He made final decisions for the crime and medico-legal labs.

"I will not let any involvement with Carcajou interfere with my normal duties."

"I know that. I promise I will speak with the director first thing Monday morning. Now go home. *Bonne fin de semaine.*"

I wished him a good weekend, too.

Quebec winters end much differently from those in the Carolina Piedmont. Back home spring slips in gently, and by the end of March and the beginning of April flowers begin to bloom and the air is soft with the warmth of summertime emerging.

Les québécois wait six weeks longer to plant their gardens and window boxes. Much of April is cool and gray, and the streets and sidewalks glisten with melted ice and snow. But when spring appears it does so with breathtaking showmanship. The season explodes, and the populace responds with an enthusiasm unmatched on the planet.

Today that vernal performance was weeks away. It was dark and a light rain was falling. I zipped my jacket, lowered my head, and made a dash for the car. The news came on as I was entering the Ville-Marie Tunnel, the Toussaint murder the lead story. That night Emily Anne was to have received an award in a lower-school writing competition. She'd titled her winning essay: "Let the Children Live."

I reached over and turned off the radio.

I thought of my plans for the evening and was glad I'd have someone to buoy my spirits. I vowed not to talk shop with Ryan.

Twenty minutes later I opened my apartment door to the sound of a ringing phone. I glanced at my watch. Six-fifty. Ryan would be here in forty minutes and I wanted time for a shower.

I walked to the living room and threw my jacket on the couch. The machine clicked on and I listened to my voice request a short message. Birdie appeared at the exact moment Isabelle came on.

"Tempe, if you're there, pick up. *C'est important.*" Pause. "*Merde!*"

I really didn't want to talk but something in her voice made me reach for the handset.

"Hello, Isa—"

"Turn on the television. CBC."

"I know about the Toussaint child. I was at the lab—"

"*Now!*"

I picked up the remote and clicked on the set.

Then I listened in horror.

31

5

"*. . . Lieutenant-détective Ryan had been under investigation for several months. He has been charged with possession of stolen goods and with trafficking and possession of controlled substances. Ryan surrendered peacefully to CUM officers this afternoon outside his home in the Old Port. He has been suspended from duty without pay pending a full investigation.*

"And now some other stories that we've been following. In financial news, the proposed merger of—"

"Tempe!"

Isabelle's bark snapped me back. I raised the receiver to my ear.

"*C'est lui, n'est-ce pas? Andrew Ryan, Crimes contre la Personne, Sûreté du Québec?*"

"It's got to be a mistake."

As I said the words my eyes flew to the message light. Ryan hadn't called.

"I'd better go. He'll be here soon."

"Tempe. He's in jail."

"I've got to go. I'll call you tomorrow."

I hung up and dialed Ryan's apartment. No answer. I called his pager and entered my number. No response. I looked at Birdie. He had no explanation.

By nine I knew he wasn't coming. I'd called his home seven times. I'd phoned his partner, with the same result. No answer. No response.

I tried grading the final exams I'd brought from UNC-Charlotte, but couldn't concentrate. My thoughts kept going back to Ryan. Time would pass and I'd find myself staring at the same essay in the same blue book, my mind absorbing nothing the student had written. Birdie nestled in the crook of my knees, but it was small comfort.

It couldn't be true. I couldn't believe it. *Wouldn't* believe it.

At ten I took a long, hot bubble bath, zapped a carton of frozen spaghetti, and took it to the living room. I chose CDs I hoped would cheer me, and placed them in the player. Then I tried reading. Birdie joined me again.

No good. Same loop. Pat Conroy might as well have been printed in Nahuatl.

I'd seen Ryan's image on the screen, hands cuffed behind his back, uniformed cops on either side. I'd watched them angle his head forward as he bent to slide into the cruiser's backseat. Still, my mind wouldn't accept it.

Andrew Ryan was selling drugs?

How could I have been so wrong about him? Had Ryan been dealing the whole time I'd known him? Was there a side to the man that I'd never seen? Or was it all a terrible mistake?

It had to be a mistake.

33

The spaghetti cooled on the table. I had no stomach for food. I had no ear for music. Big Bad Voodoo Daddy and the Johnny Favourite band played swing that could make a gulag get up and dance, but it did nothing to brighten my mood.

The rain fell steadily now, drumming the windows with a soft ticking sound. My Carolina spring seemed very far away.

I twirled a forkful of pasta, but the smell made something in my stomach recoil.

Andrew Ryan was a criminal.

Emily Anne Toussaint was dead.

My daughter was somewhere on the Indian Ocean.

I often phone Katy when I'm feeling down, but for the past few months that had been difficult. She was spending her spring on Semester at Sea, circling the world aboard the S.S. *Universe Explorer*. The ship wouldn't return for another five weeks.

I took a glass of milk to my bedroom and cracked the window and stared out, thoughts swirling like five o'clock traffic.

The trees and bushes looked like black shadows through the dark glistening mist. Beyond them I could see headlights and the shimmer of neon from the corner *dépanneur*. Now and then cars swooshed by, or pedestrians hurried past, their heels clicking on the wet sidewalk.

So routine. So normal. Just another rainy night in April.

I let the curtain fall back and crossed to my bed, doubting my world would return to normal for a very long time.

I spent the next day in constant activity. Unpacking.

Cleaning. Shopping for food. I avoided radio and television, glanced only briefly at the paper.

The *Gazette* featured the Toussaint murder: SCHOOLGIRL KILLED IN BLOODY SHOOT-OUT. Beside the headline was a blowup of Emily Anne's fourth-grade photo. Her hair was braided and bowed at both ends with large pink ribbons. Her smile showed gaps that adult dentition would never have the chance to fill.

The picture of Emily Anne's mother was equally heartbreaking. The camera had caught a slim black woman with her head thrown back, mouth wide, lips curled inward in a cry of agony. Mrs Toussaint's knees were buckled, her hands clasped below her chin, and on either side, a large black woman supported her. Unspeakable grief screamed from the grainy image.

The story gave few details. Emily Anne had two younger sisters, Cynthia Louise, age six, and Hannah Rose, age four. Mrs Toussaint worked in a bakery. Mr Toussaint had died in an industrial accident three years earlier. Born in Barbados, the couple had immigrated to Montreal, seeking a better life for their daughters.

A funeral Mass would be celebrated Thursday at 8 A.M. at Our Lady of the Angels Catholic Church, followed by burial at the Notre-Dame-des-Neiges Cemetery.

I refused to read or listen to reports about Ryan. I wanted to hear from him. All morning I left messages on his machine, but got no response. Ryan's partner, Jean Bertrand, had also gone incommunicado. I could think of nothing else to do. I was certain no one at the CUM or SQ would talk about the situation, and I knew none of Ryan's family or friends.

After a trip to the gym, I cooked a dinner of chicken breasts with prune sauce, glazed carrots with mushrooms, and saffron rice. My feline companion would no doubt have preferred fish.

Monday morning I rose early, drove to the lab, and went directly to see LaManche. He was in conference with three detectives, but told me to talk with Stefan Patineau as soon as possible.

Wasting no time, I headed down the corridor containing the offices of the medico-legal staff and the anthropology, odontology, histology, and pathology labs. Passing the Section des Documents on my left and the Section d'Imagerie on my right, I continued to the main reception area and turned left into the wing housing the administrative personnel of the LSJML. The director's office was at the very back.

Patineau was on the phone. He waved me in and I took a chair opposite his desk.

When he finished his call, he leaned back and looked directly at me. His eyes were deep brown, hooded by heavy ridges and thick brows. Stefan Patineau was a man who would never worry about thinning hair.

"Dr LaManche tells me you want to get involved with the Toussaint investigation."

"I think I could be of use to Carcajou. I've worked on several biker cases. Right now I'm sorting out the victims from the Vipers' clubhouse bombing. I'm not new to this stuff. I cou—"

He waved a hand.

"The director of Opération Carcajou has asked if I could assign one of my personnel to act as liaison to his unit. With this war heating up he'd like to be sure the crime lab, the medico-legal staff, and his investigators are all on the same page at the same time."

I didn't wait to hear more.

"I can do it."

"It's spring. Once the river thaws and the hikers and campers hit the woods your workload is going to get heavier."

That was true. The number of floaters and decomps always increased when the weather warmed and the past winter's dead came to light.

"I'll work overtime."

"I was going to assign Réal Marchand, but you are welcome to give it a try. It's not a full-time job."

He lifted a paper from his desk and handed it to me.

"There is a meeting at three this afternoon. I'll call to tell them you're coming."

"Thank you. You won't regret this."

He rose and walked me to the door.

"Is there a positive on the Vaillancourt brothers?"

"We'll know once their medical records show up. Hopefully today."

He gave a two-thumbs-up gesture.

"Go get 'em, Tempe," he said in English.

I returned the gesture and he shrugged, then retreated to his office.

In addition to being a superb administrator, Patineau filled out a shirt more impressively than most body-builders.

Mondays are busy for every coroner and medical examiner, and this one was no exception. As LaManche went through the cases I thought the meeting would never end.

A young girl had died in the hospital and the mother admitted only to shaking her. Three years is beyond the age for Shaken Baby syndrome, and a contusion suggested the child's head had been slammed against a hard surface.

A 32-year-old paranoid schizophrenic was found with his stomach open, innards spewing onto the carpet of his bedroom. The family claimed the wound was self-inflicted.

Two trucks had collided outside St-Hyacinthe. Both drivers were burned beyond recognition.

A 27-year-old Russian seaman was found in his cabin with no signs of life. He was pronounced dead by the ship's captain, and the body was preserved and brought ashore. Since the death occurred in Canadian waters, an autopsy was required.

A 44-year-old woman was beaten to death in her apartment. Her estranged husband was being sought.

Medical files had arrived for Donald and Ronald Vaillancourt. So had an envelope of snapshots.

When the pictures were passed around we knew that at least one twin lay in pieces downstairs. In a splendid Kodak moment Ronald Vaillancourt stood bare-chested, flexing his upper torso. The see-no-evil skull decorated his right chest.

LaManche assigned each of the autopsies to a pathologist, and turned the Vaillancourt documents over to me.

By ten forty-five I knew which twin had broken his fingers. Ronald "Le Clic" Vaillancourt had fractured his second and third left digits in a barroom brawl in 1993. The hospital X rays showed the injury in the same location as the irregularities I'd spotted on the meta-carpals. They also showed that Le Clic's arm bones lacked lines of arrested growth.

A motorcycle accident sent Le Clic back to the emergency room two months later, this time for hip and lower limb trauma. The radiographic picture was similar. Ronald's leg bones were normal. His record also indicated he had been thrown from a car in '95, stabbed in a street fight later that year, and beaten by a rival gang in '97. His X-ray file was two inches thick.

I also knew who had not been a healthy kid. Donald "Le Clac" Vaillancourt was hospitalized several times during his childhood. As a toddler he experienced pro-longed periods of nausea and vomiting, the cause of which was never diagnosed. At the age of six, scarlet fever nearly killed him. At eleven it was gastroenteritis.

Le Clac had also taken his lumps. His dossier, like his brother's, contained a large packet of X rays reflecting many visits to the trauma center. A broken nose and cheek. A knife wound to the chest. A blow to the head with a bottle.

As I closed the dossier I smiled at the irony. The turbulent life of the brothers would provide a diagram for sorting their bodies. Their many misadventures had left a skeletal map.

Armed with the medical files, I returned to the lower level and took up the parts identification process. I began with the tattooed segment of thorax and the fragments I'd associated with it. That was Ronald. He also got the fractured hand and all tissue containing normal long bones.

Limb bones with lines of arrested growth went to Donald. Limb bones without lines went to his brother.

Next I showed Lisa, one of the autopsy technicians, how to radiograph the remaining fragments with the bones in positions identical to those on the antemortem hospital films. This would allow me to compare details of shape and internal structure.

Since the X-ray unit was in heavy demand, we worked through lunch, finally quitting at one-thirty when the other technicians and pathologists returned. Lisa promised she would finish as the machine became available, and I hurried upstairs to change.

Opération Carcajou was headquartered in a modern three-story structure on the shore of the St Lawrence River, directly across from Old Montreal. The rest of the complex was occupied by the port police and the administrative offices of the maritime authority.

I parked facing the river. To the left I could see the Jacques Cartier Bridge arching across past Île-Notre-Dame, to the right the smaller Victoria Bridge. Enormous chunks of ice floated and bobbed on the dark gray water.

Farther up along the shore, I noticed Habitat '67, a geometric pile of residential space originally built for Expo and later converted to private condominiums. The sight of the building caused a constriction in my chest. Ryan lived in that network of boxes.

I pushed the thought from my mind, grabbed my jacket, and bolted for the building. The cloud cover was breaking, but the day was still raw and damp. An onshore breeze, carrying with it the smell of oil and icy water, flapped my clothes.

A wide staircase led to Carcajou headquarters on the third floor. Inside glass doors sat a stuffed wolverine, the totem for which the unit is named. Men and women occupied desks in a large central room, their extension numbers in block letters on signs above their heads. Framed clippings decorated every wall, stories of Carcajou investigators and their quarry.

Some looked up, most did not as I crossed to the

secretary, a middle-aged woman with overdyed hair and a mole on her cheek the size of a June bug. She dragged her eyes from her filing long enough to direct me to a conference room.

I entered to find a dozen men seated around a rectangular table, several others lounging along the walls. The unit's director, Jacques Roy, rose when he saw me. He was short and muscular, with a florid complexion and graying hair parted in the center, like the subject of an 1890s tintype.

"Dr Brennan, we are so glad you're doing this for us. It will be a great help to my investigators as well as to the folks at your lab. Please." He gestured to an empty place at the table.

I hung my jacket over the back of the chair and sat. As others drifted in, Roy explained the purpose of the meeting. Several of those present had recently rotated on to the Carcajou team. Others were old hands, but had requested a refresher session. Roy would give a quick overview of the Quebec biker scene. When Constable Quickwater arrived he would report on the major case management session he'd attended at the FBI Academy.

It felt like a time warp. It was Quantico all over again, only this time the language was French and the carnage being described was in a place I knew and of which I was fond.

The next two hours revealed a world that few will ever know. That glimpse sent a shudder through my body and a chill into my soul.

6

"First of all, a little background information."

Roy spoke from the front of the room. He had notes on the podium, but didn't use them.

"Outlaw motorcycle clubs began on the West Coast of the United States shortly after World War II. Some returning vets couldn't adjust to the social requirements of peace and took to roaming the countryside on Harley-Davidsons, harassing the citizenry and generally making themselves obnoxious. They formed loose groups with names like the Booze Fighters, the Galloping Gooses, Satan's Sinners, the Winos. Right from the start these guys weren't candidates for the College of Cardinals."

Laughter and muffled comments.

"The group to have the greatest impact was a collection of social misfits calling themselves the Pissed Off Bastards of Bloomington. The P.O.B.O.B. eventually became the Hells Angels, taking the name and the helmeted death's-head symbol from a World War II bomber squadron. From the founding chapter in San Bernardino, California—"

"Yahoo, Berdoo." A comment from the back.

"Right."

"From that chapter the Hells Angels spread across North America. Eventually other groups also went national, then international. Today the big four are the Hells Angels, the Outlaws, the Bandidos, and the Pagans. All but the Pagans have chapters outside the States, though none to the extent of the Angels."

A man sitting across the table raised his hand. He had a large paunch and receding hairline, and looked strikingly like Andy Sipowicz of *NYPD Blue*.

"How big are we talking here?"

"Figures vary, depending on the source, but the best estimate is that the Hells Angels have over sixteen hundred members throughout Europe, Australia, and New Zealand. Most are in the United States and Canada, of course, but, as of today, they have one hundred and thirty-three chapters around the globe.

"The 1998 Criminal Intelligence Service of Canada annual report estimates the Bandidos have sixty-seven chapters and about six hundred members worldwide. Other estimates bump it to eight hundred."

"*Sacrement!*"

"What qualifies as an outlaw motorcycle club?" This questioner looked about nineteen.

"Technically the OMC label designates those clubs not registered with the American Motorcycle Association or the Canadian Motorcycle Association, the North American affiliates of the Fédération Internationale de Motocyclisme, now headquartered in Switzerland. According to the AMA, these nonregistered clubs account for only one percent of all motorcyclists, but it's this deviant fringe that gives biking a bad name. And it's a tag the boys have graciously accepted, by the way. I've seen the one-percenter logo tattooed on some of the ugliest shoulders in the province."

"Yeah. The little triangle identifies the truly righteous biker." The investigator to my right wore a ponytail and a silver stud in his ear.

"The truly rat puke, you mean." Sipowicz. His French sounded exactly as I would expect if *NYPD Blue* had been set in Trois-Rivières.

More laughter.

Roy indicated a stack of notebooks in the center of the table.

"There's information in those about the structure of OMCs. Read it and we'll discuss it later. Today I want to take a look at the local scene."

He clicked on a projector. The screen filled with the image of a clenched fist, swastika tattooed on the wrist, the letters F.T.W. in red and black rippling across the knuckles.

"The basic philosophy of outlaw bikers can be summed up in one phrase."

"Fuck the World!" Shouted in unison.

"F.T.W. Fuck the World," Roy agreed. "Your colors and brothers come first and demand total loyalty. Nonwhites need not apply."

Roy clicked to the next slide. The screen showed a black-and-white photo of sixteen men arranged in three ragged rows. All were unshorn and wore sleeveless leather vests accessorized with pins and patches. Their tattoos would have impressed a Maori warrior. So would their scowls.

"At the end of the seventies the Outlaws and the Hells Angels from the States both partied hard with certain Quebec gangs they wanted to take over. In 1977 the Popeyes got asked to the prom and became the first

44

Hells Angels chapter in the province. At that time the Popeyes were the second-largest OMC in Canada, with two hundred and fifty to three hundred and fifty members. Unfortunately, only about twenty-five or thirty of the boys had impressed the Angels enough to wear the colors, so the rest got the boot. You're looking at some of the rejects here. This is the infamous North chapter. Five of these guys were liquidated by their brother Angels and the chapter became extinct."

"Why?"

"Each club has a code of conduct that applies to every member. Ever since the Hells Angels formed back in the forties their rules have prohibited heroin and the use of needles. This has become even more important in today's business atmosphere. Keep in mind, these are *not* the bikers of old. This is *not* the social rebellion of the fifties, or the subculture of drugs and revolution that danced through the sixties. Today's bikers are engaged in sophisticated organized crime. First and foremost these guys are businessmen. Junkies can cause trouble and cost the club money, and that isn't tolerated."

Roy gestured at the screen.

"Getting back to the choir here, in 1982 the Montreal chapter passed a drug law and called for death or expulsion of any Angel defying it. But the members of the North chapter were too attached to their coke, and decided to go their own way. Apparently the blow had affected their math, because they failed to note that they were strongly outnumbered on this question."

One by one, Roy tapped his pen on five of the men in the photograph.

"In June of 1985 these guys were found taking the cement siesta in the St Lawrence Seaway. One of the sleeping bags had floated up, the others had to be dredged from the bottom."

"Taking care of business." Ponytail.

"Permanently. They were killed in the Hells Angels' clubhouse out in Lennoxville. Apparently the party they'd gone out there to attend turned out not to be the one they'd expected."

"Kind of contrary to the old righteous brother outlaw doctrine." Ponytail shook his head.

"Is that what started the present war?" I asked.

"Not really. A year after the Hells Angels adopted the Popeyes, a Montreal group called Satan's Choice became the first Outlaws chapter in Quebec. They've been killing each other ever since."

Roy indicated a gaunt man squatting in the front row of the photo.

"War was declared when this Hells Angel killed an Outlaw in a drive-by. For several years after that it was open season."

"'God forgives, the Outlaws don't.' That's their slogan." Sipowicz wrote his name, "Kuricek," on a notebook as he spoke. I wondered how many people called him Sipowicz by mistake.

"True. But the Quebec Outlaws have suffered a severe reversal of fortune since then. Five or six are now in jail, and their clubhouse was burned to the ground a few years ago. The present war really involves the Angels and a Canadian group called the Rock Machine, and their puppet clubs."

"Classy guys," offered Sipowicz/Kuricek.

"But the Rock Machine also fell on hard times," Roy continued. "Until recently."

He clicked to a slide showing a man in a beret embracing a leather-jacketed comrade. Centered on the

46

embracee's back was a cartoon-like Mexican bandit, knife in one hand, pistol in the other. Red and yellow crescent-shaped banners above and below the figure identified the wearer as the national vice president of the Bandidos MC.

"The Machine was on its last legs, but appears to be undergoing a major resuscitation since members have recently been spotted wearing patches identifying them as tentative Bandidos."

"Tentative?" I asked.

"The Machine has been granted hang-around status while the Bandidos decide if they're worthy to prospect."

"I can see the advantage to the Rock Machine, but what's in it for the Bandidos?" I asked.

"For years the Bandidos were satisfied with local meth and narcotics sales, and a few bucks from prostitution. The national organization ran a pretty loose ship. Now power has shifted, and the new leadership recognizes the advantage of expansion and tight control over member chapters.

"Check out the bottom rocker." Roy pointed to the lower banner on a jacket in the background. "Quebec has been changed to Canada. That's a pretty clear indicator of where the Bandidos want to go. But it may not be that easy."

New slide. A formation of bikes on a two-lane highway.

"This was taken in Albuquerque, New Mexico, a few weeks ago. The Bandidos were on their way to a run organized by the Oklahoma chapter. When police pulled over some of the boys for traffic violations, the club's international president was among them, so investigators took the opportunity to query him about

47

all the new faces. He admitted the Bandidos were checking out wanna-be clubs around the world, but refused to answer when asked about the Rock Machine.

"Turns out the arrangement is not a done deal. The pres had just come from a meeting of the National Coalition of Motorcyclists where the Bandidos and the Hells Angels tried to hammer out an agreement about the Machine. The Angels are not thrilled about the Bandidos' expansion campaign, and offered to disband a prospect chapter in New Mexico if the Bandidos would drop negotiations with the Quebec club."

"So the Machine is really hanging out there?" Ponytail.

"Yes. But if they are patched over, a Bandidos presence could shift the balance here." Roy's voice sounded grim.

"The Rock Machine is relatively new on the scene, *n'est-ce pas*?" asked the young-looking investigator.

"They've been around since 1977," said Roy. "But they only added MC to their name in '97. Before that they didn't think of themselves as anything as conventional as a motorcycle club. It was a little surprise on their Christmas cards that year."

"Christmas cards?" I thought he was joking.

"Yeah. Tradition means a lot to these guys. It was quite the talk of the prison chat room." Kuricek.

Laughter.

"The cards allow members to keep up with each other," Roy explained. "The downside is that they also fatten the intelligence files of rival gangs."

Roy clicked to a map of Montreal.

"Currently the Rock Machine is battling the Hells Angels over control of the province's illegal drug trade

And we're talking big bucks, here. According to the solicitor general, Canada's illicit drug market is worth seven to ten billion a year to organized crime gangs. Quebec represents a big piece of that."

He indicated two areas of the city.

"The disputed turf involves the north and east sides of Montreal, and parts of Quebec City. Since 1994 there have been hundreds of bombings and arsons, and no less than one hundred and fourteen murders."

"Counting Marcotte, the Vaillancourt twins, and the Toussaint child?" I asked.

"Good point. One hundred and eighteen. At least a score of others are missing and presumed dead."

"How many of these asshole warriors are out there in the trenches?" Kuricek.

"The starting lineup is about two hundred sixty-five for the Angels, fifty for the Rock Machine."

"That's it?" I was astounded so few could wreak so much havoc.

"Don't forget the second-stringers." Kuricek leaned back and his chair whooshed softly.

"Both sides have puppet clubs that align with them. It's these losers that do all the dirty work for the organizations." Roy.

"Dirty work?" It all sounded dirty to me.

"Distribution and sale of drugs, debt collection, weapons and explosives buys, intimidation, murder. These puppet clubs are the dregs of bikerdom and they'll do anything to prove their balls to the big dogs. That's why it's so hard to nail a patch holder of a major club. The bastards are slippery as hell and always operate at arm's length."

"Then if you *do* bust them they make bond and use their baboons to terrorize or kill your witnesses." Kuricek.

I pictured the shattered flesh that had been the Vaillancourt brothers.

"The Heathens are aligned with the Rock Machine?"

"*C'est ça.*"

"And the Vipers with the Hells Angels?"

"*C'est ça.*"

"Who are the others?"

"Let's see. The Rowdy Crew, the Jokers, the Rockers, the Evil Ones, the Death Riders . . ."

At that moment Martin Quickwater appeared in the doorway. He was wearing a navy suit and crisp white shirt, and looked more like a tax lawyer than an organized crime investigator. He nodded at Roy then his eyes swept the room. When he saw me his eyes narrowed, but he said nothing.

"*Ah, bon.* Monsieur Quickwater can give us the FBI perspective."

But that was not to be. Quickwater had urgent news. The body count was about to go up.

7

By sunrise the next day I was at the Vipers' clubhouse in St-Basile-le-Grand. The building stood alone on an acre of land that was entirely enclosed by an electrified fence. Surveillance cameras dotted the barrier's upper rim, and powerful floods lit the perimeter.

Gates at the highway end of the road were electrically operated and monitored from inside the house. When we arrived they stood open, and no one questioned us via the intercom. Though I could see a remote camera focused on us, I knew no one was watching. The warrant had already been served, and unmarked cars, cruisers, coroner transport vehicles, and the crime scene van were parked along the side of the drive.

Quickwater drove through the gates and pulled in at the end of the row. As he cut the engine he glanced sideways at me, but said nothing. I returned the pleasantry, grabbed my pack, and got out.

In back the grounds were wooded, in front an open field stretched from the house to the highway. The gravel road on which we'd entered bisected the front

51

clearing and ended at a ring of asphalt encircling the building. Waist-high cement cones bordered the asphalt, placed to prevent parking within fifteen feet of any wall. The arrangement reminded me of Northern Ireland in the early seventies. Like the citizens of Belfast, the bikers of Quebec took the threat of car bombs very seriously. A black Ford Explorer was parked at the edge of the asphalt.

Sunlight mottled the horizon, bleeding yellow and pink into the pale purple of early dawn. An hour ago, when Quickwater had picked me up, the sky had been as black as my mood. I didn't want to come here. I didn't want to deal with Mr Personality. And most of all, I didn't want to unearth more dead bikers.

What Quickwater told us yesterday had caused a weight to settle over me. As I'd listened to his account I knew that what was to have been peripheral involvement on my part, undertaken only to permit me to work on Emily Anne's case, would now become a major task, and the thought of all I'd have to do was pressing me down like a school-yard bully. I reminded myself that a nine-year-old child lay in the morgue, and her shattered family would never be the same. I was there for them.

The Viper shooter who'd obliterated the Vaillancourt brothers had been willing to deal. Facing his third bust and murder-one charges, he'd offered the location of two bodies. The crown had countered with second degree. *Voilà.* Daybreak in St-Basile.

As we trudged up the drive dawn gave way to morning. Though I could see my breath, I knew the day would warm with the sun.

Gravel crunched underfoot, and now and then a pebble dislodged, skittered across the uneven roadbed, and rolled into a side trench. Birds twittered and scolded, announcing their displeasure over our arrival.

Suck eggs, I thought. My morning began before yours.

Don't be a baby, Brennan. You're annoyed because Quickwater is a jerk. Ignore him. Do your job.

Just then he spoke.

"I need to find my new partner. He's just been loaned over to Carcajou."

Though Quickwater didn't offer a name, I felt sympathy for the unlucky cop. I took a deep breath, hiked up my pack, and looked around as I followed his back.

One thing was clear. The Vipers were never going to win Landscaper of the Year. The front of the property was a good example of what nature preservationists in the U.S. Congress had fought to protect. The bottom-land that stretched to the highway was a sea of dead vegetation splayed against the reddish-brown spring mud. The scrub forest behind the house had been left to the decorating of its quadrupedal inhabitants.

When we crossed the asphalt and entered the court-yard, however, a design plan was evident. Inspired by the better prisons of America, the enclosure had all the essentials, including twelve-foot brick walls topped with surveillance cameras, motion detectors, and floodlights. Wall-to-wall cement covered the ground, with basket-ball hoops, a gas barbecue, and a doghouse with chain-link run. Steel doors had replaced the original courtyard gate, and the garage entrance was steel-reinforced and welded shut.

On the trip out, the one time Quickwater had spoken was to give me the basic history of the property. The house was built by a New Yorker who'd made his fortune running booze during the days of the Volstead

Act. In the mid-eighties the Vipers bought it from the smuggler's heirs, put four hundred thousand into renovations, and hung up their logo. In addition to the perimeter security system, the boys had installed bullet-proof glass in all first-floor windows, and steel plating on every door.

None of that mattered this morning. Like the gate, the clubhouse door stood wide open. Quickwater entered and I followed.

My first reaction was surprise at the lavish outfitting. If these guys needed to make bail or hire an attorney, all they had to do was hold an auction. The electronic equipment alone would have netted them F. Lee Bailey.

The house was built on multiple levels, with a metal staircase twisting up its core. We crossed a black-and-white-tiled hallway and started to climb. To my left I got a glimpse of a game room complete with pool and Foosball tables and a full-length bar. On the wall above the liquor collection a coiled snake with fleshless skull, fangs, and bulging eyeballs grinned down in orange neon. At the far end of the bar, a bank of video monitors provided sixteen views of the property on small black-and-white screens. The room also held a large television and a sound system that looked like a NASA control panel. A patrolman from the St-Basile PD nodded as we passed.

At the second level I noted a gym with at least half a dozen pieces of Nautilus equipment. Two weight benches and an assortment of free weights sat in front of a mirrored wall to the left. The Vipers were into body image.

On level three we crossed a living room done in late-millennium biker bilious. The carpet was deep red plush, and locked horns with the gold on the walls and the blue in the fabric of the oversized couches and love seats. The tables were brass and smoked glass, and held an assortment of snake sculptures. Wood, ceramic, stone, and metal serpents also lined the windowsills, and snarled from the top of the largest TV I'd ever seen.

The walls were decorated with posters, enlargements of snapshots taken at club soirees and runs. In shot after shot members flexed sweaty muscles, straddled cycles, or held up bottles and cans of beer. Most looked like they came from a point on the IQ curve that sloped low and very gently.

We wound our way past five bedrooms, a black marble bath with a sunken Jacuzzi and open glass shower the size of a squash court, and finally into a kitchen. There was a wall phone to my right, with an erasable message board bearing numbers, gibberish in alphabetic code, and the name of a local attorney.

To my left I noticed another staircase.

"What's up there?" I asked Quickwater.

No response.

A second uniform from St-Basile stood on the far side of the room. "It's another rec room," he said in English. "With an outside deck and ten-person spa."

Two men sat at a wooden table framed by a small bay window, one disheveled, the other pressed and groomed to perfection.

I looked at Quickwater, who nodded. My heart sank.

Luc Claudel was the nameless unfortunate newly partnered with Quickwater. Great. Now I'd have to work with Beavis *and* Butt-Head.

Claudel was speaking, now and then tapping a document that I assumed was the search warrant.

The man he was addressing looked less than pleased with his morning. He had fierce black eyes, a hooked nose that did a sharp left just below the hump, and more hair on his upper lip than a bull walrus. He scowled at his bare feet as he clenched and unclenched the hands that dangled between his knees.

Quickwater nodded at the walrus.

"The Neanderthal is Sylvain Bilodeau. Luc is explaining that we're here to do a little gardening."

Bilodeau glanced at Quickwater, then at me, his eyes hard and unsmiling, then refocused on opening and closing his fists. A tricolor serpent wound the length of his arm, and appeared to sway as the muscles tensed and eased. I suspected Quickwater's metaphor had done our Paleolithic cousins an injustice.

After a few more words Claudel stopped talking and Bilodeau shot to his feet. Though he couldn't have been over five foot three, he looked like a poster boy for steroids. For a moment he said nothing. Then, "This is shit, man. You can't just bust the fuck in here and start digging the place up." His French was so heavily accented with backcountry joual that I missed a lot of the words. But I definitely caught his drift.

Claudel rose and looked Bilodeau in the eye.

"That's exactly what this little piece of paper says we *can* do. And, as I explained, you've got two choices. You can show class and just sit tight like a good little boy, or we can haul you out of here in handcuffs and treat you to free accommodations for an indefinite period of time. It's your choice, Nose."

Claudel pronounced the nickname in a mocking tone. Good handle, I thought.

"What the fuck am I supposed to do?"

"You're going to reassure your friends that it's in the best interests of their continued good health not to drop by here today. Aside from that, your day is going to be

56

leisurely. You'll do absolutely nothing. And Caporal Berringer is going to stay here to watch you do it."

"I'm just taking care of business here. Why the fuck do you have to show up this morning?"

Claudel reached out and clapped Nose on the shoulder. "Life is timing, Nose."

Bilodeau shrugged free and stomped to the window.

"Fucking son of a bitch."

Claudel held up his hands in a "what can I do" gesture. "Maybe you've got bigger problems than we do, Nose. Guess the brothers won't be thrilled about you sleeping on watch."

Bilodeau crisscrossed the room, pacing like a caged animal. Then he stopped at the counter and pounded it with both fists.

"Fuck." His neck muscles bulged with rage and a vein throbbed like a tiny stream in the center of his forehead.

After a moment he turned, scanned from face to face, then pinned me with a look of Charles Manson intensity. He uncurled one fist and pointed a trembling finger in my direction.

"That motherfucking turncoat prick of yours better get it right the first time." His voice quivered with rage. "Because he's a walking dead man."

The turncoat prick in question had been waiting one hundred yards away in the backseat of an unmarked Jeep. As part of his plea bargain he'd agreed to take us to the grave site. However, nothing would persuade him to get out of the car until we were well clear of the house. He would be driven, or the deal was off.

We left the house and went directly to the Jeep. I took the front passenger seat and Claudel climbed in back

57

while Quickwater continued down the road to check with the recovery team. The cigarette smoke was so thick inside the vehicle I found it hard to breathe.

Our informant was a middle-aged man, with celery green eyes and dull red hair pulled into a ponytail at the back of his head. With his white skin, lank hair, and pale reptilian eyes, he looked like something that had evolved in the waters of an underground cave. Viper was an appropriate affiliation. Like Bilodeau, he was short. Unlike Bilodeau he was not interested in a prolonged stay at the clubhouse.

Claudel spoke first.

"This better be good, Rinaldi, or your folks can start planning a funeral. Looks like your approval rating has plummeted among your peers."

Rinaldi drew smoke into his lungs, held it, then blew two streams through his nose. The borders of his nostrils blanched as they expanded with the effort.

"Who's the broad?" His voice sounded odd, as though it were being scrambled to hide his identity.

"Dr Brennan will be digging up your treasure, Frog. And you're going to help her in every way you can, aren't you?"

"Pffff." Rinaldi puffed air through his lips. Like his nostrils, their edges paled with the movement.

"And you're going to be as docile as a stiff in the morgue, right?"

"Let's get the fuck on with it."

"The morgue bit was not a casual comparison, Frog. The simile will have meaning if this turns out to be a con."

"I'm not making this shit up. There are two guys eating dirt out there. Let's get this fucking show on the road."

"Let's," agreed Claudel.

Rinaldi flicked a bony finger, rattling the handcuffs connecting his wrists.

"Circle the house and watch for a dirt track off to the right."

"That sounds like a sincere start, Frog."

Frog. Another fitting moniker, I thought, listening to Rinaldi's strange, croaky voice.

Claudel stepped out and gave a thumbs-up to Quickwater, ten yards away at the crime scene van. I turned to look and caught Rinaldi staring at me as if trying to read my genetic code. When our eyes met he held on, refusing to look away. So did I.

"Do you have a problem with me, Mr Rinaldi?" I asked.

"Odd job for a chick," he said, never breaking eye contact.

"I'm an odd chick. I once peed in Sonny Barger's pool." I didn't even know if the former head of the Hells Angels had a pool, but it sounded good. Besides, the Barger reference was probably lost on Frog.

Several seconds passed, then Frog smirked, gave a half shake of the head, and reached to crush his cigarette in the tiny tray between the two front seats. When the handcuffs slipped I saw two lightning bolts tattooed on his forearm, above them the words "Filthy Few."

Claudel got back in and Quickwater joined us, taking the wheel but saying nothing. As we circled the house and cut into the woods Rinaldi gazed silently out the window, no doubt preoccupied with his own terrible demons.

Rinaldi's road was little more than two tracks, and the cars and recovery van behind us moved sluggishly through the mud and wet vegetation. At one point

Quickwater and Claudel were forced to get out and clear a tree that had fallen onto the path. As they dragged the rotted branches a pair of squirrels were startled and darted out of sight.

Quickwater returned clammy with sweat and muddy from the knees down. Claudel remained pristine and carried himself as if he were wearing a tuxedo. I suspected Claudel could look prim and tidy when walking around in his underwear, but doubted he ever did that.

Claudel loosened his tie a full millimeter and tapped on Rinaldi's window. I opened my door, but Frog was working on another cigarette.

Claudel tapped again and Frog hit the handle. The door popped open and smoke drifted out.

"Put that thing out before we're all on respirators. Are your memory cells still working, Frog? Do you recognize the terrain?" Claudel.

"They're here. If you'll just shut the fuck up and let me get my bearings."

Rinaldi got out and looked around. Quickwater gave me another of his stony stares as our informant did a visual sweep of the area. I ignored him and did my own inspection.

The spot had once been used as a dump. I could see cans and plastic containers, beer and wine bottles, an old mattress, and a rusted set of box springs. The ground was marked with the delicate tracks of deer, circling, crossing, and disappearing into the surrounding trees.

"I'm getting impatient, Frog," Claudel urged. "I'd count to three, as I do with children, but I'm sure I'd lose you with the higher math."

"Will you just shut the fuck—"

"Easy," Claudel warned.

"I haven't been out here in years. There was a shed,

man. If I can spot the fucking shed I can walk you to them."

Frog starting making sorties into the woods, probing like a hound scenting a hare. He looked less confident with each passing moment, and I was beginning to share his doubt.

I've been on many informant-led expeditions, and in a lot of cases the trip is a waste of time. Jailhouse tips are notoriously unreliable, either because the herald is lying, or because his memory has simply failed him. LaManche and I went twice in search of a septic tank reported to be the tomb of a murder victim. Two safaris, no tank. The snitch went back to jail, and the taxpayers picked up the bill.

Finally, Rinaldi returned to the Jeep.

"It's farther up."

"How much farther?"

"What am I, a geographer? Look, I'll know the spot when I see it. There was a wooden shed."

"You're repeating yourself, Frog." Claudel looked pointedly at his watch.

"*Sacré bleu!* If you'll quit riding my ass and drive a bit farther you'll get your stiffs."

"You'd better be right, Frog. Or you will be at the center of the biggest cluster fuck of the millennium."

The men climbed back into the Jeep and the procession crept slowly forward. Within twenty yards Rinaldi held up his hands. Then he gripped the seat behind my shoulders and strained forward to peer through the windshield.

"Hold it."

Quickwater braked.

"There. That's it."

Rinaldi pointed to the roofless walls of a small

wooden structure. Most of the shed had fallen in on itself, and fragments of roofing and rotten wood lay strewn around the ground.

Everyone got out. Rinaldi did a three-sixty, hesitated briefly, then set off into the woods at a forty-degree angle from the shed.

Claudel and I followed, picking our way through last year's vines and creepers, and slapping back branches still weeks from budding. The sun was well above the horizon now, and the trees threw long, spiderweb shadows across the soggy ground.

When we caught up to Rinaldi he was standing at the edge of a clearing, hands dangling in front, shoulders rounded like those of a male chimp about to put on a display. The look on his face was not reassuring.

"This place has changed, man. I don't remember so many trees. We used to come out here to light bonfires and get wasted."

"I don't care how you and your friends passed your summers, Frog. You're running out of time here. You're going to be doing twenty-five hard ones and we're all going to read about how they found you with a pipe up your ass on the shower room floor."

I'd never heard Claudel quite so colorful.

Rinaldi's jaw muscles bunched, but he said nothing. Though there had been frost that morning he wore only a black T-shirt and jeans. His arms looked thin and sinewy, and goose bumps puckered the pale flesh.

He turned and walked to the middle of the clearing. On the right the land sloped gently to a small creek. Rinaldi cut through a stand of long-needle pines to the bank, looked in both directions, then headed upstream. Quickwater, Claudel, and I followed. Within twenty yards Rinaldi stopped and waved his scrawny arms at an expanse of bare earth. It lay between the stream and a mound of boulders, and was scattered with branches, plastic containers and cans, and the usual detritus thrown up by seasonal flooding.

"There's your fucking graves."

I looked at his face. It was composed now, the look of uncertainty once again replaced by cocky insolence.

"If that's all you're offering, Frog, that pipe has your name on it." Claudel.

"Don't fuck me over, man. It's been more than ten years. If the broad knows her shit, she'll find them."

As I surveyed the area Rinaldi had indicated, the bully pressed harder on my chest. More than ten years of seasonal flooding. There wouldn't be a single indicator. No depression. No insect activity. No modified vegetation. No stratigraphy. Nothing to hint at an underground cache.

Claudel looked a question at me. Behind him the stream burbled softly. Overhead a crow cawed and another answered.

"If they're here, I'll find them," I said with more confidence than I felt.

The cawing sounded like laughter.

8

By noon we'd cleared vegetation and debris from an area approximately fifty yards by fifty yards, based on Frog's hazy recollection of the grave locations. It turned out he'd never actually seen the bodies, but was going on "reliable information." According to gang lore the victims had been invited for a lawn party, then marched into the woods and shot in the head. Terrific.

I'd marked off a search grid, then set orange plastic stakes along the boundaries at five-foot intervals. Since bodies are rarely stashed below six feet, I'd requested a ground-penetrating radar unit with a 500 MHz antenna, a frequency effective at those depths. It had arrived within the hour.

Working with the radar operator, I'd dug a test pit outside the search area to allow assessment of density, moisture content, layer changes, and other soil conditions. We had refilled the hole, burying in it a length of metal rebar. The operator had then scanned the pit for control data.

He was completing the final tuning of his equipment

when Frog got out of the Jeep and sidled over to me, followed closely by his guard. It was one of several forays he'd made, the sniper-free morning having allayed his anxiety.

"What the fuck is that?" he asked, indicating a set of devices that looked like a contraption from *Back to the Future*. Just then Claudel joined us.

"Frog, you could benefit from some new adjectives. Maybe get one of those calendars that shows you a different word every day."

"Fuck you."

In a way I appreciated the English expletives. They were like sounds of home in a foreign land.

I looked to see if Frog was merely cracking wise, but the pale green eyes suggested a genuine interest. O.K. Where he was going Frog wouldn't be having a lot of scientifically broadening experiences.

"It's a GPR system."

He looked blank.

"Ground-penetrating radar."

I pointed to a terminal plugged into the cigarette lighter of a four-wheel-drive vehicle.

"That's the GPR machine. It evaluates signals sent from an antenna, and produces a pattern on that screen."

I indicated a sledlike structure with an upright handle and a long, thick cable connecting it to the GPR box. "That's the antenna."

"Looks like a lawn mower."

"Yeah." I wondered what Frog knew about lawn care. "When an operator pulls the antenna across the ground it transmits a penetrating signal, then sends data to the GPR machine. The radar machine evaluates the strength and rebound time of the signal."

He looked as if he was with me. Though pretending disinterest, Claudel was also listening.

"If there is something in the soil, the signal is distorted. Its strength is affected by the size of the underground disturbance, and by the electrical properties at the upper and lower boundaries. The depth of the feature determines how long the signal takes to go down and back."

"So this thing can tell you where you've got a stiff?"

"Not a body specifically. But it can tell you there's a subsurface disturbance, and it can provide information about its size and location."

Frog looked blank.

"When you dig a hole and put something in it, the spot is never the same as it was before. The fill may have less density, a different mix, or different electrical properties from the surrounding matrix."

True. But I doubted that would be the case here. Ten years of water seepage has a way of obliterating soil differences.

"And the thing that's been buried, whether it's a cable, unexploded ordnance, or a human body, will not send the same signal as the soil around it."

"Ashes to ashes. What if the corpse has oozed into tomorrow's drinking water?"

Good question, Frog.

"The decomposition of flesh can change the chemical composition and electrical properties of dirt, so even bones and putrefied corpses may show up."

May.

At that moment the radar operator gave a sign indicating he was ready.

"Quickwater, you want to pull the sled?" I shouted.

"I'll do it." Claudel volunteered.

66

"O.K. Get one of the Ident guys to follow you to control the cable. It's not complicated. Start where the operator has the antenna set up just outside the cleared area. When you pass the northernmost line of stakes press the remote button twice. It's on the handle. The signal will set the boundary for that transect. Drag the sled at about two-thirds normal walking pace, keeping your sweeps as straight as possible. Each time you pass an east-west stake, press the button once. When you get to the far end give another double signal to indicate the end of the transect. Then we'll haul the thing back and start a second sweep."

"Why can't we just go back and forth?"

"Because the printouts from adjacent transects won't be comparable if they're done from opposite directions. We'll do the whole area north to south, that's thirty sweeps, then repeat the procedure east to west."

He nodded.

"I'll stay with the operator and watch the screen. If we note a disturbance I'll holler and your partner can stake the spot."

An hour later the search was done and everyone was around the van, unwrapping sandwiches and popping sodas. Twelve blue stakes formed three squares inside the survey grid.

The results were better than I'd hoped. Readings from the third and thirteenth north-south transects showed disturbances with lengths and widths roughly equal. But it was the profile from the eleventh sweep that held my attention. I'd asked for hard copy, which I studied as I ate my bologna and cheese.

The printout showed a grid. The horizontal lines indicated depth, based on our calibration with the

67

control pit, with the ground surface at the top. The vertical lines were dotted, and corresponded to the signals sent by Claudel as each grid stake was crossed.

The pattern just below the ground surface was a wavy but generally flat line. But superimposed over gridline 11 North was a series of bell-shaped curves, one inside the next, like ribs on a skeleton. The profile indicated a disturbance at the intersection of north-south line 11 and east-west line 4. It lay at a depth of approximately five feet.

I switched to profiles of the area taken on the east-west sweeps. Comparing perpendicular transects allowed me to estimate the size and shape of the disturbance. What I saw made my heart pick up a beat.

The anomaly was roughly six feet long and three feet wide. Grave size.

At grave depth.

"This will work?" I hadn't heard Claudel approach.

"We're cookin'."

"Now?"

"Yep."

I finished my Diet Coke and climbed into the Jeep. The van slogged along behind as Quickwater drove toward the 11 North 4 East coordinates. We'd decided that I would dig that location while Claudel and Quickwater investigated the other two disturbances. After I laid a simple grid around each site, they would remove the earth in thin slices, screening every shovelful.

I'd instructed the Carcajou investigators on how to watch for differences in soil color and texture. If they spotted any changes they would holler. Each of us would be aided by personnel from the Section d'Identité

Judiciaire, or SIJ, and section photographers would shoot and video the entire operation.

And that's what we did.

Claudel supervised as his team worked the disturbance at 13 North 5 East, approximately ten feet from mine. Now and then I'd glance over to see him standing above his crew, gesturing instructions or asking about something in the dirt. He'd yet to remove his sports jacket.

After thirty minutes a shovel chinked loudly in Claudel's pit. My head flew up and my stomach tightened. A blade had struck something hard and unyielding.

As Claudel watched, the technicians and I revealed the contour. The object was rusted and caked with mud, but the shape was unmistakable. Claudel's SIJ screener made the call.

"*Tabernac! C'est un Weber.*"

"Eh, Monsieur Claudel, you planning a barbecue? Throw on burgers, bring out the lawn chairs, maybe invite girls?"

"Jean-Guy, tell Luc there's an easier way. They've got these things at the Wal-Mart."

"Yes." Claudel never cracked a smile. "You are so hilarious we may need a body bag because I'm going to die laughing. Now keep digging. We still have to haul this thing out and make sure there aren't any surprises underneath."

Claudel left the grill to his teammates and walked back to 11 North 4 East with me. I resumed troweling at the north end while Claudel stood over my SIJ helper in the south. By two we were down approximately three feet and I'd spotted nothing in the pit or screen to indicate I was nearing a burial.

Then I saw the boot.

It was lying sideways, the heel projecting slightly upward. I used my trowel to clear dirt, widening the area around it. My helper watched briefly, then continued scraping at the far end of the pit. Claudel observed without comment.

Within minutes I'd found the mate. Handful by tedious handful I peeled away dirt until the pair was fully exposed. The leather was wet and badly discolored, the eyelets bent and rusted, but both boots were reasonably intact.

When the footwear was fully exposed I made notes as to level and position, and the photographer captured my find on film. As I pried each boot loose and laid it on a plastic sheet it was obvious that neither contained leg or foot bones.

Not a good sign.

The sky was delft blue, the sun strong. Now and then a breeze teased the branches overhead, tapping them gently against one another. To my right the creek purled softly as it coursed over rocks abandoned by glaciers long ago.

A drop of sweat broke from my hairline and slithered the length of my neck. I pulled my sweatshirt over my head and tossed it on the pine needles bordering our pit. I was uncertain whether my glands had kicked in due to spring warmth or due to the stress I was feeling.

It was always like this at exhumations. The curiosity. The anticipation. The fear of failure. What lies below the next layer? What if it's nothing? What if it's something but I can't get it out undamaged?

I had a desire to grab a spade and tunnel straight down. But strip-mining was not the answer. Tiresome as the process was, I knew proper technique was crucial.

70

Maximum recovery of bones, artifacts, and contextual detail would be important in a case like this, so I plodded on, loosening dirt, then transferring it to buckets for screening. On the edge of my vision I could see the SIJ tech making the same motions, Claudel silent above him. At some point he had removed his jacket.

We saw the white flecks at the same time. Claudel was about to speak when I said, "Hell-o."

He looked at me with raised brows, and I nodded.

"Looks like lime. That usually means there's somebody home."

The flecks gave way to a layer of sticky white ooze, then we found the first skull. It lay faceup, as if the dirt-filled orbits had twisted for one last look at the sky. The photographer shouted the news and the others dropped what they were doing and gathered around our pit.

As the sun moved slowly toward the horizon two skeletons emerged. They lay on their sides, one in a fetal position, the other with arms and legs bent sharply backward. The skulls and the leg and pelvic bones were devoid of flesh and stained the same tea brown as the surrounding soil.

The foot and ankle bones were encased in rotting socks, the torsos covered with shreds of putrefied cloth. The fabric enveloped each arm, clinging to the bones like some scarecrow parody of a human limb. Wire circled the wrists, and I could see zippers and large metal belt buckles nestled among the vertebrae.

By five-thirty my team had fully exposed the remains. Besides the boots, the plastic sheet held a collection of corroded cartridges and isolated teeth recovered during screening. The photographers were

71

shooting stills and videos when Frog talked his guard into another visit.

"*Allô. Bonjour*," he said, tipping the brim of an invisible hat to the skeletons in the pit. Then he turned to me. "Or maybe I should say bone *jour*, for you, lady."

I ignored the bilingual pun.

"Holy shit. Why shirts and socks and nothing else?"

I wasn't in the mood for a lecture.

"That's right," he sniggered, staring into the pit. "They made them go shoeless and carry their shoes. But where the fuck are their pants?"

"Ashes to ashes, remember?" I said curtly.

"Shit to shit is more like it." His voice was tense with excitement, as though the scrambler had been ratcheted up.

I found his callousness irritating. Death hurts. It's as simple that. It hurts those who die, it hurts those who love them, and it hurts those who find them.

"Actually, you've got it backward," I spat. "It's the shit that survives longest. Natural fibers, like cotton Levi's, decompose much sooner than synthetics. Your buddies were into polyester."

"Fuck, do they look gross. Anything else in there with them?" he asked, peering into the grave. His eyes glinted, like those of a rat sitting on a carcass.

"Bad decision about that party, eh?" he snorted.

Yes, I thought. A deadly decision.

I began cleaning the blade of my trowel, using activity to calm myself. Two bodies lay dead at our feet and this little rodent was getting high on it.

I turned to check if the photographers had finished and saw Quickwater walking in my direction.

Great. Make my day, I thought, hoping he was looking for someone else. He wasn't. I watched him approach with as much enthusiasm as I'd have for frostbite.

Quickwater drew close and drilled me with one of his looks, his face rigid as granite. He smelled of male sweat and pine, and I realized he'd worked throughout the afternoon. While others had taken breaks to check the progress at the main burial, Quickwater had stayed at his task. Maybe he just wanted to keep some distance between us. Fine with me.

"There's something you need to see."

There was a stillness about him I found unnerving. I waited for further explanation, but Quickwater merely turned and walked back toward his site, fully confident that I would follow.

Arrogant prick, I thought.

The trees were casting long shadows, and the temperature was falling by the minute. I looked at my watch. Almost six. The bologna and cheese seemed like prehistory.

This better be good, I thought.

I trudged across the cleared area to coordinates 3 North 9 East, the site of the disturbance to which Quickwater's team had been assigned. I was amazed to see they'd dug my entire grid.

The object of Quickwater's concern lay one meter down, left in place as I'd instructed. The team had excavated the rest of the square to a depth of two meters.

"That's it?"

Quickwater nodded.

"Nothing else?"

His expression did not change.

I looked around. They'd obviously been thorough. The screen still rested on its supports, flanked by cones of soggy earth. It looked as if they'd sifted every particle of dirt in the province. My eyes went back to the earthen pedestal and its macabre exhibit.

What they'd discovered made no sense at all.

9

I closed my eyes and listened to cows lowing softly in the distance. Somewhere life was calm, routine, and made sense.

When I raised my lids the bones were still there but made little sense. Dusk was closing in quickly, robbing the landscape of detail, like a slow fade in an old-time movie. We wouldn't finish the recovery that day, so answers would need to wait.

I would not risk destroying evidence by blundering around in the dark. The burials had been here for some time, and they could stay in place a few more hours. We would remove the exposed remains from each grave, but that was all. The site would be secured and work would resume in the morning.

Quickwater was still watching me. I looked around but couldn't see Claudel.

"I need to talk to your partner," I said, turning back toward my site.

Quickwater held up a finger. Then he pulled a cell phone from his jacket, punched in a number, and handed it to me. Claudel answered almost immediately.

"Where are you?"

"Behind a poplar. Should I have requested a bath-room pass?"

Stupid question, Brennan.

"Your partner didn't think two skeletons were enough so he found us a third."

"*Sacré bleu!*"

"Well, it's not exactly a skeleton. From what I can see, bachelor number three consists of a skull and a couple long bones."

"Where's the rest?"

"Very perceptive question, Detective Claudel. That's the source of some confusion on my part, as well."

"What do you want to do?"

"Let's get all the bones out, then shut it down until daylight. St-Basile will have to seal off the property and post a watch at each grave. It shouldn't be too hard to guard the place since it has tighter security than Los Alamos."

"The homeowners aren't going to be thrilled."

"Yeah, well, this isn't how I'd planned to spend my week, either."

It took less than an hour to bag the bones and dispatch them to the morgue. The grill and other physical evidence were tagged and sent to the crime lab. Then I covered the holes with plastic sheets and left them in the care of the St-Basile PD.

Predictably, Quickwater and I returned to town in silence. At home, I tried Ryan's number, but got no response.

"Why, Andy, why?" I whispered, as if he were

there to hear me. "Please don't let this be true."

My evening consisted of a bath, a pizza, and early bed.

Dawn found us all reassembled at the Vipers' picnic ground. The creek still gurgled, the birds still griped, and once again I could see my breath on the morning air. Only two things were different.

Claudel had opted to remain in town to pursue other leads.

Overnight, word of the bodies had leaked to the media, and an invasion force greeted us on our arrival. Cars and vans lined the highway, and reporters assaulted us in English and French. Ignoring them in both languages, we rolled past the cameras and mikes, identified ourselves to the officer on guard, and slipped through the gates.

I reopened each grave and began where I'd left off, starting with the double burial. I excavated to a depth of six feet, but found only a few hand bones and another pair of boots.

I did the same with Quickwater's site, growing more baffled with each scoop of dirt. Aside from the skull and leg bones the pit was completely sterile. No jewelry or clothing remnants. No keys or plastic ID cards. Not a trace of hair or soft tissue. Additional GPR scans produced no evidence of other disturbances in the cleared area.

Another thing was eerie. Though the grave with the two skeletons had been rich with insect remnants, the one at 3 North 9 East produced not a single fossilized larva or pupa casing. I could see no explanation for the difference.

By five we'd refilled the holes and loaded my equipment into the crime scene van. I was tired, dirty, and confused, and the smell of death clung to my hair and clothes. All I wanted to do was go home and spend an hour with soap and water.

As Quickwater exited the gates, a TV crew surrounded the Jeep, refusing to allow us to pass. We slowed to a stop and a middle-aged man with lacquered hair and perfect teeth circled to my side and tapped on the glass. Behind him a cameraman trained his lens on my face.

Not in the mood for diplomacy, I lowered the window, leaned out, and told them in graphic terms to clear the way. The camera light went on and the reporter began to pepper me with shotgun questions. I made suggestions as to places for storage of their live-eye equipment, and destinations they might enjoy. Then, rolling my eyes, I retracted my head and hit the button. Quickwater gunned the engine and we shot away. I turned to see the reporter standing in the road, microphone still clutched in his hand, his flawless features wide with surprise.

I settled back and closed my eyes, knowing there would be no conversation from Quickwater. It was just as well. Questions swirled in my brain, twisting and eddying like the waters of a swollen creek.

Who was this third victim? How had he died? Those answers I hoped to find in the lab.

When had the death occurred? How had part of his cadaver ended up in a clandestine grave at the Vipers' clubhouse? Those queries I figured the Vipers should field.

Most perplexing was the question of the absent body parts. Where was the rest of the skeleton? As I'd removed and packaged the bones for transport I'd watched closely for signs of animal damage. Bears, wolves, coyotes, and other predators will cheerfully dine on human corpses if given the opportunity. Ditto for the family dog or cat.

I saw nothing to indicate scavengers had absconded with the missing parts. There were no gnawed joints or shafts, no tooth scratches or puncture wounds. Nor had I seen any saw or knife marks to suggest the body had been dismembered.

So where was the rest of the deceased?

I planned Wednesday night as a modified replay of Tuesday. Bath. Microwave. Pat Conroy. Bed. Except for stage one, that's not how it went.

I'd just toweled off and slipped into a green flannel nightshirt when the phone rang. Birdie trailed me to the living room.

"*Mon Dieu*, your face is becoming better known than mine."

It was definitely not what I needed to hear. Having done theater and television for more than twenty years, Isabelle was one of the best-loved performers in Quebec. Wherever she went she was recognized.

"I made the six o'clock news," I guessed.

"An Oscar-winning performance, charged with raw anger and burning with the passion of—"

"How bad was it?"

"Your hair looked good."

"Did they identify me?"

"*Mais oui, Docteur Brennan.*"

Damn. When I dropped to the couch Birdie settled into my lap, anticipating a long conversation.

"Was the tape edited?"

"Not a thing. Tempe, I'm pretty good at reading lips. Where did you learn those words?"

79

I groaned, recalling some of my more colorful suggestions about placement of the cameras and mikes.

"But that's not why I called. I want you to come to supper on Saturday. I'm having a few friends over and I think you need some social therapy, time away from these dreadful bikers and that Ryan thing."

That Ryan thing.

"Isabelle, I don't think I'd be very good company right now. I—"

"Tempe, I am not taking no for an answer. And I want you to wear pearls and perfume and get all dressed up. It will improve your whole outlook."

"Isabelle. Tell me you're not trying another fix up."

For a moment I listened to silence. Then, "This type of work you do, Tempe, it makes you too suspicious. I told you. It will just be some of my friends. Besides, I have a surprise for you."

Oh no.

"What?"

"If I tell you it won't be a surprise."

"Tell me anyway."

"*Bon.* There's someone I want you to meet. And I know he would love to meet you. Well, actually you've met, but not formally. This man is not the least bit interested in a romantic relationship. Trust me."

Over the past two years I'd met many of Isabelle's friends, most of whom were involved in the arts. Some were boring, others captivating. Many were gay. All were unique in one way or another. She was right. A night of frivolity would do me good.

"O.K. What can I bring?"

"Nothing. Just wear your pumps and be here at seven."

After unturbaning and combing my hair, I placed a

seafood dinner in the microwave. I was programming the time when my doorbell sounded.

Ryan, I hoped suddenly, walking to the hall. It was all a mistake. But if it wasn't, did I really want to see him? Did I want to know where he'd been, what he'd say?

Yes. Desperately.

The self-examination proved unnecessary since the security monitor showed Jean Bertrand, not his partner, standing in the outer vestibule. I buzzed him into the building, then went to the bedroom for socks and a robe. When he stepped inside the condo, he hesitated, as if trying to compose himself. After an awkward moment he extended his hand. It felt cold when I shook it.

"Hello, Tempe. Sorry to surprise you like this."

Apparently surprising me was a hot thing these days. I nodded.

His face was drawn, and a dark crescent underscored each eye. Normally an impeccable dresser, he wore faded jeans tonight and a rumpled suede jacket. He started to speak again but I cut him off with a suggestion we move to the living room. He chose the sofa, and I curled into the chair opposite.

Bertrand studied me, his face tense with emotions I couldn't read. In the kitchen the microwave hummed warmth into my whitefish, carrots, and curried rice.

This is your party, I thought, refusing to break the silence. Finally.

"About Ryan."

"Yes."

"I got your calls, but I just couldn't talk about it then."

"What exactly is 'it'?"

"He's out on bail, but he's been charged wi—"

"I know the charges."

81

"Don't be angry at me. I had no idea where you stood in all this."

"For God's sake, Bertrand, how many years have you known me?"

"I knew Ryan a hell of a lot longer!" he snapped. "Evidently, I'm a lousy judge of character."

"Neither of us seems to excel in that area."

I hated myself for being so cold, but Bertrand's failure to call had hurt. When I had needed information important to me he'd blown me off like I was a drunk on the street with his hand out.

"Look, I don't know what to tell you. This thing's wrapped tighter than a deb with new tits. I hear that when they're finished with Ryan he won't qualify for a paper route."

"It's that bad?" I watched my fingers work the fringe on a throw pillow.

"They've got enough to nail him into tomorrow."

"What is it they've got?"

"When they tossed his apartment they found enough methamphetamine to fry a third world nation and over ten thousand dollars' worth of stolen parkas."

"Parkas?"

"Yeah. Those Kanuk things everyone's pissing their pants to own."

"And?" I'd twisted the fringe so tightly it sent pain up my hand and into my wrist.

"And witnesses, videos, marked bills, and a trail of stink leading right straight to the center of the dung heap."

Bertrand's voice betrayed his emotion. He took a deep breath.

"There's more. A shitload more. But I can't talk about it. Please understand, Tempe. Look, I'm sorry I

82

left you hanging. It took me a while to work through this myself. I just didn't believe it, but—"

He broke off, afraid to trust his own voice.

"I guess the guy never quite left his past behind."

As a college student Ryan had gotten into booze and pills, eventually dropping the academic life for life on the edge. A knife-wielding cokehead had nearly killed him, and the wild child reversed course, became a cop, and rose to the rank of lieutenant-detective. I knew all that. But still . . .

"I learned that someone ratted Ryan out, and for all I knew it could have been you. But it's not important now. The sonovabitch is dirty and he deserves what's coming down."

For a very long time neither of us spoke. I could feel Bertrand's stare, but refused to meet it or say a word. The microwave beeped, then shut off. Silence. Finally, I asked.

"Do you really think he did it?" My cheeks felt hot and my chest burned below my sternum.

"For the past few days I've done nothing but chase down leads to show that he *didn't* do it. Anything. Anyone. All I wanted was one tiny hint of doubt."

When he gestured with thumb and index finger, I could see a tiny tremor in his hand.

"It wasn't there, Tempe." He ran a hand over his face. "But it doesn't matter anymore."

"It does matter. It's the only thing that matters."

"At first I thought, no way. Not Andrew Ryan. Then I learned the case against him."

He took another deep breath.

"Look, Tempe, I'm sorry. I'm so sorry for this whole goddam mess I'm not sure who I am anymore or where the world's going. And I'm not sure if it's worth the price of a ticket to ride."

When I looked up Bertrand's face was filled with pain, and I knew exactly what he was feeling. He was trying not to despise his partner for succumbing to the greed, all the while hating him for the deep, cold emptiness his betrayal had created.

Bertrand promised to let me know if he learned anything. When he left I trashed the fish and cried myself to sleep.

10

Thursday I put on a dark blue suit and drove to Our Lady of the Angels. The morning was blustery, the sun appearing only infrequently among the heavy clouds scudding across the sky.

I parked and threaded through the usual collection of gawkers, journalists, and cops. No sign of Charbonneau, Claudel, or Quickwater.

Of the trickle of mourners solemnly climbing the steps, most were black. Whites arrived in couples or groups, each with at least one child in tow. Probably Emily Anne's classmates and their families.

Near the entrance, a wind gust tore the hat from the head of an old woman to my right. One gnarled hand flew to her head while the other fought the skirt whipping round her legs.

I darted forward, trapped the hat against the church wall, and handed it to the woman. She clutched it to her bony chest and gave a small smile. Her wrinkled brown face reminded me of the crab-apple dolls crafted by ladies in the Smoky Mountains.

"You be a frien' of Emily Anne?" the old woman asked in a crackly voice.

"Yes, ma'am." I didn't want to explain my involvement.

"She my gran'chile."

"I am so sorry for your loss."

"I got twenty-two gran'children, but that Emily Anne be somet'ing special. That chile do everyt'ing. She writes her letters, she does dance ballet, she does swim, she does skate on ice. I t'inking that girl be even smarter than her mama."

"She was a beautiful little girl."

"Maybe that be why God take her up."

I watched Emily Anne's grandmother totter on, remembering those same words from a long time ago. A slumbering ache stirred in my chest, and I steeled myself for what was to come.

Inside, the church was cool and smelled of incense and wax and wood polish. Light filtered through stained glass, casting a pastel softness over everything.

The pews were packed in front, with a scattering of attendees in the middle. I slipped into a back row, folded my hands, and tried to concentrate on the present. Already my skin itched and my palms felt sweaty. As I looked around, the organist finished one requiem and began another.

A miniature white casket sat below the altar, heaped with flowers and flanked by candles at either end. Balloons bobbed on strings attached to the coffin's handles. The brightly colored spheres looked jarringly out of sync with the scene.

In the front pew I could see two small heads, a larger figure between them. Mrs Toussaint was bent forward, a handkerchief clutched to her mouth. As I watched, her

86

shoulders began to heave, and a tiny hand rose and gently rubbed her upper arm.

The dormant ache within me awoke fully, and I was back at St Barnabas parish. Father Morrison was at the pulpit and my little brother lay in his own tiny coffin.

My mother's sobs were terrible, and I reached up to comfort her. She did not acknowledge my touch, just held little Harriet to her chest and cried onto her head. Feeling utterly helpless, I watched my sister's corn-silk hair grow damp with my mother's tears.

If I had been given a box of crayons and asked to draw my world at six, I would have chosen a single color. Black.

I'd been powerless to save Kevin, to stop the leukemia devastating his tiny body. He was my most treasured gift, my Christmas brother, and I adored him. I had prayed and prayed, but I could do nothing to prevent his death. Or to make my mother smile. I had begun to wonder if I were evil, because my prayers were of no effect.

Almost four decades, and the pain of Kevin's death still lingered. The sights and sounds and smells of a funeral Mass never failed to reopen that wound, allowing the buried grief to ooze into my conscious thought.

I moved my eyes from the Toussaint family and scanned the crowd. Charbonneau had concealed himself in the shadow of a confessional booth, but I recognized no one else.

At that moment the priest entered and crossed himself. He looked young, athletic, and nervous. More like a tennis player approaching a match than a priest approaching a funeral service. We all stood.

As I went through the familiar motions, my skin felt

flushed, my heart beat faster than it should have. I tried to concentrate, but my mind resisted. Images bled into my brain, taking me back to that time in my childhood.

An enormous woman took the pulpit to the right of the altar. Her skin was the color of mahogany, her hair braided atop her head. The woman's cheeks glistened as she sang "Amazing Grace." I remembered her from the newspaper photo.

Then, the priest spoke of childhood innocence. Relatives praised Emily Anne's sunny disposition, her love of family. An uncle mentioned her passion for waffles. Her teacher described an enthusiastic student, and read the essay that had won a prize. A classmate recited an original poem.

More hymns. Communion. The faithful filed up, returned to their seats. Stifled sobs. Incense. The blessing of the coffin. Soft wailing from Mrs Toussaint.

Finally, the priest turned and asked Emily Anne's sisters and classmates to join him, then seated himself on the altar steps. There was a moment of absolute stillness, followed by whispered commands and parental nudging. One by one children emerged from the pews and walked timidly toward the altar.

What the priest said was not original. Emily Anne is in heaven with God. She has been reunited with her father. One day her mother and sisters will join her, as will everyone present.

What the young priest did next *was* original. He told the children that Emily Anne was happy, and that we should celebrate with her. He signaled his servers, who disappeared into the vestry, and returned with huge bunches of balloons.

"These balloons are filled with helium," explained the priest. "That makes them fly. I want you each to take one, and we will all walk out with Emily Anne. We will say a good-bye prayer, then release our balloons to rise to heaven. Emily Anne will see them and know that we love her."

He looked at the solemn little faces.

"Is that a good idea?"

Every head nodded.

The priest rose, disentangled strings, placed a balloon in each small hand, and led the children down the steps. The organist began Schubert's "*Ave Maria.*"

The pallbearers came forward, lifted the casket, and the procession moved toward the door, the pews emptying in its wake. As the line passed, I slipped in at the end.

The mourners followed the coffin outside then circled around, children on the inside, adults forming an outer ring. Mrs Toussaint stood behind her daughters, supported by the singer.

I held back on the steps. The overcast had broken, leaving a sky filled with tumbling white clouds. As I watched balloons rise toward them, I felt a grief as sharp as anything I'd felt in my life.

I lingered a moment, then descended slowly, wiping tears from my cheeks, and reaffirming the vow I'd made on the day of Emily Anne's death.

I would find these indiscriminate butchers and put them where they could never kill another child. I could not restore the daughter but I would provide this small comfort for the mother.

Leaving Emily Anne to those who loved her, I drove toward Parthenais, in a mood to lose myself in work.

At the lab, the Carcajou investigators already had names

for the skeletons from St-Basile. Félix Martineau, age twenty-seven, and Robert Gately, age thirty-nine, rode with the Tarantulas, a now defunct OMC, but active in Montreal in the seventies and eighties. Gately was a full patch member, Martineau a prospect.

On the evening of August 24, 1987, the two had left Gately's apartment on rue Hochelaga heading for a party. Gately's ole lady did not know the name or address of the host. Neither man was seen again.

I spent the day with the bones from the double burial, sorting them into individuals and determining age, sex, race, and height. Cranial and pelvic shape confirmed both victims were male. The differences in age and height made the task of individuation considerably easier than with the Vaillancourt brothers.

As soon as I'd finished with the skulls and jaws I'd given them to Marc Bergeron for odontological analysis. I figured his job would be easy too, since both men had obvious dental work.

The taller victim had a well-healed fracture of the collarbone. I was photographing the injury when Bergeron entered my lab Friday morning. The dentist was one of the oddest-looking men I'd ever met, with wild, dandelion hair and a daddy-longlegs build. It was impossible to guess his age, and no one at the lab seemed to know.

Bergeron waited until I'd snapped the shot then confirmed the identifications as positive.

"How did you get the records so quickly?"

"Two very cooperative dentists. And, fortunately for me, the deceased had a commitment to oral health. At least Gately did. Bad teeth, lots of restorations. Martineau was less fastidious, but there were some peculiarities that made him a cinch. The big bad biker

90

was walking around with four baby teeth in his mouth. That's pretty rare for someone his age."

I turned off the lights on the copy stand.

"Have you started on the third victim?" Bergeron asked.

"Not yet, but I can finish this later. Shall we take a look?"

I'd been wanting to look at the third set of bones all morning and Bergeron provided a good excuse.

"You bet."

I returned the collarbone to the skeleton on the left side of my worktable.

"Who's who?" I asked, gesturing at the bones.

Bergeron went to his tray and checked the digits on each occipital bone, then those on the small cards I'd set beside the skeletons, and positioned the skulls accordingly. He swept a bony arm over the victim with the broken clavicle.

"Monsieur Martineau."

Then over the gentleman on his right.

"And Mr Gately."

"Was Gately an Anglophone?"

"I assume so since his dentist doesn't speak a word of French."

"Not too many of those among *les motards*."

"None that I know of," Bergeron agreed.

"Will you give the good news to Quickwater and Claudel?"

"I've already made the call."

I went to the storage shelves and pulled the box containing the third St-Basile victim. Since the remains were coated with dirt, I placed a screen in the sink, set them in it, and ran warm water over them.

The long bones cleaned easily, so I laid them on the

drainboard and began brushing mud from the outside of the skull. Its weight told me that the cranial interior was packed solid. When the facial features were clear I inverted the skull and let the tap water run over the base. Then I crossed to my desk to fill out a case identification card.

When I returned to the sink Bergeron held the skull in his hands, turning it faceup, then rotating it for a lateral view. He stared at the features a long time then said, "Oh my."

When he handed me the cranium I repeated his movements, then echoed his thought.

"Oh my."

11

One look and I knew I'd been wrong. The smooth forehead and occiput, slender cheekbones, and small mastoid processes told me that bachelor number three was clearly of my own gender.

I got my calipers and took a measurement from one of the bones that lay on the drainboard. The femoral head is a ball-like structure that fits into a socket in the pelvis to form the hip joint. This one had a diameter of only thirty-nine millimeters, placing it squarely in the female range.

And the victim had been young. I could see a jagged line across the top of the ball, indicating that fusion of the growth cap was incomplete at the time of death.

I returned to the cranium. Squiggly lines separated all the bones. I rotated the skull for a view of the base. Just in front of the foramen magnum, the hole through which the spinal cord leaves the brain, there was a gap between the sphenoid and occipital bones.

I showed Bergeron the open suture.

"She was just a kid," I said. "Probably in her teens."

He made a comment, but I didn't hear. My attention had been drawn to an irregularity on the right parietal bone. Cautiously, I ran my fingers over it. Yes, there was something there.

Taking care to cause no damage, I held the skull under the faucet and teased away dirt with a soft-bristle toothbrush. Bergeron watched as the defect came into focus. It took only moments.

What I'd spotted was a small round hole, slightly above and behind the ear opening. I estimated its diameter at approximately one centimeter.

"Gunshot wound?" Bergeron suggested.

"Maybe. No. I don't think so."

Though the proper size for a small-caliber projectile, the perforation didn't look like a bullet entrance. Its border was smooth and rounded, like the inside of a doughnut hole.

"Then what?"

"I'm not sure. Maybe some type of congenital defect. Maybe an abscess. I'll know better when I empty the skull and get a look at the endocranial surface. I'll also need X rays to see what's going on inside the bone."

Bergeron looked at his watch.

"Let me know when you've finished so I can shoot some bite-wings on this one. I didn't see any restorations, but I might spot something on the X rays. The right canine has an odd alignment which will be useful, but I'd prefer having the lower jaw."

"I'll work harder next time."

"Not necessary." He laughed.

When Bergeron left I set the skull upside down in a rubber ring and adjusted the water so it ran gently into the foramen magnum. Then I went back to

94

photographing Gately and Martineau, documenting skeletal features relevant to their identifications. I also took multiple shots of the bullet holes in the back of each man's head.

Periodically I checked the unknown female's skull, pouring off muck as the water loosened it. Just before noon, as I was draining sediment, something broke free and tapped against the cranial interior. I placed the skull back on the ring and slipped my fingers inside.

The object felt long and thin. I tried to dislodge it, but the thing had a tail of some sort still embedded in the mud. Barely able to contain my curiosity, I adjusted the tap and went back to the Gately report.

By 1 P.M. the object floated free, but the trailer was still firmly cemented. Impatient, I allowed the sink to fill, immersed the skull, and went downstairs to the cafeteria.

When I returned from lunch the soaking had liquefied the last of the dirt, and I was able to pour it off easily. Holding my breath, I inserted my fingers and delicately manipulated the object free.

The device was less than four inches long, and consisted of a length of tubing with a valve at one end. I cleaned it and placed it on a tray. Certain of its importance, but unsure as to what it was, I washed my hands and went in search of a pathologist.

According to the duty board, LaManche was at a meeting of the committee on infant mortality. Marcel Morin was at his desk.

He looked up when I tapped on the door.

"Got a minute?"

"But of course." His French was warm and lyrical, reflecting the Haiti of his boyhood. I entered the office and placed the tray in front of him.

"Ah. A surgical implant." His eyebrows rose behind

rimless glasses. They were graying, like the tightly cropped frizz of hair retreating backward on his scalp.

"I thought so. Can you tell me more about it?"

He lifted both palms. "Not much. It looks like a ventricular shunt, but I'm not a neurosurgeon. You might want to talk to Carolyn Russell. She's done some neuro consults for us."

He flipped through his Rolodex, jotted down a number, and handed it to me, saying, "She's at the MNI."

I thanked him, went to my office, and dialed the Montreal Neurological Institute. Dr Russell was in a meeting, so I left a message. I'd just hung up when the phone rang. It was Claudel.

"You've talked to Bergeron?" he asked.

"He just left."

"So two make the jump from the list of missing to the list of dead."

I waited for him to go on, but he didn't.

"And?"

A Claudel pause, then, "We've started making calls, but no one knows a thing. Not surprising, given the fact that more than a decade has passed and these people aren't geographically stable. Of course they wouldn't tell us spit if we'd hauled their grandmothers out of that hole."

"What about Rinaldi?"

"Frog's sticking to his story. He knew what he knew by word of mouth. According to club lore Gately and Martineau went to a party and walked right in on their own funeral."

"In stocking feet."

"Right. These fellows tend to underdress. But Frog wasn't there when the hit went down. It was probably his night for charity work. What about the third guy?"

"The third guy is a girl."

"A girl."

"Yes. What does Frog know about her?"

"Not a thing. But Frog would give nothing up if there wasn't a prize in it for him. What can you tell me about her?"

"She was a white female in her mid to late teens."

"She was that young?"

"Yes."

I could hear traffic in the background and figured Claudel was calling from the road.

"I'll get a list of missing teenage girls. What time frame?"

"Go back ten years."

"Why ten years?"

"I'd say the victim's been dead at least two years, but with what we recovered I can't really pinpoint an upper limit. I have a feeling this was a secondary burial."

"What does that mean?"

"I think she was buried somewhere else, then dug up and moved to the place we found her."

"Why?"

"Another perceptive question, Detective Claudel."

I told him about the surgical implant.

"What does *that* mean?"

"When I find out I'll let you know."

I'd hardly replaced the receiver when the phone rang again. Carolyn Russell could see me at three. I looked at my watch. If the parking gods smiled I could make it.

I wrote the case number on the lid of a plastic specimen container and sealed the implant inside. Pausing only to tell Bergeron that he could have the girl's skull, I hurried to my car and raced across town.

The Royal Victoria Hospital was built before the turn of the century. A sprawling gray stone complex, it lies in the heart of Montreal, looming over the McGill campus like a medieval castle on a Tuscan hillside.

At the Peel end is the Allan Memorial Institute, infamous for CIA drug experiments conducted there in the late fifties. The Montreal Neurological Institute is located to the east of the Royal Vic, across rue Université. Teaching and research units of McGill University, the MNI, the Neurological Hospital, and the new Brain Tumor Research Institute sit haunch to jowl with the football stadium, a testimonial in mortar and brick to the priorities of the modern university.

The Neuro, as the research institute and hospital are known, dates to the thirties, the brainchild of Wilder Penfield. Though a brilliant scientist and neurosurgeon, Dr Penfield was not a visionary in traffic control. Parking is a nightmare.

Following Dr Russell's suggestion, I drove onto the grounds of the Royal Vic, forked over ten dollars, and began cruising the lot. I was on my third pass when I spotted brake lights. An Audi pulled out and I shot forward and into the space, thus avoiding the necessity of tuning to FM 88.5 for a parking update. My watch said two fifty-five.

I arrived at Russell's office sweaty and panting from my dash down avenue des Pins and my trek through the hospital. It had begun to mist, and my bangs lay damp and limp across my forehead. When the doctor looked up, an expression of doubt crossed her face.

I introduced myself and she rose and held out a hand. Her hair was gray, cut short and swept to the side. Her face was deeply creased, but her grip was as strong as that of any man. I guessed she was somewhere in her sixties.

"Sorry I'm late. I had a little trouble finding you." That was an understatement.

"Yes, this building is confusing. Please sit down," she said in English, gesturing at a chair opposite her desk.

"I had no idea this place was so large," I said, seating myself.

"Oh yes. The MNI is engaged in an enormous range of activities."

"I know the institute is world famous for its epilepsy research." I slipped off my jacket.

"Yes, more epilepsy surgeries are performed at our hospital than at any other center in the world. The surgical technique of cortical resection was pioneered at this institution. Studies in the mapping of cerebral function began with epilepsy patients here more than sixty years ago. It was that work that paved the way for the MRI and PET brain mapping going on today."

"I'm familiar with Magnetic Resonance Imaging but what is PET?"

"Positron Emission Tomography. Like MRI, it's a technique used to image brain structure and physiology. Our McConnell Brain Imaging Centre is rated as one of the world's leading facilities."

"What other research do you do?"

"A tremendous amount of groundbreaking work has emanated from the MNI. The development of electro-encephalography, the concept of focal and generalized epilepsies, new methods of frameless stereotactic surgery, contributions to postglandin biochemistry in the nervous system, localization of dystrophin skeletal muscle. I could go on and on."

99

I was certain she could. Dr Russell was obviously proud of her employer. I smiled encouragement, though I understood only part of what she had listed.

She leaned back and laughed. "I'm sure you are not here for a lecture on the Neuro."

"No, but it's fascinating. I wish I had more time. But I know you're very busy and I don't want to take up any more of your day than necessary."

I took the container from my purse and handed it to her. She looked at it, then unscrewed the cap and slid the implant onto a piece of paper on the blotter of her desk.

"This is an old one," she said, turning it over with a pencil. "I don't think they've made this model for years."

"What is it?"

"It's a ventriculo-peritoneal shunt. They're implanted for the treatment of hydrocephalus."

"Hydrocephalus?" I knew the term, but was surprised to hear her say it. What other misfortunes would I learn about this child?

"It's commonly known as 'water on the brain,' but that's not really accurate, although that's a literal translation from the Greek, *hydro* being water, and *cephalus* being head. Cerebral spinal fluid is constantly produced in spaces in the brain called ventricles. Normally it circulates through the four ventricles, and flows over the brain's surface and down the spinal cord. Eventually the CSF is absorbed into the bloodstream, and the amount of fluid and pressure in the ventricles stays within acceptable limits.

"But if drainage is blocked, fluid will accumulate, causing the ventricles to swell and press on the surrounding tissue."

"So hydrocephalus refers to an imbalance in the

100

amount of CSF produced and the rate at which it drains from the ventricles."

"Exactly."

"And, as the CSF builds up, it causes the ventricles to enlarge and the pressure inside the head to increase."

"You've got it. Hydrocephalus can be acquired or congenital, which is not to say hereditary. The term simply means the condition is present at birth."

"I found the shunt in a normal-looking skull. Doesn't hydrocephalus result in increased head size?"

"Only in infants, and only if left untreated. As you know, with older children and adults the bones of the skull are already formed."

"What causes it?"

"There are lots of reasons for inadequate CSF drainage. Prematurity puts an infant at high risk. And most babies with spina bifida have hydrocephalus."

"Spina bifida involves a neural tube defect?"

"Yes. The problem occurs during the first four weeks of gestation, often before the mother knows she's pregnant. The embryo's neural tube, which develops into the brain, spinal cord, and vertebral column, fails to form properly, leading to varying degrees of permanent damage."

"How common is it?"

"Entirely too common. It's estimated that spina bifida affects one in every thousand babies born in the United States, and about one in seven hundred and fifty born in Canada."

"I recovered no vertebrae, so I have no way to know if my young lady had spina bifida."

Russell nodded in agreement, then continued her explanation.

"There are many other causes of hydrocephalus

besides spina bifida." She ticked them off on her fingers. "It can result from brain hemorrhage. The inflammation and debris resulting from brain infections, such as meningitis, can block drainage pathways. Tumors can cause compression and swelling of brain tissues and result in poor drainage. So can certain types of cysts. And hydrocephalus can be familial."

"It can be inherited?"

"Yes. Though that's rare."

"So where does the shunt come in?"

"There is no way to cure or prevent hydrocephalus. For the past forty years the most effective treatment has been the surgical insertion of a shunt. The one you've brought is a bit outdated, but it's really pretty typical.

"Most shunts are just flexible tubes placed into the ventricles to divert the flow of CSF. They consist of a system of tubes with a valve to control the rate of drainage and to prevent back flow. The early ones diverted the accumulated CSF into a vein in the neck, then into the right atrium of the heart. Those are called ventriculo-atrial, or VA shunts. Some VA shunts are still used, but there are problems associated with them, including infection, and, though rare, heart failure due to blockage of blood vessels within the lungs by particles of blood clot flaking off the shunt's catheter tip. Most shunts now drain into the peritoneal cavity. They're called VP shunts."

She indicated the device I'd pulled from the skull.

"This is a VP shunt. In the living patient you would have been able to feel the bottom tube running under the skin that overlies the ribs. That part of the device is missing."

I waited for her to go on.

"The peritoneal cavity is large and can usually handle

102

any amount of fluid delivered by the shunt. Another advantage of draining into the abdomen is that the rhythmic contractions of the intestinal organs move the tip of the catheter around. That motion prevents its becoming blocked or sequestered in scar tissue."

"When do these things go in?"

"As soon as hydrocephalus is diagnosed. As much as thirty-six inches of tubing can be placed in the abdomen of a neonate. As the child grows, the tubing unwinds to accommodate the increased length of the torso."

"I found a small hole in the skull, near the parieto-temporal junction."

"That's a burr hole. It's drilled during surgery to insert the upper end of the shunt into the brain. They're usually made behind the hairline, either at the top of the head, behind the ear, or in the back."

Russell's eyes flicked to a round metal clock on her desk, then back to mine. I was anxious to learn what difficulties might be caused by hydrocephaly, but knew the woman's time was limited. That research would be up to me.

I gathered my jacket and she returned the shunt to its jar, curling the paper and allowing the device to slide gently into place. We rose simultaneously and I thanked her for her help.

"Do you have any idea who your young lady is?" she asked.

"Not yet."

"Would you like me to send you some reading material on hydrocephalus? There are problems associated with the condition that you might find helpful."

"Yes, very much. Thank you."

12

I left the Neuro and went directly to Carcajou head-quarters for the second of Roy's review sessions. The meeting was already in progress, so I slipped into a back seat, my brain still processing what I'd learned from Carolyn Russell. Our conversation had raised as many questions as it had answered.

How had the hydrocephaly affected my unknown girl? Had she been sickly? Disabled? Retarded? How did a teenager with that condition end up buried near a biker headquarters? Was she a willing participant, or another innocent, like Emily Anne Toussaint?

This time Roy was using transparencies, and a bulleted list filled the screen. I forced myself to focus.

"Outlaw motorcycle clubs are characterized by a number of common elements. Most OMCs are organized according to the Hells Angels model. We'll come back and look at that structure in some detail."

He indicated the second item.

"All clubs have membership which is very selective,

and 'prospects' or 'strikers' are required to prove themselves to earn their colors."

He moved down the list.

"The colors, or club patch, are the member's most valued possession. Not everyone wears colors, however. Individuals who are useful to the gang are allowed to interact as associates without actually joining.

"The primary focus of an OMC is criminal activity. Each club has rules that condone violence to further the interests of the club and its members. Intelligence gathering is intensive, including the monitoring of other gangs and of law enforcement personnel."

Roy pointed his pen at the last item on the list.

"The clubhouse, which is often strongly fortified and elaborately outfitted, is the meeting place for club activities."

I thought of the Vipers' house in St-Basile, and wondered what activities could have included a sixteen-year-old girl with hydrocephaly.

Roy removed the transparency and replaced it with another, this one a tree titled "Political Structure of an OMC: National."

Roy explained the hierarchy, starting at the bottom.

"The basic element of the OMC structure is the chapter. An independent outlaw motorcycle club becomes part of a larger organization, such as the Hells Angels, only after a charter has been approved by vote of the national membership. This involves a long process that we can discuss later if we have time.

"Each chapter operates in a specific local area and maintains a certain degree of autonomy, but must live by the rules set out by the organization. These rules, either in the form of bylaws or a constitution, define the rights and obligations of the members and the gang."

Roy slid a new transparency onto the projector. This chart was labeled "Political Structure of an OMC: Chapter."

"Each chapter has its own controlling body, or executive, elected by the members. Typically there's a president, vice president, secretary-treasurer, and sergeant at arms. These are the guys responsible for maintaining order within and peace outside the group."

"Guess none of our local morons will make the Nobel short list this year." Kuricek was up to form.

Roy waved down the laughter.

"There's also an elected road captain who takes charge of the runs. Then there are the rank-and-file members—"

"And he does mean rank." Kuricek held his nose.

"—who have a say in matters affecting the group, but the president makes the final decisions. Some of the larger clubs also have a security officer whose duty it is to keep up-to-date information on rival gangs, reporters, lawyers, judges, public officials, witnesses, and, of course, on yours truly."

Roy swept his arm across the room.

"What kind of information?"

"Personal, financial, family members, girlfriends, boyfriends, phone numbers, birth dates, addresses, vehicle descriptions, license plates, places of employment, daily habits, you name it, these guys get it. Their photo collections make the National Portrait Gallery look sparse. If there's an intended victim, his dossier may include tips on the best places to kill him."

"*Merde!*"

"*Esti!*"

Roy worked his pen from left to right across three boxes on the next to lowest line of the diagram.

"At the bottom of the chapter hierarchy are the prospects, the hang-arounds, and the women."

Roy pointed to the box marked "Probationary Member."

"The 'prospect' or 'striker' must be nominated by a full patch member. He does all the shitwork around the clubhouse and during runs. Prospects can't vote and they can't attend church."

"Church?" Today the ponytailed investigator wore a silver skull in his ear.

"The mandatory weekly chapter meeting."

"How long does it take to get in?"

"The prospect period averages six months to one year. You can spot these guys because they wear only the bottom rocker of the patch."

"Which gives the chapter location." Ponytail.

"*C'est ça.* There are several pages showing club colors in the manuals I gave you. Some of them are true artistic marvels."

Roy's pen moved sideways to the box marked "Associates."

"A hang-around must also be sponsored by a full patch member. Some go on to prospect, others never do. Hang-arounds do all kinds of menial jobs, and act as a support structure for the club in the community. They are excluded from all club business."

Two boxes hung from the one at the far right marked "Female Associates."

"Women are at the lowest level of the hierarchy and fall into one of two categories. The ole ladies are wives, either common-law or legal, and are off-limits to other gang members, except by invitation. The club 'mamas' or 'sheep' are a different story. How shall I put it?" He raised eyebrows and shoulders. "They mingle freely."

107

"Warm-hearted ladies, all." Kuricek.

"Very. Mamas are fair game to any color-wearing member. While the ole ladies enjoy a certain degree of protection, have no doubt about it, outlaw motorcycle gangs are male-dominated and highly chauvinistic. Women are bought, sold, and swapped like hardware."

"The biker's idea of women's lib is to take the cuffs off after he's through. Maybe." Kuricek.

"That's pretty close. Women are definitely used and abused." Roy.

"Used how?" I asked.

"Aside from sex, there's what we might call wage sharing. They get the women into exotic dancing, drink hustling, street-level drug trafficking, prostitution, then rake back the earnings. One hooker from Halifax claimed she had to turn over forty percent of her take to the Hells Angel who pimped for her."

"How do they find these women?" I felt a knot forming in my stomach.

"The usual. They pick them up in bars, hitchhiking, runaways."

"Wanna ride my Harley, sweet thing?" Kuricek.

I pictured the skull and shunt.

"Amazingly, there's never a shortage," Roy continued. "But don't get me wrong. While many are victimized, some held against their wills, a good number of these ladies embrace the lifestyle with gusto. Macho men, drugs, alcohol, guns, round-the-mountain sex. It's a wild ride and they go along gladly.

"The women also make themselves useful in ways not strictly sexual or economic. Often it's the ladies who carry concealed drugs or weapons, and they're very good at ditching when a bust comes down. Some make very effective spies. They hire on with government

108

agencies, the phone company, records offices, any place they might have access to useful information. Some ole ladies have guns or property registered in their names, either because hubby is prohibited, or to protect his assets from seizure by the government."

Roy glanced at his watch.

"On that note, I think we'll call it a day. Some folks have just joined us from the CUM, so I may hold one more of these sessions."

CUM. Communauté Urbaine de Montréal Police. I wondered why Claudel had not been present at today's meeting.

"If so, I'll post the date."

As I drove to the lab my thoughts went back to the teenager from St-Basile, and to Russell's explanation. Could the girl have been a victim of this biker insanity? Something about her resonated in me, and I tried again to piece together what I knew about her.

She died in her teens, no longer a child but not yet a woman. Her bones revealed nothing about how she had died, but they did disclose something of how she had lived. The hydrocephalus might help identify her.

The well-healed burr hole suggested that the shunt had been there awhile. Did she hate the shunt? Did she lie in her bed at night and palpate the tube running under her skin? Was she plagued by other physical problems? Did her peers torment her? Was she an honor student? A dropout? Would we find medical records associated with a missing girl that would help identify this skull?

Unlike many of my nameless dead, I had no sense of who she was. The Girl. That's how I'd come to think of her. The Girl in the Viper pit.

And why was she buried at the biker clubhouse? Was her death linked to the murders of Gately and Martineau, or was she just another victim in the grim tradition of biker violence against women? Was her life interrupted for a premeditated reason, or had she merely been in the wrong place at the wrong time, like little Emily Anne Toussaint?

As I wound my way through rush hour traffic I again felt pain and anger. Pain over a life only partly lived, anger at the callousness of those who had taken it.

And I considered Andrew Ryan, with his sky blue eyes and burning intensity. Even the smell of him used to make me happy. How could I have missed his other side, his double life? Could it really be so? My brain told me yes. Bertrand swore it was true. Why did my heart refuse to budge?

My thoughts ran in useless circles. My neck hurt and I could feel a pounding behind my left eye.

I turned onto Parthenais and pulled into an empty spot. Then I leaned back and called a time-out. I needed a respite.

I would tell Claudel what I'd learned, then there would be no bones or thoughts of Ryan for an entire weekend. I would do nothing more serious than peruse Roy's biker manual. I would read, shop, and go to Isabelle's party. But come Monday, I would make a second vow. I would continue my search for Emily Anne's killers and I would also find a name for The Girl in the Viper pit.

13

It was after seven when I got home.

At the lab I'd secured the bones and shunt, then phoned Claudel to pass along what I'd learned from Russell. We decided that I'd research all cases from the past ten years involving partial skeletons. He'd continue with his list of missing girls. If neither of us had a hit by the end of the day on Monday, we'd enter the case into CPIC. That failing, we'd send it south into the NCIC system.

That sounded like a plan.

Following a change of clothes and a brief conversation with Birdie, I walked to McKay, climbed to the gym on the top floor, and worked out for an hour. Afterward I bought a rotisserie chicken from the butcher, and loaded up on veggies and fruit.

Back home I microwaved green beans and split the chicken, stashing half in the refrigerator for Saturday lunch. Then I got out my bottle of Maurice's Piggy Park barbecue sauce.

Montreal is a veritable smorgasbord, home to many

of the world's finest restaurants. Chinese. German. Thai. Mexican. Lebanese. No ethnic group is unrepresented. For a fast-food lunch or a lingering gourmet supper the city is unsurpassed. Its one failing lies in the art of barbecue.

In Quebec what poses as barbecue sauce is a brown gravy, as tasteless and odorless as carbon monoxide. A diligent seeker can find the tomato-based Texas variety, but the vinegar-and-mustard concoction of the eastern Carolinas is a delicacy I am forced to import. Montreal friends eyeing the golden potion are skeptical. One taste and they're hooked.

I poured Maurice's sauce into a small bowl, carried everything to the living room, and dined in front of the tube. By 9 P.M. the weekend was still going well. The hardest decision up to that point involved sports allegiance. Though the Cubs were taking on the Braves, I opted for the NBA play-offs, and cheered the Hornets to a 102–87 victory over the Knicks.

Bird was torn, attracted by the smell of chicken, but alarmed by the outbursts and arm waving. He spent the night across the room, chin on his paws, eyes flying open every time I yelled. At eleven he followed me to bed, where he circled twice before settling behind my knees. We were both asleep in minutes.

I was awakened by the sound of the doorbell. Door chirp would be more correct. When a visitor buzzes for entry to my building, the system twitters like a sparrow with hiccups.

The window shade was a pale gray, and the digits on the clock glowed eight-fifteen. Bird was no longer pressed to my legs. I threw back the covers and grabbed a robe.

112

When I stumbled into the hall I was greeted by an enormous green eye. My hands flew to my chest and I took an involuntary step back from the security monitor.

Chirrrrrrrrup.

The eye withdrew and was replaced by my nephew's face. He mugged at the camera, tipping his head from side to side and stretching the corners of his mouth with his fingers.

I pressed the button to allow him in. Birdie brushed my legs, then looked up with round yellow eyes.

"Don't ask me, Bird."

Kit rounded the corner with a duffel bag in one hand, a brown paper sack in the other, and a backpack slung from each shoulder. He wore a multicolored knit hat that looked as though it would be big in Guatemala.

"Auntie T," he boomed in his rowdy Texas drawl.

"Shhh." I held a finger to my lips. "It's Saturday morning."

I stepped back and held the door wide. As he brushed past I could smell wood smoke and mildew and something like mushrooms or moss.

He dropped the duffel and packs and gave me a hug. When he released me and pulled off the hat his hair did an Edward Scissorhands impression.

"Nice do, Auntie."

"You are *not* in a position to talk," I said, tucking strands behind my ears.

He held out the paper bag.

"A little something from the waters of Vermont." He spotted Birdie. "Hey, Bird. How's my bud?"

The cat bolted for the bedroom.

I peered down the empty hallway.

"Is Howard with you?"

113

"Nope. He headed his heinie south."

"Oh?" As I closed the door I felt a tickle of apprehension.

"Yessir. Needed to get back to the oil game. But I'm going to hang for a while, if that's cool with you?"

"Sure, Kit. That's great." Awhile? I eyed the mound of luggage and remembered my last visit from his mother. My sister Harry had come for a five-day conference and ended up staying for weeks.

"But right now I'm bushed. Is it O.K. if I shower and siesta for a few? We broke camp before the sun was even thinking about getting up."

"Sleep as long as you like. Then I want to hear about your trip." And definitely bathe, I thought.

I got towels and showed him the guest room. Then I threw on jeans and a sweatshirt and walked to the corner *dépanneur* to buy a *Gazette*. When I returned wet towels lay on the bathroom floor and the bedroom door was shut.

I went to the kitchen and sniffed Kit's package. Definitely fish. Adding an outer wrapper of plastic, I stashed it in the refrigerator pending further instructions. Then I made coffee and settled with the paper at the dining room table.

That's when the weekend went off course.

DEATH TOLL REACHES 120:
BODIES OF TWO MORE BIKERS IDENTIFIED

The story was on the third page of the front section. I'd expected some coverage. What I hadn't expected was the photo. The image was grainy, shot from a distance with a powerful telephoto lens, but the subject was recognizable.

I was kneeling by a grave with skull in hand. As usual the caption identified me as ". . . an American forensic anthropologist working for the Laboratoire de Sciences Judiciaires et de Médecine Légale."

The shot was so poorly focused I was unsure if it had been snapped at the Vipers' clubhouse, or if it was an old file photo taken at another site. My appearance and equipment vary little from dig to dig, and there was nothing in the frame to identify a specific location.

The article was accompanied by three other photos: the usual head shots of the victims, and a view of the entrance to the Vipers' clubhouse. It described the exhumation of Gately and Martineau, and recounted the story of their disappearance. There was a brief recap of the biker war, and an explanation of the revised body count.

O.K. Those facts might have been released through official channels. What followed was what shocked me.

The text went on to discuss a baffling third victim, accurately describing the partial remains found in the other pit. It concluded by stating that, to date, the young woman's identity remained a mystery.

How the hell had they gotten that?

I felt the beginnings of agitation. While I am not fond of media attention, I am particularly uneasy when it threatens to jeopardize one of my cases. Who would have released the information?

I took a long, deep breath and got up to reheat my coffee.

O.K. Someone leaked information. So what?

So that shouldn't happen, that's what.

I punched the quick-timer button on the microwave.

True. But will it compromise the case?

I thought about that.

The beeper sounded and I removed my mug.

No. In fact, the article could trigger a useful tip. Someone might come forward with a name.

So no harm done. But had there been an official decision to release that information? Probably not or I would have known about it.

Someone had talked to the press and that was unacceptable. Who knew about the girl's bones? Quickwater? Claudel? A member of the Ident section? A lab technician? Dr Russell?

You're not going to figure it out this weekend.

True again.

Intending to deal with the question on Monday, I circled my mind back to reading, shopping. And Isabelle's party.

Kit.

Oh.

I went to the phone and dialed Isabelle's number.

"*Bonjour.*"

"It's me, Isabelle."

"Tempe, don't you even think about canceling on me." I could hear *The Rite of Spring* playing in the background, and knew she must be cooking. Isabelle always cooks to Stravinsky.

"Well, something has come up—"

"The only thing that would excuse you tonight would be a fatal fall from a seven forty-seven. Yours."

"My nephew showed up this morning and he's going to be staying with me awhile."

"*Oui?*"

"I don't feel right about leaving him alone on his first day here."

116

"But of course not. You will bring this nephew with you tonight."

"He's nineteen."

"*Extraordinaire.* I think I was once that age. I believe it was the sixties. I had to go through the sixties to get to the seventies. I remember taking LSD and wearing a great many bad outfits. I will see you and this young man at seven-thirty."

I agreed and rang off.

Right. Now to convince my nephew to spend Saturday night eating lamb chops and snails with a gaggle of seniors.

As it turned out that wasn't a problem. Kit emerged around three-fifteen, rumpled and starving. He finished the leftover chicken and asked if he could do some laundry. When I mentioned the supper he readily agreed.

I made a note to call Harry. Kit's conviviality was not what I'd expected based on my daughter Katy's teenage years. But Kit was a stranger in town and probably had nowhere else to hang out.

I spent the next few hours finishing a reference letter for a student, cleaning my bedroom, and explaining detergents and fabric settings to my nephew. Around six I zipped to Le Faubourg for a bottle of wine and a small bouquet.

Isabelle lives on Île-des-Sœurs, a small chunk of land in the St Lawrence owned for generations by the gray nuns, but recently colonized by an order of Yuppies. A "mixed use" community, the island's condos, town houses, private homes, and high-rise apartments are tastefully integrated with tennis clubs, strip malls, bicycle paths, and carefully tended green spaces. The island is connected to the south shore via the Champlain Bridge, and to Montreal by two small bridges.

Isabelle's condo is on the top floor of a two-building complex at the far northern tip. Following the failure of her third marriage, she signed divorce papers, sold her home and all its contents, and sallied forth to the clean-slate Île-des-Sœurs. The only belongings she brought along were her treasured CDs and photo albums.

Wanting something in keeping with her new "what the hell" mind-set, Isabelle had chosen a safari theme. Her decorator had blended natural fabrics that looked like they'd been approved by the World Wildlife Fund with simulated leopard and tiger skin. The walls were hung with animal prints, and a collection of African carvings dotted a glass-topped coffee table, the legs of which resembled elephant feet. The king-sized bed in the master suite was swathed in a canopy of mosquito netting.

Kit was enthralled, or at least appeared to be. As Isabelle gave us a tour he asked question after question about the origin of each of her possessions. I wasn't sure of the depth of his interest, but was pleased at his social acumen.

It was not the decor but the view that captivated me. One guest was still expected, so after Kit and I had been issued drinks and had met the other attendees, I stepped onto the balcony to take it in.

A light rain was falling, and across the river the sky-line twinkled in every color imaginable. The mountain loomed over the buildings of Centre-ville, massive and black. I could see the lights of the cross high up on its flank.

118

From inside I heard the doorbell sound, then Isabelle called my name. I took one last look and went inside.

The final diner had just arrived and was handing his trench coat to Isabelle. When I saw his face my jaw dropped in surprise.

14

"*Vous!*"

It was not one of my more adroit openers. I shot Isabelle a "just wait till later" look, which she ignored.

"*Oui.* You are surprised, Tempe?" She beamed. "I said you two had met in an informal way. Now I will officially introduce you."

The journalist extended his hand. This time it held no mike, and his look was friendly, not the stunned surprise I remembered from our encounter outside the Vipers' clubhouse.

"Tempe, this is Lyle Crease. I'm sure you've seen him on television."

I could place the face now. He was an investigative reporter with CTV.

"And, Lyle, I know I don't have to tell you Dr Brennan's name. We call her Tempe. That's with the long 'e' at the end. People do have trouble with that."

When I allowed Crease to take my hand, he leaned close and kissed me first on the right cheek, then on the

120

left, in traditional Quebec fashion. I stepped back and mumbled something I hoped he'd interpret as cool but polite.

Isabelle introduced Crease to the others, and he shook hands with the men and kissed the ladies. Then she raised her champagne glass in Kit's direction.

"I think in honor of this handsome young Texan, tonight we should all practice our English."

Glasses shot up as everyone cheerfully agreed. Kit looked enormously relieved.

"May I help you with dinner?" I asked in frosty English, eager to get Isabelle alone to share some thoughts with her.

"No, no. Everything is ready. Please, everyone, come to the table. There are little cards beside each plate."

Shit.

Isabelle retreated to the kitchen while the rest of us gathered around to ascertain the seating arrangement. As I'd suspected, I was next to Crease. Kit was on my right.

There were seven in all. An elderly actor sat on Kit's other side. I'd met him on a previous occasion, but couldn't remember his name and hadn't caught it when introduced. I was unfamiliar with the other two guests. It turned out they were a couple, the wife an antiques dealer, the husband a film producer.

We made small talk as Isabelle shuttled plates from the kitchen. The actor had just finished a run as Polonius in a French production of *Hamlet* at the Théâtre du Rideau Vert. Crease recounted his most recent assignment. The story concerned a sixteen-year-old hacker who had broken into an U.S. Army network, then phoned the RCMP wanting to be caught.

"The kid wanted recognition," said the actor.

121

"He could have tried out for football," my nephew offered.

Not bad, Kit.

"And what have you two been up to?" Isabelle asked the couple as she circled the table pouring wine.

When she came to Kit she paused and looked at me. I nodded. What the hell. He was legal in Quebec and I was driving. Kit accepted with enthusiasm.

The producer's name was Claude-Henri Brault. He'd just returned from a three-month shoot in Ireland. His wife, Marie-Claire, ran a shop in Old Montreal and had spent the time buying antiques in Provence. She rambled on about the kingdom of Arles, the Angevin dynasty, and at least a dozen Louis, describing how each had changed the face of the furniture industry. Between bites of veal I stole peeks at Lyle Crease. His hair and teeth were flawless, his creases as sharp as I remembered. The only imperfection I spotted was a sprinkling of dandruff across his collar.

And Lyle was a good listener. He kept his eyes on Marie-Claire, nodding intermittently, as though the aesthetics of fabric and cabinet design were the only thing that presently mattered.

When Marie-Claire paused for breath Isabelle stepped in, redirecting the conversation like an air-traffic controller with several flights on her screen. Though I had to admire her skill, I didn't appreciate the direction she chose.

"Tempe has been working on these dreadful gang murders. Can you tell us something about them?"

"The bikers?" asked Claude-Henri.

"Yes." I wanted to glare at Isabelle, but decided it would be rude. I also wanted to strangle her, which would be still ruder.

122

"Were you involved in the discovery I read about in today's paper?"

"Yes. But as Isabelle knows"—I smiled icicles in her direction—"I can't—"

"What are you doing with bikers, Aunt Tempe?"

Kit's interest had wandered during the furniture design lesson, but he perked up at the new topic.

"You know that I work for the provincial medico-legal lab."

He nodded.

"Last week the director asked me to look at some murder cases." I mentioned nothing about my role with Opération Carcajou.

"How many?"

"Quite a few."

"More than the Bee Gees?" he persisted.

"Five."

"Five people iced in one week?" Kit's eyes were huge. Everyone else at the table had gone quiet.

"Two of them were killed in 1987. We recovered their bodies this week."

"That's what I read about," said Claude-Henri, pointing a fork in my direction. "*C'est ça.* That was you in the photograph."

"Who were the others?" Kit pressed on.

Now I wanted to strangle my nephew.

"Two were bomb victims. One was a little girl accidentally killed during a drive-by shooting."

"*Mon Dieu,*" said Marie-Claire, abandoning the commitment to English.

I reached for my Perrier, desperately wishing I'd paid attention to her so I could dodge with a question about Renaissance veneers.

123

"Are you counting the young woman whose bones were found in St-Basile-le-Grand?"

I turned at Crease's question. Though his voice sounded casual, his eyes had a glint I hadn't noticed before. If he had hopes of a story, he wouldn't get it from me.

"No."

"Have you identified her?" He reached for his wine.

"No."

"Who are you talking about?" Kit asked.

"Near the grave of two of the bikers we also found some other bones. It's a young woman, but we don't know who she is, or if she's connected with the Vipers. Her burial could predate their ownership of the property."

"Is that what you think?" Crease.

"I don't know."

"Who are the Vipers?"

I was fast restructuring my opinion of my nephew's social skills.

"They're a puppet club for the Hells Angels."

"No way!"

"Yes, way. And they and their brothers in arms are responsible for almost one hundred and twenty deaths in this province over the past five years. God knows how many others have disappeared."

"The bikers are killing each other?"

"Yes. It's a power struggle for control of the drug trade."

"Why not just let them?" asked the actor. "View it as a form of sociopath self-regulation."

"Because innocents like Emily Anne Toussaint, who was nine years old, get caught in the cross fire."

"And maybe this other girl?"

124

"Maybe, Kit."

"Do you think you'll be able to prove that?" Crease.

"I don't know. Claude-Henri, please tell us about your film."

As the producer spoke, Crease picked up the Chardonnay and reached for my empty glass. I shook my head, but he continued. When I placed my hand over the rim, he laughed, lifted it off, and filled the goblet.

Seething, I pulled my hand free from his and leaned back in my chair. I cannot tolerate people pressing liquor on those who don't want it.

My nephew's voice brought me back to the conversation. Isabelle had turned her spotlight on Kit.

"Yeah, I went with my daddy. He's in the oil business. We drove up from Texas in a big old Winnebago. Pop's idea. He wanted to do this bonding thing.

"We swung by here to drop off Auntie's cat, then east and into Vermont at Derby Line. Pop had this trip planned better than the invasion of Normandy. That's why I remember all the names.

"Anyway, we camped near this town called Westmore and fished the Willoughby River for salmon. The salmon are landlocked, and when they run in the spring it's a big deal. I guess real fishermen view it like some kind of holy place.

"Then we gunned south to Manchester and fished the Battenkill, and my daddy bought all kinds of crap at the Orvis factory. Casting rods, fly rods, and other stuff. Then he motored on to Texas in the 'Bago, and I dropped in on my aunt the biker buster." He raised his glass to me, and everyone followed suit.

"It's kind of weird," Kit continued. "Because my daddy bought me a motorcycle about a year ago."

I was dismayed but not surprised. Howard was my sister's second husband, a West Texas oilman with more money than sense, and a defect on the double helix that made him incapable of monogamy. They'd divorced when Kit was six. Howard's approach to fatherhood was to lavish toys and money on his son. At three it was ponies and motorized toy cars. By eighteen it had changed to sailboats and then a Porsche.

"What kind of motorcycle?" asked Isabelle.

"It's a Harley-Davidson. Pop's really into Harleys. My bike is a Road King Classic and he's got an Ultra Classic Electra Glide. Those are both Evos. But Pop's real love is his old knucklehead. They only made those from 1936 to 1947."

"What do those terms mean?" asked Isabelle.

"They're nicknames that refer to the design of the engine head. The Evolution V2 motor was first produced in the early eighties. Originally it was called a blockhead, but that tag never really stuck. Most folks refer to it as the Evo. A lot of the bikes you see today are shovelheads, made from 1966 to 1984. From 1948 to 1965 it was panheads, before that flatheads, which came out in '29. It's easy to identify the era of production by the design of the engine head."

Kit's interest in bikers was nothing compared with his ardor for bikes.

"Did you know that all modern Harleys descend from the Silent Gray Fellow, the first bike to roll off the line in Milwaukee back at the turn of the century? The Silent Gray Fellow had a one-cylinder twenty-five-cubic-inch motor capable of three horsepower. No hydraulic tappets, no electric starters, no V-twin engine." Kit shook his head in disbelief.

"A modern Twin Cam engine displaces upwards of

eighty-eight cubic inches. Even an old '71 FLH, at seventy-four cubic inches, has an engine compression ratio of eighty point five to one. And today they're pushing nine to one. Yeah, we've come a long way, but every hog on the road today can trace its bloodline back to that old Silent Gray Fellow."

"Aren't there other motorcycle manufacturers?" asked the actor.

"Yessir," Kit agreed, his face and voice showing disdain. "There are Yamahas, Suzukis, Kawasakis, and Hondas out there. But they're just transportation. The British made some good bikes, Norton, Triumph, BSA, but they've all gone out of business. The German BMWs were impressive machines, but for my pesos Harley is the only show in town."

"Are they expensive?" Claude-Henri.

Kit shrugged. "Harley doesn't make low-end cycles. It's not cheap equipment."

I listened as my nephew talked. He had the same reverence for and knowledge of motorcycles that Marie-Claire had for furniture. Perhaps the timing of his visit was fortunate. He could help me understand this strange world I was entering.

It was almost midnight when we said good-bye and pressed for the elevator. I felt ready for bed, but Kit was still wired, yammering on about engines and critiquing the evening's guests and events. Maybe it was wine, maybe youth. I envied him his stamina.

The rain had stopped, but a strong wind blew off the river, bouncing branches and shrubs, and swirling wet leaves across the ground. When Kit offered to get the car I carefully appraised his condition, then turned over the keys and waited inside the lobby.

In less than a minute he pulled up, then got out and circled to the passenger side. When I'd settled behind the wheel he tossed a brown envelope into my lap.

"What's this?"

"Envelope."

"I can see that. Where did it come from?"

"It was on the windshield, stuck under a wiper. You must have an admirer."

I looked at the envelope. It was a padded mailer, stapled at one end, with a pull-tab on the back for easy opening. My name appeared in red Magic Marker.

I stared at the letters, an alarm sounding deep in my brain. Who knew I would be on the island tonight? Who could have recognized my car? Had we been followed? Watched?

Gingerly, I prodded the contents. I could feel the bulge of something hard.

"Well!"

I jumped at the sound of Kit's voice. When I turned his face looked eerily pale, his features dark and distorted in the faint yellow light seeping from the lobby doors.

"Goddammit, Kit, this could be . . ." I stopped, unsure where the thought was going.

"Could be what?" Kit leaned sideways and draped his arm over the back of the seat. "Go on. Open it," he needled. "I'll bet it's a prank. One of your cop friends probably spotted the car and left something stupid to creep you out."

That was possible. Anyone on the job could have run the plate. And I *had* been the butt of jokes in the past.

"Go on." Kit reached up and turned on the interior light. "Maybe it's tickets to the Expos."

I pulled the tab and reached into the mailer. My fingers closed around a small, glass jar.

When I withdrew the container and held it up to the light I felt bile rise in my throat. The rhythmic contractions under my tongue told me I was about to be sick. I barely heard Kit as I lunged for the door handle. "Holy shit, Aunt Tempe. Who did you piss off?"

15

The eyeball rested on the bottom of the jar, pupil up, tendrils of flesh floating in the cloudy liquid. The organ was blanched and partially collapsed, and one side appeared to have a jagged tear. Though tightly sealed, the container gave off a familiar scent. A folded paper was stuck to its bottom.

Kit reached over and pulled off the note.

"*On te surveille.*" The French sounded odd with his Texas drawl. "What does that mean, Aunt Tempe?"

"We're watching you."

With shaky hands I returned the jar and note to the mailer and placed it on the floor of the backseat. The smell of formaldehyde seemed overwhelming. I knew the odor was in my mind, but that did little to allay my nausea. Fighting to bring my gag reflex back under control, I wiped damp palms on my pants and put the car in gear.

"Think it's a joke?" Kit asked as we turned onto boulevard Île-des-Sœurs.

"I don't know." My voice sounded high-pitched.

Sensing my mood, he didn't press the point.

Once home, I wrapped the jar in a series of plastic sacks and sealed it in a Tupperware canister. Then I cleaned out the vegetable drawer and placed it in the refrigerator.

Kit watched in silence, a puzzled expression on his face.

"I'll take it to the lab on Monday," I explained.

"It's a real eye, isn't it?"

"Yes."

"Think it's a joke?" He repeated his earlier question.

"Probably." I didn't believe that, but had no desire to alarm him.

"I get the feeling I shouldn't ask, but, if it's a joke, why take it to the lab?"

"Maybe it will give the merry pranksters a little scare," I said, trying to sound casual, then I hugged him. "Now, I'm off to bed. Tomorrow we'll find something fun to do."

"That's cool. Mind if I listen to some music?"

"Be my guest."

When Kit's door closed I double-checked the locks on the doors and windows, and made sure the security system was functioning. I resisted the urge to check for lurkers in my closet or under the bed.

Kit's musical choice was Black Sabbath. He played it until two-fifteen.

I lay in bed for a long time listening to the thud of heavy metal, wondering if it qualified as music, wondering how many calls I'd receive from the neighbors, and wondering who felt strongly enough about sending me a message to underscore it with a human eye.

Though I'd showered for twenty minutes, the smell of formaldehyde remained lodged in my brain. I fell

131

asleep queasy, with goose bumps still prickling my flesh.

I slept late the next morning. When I woke, still tired from having started awake repeatedly throughout the night, my thoughts turned at once to the thing in my produce crisper. Who? Why? Was it work-related? Was there a sicko in the neighborhood? Who was watching me?

I pushed the questions into the deep background, resolving to address them on Monday. In the meantime, I would be extra-vigilant. I checked my Mace, then the direct-dial buttons on the phones and security box to make sure they were set to 911.

The sun shone brightly and the thermometer on my patio said five degrees Celsius. Forty Fahrenheit at 10 A.M. It was going to be a Canadian scorcher.

Knowing the diurnal rhythm of teenagers I didn't expect to see Kit before noon, so I threw on my gear and hiked to the gym. I walked with more caution than usual, skin prickling with tension, eyes alert for anyone or anything suspicious.

After working out I picked up bagels and cream cheese, and a few goodies to go on top of the cream cheese. I also made an impulse buy at the flower cart. Birdie had largely abandoned me since Kit's arrival, so I'd lure back his affection with a catnip plant.

Neither the bagels nor the catnip were very effective. My nephew appeared around one-fifteen, the cat trailing languidly behind.

"Utter no sentence that includes the phrase 'early bird,' or 'dawn,'" said Kit.

"Bagel?"

"Acceptable."

"Cream cheese, smoked salmon, lemon, onions, capers?"

"Delete capers. Run program."

Birdie eyed the catnip but said nothing.

As Kit ate, I laid out the options.

"It's a gorgeous day out there. I suggest outdoor activities."

"Agreed."

"We can take in the Jardin Botanique, prowl around up on the mountain, or I can scare up some bicycles and we can hit the old port, or pedal the path along the Lachine Canal."

"Do they allow skates?"

"Skates?"

"Rollerblades. Can we rent some in-lines and do this bike path?"

"I think so." Oh boy.

"I'll bet you're a popper on Rollerblades. Harry's pretty good."

"Um. Huh. Why do you call your mom Harry?"

I'd always been curious. Since he first started speaking, Kit had referred to his mother by name.

"I don't know. She's not exactly *Little House on the Prairie*."

"But you've done it since you were two years old."

"She wasn't domestic back then. Don't change the subject. Are you up for in-line skating?"

"Sure."

"You're a can o' corn, Aunt Tempe. Let me grab a shower and we're on our way."

It was close to a perfect day. I started out rocky but quickly picked up the rhythm, and was soon gliding along as if born on skates. It brought back memories of roller-skating on city sidewalks as a little girl and the several times I had almost hit pedestrians or skated into the paths of cars. The sunshine brought out swarms of jocks, crowding the path with cyclists, skateboarders, and other in-line skaters. Though shaky on turns, I learned to maneuver well enough to avoid collisions. The only skill I didn't master was that of the sudden stop. Drag brakes for skates had not been invented when I was a kid.

By the end of the afternoon I was sailing along smooth as *Black Magic I* in the America's Cup. Or shit through a mallard, as Kit put it. I did insist, however, on wearing enough padding to defend an NHL goal.

It was after five when we turned in the skates and pads and headed to Chez Singapore for an Asian dinner. Then we rented *The Pink Panther* and *A Shot in the Dark* and laughed as Inspector Clouseau demonstrated how one could be both part of the solution and part of the problem. The movies were Kit's choice. He said the French immersion would acclimatize him to Montreal.

Not until I lay in my bed, tired and achy and full of popcorn, did I even remember the eye. I tossed and turned, trying not to picture the object in my refrigerator and the evil person who put it on my car.

Monday was still warm, but dark clouds had gathered over the city. They hung low, trapping a loose fog close to the ground, and forcing drivers to use headlights.

Arriving at work, I took the jar to the biology section and made a request. I didn't explain the source of the specimen, and they didn't ask. We gave the sample an unregistered number, and the technician said she'd call with results.

I had a suspicion about the eye's origin, which I

hoped was wrong. The implications were just too frightening. I held on to the note, pending the analysis.

The morning meeting was relatively brief. The owner of a Volvo dealership was found hanged in his garage, a suicide note pinned to his chest. A single-engine plane had gone down in St-Hubert. A woman had been pushed from the Vendôme métro platform.

Nothing for me.

Back in my office, I logged on to my terminal. Using *anthropologie, squelette, inconnue, femelle,* and *partiel* as my descriptors, I searched the database for cases consisting of unidentified partial female skeletons. The computer came up with twenty-six LML numbers spanning the past ten years.

Using that list, I asked for all cases lacking a skull. That worked for remains received since I'd been at the LML. Prior to that, complete bone inventories hadn't been done. Skeletal cases were simply designated partial or complete. I highlighted the cases recorded as partial.

Next, using the list of incomplete skeletons analyzed during my tenure, I requested those lacking femora.

No go. The data had been entered as skull present or absent, postcranial remains present or absent, but specific bones had not been recorded. I would have to request the actual files.

Wasting no time, I walked down the hall to the records department. A slim woman in black jeans and a peasant blouse occupied the front desk. She was almost monochromatic, with bleached hair, pale skin, and eyes the shade of old dishwater. Her only signs of color were cherry red streaks around her temples, and a sprinkling of freckles across her nose. I was unable to count the number of studs and rings displayed in each of her ears. I'd never seen her before.

"*Bonjour. Je m'appelle Tempe Brennan.*" I held out my hand, introducing myself.

She nodded, but offered neither a hand nor name.

"Are you new?"

"I'm a temp."

"I'm sorry, but I don't think we've met."

"Name's Jocelyn Dion." One shoulder shrugged.

O.K. I dropped my hand.

"Jocelyn, this is a list of files I need to review."

I handed her the printout and indicated the high-lighted numbers. When she reached for the paper I could see definition through the gauzy sleeve. Jocelyn spent time at the gym.

"I know there are quite a few, but could you find out where the files are stored and pull them for me as quickly as possible?"

"No problem."

"I need the full jacket on each one, not just the anthropology report."

Something crossed her face, just a flicker of change and then it was gone.

"Where would you like them?" she asked, dropping her eyes to the list.

I gave her my office number, then left. Two strides down the corridor I remembered that I hadn't mentioned pictures. When I turned back I could see Jocelyn's head bent low over the printout. Her lips moved as a lacquered finger worked its way down each side of the paper. She seemed to be reading every word.

When I mentioned the photos, she started at my voice.

"I'm on it," she said, sliding from her stool.

Weird one, I thought as I headed back to work on the Gately and Martineau reports.

136

Jocelyn brought me the dossiers within an hour, and I spent the next three going through them. In all, I'd worked on six headless women. Only two had lacked both thigh bones, and neither was young enough to be the girl in the pit.

From the years before I'd arrived in Montreal, seven female skeletons without crania remained unidentified. Two were young enough, but the descriptions of the remains were vague, and without skeletal inventories there was no way to know what bones had been recovered. Neither folder contained photographs.

I went back to the computer and checked the disposition of the earliest case. The bones had been held five years, rephotographed, then released for burial or destruction.

But the file contained no pictures. That was odd.

I asked for site of recovery. The bones had come in from Salluit, a village around twelve hundred miles north on the tip of the Ungava Peninsula.

I entered the more recent LML number and asked for site of recovery.

Ste-Julie. My pulse quickened. That was not twelve miles from St-Basile-le-Grand.

Back to the folder. Again, no photos.

I checked on the disposition and found nothing to indicate the case had been cleared.

Could I be that lucky?

When I began at the LML, I inherited a collection of skeletal cases. While I'd disposed of some, much of this material remained in my storeroom.

I unlocked the door and dragged a chair to the far end of the small room. Brown cardboard boxes lined both walls, arranged chronologically by LML number. I went to the section containing the oldest codes.

The case was on the top shelf. I climbed onto the chair, lifted it down, and carried it out to my worktable. Brushing off dust, I raised the lid.

To the left lay a mound of vertebrae and ribs, to the right a stack of long bones. Though most joint surfaces had been gnawed by animals, it was clear that both femora were there.

Damn.

I took everything out and checked for inconsistencies, but nothing seemed amiss. Disappointed, I replaced the bones and reshelved the box. After washing my hands I crossed to my office, planning to regroup over a tuna sandwich and carton of Jell-O pudding.

Swiveling my chair, I crossed my feet on the window ledge and peeled the cover from the pudding container. A colleague at UNC-Charlotte had a sticker on her door that read: *Life is uncertain. Eat dessert first.* I'd always considered that good advice.

Gazing at the river, I slurped butterscotch, my thoughts adrift. Sometimes my mind works better that way, mingling associations freely rather than herding them into the center of my consciousness.

The skull and leg bones we'd found in St-Basile were not the missing parts of a body recovered earlier. That was clear. At least not a body recovered in Quebec.

O.K.

Unless Claudel came up with a name, the next step would be CPIC.

Easy enough.

If that failed, we'd go to NCIC. There was nothing to suggest that the girl was local. She could have traveled north from the States.

Ally McBeal's therapist was right. I needed a theme song for times when I felt stressed.

138

Runnin' down the road tryin' to loosen my load
Got a world of trouble on my mind . . .

Maybe.

Slow down, you move too fast.
Got to make the morning last . . .

As I reached for the sandwich an image of Saturday night's grotesque offering flashed across my mind. Again my skin went cold and prickly.

Forget it. It could be a pig's eye. Your picture was in the paper, and any moron could have stuck it on the car for laughs. If anyone is out there watching, it's some twisted nitwit without a life.

I am woman watch me—

Definitely no.

It's a beautiful day in the neighborhood . . .

Oh boy.

Game plan. Finish the reports on Gately and Martineau, finalize those on the Vaillancourt twins. Talk to Claudel. Based on his report, CPIC, then NCIC.

Life is under control. This is my job. There is no reason to feel stressed.

That thought had hardly materialized when the phone rang, destroying the calm I had worked so hard to achieve.

16

A female voice said, "I have a call from Mr Crease. Hold, please."

Before I could stop her he was on the line.

"I hope you don't mind my calling you at work."

I did, but held my tongue.

"I just wanted to say that I really enjoyed Saturday night, and hoped the two of us might get together."

Original.

"Would you be free to have supper some night this week?"

"I'm sorry, but that's not possible right now. I'm really swamped."

I could be free until the end of the next millennium and I wouldn't dine with Lyle Crease. The man was too glib for my taste.

"Next week?"

"No, I don't think so."

"I understand. Can I have your nephew as a consolation prize?"

"What?"

"Kit. He's a fabulous kid."

Fabulous?

"I have a friend who owns a motorcycle shop. He must stock five thousand items of Harley-Davidson paraphernalia. I think Kit would find it interesting."

The last thing I wanted was my impressionable young nephew under the influence of a media smoothie. But I had to agree, Kit would enjoy it.

"I'm sure he would."

"Then it's cool with you if I give him a call?"

"Sure." Cool as dysentery.

Five minutes after I hung up Quickwater appeared at my door. He gave me his usual stony stare, then flipped a folder onto my desk.

I really needed to settle on a theme song.

"What are these?"

"Forms."

"For me to fill out?"

Quickwater was preparing to ignore my question when his partner joined us.

"I take it this means you came up empty."

"As Al Capone's vault," Claudel replied. "Not a single match. Not even close."

He gestured at the packet on my desk.

"If you get the papers filled out, I can access CPIC while Martin does NCIC. Bergeron's working on the dental descriptors."

CPIC is the acronym for the Canadian Police Information Centre, NCIC for the National Crime Information Center operated by the FBI. Each is a national electronic database providing quick access to information crucial to law enforcement. Though I'd used CPIC a few times, I was much more familiar with the American system.

NCIC first went on line in 1967 with data on stolen autos, license plates, guns, and property, and on wanted persons and fugitives. Over the years more files were added, and the original ten databases expanded to seventeen, including the interstate identification index, the U.S. Secret Service protective files, the foreign fugitive file, the violent gangs/ terrorist file, and files on missing and unidentified persons.

The NCIC computer is located in Clarksburg, West Virginia, with connecting terminals in police departments and sheriffs' offices throughout the United States, Canada, Puerto Rico, and the U.S. Virgin Islands. Entries can be made only by law enforcement personnel. And they definitely make them. In its first year NCIC recorded two million transactions. It currently handles that many each day.

The NCIC missing persons file, created in 1975, is used to locate individuals who are not "wanted," but whose whereabouts are unknown. A record can be entered for missing juveniles, and for people who are disabled or endangered. Victims of abduction and those who have disappeared following a disaster also qualify. A form is completed by the missing person's parent or guardian, physician, dentist, and optician, and entered by a local department.

The unidentified persons file was added in 1983 to provide a way to cross-reference recovered remains against missing persons records. Entry into the system is permitted for unidentified bodies and body parts, for living persons, and for catastrophe victims.

It was this packet that Quickwater had tossed onto my desk.

"If you'll fill out the NCIC form we can work both

networks. It's basically the same data, just different coding systems. How long will you need?"

"Give me an hour." With only three bones I'd have little to say.

As soon as they left I began working my way through the form, periodically checking the data collection entry guide for codes.

I checked the box for EUD for unidentified deceased.

I placed an "S" in boxes 1, 9, and 10 of the body parts diagram, indicating that a skeletonized head and right and left upper leg bones had been recovered. All others boxes got an "N" for not recovered.

I marked "F" for female, "W" for white, and wrote in the approximate height range. I left empty the space for estimated year of birth and estimated date of death.

In the personal descriptors section I wrote SHUNT CERB, for cerebral ventricular shunt, and checked that item on the supplemental form. That was it. No fractures, deformities, tattoos, moles, or scars.

Since I hadn't any clothing, jewelry, eyeglasses, fingerprints, blood type, or information as to cause of death, the rest of the document remained blank. All I could add were a few comments about where the body was found.

I was completing the sections on agency name and case number when Quickwater reappeared. I handed him the form. He took it, nodded, and left without a word.

What was it with this guy?

An image flicked through my mind and was gone. A bloated eyeball in a jelly jar.

Quickwater?

No way. Nevertheless, I decided to make no mention of the incident to Claudel or his Carcajou partner. I might have asked Ryan, might have turned to him for advice, but Ryan was gone and I was on my own.

I completed the Gately and Martineau reports and walked them to the secretarial office. When I returned, Claudel was seated in my office, a computer printout in his hand.

"You were right with the age but a bit off on the date of death. Ten years wasn't enough."

I waited for him to go on.

"Her name was Savannah Claire Osprey."

In French it came out Oh-spree, with the accent on the second syllable. Nevertheless, the name told me that the girl was probably Southern, or at least had been born Southern. Not many people outside the Southeast named their daughters Savannah. I lowered myself into my chair, relieved but curious.

"From?"

"Shallotte, North Carolina. Isn't that your hometown?"

"I'm from Charlotte."

Canadians have difficulty with Charlotte, Charlottesville, and the two Charlestons. So do many Americans. I'd given up explaining. But Shallotte was a small coastal town that didn't qualify to be part of the confusion.

Claudel read from the printout. "She was reported missing in May of 1984, two weeks after her sixteenth birthday."

"That was a quick turnaround," I said, digesting the information.

"*Oui.*"

I waited, but he did not go on. I kept the annoyance from my voice.

144

"Monsieur Claudel, any information you have will help me confirm this ID."

A pause. Then, "The shunt and the dentals were unique so the computer spit the name right out. I called the Shalotte PD and actually talked to the reporting officer. According to her, the mother got the case entered, then dropped it cold. There was the usual media frenzy at first, then things died down. The investigation went on for months, but nothing ever turned up."

"Troubled kid?"

A longer pause.

"There is no history of drug or discipline problems. The hydrocephaly caused some learning disabilities and affected her eyesight, but she wasn't retarded. She went to a normal high school and did well. She was never considered a potential runaway.

"But the child was hospitalized frequently because of problems with the shunt. Apparently the apparatus would get blocked and they'd have to go in and fix it. These episodes were preceded by periods of lethargy, headache, sometimes mental confusion. One theory is that she became disoriented and wandered off."

"Off what, the planet? What's the other theory?"

"The father."

Claudel flipped open a small spiral notebook.

"Dwayne Allen Osprey. A real charmer with an arrest record longer than the Trans-Siberian Railway. Back then Dwayne's domestic routine revolved around drinking Jim Beam and beating up his family. According to the mother's original statement, which she later retracted, her husband always disliked Savannah, and things got worse as the child grew older. It wasn't beyond him to slam her into a wall. Seems Dwayne found his

145

daughter a disappointment. Called her Water Brain."

"They think he murdered his own daughter?"

"It's a possibility. Whiskey and rage are a deadly cocktail. The theory was that things got out of hand, he killed her, then disposed of the body."

"How did she end up in Quebec?"

"An insightful question, Dr Brennan."

With that he rose and shot the cuffs on the crispest, whitest shirt I'd seen in decades. I gave him a drop-dead-peckerhead look, but he was already out the door.

I sighed and leaned back in my chair.

You bet your prim little ass it's an insightful question, Monsieur Claudel.

And I'm going to answer it.

146

17

I took a deep breath. As usual, Claudel had made me furious.

When I felt calmer, I looked at my watch. Four-forty. It was late, but maybe I could catch her.

Checking my Rolodex, I dialed SBI Headquarters in Raleigh. Kate Brophy picked up on the first ring.

"Hi, Kate. It's Tempe."

"Hey, girl, are you back in Dixie?"

"No. I'm in Montreal."

"When are you going to get your skinny tail down here so we can tip a few?"

"My tipping days are over, Kate."

"Oops. Sorry. I know that."

Kate and I had met at a time when I was as committed to alcohol as a college freshman on spring break. Only I wasn't eighteen and I wasn't at the beach. Past thirty, I was then a wife and mother, and a university professor with exhausting teaching and research responsibilities.

I never noticed when I joined the rank of brothers and

sisters in denial, but somewhere along the way I became a champion rationalizer. A glass of Merlot at home in the evening. A beer after classes. A weekend party. I didn't need the booze. I never drank alone. I never missed work. It wasn't a problem.

But then the glass became a bottle, and the late-night binges required no company. That's the beguiling thing about Bacchus. He has no entrance fee. No minimum drink order. Before you know it you're in bed on a sunny Saturday afternoon while your daughter plays soccer and other parents cheer.

That show had closed down, and I wasn't about to re-raise the curtain.

"It's funny you called," said Kate. "I was just talking to one of our investigators about the biker boys you glued together back in the eighties."

I remembered those cases. Two entrepreneurs had made the mistake of dealing drugs on turf claimed by the Hells Angels. Their body parts were found in plastic bags, and I'd been asked to sort dealer A from dealer B.

That foray into fresh forensics had been a catalyst for me. Until then I'd worked with skeletons unearthed at archaeological sites, examining bones to identify disease patterns and estimate life expectancies in prehistoric times. Fascinating, but minimally pertinent to current events.

When I began consulting to the North Carolina medical examiner, I felt an excitement not present in my early work. Kate's bikers, like the cases that followed, had an urgency that ancient deaths did not. I could give a name to the nameless. I could provide a family with closure. I could contribute to law enforcement's efforts to reduce the slaughter on America's streets, and to identify and prosecute perpetrators. I'd shifted my professional focus, gone dry in my personal life, and never looked back on either front.

"How did you end up in Tulio's case review session?" I asked.

"I drove a couple of my analysts up to Quantico for a VICAP training session. Since I was there, I decided to sit in to see what's new."

"What was?"

"Other than the fact that your biker boys are knocking each other off with greater alacrity than most social clubs, looks like the same old."

"I don't think I've worked a Carolina biker case in years. Who's down home these days?"

"We've still got three of the big four."

"Hells Angels, Outlaws, and Pagans."

"Yes, ma'am. No Bandidos yet. And it's been quiet for some time, but you never know. Things could heat up next month when the Angels hold their run at Myrtle Beach."

"It's still pretty wild up here, but that's not why I'm calling."

"Oh?"

"Ever hear of a young girl named Savannah Claire Osprey?"

There was a long silence. Across the miles the connection sounded like the ocean in a seashell.

"Is this a joke?"

"Absolutely not."

I heard her take a deep breath.

"The Osprey disappearance was one of the very first cases I worked for the bureau. It was years ago. Savannah Osprey was a sixteen-year-old kid with a lot of medical problems. Didn't hang with a wild crowd, didn't do drugs. One afternoon she left her house and was never seen again. At least that was the story."

"You don't believe she ran away?"

"The local police suspected the father, but no one could find a thing to prove it."

"Do you think he was involved?"

"It's possible. She was a timid kid, wore thick glasses, rarely went out, didn't date. And it was common knowledge the old man used her for a punching bag." Her voice was filled with contempt. "The guy should have been locked up. Actually he was, but not until later. Got busted on a drug charge, I think. Died about five years after his daughter disappeared."

What she said next hit me like a blow to the chest.

"He was such a peckerwood shit and she was such a pathetic little thing that the case really bothered me. I've kept her bones all these years."

"What did you say?" I gripped the phone, barely breathing.

"The parents never accepted it, but I know they're hers. I still have them stored at the ME office. Doc calls every now and then, but I always ask him to hang on to the stuff."

"Her remains were found?"

"Nine months after Savannah disappeared a female skeleton turned up near Myrtle Beach. That was the thing that shined the light on Dwayne Osprey. While he was never what you'd call a steady worker, around the time she went missing he was making deliveries for a local cheesecake company. The day of his daughter's disappearance Daddy made a trip to Myrtle Beach."

I was so shocked I could hardly formulate a question.

"But did you ever get a positive on the remains?"

"No. There was too much missing and what was recovered was too damaged. And of course we weren't

150

doing DNA back then. Why are you asking about Savannah Osprey?"

"Did you recover a skull?"

"No. That was the main problem. The victim had been dumped in the woods then covered by a sheet of corrugated tin. Animals pulled parts of the body out and scattered them all over creation. The skull and jaw were never found, and we figured they'd dragged them off. The bones left under the tin were intact but weren't very useful, and the rest of the skeleton was so badly chewed that it was hard to tell much except gender. Some pathologist was doing the anthropology back then. His report stated that nothing remained to indicate age, height, or race."

A pathologist would not have known about microscopic aging, or about calculation of stature from partial long bones. Not a good job, Doc.

"Why do you think it's Savannah?" I asked.

"We found a small silver charm in the vicinity of the bones. It was a bird of some sort. Though she denied it, I could tell from the mother's reaction that she recognized the thing. Later I did some research. The charm was an exact replica of a fish hawk."

I waited.

"The fish hawk is also known as the osprey."

I told her about the skull and leg bones in Montreal.

"Holy shit."

"Is the mother still around?"

"Anything's possible since they cloned that sheep. I'll find out."

"Do you still have the file?"

"You bet."

"Antemortem X rays?"

"Zillions."

151

I made a quick decision.

"Get those bones, Kate. I'm coming down."

Patineau authorized the trip, and I booked a morning flight to Raleigh. Kit and I had a late dinner that night, both of us avoiding mention of the bundle in the entrance hall that I had brought from the lab and would be taking with me. He was looking forward to tomorrow's outing with Crease and had no problem with my absence.

The plane was crowded with the usual assortment of students, businessmen, and weekend golfers. I stared out the window as attendants served coffee and soft drinks, wishing I, too, were off to a course – Pinehurst, Marsh Harbor, Oyster Bay, anything but the grim analysis of a teenage girl's bones.

My eyes dropped to the athletic bag under the seat in front of me. It looked innocuous enough, but I wondered what my fellow passengers would think if they knew the nature of its contents. I have flown out of Dorval often enough that the X-ray machine operators no longer ask for an explanation. I wondered how it would be leaving Raleigh.

Outside, the morning sun was painting the clouds a luminescent pink. When we broke through I could see a tiny shadow plane paralleling the one in which I rode.

Yes, that was it, I thought. That's how I saw the girl at my feet. Though I now had a name, in my mind's eye she remained a shadowy ghost on a formless landscape. I hoped this trip would change that image into a firm identification.

18

Kate met me at the Raleigh-Durham airport and we drove directly to the SBI lab. She'd already brought the remains from the medical examiner's office in Chapel Hill, and secured a room where we could work. If samples were to be taken for DNA analysis, all parties agreed that this arrangement was the most efficient.

I gloved my hands and unwrapped my parcel as Kate retrieved hers from a locked closet. She placed a long white box on the table and stepped away. I could feel the familiar tension in my chest as I unwound the string and folded back the cardboard flaps.

One by one I arranged the bones, placing each in its correct anatomical position. Ribs. Vertebrae. Pelvis. Long bones.

The pathologist had been right in his assessment of animal damage. Scavengers had gnawed away so much that not a border, crest, or joint remained on any but the smallest bones. The pubic symphyses and iliac crests were completely gone, and only fragments of clavicle had survived. But one fact was immediately clear.

Both femora were missing.

I added the bones from St-Basile to those that lay on the table. While they did not complete the skeleton, neither did they duplicate any element.

Kate spoke first.

"Looks like a match for size and muscular development. She must have been a tiny thing."

"Using a femur I calculated a height of five foot two, plus or minus. Let's see what your tibia gives us." I indicated two landmarks on the shaft. "There's a regression formula that allows the use of just this segment."

I took the measurement then did the math. The error range was large but bracketed the estimate I'd gotten with the femur. When I showed her the figure, Kate went to the side counter and riffled through a file that was thicker than a Manhattan phone book.

"Here it is. Savannah was five-one and three-quarter inches."

She riffled some more, then withdrew a five-by-seven envelope and shook free several pictures. She spoke as she studied an image.

"It was so sad. Most of Savannah's classmates had no idea who she was. And Shallotte is *not* that big a place. The kids that did recognize her name or photo couldn't tell us a thing about her. She was one of those people that no one remembers. Born 1968. Died 1984."

Kate held out a snapshot.

"The kid got a really bum deal. Miserable family. No friends. Anyway, you can tell she wasn't very big."

I looked at the photo and felt a surge of pity.

The girl sat on a blanket, one scarecrow arm clutching her middle, the other held palm out to fend off the picture taker. She wore a one-piece bathing suit that showed skin so pale it was almost blue. She'd been hiding her face, but the camera caught her looking up, eyes enormous behind thick lenses. In the distance I could make out the horizontal slash of waves meeting shore.

As I stared at the wan little face, I ached inside. What could have prompted an attack on someone so fragile? Did a stranger force her at knifepoint, then strangle and leave her to the dogs? When did she realize she was going to die? Did she scream in terror, knowing no one would hear her cries? Had she died in her own home, to be hauled off and dumped? As her eyes closed for the last time did she feel terror or resignation or hatred or numbness, or merely bewilderment? Had she felt pain?

"—compare cranial features."

Kate was pulling X rays from a large brown envelope and popping them onto a wall illuminator.

"This is a cranial series taken just four months before Savannah disappeared."

I got my X rays from the athletic bag and clipped them next to the hospital films. Starting with the facial views, I compared the shape of the frontal sinuses. Varying from small and simple to large and multi-chambered, these hollow spaces above the orbits are as unique to an individual as his or her fingerprints.

Savannah's sinuses rose into her forehead like a crest on the head of a cockatoo, the configuration on her hospital X rays matching exactly the one in the skull on my film. And the surgical burr hole was clearly visible in every view, the shape and position identical on the antemortem and postmortem films.

There was no doubt that the skull unearthed in St-Basile was Savannah Claire Osprey. But could we link the skull and femora to the partial skeleton found near Myrtle Beach?

Before leaving Montreal I'd removed a sliver of bone from the shaft of one of the femora and extracted a molar from the upper jaw in the skull, thinking that if relatives could be located, or antemortem samples of the victim's tissue or blood could be recovered, DNA sequencing might confirm the suspected identity. While the dental and radiographic evidence now rendered DNA testing unnecessary for purposes of identifying the bones from Montreal, I had another goal in mind.

Using a bone saw, I cut a one-inch chunk from all of the tibiae and fibulae that Kate had been saving all these years. She watched in silence as the circular blade buzzed through the dry bone, sending up a powdery white spray.

"It's not likely the hospital will come up with samples after all this time."

"No," I agreed. "But it happens."

It was true. Gallstones. Pap smears. Blood spots. Old DNA had been found in all sorts of strange places.

"What if there are no relatives?"

"By comparing the sequencing from the Myrtle Beach bones to that found in the St-Basile-le-Grand bones we'll at least know if all the remains come from the same individual. If they do we have essentially identified the Myrtle Beach bones because we have a firm ID on the Montreal skull. But I would like to get a DNA."

"What if there's no DNA?"

"I've already had microscope slides made from one of the St-Basile thigh bones. When I get back I'll do the same with these samples, then I'll examine everything under high-powered magnification."

156

"What will that tell you?"

"Age, for one thing. I'll see if that's consistent between the two sets of remains. I'll also look for details in microstructure that might be useful."

It was almost one when we'd labeled and numbered the four specimens and Kate had done the paperwork necessary to release them to me. We decided to grab a quick lunch before tackling the case file. Over cheeseburgers and fries at the local Wendy's she related what was known of Savannah Osprey's last hours.

According to the parents, Savannah had had a routine week. Her health was good and she was looking forward to an event at her school, though they couldn't remember what it was. On the day of her disappearance she spent the early afternoon studying for a math exam, but didn't appear particularly anxious about it. Around two she said she needed something at the drugstore, and left the house on foot. They never saw her again.

"At least that was Daddy's version," Kate concluded.

"He was at home that day?"

"Until around three-thirty, when he made a pickup in Wilmington, then set out for Myrtle Beach. The departure time was confirmed by his employer. He showed up a little late with the delivery, but blamed the delay on traffic."

"Were you able to search the house or truck?"

"Nope. We had nothing on him, so we could never get a warrant."

"And the mother?"

"Brenda. She's another piece of work."

Kate took a bite of burger then wiped her mouth with a paper napkin.

"Brenda was working that day. I think she cleaned motel rooms. According to her statement, when she returned at five the house was empty. She didn't begin to worry until it got dark and Savannah didn't call or show up. By midnight Mama was panicked and reported her daughter missing."

She drained her Coke.

"Brenda was cooperative for about two days, then did a complete reversal and decided her daughter had taken off with friends. From then on it was like talking to a frozen pork roast. It was the Shallotte PD that contacted us and eventually got the NCIC info from Savannah's doctors and dentist. That's normally the job of the parent or guardian."

"Why the about-face?"

"Dwayne probably threatened her."

"What happened to him?"

"About five years after Savannah disappeared Dwayne must have developed a yearning for the mountains. He drove all the way up to Chimney Rock to celebrate July Fourth by camping and drinking with his buddies. On his second night there he made a beer run into town and Yankee Doodle Dandied himself right off the highway and into Hickory Nut Gorge. He was thrown out and the car rolled over him. I understand that when they found him the diameter of Dwayne's head exceeded that of the spare tire."

Kate bunched up her wrappers, centered them on her tray, and pushed back from the table.

"The investigation pretty much died with Dwayne," she said as she slid everything into a waste container.

We emerged from the restaurant and onto a small patio where an ancient black man in a Yankees cap greeted us with the standard "Hey." He was watering flowers with a garden hose, and the scent of wet earth and petunias mingled with the odor of cooking grease.

Afternoon sun glared off cement and warmed my head and shoulders as we crossed the parking lot to Kate's car. When we were buckled in I asked, "Do you think he did it?"

There was a silence before she answered.

"I don't know, Tempe. Some things didn't add up."

I waited as she sorted through her thoughts.

"Dwayne Osprey had a drinking problem and was mean as a snake, but the fact that he lived in Shallotte meant some village was deprived of its rightful idiot. I mean this guy was stupid. I never thought he could kill his child and transport her body to another city, then cover his tracks completely. He just didn't have the neurons. Besides, a lot was going on that week."

"Such as?"

"Every year in mid-May there's a huge motorcycle rally in Myrtle Beach. It's a mandatory run for Hells Angels chapters in the South, and a lot of Pagans usually show up, as well. The place was crawling with bikers that week, everything from outlaw to Rubbie."

"Rubbie?" She couldn't mean it in the Montreal sense, where the term was slang for wino.

"Rich Urban Bikers. Anyway, that's how I ended up on the case. My boss thought there might be a gang connection."

"Was there?"

"We never found one."

"What do you think?"

"Hell, Tempe, I don't know. Shallotte is right on Highway 17 en route to Myrtle Beach and there are dozens of motels and fast-food joints along there. With all the traffic heading to and from South Carolina that week she could have just bumped into some psychopath pulling off the highway for chicken and biscuits."

"But why murder her?" I knew it was stupid as soon as I asked it.

"People are shot for driving too close, for wearing red where the blue gang hangs, for getting product from the wrong supplier. Maybe someone killed her just for wearing glasses."

Or for no reason at all, like Emily Anne Toussaint.

Back at the SBI lab we spread out the dossier and began examining documents. Medical records. Dental records. Phone records. Arrest records. Transcripts of interviews. Reports of neighborhood canvassing. Handwritten notes taken on stakeouts.

The SBI and Shallotte investigators had pursued every lead. Even the neighbors had pitched in. Parties searched ponds, rivers, and woods. All to no avail. Savannah Osprey had left her house and disappeared.

Nine months after Savannah's disappearance, remains were found in Myrtle Beach. Suspecting a link to the Osprey case the Horry County coroner contacted North Carolina authorities and sent the bones to Chapel Hill. The medical examiner's report noted consistency, but concluded that positive identification of the skeleton was not possible. Officially, no trace of Savannah was ever found.

The last entry in the file was dated July 10, 1989. Following Dwayne Osprey's death his wife had again been questioned. Brenda held to the story that her daughter had run away.

We finished with the file after seven. My eyes burned and my back screamed from hours of bending over small print and bad handwriting. I was tired, discouraged, and I'd missed my flight. And I'd learned almost nothing. A sigh from Kate told me she was on the same page.

"Now what?" I asked.

"Now let's get you a place to stay, have a nice dinner, and figure where to go from here."

Seemed like a plan.

I reserved a room at a Red Roof Inn on I-40 and booked a morning flight. Then I tried Kit but got no answer. Surprised, I left a message and the number for my cell phone. When I'd finished, Kate and I packed our respective bones and drove up Garner Road to her office.

The structure housing the SBI stood in stark contrast to its ultramodern crime laboratory. While the latter is high-rise cement, all sterile and efficient, the head-quarters building is only two stories, a genteel redbrick affair with cream-colored trim. Surrounded by mani-cured grounds and approached by an entrance lane of stately oaks, the complex blends better with the tiny antiques store it faces than with the megalith down the road.

We parked on the main avenue, retrieved our packages, and headed toward the building. To the right lay a circular hedge with border plantings of marigolds and pansies. Three poles rose from the garden's center, like the masts on a square rigger. I could hear the flap of fabric and the clink of metal as a uniformed officer lowered the last of the flags. He was backlit by a partial sun dropping below the roof of the Highway Patrol Training Center.

We passed through the glass door with its North Carolina Department of Justice, State Bureau of Investigation crest, cleared security, and climbed to the second floor. Once again we secured the bones, this time in a locked cabinet in Kate's small office.

"What would you like to eat?"

"Meat," I said without hesitating. "Red meat marbled with real fat."

"We had cheeseburgers for lunch."

"True. But I just read a theory about the evolution of Neanderthals into modern human beings. Seems the key to the transition was increased fat in the diet. Maybe a pair of big prime ribs will help our thought processes."

"I'm convinced."

The beef turned out to be a good idea. Or maybe it was just the break from blurry print on photocopied documents. By the time our cobbler arrived we'd focused on the central question.

The bones in Montreal were without a doubt Savannah's. For the bones found here the jury was still out. Did a sickly sixteen-year-old girl with bad eyesight and a timid personality travel fifteen hundred miles north of her home to another country and die there? Or did some, but not all, of the bones belonging to a dead girl get taken from the Carolinas to Montreal and buried there?

If death occurred in Montreal, the Myrtle Beach bones *were not* Savannah's.

Though Kate didn't buy this theory, she did admit to its possibility.

If the Myrtle Beach bones *were* Savannah's, part of the skeleton had been moved.

I'd studied the scene photos and found nothing disturbing. The decomposition appeared consistent with a period of nine months, and a postmortem interval that tallied with the date of Savannah's disappearance. Unlike the pit at the Vipers' clubhouse, this scene gave no indication of a secondary burial.

This assumption presented several possibilities.

Savannah died in Myrtle Beach.

Savannah died elsewhere, then her body was brought to Myrtle Beach.

Savannah's body was dismembered, parts either brought to or left in Myrtle Beach, then the skull and leg bones separated and transported to Canada.

But if the body had been deliberately separated, why were there no cut marks on any of the bones?

The key question remained: How did Savannah, either in whole or part, alive or dead, end up in Quebec?

"Do you think they'll reopen the case?" I asked as we waited for the bill.

"It's doubtful. Everyone was pretty well convinced Dwayne did it. The investigation had stalled long before his accident, but his death really capped it."

I handed the waiter my Visa card, ignoring Kate's protests.

"What now?"

"Here's my thinking," she said. "First of all, that was a sneak play on the check."

Yeah. Yeah. I urged her on with a hand gesture.

"Savannah's skull was found on biker property in Quebec."

She enumerated points by raising fingers.

"The Vipers are a puppet club for the Hells Angels, correct?"

I nodded.

"The Angels were gathering just down the highway from Savannah's hometown the week she disappeared."

A third finger joined the other two.

"Her skeleton turned up in Myrtle Beach State Park, a stone's throw from the party venue."

Her eyes met mine.

"Seems worth looking into."

"But you did that."

"We didn't have the Quebec link."

"What do you propose?"

"The early eighties were a wild ride for Carolina bikers. Let's pull out my gang files and see what we can see."

"They go back that far?"

"The gathering of historic information is one of my mandates. Predicate acts are often important in RICO investigations, especially old homicides."

She referred to the Racketeering Influenced and Corrupt Organizations Act signed by Nixon in 1970. The statute was often used in the prosecution of organized crime.

"Also, gang members often shift between chapters and it's helpful to know who was at what location at what time when you're looking for witnesses. I have tons of information, including photos and videos."

"I've got all night," I said, spreading my hands.

"Let's go look at bikers."

And that's what we did until my cell phone rang at 5:23 A.M. The call was from Montreal.

19

Les Appartements du Soleil were anything *but* sunny, contrary to their name. But naming the place after its actual attributes would have been bad marketing. The building was dark and cheerless, its windows clouded by grime and painted shut by decades of careless maintenance. The tiny balconies jutting from each of its three floors were wrapped in turquoise siding and packed with rusted grills and cheap lawn chairs, plastic garbage cans, and assorted types of athletic equipment. One or two had flowerpots, the contents brown and withered from seasons past.

But no one could fault the heating system. In the day I'd been gone in North Carolina spring had finally made it to Quebec, and I touched down to a report of sixty-eight degrees Fahrenheit. It was above that now, but the Soleil's radiators soldiered on, raising the temperature inside to well over eighty. The heat and the odor of putrefaction combined to make one queasy and inclined toward shallow breathing.

From where I stood I could see into each of the rooms

that made up the squalid little flat. The kitchen lay to my left, the living room to my right, the bedroom and bath straight ahead. The place looked as if its occupant had been holding a garage sale, though the filth and stench would have discouraged even the most ardent bargain hunter.

Every elevated surface was heaped with tools, magazines, paperback books, bottles and broken appliances, and the floor was crammed with camping equipment, automobile and motorcycle parts, tires, cardboard boxes, hockey sticks, and plastic bags tied with metal twisters. A pyramid of beer cans rose almost to the ceiling at the far end of the living room, with torn and curling posters tacked to the wall on either side. The poster on the right advertised a Grateful Dead concert. July 17, 1983. Below it a White Power fist advocated Aryan purity.

On the top left a poster entitled *Le Hot Rod* showed a penis in Ray-Bans, a smoking cigarette tucked between it and its companion genitalia. The image below featured an upright phallus, the words *Astro-Cock* in bold letters across the top. The organ was circled by the symbols of the Zodiac, a message of wisdom under each. I took a pass on consulting my sign.

As far as I could see, the only furniture available for practical use consisted of a Formica table and single chair in the kitchen, a twin bed in the bedroom, and an armchair in the living room. A body now occupied the armchair, its head a distorted red mass above a blackened torso and limbs. Embedded in the flesh I could see a shattered skull and facial bones, a partial nostril with mustache skirt, and one complete eye. The lower jaw hung slack but intact, showing a purpled tongue and rotten teeth stained brown.

Someone had collected shards of bone and brain

pudding and sealed them in a Ziploc bag. The plastic sack lay in the man's lap, as though he'd been put in charge of watching over his own brain. A large flap of skin clung to the edge of the chair, smooth and shiny as the belly of a perch.

The deceased sat opposite a small TV on which a coat hanger had been rigged to replace the broken antenna. One twisted end projected toward his head, like the finger of an eyewitness pointing to its find. No one had bothered to turn the set off and I could hear Montel talking with women whose mothers had stolen their lovers. I wondered what the discussants would think of their grisly viewer.

A member of the Ident section dusted the bedroom for latent prints, while another did the same in the kitchen. A third worked a camcorder, slowly sweeping each room, then zooming in for close-ups of the jumbles of junk. Before I'd gotten there, she'd shot dozens of stills of the victim and his gloomy surroundings.

LaManche had been and gone. Since the body wasn't badly burned and decomposition was only moderate I wasn't really needed, but that hadn't been clear in the early stages. Initial reports described a body and a fire, so I'd been called and transport arrangements had been made. By the time the scene was assessed, I was in transit from Raleigh and the simplest thing was to follow through with the original plan. Quickwater had picked me up at the airport and brought me here.

Les Appartements du Soleil were located southwest of Centre-ville, on a small street running east from rue Charlevoix. The neighborhood, known as Pointe-St-Charles, was on the island of Montreal, so the murder fell to the CUM.

Michel Charbonneau stood across the room, his face

167

the color of Pepto-Bismol, his hair projecting in clammy spikes. He was jacketless, his collar soaked with sweat, his tie hanging below the open top button of his shirt. Even loosened it was much too short. I watched him pull a hankie from his pocket and wipe it across his forehead.

Charbonneau once told me that as a teen he'd worked in the Texas oil fields. Though he loved the cowboy life, the heat won out and he'd returned to his home in Chicoutimi, eventually drifting to Montreal, where he joined the city police force.

At that moment Quickwater emerged from the kitchen. The victim was known to have gang connections, so Carcajou would also be involved.

The constable joined Charbonneau and the two stood watching a team examine bloodstains in a corner behind the victim. Ronald Gilbert held a gray-and-white L-shaped ruler against the wall while a younger man shot videos and prints. They repeated the shots with a plumb line, then Gilbert switched to sliding calipers and took a series of measurements. He entered the data into a laptop computer, then went back to the ABFO ruler and plumb line. More video footage. More photos. More measurements. Blood was everywhere, speckling the ceiling and walls and mottling objects stacked against the baseboards. The two looked like they'd be at their task a long time.

I took a deep breath and approached the detectives.

"*Bonjour. Comment ça va?*"

"Eh, Doc. How's tricks?" Charbonneau's English was an odd blend of québécois and Texas slang, most of the latter out-of-date.

"*Bonjour, Monsieur Quickwater.*"

Quickwater rotated slightly, looking annoyed at having to acknowledge my presence, then returned his attention to the blood-spatter team. They were filming an acoustic guitar propped upright on a rusted birdcage. Behind the cage I could see an athletic cap jammed against the wall, the letters "-cock-" visible in the center of a wine-colored blotch. I thought of the posters and wondered what lewd macho message we'd been spared by the gore.

"Where's Claudel?" I asked Charbonneau.

"Checking out a suspect, but he'll be here soon. These guys are really something, aren't they?" Charbonneau's voice filled with disgust. "Got the moral qualities of dung beetles."

"This is definitely gang-related?"

"Yeah. The guy that's not looking too good over there is Yves Desjardins, street name 'Cherokee.' He was a Predator."

"Where do they fit in?"

"The Predators are another Hells Angels puppet club."

"Like the Vipers."

"You got it."

"So this was a Rock Machine hit?"

"Probably. Though I understand Cherokee hadn't been active in years. He had a bad liver. No. Colon cancer. That was it. Not surprising given the shit these guys usually have on board."

"What had he done to anger the opposition?"

"Cherokee ran some kind of spare-parts business." When Charbonneau made a sweeping gesture I could see a dark crescent under his armpit. "But apparently sprockets and carburetors weren't profitable enough. We found about two kilos of coke hidden in the big brave's underwear drawer. No doubt a safe spot since the guy looks like he never changed his shorts. Anyway,

169

that's probably what inspired the surprise visit. But who knows? Maybe it was retaliation for the Marcotte hit."

"Spider."

Charbonneau nodded.

"Were there signs of forced entry?"

"There's a broken window in the bedroom, but that's not how they got in."

"It's not?"

"Most of the fragments are in the alley. Looks like the window was popped from inside."

"By whom?"

He gave a palms-up gesture.

"So how did the killer get in?"

"He must have let them in."

"Why would he do that?"

"Cherokee was wily as a pit bull and just a little less friendly. But he'd outlived the stats and was probably starting to feel immortal."

"Except for the cancer."

"Right. Let me show you something."

Charbonneau crossed to the body and I followed. Close up the smell was stronger, a nauseating blend of charred wool, gasoline, excrement, and putrefying flesh. He pulled out his hankie and held it across his nose.

"Check out the tattoos." Muffled.

Cherokee's right hand was in his lap, his left flung at an odd angle across the arm of the chair, fingers hanging toward the carpet. Despite a thick layer of soot, a cluster of skulls was clearly visible on his right wrist. There were fifteen in all, arranged in a pyramid like the mysterious offerings found in European caves. But these trophies showed a distinction our Neanderthal ancestors had failed to make. Thirteen of the skulls had black eyes, two had red.

"They're like notches on a gun." Charbonneau took the cloth from his mouth just long enough to speak. "Black means he killed a male, red a female."

"Pretty stupid to advertise."

"Yeah, but our boy here was old school. Today they're listening more to their lawyers."

From the amount of bloating and skin slippage I guessed the victim had been dead a couple of days.

"How was he found?"

"The usual. A neighbor complained about a foul odor. Amazing anyone would notice in this shithole."

I looked at the body again. Other than the bad teeth and mustache it was impossible to tell what the man had looked like. What was left of his head rested against the back of the chair, a dark blossom staining the upholstery around it. I could see shotgun pellets in the flesh that had been his face.

"Like the special effects?"

Charbonneau pointed at the small braided carpet below the victim's feet. It was badly charred, as was the underside of the chair. Cherokee himself was smoke-blackened, and his dangling left hand, jean cuffs, and boots were singed. But beyond that there was little damage due to burning.

A fire had been set in front of the chair, and the lingering smell of gasoline suggested the use of an accelerant. Flames had probably engulfed the body, but then, lacking fuel, petered out. By then the killers were long gone.

Charbonneau lifted the hankie again.

"Typical biker shit. Blast the target then torch the body. Only this team must have failed Arson 101."

"Why would this guy open the door if he was dealing coke in someone else's backyard?"

"Maybe his colon backed up into his brain. Maybe he was smacked on drugs. Maybe he suffered from delusions of normalcy. Hell, who knows how they think? Or if they think."

"Could it have been his own club?"

"Ain't without precedent."

Claudel arrived at that moment and Charbonneau excused himself to join his colleagues. While I was curious about the suspect he'd been interrogating, I didn't want to take on a Claudel-Quickwater tag team, so I moved to the far side of the room and resumed observation of the blood-spatter analysts. By now they'd finished the west wall and were rounding the corner onto the north.

Though I'd positioned myself as far from the body as I could get, the smell in the room was becoming unbearable. And Charbonneau was right. The corpse was only one element in the sickening cocktail of mildew, motor oil, stale beer, perspiration, and years of bad cooking. It was hard to imagine how anyone could have lived in such a putrid atmosphere.

I looked at my watch. Two-fifteen. Starting to think about a taxi, I turned to the window at my back.

Cherokee lived on the first floor, his balcony not six feet above the sidewalk. Through the filthy glass I could see the usual armada of cruisers, vans, and unmarked cars. Neighbors stood in clumps or observed from the stoops of neighboring buildings. Press cars and mini-vans added to the confusion on the small street.

The morgue vehicle pulled up as I was surveying the assemblage, and two attendants hopped out, released the rear doors, and withdrew a gurney. They snapped the wheels into place and pushed the cart up the short front walk to the building's entrance, passing between rutted patches of mud, each furrow filled with standing water. An iridescent slick shone atop the surface of each. Nice. The front yard du Soleil.

In seconds the transport team knocked on the door. Claudel admitted them, then rejoined the group. Steeling myself, I crossed to the detectives. Claudel did not interrupt his account of the interview with the prime suspect.

"You think that wall is a mess?" Claudel gestured toward the northwest corner where the recovery team was still measuring and filming bloodstains. "This guy's jacket looks like he wore it in the slaughtering house at a stockyard. Of course the little roach hasn't the brains to pull the wings off a moth."

"Why did he hang on to it?" Charbonneau.

"He was probably too cheap to part with the leather. And he figured we'd never link him. But he'd taken the time to wipe it off and stash it under the bed, just in case."

"He was spotted here Monday night?"

"Just after midnight."

"That squares with LaManche's estimated time of death. What's his story?"

"He's having a little trouble remembering. It seems George drinks a bit."

"Any ties to the vic?"

"George has been a Heathens hang-around for years. They let him drive and deal a little grass, so he thinks he's hot stuff. But he's so low in the hierarchy he needs a snorkel just to breathe."

A transporter called to Claudel, and the detective gave a go-ahead gesture. One of the men unfolded a body bag and laid it on the gurney, while the other placed a brown paper bag on Cherokee's left hand.

Watching Claudel, I was struck by how out of place

he appeared. His brow was sweat free, his hair perfect, the creases on his trousers sharp as razor blades. A spot of Armani in the midst of a nightmare.

"Maybe he saw the hit as his big chance for upward mobility," said Charbonneau.

"Undoubtedly. But George Dorsey isn't going to be mobile for a long time." Claudel.

"Is there enough to hold him?" Quickwater.

"I'll hold him on suspicion of spitting if I have to. My sources tell me Dorsey recently sent out word he was looking for work, and that no job was off-limits. We've got him pegged for another hit, so I showed his picture around. A witness put Dorsey right here when the shoot went down, and when I dropped in to discuss this fact, I found Dorsey's outerwear covered with blood. Does that sound dirty to you?"

At that moment Claudel's radio erupted in static. He stepped toward the door, listened, spoke into the mouthpiece, then gestured to Quickwater. The two men exchanged words, then Quickwater turned to Charbonneau, pointed at me then at the door. When Charbonneau gave a thumbs-up Quickwater waved and exited into the hall, and Claudel rejoined us.

Great. I'd been passed off like someone's kid sister.

There are two emotions that cause me agitation: feeling trapped and feeling useless. I was experiencing both, and it was making me restless.

And something about the scene bothered me. I knew I was out of my element, but I kept remembering the slides I'd seen at Carcajou headquarters. What I was seeing didn't ring true.

What the hell. I hadn't asked to come here.

"Isn't this a little different from their normal method of dispatch?"

174

Claudel turned in my direction, his face pinched into its usual chilly expression.

"Excuse me?"

"Isn't the shotgun off from the MO for a biker hit? And the botched fire?"

Charbonneau cocked an eyebrow and shrugged both shoulders. Claudel said nothing.

"This seems so messy," I pressed on, determined to make a contribution. "In the cases I've reviewed the hits were pretty efficient."

"Things happen," said Charbonneau. "Maybe the perp was interrupted."

"I guess that's my point. Don't bikers research their victims and pick settings where they know they won't be interrupted?"

"With a dead biker who was freelancing in the drug trade, we do not need to search the membership roster at the Unitarian church to find our hit man." Claudel's voice was cool.

"Nor should we slam our brains shut after the first theory drifts into them," I said caustically.

Claudel gave me a look implying infinitely strained patience.

"You may be very good at digging up bodies and measuring bones, Ms Brennan. But those skills are not at the heart of this homicide investigation."

"It's hard to find a hit man if you don't know who's been hit, Monsieur Claudel. Are *you* going to put his face back together?" Anger made my face burn.

"That will not be a problem here. Fingerprints should suffice."

I knew that, but Claudel's arrogance was bringing out the worst in me.

175

Charbonneau crossed his arms and blew out a deep breath.

Claudel checked his watch and I saw the flash of a gold cuff link. Then the arm dropped to his side.

"Sergent-détective Charbonneau and I will drop you off." His voice indicated he would not be discussing the case further on this occasion.

"Thank you."

We crossed the room and I took one last look at the chair where Yves "Cherokee" Desjardins had died. It was empty now, but a port-colored cloud marked the place where his head had rested. Dark rivulets curved from each lobe, like the talons on a raptor greedy for a kill.

Claudel held the door and I exited to the corridor, gripping my bags so tightly my nails bit into the heels of my hands. Still annoyed with Claudel's superior attitude, as I swept past him I couldn't resist one last gibe.

"As you know, Monsieur Claudel, I am the lab's liaison to Carcajou. You have a professional obligation to share ideas and information with me, like it or not, and I expect nothing less."

With that I strode down the hall and descended into sunlight.

20

Though we drove through bright sunshine, my thoughts were dark. When I had volunteered for the Carcajou unit it had been to help solve the Emily Anne shooting, not to join the murder-of-the-day club. I rode in back, my mind shifting between Yves "Cherokee" Desjardins and Savannah Claire Osprey, victims as different as Charlie Manson and the Sugarplum Fairy.

But Savannah hadn't danced off with Ariel or Puck, and I couldn't shake the image of the spider-legged girl in the baggy swimsuit. I kept wondering about the poisonous web into which she'd been drawn.

I was also haunted by the horror we'd just left. Though the dynamic duo in the front seat were convinced Cherokee's killing was a biker hit, something about the scene seemed out of sync. It was not my call, but my uneasiness remained, prickling my brain.

Savannah and Cherokee. Cherokee and Savannah. And Ronald and Donald Vaillancourt, Robert Gately and Félix Martineau. And Emily Anne Toussaint, the little girl who danced, and skated, and loved waffles.

These lives seemed unconnected, the only tie a post-humous one, created by homicide files.

No one spoke. Now and then the radio sputtered as it scanned channels, diligent in its attention to police matters.

In the Ville-Marie Tunnel we were snared briefly by the clog of traffic exiting onto Berri. I looked at the flow of cars heading toward the old city and experienced a return to melancholy. Why was I trapped with Señor Surly and his partner, the bones of a dead girl at my feet and visions of mutilated bikers in my head? Why wasn't I heading for Place Jacques Cartier, thinking about dinner, dancing, or drinks with a lover?

But I couldn't handle the pleasure of drink.

And I had no lover.

Ryan.

Put it away, Brennan. That line of thought will take you from melancholy to depression. The simple fact is you chose this life. You could be limiting your bone analysis to archaeological digs and your professional commentaries to textbooks or classrooms in which you talk and they listen. You asked for this and you got it, so stop brooding and do your work.

When Charbonneau pulled up at the SQ building I said a terse thank you, slammed the door, and headed up the block toward the main entrance. Before I got to the end of the wrought-iron fence my cell phone rang, so I set the athletic bag on the sidewalk and dug the phone out of my purse.

"Aunt Tempe?"

"Hey, Kit."

I was relieved and annoyed to hear his voice. Though I'd called several times since leaving for Raleigh, Kit hadn't once picked up.

"Did you get my messages?"

"Yeah. Bad timing. I was out, then when I got in I hit the sack. Figured you wouldn't want me to call that late."

I waited.

"I was with Lyle."

"For two days?"

"The guy's O.K."

O.K.?

"We went to that cycle shop. Man, he wasn't exaggerating. They've got more shit than the Harley factory. Oops, sorry."

"Hm."

I placed the briefcase next to the athletic bag and rotated my shoulder to work out a kink. Hip-hop music pounded from a Caravan on the opposite side of Parthenais. The driver sat sideways, one arm draped around the wheel, the other drumming the back of the seat.

"I'll be home by six," I told Kit. "Tell me what you'd like and I'll throw something together for dinner."

"That's why I'm calling. Lyle said he'd take me to the TV studio so I can watch them do the show tonight."

A man emerged from an apartment building across the street and did a slow crawl down the steps, a cigarette dangling from his mouth. His hair looked as if he'd gotten his head too close to an explosion. Some of it stuck out in clumps, some strands lay in knots against his head. He wore a sleeveless denim jacket that showed arms so fully tattooed that from where I stood they looked blue.

The man took a deep drag as he scanned the street. His eyes locked onto me then narrowed, like those of a terrier sighting on a rat. Two smoke streams shot from his nose, then he flicked the butt, crossed the sidewalk, and climbed into the van with the music lover. As the pair drove off I felt a chill, despite the warmth of the afternoon sun.

". . . ever seen it in person?"

"What?"

"The news. Have you ever been at the station when they actually do it?"

"Yes. It's very interesting."

"So if you don't mind, I'd really like to go."

"Sure. That sounds like fun. I'm pretty beat anyway."

"Did you find out who she is?"

The switch left me behind.

"The girl. Did she turn out to be who you thought she was?"

"Yes."

"That's cool. Can I tell Lyle?"

"It's not official yet. Better wait until the coroner releases her name."

"No sweat. So, I'll see you later."

"O.K."

"You're sure?"

"Kit, it's fine. I've been ditched by tougher men than you."

"Ooh. Hit me where I bleed."

"Bye."

Lyle Crease. Was that bastard going to use my nephew to wheedle information that he couldn't get directly from me?

Upstairs, I secured Savannah's remains in my evidence locker, and gave one set of bone samples to Denis, the

180

histology technician. He would use a microtome to cut slices less than a hundred microns thick, then stain them and mount them on slides for analysis.

I took the other set to the DNA section. While there I asked about the eyeball. As I waited I felt a band of tension move slowly up the back of my head, and I began to rub my neck.

"Headache?" asked the technician when she returned.

"A little."

The results were not yet in.

Next I reported to LaManche. He didn't interrupt as I told him of my meeting with Kate, and showed him photos and copies of hospital records.

When I'd finished he removed his glasses and kneaded two red ovals on the bridge of his nose. Then he leaned back, his face devoid of the emotions normally created by death.

"I will call the coroner's office."

"Thank you."

"Have you discussed this with the people at Carcajou?"

"I mentioned it to Quickwater, but right now everyone is focused on the Cherokee Desjardins murder."

That was an understatement. When I'd told him in the car, Quickwater had hardly listened.

"I'll talk to Roy tomorrow," I added.

"The agent in North Carolina believes this child was killed by gang members?"

"Kate Brophy. She believes it's a good possibility."

"Does she know of any ties between Quebec and Myrtle Beach gangs?"

"No."

LaManche inhaled deeply, exhaled.

"Nineteen eighty-four is a long time ago."

Sitting across from my boss, listening to his precise French and seeing him backlit by the St Lawrence River, I had to admit the Carolina theory sounded bizarre even to me. What had seemed so right in Raleigh now felt like a remembered dream in which I couldn't sort reality from fantasy.

"We had to cut it short when I got the call about Cherokee's body in the fire, but Agent Brophy lent me a great deal of material from the SBI files, including old photos. Tomorrow I'll take everything over to Carcajou and we'll see what falls out."

LaManche replaced his glasses.

"This Carolina skeleton may be unrelated."

"I know."

"How soon will they have the DNA results?"

I avoided the impulse to roll my eyes, but I'm sure the frustration showed in my voice.

"They're backed up because of the bomber twin case, and wouldn't give me an estimate." I remembered the look I'd gotten when the technician spotted Savannah's DOD. "And, as you said, it's not exactly a recent death."

LaManche nodded.

"But it is an unexplained death, and the remains were found in Quebec, so we will treat it as a homicide. Hopefully the SQ will do the same," he said.

At that moment his phone rang. I gathered papers as he spoke. When he'd hung up I said, "The Cherokee case doesn't fit the recent pattern here, but who knows why people kill."

He answered as he scribbled something on a small yellow pad, his mind still on the phone conversation. Or perhaps he thought I was talking about something else.

"Occasionally Monsieur Claudel can be abrupt, but in the end he will get it right."

What the hell did that mean?

Before I could ask, the phone rang again. LaManche reached for the receiver, listened, then held it to his chest.

"Was there anything else?"

A polite dismissal.

I was so preoccupied by LaManche's comment about Claudel that I almost collided with Jocelyn the temp as I left his office and headed toward my own. She wore large beaded loops in her ears, and the hair streaks were now the color of purple African violets.

As we circled each other, readjusting our armloads of papers, I again was struck by the whiteness of her skin. Under the harsh fluorescent light, her lower lids looked plum, her skin as pale as the underbelly of a lemon peel. It crossed my mind Jocelyn might be albino.

For some reason, I felt compelled to speak to her.

"How are you getting along, Jocelyn?"

She stared at me with a look I couldn't interpret.

"I hope you're not finding the lab too over-whelming."

"I can do the job."

"Yes, of course you can. I just meant it's hard to be the new kid on the block."

As she opened her mouth to say something, a secretary emerged from an adjacent office. Jocelyn hurried off down the hall.

Jesus, I thought. This one could use a bit of charm school. Maybe she could get a two-for-the-price-of-one deal for her and Quickwater.

I spent the rest of the afternoon clearing my desk of

183

message slips. Calls from the media I threw away, those from law enforcement I returned.

I scanned a request from Pelletier, the oldest of the lab pathologists. Bones had been found by a homeowner in Outremont when he dug a hole in his cellar floor. The remains were old and brittle, but Pelletier was unsure if they were human.

Nothing urgent.

My desk reasonably clear, I drove home and spent another glamorous evening in the oldest French city in North America.

Pizza. Bath. Baseball.

Birdie stayed through the eighth inning, then curled into a ball on the guest room bed. When I turned in at eleven-fifteen he stretched and relocated to my bedroom chair.

I fell asleep almost immediately and dreamed piece-meal scenarios that made no sense. Kit waved from a boat, Andrew Ryan by his side. Isabelle served dinner. A headless Cherokee Desjardins tweezered pieces of flesh and dropped them into a plastic sack.

When Kit came in I floated to the surface, but was too groggy to call out. He was still fumbling in the kitchen when I sank back into oblivion.

The next morning I was going through Pelletier's bones when Denis came into my lab.

"*C'est la vedette!*"

The star?

Oh no.

He opened a copy of *Le Journal de Montréal* and showed me a picture of myself at the Vipers' clubhouse. Beside it was a short story recounting the recovery of Gately and Martineau, and identifying the mysterious third skeleton as that of sixteen-year-old Savannah Claire Osprey, according to the coroner, an American missing since 1984. The caption described me as a member of the Carcajou unit.

"*C'est une promotion ou une réduction?*"

I smiled, wondering if Quickwater and Claudel would see the error as a promotion or demotion, then resumed sorting. So far I was up to two lamb dinners, a pot roast, and more grilled chicken than I planned to count.

By ten I'd finished with the bones and written a detailed narrative saying that the remains were not human.

I took the report to the secretarial pool, then returned to my office and dialed Carcajou headquarters. Jacques Roy was in a meeting and wouldn't be free until late afternoon. I left my name and number. I tried Claudel, left the same message. Charbonneau. Same name, same number. Please call. I thought of using pagers, decided the situation was not that urgent.

Frustrated, I swiveled my chair and surveyed the river.

I couldn't examine the microstructure of the Myrtle Beach bones because the slides weren't ready. God knew when I'd have DNA results, or if there would be anything there to sequence.

I thought of calling Kate Brophy, but didn't want to pressure her. Besides, she was as concerned about the Osprey case as I was. More so. If she discovered anything she'd let me know.

Now what?

LaManche was downstairs performing an autopsy on Cherokee. I could drop in, maybe assuage my doubts about the killing.

185

Pass. I was not enthused at the thought of studying another biker spread out on a table.

I decided to organize the material Kate had given me. I'd left in such a rush that I hadn't gone through it. We'd done a quick triage, packed everything into my briefcase, signed for possession, and raced to catch a flight.

I emptied the case onto my desk and stacked the photos to my left, the folders to my right. I picked a brown envelope, shook several five-by-sevens onto the blotter, and flipped one over. It was labeled on the back with a date, location, event, name, and several reference numbers.

I reversed the photo and stared into the face of Martin "Deluxe" DeLuccio, immortalized on July 23, 1992, during a run to Wilmington, North Carolina.

The subject's eyes were hidden by dark lenses the size of quarters, and a twisted bandanna circled his head. His sleeveless denim jacket bore the grinning skull and crossed pistons of the Outlaws motorcycle club. The bottom rocker identified its owner as a member of the Lexington chapter.

The biker's flesh appeared puffy, his jawline slack, and a large gut bulged below the jacket. The camera had caught him straddling a powerful hog, a Michelob in his left hand, a vacuous expression on his face. Deluxe looked as if he'd need instructions to use toilet paper.

I was moving on when the telephone rang. I laid Eli "Robin" Hood next to Deluxe and picked up, hoping it was Roy.

It wasn't.

A gravelly voice asked for me, dropping the final long "e" from my first name, but correctly pronouncing the second. The man was a stranger, and obviously an Anglophone. I answered in English.

"This is Dr Brennan."

There was a long pause during which I could hear clanging, and what sounded like a public address system.

"This is Dr Brennan," I repeated.

I heard a throat cleared, then breathing. Finally a voice said, "This is George Dorsey."

"Yes?" My mind scanned, but got no hits.

"You're the one dug up those stiffs?"

The air had gone hollow, as if George Dorsey had cupped his hand around the mouthpiece.

"Yes." Here we go.

"I saw your name in today's pap—"

"Mr Dorsey, if you have information about those individuals you should speak with one of the investigating officers."

Let Claudel or Quickwater deal with the postmedia circus parade.

"Ain't you with Carcajou?"

"Not in the sense you mean. The investigating officer—"

"That fuck has his head so far up his ass he's going to need sonar just to find it."

That got my attention.

"Have you spoken with Constable Quickwater?"

"I can't speak with fuck-all while this moron Claudel is squeezing my nuts."

"Excuse me?"

"This ass wipe has aspirations to higher rank, so I sit here sucking shit."

For a moment no one spoke. The call sounded like it was coming from a bathysphere.

187

"He's probably putting something together for CNN."

I was growing impatient, but didn't want to risk losing information that might be useful.

"Are you calling about the skeletons unearthed in St-Basile?"

I heard choking noises, then, "Shit, no."

It was then that my brain locked on to the name.

George Dorsey was the suspect Claudel had locked up.

"Have you been charged, Mr Dorsey?"

"Fuck, no."

"Why are they holding you?"

"When they popped me I was holding six bumps of meth."

"Why are you calling me?"

"Because none of these other fucks will listen. I didn't whack Cherokee. That was unskilled labor."

I felt my pulse increase.

"What do you mean?"

"That ain't how brothers take care of business."

"Are you saying Cherokee's murder wasn't gang-related?"

"Fuckin' A."

"Then who killed him?"

"Get your ass over here and I'll lay it all out."

I said nothing. Dorsey's breath was loud in the silence.

"But this ain't going to be a one-sided shuck."

"I've got no reason to trust you."

"And you ain't my choice for Woman of the Year, but none of these jag-offs will listen. They've launched the D day of police fuck-ups and parked me right on Omaha Beach."

"I'm impressed with your knowledge of history, Mr Dorsey, but why should I believe you?"

"Got a better lead?"

I let the question dangle a moment. Loser though he was, George Dorsey had a point. And no one else appeared inclined to talk to me today.

I looked at my watch. Eleven-twenty.

"I'll be there in an hour."

21

For policing purposes, the Communauté Urbaine de Montréal is divided into four sections, each with a headquarters housing intervention, analysis and investigation divisions, and a detention center. Suspects arrested for murder or sexual assault are held at a facility near place Versailles, in the far eastern end of the city. All others await arraignment at one of the four sectional jails. For possession of methamphetamine, Dorsey went to his local facility, Op South.

The Op South headquarters is located at rue Guy and boulevard René Lévesque, on the outskirts of Centre-ville. This section is predominantly French and English, but it is also Mandarin, Estonian, Arabic, and Greek. It is separatist and federalist. It holds the vagrant and the affluent, the student and the stockbroker, the immigrant and the "*pur laine*" québécois.

The Op South is churches and bars, boutiques and sex shops, sprawling homes and walk-up flats. The murders of Emily Anne Toussaint and Yves Cherokee Desjardins had taken place within its borders.

As I turned off Guy into the lot, I passed through a group carrying placards and wearing signs. They'd spread down the sidewalk from the building next door, blue-collar workers picketing for higher pay. Good luck, I thought. Perhaps it was the political instability, perhaps the Canadian economy in general, but Quebec Province was in a financial squeeze. Budgets were being cut, services curtailed. I hadn't had a raise in seven years.

I entered at the main door and stepped to a counter to my right.

"I'm here to see George Dorsey," I said to the guard on duty. She put down her snack cake and eyed me with boredom.

"Are you on the list?"

"Temperance Brennan. The prisoner asked to see me."

She brushed chubby hands together, checked for crumbs, then entered something into a keyboard. Light reflected off her glasses as she leaned forward to read the monitor. Text scrolled down each lens, froze, then she spoke again without raising her eyes.

"Carcajou?" Ralph Nader couldn't have sounded more dubious.

"Mm." *Le Journal* thought so.

"Got an ID?"

She looked up and I showed her my security pass for the SQ building.

"No badge?"

"This was handy."

"You'll have to sign in and leave your things here."

She flipped pages in a ledger, wrote something, then handed me the pen. I scribbled the time and my name. Then I slipped my purse off my shoulder and handed it across the counter.

"It'll be a minute."

Ms Cupcake secured my bag in a metal locker, then picked up a phone and spoke a few words. Ten minutes later a key turned in a green metal door to my left, then it opened and a guard waved me in. He was skeletal, his uniform drooping from his bones like clothes on a hanger.

Guard number two swept me with a handheld metal detector, then indicated I should follow. Keys jangled on his belt as we turned right and headed down a corridor lighted by fluorescents and surveilled by wall and ceiling cameras. Straight ahead I could see a large holding cell, with a window facing the hall I was in, green bars facing the other. Inside, a half-dozen men lounged on wooden benches, sat or slept on the floor, or clung to the bars like captive primates.

Beyond the drunk tank was another green metal door, the words *Bloc Cellulaire* in bold white to its right, beside that another counter. A guard was placing a bundle in one of a grid of cubicles, this one marked XYZ. I suspected a Mr Xavier was arriving. He would not see his belt, shoelaces, jewelry, glasses, or other personal possessions until checkout.

"Man's in here," said the guard, thrusting his chin toward a door marked *Entrevue avocat*, the door attorneys used. I knew Dorsey would pass through an identical door marked *Entrevue détenu*, for the prisoners.

I thanked him and brushed past into a small room not designed to lift prisoner or visitor morale. The walls were yellow, the trim green, the only furnishings a red vinyl counter, a wooden stool fixed to the floor, and a wall phone.

George Dorsey sat on the opposite side of a large

rectangular window, back rounded, hands dangling between his knees.

"Push the button when you're done," said the guard. With that he closed the door and we were alone.

Dorsey didn't move but his eyes locked on me as I crossed to the counter and picked up the handset.

I flashed on Gran's painting. Jesus, skull circled with thorns, forehead covered with droplets of blood. No matter where I went the gaze followed. Look, the eyes were open. Blink, they were closed. The picture was so unnerving I avoided my grandmother's bedroom my entire childhood. Dorsey had the same eyes.

Inwardly trembling, I sat and folded my hands on the countertop. The man across from me was thin and wiry, with a hump nose and razor-blade lips. A scar started at his left temple, looped his cheek, and disappeared into a circle of plumage around his mouth. His head was shaved, his only hair a dark bolt of lightning that touched down just above the scar's terminus.

I waited for him to pick up the phone and break the silence. Outside our little room I heard voices and the clang of steel against steel. Despite the intensity of his stare, Dorsey looked as though he hadn't slept in a while.

After several birthdays Dorsey smiled. The lips disappeared and small, yellow teeth took their place. But there was no mirth in his eyes. With a jerky motion he yanked the receiver from its cradle and placed it to his ear.

"You've got balls coming here, lady."

I shrugged.

"Got cigarettes?"

"Don't smoke."

He drew both feet in, flexed his toes, and jiggled one

leg up and down on the ball of his foot. Again he went mute. Then, "I had nothing to do with that piece of work in Pointe-St-Charles."

"So you said." I pictured the gruesome scene at Les Appartements du Soleil.

"This asshole Claudel is trying to cut my dick off. Figures if he sweats me hard enough I'll cop to burning Cherokee."

The jiggling intensified.

"Sergeant-Detective Claudel is simply doing his job."

"Sergeant-Detective Claudel couldn't blow a fart and get it right."

There were times I agreed with that assessment.

"Did you know Cherokee Desjardins?"

"I've heard of him."

He ran a finger back and forth along a groove on the countertop.

"Did you know he was dealing?"

Now Dorsey shrugged.

I waited.

"Maybe the stuff was for personal use. You know, medicinal. I heard he had health problems."

He ran the finger through the hair on his chin, then went back to working the groove.

"You were seen at Desjardins' building around the time he was shot. They found a bloody jacket in your apartment."

"The jacket ain't mine."

"And O.J. never owned the gloves."

"What kind of moron is gonna keep souvenirs after a hit?"

He had a point.

"Why were you in that neighborhood?"

"That's my business."

194

He shot forward and spread his elbows on the counter. My heart did a hop, but I didn't flinch.

"And it had nothing to do with wasting Cherokee."

I noticed a tightening around his eyes, and wondered what scenario he was constructing for my consumption.

More silence.

"Do you know who killed him, George?"

Mistake.

"Ohh, whee!" He curled his fingers and rested his chin on the back of one hand. "And can I call you Tempe?"

"This isn't a social call. You asked to meet."

Dorsey turned sideways and stretched a leg toward the wall. One hand played with the phone cord as he kicked at the baseboard with a laceless boot. Outside the door a man's voice called to someone named Marc. I waited. Finally, "Look, I'm telling you. That hit was *Amateur Hour*. The only thing missing was Ted Mack."

Dorsey swiveled back and tried to stare me down. Then his gaze dropped and he opened and closed his fingers several times. I watched the letters F.T.W. change shape across his knuckles.

"And?"

"That show was not four star, that's all I'll give up right now."

"Then I can't help you. We've already determined it was a sloppy hit."

Dorsey lunged forward again and spread his forearms on the counter.

"Your boy Claudel may think I'm just some Heathens coolie ass wipe, but he's got one thing wrong. I'm not stupid. And neither are they."

I didn't point out that he'd listed two points of error.

"He likes you for this one."

195

Dorsey leaned so close to the glass I could see dirt in the pores on his nose.

"It's a goddam lie. I didn't kill Cherokee."

I looked into the face that was inches from mine, and for one heartbeat the mask slipped. In that fraction of an instant I saw fear and uncertainty. And something else in those bitter, dark eyes. I saw candor.

Then the lids narrowed and the bravado was back.

"I'm going to cut right to it. You don't like the way my friends and me do business. Fair enough. I don't like your righteous bullshit. But know this. Keep grinding me and whoever did Cherokee is going to walk."

"Is that all you can tell me, Mr Dorsey?"

The eyes bored into mine and I could almost smell his hatred.

"I might be privy to additional knowledge," he said, inspecting his fingernails with feigned nonchalance.

"About what?"

"I'm not telling you nothing. But Cherokee's not the only stiff in the news lately."

My mind raced. Was he talking about Spider Marcotte? Did he know the identity of Emily Toussaint's killers?

Before I could ask, Dorsey slumped back again, an amused expression curling the corners of his mouth.

"Is there something funny you'd like to share?"

Dorsey ran a hand under his chin and the goatee curled around his fingers. He shifted the receiver to the other ear.

"Tell pus butt to ease off my case."

I stood to leave, but his next words froze me in place.

"Work with me and I'll give you the girl."

"What girl?" I asked, forcing calm into my voice.

"That sweet little thing you dug up."

I stared at him, so angry my heart pounded.

"Tell me what you know," I hissed.

"Are we dealing?" Though the little rat teeth were out, the eyes were dark as Dante's ninth ring.

"You're lying."

He raised his eyebrows and the palm of his free hand.

"But truth is the cornerstone of my life."

"Peddle it elsewhere, Dorsey."

Trembling with anger, I slammed home the phone, whirled and hit the button. I couldn't hear Dorsey's last mocking addendum, but I saw his face as I stormed past the guard. His lips were clear.

He'd be in touch.

The drive back took almost an hour. An accident had closed all but one of the eastbound lanes of 720, and traffic in the Ville-Marie Tunnel was backed up for miles. By the time I realized the situation, reversing up the ramp was not an option, and there was nothing to do but creep along with the other frustrated motorists. The concrete tunnel blocked radio reception so there were no diversions. Dorsey had the floor in my head.

He'd been jumpy as cold water on a hot griddle, but could the man be innocent?

I remembered the eyes, and that moment the veil dropped.

I palmed the gearshift, inched forward, dropped back to neutral.

Was Claudel on the wrong track?

Wouldn't be the first time.

I watched an ambulance squeeze past along the right shoulder, its light pulsing red against the tunnel walls.

What would Claudel say when he learned I'd been to the jail?

That one was easy.

I drummed my fingers on the wheel.

Did Dorsey really know something about Savannah Osprey?

I shifted and advanced a car length.

Was he just another con scamming a deal to save his ass?

No answer.

I saw Dorsey's face, a study in macho contempt and antisocial scorn.

The man was repulsive. Yet, in that single nanosecond, I was certain I saw truth. Could I believe him? Did I need to believe him? If he would provide verifiable information on Savannah Osprey in return for the police casting a wider investigative net around the Cherokee murder, what was lost? But could that be done? Certainly not through Claudel.

After forty minutes I drew abreast of the accident. One car lay on its side, another rested against the tunnel wall, headlights pointed in the wrong direction. The pavement glistened with shattered glass, and police and rescue vehicles had circled the wreckage like a wagon train. As I watched workers position the jaws of life over the upturned car I wondered if its occupant would be heading for the same place as I.

I finally broke free, raced down the tunnel, exited at de Lorimier, and drove the last few blocks to the lab. When I got off the elevator on the twelfth floor I knew something was wrong.

The front desk was unattended, the phone clamoring for attention. I counted as I crossed the lobby. Five. A pause, then the ringing started again.

I inserted my security pass and the glass doors opened. Inside, the receptionist stood near the women's

198

lavatory, eyes red, Kleenex bunched into a tight ball. A secretary comforted her, one arm draped around her shoulders.

Along the hall people in clumps spoke to one another, voices muted, faces tense. The scene was like a surgical waiting area.

Another flashback.

Fifteen years ago. I'd left Katy in the care of my sister while I ran errands. Rounding the corner to my street, the same hair-trigger fear, the same adrenaline rush.

Fragmented memory bytes. Harry and the neighbors standing on the drive. So wrong together. They didn't know each other. My sister's face, mascara running down blanched cheeks. Hands twisting.

Where was Katy?

Bargaining.

Dear God. Not Katy. Anything. Not my baby.

The neighbors' eyes, wide with sympathy, watching as I climbed from the car.

McDuff had bolted and run in front of a Buick. The dog was dead. Relief, later sorrow. Bad, but I'll take it. My poodle was dead but my daughter was not.

I felt that same dread as I looked at my colleagues.

What had happened here?

Through the second set of glass doors I could see Marcel Morin in conversation with Jean Pelletier. I keyed in and hurried down the hall.

At the sound of my footsteps they fell silent and looked in my direction.

"What is it?" I asked.

"Dr LaManche." Morin's eyes shone with emotion. "He collapsed while doing the Cherokee Desjardins autopsy."

"When?"

"He was working alone during the lunch hour. When Lisa returned she found him on the floor. He was unconscious and barely breathing."

"Is it bad?"

Pelletier made a sound in his throat.

Morin shook his head.

"It is in God's hands."

22

First thing Friday I called the hospital. LaManche had stabilized, but remained in intensive care, with no visitors allowed. The nurse would say nothing more about his condition.

Feeling helpless, I ordered flowers, then showered and dressed.

Kit's door was closed. I hadn't spoken to him since Wednesday, and wasn't sure where he'd been the night before. On arriving home I had found a note on the fridge. He'd be out late. I shouldn't wait up.

I didn't.

As I made coffee I reminded myself to call Harry. While my nephew was nineteen and past the age for active shepherding, I wanted to be clear on how much parenting was expected. And for how long.

Kit was slowly spreading. The refrigerator was crammed with frozen pizzas and pita-pocket sandwiches, hot dogs, jars of baked beans, and cans of Mellow Yellow. Cheese doodles, nacho chips, doughnuts, Lucky Charms, and Cocoa Puffs lined the counter.

In the living room my TV had been converted to a Sony PlayStation, and wires crisscrossed the floor like tangled spaghetti. CD's were stacked on the sideboard and scattered across the hearth. A heap of crumpled jeans, socks, and jockey shorts filled one chair, a Stetson hung from the wing of another. In the hall, two pairs of cowboy boots lay where they'd been kicked.

The place looked like I was living with Garth Brooks.

I replaced Kit's note with a reply, stating that I'd be home by five and requesting the pleasure of his company at dinner. Then I went to work.

The atmosphere at the lab was as somber as before. Morin announced in the morning meeting that he had spoken with LaManche's wife. Her husband was still comatose, but his vital signs were stable. They were attributing his state to cardiogenic shock. She would call if there was any change. The day's cases were discussed quickly and quietly, without the usual banter.

A tree had fallen on a man in Dollard-des-Ormeaux, crushing him. A couple was found dead in bed in Pointe-aux-Trembles, victims of an apparent murder-suicide. A woman's body had washed ashore near Rivière-des-Prairies.

Nothing for the anthropologist. Perfect. That would leave me free to go through the material Kate Brophy had loaned me. If Jacques Roy was available I'd drive over to Carcajou headquarters and see what he thought.

When the meeting ended I got my mug and went for coffee. Ronald Gilbert was at the counter, talking with one of the new technicians from his section. Though I didn't know the younger man's name I recognized him from the Cherokee murder scene. He'd assisted Gilbert with the blood spatter.

As I waited my turn at the coffee machine I heard

snatches of their conversation and realized they were discussing Cherokee's case. I lowered my breathing, straining to hear.

"No, thank God. They're not all this complicated. You pulled a real pot of soup for your first time out."

"Beginner's luck, I guess."

"I'd like to have a heart-to-heart with LaManche before I write this up, but I guess that's not going to happen."

"How's he doing?"

Gilbert shrugged, stirred his coffee, then arced the little wooden stick into the trash.

As I watched them leave I thought of Cherokee's apartment and again sensed uneasiness. None of the others had felt the murder was atypical. Why was I suspicious? What was it that didn't seem right? I had no answers to my questions.

I filled my cup, added cream, and returned to my office, where I sipped and pondered, feet on the sill, eyes fixed on a barge moving slowly up the river.

What was not right about the Cherokee scene? No forced entry? So the victim had grown complacent. So what? It happens. The bungled fire? Charbonneau was probably right. Something went haywire and the perp fled. Even good plans can fail from faulty execution. Look at Watergate.

I took a sip.

What did Gilbert mean by "a real pot of soup"?

I took another sip.

What was so complicated?

Sip.

What did he want to discuss with LaManche?

Never hurts to ask.

Look at Watergate.

I found Gilbert in front of a computer screen. When I knocked he swiveled and looked at me over wire-rimmed glasses. His head, cheeks, and chin were covered with curly brown hair, giving him the look of a hero from Greek mythology.

"Got a minute?"

"As many as you like."

He waved me in and pulled a chair next to his.

"It's about the Cherokee Desjardins case."

"Yes. I saw you at the scene. Why are you working that one?"

"I'm not, exactly. I was there because initial reports described a burned body. As it turned out the victim was not in bad shape."

"Not in bad shape? He looked like a still life in brain tissue."

"Well, yes. Actually, that's what I'd like to talk to you about. I was going to ask Dr LaManche but, of course, that's not possible right now."

He looked puzzled.

"The investigators working the Cherokee case are convinced it's a biker hit." I hesitated, unsure how to put my reservations into words. "I can't nail it down, but something about the scene struck me as being off."

"Off?"

I explained my assignment with Opération Carcajou, and what I'd seen at the briefing session.

"I realize I'm a novice, but maybe that's it. Maybe I'm seeing things through different eyes."

"And what do your eyes tell you?"

"That the Cherokee murder was sloppy."

"Anything else?"

"That the victim was sloppy. Apparently Cherokee

204

admitted his killer. Does that sound like a former member freelancing drugs on gang turf?"

I didn't mention Dorsey, or his claims of innocence. I figured the less said about my prison visit the better.

Gilbert looked at me a long time, then smiled.

"Claudel thinks you're an interfering pain in the ass."

"I think highly of him, as well."

He threw back his head and laughed, then his face grew serious.

"How much do you know about blood-spatter analysis?"

"Not much," I admitted.

"Ready for a crash course?"

I nodded.

"O.K. Here goes."

He leaned back and raised his eyes to the ceiling, no doubt deciding where to begin and how to condense years of training into a brief lecture. I could picture him doing the same for a jury.

"A free-falling drop of blood is spherical due to the effects of gravity and surface tension. Think about when you prick your finger. Blood builds up on the down side until the drop is able to break free and fall. Seems simple, right?"

"Yes."

"It's not. All kinds of opposing forces are at work. Gravity and the increasing weight of the blood are 'pulling' the drop downward. At the same time the surface tension of the blood is trying to reduce the exposed surface of the drop and is 'pushing' it upward."

He gestured quotation signs around the verbs.

"Only when the 'pulling' forces exceed the 'pushing' forces will the drop break free. Initially it's elongated, but as it falls the drop flattens due to air resistance. The attractive forces of surface tension within the drop cause it to assume a shape with the least amount of surface area. Thus, drops of blood are shaped like spheres, not like teardrops as they're usually drawn. And shape is one of the things we consider in spatter-pattern analysis.

"A blood spatter is produced as a result of a force striking static blood. It could be in a pool on the sidewalk, or inside a victim's head. When hit, the blood breaks into drops, called spatter, which travel through the air as spheres."

I nodded.

"When these spheres strike a surface they leave predictable types of trails. Bloodstain-pattern interpretation is concerned with examining stains produced by drops of blood that are *not* typical. The stains and trails have been altered in some way, usually by violent activity.

"The goal of bloodstain-pattern interpretation is to work backward from a crime scene and reconstruct the events that took place. What happened? In what sequence? Who was where? What weapon was used? What objects have been moved? To answer these questions we look at what has altered the drops of blood present.

"And it's very complex." He began ticking points off on his fingers. "For example, we have to take into account the properties of the target. Blood will act differently when striking a smooth versus a textured surface."

Tick.

"Shape. Since the ratio of a stain's width and length accurately reflects its angle of impact, regardless of striking surface, we look carefully at the shape of the stains."

Tick.

"Spatter size. Smaller or slower-moving forces produce large spatters, while larger or faster-moving forces produce smaller spatters."

He stopped, thumb pressed to his fourth finger.

"Still with me?"

"Yep."

"We talk about low-, medium-, and high-velocity-impact spattering, although these terms are really relative."

"Give me examples."

"I'll do better than that. Come with me."

He led me down the hall to a stainless steel refrigerator and withdrew a one-liter bottle labeled *Sang du boeuf*.

"Beef blood," he explained.

I followed him along a narrow side corridor to an unmarked door, and we entered a windowless room where large sheets of white paper were taped to most surfaces.

The small chamber looked like a massacre site. Blood was pooled along one baseboard, streaked and splattered on the walls, and dripping from various-sized spots at knee level in the far corner. Above each stain I could see pencil notations.

"This is our blood-spatter experiment room," said Gilbert, placing the bottle on the floor. "Watch."

He removed the cap, dipped a wooden rod into the blood, then allowed it to drop onto the paper under his feet.

"Low-velocity-impact spatters are associated with drops passively falling onto a surface. Dripping blood, for example. The characteristic spatter size is greater than three millimeters in diameter. In these situations

207

the blood is moving slowly, from normal gravitational pull to up to five feet per second."

I examined the small round stains he'd created.

"Medium-velocity blood spatter results from activities such as beatings, blunt trauma injuries, or stabbings. The blood is moving faster, with a force velocity between five feet and twenty-five feet per second."

As he said this he poured a small amount of blood into a dish, signaled me to step back, then swung the rod into it. The blood flew up and struck the wall. Gilbert gestured me over and pointed to several of the stains. They were smaller than the ones at his feet.

"See these spatters? The size range for medium-velocity spatter is typically less, averaging between one and four millimeters in diameter."

He lay down the rod.

"But the spots aren't as fine as with high-impact spatters. Come look at this."

We moved to the far wall, where he indicated an area that looked as if it had been spray-painted.

"High-velocity-impact spattering means a force velocity greater than one hundred feet per second and results from gunshots, explosions, and mechanical accidents. It's more like a mist, with individual spatters averaging less than one millimeter in diameter.

"But don't get me wrong. Not every spatter falls neatly into one of these categories. Blood that is splashed, cast off, or projected can really complicate a picture."

"How so?"

"These are actually forms of low- to medium-velocity spatter, but they differ from the ones I just described. For example, splashed blood results from someone stepping into already-pooled blood. This leaves long, narrow spatters surrounding a central stain, with very few round stains present.

"Projected blood results from someone running through, stamping into, or slapping a pool of blood. Or from arterial gushing, or beating a head on the floor. Again there are long, spiny spatters radiating from a central stain. But in this case the borders of the central stain are also distorted.

"Blood cast off from a weapon leaves yet another pattern. Let me show you."

He went back to the rod, dipped, and swung it in an arc. Blood flew from the tip and struck the wall to his right. I drew close and studied the stain.

"Cast-off drops are smaller than those in typical low-velocity spatter, and the greater the force the smaller the drops. Also, since the blood is being thrown from a moving object, cast-off spatter occurs in straight or slightly curved trails, and the drops are fairly uniform throughout."

"So you can determine the nature of an assault based on the size and shape of the spatter?"

"Yes. And in most cases we can pinpoint where the attack took place. Let's go back to my office and I'll show you something else."

When we were once again in front of the computer he placed his hands on the keyboard and entered a command.

"You saw us taking videos of the bloodstains in the victim's apartment, right?"

"Yes."

"We used a simple video camera, but you can also use digital. We recorded each area of spatter using a scale and a plumb line."

"Why a plumb line?"

"The program uses that to determine the vertical direction of the stain."

Gilbert hit a key and a cluster of elliptical brown forms came up on the monitor.

"The images on the videotape are entered into the computer and can be played back on the monitor. Single frames are grabbed and recorded on the hard disk as bitmaps. A program then displays the image of each stain so we can take measurements. The measurements are used to calculate two angles: the angle of directionality, and the angle of impact."

More keystrokes, and an oval-shaped white outline appeared superimposed over the stain at center screen. Gilbert pointed at it.

"The direction of the main axis of the ellipse with respect to the plumb line defines the directionality angle, or gamma of a stain. That can range from zero to three-sixty.

"The impact angle, or alpha, can range from zero to ninety degrees. That's calculated from the shape of the ellipse."

"Why is that?"

"Remember, when a drop of blood travels through space it's spherical. But when it strikes a target it flattens and leaves a trail. That's because the bottom of the drop is actually wiping across the surface."

He made a swiping gesture with his hand.

"The trail is small at first as the drop strikes, then widens, with the widest point of the trail corresponding to the center, or widest part of the drop. The trail then narrows and eventually tapers off. See this one here?"

He pointed to an elongated oval with a small dot at one end. It looked like many I'd seen in the blood-spatter room.

"It looks like an exclamation point."

"That's exactly what it's called. Sometimes a small dot of blood detaches from the original drop and hops to the head of the trail. So looking at a spatter from above, it resembles either a tadpole or an exclamation point, depending on whether the far end is merely elongated, or a small portion detached completely. In either case the direction of travel is clear."

"The dot points toward the direction the drop was moving."

"Exactly. The program produces a file containing the values of the angles for each stain analyzed. It's from that data that point of origin is calculated. And believe me, using the computer is a lot quicker than the old string method."

"Back up."

"Sorry. With the string method one end of a string is fastened to the surface at the position of the stain, then stretched in the estimated direction of motion. This is repeated for a number of bloodstains around the scene. The result is a pattern of strings extending away from the spatter toward the source of the blood. Home plate is the point where all the strings converge. The procedure is time consuming and leaves a lot of room for error. Instead of doing it by hand the computer draws virtual strings computed from the data."

His fingers flew over the keys and a new image appeared. X and Y coordinates ran down the left side and across the bottom of the screen. A dozen lines formed an X-shaped pattern, crossing each other in a geometric bow.

"This is a bird's-eye view of a set of virtual strings based on twelve spatters. It's hard to get this point of view with real strings, yet it's the most useful one."

211

More key clicking and a new image appeared. The lines now plunged together from upper left to lower right, converging at a point two thirds of the distance from the bottom of the screen, then spreading slightly, like stems on a bunch of dried flowers.

"The program can also produce a side view, which is necessary to estimate the height of the source of blood. By combining the two views you have a pretty accurate idea of point of convergence and, therefore, of victim position."

Gilbert leaned back and looked at me.

"So what do you want to know about the Cherokee scene?"

"Anything you can tell me."

For the next forty minutes I listened and watched, interrupting only for clarification. Gilbert was patient and thorough as he walked me through the bloodbath in the apartment.

What he said increased my conviction that Claudel was leading us in a dangerously wrong direction.

23

The screen was filled with hundreds of tiny dots, like the spray-paint mist in Gilbert's test room. Scattered among them were small bits of flesh and bone.

"You're looking at a section of the north wall, right behind the victim's chair. That's forward spatter."

"Forward spatter?"

"From the pellets exiting Cherokee's head. Blood from an entrance wound is called back spatter. Look at this."

Gilbert hit the keys and a new image filled the screen. It was a similar spray of aerosolized blood, though less densely packed, and lacking the larger globs of tissue.

"That's from the TV. When the pellets struck Cherokee, blood flew backward."

"He was shot sitting in the chair?"

"Yes."

He entered several more keystrokes and the image was replaced by a view of the chair where the body had been found. Lines ran diagonally from the wall and the TV, and crossed at a point head-high above the seat.

"But the gunshot was icing on the cake. If he wasn't dead already, he was well on his way. Look at this."

More keystrokes. Another image, this one with larger spots and more variation in their size.

"That's medium-velocity spatter. It was all over the northwest corner of the apartment."

"But—"

"Just wait."

He brought up another frame. This one showed spots slightly larger than those in the previous image, but of roughly uniform size. They varied in shape from round to ovoid.

When Gilbert hit a key and zoomed out I could see that most of this spatter was distributed in a long curving line, with some drops lying to either side of the arc.

"That's from the ceiling."

"The ceiling?"

"It's what we call a cast-off pattern. It results from blood being thrown from a moving object, like my stick. When swinging a weapon, the attacker terminates his backstroke abruptly, then reverses direction to deliver the next blow. Most blood flies off on the backstroke, at least if there's enough force, but some can be thrown on the downward stroke, too."

He pointed to drops in the center of the trail.

"These spatters are due to the backswing."

He indicated several drops lying along the edge of the arc.

"And these are downswing trails."

I took a moment to digest that.

"So you're saying that he was beaten before he was shot?"

"This trail is one of five we were able to identify. Generally, assuming the blunt injury trauma is the only

214

source of blood, or at least the first, the number of trails equates to the number of blows plus two."

"Why plus two?"

"There wouldn't have been any blood on the first blow. On the second blow blood is picked up by the weapon and thrown off as the attacker makes the backswing for the third blow."

"Right."

"This medium-velocity spatter was found down low on the walls, and on the crap stacked in the corner."

He worked the keys again and more strings appeared, these converging on a point less than two feet above the floor.

"My opinion is that he was struck near the corner of the room, fell to the floor, and was then hit repeatedly. After that he was placed in the chair and shot."

"Struck with what?"

Gilbert pooched out his lips. "Pfff. Not my call."

"Why bludgeon him then shoot him?"

"Definitely not my call."

"If he was dragged, wouldn't that have left a trail?"

"The assailant may have wiped it up. Besides, there was so much blood everywhere, and so many people on the scene the floor was useless."

"And the burning may have disguised some of it."

"At least on the carpet. We may go in with Luminol, but it's not going to change what the spatters tell me."

I was thinking about that when he spoke again.

"There's something else."

"There's more?"

Again he worked the keys. Again a mist of high-velocity blood spatter filled the screen. But a portion of the cloud was missing, like a stencil with a cut out pattern.

"This is another shot of the wall behind the victim's head."

"It looks like someone took a cookie cutter to it."

"This is called a void pattern. It's produced when an object blocks the path of blood and is then removed."

"What object?"

"I don't know."

"Who removed it?"

"I don't know."

As I hurried back to my office, Dorsey's words provided voice-over for Gilbert's images.

Amateur Hour. Whoever did Cherokee is going to walk.

I grabbed my phone and punched in a number. A secretary told me Jacques Roy had flown to Val-d'Or and would be unavailable until Monday. Impatient, I asked for Claudel. Neither he nor his Carcajou partner was in. I thought of pagers, again decided the situation was not sufficiently urgent, and left messages for everyone.

I had just replaced the receiver when the phone rang.

"Should I be sending the world's biggest fruit basket?"

"Hi, Harry."

As usual my sister sounded as though she'd just completed some event requiring intense exertion.

"Why are you out of breath?"

"Akido."

I didn't ask.

"Is my baby boy driving you back to the solace of drink?"

"He's fine, Harry."

"Are you always this cheerful on Fridays?"

"I just heard something disturbing. What's up?"

"I suppose you know that Kit and Howard went at it again."

216

"Oh?" I suspected as much, but hadn't pressed my nephew.

"It's the golf cart all over again."

I remembered that episode. When Kit was fifteen he'd stolen a cart from the pro shop at Howard's country club. It was found the next morning, half-submerged in a water hazard on the fifteenth hole, with half a bottle of tequila in the back compartment. Daddy went ballistic and son lit out. A week later Kit showed up in Charlotte. The last leg of hitchhiking had not gone well, and he owed ninety-six dollars to a taxi driver. Katy and Kit bonded immediately, and my nephew stayed the summer.

"What was the fight about?"

"I'm not sure, but it involved fishing gear. Is he behaving himself?"

"Actually, I haven't seen that much of him. I think he's made friends here."

"You know Kit. Well, if you could let the little buckaroo stay just a little while I'd appreciate it. I think he and his daddy need some distance and some time."

"Doesn't Howard live near Austin?"

"Yes."

"And Kit's in Houston with you?"

That seemed like distance to me.

"See, that's the problem, Tempe. I've had this trip to Mexico planned for a long time, and I'm supposed to leave tomorrow. If I cancel I'll lose my deposit, and Antonio will be really torqued. Of course, say the word and that's what I'll do."

"Uh. Hm."

I wondered if Antonio was the akido link. With Harry, a new man usually meant a new interest.

"I would hate to leave Kit unsupervised and in my

217

home for a week, and at the moment I can't send him to his daddy. And as long as he's with you anyway, and you say he's no problem . . ."

She let the sentence dangle.

"You know I love having Kit." But not necessarily this week, I thought.

"Tempe, if this is just the least little tiny bit inconvenient you just say so and I'll cancel this trip quicker than—"

"I do want to know how much parental control is expected."

"Parental control?" She sounded completely at a loss.

"Guidance? Parenting? It's a lonely job, but does someone have to do it?"

"Get real, Tempe. Kit's nineteen. You can parent until Tinkerbell bites the Pope, but that boy's born to boogie and that's what he's gonna do. I just need to have him check in daily and verify that he is physically fit and not wanted by the authorities. And that he is not using my home as a convention center for underage boozers. He didn't grow up in the Partridge family, you know."

The Partridge family had not entered my mind.

"But that doesn't mean you shouldn't make him chop cotton. Make sure he keeps his belongings orderly and does the dishes now and again."

I pictured the clothing heaped in my living room.

"In fact, I'm gonna call him myself and make sure he understands that your home is not a port of entry for any old thing he wants to drag in."

"How long will you be in Mexico?"

"Ten days."

"What if he wants to head home before you get back?"

"No problemo. Howie's given him about eleven

218

hundred credit cards. Just make him understand that an early return means Austin, not Houston, and don't let him go off all depressed. You're good at that, big sister. And you know how crazy he is about you."

Sweet-talkin' Harry.

"I'll keep that in mind when he pawns Gran's silver. Have a good time. And leave a number where you can be reached."

As I was hanging up Claudel appeared in the doorway, his face so taut the bones seemed to push out on the tissue. I watched him cross to the chair opposite my desk.

Great.

"*Bonjour, Monsieur Claudel.*"

I didn't expect a greeting. I didn't get one.

"You made an unauthorized visit to the jail."

"Did Mr Dorsey tell you about our conversation?" I asked innocently.

"You interrogated my prisoner."

"He's your personal property?"

"You are not homicide, you are not even a detective." Claudel fought to keep his voice even. "You have no business involving yourself in my case."

"Dorsey called me."

"You should have referred him."

"He called me because he felt you would not listen."

"He is just using you to interfere with my investigation."

"Why won't you even consider that you may be on the wrong track, Claudel?"

"You are out of your league and I don't have to explain to you."

"This thing with Dorsey is a very weak bust."

"But it is *my* weak bust, madam, and not yours."

219

"You are convinced Cherokee was murdered by bikers," I said evenly. "And I am on temporary assignment to Carcajou."

"I am doing what I can to alter that," said Claudel, his outrage barely concealed.

"Really." I felt blood rise to my cheeks.

"I'm not going to argue the point, Ms Brennan. Stay out of my investigation."

"I do not take my orders from you!"

"We will see."

"We worked together once, with good success."

"That does not make you a detective, or entitle you to act directly in a case assigned to me."

"You cannot overestimate how much you underestimate me, Monsieur Claudel."

He straightened, dropped his chin, and took a deep breath. When he spoke again his voice was calm.

"Any further exchange is pointless."

I agreed.

He walked toward the door, his back stiff as a dressage rider's. Before leaving, he turned, raised his chin, and spoke down his nose.

"There is one other thing that I should tell you, Ms Brennan."

I waited.

"George Dorsey was charged with first-degree murder this morning."

Though his words were ice, I could feel the heat all the way across the room. Then he was gone.

I took a long breath that caught several times on the way up. Then I uncurled my fingers, sat, and stared at children playing in the school yard twelve floors down.

I was angry for Dorsey. I was frustrated by Claudel's pigheaded refusal to listen. I was mortified that the man had taken steps to annul my appointment to Carcajou.

I was furious with Claudel, but I was equally angry with myself. I detest losing my temper, but seemed unable to control it in arguments with Claudel. But it was more than that.

While I hated to admit it, Claudel still intimidated me. And I still sought his approval. Though I thought I'd gained ground in the past, the man obviously continued to regard me with disdain. And it mattered. And that irked me. Also, I knew it had been wrong not to at least notify him of the Dorsey interview. Investigative teams demand that all information be contributed to the common pool, and rightly so. Because I knew Claudel would not include me in the loop, I had elected not to inform him. Only, he was one of the chief investigators on the Cherokee case. By my actions, I had handed him a weapon to use against me.

"The hell with him."

I turned my gaze from the kick ball below and surveyed the contents of my office. Articles to be filed. Forms to be signed for destruction of remains. Phone messages. A briefcase filled with biker info.

My scanning stopped at a pile of photocopies stacked on a corner cabinet. Perfect. I'd been putting it off for months. I decided to distance myself from the current quagmire of bones and bikers and surly detectives by updating my database on old cases.

And that's what I did until it was time to go.

On the way home I swung by the Métro store on Papineau and picked up the ingredients for puttanesca sauce. I wondered if Kit would like anchovies, bought them anyway. I'd proceed as I had when serving Katy a foreign dish. I wouldn't tell him.

The evening's cuisine was a moot point. When I

arrived at the apartment no one greeted me but Birdie. The boots and clothing had been cleared, and a floral arrangement the size of Rhode Island filled the dining room table. A note had been placed on the refrigerator door.

My nephew was so, so sorry. He'd made plans that couldn't be changed. Sad face. He promised me the entire day on Saturday. Smiley face.

I slammed the bags on the kitchen counter, stomped to the bedroom, and kicked off my pumps.

Hell. What kind of life is this? Another Friday with the cat and the tube.

Maybe Claudel would like dinner. That would make my day.

I pulled off my work clothes, threw them on the chair, and slipped into jeans and a sweatshirt.

It's your own fault, Brennan. You're not exactly Miss Congeniality.

I dug around on my closet floor, located my Top-Siders, and broke a nail yanking them on.

I couldn't remember when I'd felt so down. And so very alone.

The idea popped up without warning.

Call Ryan.

No.

I went to the kitchen and began emptying groceries, Ryan's face filling my mind.

Call.

That's past.

I remembered a spot just below his left collarbone, a hollowed-out muscle that cradled my cheek perfectly. Such a safe spot. So quiet. So protected.

Call him.

I did that.

Talk to him.

I don't want to listen to lame excuses. Or lies.

Maybe he's innocent.

Jean Bertrand said the evidence is overwhelming.

My resolve crumbled with the canned tomatoes, but I finished emptying the bags, balled and stuffed them under the sink, and filled Birdie's dish. Then I went to the living room phone.

When I saw the light my stomach did a mini-flip.

I pushed the button.

Isabelle.

The landing was like that of a gymnast after a bad vault.

The machine told me I had two entries that had not been erased.

I pushed again, hoping Kit had played them and forgotten.

The first was Harry, looking for her son.

The second message was also for Kit. As I listened, the small hairs rose at the back of my neck, and my breath froze in my throat.

24

After unsuccessfully attempting to decode the garbled message for Kit from a person named Preacher about a meet, I concluded that this probably involved Harleys, and not those owned by a suburban motorcycle club. I thought of waiting up, decided against it.

Impulsively, I dialed Ryan's number. The answering machine replied. My despondency complete, I went to bed.

I slept fitfully, my thoughts like colored chips in a kaleidoscope, congealing to form clear images, then drifting apart into meaningless patterns. Most of the tableaux involved my nephew.

Kit, driving his pickup through a tunnel of trees. Kit, arms overflowing with flowers. Kit on a Harley, Savannah Osprey riding the back, bookend bikers to either side.

At one point I heard the beep of the security system. Later, vomiting, then the sound of a toilet.

In between cameos of my nephew, my unconscious presented theme song suggestions. *Lord of the Dance* kept repeating. The music was like fleas in the carpet: Once in, it was impossible to dislodge.

Dance, dance, wherever you may be . . .

I awoke to pale gray lighting the edges of the window shade. Slamming a pillow across my head, I threw an arm over it and pulled my knees to my chest.

I am the lord of the dance, said he . . .

At eight I gave up. Why be annoyed? I reasoned. It isn't rising early that's a pain. It's *having* to rise early. I didn't *have* to get up, I was choosing to do so.

I threw back the covers and slipped on the same outfit I'd featured for my Friday evening with Bird. A Brennanism: When in doubt as to where the day will take you, underdress.

While the Krups pot brewed my 100 percent Kona I peeked out the French doors. Rain fell steadily, turning trunks and branches shiny, jiggling leaves and shrubs, and puddling in low spots on the courtyard brick. Only the crocus sprouts looked happy.

Who was I kidding? This was a morning to sleep.

Well, you're not. So do something else.

I threw on a jacket and sprinted to the corner for a *Gazette*. When I got back, Birdie was curled on a dining room chair, ready for our Saturday ritual.

I poured myself some Quaker Harvest Crunch, added milk, and set the bowl next to the paper. Then I got coffee and settled in for a long read. Birdie watched, secure in the knowledge that all cereal leavings would be his.

A United Nations human rights panel had blasted Canada for its treatment of aboriginals.

Dance, dance . . .

The Equality Party was celebrating its tenth birthday. What's to celebrate? I wondered. They hadn't won a single National Assembly seat in the last election. Equality had been born of a language crisis, but the issue had been relatively quiet over the past decade, and the party was hanging on by suction cups. They needed another linguistic flare-up.

The Lachine Canal would be undergoing a multimillion-dollar face lift. That was good news.

As I refilled my cup and gave Bird his milk, I pictured the place where Kit and I had skated last Sunday. The bike path ran along the canal, a nine-mile waterway filled with toxins and industrial sludge. But it had not always been a sewer.

Built in 1821 to bypass the Lachine rapids and allow ships direct passage from Europe to the Great Lakes, the canal was once an integral part of the city's economy. That changed when the St Lawrence Seaway opened in 1959. The canal's mouth and several basins were filled with earth displaced by construction of the métro system, and it was eventually closed to navigation. The surrounding neighborhoods were neglected and, save for the creation of the bicycle path, the canal was ignored, tainted by a century of industrial dumping.

Now plans were afoot to revitalize the city's southwest side. Like Mont-Royal Park, designed by Frederick Law Olmsted one hundred and twenty-five years ago, the canal was to be the centerpiece for a renaissance of the entire sector.

Maybe it's time to buy a new condo.

I resettled at the table and opened to another section.

The RCMP had to squeeze more than twenty-one million dollars from its budget to cover salary raises. The federal government would cough up only a portion.

I thought of the blue-collar workers picketing on Guy.

Bonne chance.

The Expos lost to the Mets, 10–3.

Ouch. Maybe Piazza was worth the ninety-one million the Big Apple had forked out.

Dorsey's rearraignment on new charges was on page five, next to a story about Internet crime. The only thing I learned was that he'd been arraigned late Friday afternoon, then transferred from Op South to the provincial prison at Rivière-des-Prairies.

At ten I phoned the hospital. Madame LaManche reported that her husband was stable, but still uncommunicative. Thanking me politely, she refused my offer of help. She sounded exhausted, and I hoped her daughters were there for support.

I sorted clothes and ran a load of whites. Then I changed to basketball shorts and a T and laced up my cross-trainers. I walked to McKay and Ste-Catherine, and took an elevator to the top-floor gym.

I ran the treadmill for twenty minutes, finished with another ten on the StairMaster. Then I lifted weights for half an hour and left. My usual routine. In. Exercise. Out. That's why I liked Stones Gym. No high-tech glitz. No personal trainers. A minimum of spandex.

When I emerged, the rain had stopped and the cloud cover was losing its hold. An especially promising patch of blue had appeared over the mountain.

I arrived home to the same quiet I'd left. Birdie was sleeping off the cereal milk, my nephew was sleeping off something I didn't want to contemplate.

Dance, dance . . .

I checked the answering machine, but the message light was dark. No response from Ryan. As with all recent calls to his number, his machine was not calling back.

O.K., Ryan. Message received loud and clear.

I showered and changed, then arranged myself at the dining room table. I sorted everything Kate had loaned me. Photos to the left, documents to the right. Again I began with the photos.

I glanced briefly at Martin "Deluxe" Deluccio and Eli "Robin" Hood, then at a dozen members of the same species, bearded, mustached, goateed, and stubbled. I moved on to the next envelope.

Color prints fell to the table. In most the focus was blurry, the subjects badly framed, as though each was shot quickly and covertly. I sifted through them.

The settings were predictable. Parking lots. Motel pools. Barbecue joints. Yet the amateur quality made these scenes somehow more compelling, gave them a vitality lacking in the police surveillance photos.

Going from picture to picture, I noted accidental events captured by tourists, salesmen, passing motorists. Each told the story of a chance encounter, a random intersection of the ordinary and the dark. Kodak moments of fascination and fear. Heart racing, palms sweaty, reaching for the camera before the wife and kids returned from the toilet.

I picked one up and studied it closely. An Esso station. Six men on chopped-down Harleys, twenty yards from the lens yet a universe away. I could feel the shooter's awe, his seduction-repulsion by the aura of the motorcycle outlaw.

For the next hour I worked my way through the stack of envelopes. From Sturgis, South Dakota, to Daytona Beach, Florida, whether shot by police or Joe Citizen, the events and participants were tediously similar. Runs. Campgrounds. Swap meets. Bars. By one o'clock I'd seen enough.

It was time to talk to Kit.

Bracing myself for the conversation, I went to the guest room door and knocked.

Nothing.

I knocked harder.

"Kit?"

"Yo."

"It's after one. I'd like to talk to you."

"Mmmm."

"Are you up?"

"Uhm. Hum."

"Don't go back to sleep."

"Give me five."

"Breakfast or lunch?"

"Yeah."

Taking that as an affirmative for the latter, which was my preference, I made ham and cheese sandwiches and added deli dills. As I was consolidating Kate's material to make space at the table, I heard the bedroom door open, then activity in the bathroom.

When my nephew appeared I almost lost my resolve. His eyes were red-rimmed, his face the color of cooked oatmeal. His hair was doing Jim Carrey.

"Mornin', Aunt T."

When he raised both hands and rubbed them up and down over his face, the border of a tattoo peeked from the hem of his T-shirt sleeve.

"It's afternoon."

"Sorry. I got in kind of late."

"Yes. Ham sandwich?"

"Sure. Got any Coke?" he asked in a thick voice.

"Diet."

"That's cool."

I got two sodas and joined him at the table. He was

229

regarding the sandwich as one might a squashed cockroach.

"You'll feel better if you eat," I encouraged.

"I just need to wake up a little. I'm fine."

He looked as fine as a smallpox victim. Up close I could see tiny veins threading through the whites of his eyes, and smell the smoke that clung to his hair.

"This is me, Kit. I've been there."

I had, and I knew what he was going through. I could remember the feel of residual booze slugging through my bloodstream, churning my stomach and pounding the dilated vessels in my brain. The dry mouth. The shaky hands. The sense that someone had poured lead shot in the space below my sternum.

Kit rubbed his eyes, then reached over and stroked Bird's head. I knew he was wishing he were someplace else.

"Food will help."

"I'm fine."

"Try the sandwich."

He raised his eyes to me and smiled. But as soon as he relaxed the corners of his mouth hooked downward, unable to sustain the effort without conscious direction. He took a bite the size of a dime.

"Umm." He popped open the Diet Coke, tipped back his head, and gulped.

It was obvious that he didn't want to travel in the direction I was headed. Well, neither did I. Perhaps there was no issue. He was nineteen. He'd had a big night. He was hungover. We'd all been there.

Then I remembered the phone message. And the new tattoo.

There were issues, and we needed to discuss them.

I knew what I said would make little difference. Probably none. He was young. Invulnerable. And "born to boogie," according to Harry. But I owed it to him to try.

"Who's the Preacher?" I asked.

He looked at me as he rotated his Diet Coke can on the table.

"Just a guy I met."

"Met where?"

"At the Harley shop. When I went with Lyle."

"What kind of guy?"

He shrugged the question off.

"No one special. Just a guy."

"He left you a message."

"Oh?"

"You listen. I can't translate it."

"Yeah. The Preacher's kind of a head case."

That was an understatement.

"How so?"

"I don't know. He's just out there. But he rides this chopped '64 panhead that is truly righteous." He took a long swig of Diet Coke. "I'm sorry I stood you up last night. Did you find my note?" He was looking for a new topic.

"Yes. What was this event that was so important?"

"A boxing match," he said without expression. His face had the consistency of bread dough. And about as much color.

"Do you follow boxing?"

"Not really. These guys do, so I went along."

"What guys?"

"Just these guys I met."

"At the Harley shop."

He shrugged.

"And the tattoo?"

231

"Pretty cool, eh?"

He raised his sleeve. A scorpion wearing some sort of helmet spread its legs across his left biceps.

"What is it supposed to mean?"

"It doesn't mean anything. It just looks kick-ass."

I had to agree.

"Your mother is going to kill me."

"Harry has a tattoo on her left buttock." He pronounced the last with a British inflection.

I am the lord of the dance, said he . . .

For a while neither of us spoke. I ate my sandwich while Kit picked at his, nibbling off a gram at a time then washing each down with Diet Coke.

"Do you want another?" he asked, pushing back his chair and wiggling his empty can.

"No thanks."

When he returned I plunged in again.

"How much did you drink last night?"

"Too much." He scratched his head roughly with both hands and the hair went from Carrey to Alfalfa. "But it was just beer, Aunt T. Nothin' hard. And I'm legal here."

"Just beer?"

He lowered his hands and looked at me, making sure he understood my meaning.

"If there's one thing you can count on with this boy, it's a negatory on pharmaceuticals. This body ain't much, but I'm keeping it a drug-free zone."

"I'm very glad to hear that." I was. "What about the Preacher and his flock?"

"Hey. Live and let."

"It doesn't always work that way, Kit."

Go ahead. Ask.

"Are these guys bikers?"

"Sure. That's why it's Disneyland for me. They all ride Harleys."

Try again.

"Are they affiliated with a club?"

"Aunt T, I don't ask them a lot of questions. If you mean do they wear colors, the answer is no. Do they hang with guys that do? Yeah, probably. But I'm not going to sell my boat and strike for the Hells Angels, if that's what worries you."

"Kit. Outlaw bikers don't draw lines between gawkers and those wanting charter memberships. If they perceive you as even the most minor of threats, or even a slight inconvenience, they'll chew you up and spit you into tomorrow. I don't want that to happen to you."

"Do I look like an idiot?"

"You look like a nineteen-year-old kid from Houston with a fascination for Harleys and a romanticized image of the *Wild Ones*."

"What?"

"The Stanley Kramer movie?"

A blank look.

"Marlon Brando?"

"I've heard of Brando."

"Never mind."

"I'm just feeling free. Having some fun."

"So is a dog with its head out the car window. Until it leaves its brains on a utility pole."

"They're not that bad."

"Bikers are moral cretins, and they not only are that bad, they're worse."

"Some of what they say makes sense. Anyway, I know what I'm doing."

"No, you don't. I've learned more about these guys in the past two weeks than I ever wanted to know, and none of it is good. Sure, they give toys to tots once a year, but bikers are hoodlums with a contempt for the law and a predisposition for violence."

"What do they do that's so bad?"

"They're reckless and treacherous and they prey on the weak."

"What do they do? Abort babies with coat hangers? Rape nuns? Machine-gun seniors in fast-food joints?"

"For one thing, they sell drugs."

"So does Eli Lilly."

"They set bombs that butcher women and children. They lock men into trunks, drive them to remote areas, and blow their brains out. They chainsaw rivals, pack what's left into garbage bags, and toss them off ferry docks."

"Jesus. We had a few beers."

"You don't belong in that world."

"I went to a bloody boxing match!"

The deep, green eyes bore into mine. Then a lower lid twitched and he squeezed them shut, dropped his chin, and rotated two fingers on each temple. I figured the blood was doing double-time behind his sockets.

"I love you as much as my own child, Kit. You know that."

Though he refused to meet my gaze I could sense discomfort in the curve of his spine.

"I trust you. You know that, too," I went on. "But I want you to be aware of who these people are. They will feed your interest in Harleys, get you to trust them, then ask for some small favor that will be part of some illegal transaction, only you won't even know it."

For a very long time neither of us spoke. Outside, sparrows battled over a seed bell I'd hung in the court-

234

yard. Finally, without looking up, "And what are you walking into, Aunt Tempe?"

"I'm sorry?"

"You're on some kind of ride these days."

I had no idea where he was going.

"Hello from the cesspool. Welcome on in."

"What are you talking about?"

"You play me like the old shell game. Allow me to see this. Hide that."

"What am I hiding?"

He was staring straight at me now, the whites of his eyes like bloody water.

"I followed that conversation at dinner last week. I saw the eyeball. I saw your mysterious little package, watched you slip off on your secret trip. You said it yourself. You've seen more of this shit in the past few weeks than most people see in a lifetime."

He turned away, went back to twirling the Diet Coke can.

"You want to know all about me, but when I ask what you're doing you shut me down."

"Kit, I—"

"And it's more than that. Something's going on with this guy Ryan that's got you jumpier than an evangelist at tax time."

I felt my lips part, but nothing came out.

"You put *me* in the crosshairs 'cause you think I'm shooting chemicals into my veins, but you don't let me ask *you* jack shit."

I was too stunned to speak. Kit dropped his eyes and clamped his upper teeth on his lower lip, embarrassed by the emotion he'd allowed to surface. The sun shone through the muslin behind him, silhouetting his head against the brightness.

"I'm not complaining, but when I was growing up, you were the only one who listened. Harry was" – he turned his palms up and curled his fingers, as if groping for the proper words – "well, Harry was Harry. But you listened. And you talked to me. You were the only one who did. Now you're treating me like some kind of dimwit."

He had a point. When Kit had shown interest, I'd been evasive and distant, avoiding disclosure of any meaningful information. I live alone and don't discuss casework with anyone not part of the lab. I automatically deflect questions that may arise in a social setting. Then this morning, out of the blue, I'd asked for an accounting of his activities.

"What you say is both fair and unfair. I have put off answers I could have given, but I also am obligated not to discuss open cases or ongoing investigations. That is a requirement of my job and not a matter of personal discretion. Do you really want to know what I've been doing?"

Shrug. "Whatever."

I looked at my watch.

"Why don't you shower while I clean up here. Then we'll take a walk on the mountain and I'll lay some things out. All right?"

"All right." Barely audible.

But my decision was far from all right.

25

Locals call it "the mountain," but the small elevation is a far cry from the craggy spires of the Rockies, or the lush peaks of my Carolina Smokies. Mont-Royal is the vestige of an ancient volcano, smoothed by aeons to gentle curves. It lies at the heart of the city like the body of a giant slumbering bear.

Though lacking in height and geologic drama, the mountain gives more than its name to Montreal. It is the spinal cord on which the city is strung. McGill University lies on its eastern slope, with the predominantly English-speaking suburb of Westmount directly opposite. L'Université de Montréal and the largely French neighborhood of Outremont claim the northern flanks. Directly below lies Centre-ville, a polyglot fusion of the industrial, financial, residential, and frivolous.

The mountain is promontories, parks, and cemeteries. It is wooded trails and old mossy rocks. It is tourists, lovers, joggers, and picnickers during the precious summer months; snowshoers, skaters, and tobogganers in winter. For me, as for every Montrealer, the mountain is sanctuary from the urban tumult at its feet.

By early afternoon the temperature was windbreaker warm, the sky immaculate. Kit and I walked across de Maisonneuve, and turned uphill on Drummond. To the right of a tall round building with a sweeping curvilinear base that looks like the prow on a cement frigate, we ascended a wooden staircase to avenue des Pins. Pine Avenue.

"What is that building?" asked Kit.

"McIntyre Medical. It's part of McGill."

"Looks like the Capitol Records Building in L.A."

"Hmm."

Halfway up the stairs, the air grew thick with the sharp, musky smell of skunk.

"*Une mouffette*," I explained.

"Sounds good in French, but it stinks like plain old Texas varmint," said Kit, wrinkling his nose. "How 'bout we pick up the pace."

"Right." I was already panting from the steep climb.

At the top we crossed Pine, followed a serpentine dirt road to a cement staircase, climbed, took a hard right, more road, then another set of wooden stairs that shot straight up the escarpment.

By the time we arrived at the summit I was seriously thinking about defibrillation. While I paused to catch my breath Kit charged to the overlook. I waited for my heartbeat to descend from the troposphere, then I joined him at the balustrade.

"This is awesome," said Kit, squinting down a pair of brass pointers lined up on the McTavish Reservoir.

He was right. The view from the top is pure spectacle, a theater-in-the-round of a city in progress. In the foreground rise the skyscrapers and flats and smokestacks and church spires of downtown, beyond that the docks of the port and the city's main artery, the St Lawrence River. In the far distance loom the peaks of St-Bruno and St-Hilaire, with the Eastern Townships at their feet.

Kit sighted down each indicator, and I pointed out landmarks I thought would interest him. Place Ville-Marie. The McGill football field. The Royal Victoria Hospital. The Montreal Neurological Institute and Hospital.

The complex reminded me of Carolyn Russell and our conversation concerning the shunt. Thinking of Savannah Osprey brought the familiar twinge of sadness.

"Come on, Kit. I'll tell you what I've been up to."

We strolled up broad stone steps, wending between bicycles lying on their sides, and settled on one of the wooden benches flanking the entrance to the chalet. Above us pigeons cooed softly in the heavy wooden beams.

"Where should I start?"

"At the beginning."

"O.K., wise one."

What was the beginning?

"Quebec Province has the dubious distinction of hosting the only active biker war in the world right now."

"That Hells Angels thing you talked about at Isabelle's dinner."

"Exactly. These gangs are fighting over control of the drug trade."

"What drugs?"

"Mostly cocaine, some pot and hash."

A busload of Japanese tourists appeared from the parking lot, worked its way toward the railing, then began photographing itself in varying combinations.

"I became involved about two weeks ago. Two members of the Heathens, that's a puppet club to the Rock Machine, were blown up while trying to bomb a Vipers clubhouse on the southwest side of the city."

"Who were the bombed-out bombers?"

"Twin brothers, Le Clic and Le Clac Vaillancourt."

"The Vipers are with the Hells Angels?"

"Yes. The sniper who took them out was arrested—"

"A Viper sniper. I like that."

"The sniper investigation led to the recovery of two of the bodies we discussed at dinner."

"The guys buried near the Vipers' clubhouse?"

"Yes."

"Where is this clubhouse?"

"St-Basile-le-Grand." An odd look crossed his face, but he said nothing.

"The two skeletons were later identified as members of an OMC called the Tarantulas, defunct now, but active in the seventies and eighties."

"What about the girl's bones you found out there?"

"She has since been identified as Savannah Claire Osprey, from Shallotte, North Carolina. That's why I went to Raleigh. Savannah was sixteen when she disappeared in 1984."

"Who killed her?"

"I wish I knew."

"How did she end up here?"

"Same answer. Let me backtrack a minute. Before the discoveries at St-Basile-le-Grand, there was another murder. The sergeant at arms for the Vipers, a gentleman named Richard 'Spider' Marcotte, was shot in a drive-by outside his home. It may have been a Heathens hit in retaliation for Clic and Clac."

"That saved the taxpayers some money."

"Yes, but remember there was a toll exacted on the public. A child got caught in the cross fire."

"That's right. She was nine years old." His eyes were focused on my face. "She died, didn't she?"

I nodded.

"Emily Anne Toussaint was killed the day you and Howard dropped off Bird."

"Holy crap."

"Since that time I have been pursuing forensic evidence pertaining to these biker crimes. So you can understand my lack of enthusiasm for your newly acquired friends."

"And tattoo. You've seen some rough shit."

"There's more."

I glanced at his face. Though shadowed by the eaves, his eyes were bright as a songbird's.

"This past week another biker was killed. Yves 'Cherokee' Desjardins."

"Which side?"

"He was a Predator. That's the Angels."

"So the Heathens were still evening the score for the twins?"

"Maybe. The problem is Cherokee was an older guy who hadn't been active for a while. Also, it seems he was running his own coke concession."

"So he might have been snuffed by his own side?"

"It's possible. We don't have all the evidence. We just don't know. Right now our investigation has slowed."

I told him about LaManche.

"Holy shit. Maybe they got to him, too."

"Who?"

"The Angels. Maybe he was going to find something in that body they didn't want found."

241

"I don't think so, Kit."

"Maybe they slipped him something. You know, one of those poisons that leave no trace."

"He was in the autopsy room. That's a secure area."

"There could be a mole at your lab. They do that, you know. Position their people on the inside."

"Whoa." I laughed. "Let's not get carried away."

He turned and looked past the Japanese tourists to the misty peaks in the far distance. Someone opened a door behind us and pigeons startled from the steps.

"Jesus, Aunt Tempe, I feel like a real lowlife. Your boss is sick, and you're trying to juggle a zillion separate murders all at once. And what do I do? I show up, dump a dead fish on your counter, then run around town having fun."

The Japanese were moving our way.

"And I was too distracted to follow what you were doing. Anyway, ready to hike?"

"I live to ramble."

We circled the chalet and set off on one of the many dirt trails that honeycomb the mountain. We walked in silence for a while, watching squirrels scuttle among last year's leaves, excited by the arrival of spring. The trees overhead were loud with chirps and trills and warbles and shrieks. At one point we stopped to listen to an old man perform a recorder adaptation of "Ode to Joy." Wearing a long overcoat and ear-flapped beret, he played with all the concentration of a symphonic virtuoso.

As we strolled west, the dome of l'Oratoire St-Joseph appeared on the horizon. I told Kit the story of Frère André's heart. Stolen from its altar crypt, the organ became the focus of a massive manhunt. Eventually it showed up at our lab, and was now ensconced in safer quarters deep within the church.

To the south rose the pale yellow tower of l'École Polytechnique at l'Université de Montréal, site of the 1990 slaughter of thirteen women. The day was too lovely to share that story.

We were heading downhill when Kit broached an equally unpleasant topic.

"So who's this guy Ryan?"

"Just a friend," I hedged.

"Harry talked about him. He's a detective, right?"

"Yes. With the provincial police."

I'd introduced my sister to Ryan during her stay in Montreal. Sparks had flown, but I'd left town almost immediately and didn't learn if there was liftoff. I'd avoided Ryan for a long time after that, but I'd never asked.

"So what's the deal?"

"He's gotten into some trouble."

"What kind of trouble?"

A *calèche* passed on the road above, moving in the direction from which we'd come. I heard the driver cluck, then the slap of reins on the horse's neck.

"He may have gotten involved in drugs."

"Using?"

"Selling." Though I was trying hard, my voice sounded wavery.

"Oh."

The clop of hooves receded, grew quiet.

"You care about this guy, don't you?"

"Yes."

"More than Uncle Pete?"

"That's not a fair question, Kit."

"Sorry."

"Whatever happened to that fish?" I said, changing the subject.

"It's in the freezer."

"Here's a plan. We zap Mr Trout, then peruse les *motards* while he finishes defrosting. Tonight we throw him on the grill, then slide over to Hurley's for a few beers."

"It's a salmon. Otherwise the plan is sound."

We descended the rest of the way, cut through the Montreal General, and continued downhill on Côtedes-Neiges. At the bottom I turned and looked back up at the peak.

"Did you ever notice the cross at night?"

"Sure. It's pretty."

"From down here, yes. From nearby it's just a pile of steel mesh and bare bulbs. I think Andrew Ryan's like that. Nice at a distance, but up close he's a tangled mess."

26

The Berawan are a horticultural people living in longhouse villages on the island of Borneo. When I taught introductory anthropology, I used them as an illustration of the absurdity of Western funerary practices.

According to Berawan beliefs, the souls of the dead are released to the afterlife only when the flesh has decomposed. Until that point, the deceased hover in limbo, no longer part of the living, but unable to join the dead. And there's a hitch. Their bodies can be reanimated by malevolent spirits roaming the world in search of housing. Once revived, these living-dead cannot be killed. Needless to say, the villagers are not wild about having them around.

The Berawan were repulsed and horrified when their ethnographer responded to questions about American customs. In their view, embalming, treatment with cosmetics and waxes, and burial in watertight coffins and vaults are actions of pure folly. Not only are we prolonging the transition of our loved ones, but our cemeteries provide vast storehouses for potential zombies.

I wondered how the Berawan would react to Bernard Silvestre, centerpiece of the photo in my hand. The fish was taking forever to defrost, and in the interim Kit and I were working our way through Kate's collection.

Silvestre lay in his coffin, mustache and sideburns spread symmetrically on each cheek, hands folded piously on his black leather jacket. Ten men crouched in a semicircle below, denimed and booted, while four stood flanking the open casket. Except for the dress and mangy appearance, they looked like a fraternity at a Paddy Murphy party.

Elaborate bouquets stretched from one side of the photo to the other, a mini Rose Bowl of floral condolences. One said "Slick" in blue on yellow, another "Good-bye BS," in shades of red and pink. Carnations forming the number "13" rose directly behind the coffin, flaunting "Slick's" connection to pot or meth.

But best of show was the rectangle on the upper right, a petal mosaic of cycle and rider, complete with whiskers, shades, and angel's wings. I tried, but was unable to read the banners above the helmet and below the front tire.

"Know anything about Slick?" asked Kit.

"He doesn't look like the pick of the litter."

"Yeah, even from that motley litter." He flipped the picture. "Heck, this guy croaked when I was three years old."

There were two more photos of Slick's funeral, both taken from a distance, one at the cemetery, the other on the church steps. Many of the mourners wore caps riding their eyebrows, and bandannas stretched to cover their mouths.

246

"The one you've got must be from a private collection." I handed Kit the other pictures. "I think these two are police surveillance photos. Seems the bereaved weren't anxious to show their faces."

"Man, this chopper is one statement in chrome and steel. No wonder the dude rode it right up to the grave."

I walked around the table and peered over his shoulder.

"It looks pretty stark to me."

"That's the point. Raw power. The guy probably started with a garbage wagon and—"

"Garbage wagon?"

"An old police cycle, probably an FLH touring model. He stripped away all the nonessential crap like the windshield, roll bars, and fiberglass luggage bags, and replaced the stock items with streamlined custom parts."

"Such as?" It looked like a cycle without any of the good stuff.

Kit pointed out items on the graveside bike.

"A thin front wheel, coffin-shaped gas tank, bobbed rear fender, and tapered soda seat. Those are the coolest. Makes it look like you're straddling the motor."

He pointed at the front wheel.

"And he extended the front end and added ape hangers."

I assumed those were the long, backward-projecting handlebars.

"And check out the molding and custom paint job! Man, I wish I could see that up close. This machine is a work of art. All it needs to achieve perfection is a sissy bar."

"From which to serve beer and mixed drinks?"

"It's a backrest."

The bike *was* bizarre, but no more so than its owner. He had leather wristbands, a denim vest with assorted Harley-Davidson pins and patches, riding chaps, and more hair than a Wookie. He looked like a walking threat display.

"I'm going to poke Mr Salmon again. If he's still cryogenic, we'll nuke him."

He was and we did, then laid him on the grill for a charcoal finish. Then I buttered green beans and tossed a salad while Kit carved and served the fish.

We'd just opened our napkins when the phone rang. I answered, and a rough male voice asked for my nephew. Wordlessly, I handed him the phone.

"Hey, man, what's up?"

Kit stared at a spot on the glass tabletop.

"No go. Can't do."

Pause.

"No way." He shifted position, and worked at the spot with his thumbnail.

"Not this time."

Though muted by my nephew's ear, I could hear the voice on the other end. It sounded harsh, like an angry dog locked in a cellar. The nerves in my stomach tightened.

"Well, that's how it is."

The muffled response rose and fell in agitation.

Keeping his eyes averted, my nephew left the table and moved down the hall out of earshot.

I speared a green bean, chewed, swallowed. Mechanically, I repeated the action, but my appetite had evaporated. After five forkfuls he was back.

The look on his face brought a feeling like physical pain to my chest. I wanted to put my arms around him, to brush back his hair and comfort him the way I had

248

when he was a little boy. But whatever had happened was not a skinned knee, and I couldn't do that now. Even if he allowed it, I knew the gesture would only discomfort him. I sensed his distress, but was helpless to ease it.

He gave me a big smile, shrugged palms and shoulders, then sat and dived into his fish.

I stared at the top of his head. Finally, he looked up.

"This is great." He swallowed and reached for his iced tea. "Yes, that was one of them. And no, I'm not going."

I was suddenly ravenous.

The next call came as we were finishing cleanup. Kit answered, but I could hear nothing over the chugging and sloshing of the dishwasher. In a few minutes he reappeared at the kitchen door.

"It's Lyle. I guess I told him I like swap meets, so he's inviting us to an estate sale tomorrow."

"An estate sale?"

"Well, it's a flea market in some place called Hudson. He thought if I called it an estate sale you might be more inclined to go."

The doublespeak had little impact on my response. While I would have enjoyed a trek to Hudson, it was not worth the price of an afternoon with Crease.

"You go ahead, Kit. It's really very pretty out there. Horse country. I should stay and finish some things I've been putting off."

"Like what?"

"Actually, I think I'm having my hair cut tomorrow."

"Uh-huh."

He returned to the living room and I finished wiping the counters. I couldn't believe I was feeling relief that my nephew would be with Lyle Crease. The guy was as smarmy as a snake-oil salesman from Matamoros.

And what was Crease's interest in a nineteen-year-old kid? I had no doubt that Kit could handle the little twerp, but I vowed to call Isabelle and ask a few questions.

Easy does it, I told myself. Brush your hair and go see the fiddlers.

Hurley's is the closest thing to an Irish pub that Montreal has to offer. Though I don't imbibe, my Gaelic genes still enjoy the atmosphere.

The place was as big a hit with Kit as it had been with his mother. But then, it's hard to be gloomy with a fiddle and mandolin belting out reels, and dancers jigging up and down like Nijinsky with a neurological disorder. We stayed until well past midnight.

When Lyle Crease showed up the next morning I was idly flipping through the photos Kit and I had left on the table the night before.

"How's it going?" Crease asked, as I let him into the entrance hall. He wore khakis, a long-sleeved white shirt, and a windbreaker with *CTV News* printed on the left breast. His hair looked like molded plastic.

"Good. And yourself?" We spoke English.

"Can't complain."

"Kit said he'd be just a minute. He overslept a bit."

"No problem." Crease chuckled, then gave me a knowing grin.

I did not return it.

"Can I offer you some coffee?"

"Oh no, thanks. I've already had three cups this morning." He showed miles of capped teeth. "It's a gorgeous day out there. Sure you won't change your mind?"

"No, no. I have things I have to do. But thanks. Really."

"Maybe next time."

When Moses does another bush, I thought.

We stood for a moment, unsure where to go from there. Crease's eyes roamed the hall, then came to rest on a framed photo of Katy.

"Your daughter?"

"Yes."

He walked over and picked it up.

"She's lovely. Is she a student?"

"Yes."

He replaced the portrait and his eyes moved on to the dining room.

"That's quite a bouquet. You must have a serious admirer."

Nice try.

"May I?"

I nodded, though Crease was as welcome in my home as the *Exorcist* demon. He crossed to the flowers and sniffed.

"I love daisies." His eyes drifted to Kate's photos. "I see you're doing some research."

"Would you like to sit down?" I indicated the living room sofa.

Crease helped himself to a picture, replaced it, chose another.

"I understand you're involved in the Cherokee Desjardins investigation," he said without looking up.

"Only peripherally," I said, and moved quickly to stack the photos.

He gave a deep sigh. "The whole world's going crazy."

"Perhaps," I noted, reaching out my hand for him to

251

surrender the picture of the Silvestre funeral.

"Please," I said, gesturing toward the sofa. "Make yourself comfortable."

Crease sat and crossed his legs.

"I understand Dorsey's been charged and moved to Rivière-des-Prairies?"

"So I've heard."

"Think he did it?"

This guy never gave up.

"I'm really not involved in the investigation."

"How about the Osprey girl. Anything breaking on that front?"

How about your face, I thought.

At that moment my nephew appeared, looking pure urban cowboy in his Levi's, boots, and ninety-gallon hat. I popped to my feet.

"I'm sure you two want to get there early before the good stuff's gone."

"What good stuff?" asked Kit.

"The bass fishing lures and Elvis T-shirts."

"I'm actually looking for a plastic Madonna."

"Try the cathedral."

"The other Madonna."

"Be careful," I said, pointing a finger at him.

"Careful is my middle name. Christopher Careful Howard, C.C. to my close friends." He tapped two fingers to the brim of his hat.

"Right."

As Crease said good-bye he placed a hand on my shoulder, ran it down my arm, and squeezed just above my elbow.

"You take care," he said with a meaningful look.

What I took was a long shower.

Later, scrubbed and smelling of sandalwood, I

checked my e-mail. There was nothing earth-shattering. I offered suggestions for problems submitted by students, sent an opinion to a pathologist inquiring about an oddly shaped skull, and replied to my three nieces in Chicago. Daughters of Pete's sisters, the teenagers were avid computer buffs, and kept me informed of happenings within my estranged husband's extended Latvian family.

Finally, I thanked a colleague at the Armed Forces Institute of Pathology who'd forwarded a particularly amusing photo. The case involved a pig and a high-rise building.

At one-thirty I logged off and tried Isabelle. Predictably, she was not in.

Looking for an excuse to be outside, I set out to buy jumbo shrimp at the *poissonnerie*. I'd gone less than a block when I was stopped dead, distracted by photos at *Coiffure Simone*.

I stared at the woman in the black and white. She looked good. Stylish, but neat. Professional, but jaunty.

Jesus, Brennan. You sound like copy for a shampoo ad. Next you'll be telling yourself you're worth it.

I *had* told Kit I'd scheduled a haircut.

I studied the poster, estimating the amount of maintenance the style would require. I thought it could pass my ten-minute rule.

I started to move on, caught my reflection in the glass. What I saw was light-years from poster lady.

How long had it been since I'd tried a new do?

Years.

And the salon was offering a special Sunday discount.

Five dollars off. Right. You'll save about three-fifty U.S.

A new haircut could boost your spirits.

253

It could be a disaster.

Hair grows back.

That last came straight from my mother.

I pushed open the door and went in.

Hours later I was eating dinner with the Discovery channel. On the screen, male kangaroos kickboxed over control of the mob. On the hearth, Birdie eyed me silently, curious, but keeping his distance.

"Hair grows back, Bird."

I dipped a shrimp and popped it into my mouth, wishing it would happen before Kit got home.

"And I could use your support," I informed him.

If the new look was to have buoyed my spirits, the experiment had been a catastrophe. Since returning home I'd been thinking of ways to avoid public contact. Thanks to developments in telecommunication I had many options. I'd use telephone, fax, and e-mail. And lots of hats.

By ten I was feeling as low as I had on Friday evening. I was overworked, underappreciated, and my never-was lover turned out to prefer the robbers over the cops. My boss had collapsed, my nephew was out with the sleaze of the year, and I now looked like I'd been attacked by a Weed Eater.

Then the phone rang and things got terribly, terribly worse.

"*Claudel ici.*"

"Yes," I answered, too surprised to switch to French.

"I thought you should know. George Dorsey was attacked about two hours ago."

"Attacked by whom?"

"He's dead, Ms Brennan. Murdered because of your meddling."

254

"Me?"

I was speaking to a dial tone.

The rest of the evening I was too distracted to focus on coherent thought. I barely acknowledged Kit's return and report that he had had a really good time.

"Murdered because of your meddling." That was unfair. Dorsey had asked to see me. What if he had asked for Claudel or Charbonneau or Quickwater? This was a prison murder of someone who was a threat to others. Those things happen. I didn't cause it. Claudel was unfair. I tossed and turned all night and repeated "unfair."

27

The next morning I was at work by seven-thirty. Others wouldn't arrive for an hour, and the building was graveyard quiet. I cherished the calm and planned to take full advantage of it.

I let myself into my office, slipped on a lab coat, and crossed to the anthropology lab. Unlocking the door to the storage room, I pulled out the box containing Savannah's remains. I intended to get straight to work and let the Claudel matter arise in whatever manner he chose to raise it.

I laid the skull and femora on the table, and began the painstaking process of reinspecting every millimeter of bone under magnification and strong light. Though doubtful, I hoped to find something I'd missed. Perhaps a tiny nick or scrape that would tell me how the bones had been separated from the rest of the body.

I was still at it when someone knocked at the door. When I looked up Claudel stood framed in the glass. As usual his spine was ramrod straight, his hair as perfect as a studio shot of Douglas Fairbanks.

"Nice tie," I said, opening the door.

It was. Pale violet, probably designer silk. A good choice with the tweed jacket.

"*Merci,*" he mumbled with all the warmth of a pit bull.

I laid down the femur, clicked off the fiber-optic light, and stepped to the sink.

"What happened to Dorsey?" I asked as I washed my hands.

"A Philips screwdriver happened to him," he replied. "The guard was outside reading while Dorsey showered. Probably catching up on his professional journals."

I pictured the man with the little rat teeth.

"The guard heard a change in the noise of the water, so he took a look-see. Dorsey was facedown in the drain with twenty-eight holes in his upper body."

"Jesus."

"But Dorsey didn't die right away," Claudel continued. "He shared a few thoughts on the ride to the hospital. That's why I felt I should come by."

I reached for a paper towel, surprised that Claudel was being so open.

"The paramedic didn't get it all, but he caught one thing."

Claudel lifted his chin a little.

"Brennan."

My hands froze.

"That's it?"

"He said he was busy keeping Dorsey alive. But he noticed the name because of his dog."

"His dog?"

"He's got an Irish setter named Brennan."

"It's a common name."

"Maybe in Galway, but not here. You did talk to Dorsey about Cherokee Desjardins, did you not?"

"Yes, but nobody knows that."

"Except everyone at Op South."

"We were in a private interrogation room."

Claudel was silent. I pictured the corridor, with the holding tank just ten feet away.

"I suppose I could have been spotted."

"Yes. These things have a way of getting back."

"Getting back to whom?"

"Dorsey was a Heathens hang-around. The boys wouldn't be happy if they thought he was launching a self-preservation movement."

I felt tension rise up my neck at the thought I might have triggered the attack.

"I don't think Dorsey killed Cherokee," I said, bunching up the towel and tossing it into the trash.

"You don't."

"No."

"I suppose Dorsey claimed he was innocent as the Easter Bunny."

"Yes. But there's more."

He gave me an uncertain look, then folded his arms across his chest.

"All right. Let's hear it."

I told him about the blood spatter.

"Does that sound like a biker hit?"

"Things go wrong."

"Bludgeoning? Don't hit men usually come in shooting?"

"The last biker pulled from the river was hammered to death. So was his bodyguard."

"I've been thinking about that void pattern behind

258

Cherokee's head. What if he was killed for whatever was removed?"

"There were a lot of people milling around that scene. Someone could have knocked the thing out of position. Or maybe the neighbor snatched it."

"It was covered with blood."

"I'll talk to her anyway." Finite at the best of times, Claudel's patience was clearly evaporating.

"And why would Cherokee let someone in?" I pressed on.

"Maybe the hit man was a buddy from the old days."

That made sense.

"Has ballistics gotten anything?"

He shook his head.

"Who's heading the Spider Marcotte investigation?"

"That and the little girl fell to Kuricek."

Sipowicz.

"Any progress?"

Claudel raised both palms.

"Dorsey hinted he had something he'd trade on that."

"These degenerates will say anything to save themselves."

He dropped his eyes and picked a nonexistent fleck from his sleeve.

"There's something I need to discuss with you."

"Oh?"

At that moment we heard the door open in the adjacent lab, announcing the arrival of the technicians.

"May we . . . ?" He tipped his head toward my office.

Curious, I led him across the hall and slipped behind my desk. When he'd settled across from me Claudel withdrew a picture from his inside pocket and placed it on the blotter.

It differed little from Kate's biker photos. The vintage was more recent, the quality better. And one other thing.

Kit stood among the group of leather-jacketed men centered in the image.

I looked a question at Claudel.

"That was taken last week at an establishment called La Taverne des Rapides." He looked away. "That's your nephew, right?"

"So? I don't see any patches," I said curtly.

"They're Rock Machine."

He placed a second photo in front of me. I was getting very tired of celluloid bikers.

Again I saw Kit, this time straddling a Harley, engaged in conversation with two other cyclists. His companions were clean-cut but wore the standard bandannas, boots, and sleeveless denim jackets. On each back I could see a heavily armed figure in a large sombrero. The upper rockers said *Bandidos*, the lower, *Houston*.

"That was taken at a swap meet at the Galveston County fairgrounds."

"What are you suggesting?" My voice came out high and stretched.

"I'm not suggesting anything. I'm just showing you pictures."

"I see."

Claudel frowned, then crossed his ankles and regarded me intently.

I folded my hands to disguise the shaking.

"My nephew lives in Texas. Recently his father bought him a Harley-Davidson motorcycle, and he's become enamored with the two-wheeled culture. That's it."

"Riding in the wind is not what bikers live for these days."

"I know that. I'm sure these were chance encounters, but I will speak to him."

I handed back the photos.

"The Houston PD has a jacket on Christopher Howard."

If I could have laid hands on Harry at that moment I would have committed a felony.

"He's been arrested?"

"Four months ago. Possession."

No wonder his father had hauled him up to the north woods.

"I know what advice is worth on the open market," Claudel went on. "But be careful."

"Be careful of what?"

He looked at me a long moment, no doubt deciding whether to confide.

"The paramedic actually picked out two words."

The phone rang but I ignored it.

"Brennan's kid."

I felt someone light a match in my chest. Could they know about Katy? Kit? I looked away, not wanting Claudel to see my fear.

"Meaning?"

Claudel shrugged.

"Was it a threat? A warning?"

"The paramedic says he doesn't listen to patients while he's working on them."

I studied the wall.

"So what are you suggesting?"

"I don't want to alarm you, but Constable Quickwater and I think—"

"Oh, yeah. Quickwater. He's a lot of laughs." I cut him off, my sarcasm triggered by anger and fear.

"He's a good investigator."

261

"He's an asshole. Every time I talk to him he acts like he's deaf."

"He is."

"What?"

"Quickwater is deaf."

I searched for a response, but couldn't come up with a single word.

"Actually, he's deafened. There's a difference."

"Deafened how?"

"He took a cast-iron pipe in the back of the head while breaking up an alley fight. Then they shot him with a stun gun until the batteries died."

"When?"

"About two years ago."

"That destroyed his hearing?"

"So far."

"Will it come back?"

"He hopes so."

"How does he function?"

"Extremely well."

"I mean, how does he communicate?"

"Quickwater is one of the quickest studies I've ever met. I'm told that he learned to lip-read in no time, and he's crackerjack. For distance communication he uses e-mail, fax, and TTY."

"TTY?"

"It's an acronym for teletypewriter. Essentially, it's a keyboard and acoustic coupler built into one device. At home he has a special modem in his PC that communicates at the same band Baudot code as a regular TTY. He's got his fax and TTY on the same phone line and uses a switching device that recognizes an incoming fax tone. It sends faxes to the fax machine and all other calls to the TTY. We've got the same setup and software

262

at headquarters, so calling back and forth is no problem."

"What about when he's out?"

"He has a portable TTY. Battery-operated."

"How does he talk to someone without a TTY, or to you if you're not at headquarters?"

"There's a relay service that acts as intermediary. The service takes the call, then types what the hearing person says. For someone who's also mute, they read aloud what the deaf person types. Quickwater speaks fine, so he doesn't need to type his words."

My mind was struggling to take this in. I pictured Quickwater at the Vipers' clubhouse, then in the conference room at Quantico.

"But part of his assignment in Quantico was to report back on what he'd learned. How can he take notes and lip-read at the same time? And how does he know what's being said when the lights are dimmed, or when he can't see the speaker?"

"Quickwater explains this a lot better than I. He uses something called CARTT, Computer Assisted Real Time Translation. A reporter transcribes what's being said into a stenotype machine, then a computerized translation is performed and the words are displayed on a video monitor in real time. It's the same system used for closed-captioning of live television. The FBI has someone down there that can do it, but a hookup can be made from anywhere, with the reporter in one location and Quickwater in another."

"By phone and PC?"

"Exactly."

"But what about his other duties?"

I didn't voice what I was really thinking. Reporting on a conference or meeting is one thing, but how does a deaf officer cover himself when someone goes for the jugular?

"Constable Quickwater is a skilled and dedicated officer. He was injured in the line of duty and no one can say if the hearing loss is permanent or not. Obviously he can't do everything he used to do, but for now, the force is working with it."

I was about to circle back to Dorsey when Claudel stood and placed a paper on my desk. I braced myself for more bad news.

"This is the DNA report on the blood found on Dorsey's jacket," he said.

I didn't have to look. The expression on his face told me what the form would say.

28

When Claudel left I just sat there, my thoughts slip-streaming in and out of the conversation just concluded.

DNA doesn't lie. The victim's blood was all over the jacket, meaning Dorsey had killed Cherokee just as Claudel suspected. Or had he? Dorsey had said the jacket was not his.

The man knew nothing about Savannah Osprey. He'd been scamming me to save himself, and I had fallen for it.

And my visit to the jail had gotten Dorsey killed. Or had it? Was he killed because he was the killer or because he was not the killer? Either way, he was dead because someone feared what he would tell me.

I felt burning behind my eyelids.

Don't cry. Don't you dare cry. I swallowed hard.

And there was Quickwater. He hadn't been glaring, he'd been reading my lips. Who had treated whom badly? But how was I to know?

And Kit. Were the surveillance shots truly chance encounters as I'd said, or was Kit involved with the

Bandidos? Did that explain the Preacher? Was the real reason he'd come here something other than anger with his father? Or fondness for his dim-witted aunt?

And the eyeball. *Did* Kit find it on the windshield?

Claudel had gotten his report. Dammit, where was mine?

I slammed my palms on the blotter and shot to my feet. Weaving through clerical staff carrying papers and folders and technicians pushing specimen carts, I strode down the hall, took the stairs to the thirteenth floor, and went straight to the DNA section. I spotted my target bending over a test tube at the far end of the lab, and closed in.

"*Bonjour, Tempe. Comment ça va?*" Robert Gagné greeted me.

"*Ça va.*"

"Your hair is different." His own was dark and curly, though graying at the temples. He kept it short and carefully combed.

"Yes."

"Are you going to let it grow?"

"It's difficult to stop it," I replied.

"It looks good, of course," he mumbled, laying down a glass pipette. "So, I guess that jacket will nail this Dorsey character. Claudel actually smiled when I gave him the news. Well, almost. He twitched."

"I'm wondering if you've had time to do the comparison I requested."

"Unnumbered, right?"

I nodded.

"Eyeball?"

I nodded again.

"To be compared with sequencing from LML 37729."

266

"Yes." His memory for case numbers always impressed me.

"Hold on."

Gagné walked over to a honeycomb of folders, riffled through those in a middle cell, and pulled one out. I waited as he scanned the contents.

"The comparison is done, but the report isn't written."

"And?"

"It's a match."

"Without question?"

"*Mais, oui.*" His eyebrows shot up. "The eye and the tissue sample come from the same person."

Or persons, I thought, if they happen to be twins. I thanked him and hurried back to my office.

My suspicion had been right. The eyeball belonged to one of the Vaillancourts. A member of the Vipers had probably found it at the scene and kept it for some macabre reason. But who had placed it on my car?

I heard the phone before I reached my door, and bolted the last few steps. Marcel Morin was calling from downstairs.

"We missed you at the morning meeting."

"Sorry."

He went straight to the point. In the background I could hear voices and the sound of a Stryker saw.

"A ship arrived at the port two weeks ago and several cargo containers were off-loaded for repair."

"The big ones that go onto eighteen-wheelers?"

"*C'est ça.* Yesterday workers opened the last of the containers and found a body. The captain thinks the deceased is probably a stowaway, but has no explanation beyond that."

"Where is the ship registered?"

"Malaysia. I've begun the autopsy, but the remains are so badly decomposed I'm not going to be able to do much. I'd like you to take a look at them."

"I'll be down shortly."

When I hung up and crossed to the lab I found Jocelyn the temp bending over my worktable. Ms Charm School wore fishnets and a leather skirt that rode high enough to show dark at the top of each stocking. At the sound of the door she straightened and turned.

"Dr Morin asked me to give you this."

She extended an arm, and her earrings oscillated like tiny school-yard swings. Each hoop was large enough to perch a finch.

I crossed to her and took the request form, wondering why Morin hadn't left it on my desk.

"Killer haircut." She spoke in a low, monotone voice, and I couldn't tell if she was being sarcastic. Her face looked more pallid than normal, her eyes red-rimmed and underlined by dark commas.

"Thank you, Jocelyn." I hesitated, not wanting to pry. "Are you all right?"

She reacted as though the question totally confused her. Then she hitched a shoulder and mumbled, "Allergies kick me around in the spring. I'm fine."

With one last puzzled look, she scurried out of the lab.

I reboxed the Osprey remains and spent the rest of the morning with the Malaysian stowaway. Morin had not exaggerated. The bulk of the soft tissue in the body bag belonged to maggots.

At noon I went back upstairs to find Kit seated in my chair, boots crossed on the windowsill, a Frank Sinatra fedora on the back of his head.

268

"How'd you get onto this floor?" I asked, trying to hide my surprise. I'd totally forgotten the lunch date we'd arranged via the refrigerator door.

"I left my driver's license with the guard and he let me come up." He flipped the blue visitor's pass that was clipped to his collar. "I was sitting in the lobby, then a lady took pity and brought me here."

He swung his feet down and swiveled toward me.

"Whooaa! Let me get a bead on that."

He must have seen something in my face.

"Don't take me wrong. That is one rad haircut." He leveled two index fingers at me. "Makes you look younger."

"Let's go," I said, retrieving a sweater from the hall tree. I'd had more than enough comments on my hair.

Over brasserie subs and fries my nephew described his Sunday with Lyle Crease, the highlight of which had been the purchase of the fedora. No Madonna or fishing lures. After returning to Montreal, they'd dined on smoked meat at Ben's, then Crease took him to the newsroom.

"What do you two talk about?"

"The dude's really heads-up." Muffled through cold cuts and cheese. "It's awesome how much he knows about broadcasting. And he's pretty tight on cycles, too."

"Does he ask you a lot of questions?"

I wondered how much Crease was using Kit to get information about my cases. The biker war was hot news just now.

"Some."

Kit yanked a paper napkin from a metal box at the end of the table and wiped grease from his chin.

"About what?"

He bunched up the napkin and reached for another.

"All kinds of stuff. Lyle's amazing. He's interested in everything."

Something in his voice told me my nephew had begun to worship Lyle Crease. O.K., I thought. I can live with that. Oily as the guy is, he beats the Preacher sight unseen.

After lunch Kit insisted on returning with me to the lab. Though anxious to get back to my skeletal autopsy, I obliged him with a short tour. I could be heads-up, too.

During our rounds Kit made only two comments. I would recall them later, and chastise myself for taking no notice.

"Who's the freak show?" he asked, after passing Jocelyn at the Xerox machine.

"She works in records."

"Bet that's a head full of slash and burn."

"She has allergy problems."

"Right. Nasal spray."

The other remark was made in the ballistics section. He called their collection of firearms "sweet."

When Kit had gone I went back to the stowaway. By four-thirty I'd finished my preliminary examination, concluding that the remains were those of a male in his late twenties. I'd dissected out the bones and sent them upstairs for boiling. Then I'd washed up, changed, and returned to my office.

I was reaching for my sweater when I noticed a color print centered squarely on my blotter.

Oh, great, I thought. Here's something new. I haven't scoped a photo in at least two hours.

I reached for the picture, thinking that perhaps it belonged to Claudel.

It didn't.

Though the snapshot was old, and a network of cracks marred its surface, the color and focus were relatively good. It was a group shot, taken in a camping or picnic area. In the foreground a crowd of men and women milled around wooden tables jammed together to form a U. The earth was littered with empty cans and bottles, the tables heaped with backpacks, coolers, bundles, and paper bags. Loblolly pines rose in the background, truncated by the picture's upper border.

One large bag lay upright against a table leg, its print square to the camera lens. The logo caught my attention.

"—ggly Wiggly."

I flipped to the back of the print. Nothing.

I rehung the sweater, dug out a magnifying glass, and sat down to examine the image. Within seconds I found confirmation on a gorilloid oaf in denim vest and finger-less leather gloves. An arm wider than a state highway reached across his chest, displaying swastika, lightning bolts, and the poetic acronym "F.T.W." While Kong's upper limb obliterated part of his T-shirt, the bottom words were fully legible.

"Myrtle Beach."

Barely breathing, I began a close inspection of the persons pictured. Slowly, I worked the lens across the image, checking each face as it took form.

Within seconds I found her. Half hidden in a sea of caps and bushy heads, a frail figure leaned against a tree, little twig arms wrapped around her waist. Her head was tipped, and a ray of sunlight flashed off one of the huge lenses dwarfing her features.

Savannah Claire Osprey.

While I couldn't read her expression I could sense the

tension in her body. From what, I wondered. Excitement? Fear? Self-consciousness?

I moved on.

The man to Savannah's right looked like a character from *The Life and Death of Cormac the Skald*. He had shoulder-length hair and a beard that hung to mid-chest. Cormac was caught with chin raised, a can of Miller pressed to his lips.

The companion on her other side was very tall, with short hair and scraggly beard and mustache. His face was obscured in shadow, making his belly the most conspicuous trait. It had the tone of a used Ace bandage, hanging in fleshy rolls over a large, oval belt buckle. On it I could see letters. I raised and lowered the lens trying to make out the message, but too much was obscured by paunch.

Frustrated, I slid the lens up the torso and studied the face, hoping something would click. No go. I dropped back to the buckle and brought my face close to the glass.

A random synaptic firing, and there it was. Back to the face. Could it be?

No. This man was much larger.

But maybe. I couldn't tell. I'd gotten there too late. Too much damage.

Yet, there was a resemblance.

Had George Dorsey known something after all?

Heart pounding, I reached for the phone.

29

When Claudel answered I identified myself and dived right in.

"There's something I didn't tell you. Spider Marcotte wasn't the only one Dorsey mentioned. He claimed to have information about Savannah Osprey."

"The young girl we found in St-Basile-le-Grand?"

"Yes. I think he may have been telling the truth."

"Dorsey's trademark."

I ignored the sarcasm.

"Did you leave a picture on my desk?"

"No."

"Someone did. It's an old snapshsot taken at a biker gathering."

"Probably a prayer meeting."

"It looks like a picnic or camp-out."

"Uh-huh."

I took a deep breath to steady my voice.

"Savannah Osprey is there."

"She is?" His tone told me he didn't believe it.

"Absolutely."

"What does that have to do with Dor—"

"The picture was taken in Myrtle Beach."

"How do you know?"

"At least one of the believers is wearing a Myrtle Beach T-shirt."

"My son has a Kansas City Chiefs' shirt."

"I know honeysuckle and kudzu when I see it. And I recognized a Piggly Wiggly logo on one of the grocery bags."

"What's a Piggly Wiggly?"

"It's a chain of supermarkets, with several in the Myrtle Beach area."

"Why would anyone call a supermarket Piggl—"

"And one of the picnickers may be Cherokee Desjardins."

There was a moment of dead air.

"What makes you think that?"

"He's wearing a belt buckle that says 'Cherokee.'"

"What does the man look like?"

"Something Jack Hanna would keep on a chain and pacify with small chunks of meat," I spat. His skepticism was irritating me.

"I mean does the man in the buckle resemble Cherokee Desjardins?"

"His features aren't clear. Besides, I never got a look at Desjardins when he was wearing a face."

There was another moment of silence, then the sound of an exhaled breath.

"I'll get photos of Desjardins and come by in the morning."

"We can try enhancing the image."

"Set it up. But it will have to be quick. We're expecting difficulties because of the Dorsey murder, and the whole squad is on alert."

I drove home plagued by feelings of self-doubt.

I'd been fooled by Dorsey, and my naiveté had gotten him killed.

What if the man in the photo wasn't Cherokee? Claudel obviously had reservations. If I was wrong he'd be even more convinced I was an idiot.

As I had been with regard to his Carcajou partner. I'd entirely misread Quickwater. Had I also misjudged Ryan? My nephew?

Where had the picture on my desk come from? Why no note, no phone call? It had to be one of the detectives or lab people. No one else would have an opportunity to leave it there.

I steered and shifted robotically, barely noticing the traffic around me.

Should I make a surprise call on Ryan? Would he answer the door? Probably not. Ryan had cut himself off because he preferred it that way. But how could it be true? I still couldn't believe the man was a criminal.

Was Kit involved with the Bandidos? With drugs? Was he in danger? What had Dorsey been trying to say to the paramedic?

Was it possible Katy was in danger from the biker gangs thousands of miles away on a ship? Her last letter had come from Penang.

Who was I kidding? Dorsey had been killed while under armed guard in a provincial prison. If *les motards* wanted you to be in danger, you were there.

"Dammit!" I slapped the steering wheel with the heel of my hand.

Ryan and Katy were out of my reach, but I could do something about my nephew. I vowed to have it out with Kit before the sun set.

Or rose, I thought, turning onto the ramp that led under my building. I had no idea how late he'd get in, but resolved to wait up.

It wasn't necessary.

"Hey, Auntie T," he greeted me when I entered the condo, as did the aroma of cumin and turmeric.

"Something smells good," I said, dropping my briefcase in the entrance hall.

My nephew and cat were sprawled on the sofa, surrounded by remnants of that morning's *Gazette*. The Sony PlayStation had been reattached to the TV and wires squiggled across the floor.

"I stopped by La Maison du Cari. Figured it was my turn to cook."

He'd removed his earphones and draped them around his neck. I could hear the tinny sounds of the Grateful Dead.

"Great. What did you get?"

"*Uno momento.*"

He swung his feet to the floor and tossed the headset onto the couch. Bird bolted at the sudden proximity to Jerry Garcia. Kit retrieved a receipt from the kitchen and read off nine items.

"Are you expecting your state legislature?"

"No, ma'am. I wasn't sure what you like, so I got a cross section of regional cuisines."

He pronounced the last in an accent that mimicked perfectly that of the restaurant's owner.

"Don't you worry. We'll graze right through it," he added, reverting to Texan.

"Let me change and then we'll eat."

"Wait. First you gotta see this."

He dug through the scattered *Gazette* and came up with the front section. Opening to a middle page, he

276

folded the paper in half and handed it to me, indicating a headline.

PRISONER SLAIN IN GANG ASSASSINATION

The article summarized the facts surrounding the Dorsey murder, referring to him as a prime suspect in the execution-style killing of Yves "Cherokee" Desjardins. It described Dorsey as a Heathens associate, Cherokee as a member of the Predators, though inactive in recent years.

The story went on to speculate that Dorsey's death may have been ordered in retaliation for the Desjardins killing, and recounted the murders of the Vaillancourt twins, Richard "Spider" Marcotte, and Emily Anne Toussaint. It reported that Dorsey's funeral would be held as soon as the coroner released the body.

The piece concluded by stating that the authorities were concerned that an escalation in violence was on the horizon, and that the Dorsey funeral might be used as an opportunity for revenge by Heathens sympathizers. Police would be taking extra precautions in the coming weeks.

I looked up to see Kit regarding me intently.

"It would be rockin' to go to that funeral."

"No way."

"The cops will have these guys so boxed in they'll be like altar boys heading to Mass."

"No."

"The bikes will be solid Harley."

"You're not going anywhere near that funeral."

"All that juice pounding along in formation." He mimicked steering handlebars. "Rolling thunder."

"Kit."

"Yeah?" His eyes were bright as a Pentecostal zealot's.

"I don't want you there."

"Aunt Tempe, you worry too much."

How many times had Katy said that?

"I'll throw on jeans, then let's have dinner. I want to ask you about something."

I broached the subject during dessert.

"A Carcajou investigator came to see me today."

"Yeah?" Kit scraped the top off then scooped a spoonful of rice pudding.

"You're supposed to eat the frosting."

"It looks like silver."

"It is."

I was stalling.

"He brought a set of police surveillance photos."

A quizzical look. More pudding.

"Of you."

My nephew lowered his chin and raised his brows.

"The pictures were taken at the Galveston County fairgrounds. You're with members of the Bandidos motorcycle club."

"Uh-oh," he said, giving a goofy grin. "Hanging out with bad companions."

"Do you?"

"Do I what?"

"Hang out with the Bandidos?"

"Just that once. But the big kids made me do it."

"This isn't funny, Kit! You were caught on film with drug dealers!"

He lay down his spoon and gave me another brilliant smile. I did not return it.

"Aunt Tempe. I go to flea markets. Bikers go to flea markets. Sometimes we go to the same flea markets. We talk about Harleys. That's all it is."

"The detective said you'd been arrested on a drug charge." I forced myself to speak calmly.

He slumped back and threw out his legs.

"Oh, great. That shit again."

"What shit?"

"Jesus. You'd think I was supplying a preschool." His voice was hard, the humor gone.

I waited.

"I bought a ten-dollar bag for a friend because she left her wallet at home. Before I could give her the weed a cop pulled me over for an illegal left and found the stuff in my pocket. How's that for a seasoned dope dealer?"

"Why did the cop search you?"

"I'd had a little beer."

He scuffed at the rug with one big toe. A long thin toe, knobby at the joints, oblong under the nail. My father's big toe. As I looked at him my heart ached. Every cell in his body reminded me of Daddy.

"All right, I'd had a lot of beer. But I don't do drugs. I told you that. Christ, you're acting just like my father."

"Or any concerned parent." Love and anger battled for control of my voice.

"Look, I did my community service and went to their lame substance abuse program. Aren't you people ever going to ease up?"

With that he lurched from the chair and slouched out of the room. In seconds I heard the slam of the guest room door.

Well-done, Brennan. Take a gold star for effective parenting.

I cleared the table, repackaged the uneaten portions of food, loaded the dishwasher, and tried Howard's number.

No answer.

Damn you, Harry, for not telling me about this. And damn you for being in Mexico.

I tried Isabelle, hoping to ask about Lyle Crease.

Machine.

I spent the rest of the evening with the Pat Conroy book I'd laid down a week earlier. Nothin' could be finer than to be in Carolina.

Predictably, Kit was sleeping when I left for work. This day, I attended the morning meeting.

When I returned to my office, Claudel was there.

"Figure out who killed Dorsey?" I asked as I threw the morning's case log on the desk.

He gave me a look that could freeze molten lava, then held out an envelope.

I sat, unlocked my desk drawer, and handed him the Myrtle Beach photo.

"Where did you say this came from?"

"I didn't." I gave him the lens. "Because I don't know."

"It just appeared?"

"Yes."

His eyes roved the print.

"I noticed it yesterday. I can't say for certain when it arrived on my desk."

After several seconds the lens froze and he drew closer to it. Then, "You're talking about the man next to Z. Z. Top?"

"Show me," I said, surprised at the musical reference. I would have pegged Claudel as strictly classical.

He turned the photo and pointed.

"Yes. The girl next to him is Savannah Osprey."

Back to the lens.

"You're sure?"

I dug out the yearbook portrait Kate had given me. He studied it, then the picnic shot, going back and forth like a fan at Wimbledon.

"You're right."

"What about Buckle Boy?"

He indicated the envelope in my hand. "Desjardins was a large man before his illness."

I shook out the photos and Claudel circled the desk so we could view them together.

Large was an understatement. The partially headless form I'd seen in the chair was a feeble reminder of the body that once had housed Cherokee Desjardins. Before cancer had parched his innards, and drugs and chemo had done their magic, the man had been massive, though in a spongy, gut-bulging sort of way.

The file photos spanned a period of years. Beards came and went and the hairline crept backward, but the belly and facial features changed little.

Until the cancer struck.

Six months before his death Cherokee was a shadow of his former self, bald and death-camp thin. Had the picture been unlabeled, I would not have recognized the subject as the same man.

As I studied the face from shot to shot I remembered an old Brando quote. I have eyes like those of dead pig, the aging actor had said of himself.

Not to worry, Marlon. They served you well. This guy looked merely baleful, and mean as a pack dog with a stolen flank steak.

But try as we might we could not determine for sure if our late but unlamented Cherokee was the one wearing the buckle at Myrtle Beach.

30

I gathered the Cherokee photos, and we moved down the hall to a section labeled Imagerie. We'd decided that I would manipulate the image using Adobe Photoshop, since I was familiar with the program. Should that prove inadequate, a technician would help us with more sophisticated graphics software.

We were expected, and the equipment was immediately available. The technician clicked on the scanner, keyed the computer to the proper program, then left us to our task.

I placed the snapshot on the flatbed scanner, cropped to include the full scene, then digitized the image and saved it to the hard drive. Then I opened the file to the Myrtle Beach picnic.

I clicked on Buckle Boy's face and zoomed in until his features filled the screen. Then I cleaned up the "noise" of dust and cracks, modified the curves that control the contribution of red, green, and blue tones, adjusted the brightness and contrast, and sharpened the edges of the image.

Claudel watched as I worked the keys, silent at first, then making suggestions as his interest grew, despite his initial cynicism. Each correction morphed the highlights, shadows, and midtones, mutating the curves and planes of the face, and bringing out detail invisible in the original shot.

In less than an hour we sat back and studied our work. There could be no doubt. Buckle Boy was, in fact, Yves "Cherokee" Desjardins.

But what did that mean?

Claudel spoke first.

"So Cherokee knew the Osprey girl."

"Looks that way," I agreed.

"And Dorsey killed him." Claudel was thinking aloud. "What do you suppose Dorsey had to trade?"

"Maybe Cherokee killed Savannah and Dorsey knew that."

"Could she have traveled up here with him?" Again, it was verbalized thought, not conversation.

I pictured the puzzled little face, the wide eyes taking in the world through clock-face lenses. I shook my head.

"Not voluntarily."

"He could have killed her in Myrtle Beach then displaced the body to Quebec." This time he was addressing me.

"Why transport it all that way?"

"Less chance of discovery."

"Does that sound typical of these guys?"

"No." Behind his eyes I could see confusion. And anger.

"And where's the rest of her?" I pressed.

"Perhaps he cut off her head."

"And legs?"

"This is not a question for me." He flicked at an

invisible speck on his sleeve, then straightened his tie.

"And how did she end up buried near Gately and Martineau?"

Claudel did not answer.

"And whose skeleton did they find in Myrtle Beach?"

"That's one for your SBI friends."

Since Claudel seemed willing to talk for once, I decided to up the ante. I switched direction.

"Maybe Cherokee's murder wasn't a revenge killing at all."

"I'm not clear where you're going."

"Maybe it was connected to the discovery of Savannah's grave."

"Maybe." He checked his watch, then stood. "And maybe I'll be invited to join the Dixie Chicks. But until then I had better collar some bad guys."

What was it with the pop music references?

When he'd gone I saved the original and modified versions of the Myrtle Beach snapshot to a compact disc. Then I scanned and added selections from Kate's collection, thinking maybe I'd play with the images at home.

Back in my office I called the DNA section, knowing the answer but unable to bear the thought of another stroll through a biker-happy album.

I was right. Gagné was sorry, but the tests I'd requested had not been completed. An '84 case could not be given high priority, but they hoped to get to it soon.

Fair enough. You jumped the eyeball to the front of the line.

I hung up and reached for my lab coat. At least the slides should be ready.

I found Denis logging cases into the computer in the

histology lab. I waited as he read the label on a plastic jar in which chunks of heart, kidney, spleen, lung, and other organs floated in formaldehyde. He made a few keystrokes, then returned the container to the collection on the cart.

When I made my request he went to his desk and brought me a small white plastic box. I thanked him and took it to the microscope in my lab.

Denis had prepared slides from the bone samples I'd brought from Raleigh. I placed a tibial section under the lens, adjusted the light, and squinted through the eyepiece. Two hours later I had my answer.

The samples I'd taken from the tibiae and fibulae in Kate's unidentified skeleton were indistinguishable histologically from those I'd cut from Savannah's femora. And each thin section yielded an estimate consistent with Savannah's age at the time of her disappearance.

Consistent. The favorite word of the expert witness.

Can you state with a reasonable degree of scientific certainty that the bones recovered in Myrtle Beach belong to Savannah Claire Osprey?

No, I cannot.

I see. Can you state that the bones recovered in Myrtle Beach come from an individual of exactly the same age as Savannah Claire Osprey?

No, I cannot.

I see. What can you tell this court, Dr Brennan?

The bones recovered in Myrtle Beach are consistent in histological age and microstructure with other bones identified as belonging to Savannah Claire Osprey.

I clicked off the light and placed the plastic hood over the scope.

It was a start.

After a lunch of vegetarian pizza and a Mr Big ice cream bar, I reported to Carcajou headquarters. Morin had completed his autopsy and was releasing Dorsey's body. Jacques Roy had called a meeting to discuss security measures for the funeral, and had requested my presence.

Dorsey's roots were in a neighborhood just southeast of Centre-ville, an area of narrow streets and narrower alleys, of crowded flats trimmed with steep stairs and tiny balconies. To the west lies the Main, to the east Hochelaga-Maisonneuve, site of some of the fiercest battles in the current gang war. The district boasts the highest rate of car theft in the city. Unlike most in Montreal, it has no name.

But it has notoriety. The quarter is the heartland of the Rock Machine, and it is home to the Sûreté du Québec. I often gaze onto its streets, its playgrounds, its riverfront, its bridge, for the Laboratoire de Sciences Judiciaires et de Médecine Légale sits at its core.

Dorsey's funeral was to take place not six blocks from our door. Given that, and the fact that the streets would be crawling with local hoods, the police were taking no chances.

Roy used a map of the island to explain the deployment of personnel. The service was to begin at 8 A.M. Friday at the family parish at Fullum and Larivière. Following Mass, the cortege would move north on Fullum to avenue Mont-Royal, then proceed west and up the mountain to the Cimetière de Notre-Dame-des-Neiges.

Roy outlined the positioning of barricades, cruisers, foot patrolmen, and surveillance personnel, and described the procedures to be followed for the event.

The area around the church would be under tight security, side streets blocked at their intersections with Mont-Royal during the funeral procession. The entourage would be limited to the eastbound lanes of Mont-Royal and surrounded by a police escort. Security at the cemetery would also be maximal.

All leaves were canceled. Everyone would report for work on Friday.

The slide show opened to a chorus of "*Sacré bleu!*" and "*Tabernac!*" but the complaints petered out as the screen filled with scenes of funerals past. Frame by frame we observed the cast of characters, smoking on church steps, riding in columns behind flower-laden hearses, clustered at gravesides.

The faces around me shifted from rose to blue to yellow as each new slide dropped into place. The projector hummed and Roy droned on, giving the date and location of each event, and pointing out the relevant players.

The room was warm, and a good portion of my blood had deserted my brain to work on the Mr Big. After a while I felt myself yielding to the monotony. My upper lids reached for my lower, and the weight of my head approached the carrying capacity of my neck muscles. I began to nod off.

Then the projector clicked again and I was wide awake.

The screen showed bikers at a police road check. Some straddled Harleys, others had dismounted and were milling about. Though all wore the skull and winged helmet of the Hells Angels, I could read only two bottom rockers. One said *Durham*, the other *Lexington*. The words *Metro Police* were visible on a yellow van in the background, but the rest of the identifier was blocked by a bearded figure photographing the photographer. At his side, Cherokee Desjardins stared insolently into the lens.

"Where was that taken?" I asked Roy.

"South Carolina."

"That's Cherokee Desjardins."

"The big chief spent time down South in the early eighties."

My eyes roved over the pictured group, then came to rest on a bike and rider on the outer edge. His back was turned, his face obscured, but the cycle was visible in full profile. It looked familiar.

"Who's the guy on the far left?" I asked.

"On the chop job?"

"Yes."

"Don't know."

"I've seen that guy in a couple of old photos," Kuricek offered. "Nothing recent, though. He's ancient history."

"What about the bike?"

"A work of art."

Thanks.

A discussion of Friday's operation followed the slides. When the investigators had gone I approached Roy.

"Could I borrow that shot of Cherokee Desjardins?"

"Would you prefer a print?"

"Sure."

"Spot something interesting?"

"I just thought the bike looked familiar."

"It's a hummer."

"Yeah."

We went to his office and he pulled a file from a metal cabinet, then leafed through until he located the picture.

"They sure as hell don't all look like this anymore," he said, handing it to me. "Now some of them wear Versace and own fast-food franchises. Made our job easier when they were drunk and filthy."

"Did you leave another South Carolina print on my desk in the last couple of days?"

"Not I. Is it something I should see?"

"It's like the one you just gave me, but it includes the Osprey girl. I've shown it to Claudel."

"Now that's interesting. I'll be curious to hear what he says."

I thanked him and left, promising to return the print.

When I got to the lab I went directly to Imagerie and added the photo to my compact disc. It was just a hunch, probably a dead end, but I wanted to make a comparison.

I left work at four-thirty and swung by the Hôte-Dieu Hospital, hoping LaManche had improved enough to receive visitors. No go. He was still unresponsive, and his doctors were keeping him in cardiac intensive care, with no visitors except immediate family. Feeling helpless, I ordered a small bouquet in the hospital gift shop, and headed for the parking lot.

In the car I turned on the radio and hit scan. The channel selector ran the band, pausing briefly on a local talk show. Today's topic was the biker war and the upcoming funeral for its latest victim. The host was soliciting comments on police performance. I clicked in to listen.

While opinions varied as to police handling of the gang situation, one thing was clear. Callers were nervous. Whole neighborhoods were being avoided. Mothers were walking their kids to school. Late-night carousers were changing watering holes, looking over their shoulders as they scurried to their cars.

And the callers were angry. They wanted their town released from the threat of these modern-day Mongols.

When I got home Kit was on the phone. He held the mouthpiece to his chest, and informed me that Harry had called from Puerto Vallarta.

"What did she say?"

"*Buenos días.*"

"Did you get a number?"

"She said she was moving around. But she'll call again later in the week."

Then he resumed his conversation, disappearing into his room.

Good going, Harry.

Wasting no time worrying about my sister, I pulled out the print Roy had loaned me and laid it on the table. Then I sorted through Kate's photos for the shots of Bernard "Slick" Silvestre's biker funeral down South. I was particularly interested in the graveside scene Kit and I had studied.

I went through the stack three times and came up empty. I checked everything in my briefcase. Then the desk in my bedroom. The papers around my computer. Every folder Kate had given me.

The photos were nowhere to be found.

Puzzled, I stuck my head into Kit's room to ask if he'd borrowed them.

He hadn't.

O.K., Brennan. Play the remembering game. When did you last see them?

Saturday night with Kit?

No.

Sunday morning.

In the hands of Lyle Crease.

The anger hit me like a sucker punch, sending heat up my neck, and curling my fingers into fists.

"Goddammit! Sonovabitch!"

I was furious with Crease and more furious with myself. Living alone, I had gotten into the habit of working investigative material at home, a practice discouraged by the lab. Now I was missing a piece of potential evidence.

Slowly, I calmed down. And I recalled something a detective once told me while working a homicide in Charlotte. Media vans surrounded the charred suburban colonial where we were bagging what remained of a family of four.

"Our free press is like a sewer system," he said, "sucking in everyone and grinding them to shit. Especially those who ain't paying attention."

I hadn't paid attention, and now I would have to retrieve those photos.

31

To work off my anger at Crease, my disgust with myself, and my fear for LaManche, I pounded out three miles on the treadmill at the gym. Then I lifted for thirty minutes, and sat in the steam room for another ten.

Walking home along Ste-Catherine I felt physically tired, but still mentally anxious. I forced my thoughts to innocuous things.

The weather had turned heavy and humid. Seagulls screamed at the dark clouds that hung low over the city, trapping the smell of the St Lawrence and bringing on a premature dusk.

I thought about city gulls. Why fight pigeons for urban scraps when a world-class river flows a mile away? Are gulls and pigeons variations of the same bird?

I thought about dinner. I thought about the pain in my left knee. I thought about a tooth in which I suspected a cavity. I thought about ways to conceal my hair.

Mostly I thought about Lyle Crease. And I understood the rage of Islamic fundamentalists and postal workers. I would call him and demand the return of the photos. Then, if the little reptile crossed my path again I would probably get my name in the papers.

As I rounded the corner onto my street I saw a figure moving toward me, a leather-vested white-trash redneck who looked like a hyena pack of one.

Had he come from my building?

Kit!

I felt a constriction in my chest.

I quickened my pace and kept to the center of the sidewalk. The man held his path, banging into me as we passed. His bulk was such that the impact knocked me off balance. Stumbling, I looked up into dark eyes, made darker by the brim of a baseball cap. I stared into them.

Look at me, asshole. Remember my face. I'll remember yours.

He met my gaze, then puckered his lips in an exaggerated kiss.

I offered a digit.

Heart pounding, I raced to the complex and into the vestibule, taking the steps two at a time. With shaking hands I unlocked the front door, hurried down the hall, and inserted the key to my condo.

Kit was in the kitchen adding pasta to boiling water. There was an empty beer bottle by the sink, a half-full one at his elbow.

"Kit."

His hand jumped at the sound of my voice.

"Hey. What's up?"

He poked the noodles with a wooden spoon, and took a swig of beer. Though the greeting was casual, his jerky movements belied tension.

I was silent, waiting for him to go on.

"I found some store-bought sauce. Roasted garlic

and black olive. It ain't gourmet, but I thought you'd like a home-cooked."

He gave a brilliant Kit smile, then tossed back another mouthful of Molson.

"What's going on?"

"NBA play-off game tonight."

"You know what I mean."

"I do?"

"Kit." I did not disguise my annoyance.

"What? Just ask, ma'am."

"Was someone here while I was gone?"

He swirled the linguine, tapped the spoon on the edge of the pot, and looked straight at me. For several moments the steam rose between us. Then the corners of his eyes pinched, and he tapped again.

"No."

He dropped his gaze, stirred, flicked back to me.

"What's the deal?"

"I saw someone on the sidewalk and thought he might have been coming from here."

"Can't help you." Another shit-eating grin. "You like your linguine *al dente*, madam?"

"Kit—"

"You worry too much, Aunt Tempe."

It was becoming a familiar refrain.

"Are you still seeing those men from the bike shop?"

He extended his hands, wrists pressed together.

"O.K. I give up. Arrest me on suspicion of involvement with organized pasta."

"Are you?"

His voice grew stern. "Who hired you to ask these questions, ma'am?"

It was clear he would tell me nothing. I pushed the fear to a corner of my mind, knowing that it wouldn't stay there, and went to my room to change. But I'd made a decision.

Kit was going back to Houston.

After dinner Kit settled in front of the TV and I went to my computer. I'd just pulled up the jpg files that contained Kate's photos and the one I'd borrowed from Jacques Roy, when the phone rang.

Kit answered, and I heard laughter and banter through the wall, then the tone changed. Though I could make out no words, it was clear Kit was upset. His voice grew loud and angry, and at one point I heard something slammed.

In a moment Kit appeared at my door, his agitation apparent.

"I'm going out for a little bit, Auntie T."

"Out?"

"Yep."

"With?"

"Just some guys." Only his mouth smiled.

"That's not good enough, Kit."

"Oh hell, don't you start in."

With that he stormed down the hall.

"Shit!"

I leaped to my feet, but Kit was already out the door when I rounded the corner into the living room.

"Shit!" I repeated for emphasis.

I was about to go after him when the phone rang. Thinking it was Kit's earlier caller, I grabbed the handset.

"Yes!" I seethed.

"Jesus, Tempe. Maybe you need to get into some kind of exercise program. You are becoming consistently rude."

"Where the hell are you, Harry?"

"The great state of Jalisco. *Buenos noch*—"

"Why didn't you tell me about Kit's trouble in Houston?"

"Trouble?"

"The tiny matter of the drug bust!" I was almost shouting.

"Oh, that."

"That."

"I really don't believe that was Kit's fault. If it weren't for the pasty-faced little pricks he was hanging out with, he'd never have gotten involved with that stuff."

"But he did, Harry. And now he has a police record."

"But he didn't have to do any jail time. Howard's lawyer got him off with probation and some community service. Tempe, that boy worked at a homeless shelter for five nights, ate there and slept there and everything. I think it gave him a real good understanding of how the less fortun—"

"Did you get him into counseling?"

"It was just wild oats. Kit's fine."

"He could have a serious problem."

"He just took to runnin' with the wrong crowd."

I wanted to explode from sheer exasperation. Then another thought occurred to me.

"Kit is on probation?"

"Yes, that's all. So it didn't seem worth mentioning."

"What are the terms of his probation?"

"What?"

"Are there restrictions on what Kit is allowed to do?"

"He can't drive after midnight. That's been a real pisser. Oh, yeah. And he can't associate with criminals." She said the last with exaggerated drama, then snorted. "As if he roams with Bonnie and Clyde."

Harry's inability to grasp the obvious never ceased to amaze me. She talked to houseplants, but had no inkling of how to communicate with her son.

"Are you supervising what he does, whom he sees?"

"Tempe, it's not like the boy's gonna rob a bank."

"That's not the point."

"I really don't want to discuss this anymore."

Harry was a grand master at "I really don't want to discuss this."

"I've got to run, Harry." The conversation was degenerating into an argument, and I had no desire to go there.

"Okeydokey. Just wanted to make sure y'all are doing fine. I'll keep in touch."

"Do that."

I disconnected and stood for a full five minutes, considering my options. None was appealing, but I finally settled on a plan.

After checking the phone book for an address, I grabbed my keys and headed out.

Traffic was light, and within twenty minutes I pulled to the curb on rue Ontario. I cut the engine and looked around, while butterflies took flight in my stomach. I'd have preferred a decade of laser resurfacing to the enterprise I was about to undertake.

La Taverne des Rapides was directly across from me, sandwiched between a tattoo parlor and a motorcycle atelier. The place looked as seedy as I remembered from the photos of Kit that Claudel had brought to my office. Neon signs promised Budweiser and Molson through window glass last washed in the Age of Aquarius.

Zipping a can of Mace inside my jacket pocket, I got

out, locked the car, and crossed the street. From the sidewalk I could feel the throb of music vibrating the tavern. Opening the door, I was blasted by the smell of smoke and sweat and stale beer.

Inside, a bouncer looked me up and down. He wore a black T-shirt with the words *Born to Die* emblazoned across a screaming skull.

"Sweet darling," he said with an oily purr, leering at my chest. "I think I'm in love."

The man was missing several teeth, and looked like a member of Thugs Anonymous. I did not return his greeting.

"You come back to Rémi when you're ready for something special, honey."

He ran a hairy hand down my arm, then signaled me to proceed.

I moved past, wanting to reduce Rémi's dentition by another two or three incisors.

The place had the feel of an Appalachian hooch house, complete with pool table, jukebox, and TV's bolted to corner shelves. A bar occupied one wall, booths another. The rest of the room was filled with tables. It was dark except for Christmas lights framing the bar and front windows.

When my eyes adjusted, I did a sweep. The clientele were alpha male, scruffy and longhaired, looking like Visigoth extras from central casting. The women had swirled their hair into styling-gel do's, and stuffed their breasts into halters with rock-my-world cleavage.

I did not see Kit.

I was threading my way toward the back of the room when I heard shouts and the sound of scuffling feet. Lowering my head, I plowed a course through a sea of beer bellies and flattened myself against a wall.

298

Near the bar, a goon with Rasputin brows and concave cheeks bellowed and shot to his feet. Blood streamed down his face, staining his sweatshirt and darkening the chains around his neck. A puffy-faced man glared at him from the opposite side of a small table. He was holding a Molson bottle by the wrong end, jabbing it forward to keep his opponent at bay. With a yell, Rasputin grabbed a chair and slammed it into his rival. I heard glass shatter as man and bottle hit the cement.

Tables and bar stools emptied as patrons surged forward, eager to join in whatever was happening. Rémi the bouncer appeared with a baseball bat, and boosted himself onto the bar.

That was enough for me. I decided to wait for Kit outside.

I was halfway to the door when a pair of hands clamped my upper arms. I tried to wrench free but the grip tightened, squeezing my flesh hard against my bones.

Furious, I twisted, and looked into a face strikingly like that of a swamp gator. It sat atop a thick neck, with protruding beady eyes, jaw long and narrow and slung forward at an obtuse angle.

My captor curled his lips and split the air with a piercing whistle. Rasputin froze, and there was a moment of surprised silence as he and his spectators located the source of the whistle. George Strait crooned in the sudden quiet.

"Hey, cut the shit, I got some show-and-tell." The man's voice was surprisingly high. "Rémi, get the goddam bottle from Tank."

Rémi dropped from the bar and stepped between the combatants, the bat resting lightly on his shoulder. He

299

placed a foot on Tank's wrist, applied weight, and what remained of the bottle rolled free. Rémi kicked it away, then pulled Tank to his feet. Tank started to sputter but the man holding me cut him off.

"Shut the fuck up and listen."

"You talking to me, JJ?" Tank swayed, then spread his feet for better balance.

"You fucking bet your ass I am."

Again Tank opened his mouth. Again JJ ignored him.

"Look what we have here, gents."

A few listened, faces vacant from booze or boredom, most turned away. George finished his song and the Rolling Stones took over. The bartender went back to pouring drinks. The hubbub began to swell.

"Big fuckin' deal," yelled a man at the bar. "You found a broad who don't puke when she looks at you."

Laughter.

"Take a good look, dick brain," JJ replied in an adenoidal whine. "Ever hear of the bone lady?"

"Who the fuck cares?"

"The one what did a little yard work for the Vipers?" He was shouting now, the tendons in his neck taut as guy wires.

A handful of customers turned back to us, confusion floating across their faces.

"Don't any of you assholes read the papers?" JJ's voice cracked with the effort to be heard.

While others went back to their drinks and conversation, Tank picked his way toward us, moving with the exaggerated care of the very drunk. Breathing heavily, he planted himself in front of me, and ran a hand down my cheek.

I turned away, but he cupped my chin and twisted my face to his. His beery breath made my stomach lurch.

300

"She don't look like such a ball buster to me."

I said nothing.

"You out slummin', *plotte*?"

Ignoring the whore reference, I looked him straight in the eyes.

With his free hand Tank fumbled with the zipper of his jacket. When it opened I could see the butt of a .38 tucked into his waistband. Fear slithered along my nerves.

On the edge of my vision, I saw a man slide from a bar stool and move in our direction. He stepped close and gave Tank a shoulder-jab greeting.

"*Tabernouche*, I could definitely get a bone on for this."

The man wore baggy black trousers, gold neck chains, and an open vest showing skin that was fish-belly white. Jailhouse art decorated his chest and arms, and wraparound shades covered his eyes. His muscles were swollen with steroids, and he spoke in heavily accented French.

Tank released my chin and stepped back, staggering slightly.

"She's the bitch dug up Gately and Martineau."

Stay calm, I told myself.

"You dig Pascal, sugar, you come up with something really big."

When Pascal removed his shades my fear escalated. His eyes had the bright, glazed look of omnipotence only meth or crack can bestow.

Pascal reached toward me, and I yanked an arm free and parried his move.

"What the fuck?" He glared at me, all pupil.

"Somebody put this guy on his leash." I said it with much more bravado than I felt.

Pascal's flush deepened and the muscles in his neck and arms corded.

"Who the fuck is this bitch?"

Again he reached for me. Again I knocked his hand away. I was almost numb with fear, but I couldn't let them see it.

"You probably come from a dysfunctional home where no one can spell the word polite, so the lack of manners may not be your fault. But don't ever touch me again," I hissed.

"*Sacré bl—*" Pascal's fingers balled into fists.

"Want me to shoot her ass?" asked Tank, reaching for the .38.

"Be cool, bitch, or these guys'll leave your brains on a wall." JJ giggled, shoved me forward, then melted into the crowd.

I started to bolt, but Pascal grabbed and spun me, angling my arm up hard against my back. Pain shot to my shoulder, and tears blurred my vision.

"Not in here, Pascal." Rémi spoke in a low, bloodless voice. He'd positioned himself behind my assailant, the bat still on his shoulder. "Take it somewhere else."

"No problem." Pascal wrapped an arm around my throat and pressed his body into mine. I felt something cold and hard against my neck.

I flailed and twisted as best I could, but I was no match for the drugs pumping through his veins.

"*Allons-y,*" Pascal snarled, half-pushing, half-dragging me toward the back of the bar. "This bitch is going to the opera."

32

"No!" I protested, terror overcoming my resolve to stay cool.

One arm compressing my trachea, the other bending my elbow at an excruciating angle, Pascal drove me through the crowd. His blade jumped with each step, and I felt blood ooze down the side of my neck.

Rage and fear rocketed my adrenaline, and my mind screamed conflicting orders.

Do as he tells you!

Don't go with him!

Frantic, I looked around for sources of help. The bartender just watched our progress, smoke curling across his face. Rockabilly music pounded from the jukebox. I heard catcalls and hoots, but the faces we passed were passive, carvings in apathy. No one showed interest in what happened to me.

Don't let him take you outside!

I struggled and twisted, but my efforts were useless against Pascal's strength. Increasing the pressure on my throat, he forced me out a back door and down a set of metal steps. Bootfalls told me Tank was right behind.

When my feet hit gravel, I took a deep breath, ducked and twisted, but Pascal only tightened his choke hold. Desperate, I dipped my chin and bit his hand with all the strength my jaws could muster.

Pascal bellowed and threw me to the ground. I scrabbled through soggy wrappers, condoms, beer caps, and cigarette butts, my stomach curdling at the smell of sludge and urine, trying to unzip the pocket that held the Mace.

"No such fucking luck," Pascal snarled, coming down hard with a boot to my back.

My chest slammed into gravel. Air burst from my lungs, and white light exploded in my brain.

Scream!

My thorax was on fire. I couldn't make a sound.

The boot withdrew, then I heard footsteps, and a car door opening. Gasping for air, I started hitching forward, elbows and knees sliding in the reeking mud.

"Is today the day, cunt?"

Feeling a gun barrel against my temple, I froze. Tank's face was so close I could smell his breath again.

I heard boots on gravel.

"Your limo's here, bitch. Tank, get her fuckin' feet."

Rough hands lifted me like a rolled carpet. I squirmed and bucked as best I could, but it did no good. Panicked now, I cast desperate looks up and down the alley. There was no one in sight.

Stars and rooftops wheeled out of sight as I was turned and thrown into a car. Tank climbed in back, placed a boot across my shoulders, and forced my face into the carpet. Smells of dust, dried wine, stale smoke, and vomit sent a wave of nausea through my body.

Doors slammed, tires spun, and the car sped down the alley.

I was trapped! I was suffocating!

I maneuvered my hands to shoulder level and raised my head. The boot lifted, and a heel struck my back.

"Make a sound and you get a bullet up your ass." Tank's voice had grown hard, less slurry than in the bar.

With the booze and pills to stoke their ordinarily malevolent dispositions, I had no doubt these men would kill me without a hitch in their thoughts. Don't provoke them while there's no opportunity for escape, I thought. Look for an opening. I lowered my head and waited.

Pascal drove erratically, hitting the gas and brake pedals with quick, jerky movements. The car rolled and lurched, intensifying my nausea. Unable to see out, I counted the stops and turns, trying to memorize the route.

When we stopped, Tank's boot withdrew, and doors opened and slammed. I heard voices, then the back door opened again. Pascal grabbed my arms and dragged me from the car.

As I struggled for balance my gaze fell on Tank, and a wave of terror traveled up my spine. He held the .38 aimed directly at my head. His eyes gleamed black in the pale pink of the streetlight, feral with anticipation. I resisted the impulse to beg, knowing my pleas would only fuel his blood lust.

Pascal shoved me up a short walk toward a building with a green roof and brick exterior wall. When he withdrew a key, unlocked the gate, and pushed me through, my painfully constructed calm crumbled.

Run! Don't go inside!

"No!"

"Move your ass, bitch."

305

"Please no!" My pulse beat at a ferocious pace.

I tried to plant my feet against the advance, but Pascal forced me across the courtyard toward the house. Tank followed closely. I could feel his gun on the back of my head, and knew escape was impossible.

"What do you want from me?" I was almost sobbing.

"All you got and then some, bitch," Pascal snarled. "Shit you ain't even dreamed of."

He spoke into an intercom. I heard a metallic voice followed by a click, then he shouldered open the steel-reinforced door and pushed me inside.

There are moments in life when it seems clear the wrap-up is at hand. Your heart pounds and your blood pressure rises, but you know the blood will soon be spilled, never to flow again. Your mind flip-flops between an urge to launch one last desperate effort and a sense of resignation, a desire to just give in.

I've had this feeling a time or two, but never as vividly as at that moment. As Pascal shoved me down the hall, I knew with certainty I would not leave that house alive. My brain opted for furious action.

I turned and drove my fist as hard as I could into Pascal's face. I felt something crunch, but swung back with my elbow and brought it up under his chin. Pascal's head flew back and I slipped below his arm and bolted through a doorway on my left.

I found myself in a game room similar to that at the Vipers' clubhouse in St-Basile-le-Grand. Same bar. Same neon art. Same video monitors. The only difference was that these were working, throwing a cool blue light over the bar and its occupants.

I ran to the far side of the pool table, grabbed a cue in one hand, and fumbled for the Mace with my other, my eyes searching for any door or window.

Two men sat at the bar, another stood behind it. All three had turned at the sound of Pascal's roar. They watched me tear across the room, then shifted their attention back to the door when Pascal burst through it.

"I'll kill that little bucket of shit! Where the fuck is she?"

Light from the neon sign angled obliquely across Pascal's face, deepening the furrows and casting shadows across his eyes and cheeks.

"Hold it right there."

The voice was low and hard as quartz, and stopped Pascal dead. The sound of the outer door suggested Tank had opted out of further involvement. I stole a look at the man who had spoken.

He wore a double-breasted tan suit with a pale peach shirt and matching tie. His skin was tanning-booth bronze, and he probably paid his hairstylist eighty dollars per visit. Large rings adorned each of his hands.

It was the man beside him who caused my heart to stop.

Andrew Ryan wore black jeans, boots, and a gray sweatshirt with the arms razored off. The muscles in his face looked hard and tense, and stubble roughened his cheeks and chin.

Ryan's eyes met mine and the flesh underneath tensed slightly, then he looked away.

I felt heat rise up my neck and spread across my cheeks. My legs trembled, and I leaned into the pool table to steady myself.

After several seconds Ryan swiveled on his bar stool and stretched his legs in my direction. A smirk spread across his face.

"Well, if it ain't shit for brains."

"You know this fuckin' cunt?" Pascal's voice

trembled with rage. Blood trickled from his nose, and he wiped it on his sleeve.

"It's Dr Too Goddam Many Degrees," Ryan said, drawing a pack from his pocket and tapping out a Marlboro.

The others watched as Ryan placed the cigarette between his lips, drew a wooden match from under the cellophane, lit up, and exhaled.

So did I. Ryan's hands looked so familiar on the match and cigarette I felt tears behind my lids. My chest gave a small heave.

Why is he here?

Ryan took his cigarette between thumb and forefinger, upended the matchstick between his teeth, then arched and sent it winging across the room toward me. I watched the match drop onto green felt, and fury exploded inside me.

"You turncoat bastard! You contemptible son of a bitch! Read my lips, Ryan. Drop dead!"

"See what I mean." Pascal wiped his nose again. "We're gonna teach this cunt some manners."

"Bad idea," said Ryan, taking a long drag.

The man in the gabardine suit stared at the side of Ryan's face. Several long seconds passed. The tension in the room was enough to launch arrows. Then, "Why do you say that?" he asked quietly.

"She's a cop." Another drag. "And the cops already have a two-by-four up Pascal's ass for exactly this kind of shit."

"So? You got no balls?" Pascal challenged.

Ryan blew smoke out both nostrils.

"Here's the news flash, asshole. You've already screwed up big time messing up one of your tramps, and now you drag a cop in here. You mess up a cop, particularly a dame, and the whole force comes screaming up your butt. Now, you may not mind taking the bounce for Goldilocks here, but the rest of us sure as hell will. All the shit we have in the works goes into the deep freeze while the cops dissect us top to bottom."

Pascal looked at Ryan, his eyes blazing with fury and speed.

"The fucking bitch hit me! I'm gonna tear her a new asshole." The muscles in his face jumped and his eye and mouth twitched.

The man in the suit continued to study Ryan, his face devoid of expression. Then he turned to Pascal.

"No," he said calmly. "You are not."

Pascal started to bluster, but Ryan held up a hand.

"You want to bloody her up? Watch this."

Walking to the end of the bar, Ryan snatched a red plastic bottle, circled the pool table, and held it over me. Then he squeezed, making circular movements with his hand. I didn't budge.

"Read *that*, Shakespeare." He slammed the bottle onto the table.

I looked down. Ketchup swirled across my shirt. As my eyes crawled back to Ryan's face, words eddied in my head I knew I wouldn't use.

The smirk was gone, and for a long moment the Viking blues held mine. Then Ryan's gaze left me and slid back to Pascal.

"This party's over."

"The party's over when I say it is." Pascal's pupils were wider than a sewer main. He appealed to Ryan's companion.

"This puke can't talk to me like that. He's not ev—"

"But I can. This party's over. Now get the fuck out of here." Barely above a whisper.

Pascal's brow furrowed, and a vein bulged along his temple. With one last "Sonovabitch!" he turned and exited the room.

The man in the gabardine suit watched in silence as Ryan swung back to me.

"You keep your sorry ass, slut, but don't get any wrong ideas. This wasn't for you." He emphasized each word with a jab to my chest. "For all I care you could be upstairs doing the dirty boogie on all fours with Pascal. And take note."

He stood so close I could smell his perspiration, a scent as familiar as my own body.

"Tonight's adventure is one big black hole in your memory bank. It didn't happen." He grabbed my hair and pulled my face to his. "You talk, and I'll personally lead Pascal to you."

He released me with a shove to the chest, and I staggered backward.

"We'll buzz the gate. Now disappear."

Ryan rejoined the man at the bar, sucked once on his cigarette, then flipped the butt against the stainless steel below the counter.

As I watched the spray of sparks, I felt something inside me curl into a cold, hard ball.

Without a word I lay down the pool cue, and fled on shaking legs. Outside the gate, I finally got the Mace out of my pocket and in a venting of frustration, humiliation, relief, and rage, I turned and sprayed the house. Sobbing, teeth chattering, I clutched the cylinder to my chest and bolted into the dark.

The clubhouse was less than six blocks from La Taverne des Rapides, and, after half-stumbling, half-running that distance, it did not take long to find my car. Once inside, I locked the doors, then sat a moment, legs trembling, hands shaking uncontrollably, my mind numb. I took a deep breath and forced myself to move with slow, deliberate motions. Belt. Ignition. Shift. Gas.

Though lightning flickered, and raindrops battered the windshield, I broke all speed laws getting home. My thoughts were chaos.

Ryan had given his companion sound advice. An outlaw enterprise needs a strong reason to mess up even an adjunct cop like me. Retribution would be powerful and the organization would be out of business for an extended time. Unless the cop was wreaking major havoc, it made no sense and the man in the suit had understood that. But what about Ryan? Had sound *consigliere* advice been his sole motive?

What had just taken place? Had I stumbled onto Ryan in his new life? Was he there as a member of the pack, or did he have other motives? What did his actions mean? Had he humiliated me as a message that his past life was done and he now belonged to the other side, or had he done it as part of a scene designed to get me out of there safely? Had he put himself at risk?

I knew I should report the incident. But what would be gained? Carcajou knew of the clubhouse, no doubt had files on Pascal and Tank.

Carcajou. Claudel and Quickwater. My stomach knotted. What would they say when they learned how I'd literally thrown myself in jeopardy? Would the incident reinforce Claudel's desire to have me removed as liaison to the unit?

What if Ryan was undercover? Could a police report threaten his cover?

I didn't have answers, but I made a choice. Regardless of the man's motives, I would do nothing to hurt

Andrew Ryan. If the slightest chance existed that an incident report could harm him, I would make no report. Tomorrow I would decide, I thought.

When I got home Kit's door was closed, but I could hear music through the wall.

Good call, Auntie. This is why you're not a cop.

I threw my clothes on a chair and dropped into bed. As I did so, the thought hit me. What if Pascal had taken me someplace else? Sleep came much, much later.

33

The next morning I slept late, finally waking around ten, sore and achy. I spent the morning nursing myself with aspirin, tea, and hot baths, fighting off flashbacks to the night before. Though I had bruises on my legs and back, and a small cut on my neck, my face had escaped largely unmarked. After a late lunch I applied extra makeup, chose a turtleneck sweater, then went into the lab and spent the day on routine matters. I made no report.

When I got home Kit and I had a quiet dinner. He had no questions about my previous night's outing, and I assumed he was unaware that I'd been gone. I did not bring up his storming out, and he offered no explanation.

After dinner I decided to do laundry. Pulling the basket from the bedroom closet, I added the clothing I'd worn the night before. I sorted, then loaded the washer, holding back items requiring special treatment. My stomach tightened when I lifted the shirt with the ketchup blotch, the scene still vivid in my mind.

I spread the shirt and began spraying the stain, the

product jingle for the spot remover bouncing through my head.

I'll Shout *you* out, you sonovabitch. I squeezed the handle. Phhht!

I pictured the smirk on Ryan's face, remembered his finger jabbing my chest.

I squeezed again. Phhht!

Read that, Shakespeare! Phhht!

My hand froze and I stared at the pattern. The squiggles were not random, but formed two perfect sixes.

Read that, Shakespeare. Shakespeare. The sonnets were a passion with Ryan.

I recalled something from a long time ago. High school. Mr Tomlinson. Senior Honors English.

Was it possible?

I raced to the bedroom bookshelf and pulled out a volume. *The Complete Works of William Shakespeare.* Hardly breathing, I opened to the sonnets and flipped to number sixty-six.

Come on, Bill, let it be there.

Tears welled when I read the line.

And right perfection wrongly disgraced . . .

Wrongly disgraced.

It was a message. Ryan was saying that all was not as it seemed.

Right perfection.

Ryan was not a point man for the dark side! He had not gone over!

What then?

Undercover?

But why hadn't he contacted me?

314

He couldn't, Brennan. You know that.

It didn't matter. Suddenly I was certain that whatever Ryan was doing, the man I knew remained beneath. In time I would know the full story.

And I was equally certain I would never report the previous night's events. I would do nothing to compromise Ryan's cover.

I closed the book and went back to the laundry. Though I understood that covert operations could last months, or even years, at least now I knew.

A smile spread across my face as I bunched the shirt and tossed it into the washer. I can wait, Andrew Ryan. I can wait.

Feeling happier than I had in weeks, I shook off the vision of Pascal and Tank and went back to the photos I'd abandoned the night before. I'd just booted up the disc when Kit appeared in the doorway.

"I forgot to tell you that Isabelle phoned. She's going out of town and wanted to return your call before she left."

"Where is she going?"

"I forget. Something to do with an award."

"When is she leaving?"

"I forget."

"Thanks."

His eyes shifted to the screen.

"What are you doing?"

"I'm trying to clean up some old photographs so I can view the faces."

"Whose?"

"Savannah Osprey is in one shot. And the man who was killed last week."

"The guy who was stabbed in jail?"

"No. The person the police think was his victim."

315

"Awesome."

He moved into the room.

"Can I see?"

"Well, I guess there's nothing in the way of sensitive information here. As long as you promise not to discuss these things with anyone but me, you can pull up a chair."

I brought up the Myrtle Beach photo and indicated Savannah and Cherokee Desjardins.

"Man. That dude looks like a reject from the W.W.F."

"World Wrestling Federation?"

"World Wildlife Fund." He pointed at Savannah. "She's sure no ole lady."

"No. But it's not uncommon for bikers to drug young girls and hold them against their will."

"And she's no beach bunny. Man, her skin's the color of a bedsheet."

I had a thought.

"I want you to take a look at something."

I closed the picnic photo and opened the police-check photo.

Kit leaned in and studied the scene.

"Is that the same dude?" He indicated Cherokee.

"Yes."

"We still in Dixie?"

"South Carolina."

"Looks like a road bust."

His eyes moved across the group, then locked onto the cycle at the periphery.

"Holy shit. Sorry. When was this taken?"

"That's unclear. Why?"

"That's the same chopped hog we saw in the funeral picture."

316

My pulse stepped up.

"Are you sure?"

"Auntie T, that is the sweetest piece of Milwaukee iron I have ever seen. You could really ride the edge on those wheels."

"That's why I was asking about the other picture."

"Did you find it?"

"No."

"Doesn't matter. That's the same bike."

"How can you be sure?"

"Can you zoom it up?"

I magnified that part of the photo.

"Jesus. That is five hundred pounds of thunder."

"Tell me how you know it's the same bike."

"Like I said before, it's an old FLH, a police touring cycle that's been stripped and customized. That's no big deal. But it's the way he did the chop that's so bitching."

One by one he again pointed out the bike's wonders. "This dude wanted a truly raw machine, so he changed the power-to-weight ratio."

His finger touched the front of the bike.

"He lengthened the wheel base and raised the front end by installing longer front forks. Man, those puppies must be twenty inches over stock. He probably cut out a section of the neck of the frame. You've really got to know your shit to pull that off."

"Why?"

"If you screw it up the bike will split and you'll find yourself eating cement at high speed."

He indicated the handlebars.

"He used dog bones, steel struts to raise the handlebars."

"Mm."

"The guy that did this was definitely not interested in

comfort. He's riding a springer front end, that's one with external springs, not hydraulic shock absorbers, and a 'hard tail' frame."

"A hard tail?"

"It's a rigid frame with no rear shock absorbers. It's called a 'hard tail' because your ass really takes a beating."

He pointed to a set of pins at the front of the bike.

"Check out the highway pegs."

I must have looked blank.

"He's got extra foot pegs up front, and a forward-positioned custom-shift-and-brake assembly so he can stretch out his feet. This guy is into serious puttin'."

"And you're sure this is the same bike we saw at Silvestre's grave?"

"Same righteous hog. But that's not my only clue."

I knew I was in over my depth, and said nothing.

"Look at this." He pointed at the gas tank. "He's sculpted the tank with some kind of molding material. What does that look like to you?"

I bent close. The front end did look odd, but the shape brought nothing to mind. I peered at it, forcing my brain cells to draw meaning from the tapered form.

Then I saw it.

"Is that unusual?" I asked.

"It's the only one I've ever seen. The guy's a regular Rodin with bondo."

He stared at the screen, mesmerized. Then, "Yeah! Jammin' in the wind sitting on a snake's head. Hee ha—"

He stopped short and an odd look crossed his face. Then he leaned in, back, then in again, like a bird sighting on a curious insect.

"Can you bring that guy's face up?"

"The one on the bike?"

"Yeah."

"It will blur as I enlarge it."

"Try."

I did, then went through the same manipulations I'd performed with Claudel. As lines and shadows shifted, congealing pixels into recognizable features, then reordering them into meaningless patterns of color and shape, I gradually realized what my nephew had spotted.

In twenty minutes I'd done what I could do. During that time we had not spoken. I broke the silence.

"What made you recognize him?"

"I'm not sure. Maybe the jaw. Maybe the nose. It grabbed me as I was pointing out the snake's head. Before that I hadn't even noticed the rider."

We stared at the man on the marvelous hog. And he looked into space, intent on a happening long since past.

"Did he ever mention riding with the Angels?"

"He's not wearing colors."

"Did he, Kit?"

My nephew sighed.

"No."

"Does he hang with them now?"

"Oh, please. You've seen the guy."

Yes. I'd seen the guy. On a country road in St-Basile-le-Grand. Across a dinner table. On the late-night news. And in my own home.

The man on the bike was Lyle Crease.

34

Words and images flashed in my brain. Pascal's face in neon and shadow. George Dorsey mumbling my name to a paramedic. A glossy eyeball.

". . . are you going to do?" Kit asked.

"Call Isabelle, then go to bed." I closed down the program and slid the CD into its holder.

"That's it?"

"That's it."

Sometimes when thoughts are ricocheting inside my head, the best strategy is to lay back and let them find their own patterns.

"Aren't you curious?"

"Very. And I *will* find out if Crease has ties to the Hells Angels. But not tonight."

"I could ask around."

"That is precisely what you will not do," I snapped. "He could be a dangerous man with dangerous friends."

Kit's face froze. Then his eyes dropped and he turned away.

"Whatever." He shrugged.

I waited for the click of his bedroom door, then dialed Isabelle's number. She answered after four rings, sounding slightly out of breath.

"*Mon Dieu*, I was buried in the back of the closet. I've misplaced my Vuitton overnighter and can't imagine where it is. And, really, nothing else will do."

"Isabelle, I need some information."

My tone suggested I was not in the mood for a luggage discussion.

"*Oui?*"

"I'd like to know about Lyle Crease."

"Ahhh, Tempe, you little pixie. I knew you would change your mind."

Like hell. "Tell me about him."

"He's cute, eh?"

As a mealworm, I thought, but said nothing.

"And you know he is an investigative reporter with CTV. Very glamorous."

"How long has he done that?"

"How long?"

"Yes. How long?"

"*Mon Dieu*, forever."

"How many years?"

"Well, I'm not sure. But he's been on the air as long as I can remember."

"What did he do before that?"

"Before that?"

"Yes. Before CTV." This was harder than questioning George Dorsey.

"Let me think." I heard a soft ticking, and pictured lacquered nails tapping the handset. "I know the answer to this, Tempe, because Véronique told me. Véronique hosts a talk show on Radio-Canada now, interviews

321

celebrities, but she started out doing the weather at CTV. Do you know her?"

"No." My left eye was beginning to throb.

"She dated Lyle briefl—"

"I'm sure I've seen her."

"I think she told me Lyle was hired away from an American newspaper. No. Wait, this is coming back to me." Tick. Tick. Tick. "It was a paper somewhere out west. Alberta, I think. But originally he comes from the States. Or maybe he went to school down there."

"Do you know which state?"

"Somewhere in the South, I think. You should like that."

"When did he come to Canada?"

"Oh my goodness, I have no idea."

"Where does he live?"

"Off the island, I think. Or maybe downtown."

"Does he have family here?"

"Sorry."

"How well do you know Lyle Crease?"

"I am not his confidante, Tempe." Her tone was becoming defensive.

"But you tried to pair me up with him!" I tried to keep my voice neutral but the irritation curled around the edges.

"You needn't put it like that. The gentleman asked to meet you, and I saw no reason to refuse. It's not as though your love life has been bountiful this year."

"Hold it. Back up. It was Crease's idea that we meet?"

"Yes." Guarded.

"When was this?"

"I don't know, Tempe. I ran into him at *L'Express*, you know, that bistro on rue St-Denis th—"

"Yes."

322

"Lyle saw your picture in the paper and was absolutely smitten. Or so he said, though not in those exact words. Anyway, we were talking, and one thing led to another, and before I could help myself I'd invited him to dinner."

Tick. Tick.

"And really, he wasn't so bad. In fact, he was quite charming."

"Um." So was Ted Bundy.

For a few moments no one spoke.

"Are you angry with me, Tempe?"

"No, I'm not angry."

"I'll see what I can find out. I'll phone Véronique an—"

"No. Never mind. It's not important."

The last thing I needed was an alert to Lyle Crease.

"I was just curious. Have a good trip, Isabelle."

"*Merci*. Where do you suppose that overnighter has gone?"

"Try your storage locker."

"*Bonne idée. Bonsoir, Tempe.*"

When we disconnected, I realized I hadn't asked where she was going.

An hour later the mental commingling began. As I lay in bed, trying to block out Kit's music, images, facts, and questions floated to the surface then sank into the deep, like tropical fish in a subliminal tank.

Image. Lyle Crease pouring wine.

Fact. Crease had finagled the introduction. He was at St-Basile-le-Grand and knew about the skeletons, and had seen the article in the *Gazette*, before Isabelle's dinner party.

Questions. Why did he want to meet me? Was his

request linked to the discovery of the burials? Was he simply looking for an inside scoop, or did he have other reasons for wanting information?

Image. A young Lyle Crease on a chopped hog.

Fact. Crease had ties to the Southern states.

Questions. What was Crease doing with the homeboys? Had he stolen the Silvestre funeral photo from me? If so, why? Could his past somehow endanger him now? Whom did he fear?

Image. A hyena redneck lumbering up my block.

Fact. Besides initial fear, the man had triggered something in my psyche.

Questions. Had Kit been lying when I asked about visitors? Why? Who was the goon in the baseball cap? Why did the man provoke such a strong reaction in me?

Image. LaManche on tubes and life support.

Fact. The pathologist was in his sixties and had never taken time for exercise or a proper diet.

Questions. Would he survive? Would he ever return to work?

Image. Ryan slouching on a barroom stool.

Fact. He was undercover, and hadn't gone over.

Questions. Had his actions on my behalf jeopardized his cover? Was he in danger? Had I contributed to that?

These musings mingled with more mundane considerations. How to relocate Kit to Houston. Birdie's overdue vaccinations. The cavity. Hair growth.

But underlying all my thoughts was the nagging signal from my subconscious, unrelenting, yet out of reach. The redneck in the baseball cap. I tossed and turned, frustrated that my psyche was beaming a message I could not decipher.

I was sleeping fitfully when the phone shrilled.

"Hello." Groggy.

324

"Oh, were you in bed?"

The digits on my clock glowed one-fifteen.

"Mm."

"It was the University of South Carolina," Isabelle chirped.

"What?"

"Lyle is from London, Ontario, but he went to school in South Carolina." Her voice beamed with satisfaction. "And don't worry about my source. I was *très discreet*."

Oh boy.

"Thank you, Isabelle." Mumbled.

"Now, go back to sleep. Oh, and I found the suitcase in the bathroom closet. Silly me. Bonsoir."

Dial tone.

I clicked off and flopped back on the pillow, noticing that the bedroom wall no longer vibrated. Had Kit gone out?

As I began to drift off my id made one more try at sending up images. The hyena took form with his leather vest and grungy long hair. Boots. Cap.

Cap.

My eyes flew open and I shot to a sitting position, searching my stored memories for another image.

Could it be?

The next morning I was up before the alarm. A peek told me Kit was asleep in his bed. I showered, dressed, and puttered until it was time to go to the lab.

I went directly to Ronald Gilbert's office and made my request. Without a word he crossed to a shelf, selected a videotape, and handed it to me. I thanked him and hurried to the conference room.

Nervously, I inserted the plastic box into a VCR and clicked on the monitor. Not knowing at what point I'd find the scene, I started at the beginning and hit fast-forward.

Views of the Cherokee Desjardins apartment jerked across the screen. The living room, the kitchen, the faceless corpse. Then the tape focused on bloody walls.

The camera swept across a corner, zooming in, then drawing back. I hit play and the pace slowed to normal.

Two minutes later I spotted the object wedged between the wall and a rusted birdcage supporting a guitar. I hit freeze and read four letters peeking from a wine-colored stain.

"-cock-"

I studied the cap closely. It was red and white, and I could see portions of a familiar logo that hadn't registered while I was at the scene. My mind completed the letters obliterated by Cherokee's blood.

G-a-m-e - - - - s.

Yes.

Gamecocks.

The cap hadn't proclaimed some macho obscenity. It had broadcast the name of an athletic team. The Gamecocks.

The University of South Carolina Gamecocks.

The hyena's cap had nudged my id. Isabelle's call had allowed my brain's summons to assemble and organize to breakthrough.

Just then the door opened and Michel Charbonneau stuck his spiky head into the room. He held up a brown envelope.

"Claudel asked me to give you this. It's the official game plan for tomorrow, and Roy wanted you to have it."

"I guess Monsieur Claudel is too busy."

326

Charbonneau gave one of his shrugs. "He's working these homicides for both agencies."

His eyes drifted to the monitor.

"Desjardins?"

"Yes. Look at this."

He circled the table and stood behind me. I pointed at the cap.

"It's from the University of South Carolina."

"You can't lick our Cocks."

"You've heard of the team."

"With a motto like that, who hasn't?"

"That's not the official slogan."

"Cherokee's decor suggested he was an athletic supporter."

I ignored that.

"In all the photos you've seen of him, was Cherokee ever wearing headgear?"

Charbonneau thought a moment.

"No. So what?"

"Maybe the cap isn't his. Maybe it belongs to his killer."

"Dorsey?"

I told him about the pictures of Lyle Crease.

"So the guy spent some time in South Carolina. Big deal. Half the population of Quebec vacations down there."

"Why would Crease take a sudden interest in me after I dug up those bodies?"

"Aside from the fact that you're cute as a sea monkey?"

"Aside from that."

"O.K., when things quiet down we might reel Crease in and query him on Gately and Martineau. But there's nothing to tie him to the Cherokee hit."

I told him about the Myrtle Beach photo.

"Crease and Cherokee knew each other, and that photo was not of a Boy Scout camporee."

"A trip through Dixie back in the Ice Age. Crease is a journalist. He might have been covering a story."

Charbonneau flipped the envelope onto the table.

"Look, Cherokee had chemo. He probably got the cap when comb-overs were no longer an option. But if it makes you feel better, I'll check Crease out."

When he'd gone, I turned back to the tape, my mind zigzagging through a labyrinth of explanations. The cap could belong to Dorsey. He claimed to have knowledge of Savannah Osprey. Maybe he'd been to South Carolina.

When the camera moved off along the wall I hit rewind and did another sweep through the corner. Bloodstains. Guitar. Birdcage. Cap.

Then the lens drew very close, and I felt movement in the tiny hairs at the back of my neck. I leaned in and squinted at the screen, hoping to make sense of what I'd spotted. It was fuzzy, but definitely there.

I rewound the tape, switched off the VCR, and hurried from the room. If what I saw was real, Claudel and Charbonneau would have to find another theory.

I took the stairs to the thirteenth floor and went to a large window opening onto a room filled with shelves and lined by storage lockers. A small blue sign identified it as the *Salle des Exhibits*. The property room.

A uniform from the SQ was sliding a deer rifle across the counter. I waited while the clerk filled out forms, handed the officer a receipt, then tagged the gun and carried it to the storage area. When she returned I showed her the Cherokee case numbers.

"Could you check to see if the evidence inventory includes an athletic cap?"

"There was a long list for that case," she said, entering the number into a computer. "This may take a moment."

Her eyes scanned the screen.

"Yes, here it is. There was a cap." She read the text. "It went to biology for testing on a bloodstain, but it's back."

She disappeared into the shelves and returned after several minutes with a Ziploc plastic bag. In it I could see the red cap.

"Do you need to sign it out?"

"If it's all right I'll just take a look at it here."

"Sure."

I zipped open the seal and slid the cap onto the counter. Gently raising the brim, I studied the hat's interior.

There it was. Dandruff.

I resealed the cap and thanked the technician. Then I flew to my office and snatched up the phone.

35

Claudel and Quickwater were not at Carcajou headquarters. Neither Claudel nor Charbonneau was at CUM headquarters. I left messages, and returned to Ronald Gilbert's office.

"Thanks for the tape."

"Did it help?"

"May I ask you about something?"

"Please."

"Do you remember the corner of the room with the guitar and birdcage stacked against the wall?"

"Yes."

"There was a cap there."

"I remember it."

"Did you make observations on the bloodstaining?"

"Certainly."

"I'm interested in the cap's position at the time of the murder. Would your notes have anything on that?"

"I don't need my notes. I recall perfectly. The stain and spatter on the cap came from the blunt object attack near that corner."

"Not the gunshot."

"No. That would look quite different. And the orientation of the spatter was consistent with the type of assault we discussed."

"With Cherokee lying on the floor."

"Yes."

"Was he wearing the cap?"

"Oh my, no. That's impossible. The cap was behind the birdcage when struck by most of the spatter."

"How did it get there?"

"It was probably flung there during the struggle."

"How do you know that?"

"There was blood under as well as on the cap. The assailant probably lost it in the frenzy of the attack."

"Cherokee was not wearing it?"

"I'd bet my life on it."

"Thanks."

Back in my office I looked at the clock. Ten-thirty. I had no message slips. I had no case requests.

I drummed my fingers and stared at the phone, willing it to ring. It didn't. Not optimistic, I dialed Harry's number in Houston, then listened to a recording in very bad Spanish. I tried Kit, got my own voice.

Damn. Where was everybody?

I called Claudel again, this time leaving my cell number. Ditto Charbonneau. Then I grabbed my purse and bolted, unable to bear the waiting.

When I stepped outside I was blinded for a moment. Sunlight bathed the day and sparrows twittered in the branches overhead. Lab and SQ staff chatted along the drive and relaxed at picnic tables on the lawn, enjoying a midmorning smoke or coffee.

I inhaled deeply, and started up Parthenais,

wondering how I could have lost track of spring. For a moment I had an odd fantasy. The Dorsey funeral would take place in less than twenty-four hours. If I could freeze time I could hold it at bay, keep the birds singing, the sun shining, and the ladies on the lawn with their shoes kicked off.

But I couldn't, and the tension was making me jumpier than a proton in a particle accelerator.

Jesus, Brennan. Upstairs you wanted things to move faster. Now you want a freeze-frame. Clear your neurons.

The situation called for a hot dog and fries.

I hung a left on Ontario, walked east a block, and pushed open the door to Lafleur. At 11 A.M. there was no line, and I stepped directly to the counter.

Lafleur is Quebec's version of the fast-food joint, offering hot dogs, burgers, and poutine. The decor is chrome and plastic, the clientele largely blue collar.

"*Chien chaud, frites, et Coke Diète, s'il vous plaît,*" I told the man at the cash register. Why did the literal translation of hot dog in French still sound strange to me?

"*Steamé ou grillé?*"

I chose steamed, and in seconds a cardboard container was slapped in front of me. Grease from the fries already stained the left side.

I paid and carried my food to a table with an excellent view of the parking lot.

As I ate my eyes roved over the other patrons. To my left were four young women in nurse's white, students from the technical school across the street. Tags identified them as Manon, Lise, Brigitte, and Marie-José.

Two painters ate in silence beyond the students.

332

They wore coveralls, and their arms, hair, and faces were speckled like the walls of Gilbert's spatter lab. The men worked on platters of fries topped with curd cheese and brown gravy. In a city renowned for its fine cuisine, I have never understood the appeal of poutine.

Across from the painters sat a young man trying his best to grow a goatee. His glasses were round and he was overweight.

I finished my fries and checked my cell. The phone was on, the signal strong, but there were no messages. Damn! Why wasn't anyone returning my call?

I needed release. Physical release.

I spent two hours running, lifting, rolling around on a large rubber ball, and taking a high-impact aerobics class. By the time I finished I could hardly drag myself to the showers. But the exercise was an effective anti-venin. My anger had dissipated along with the toxins from the hot dog and fries.

When I returned to the lab two messages lay on my desk. Charbonneau had called. Morin wanted to talk about LaManche. That didn't sound good. Why hadn't Madame LaManche phoned?

I hurried down the hall, but Morin's door was already closed, indicating he'd left for the day. I went back to my office and dialed Charbonneau.

"There may be more to this Crease than I thought."

"Such as?"

"Seems he and the Angels go back a ways. Crease is Canadian, but he did his undergraduate studies at South Carolina. Go Cocks."

"You're really hung up on that."

"Hey, beats the Redmen."

"I'll pass on your opinion to the McGill board."

"Politically it's more correct."

I waited.

"Newsboy completed a B.A. in journalism in '83 and decided to go on for a master's degree, using outlaw bikers as his thesis topic. By the way, he was calling himself Robert then."

"Why would anyone choose Lyle over Robert?"

"It's his middle name.

"Anyway, Robby got a hog and a nod from the brothers, and roared off with the pack."

"Did he finish the degree?"

"He completely dropped from sight. He attended classes for a month or two, then his professors never heard from him again."

"There's no record of where he was? Driver's license? Tax return? Credit card application? Blockbuster membership?"

"Nada. Then Crease resurfaced in Saskatchewan in '89, working the crime beat for a local paper and doing some on-air stories for the evening news. Eventually he was offered the job at CTV and relocated to Quebec."

"So Crease was interested in bikers as a student. That was the Ice Age, remember?"

"Apparently Crease left Saskatchewan in a bit of a hurry."

"Oh?"

"Ever hear of Operation CACUS?"

"Wasn't that an FBI sting using informants inside the Hells Angels?"

"Informant. Tony Tait joined the Alaska chapter in the early eighties then rose through the ranks to national prominence. He wore a wire for the bureau the whole time."

"Angels Forever, Forever Angels."

"I guess Tony preferred cash."

"Where is he now?"

"In witness protection if he's smart."

"What does this have to do with Crease?"

"It seems the Mounties had their own investigation going in the eighties."

"Are you telling me Lyle Crease was an RCMP informant?"

"No one will talk and I've found nothing on paper, but I've always heard we had someone inside for a while. When I leaned on a couple of long-timers, they wouldn't confirm, but they didn't deny."

He paused.

"And?" I prodded.

"This is just for us, Brennan."

"But I share everything with my hairstylist."

He ignored that.

"I run my own sources on the street. Shit, I can't believe I'm telling you this."

I heard rattling as he switched the receiver to his other hand.

"Word is someone was definitely going to church with the Angels back then, and the guy was American. But it was a two-way street."

"The snitch was working both sides?"

"That's the story my sources gave up."

"Risky."

"As a cerebral hemorrhage."

"Do you think the plant was Lyle Crease?"

"How else does a guy completely bury six years of his life?"

I thought about that.

"But why would he reappear in such a public line of work?"

"Maybe he figures visibility confers protection."

For a moment no one spoke.

"Does Claudel know this?"

"I'm about to give him a call."

"Now what?"

"Now I dig deeper."

"You'll question Crease?"

"Not yet. We don't want to spook him. And Roy owns Claudel's ass until this funeral is over. But then I'll get him to help me take a run at the guy."

"Do you think Crease was involved in the Cherokee murder?"

"There's no evidence of that, but he may know something."

"That cap didn't belong to Cherokee or Dorsey."

"How do you know that?"

"The inside is covered with dandruff."

"So?"

"Dorsey shaved his head and Cherokee was bald from chemo."

"Not bad, Brennan."

"Gately and Martineau were killed during the time Crease was underground."

"True."

"And Savannah Osprey."

Silence hummed across the wire.

"What about asking Rinaldi?"

"Frog?"

"Yeah, Frog. He was willing to spill his guts about the Gately and Martineau graves. Why not ask him about Cherokee? He might know something."

"Claudel says they've questioned Frog until they're blue in the face. He was willing to trade the St-Basile-le-Grand bodies because they're old news. He doesn't

336

think the brothers will take him out for that. On anything recent he turns into a potted palm.

"Look, I'll get Claudel to help me flush Crease once the circus is over tomorrow. And, by the way, Brennan, keep your head low. Bandidos patches have been spotted in town, and there are rumors the Angels may make a move. Don't—"

He hesitated.

"Yes?"

"Well, your nephew might want to check out the action."

My cheeks burned. Claudel had discussed Kit with his CUM buddies.

"My nephew won't be anywhere near that funeral."

"Good. A Bandidos presence could force a show of strength by the Angels. Might turn hairy."

We'd hardly hung up when I started worrying. How could I keep Kit away if he was intent on going?

What did Morin want to say about LaManche? Had my old friend died?

Could Ryan be in immediate danger? Had helping me compromised his cover? Had I put him in peril as I had George Dorsey?

I laid my head on the fuzzy green surface of my desk blotter and slowly closed my eyes.

36

I was under water and Lyle Crease was speaking to me.
Seaweed undulated from below, like strands of hair on
a submerged corpse. Here and there a shaft of sunlight
penetrated the murky gloom, illuminating tiny particles
floating around us.

My neck hurt. I opened my eyes then lifted and
rotated my head, gingerly working the kink from my
cervical vertebrae. My office was dark except for a pale
fluorescence oozing through the glass beside the door.

How long had I slept? I strained to see my watch.

When I noticed the figure outside my door an alarm
went off in my head. I froze, watching and listening.

The floor was still, except for my heart drumming
against my ribs.

The figure stood motionless, a silhouette framed by
low-level light spilling from my lab.

My eyes dropped to the phone. Should I call security?

My hand was on the receiver when the door swung
inward.

Jocelyn's face looked ghostly. She was dressed in black,

and the pale oval head seemed to float, a disembodied jack-o'-lantern with dark holes for eyes and mouth.

"*Oui?*"

I stood, not wanting to give her the advantage of height.

She didn't answer.

"*Puis-je vous aider?*" I asked. May I help you?

Still, she said nothing.

"Please turn on the light, Jocelyn."

The command brought forth a response where the questions had failed. Her arm rose, and the office was thrown into brightness.

Her hair clung damply to her neck and face, and her clothes were corrugated, as if she'd been sitting a long time in a hot, cramped space. She sniffed and ran the back of a hand under her nose.

"What is it, Jocelyn?"

"You're just letting them slide." Her voice was hard with anger.

"Who?" I asked, confused.

"I thought you might be different."

"Different from whom?"

"Nobody gives a shit. I hear cops joke about it. I hear them laugh. Another dead biker. Good riddance, they say. It's cheap trash removal."

"What are you talking about?" My mouth felt dry.

"It's these cops who are a joke. Wolverines. Pfff." She puffed air through her lips. "Dickheads would be more like it."

I was stunned by the hatred in her eyes.

"Tell me why you're upset."

There was a long silence while she studied my face. Her gaze seemed to focus then withdraw, as if grabbing my image for testing in some mental equation.

"He didn't deserve what he got. No fuckin' way."
The obscenities sounded odd in French.

Quietly I said, "If you don't explain I can't help you."

She hesitated, taking a final tally, then the angry eyes fixed on mine.

"George Dorsey didn't kill that old man."

"Cherokee Desjardins?"

She answered with a shrug.

"How do you know?"

She frowned, deciding if the question was a trap.

"Anyone with the IQ of celery would know that."

"That's not terribly convincing."

"A real mechanic would have done it right."

"What does that mea—"

She cut me off. "Do you want to hear this or not?"

I waited.

"I was there that night."

She swallowed.

"I was hardly in the door when some guy showed up, so I went into the bedroom. He and Cherokee started talking, friendly at first, but pretty soon I heard shouting, then slamming and banging. I knew something was coming down, so I hid in the closet."

"Why were you there, Jocelyn?"

"Cherokee was gonna sponsor me in the Kiwanis," she sneered.

"Go on."

"I hunkered in until things quieted down, then when I thought the guy was gone, I started to split. That's when I heard the gunshot. Jesus."

Her eyes slipped past me to a spot somewhere over my shoulder. I tried to imagine what for her was memory.

"Then I heard the guy banging drawers and flinging

340

crap around. I figured he was a smackhead looking for Cherokee's rock, and I nearly shit my shorts, 'cause I knew the stuff was in the bedroom with me.

"When I smelled smoke it was time to haul ass, junkie or no junkie. I smashed the window, dropped to the alley, and ran to the corner. Now here's the weird part. When I cut around the building and looked up the block, the little roach was still outside Cherokee's pad, scratching at something in the mud. Then a car turned onto the street and he took off."

"What was he looking for?"

"How the hell should I know?"

"Then what?"

"When I was sure he wasn't coming back I walked over and poked around."

There was a long silence. Then she dropped a purse strap from her shoulder, dug inside, and withdrew a small, flat object.

"I found this where the guy was squatting." She thrust it at me.

I unfolded a pharmacy sack and removed a photograph framed in cheap plastic. Two men smiled through a mist of spattered blood, inner arms entwined, outer arms raised, middle fingers pointing skyward. The one on the right was Cherokee Desjardins, robust and full of life.

When I recognized the man on the left my throat tightened and my breath came in short, quick spurts. Jocelyn went on speaking but I didn't hear her.

". . . torn bag beside it. When the headlights hit him he bolted like a jackrabbit."

My thoughts raced. Images flashed.

". . . why the fuck he wanted it. But go figure what burns in a junked-out head."

I saw a face.

341

". . . wish I'd gotten a look at him."

I saw a baseball cap.

". . . this son of a bitch get away with it."

I saw flecks of gold circling in a watery vortex.

". . . didn't deserve a shiv up his ass."

I pulled myself back to the present and willed my face neutral.

"Jocelyn, do you know a newscaster named Lyle Crease?"

"English?"

"Yes."

"I don't watch English TV. Why are you asking me that? Look, I'm trying to tell you Dorsey didn't whack Cherokee."

"No," I agreed. "He didn't."

But I had a pretty good idea who did.

When Jocelyn left I phoned Claudel. He was not in, but this time I hung up and dialed his pager.

Urgent enough, I thought, as I entered my number.

When Claudel called back I relayed Jocelyn's story.

"Can she identify the man?"

"Never saw his face."

"*Fantastique*."

"It's Crease."

"How can you be sure?"

"The cap found in Desjardins' apartment had a USC logo. Crease went to school there."

"We've alread—"

"Did Charbonneau tell you about the dandruff?"

"Yes."

"I had the pleasure of dining with Crease not too long ago. He has enough dandruff to open a ski hill."

"Motive?"

342

I described what I'd seen in the photo.

"Holy Mother of Christ."

Rarely had I heard Claudel blaspheme.

"What's this woman's relationship to Dorsey?"

"She was not receptive to personal inquiries."

"Can she be trusted?" His breath sounded moist against the mouthpiece.

"She obviously has a habit, but I believe her."

"If she was terrified, why hang around?"

"She probably thought the intruder dropped drugs and she had a shot at a free score."

"Michel Charbonneau told me of your conversation." More breathing. "I think it's time to net this Mr Crease."

When we disconnected I phoned for air reservations. Willing or not, Kit was on his way to Texas. Until then, I wasn't going to let him out of my sight.

I arrived home to find Kit in the shower.

"Have you eaten?" I shouted through the door when I heard the sound of the water stop.

"Not much."

O.K, podna. I, too, can cook pasta.

I made a run to Le Faubourg for scallops and greens. Back home I sautéed the seafood with onions and mushrooms, then mixed and added a yogurt-mustard-lemon-dill sauce. I ladled the mollusk concoction over angel-hair pasta, and served it with a baguette and tossed salad.

Even Kit was impressed.

We talked as we ate, but said little.

"How was your day?" I asked.

"Pretty good."

"What did you do?"

343

"Not much."

"Did you stay here?"

"I rode the subway to some island and cruised around the parks."

"Île-Ste-Hélène."

"Yeah. There's a beach out there and lots of trails. It's pretty slick."

That explained the skateboard in the entrance hall.

"How 'bout your day?" he asked, picking a crouton from the salad remains.

"Pretty good."

A cokehead security risk in our own lab accused me of indifference to bikers, and I discovered one of your *Easy Rider* playmates may be a killer.

"Cool," he said.

I took a deep breath.

"I made airline reservations today."

"Off on another trip?"

"The flight is for you."

"Uh-oh. The bum's rush." He kept his eyes on the salad bowl.

"Kit, you know I love you, and I love having you here, but I think it's time you went home."

"What is it they say about houseguests and old fish? Or is it relatives?"

"You know that isn't it. But you have been here almost two weeks. Aren't you bored? Don't you want to see your friends and check on the boat?"

He shrugged. "They're not going anywhere."

"I'm sure Harry and your father both miss you."

"Oh, yeah. They've been burning up the phone wires."

"Your mother's in Mexico. It's not eas—"

"She arrived in Houston yesterday."

344

"What?"

"I didn't want to tell you."

"Oh?"

"I knew you'd hustle me off when she got back."

"Why would you think that?"

His hand dropped, fingers curling over the bowl's edge. Outside, a siren wailed, soft, loud, soft. When he answered he didn't look at me.

"When I was a little kid, you always stayed just out of reach, afraid Harry might feel jealous. Or angry. Or resentful. Or inadequate. Or, or—"

He picked a crouton, threw it back. Drops of oil jumped onto the table.

"Kit!"

"And, you know what? She *ought* to feel inadequate. The only thing I should thank Harry for is not burying me in a goddam shoe box when I was born." He got to his feet. "I'll pack my stuff."

I stood and grabbed his arm. When I looked up his face was tight with anger.

"Harry has nothing to do with this. I'm sending you home because I'm frightened for you. I'm frightened over the people you've been seeing and what they may be doing, and I'm afraid you're involved with things that could place you in jeopardy."

"That's bullshit. I'm not a baby anymore. I make my own decisions."

I flashed on Frog Rinaldi, his shadow rippling across a grave. Gately and Martineau had made a decision. A deadly decision. So had Savannah Osprey. And George Dorsey. I would not permit Kit to do the same.

"If something happened to you I'd never forgive myself."

"I'm not going to get hurt."

345

"I can't take that chance. I think you've been putting yourself in dangerous circumstances."

"I'm not six years old, Aunt Tempe. You can kick me out of here, but you can't tell me what to do anymore." His jaw muscles bunched, then his Adam's apple rose and dropped.

We both fell silent, realizing our proximity to words that, once spoken, would wound. I released my grip, and Kit disappeared down the hall, bare feet swishing softly on the carpet.

I slept fitfully, then woke and lay in the dark, thinking about my nephew. The window shade changed from black to charcoal. I gave up on sleep, brewed tea, and took it to the patio.

Bundled in Gran's quilt, I watched stars fade overhead, and remembered evenings in Charlotte. When Katy and Kit were small we would identify constellations and christen patterns of our own. Katy would see a mouse, a puppy, a pair of skates. Kit would see a mother and child.

I tucked my feet and sipped the hot liquid.

How could I make Kit understand my reasons for sending him away? He was young, and vulnerable, and desperate for recognition and approval.

But recognition and approval from whom? Why does he want to stay with me? Do I provide a base from which he can pursue activities he won't disclose to me?

From the day of Kit's arrival his apathy had puzzled me. While Katy would have craved constant peer contact, my nephew seemed satisfied with limited sightseeing, video games, and the company of an aging aunt and her aging cat. The current Kit was jarringly at odds with the youngster I remembered. Skinned knees. Stitches. Broken bones. Kit's perpetual motion had kept

346

Harry on a first-name basis with her local paramedics for the duration of his childhood.

Had Kit been staying in, or had he been out and about with Lyle Crease? Or the Preacher? Or the hyena? Was he lethargic around me because he was tired?

More tea. Tepid now.

I pictured two men behind blood-spattered plastic, and even the tea couldn't warm my chill.

Was I making a mistake? If Kit was going through a rough patch could I have some positive influence? If he was involved in something precarious would it be safer to keep him with me?

No. The overall situation made it too risky. I would stick to my plan. My nephew would be in Texas before George Dorsey's body was underground.

As dawn crawled up from the horizon, a gentle wash spread across my yard, tinting trees, hedges, and the old brownstones across the street. Edges softened, until the city resembled a Winslow Homer landscape. A gentle watercolor, a perfect backdrop for a gangland funeral.

I poured the last of my tea onto the lawn, and went to wake my nephew.

His room was empty.

37

A note was stuck to the refrigerator. I read it in place, afraid to trust my unsteady hands.

Thanks for everything. Don't worry. I'm with friends.

Friends?

My heart felt dead in my chest.

I looked at the clock. The Dorsey funeral would start in a little more than an hour.

I dialed Claudel's pager, then made coffee, dressed, and made the bed.

Seven-fifteen.

I sipped and picked at a cuticle.

The earth rotated. Tectonic plates shifted. Twelve acres of rain forest disappeared from the globe forever.

I went to the bathroom, combed my hair, dabbed on makeup, added blush, returned to the kitchen for a second cup.

Seven-thirty. Where the hell was Claudel?

Back to the bathroom, where I wet and recombed my

hair. I was reaching for dental floss when the phone rang.

"I wouldn't have thought you an early riser." Claudel.

"Kit's gone."

"*Cibole!*"

I could hear traffic in the background.

"Where are you?"

"Outside the church."

"How does it look?"

"Like a theme park of deadly sins. Sloth and gluttony are well represented."

"I don't suppose you've seen him."

"No, but I might not spot Fidel Castro in this crowd. Looks like every biker on the continent is here."

"Crease?"

"No sign."

I heard a hitch in his breathing.

"What?"

"Charbonneau and I did some more checking. From '83 to '89 Lyle Crease was playing foreign correspondent, not secret agent. But the only reports he was filing were with the guard on his cell block."

"He did time?" I asked, unnerved.

"Six years, south of the border."

"Mexico?"

"Juárez."

My heart came back to life and thumped inside my chest.

"Crease is a killer and Kit may be with him. I've got to do something."

Claudel's voice went cop cold.

"Don't even think about freelancing, Ms Brennan. These bikers look like sharks smelling the water for blood, and it could get rough down here."

"And Kit could get sucked into the feeding frenzy!" I heard my voice catch, and stopped to steady myself.

"I'll send a patrol car to pick Crease up."

"Suppose he has funeral plans?"

"If he shows his face, we'll arrest him."

"And if a nineteen-year-old kid gets nailed along the way?" I was almost yelling.

"All I'm saying is don't come down here."

"Then find this bastard!"

I'd hardly disconnected when I heard my cell phone. Kit!

I raced to the bedroom and pulled it from my purse.

The voice was quavery, like a child after a long cry.

"You need to know what they're doing."

At first I felt confusion, then recognition, then apprehension.

"Who, Jocelyn?"

"Someone needs to know what these Heathen scum are doing." She inhaled sharply through her nose.

"Tell me."

"This town is turning into a slaughterhouse, and your kid is ambling right down the chute."

My stomach went tight with fear.

"What do you mean?"

"I know what's coming down."

"How does this involve my nephew?"

"I need money and I need cover." Her voice was stronger now.

"Tell me what you know."

"Not till we deal."

"I don't have that kind of authority."

"You know who does."

"I will try to help you," I said. "But I need to know if my nephew is in danger."

Silence. Then, "Fuck, I'm dead anyway. Meet me in the Guy métro in twenty minutes. Westbound platform."

Her voice was leaden with defeat.

"I'll wait ten minutes. If you're late, or bring a buddy, I'm gone, and the kid'll be a footnote when this whole thing is written up."

Dead air.

I dialed Claudel's pager and left my number. Then I stared at the phone, ticking through options.

Claudel was unreachable. I couldn't wait for a return call.

Quickwater.

Ditto.

Claudel hadn't told me to avoid the underground. I'd meet with Jocelyn, then ring him when I had information.

I punched in the number at Carcajou headquarters, but didn't hit send. Then I slid the phone into my purse, and bolted for the door.

Jocelyn was seated at the end of the tunnel, a canvas duffel in her lap, another at her feet. She had chosen a corner bench, as if concrete backing conferred protection from whatever menace she feared. Her teeth worked a thumbnail as she scanned the commuters standing to either side of the tracks.

She spotted me and followed my approach. I stayed to the middle of the platform, my pulse louder in my ears than any competing noise. The air was warm and stale, as though breathed and rebreathed by legions of subterranean travelers. I felt an acrid taste and swallowed hard.

Jocelyn watched in silence as I sat on the bench. Her

chalky skin looked violet in the artificial light, the whites of her eyes yellow.

I started to speak but she stopped me with a hand movement.

"I'm going to say this once, then I'm taking off. I talk. You listen."

I said nothing.

"I'm a junkie, we both know that. I'm also a whore and a liar." Her eyes roved the faces lining the tracks, her movements ragged and jerky.

"Here's the mind-fuck. I come from a Girl Scout – summer camp – tuna casserole background just like you. Only somewhere along the way I joined a freak show I can't escape."

Purple shadow turned her eyes cadaverous.

"Lately I've been doing some hard time with hate. I hate everyone and everything on the planet. But mostly I hate myself."

She backhanded a sheen of liquid from below her nostrils.

"You know it's closing time when you can't look in a pond or pass a mirror or storefront because you despise what you see looking back."

She turned to me, the lobotomy eyes burning with rage and guilt.

"Talking to you may get me killed, but I want out. And I want these guys to pay."

"What are you offering?"

"Spider Marcotte and the little girl."

"I'm listening."

"It was George Dorsey. He's dead now, so it don't matter." She looked away, then focused again on my face.

"Marcotte was Heathen payback for the Vipers

352

blowing up the Vaillancourts. George and a full-patcher named Sylvain Lecomte took him out. The kid was a mistake."

She braced a booted foot against the duffel.

"George thought the hit was his ticket to stardom. But the Heathens burned George because they thought he was going to give up Lecomte." She snorted and tipped her chin. "George was actually waiting for me near the Cherokee hit scene. When he got busted by the Carcajou and then set up a meet with you, the Heathen brothers decided to do George before he could finger Lecomte. Big man, Lecomte. Wasted a little girl. Big turd," she spat.

"Anything else?"

She shrugged.

"The St-Basile burials. I've been on the scene nine years. I've got plenty to trade."

"Are you talking about witness protection?"

"Money and out."

"Rehab?"

She shrugged.

"What about Cherokee?"

"He brought the girl's bones up North, but I've put his story on paper. I give it up when my ass is safe and a long way from here."

She sounded like the thought was collapsing even as she voiced it.

"Why now?"

"They wasted Dorsey. He did their work, and they wasted him."

She shook her head and turned back to her surveillance.

"And I've become them." Her voice dripped with self-loathing. "I set that reporter up."

"What reporter?"

"Lyle Crease. I figured something was up when you asked about him, so I tuned into the news that night. Sure enough, he was the one I saw at Cherokee's place. I dropped his name to the Vipers for a bag of flake."

"Jesus Christ."

"I'm a goddam junkie, all right?" It was almost a shriek. "When you're coming down and the world is closing in, you'll dime your mother for a score. Besides, I had other reasons."

Her hands began to tremble, and she pressed her fingertips to her temples.

"Later, I phoned Crease to set up a meet at the cemetery." Again the self-deprecating laugh. "Back on big rock candy mountain."

"Did they ask you to arrange a meeting?"

"Yeah. They plan to take Crease out, and some Heathens, too."

"What does this have to do with my nephew?" My mouth was so dry I could hardly speak.

"Crease said not to try anything funny because he would have the kid with him."

I heard the rumble of a train far up the tunnel.

Again, the head shake. Her face looked hard in profile.

"This funeral's going to be one big snuff film, and your nephew could have a starring role."

I felt a change in air pressure as the train grew louder. Passengers on the far side moved toward the platform's edge.

Jocelyn's gaze froze on something across the tracks. The hooded eyes grew puzzled a moment, then widened in recognition. Her mouth opened.

"Lecom—!" she screamed, and her hand shot to the duffel's zipper.

The train thundered in.

Jocelyn's head flew backward, and a dark cumulus spread around it on the wall. I threw myself to the concrete, and covered my head with both hands.

Brakes shrilled, whooshed.

I tried to scramble behind the bench, under it, anywhere. It was bolted to the wall! There was nowhere to go!

Doors opened. Commuters both boarded and left the train.

On our side, screams. Faces turning. Bewilderment. Horror.

The train barreled off.

Then the sounds changed. Panicked retreat. People running.

After a full minute with no more shots, I cautiously rose to my feet, bone and brain matter on my jacket. My stomach lurched and I tasted bile.

Voices. English. French.

"*Attention!*"

"*Sacrifice!*"

"Call the police."

"*Elle est morte?*"

"They're on the way."

"*Mon Dieu!*"

Confusion. A rush for the escalators.

Jocelyn's body twitched, and a thread of saliva trailed from the corner of her mouth. I could smell urine and feces, and see blood pooling on the bench and floor.

I had a vision of Cherokee. Others, fast, like flashbulbs. Gately. Martineau. Savannah Osprey. Emily Anne Toussaint.

I could not have stopped those deaths, nor had I done anything to bring them about. And I could do nothing

355

for Jocelyn. But I would not allow my nephew to be the next casualty. I would not permit that. Death dealt out by bikers would not happen. Not to Kit. Not to Harry. And not to me.

On rubbery legs I staggered to the escalators, rode to ground level, and was carried along by the crush of pedestrians distancing themselves from tragedy. Already two cruisers blocked the entrance, doors open, lights flashing. Sirens foretold the arrival of others.

I should have stayed, given my story, and let the police handle the rest. I felt sick, and repulsed by the carnage we seemed powerless to stop. Fear for Kit twisted in my gut like a physical pain, overriding judgment and sense of duty.

I broke from the crowd and ran.

38

My hands still trembled as I let myself into my silent condo. I called out, not expecting an answer.

From my briefcase, I dug out the envelope Charbonneau had delivered from Roy. I scanned the protocol, checked my watch, and raced to the garage.

Though rush hour was tapering off, Centre-ville remained clogged. I crawled along, engine idling, heart racing, hands sweaty on the wheel, until I finally broke free, shot up the mountain, and pulled into a car park opposite Lac aux Castors.

The cemeteries sprawled along the uphill side of Chemin Remembrance, cities of the dead flowing toward the horizon. According to Roy's map, the Dorsey plot was just inside the perimeter fence, twenty yards from the south gate. The cortege would arrive from the east and enter the cemetery opposite where I sat.

I wiped my hands on my jeans and checked the time. Soon.

Normally, early morning meant few people on the mountain, but today mourners lined the shoulder and

357

stood along the drive leading through the gate. Others wandered among the trees and headstones inside the cemetery grounds. The ritual hypocrisy struck me as surreal. Heathens and Rock Machine, burying with great ceremony the comrade they themselves had killed.

Manned cruisers were parked on both sides of Remembrance, lights flashing, radios sputtering. I locked the car and ran across the road, slipping on new grass beginning to green the median. Hurrying along the shoulder, I inspected those milling about. Most were male, young, and white. I saw Charbonneau leaning on a squad car, but there was no sign of Crease or Kit.

A uniformed officer stopped me at the gate.

"Whoa, there. Slow down, madam. I'm sorry, but there is a funeral expected shortly, and this entrance is closed. You'll have to move on."

He held out both arms, as if physical restraint might be necessary.

"Dr Temperance Brennan," I identified myself. "Carcajou."

His face crimped with suspicion. He was about to speak when a sharp whistle split the air, like someone calling a dog. We both turned.

Claudel stood on a knoll a short distance back from the Dorsey grave site. When he had our attention he gave a crisp come-on signal with one hand. The guard pointed to me, and Claudel nodded. With a disapproving look, he passed me through the gate.

The Mont-Royal cemeteries are strange and beautiful places, acres of elegant landscaping and ornate funerary architecture rising and falling across the curves of the mountain. Mont-Royal. The Jewish. Notre-Dame-des-Neiges.

The latter is for the Catholic dead. Some are buried

with elaborate tombs and monuments, others with simple plaques and ten-year leases. Since the mid-nineteenth century, over a million souls have been laid to rest within the cemetery's wrought-iron fence. The complex contains mausoleums, crematoria, columbaria, and interment sites for the more traditional.

There are sections for the Polish. The Vietnamese. The Greek. The French. The English. Visitors can obtain maps pinpointing the graves of Montreal's famous. The Dorsey family lay in the Troie section, not far from Marie Travers, the thirties singer known as La Bolduc.

More relevant was the fact that today's burial would take place less than ten yards from Chemin Remembrance. Roy's advisers felt that if a hit was planned the cemetery was the most likely location. And the most difficult to secure.

I sprinted up the gravel path and scrambled uphill to join Claudel. His greeting was not warm.

"What the hell do you think you're doing?"

"Kit is with Crease and they're coming here," I panted.

"You just don't listen, do you, Ms Brennan?" His eyes swept the crowd as he spoke. "There's already been one homicide today."

My mind flashed to the métro. Jocelyn, searching. Jocelyn, in agonal spasm.

"I was with her."

"What?" Claudel's eyes flew to my face, then dropped to the blood and brain matter on my jacket.

I told him.

"And you left the scene?"

"There was nothing I could do."

"I'm not going to point out the obvious."

"She was dead!" I snapped. Fear, anger, and guilt

churned in my head, and his unfeeling attitude did nothing to calm me. A sob welled in my chest.

No. No tears!

At that moment his Carcajou partner appeared over the edge of the hillock. Quickwater approached Claudel, spoke in a low voice, and left without acknowledging my presence. In seconds he reappeared below, wove through a grouping of ornamental headstones, and positioned himself behind a pink granite obelisk.

"If I say dive, you take cover. No questions. No heroics. Do you understand?"

"Fine."

He did not resume our conversation.

That was fine, too. I recoiled from voicing my fear for Kit, afraid that shaping the threat into words might cause it to be realized. I would tell him later about Lecomte.

Five minutes passed. Ten. I scanned the bereaved. Business suits mixed with chains, swastikas, studs, and bandannas.

I heard the noise before I saw the procession. It started as a low rumble and grew to a roar as two police cruisers rounded the curve, then a hearse, limo, and a half-dozen cars. A phalanx of cycles followed, four abreast behind the cars, in twos and threes farther back. Soon the road was dense with bikes, and I could not see the end of the line.

Sun flashed off chrome as the cortege slowed and turned into the cemetery. The air filled with the sound of engines and shifting gears as bikers broke formation and massed around the entrance. Men in greasy Levi's, beards, and shades began to dismount and move toward the gate.

Claudel's eyes narrowed as he watched the graveyard below become a human zoo.

"*Sacré bleu*. We should keep this outside the fence."

"Roy says that's not possible."

"Civil rights be damned. Bar the vermin, and let their lawyers sue."

The cortege turned left and crept along the tree-lined road skirting the Troie section. When it pulled to a stop a suited man moved to the limo and opened the rear door. People emerged wearing the bewildered expressions of those unfamiliar with personal service.

I watched the funeral director lead the family to folding chairs beneath a bright green canopy. An old man in an old suit. Two matrons in black dresses, faux pearls around their necks. A young woman in a floral print. A boy in a jacket with sleeves that did not reach his wrists. An elderly priest.

As friends and relatives climbed from cars, Dorsey's other family drew together. Joking and calling, they formed a ragged horseshoe outside the canopy. Under it, the new grave lay draped like a patient awaiting surgery.

A detachment of eight slowly gathered at the hearse, all in denim and shades. At a sign from the director, an assistant offered gloves, which a behemoth in a do-rag batted aside. Barehanded, the pallbearers slid the casket free and carried it toward the canopy, struggling under the weight of the deceased and his packaging.

The branches above me lifted and fell, and I caught the scent of flowers and freshly turned earth. The bikes had gone still. A sob drifted from under the canopy, slipping free on the breeze to ride over the graves of the surrounding dead.

"*Sacré bleu!*"

When I turned, Claudel was staring at the gate. I followed his gaze, and fear shot through me.

Crease and Kit were making their way through those

lingering at the entrance, moving past the semicircle of mourners, and stepping into the shadow of a life-sized bronze angel, its arms perpendicularly outstretched, as if treading water.

I started to speak but Claudel silenced me with a hand. Lifting his radio, he looked down at his partner. Quickwater made a subtle gesture, first to his right, then straight ahead.

I looked where Quickwater had indicated. Beyond the mourners, partially hidden among the tombstones and trees, were men whose attention was not on the service. Like Claudel and Quickwater their eyes never rested, and they carried handsets. Unlike the Carcajou investigators, these men were tattooed and booted.

I looked a question at Claudel.

"Rock Machine security."

Under the canopy the priest stood and opened his prayer book. Hands rose and fell, crossing chests. Missal pages fluttered as the old priest began the rites for the dead, and he extended a gnarled finger to hold them still. The breeze played with his words, stealing some, sharing others.

"—*who art in heaven, hallow*—"

Beside me, Claudel tensed.

A man had appeared among a cluster of cement crypts sixty feet to the west. Head down, he walked toward the canopy.

"*Thy kingdom— thy will*—"

I looked down at Quickwater. His eyes were fixed on the Rock Machine sentries. One spoke into his walkie-talkie. Across the grounds, another listened. Quickwater stared at them, then raised his radio.

Claudel keyed his partner, eyes glued to the man closing in on the grave site.

"—forgive— who trespass against us—"

"Trouble?" I asked when the transmission ended.

"He's not Rock Machine. He could be Bandidos, but the lookouts aren't sure."

"How—?"

"He reads lips."

"Do you recognize the guy?"

"He's not a cop."

My nerves prickled. As with many in the crowd, a bandanna covered the lower face of the approaching figure, and a cap shadowed his eyes. But this man looked wrong. His jacket was too heavy for the day, his arms held too tightly to his sides.

Suddenly a Jeep roared up Remembrance and veered toward the fence. At the same moment a motor flared and a Harley shot through the gate.

The next events seemed to continue forever, each unfolding in slow motion. They told me later that the entire episode lasted two minutes.

In the horseshoe of bikers a man spun sideways and flew into a canopy support pole. Screams. Gunfire. The tent collapsed. The crowd froze momentarily, then scattered.

"Down!"

Claudel pushed hard on my back, slamming me to the ground.

A bearded man crawled from the heap of canvas and ran toward a stone Jesus with outstretched arms. Halfway there his back arched, and he fell forward. He was dragging himself across the ground, when his body jerked again and collapsed.

I spit dirt from my mouth and tried to see. A bullet whacked into the chestnut behind me.

When I looked again the jacketed man with the

bandanna-covered face was behind a vault, bending toward the base of the crypt. He stood, and sun glinted off steel as he pulled back the slide on a semiautomatic. Then he dropped his hand straight to his side and walked toward the swimming angel.

Fear shot through me.

Without thinking, I began to crawl toward the path.

"Get back here, Brennan," Claudel shouted.

Ignoring him, I pushed to my feet and scrabbled down the hill, keeping to the far side to avoid gunfire. Crouching low and darting from monument to monument, I worked my way toward the statue sheltering my nephew.

Pistols and semiautomatics barked around me. The Angels were reaping their vengeance, and the Machine were returning fire. Bullets sparked off tombs and headstones. A granite splinter struck my cheek, and something warm trickled down my face.

As I rounded the statue on one side, the jacketed man appeared on the other. Crease and Kit stood directly between us. The gunman raised his arm and aimed.

Crease swung Kit around to shield himself.

"Get down!" I screamed. Sweat trickled from my hairline, and the wind felt cold on my face.

It took Kit a moment to realize his situation. Then he spun and brought his knee up hard between the reporter's legs. Crease's hand flew up and his mouth opened in a perfect O, but one hand held tight to Kit's shirt.

Kit twisted to his right, but Crease yanked hard just as the shooter squeezed the trigger. A deafening sound reverberated off the bronze torso and wings above us. My nephew fell to the ground and lay still.

"No!" My scream was drowned by the sound of engines and gunfire.

Another thunderous roar. I saw a hole open in Crease's chest, and a liquid river of red streamed down his front. He went rigid for a moment, then dropped next to Kit.

I sensed a figure moving around the monument, and threw myself forward to cover Kit. His hand moved feebly and a burgundy stain was spreading across his back.

The figure loomed larger and filled the gap between the angel and the neighboring tomb, feet spread, pistol extended in a two-handed grip toward the gunman above us. The muzzle flashed. Another deafening crack. The gunman's eye exploded, blood bubbled from his mouth, and he crumpled to the ground beside me.

My eyes met eyes bluer than a butane flame. Then Ryan whirled and was gone.

At that instant Quickwater flung himself under the angel and dragged and shoved Kit and me toward the base. Crouching in front of the supine bodies of Crease and his assassin, he swept his gun in wide arcs, using the monument for cover.

I tried to swallow, but my mouth was a desert. Bullets strafed the earth beside me, and again I was conscious of the smell of dirt and flowers. Outside our tiny cave I could see figures running in all directions.

Quickwater's eyes scanned, his body coiled and ready to spring. In the distance I heard sirens and engines, then the sound of an explosion.

Adrenaline pumping, I pressed a hand to the hole in my nephew's back, and tried to stuff a hankie into the one in his chest. Time lost all meaning.

Then it was silent. Nothing appeared to move.

Beyond Quickwater I saw people crawl from under the canopy, disheveled and sobbing. Bikers emerged from hiding and coalesced into groups, faces furious, fists pistoning as if they were angry hip-hop artists. Others lay motionless on the ground. Ryan was nowhere to be seen.

Far down the mountain sirens wailed. I glanced at Quickwater, and our eyes locked. My lips trembled, but no words came.

Quickwater reached down and wiped blood from my cheek, then gently brushed the hair from my face. His eyes went deep into mine, acknowledging what we had just seen, the secret we shared. My chest heaved and tears burned my lids. I turned away, not wanting a witness to my frailty.

My gaze fell on a tiny portrait, encased in plastic and secured to the angel's pedestal. A solemn face stared out, separated by death and faded by years of rain and sun.

No, God. Please, no. Not Kit.

I looked down at the blood oozing through my fingers. Openly weeping, I applied more pressure, then closed my eyes and prayed.

39

"What the hell did you plan to do?" Charbonneau asked.

"I didn't plan. I acted on instinct."

"You were unarmed."

"I was armed with righteous fury."

"Rarely wins against a semiautomatic."

A week had passed since the shoot-out at Notre-Dame-des-Neiges, and we'd been over it a dozen times. Charbonneau was in my lab, watching me prepare Savannah Osprey's bones for shipment.

DNA sequencing had come back positive, linking the Myrtle Beach skeleton to the remains from St-Basile-le-Grand. Kate Brophy had established that Savannah's mother was dead, but had located a maternal aunt. Burial would take place in North Carolina.

I felt melancholy each time I pictured that lonely, little ceremony. My satisfaction at finding and identifying Savannah was tempered by sadness over her life. She was so young and frail, hampered by physical disability, lonely, loathed by her father, abandoned in death by her

367

mother. I wondered if there was anyone left who would care for her grave.

"Do you think Savannah chose to go to Myrtle Beach that day?" I asked, changing the subject.

"According to Crease the kid went willingly."

"Bad decision." I pictured the pale little waif and wondered what had led her to it.

"Yeah. A deadly decision."

I looked at Charbonneau, surprised at how closely his thought echoed mine. There had been so many fatal decisions. Gately and Martineau. Jocelyn Dion. George Dorsey. The Hells Angels responsible for the cemetery attack. And near-fatal decisions. Kit and Crease, both of whom had managed to survive.

A Hells Angels death squad had been sent from the States to blow away Crease because Jocelyn had fingered him as Cherokee Desjardins' killer. The Angels had intended to send a message that killing one of their own meant certain retribution, and had chosen a very public forum to deliver that message. The gunman assigned to Crease was to have escaped by cycle. The cycle did get away, but the shooter didn't. Ryan and Quickwater saw to that, though the public version would be different.

Unfamiliar with the local terrain, the shooters in the Jeep went off the mountain while speeding from police. The two in front were killed in the crash, the third hospitalized with multiple injuries. A routine check turned up a New York warrant for murder. The man was providing limited cooperation, preferring the non-death penalty attitude of our northern neighbors to the laws of his home state. His thinking was that a life sentence in Canada was preferable to a lethal injection in New York, even though the state hadn't executed anyone since 1963.

Six hours of surgery had pulled Crease through, but the reporter was still in intensive care. The story of his involvement was emerging piecemeal as his periods of lucidity lengthened.

Crease and Cherokee traveled with the Angels in the early eighties, the latter aspiring to brotherhood, the former a wanna-be academic charmed by the biker lifestyle. The two were drawn together by their shared Canadian roots.

According to Crease, he and Cherokee encountered Savannah Osprey on the Myrtle Beach run and invited her to ride along. Later, a party turned ugly and Savannah wanted to leave. Things got out of hand, the girl was strangled, and Cherokee hid the body in the woods.

"Has Crease admitted to a part in the murder?"

"He denies that, but admits to the return visit, when Cherokee decided to collect bones to decorate the clubhouse."

"The bastards."

I glanced at Savannah's remains and experienced the same anger and repulsion I'd felt on seeing the photo Jocelyn had taken from Cherokee's apartment. I'd recognized the cranium instantly by the tiny burr hole in its side. The skull was mounted on a wall, the leg bones crossed below like the symbol on a pirate flag. Crease and Cherokee were posed below the macabre Jolly Roger, hands raised in a one-finger salute.

"Where was that snapshot taken?" Until then, I hadn't asked.

"At the Vipers' clubhouse in St-Basile. Crease and Cherokee went back to Myrtle Beach the winter after Savannah was killed. They checked out the body, found the skull and leg bones still under the tin, the rest skeletonized and scattered by animals. Thinking a human skull would be a hit with the brothers, they decided to haul the undamaged parts back to Quebec."

I was too disgusted to respond.

"Savannah's bones decorated the bar for several years before the Vipers, worried about heat from the police, buried them in the woods."

"Why so close to Gately and Martineau?"

"The proximity of the graves was coincidental. Gately and Martineau were strictly business. Back in '87 the Angels wanted a bar that Gately owned. That was their way of getting it. Martineau was a friend of Gately's, and had taken a shot at an Angel who was hassling Gately about the bar."

"Bad move."

"Indeed."

"If Crease is innocent of the Osprey murder, why was he so desperate to get that picture?"

"He figured that with the bones becoming front-page news, his past might come out and his career would be over."

"So he killed Cherokee for it."

"We haven't worked that out, but we will. And the blood on the thing is gonna put him away for the rest of his worthless life."

"He'll deny any link to that photo, and your sole eyewitness won't be testifying."

Jocelyn had arrived at the Montreal General DOA.

"Then the dandruff will nail him."

"What if the DNA is inconclusive?"

"It won't matter. He's dirty and he'll give it up."

So we believed, for another nine hours.

At the hospital the blinds were drawn, the room filled with slatted sunlight. Kit was staring at a talk show, the sound turned completely down, while Harry flipped through a fashion magazine. Though he'd been moved from intensive care four days earlier, his face was still white, and his eyes looked as though they'd been under-brushed with violet paint. His chest was bandaged, and an IV needle ran into a vein in his left arm.

He brightened when he saw me.

"How's it going?" I rubbed the back of his arm.

"Acey, peachy."

"I brought more flowers," I chirped, holding out the selection I'd grabbed at the hospital florist. "The Spring Daisies Bouquet. Guaranteed to freshen the most sagging spirit."

"Pretty soon we're going to need some kind of permit with all the photosynthesis going on in here."

Wriggling to sit higher, he reached for the orange juice on his tray, winced and pulled back.

"Let me help with that."

I handed him the glass, and he settled into his pillows, closing his lips around the straw.

"How's the breathing?"

"O.K." He rested the glass on his chest.

The bullet intended for Crease had caught Kit at a high angle. It fractured two ribs, nicked a lung, and exited through muscle. A complete recovery was expected.

"Have they busted these sons of bitches yet?"

I turned to my sister. She sat in a corner chair, her long legs braided like a Chinese contortionist's.

"The getaway cycle got away. The guy who survived the Jeep crash has been charged with attempted murder, among other things. He's cooperating with the police."

"Tempe, if I get my h—"

371

"Harry, do you think you could ask the nurse for another vase?"

"I get it. Time for an auntie-nephie chat. I'll scoot for a nicotine hit." She gathered her purse, kissed her son on the top of the head, and stepped into the corridor, leaving behind a trail of Cristalle.

Perching on the side of the bed, I squeezed Kit's hand. It felt cool and pliant.

"Acey, peachy?"

"It's a drag, Aunt Tempe. Every five minutes some nurse sticks me with a needle or shoves a thermometer up my butt. And we're not talking 'Hot Lips' Houlihan here. These women feed on small furry things."

"Uh-huh."

"And they're saying I have to stay another two or three days."

"The doctors want to be sure that lung won't collapse again."

He hesitated, then, "What was the count?"

"In addition to you and Crease, two family members were wounded, and three Heathens and Rock Machine bikers were killed. Of the attackers, one got away, one was killed, two died in a crash, and one was captured. It was a bloodbath the likes of which has seldom been seen in Canada."

He dropped his eyes and picked at the blanket with his free hand.

"How's he doing?"

"He'll make it. But he's about to be charged with the Cherokee Desjardins murder."

"I know Lyle didn't kill that guy. He couldn't."

"He tried to sacrifice you to protect himself."

Kit said nothing.

"And he was using you to get information."

"He may have done that, but he would never murder anyone."

I pictured the skull and crossbones, but said nothing to contradict him.

"Why did he bring you to that funeral?"

"He didn't want to, but I was crazy to see the bikes. I told him I'd go on my own if he didn't take me. Hell, except for going to that cycle shop, Lyle didn't even hang around with those guys. When we went there he tried to look cool, but I could tell nobody really knew him."

I remembered my conversation with Charbonneau, and our initial suspicion that Crease had been a double agent. In retrospect the idea seemed ludicrous. It was ironic, however, that my worry for Kit had been based on fear of his involvement with bikers. I should have worried about Lyle Crease.

Kit worked a thread loose with his finger.

"Look, Aunt Tempe, I'm sorry for all the grief I've caused you."

He swallowed, doubled back on his finger with the thread.

"The Preacher and those other guys are losers who can't even get it together to buy their own wheels."

I'd already learned this from Claudel, but let him go on.

"I let you think they were big-ass bikers to make myself look cool. Instead I almost got you killed."

"Kit, who was the man outside my condo?"

"I really, honestly don't know. He was probably some goof just passing by." A grin teased the corners of his mouth. "Maybe he was applying for a job at the place that cut your hair."

I gently punched his good shoulder. This time I believed him.

"Hey, careful with the rough stuff. I'm an invalid."

He took a sip of juice and handed me the glass.

"What about that eyeball?"

"The police think the Vipers put it on my car to discourage further interest in their history."

A pause. On-screen, a man mouthed the news while stock prices ticked by below.

"I think I'm going to look into school when I get back home. Try a few courses. See how it goes."

"I think that's a wonderful idea, Kit."

"You must think I'm about as dumb as a largemouth bass."

"Maybe a perch."

"I hope you don't give up on me."

"Never."

Embarrassed, he changed the subject.

"How's your boss?"

"Much better. He's starting to give the nurses a hard time."

"I'm with him there. And Ryan?"

"Don't push it, fish brain."

"How long do you think he'll be moonin' around here, expecting flowers and caramel clusters?" Harry stood in the doorway, a smile on her lips, a vase in her hand. Both were the same geranium red.

Leaving the hospital, I drove home, had dinner with Birdie, and began a series of household tasks. A return to normalcy by immersion in the mundane. That was the plan and it was working.

Until the doorbell chirped.

Dumping an armload of dirty sweaters, I glanced at my watch. Eight-fifteen. Too early for Harry.

Curious, I went to check the security screen.

What the hell?

Sergeant-Detective Luc Claudel stood in my vestibule, hands clasped behind his back, weight shifting from the heels to the balls of his feet.

"So much for normalcy," I muttered as I buzzed him in.

"*Bonsoir, Monsieur Claudel.*"

"*Bonsoir.* I apologize for disturbing you at your home, but there has been a development." His jaw tensed, as though what he had to say was pushing him to the limits of civility. "I thought that you should know."

Courtesy from Claudel? In English? What now?

Birdie did a figure eight around my ankles, but offered no conjecture.

I stepped back and gestured the detective inside. He entered and waited stiffly as I closed the door, then followed me to the living room sofa. Settling into the armchair opposite, I remembered my conversation with Ryan's partner, Jean Bertrand, and the thought of Ryan brought the usual stomach clutch.

God, please let him be safe!

I pushed the thought aside and waited for Claudel to speak.

He cleared his throat and looked away from me.

"You were right about George Dorsey. He did not kill Cherokee Desjardins."

There was a revelation.

"Nor did Lyle Crease."

I stared at him, too surprised to respond.

"Shortly before her death Jocelyn Dion mailed a letter to her mother giving information about a number of illegal biker activities. Among the subjects discussed were the shooting of Emily Anne Toussaint and Richard 'Spider' Marcotte, and the murder of Cherokee Desjardins."

"Why did she do that?"

"Her motives were complex. First and foremost, she feared for her own life and felt the letter might confer protection. In addition, she was angry over Dorsey's murder, which, by the way, was ordered by his own gang. Jocelyn Dion was living with George Dorsey at the time of his death."

I felt heat climb the sides of my neck, but did not let on what Jocelyn had said about Dorsey's death.

"Was Dorsey killed because he spoke with me?"

Claudel ignored the question.

"Dion also felt remorse for certain of her own actions, including the killing of Cherokee Desjardins."

"What?" I blurted in astonishment.

"That is correct. Jocelyn Dion killed Desjardins."

"But Jocelyn told me she heard Crease bludgeon and shoot him."

"It seems your clerk was somewhat economical with the truth."

He tented his fingers under his chin.

"According to the young lady's letter, she'd gone to Desjardins for drugs when Crease showed up, wanting the infamous barroom photo. The men argued, Crease knocked Cherokee unconscious with a pipe, then began ransacking the apartment. Hearing noises in the bedroom, he panicked and fled.

"It seems your Jocelyn had a big habit and a short budget. She went over there high on drugs, and saw the situation as an opportunity to stock her medicine chest. When Crease left, she battered Desjardins' unconscious body, dragged it to a chair, and used a shotgun to remove his face."

"Why bother to shoot him?"

"She didn't want Desjardins coming after her. Also, she was stoned, but sober enough to realize that she had to cover her tracks, so she made it look like a biker hit." Claudel dropped his hands. "On that point you were correct."

More throat clearing, then he went on.

"Thinking it contained more pharmaceuticals, Dion retrieved a package Crease had dropped. It contained an old photograph of Crease and Desjardins. Later, she cooked up a blackmail scheme, figuring that if Crease wanted the picture badly enough to fight for it, he might be willing to pay."

"In the meantime, the Heathens heard about my meeting with Dorsey and ordered his death." Again the tension in my neck.

"Yes. Fearing for her own safety, Dion cooked up and floated the story that Crease had murdered Desjardins. The Vipers got wind and decided payback was due. Desjardins had been an Angel, his killer was an Angel dropout, despised by the brothers, and his killer had to die. Also, they had not settled the Spider Marcotte account, as far as they were concerned. They phoned New York for outside help, persuaded Dion to lure Crease to Dorsey's funeral, and decided they would settle several Heathen scores at the same time."

A pause.

"It must have been Jocelyn who left the picture on my desk."

"To throw suspicion toward Crease."

I thought of something else.

377

"That's why Cherokee's blood was on that jacket."

"For once the little lizard was telling the truth. The jacket belonged to Jocelyn, but Dorsey couldn't admit that if he wanted to protect her."

"And meeting with me got him killed." I bit down on my lip.

"Dorsey was killed because his brothers feared he was about to turn on them. Had it not been you, he'd have contacted someone else."

I felt myself swallow.

"Do you believe Dion's letter?"

"Largely, yes. We'd already had reason to suspect Lecomte in the Marcotte-Toussaint murders. We are keeping him under close surveillance. The prosecutor feels that what you heard Dion scream as she was shot is not enough to arrest him now, but in time, we will know."

"Undoubtedly Jocelyn was the leak at our lab."

"She got the position there to spy for the Heathens, but wasn't averse to an occasional chat with the press."

"When approved by the home office."

"Yes."

Claudel drew air through his nose, exhaled.

"These biker gangs are the mafia of the new millennium, and have tremendous power over those attracted to them. Jocelyn Dion was among those who feed at the bottom of the chain, the hookers, the pimps, the strippers, the petty street dealers. She probably needed clearance to take her mother to Sunday Mass.

"One rung up are the more successful entrepreneurs, the chop shop operators, the fences, the bar owners, those who are allowed to hang around because they wash dirty money or perform some service useful to the club. Climb higher and one finds the full-patchers who run their own drug cells. At the very top are men with links to cartels in Mexico and Colombia, and to their counterparts in gangs worldwide."

I'd never seen Claudel so animated.

"And who are these degenerates who make their living off the weak? Most have neither the moral nor intellectual ability to complete a traditional educational process or function in an open market. They use women because, deep down, they fear them. They are unedu-cated, self-deluded, and, in many cases, physically inadequate, so they have themselves tattooed, create nicknames, and band together to reinforce their shared nihilism."

He took a deep breath and slowly shook his head.

"Sonny Barger is in retirement, probably writing his autobiography. Millions will buy the book, and Hollywood will make a film. *The Wild Ones* will be romanticized anew, and the myth will deceive another generation."

Claudel rubbed his face in his hands.

"And the flow of drugs will continue to our school yards, and to the ghettos of the hopeless."

He shot his sleeves, straightened each gold cuff link, and stood. When he spoke again, his voice was hard as tempered steel.

"It is ironic. As the Angels carried out their slaughter at the cemetery, their opponents were sending forth assassins of their own. I do not know which of these subhumans killed George Dorsey, and I do not have the evidence to prove that Lecomte shot Jocelyn Dion, Spider Marcotte, and Emily Anne Toussaint, but I will. One day I will."

He looked me dead in the eyes.

"And I will not rest until this evil is driven from my city."

"Do you believe that can be done?"

He nodded, hesitated, then, "We will be a team?"

Without hesitation, I nodded back.

"*Oui*."

40

The next morning I slept late, went to the gym, then brought coffee and doughnuts home and shared them with my sister. When Harry left for the hospital, I phoned the lab. There were no anthropology cases, so I was free to reactivate the plan interrupted by Claudel's visit.

I soaked the sweaters, then launched myself full speed at the refrigerator. Items older than one month, I threw away. Ditto for anything that could not be identified.

My mood was better than it had been in weeks. Claudel had come around once again to admitting my value as a colleague. I was confident that he, Charbonneau, and Quickwater would pursue the investigation until the Dorsey and Dion killers were behind bars.

I had apologized to Martin Quickwater, and the man seemed to hold no grudge. He'd even smiled in my direction.

LaManche was recovering.

Savannah Osprey's murder had been resolved, and her bones were heading to her family.

Katy would be home in two weeks. My nephew was going to be fine, in every sense of the word.

And my hair was showing signs of growth.

The only shadow in my life was cast by worry over Ryan's safety. He had broken cover to save my life, and I prayed that action would not cost him his. I hoped fervently it had not been another deadly decision.

Right perfection wrongly disgraced.

The line still brought tears to my eyes.

I knew Ryan couldn't contact me, and had no idea when I would see him again.

It didn't matter. I could wait.

I tossed a lump of old Cheddar into the garbage bag.

But it might take time.

Two jars of congealed jelly. Out.

I would definitely need that theme song.

I've got sunshine on a cloudy day . . .

Kathy Reichs's new novel featuring Dr Temperance Brennan, *Fatal Voyage*, will be published in hardback by William Heinemann in August 2001. Read on for an exclusive extract.

1

I stared at the woman flying through the trees. Her head
was forward, chin raised, arms flung backward like the tiny
chrome goddess on the hood of a Rolls Royce. But the tree
lady was naked, and her body ended at the waist. Blood-
coated leaves and branches imprisoned her lifeless torso.

Lowering my eyes, I looked around. Except for the
narrow gravel road on which I was parked, nothing but
dense forest. The trees were mostly pine, the few
hardwoods like wreaths marking the death of summer,
their foliage every shade of red, orange, and yellow.

Though it was hot in Charlotte, at this elevation the
early October weather was pleasant. But it would soon
grow cool. I took a windbreaker from the back seat,
stood still, and listened.

Birdsong. Wind. The scurrying of a small animal.
Then, in the distance, one man calling to another. A
muffled response.

Tying the jacket around my waist, I locked the car
and set off toward the voices, my feet swishing through
dead leaves and pine needles.

384

Ten yards into the woods I passed a seated figure leaning against a mossy stone, knees flexed to his chest, lap top computer at his side. He was missing both arms, and a small china pitcher protruded from his left temple.

On the computer lay a face, teeth laced with orthodontic wiring, one brow pierced by a delicate gold ring. The eyes were open, the pupils dilated, giving the face an expression of alarm. I felt a tremor beneath my tongue, and quickly moved on.

Within yards I saw a leg, the foot still bound in its hiking boot. The limb had been torn off at the hip, and I wondered if it belonged to the Rolls Royce torso.

Beyond the leg, two men rested side by side, seat belts fastened, necks mushrooming into red blossoms. One man sat with legs crossed, as if reading a magazine.

I picked my way deeper into the forest, now and then hearing disconnected shouts, carried to me at the wind's whim. Brushing back branches and climbing over rocks and fallen logs, I continued on.

Luggage and pieces of metal lay among the trees. Most suitcases had burst, spewing their contents in random patterns. Clothing, curling irons, and electric shavers were jumbled with containers of hand lotion, shampoo, after shave, and perfume. One small carry-on had disgorged hundreds of pilfered hotel toiletries. The smell of drug store products and airplane fuel mingled with the scent of pine and mountain air. And from far off, a hint of smoke.

I was moving through a steep-walled gully whose thick canopy allowed only mottled sunlight to reach the ground. It was cool in the shadows, but sweat dampened my hairline and glued my clothing to my skin. I caught my foot on a backpack and went hurtling forward, tearing my sleeve on a jagged bough truncated by falling debris.

I lay a moment, hands trembling, breath coming in ragged gulps. Though I'd trained myself to hide emotion, I could feel despair rising in me. So much death. Dear God, how many would there be?

Closing my eyes, I centered mentally, then pushed to my feet.

Eons later, I stepped over a rotting log, circled a stand of rhododendron, and, seeming no closer to the distant voices, stopped to get my bearings. The muted wail of a siren told me the rescue operation was gathering somewhere over a ridge to the east.

Way to get directions, Brennan.

But there hadn't been time to ask questions. First responders to airline crashes or other disasters are usually well-intentioned, but woefully ill-prepared to deal with mass fatalities. I'd been on my way from Charlotte to Knoxville, nearing the state line, when I'd been asked to get to the scene as quickly as possible. Doubling back on I-40, I'd cut south toward Waynesville, then west through Bryson City, a North Carolina hamlet approximately 175 miles west of Charlotte, 50 miles east of Tennessee, and 50 miles north of Georgia. I'd followed county black top to the point where state maintenance ended, then proceeded on gravel to a Forest Service road which snaked up the mountain.

Though the instructions I'd been given had been accurate, I suspected there was a better route, perhaps a small logging trail that allowed a closer approach to the adjacent valley. I debated returning to the car, decided to press on. Perhaps those already at the site had trekked overland, as I was doing. The Forest Service road had looked like it was going nowhere beyond where I'd left the car.

After an exhausting uphill scramble, I grabbed the trunk of a Douglas fir, planted one foot, and heaved myself onto a ridge. Straightening, I stared into the button eyes of Raggedy Ann. The doll was dangling upside down, her dress entangled in the fir's lower branches.

An image of my daughter's Raggedy flashed to mind, and I reached out.

Stop!

I lowered my arm, knowing that every item must be mapped and recorded before removal. Only then could someone claim the sad momento.

From my position on the ridge I had a clear view of what was probably the main crash site. I could see an engine, half-buried in dirt and debris, and what looked like pieces of wing flap. A portion of fuselage lay with the bottom peeled back, like a diagram in an instructional manual for model planes. Through the windows I could see seats, some occupied, most empty.

Wreckage and body parts covered the landscape, like refuse discarded at a dump. From where I stood, the skin covered body portions looked starkly pale against the backdrop of forest floor, viscera, and airplane parts. Articles dangled from trees, or lay snarled in the leaves and branches. Fabric. Wiring. Sheet metal. Insulation. Molded plastic.

The locals had arrived and were securing the site and checking for survivors. Figures searched among the trees, others stretched tape around the perimeter of the debris field. They wore yellow jackets with *Swain County Sheriff's Department* printed on back. Still others just wandered or stood in clumps, smoking, talking, or staring aimlessly.

Way off through the trees I noticed the flashing of red, blue, and yellow lights, marking the location of the access route I'd failed to find. In my mind I saw the police cruisers, fire engines, rescue trucks, ambulances, and vehicles of citizen volunteers that would clog that road by tomorrow morning.

The wind shifted and the smell of smoke grew stronger. I turned and saw a thin, black plume curling upward just beyond the next ridge. My stomach tightened, for I was close enough now to detect another odor mingling with the sharp, acrid scent.

Being a forensic anthropologist, it is my job to investigate violent death. I have examined hundreds of fire victims for coroners and medical examiners, and know the smell of charred flesh. One gorge over, people were burning.

I swallowed hard, and refocused on the rescue operation. Some who had been inactive were now moving across the site. I watched a sheriff's deputy bend and inspect debris at his feet. He straightened, and an object flashed in his left hand. Another deputy had begun stacking debris.

"Shit!"

I started picking my way downward, clinging to underbrush and zig-zagging between trees and boulders to control my balance. The gradient was steep, and a stumble could turn into a headlong plunge.

Ten yards from the bottom I stepped on a sheet of metal that slid and sent me into the air like a snowboarder on a major wipeout. I landed hard and began to half-roll, half-slide down the slope, bringing with me an avalanche of pebbles, branches, leaves, and pine cones.

To stop my fall, I grabbed for a handhold, skinning my palms and tearing my nails before my left hand struck something solid and my fingers closed around it. My wrist jerked painfully as it took the weight of my body, breaking my downward momentum.

I hung there a moment, then rolled onto my side, pulled with both hands, and scooched myself to a sitting position. Never easing my grasp, I looked up.

The object I clutched was a long metal bar, angling skyward from a rock at my hip to a truncated tree a yard upslope. I planted my feet, tested for traction, and worked my way to a standing position. Wiping bleeding hands on my pants, I re-tied the jacket, and continued downward to level ground.

At the bottom, I quickened my pace. Though my *terra* felt far from *firma*, at least gravity was now on my side. At the cordoned off area, I lifted the tape and ducked under.

"Whoa, lady. Not so fast."

I stopped and turned. The man who had spoken wore a Swain County Sheriff's Department jacket.

"I'm with DMORT."

"What the hell is DMORT?" Gruff.

"Is the sheriff on site?"

"Who's asking?" The deputy's face was rigid, his mouth compressed into a hard, tight line. An orange hunting cap rested low over his eyes.

"Dr. Temperance Brennan."

"We ain't gonna need no doctor here."

"I'll be identifying the victims."

"Got proof?"

In mass disasters, each government agency has specific responsibilities. The Office of Emergency Preparedness, OEP, manages and directs the National Disaster Medical System, NDMS which provides health and medical response, and victim identification and mortuary services in the event of a mass fatality incident.

To meet its mission, NDMS created the Disaster Mortuary Operational Response Team, DMORT, and Disaster Medical Assistance Team, DMAT, systems. In officially declared disasters, DMAT looks after the needs of the living, while DMORT deals with the dead.

I dug out and extended my NDMS identification.

The deputy studied the card, then tipped his head in the direction of the fuselage.

"Sheriff's with the fire chiefs." His voice cracked and he wiped a hand across his mouth. Then he dropped his eyes and walked away, embarrassed to have shown emotion.

I was not surprised at the deputy's demeanor. The toughest and most capable of cops and rescue workers, no matter how extensive their training or experience, are never psychologically prepared for their first major.

Majors. That's what the National Transportation Safety Board dubbed these crashes. I wasn't sure what was required to qualify as a major, but I'd worked several and knew one thing with certainty. Each was a horror. I was never prepared, either, and shared his anguish. I'd just learned not to show it.

Threading toward the fuselage, I passed a deputy covering a body.

"Take that off," I ordered.

"What?"

"Don't blanket them."

"Who says?" I showed ID again.

"But they're lying in the open." His voice sounded flat, like a computer recording.

"Everything must remain in place."

"We've got to do something. It's gettin' dark. Bears

are gonna' scent on these . . ." he stumbled for a word, ". . . people."

I'd seen what *Ursus* could do to a corpse and sympathized with the man's concerns. Nevertheless, I had to stop him.

"Everything must be photographed and recorded before it can be touched."

He bunched the blanket with both hands, his face pinched with pain. I knew exactly what he was feeling. The need to do something, the uncertainty as to what. The sense of helplessness in the midst of overwhelming tragedy.

"Please spread the word that everything has to stay put. Then search for survivors."

"You've got to be kidding." His eyes swept the scene around us. "No one could survive this."

"If anyone *is* alive they've got more to fear from bears than these folks do." I indicated the body at his feet.

"And wolves," he added in a hollow voice.

"What's the sheriff's name?"

"Crowe"

"Which one?"

He glanced toward a group near the fuselage.

"Tall one in the green jacket."

I left him and hurried toward Crowe.

The sheriff was examining a map with a half dozen volunteer fire fighters whose gear suggested they'd come from several jurisdictions. Even with head bent, Crowe was the tallest in the group. Under the jacket the shoulders looked broad and hard, suggesting regular workouts. I hoped I would not get at cross purposes with Sheriff Mountain Macho.

When I drew close the firemen stopped listening and looked in my direction.

391

"Sheriff Crowe?"

Crowe turned, and I realized that macho would not be an issue.

Her cheeks were high and broad, her skin cinnamon. The hair escaping her flat-brimmed hat was frizzy and carrot red. But what held my attention were her eyes. The irises were the color of glass in old Coke bottles. Highlighted by orange lashes and brows, and set against the tawny skin, the pale green was extraordinary. I guessed her age at around forty.

"And you are?" The voice was deep and gravelly, and suggested its owner wanted no nonsense.

"Dr. Temperance Brennan."

"And you have reason to be at this site?"

"I'm with DMORT."

Again the ID. She studied the card and handed it back.

"I heard a crash bulletin while driving from Charlotte to Knoxville. When I phoned Earl Bliss, who's leader of the Region Four team, he asked me to divert over, see if you need anything."

A bit more diplomatic than Earl's actual comments.

For a moment the woman did not reply. Then she turned back to the fire fighters, spoke a few words, and the men dispersed. Closing the gap between us, she held out her hand. The grip could injure.

"Lucy Crowe."

"Please call me Tempe."

She spread her feet, crossed her arms, and regarded me with the Coke bottle eyes.

"I don't believe any of these poor souls will be needing medical attention."

"I'm a forensic anthropologist, not a medical doctor. You've searched for survivors?"

She nodded with a single upward jerk of her head, the type gesture I'd seen in India. "I thought something like this would be the ME's baby?"

"It's everybody's baby. Is the NTSB here yet?" I knew the National Transportation Safety Board never took long to arrive.

"They're coming. I've heard from every agency on the planet. NTSB, FBI, ATF, Red Cross, FAA, Forest Service, TVA, Department of the Interior. I wouldn't be surprised if the pope himself came riding over Wolf Knob there."

"Interior and TVA?"

"The feds own most of this county, about eighty-five percent as national forest, five percent as reservation." She extended a hand at shoulder level, moved it in a clockwise circle. We're on what's called Big Laurel. Bryson City's off to the northwest, Great Smoky Mountains National Park's beyond that. The Cherokee Indian Reservation lies to the north, the Nantahala Game Land and National Forest to the south."

I swallowed to relieve the pressure inside my ears.

"What's the elevation here?"

"We're at forty-two hundred feet."

"I don't want to tell you how to do your job, Sheriff, but there are a few folks you might want to keep ou—"

"The insurance man and the snake-bellied lawyer. Lucy Crowe may live on a mountain, but she's been off it once or twice."

I didn't doubt that. I was also certain that no one gave lip to Lucy Crowe.

"Probably good to keep the press out, too."

"Probably."

"You're right about the ME, sheriff. He'll be here. But the North Carolina emergency plan calls for DMORT involvement for a major."

I heard a muffled boom, followed by shouted orders. Crowe removed her hat and ran the back of her sleeve across her forehead.

"How many fires are still burning?"

"Four. We're getting them out, but it's dicey. The mountain's mighty dry this time of year." She tapped the hat against a thigh as muscular as the shoulders.

"I'm sure your crews are doing their best. They've secured the area and they're dealing with the fires. If there are no survivors, there's nothing else to be done."

"They're not really trained for this kind of thing."

Over Crowe's shoulder an old man in a Cherokee Volunteer PD jacket poked through a pile of debris. I decided on tact.

"I'm sure you've told your people that crash scenes must be treated like crime scenes. Nothing should be disturbed."

She gave her peculiar down-up nod.

"They're probably feeling frustrated, wanting to be useful, but unsure what to do. A reminder never hurts."

I indicated the poker.

Crowe swore softly, then crossed to the volunteer, her strides powerful as an Olympic runner. The man moved off, and in a moment the sheriff was back.

"This is never easy," I said. "When the NTSB arrives they'll assume responsibility for the whole operation."

"Yeah."

At that moment Crowe's cell phone rang. I waited as she spoke.

"Another precinct heard from," she said, hooking the handset to her belt. "Charles Hanover, CEO of Sun Air."

Though I'd never flown it, I'd heard of the airline, a small regional carrier connecting about a dozen cities in the Carolinas, Georgia, and Tennessee with Washington D.C.

"This is one of theirs?"

"Flight 228 was late leaving Atlanta for Washington, D.C. Sat on the runway forty minutes, took off at 12:45 pm. The plane was at about twenty-five thousand feet when it disappeared from radar at 1:07. My office got the 911 call around 2."

"How many on board?"

"The plane was a Fokker-100 carrying eighty-two passengers and six crew. But that's not the worst of it."

Her next words foretold the horror of the coming days.

fatal voyage

Dedicated with button-bursting pride to:

Kerry Elisabeth Reichs, J.D., M.P.P.,
Duke University, Class of 2000

Courtney Anne Reichs, B.A., University of Georgia,
Class of 2000

Brendan Christopher Reichs, B.A. (*cum laude*),
Wake Forest University, Class of 2000

Yippee!!!

Acknowledgments

As always, I owe many thanks to many people:

To Ira J. Rimson, P.E., and Captain John Gallagher (retired), for input on aircraft design and accident investigation. To Hughes Cicoine, C.F.E.I., for advice on fire and explosion investigation. Your patience was amazing.

To Paul Sledzik, M.S., National Museum of Health and Medicine, Armed Forces Institute of Pathology, on the history, structure, and operation of the DMORT system; Frank A. Ciaccio, M.P.A., Office of Government, Public, and Family Affairs, United States National Transportation Safety Board, for information on DMORT, the NTSB, and the Family Assistance Plan.

To Arpad Vass, Ph.D., Research Scientist, Oak Ridge National Laboratories, for a crash course on volatile fatty acids.

To Special Agent Jim Corcoran, Federal Bureau of Investigation, Charlotte Division, for outlining the workings of the FBI in North Carolina; Detective Ross Trudel (retired), Communauté Urbaine de Montréal Police, for information on explosives and their regulations: Sergent-détective Stephen Rudman (retired), Communauté Urbaine de Montréale Police, for details on police funerals.

To Janet Levy, Ph.D., University of North Carolina-Charlotte, for specifics on the North Carolina Department of Cultural Resources, and answers to questions archaeological; Rachel Bonney, Ph.D., University of North Carolina-Charlotte, and Barry Hipps, Cherokee Historical Association, for knowledge about the Cherokee.

To John Butts, M.D., Chief Medical Examiner, State of North Carolina; Michael Sullivan, M.D., Mecklenburg County Medical Examiner; and Roger Thompson, Director, Charlotte-Mecklenburg Police Department Crime Laboratory.

To Marilyn Steely, M.A., for pointing me to the Hell Fire Club; Jack C. Morgan Jr., M.A.I., C.R.E., for enlightening me on property deeds, maps, and tax records; Irene Bacznsky, for help with airline names.

To Anne Fletcher, for accompanying me on our Smoky Mountain adventure.

A special thanks to the people of Bryson City, North Carolina, including Faye Bumgarner, Beverly Means, and Donna Rowland at the Bryson City library; Ruth Anne Sitton and Bess Ledford at the Swain County Tax and Land Records Office; Linda Cable, Swain County Administrator; Susan Cutshaw and Dick Schaddelee at the Swain County Chamber of Commerce; Monica Brown, Marty Martin and Misty Brooks at the Fryemont Inn; and, especially, Chief Deputy Jackie Fortner, Swain County Sheriff's Department.

Merci to M. Yves St. Marie, Dr. André Lauzon, and to all my colleagues at the Laboratorie de Sciences Judiciaires et de Médecine Légale; Chancellor James Woodward at the University of North Carolina-Charlotte. Your continued support is greatly appreciated.

To Paul Reichs, for his valuable comments on the manuscript.

To my superb editors, Susanne Kirk and Lynne Drew.

And, of course, to my miracle-worker agent, Jennifer Rudolph Walsh.

My stories could not be what they are without the help of friends and colleagues. I thank them. As always, all mistakes are of my making.

fatal voyage

fatal voyage

1

I stared at the woman flying through the trees. Her head was forward, chin raised, arms flung backward like the tiny chrome goddess on the hood of a Rolls-Royce. But the tree lady was naked, and her body ended at the waist. Blood-coated leaves and branches imprisoned her lifeless torso.

Lowering my eyes, I looked around. Except for the narrow gravel road on which I was parked, there was nothing but dense forest. The trees were mostly pine, the few hardwoods like wreaths marking the death of summer, their foliage every shade of red, orange, and yellow.

Though it was hot in Charlotte, at this elevation the early October weather was pleasant. But it would soon grow cool. I took a windbreaker from the backseat, stood still, and listened.

Birdsong. Wind. The scurrying of a small animal. Then, in the distance, one man calling to another. A muffled response.

Tying the jacket around my waist, I locked the car

and set off towards the voices, my feet swishing through dead leaves and pine needles.

Ten yards into the woods I passed a seated figure leaning against a mossy stone, knees flexed to his chest, laptop computer at his side. He was missing both arms, and a small china pitcher protruded from his left temple.

On the computer lay a face, teeth laced with orthodontic wiring, one brow pierced by a delicate gold ring. The eyes were open, the pupils dilated, giving the face an expression of alarm. I felt a tremor beneath my tongue, and quickly moved on.

Within yards I saw a leg, the foot still bound in its hiking boot. The limb had been torn off at the hip, and I wondered if it belonged to the Rolls-Royce torso.

Beyond the leg, two men rested side by side, seat belts fastened, necks mushrooming into red blossoms. One man sat with legs crossed, as if reading a magazine.

I picked my way deeper into the forest, now and then hearing disconnected shouts, carried to me at the wind's whim. Brushing back branches and climbing over rocks and fallen logs, I continued on.

Luggage and pieces of metal lay among the trees. Most suitcases had burst, spewing their contents in random patterns. Clothing, curling irons, and electric shavers were jumbled with containers of hand lotion, shampoo, aftershave, and perfume. One small carry-on had disgorged hundreds of pilfered hotel toiletries. The smell of drugstore products and airplane fuel mingled with the scent of pine and mountain air. And from far off, a hint of smoke.

I was moving through a steep-walled gulley whose thick canopy allowed only mottled sunlight to reach the ground. It was cool in the shadows, but sweat dampened my hairline and glued my clothing to my

2

skin. I caught my foot on a backpack and went hurtling forward, tearing my sleeve on a jagged bough truncated by falling debris.

I lay a moment, hands trembling, breath coming in ragged gulps. Though I'd trained myself to hide emotion, I could feel despair rising in me. So much death. Dear God, how many would there be?

Closing my eyes, I centered myself mentally, then pushed to my feet.

Aeons later, I stepped over a rotting log, circled a stand of rhododendron, and, seeming no closer to the distant voices, stopped to get my bearings. The muted wail of a siren told me the rescue operation was gathering somewhere over a ridge to the east.

Way to get directions, Brennan.

But there hadn't been time to ask questions. First responders to airline crashes or other disasters are usually well intentioned, but woefully ill-prepared to deal with mass fatalities. I'd been on my way from Charlotte to Knoxville, nearing the state line, when I'd been asked to get to the scene as quickly as possible. Doubling back on I–40, I'd cut south towards Waynesville, then west through Bryson City, a North Carolina hamlet approximately 175 miles west of Charlotte, 50 miles east of Tennessee, and 50 miles north of Georgia. I'd followed county blacktop to the point where state maintenance ended, then proceeded on gravel to a Forest Service road that snaked up the mountain.

Though the instructions I'd been given had been accurate, I suspected there was a better route, perhaps a small logging trail that allowed a closer approach to the adjacent valley. I debated returning to the car, decided to press on. Perhaps those already at the site had trekked overland, as I was doing. The Forest Service road had looked like it was going nowhere beyond where I'd left the car.

After an exhausting uphill scramble, I grabbed the trunk of a Douglas fir, planted one foot, and heaved myself on to a ridge. Straightening, I stared into the button eyes of Raggedy Ann. The doll was dangling upside down, her dress entangled in the fir's lower branches.

An image of my daughter's Raggedy flashed to mind, and I reached out.

Stop!

I lowered my arm, knowing that every item must be mapped and recorded before removal. Only then could someone claim the sad memento.

From my position on the ridge I had a clear view of what was probably the main crash site. I could see an engine, half buried in dirt and debris, and what looked like pieces of wing flap. A portion of fuselage lay with the bottom peeled back, like a diagram in an instructional manual for model planes. Through the windows I could see seats, some occupied, most empty.

Wreckage and body parts covered the landscape like refuse discarded at a dump. From where I stood, the skin-covered body portions looked starkly pale against the backdrop of forest floor, viscera, and airplane parts. Articles dangled from trees or lay snarled in the leaves and branches. Fabric. Wiring. Sheet metal. Insulation. Molded plastic.

The locals had arrived and were securing the site and checking for survivors. Figures searched among the trees, others stretched tape around the perimeter of the debris field. They wore yellow jackets with *Swain County Sheriff's Department* printed on the back. Still others just wandered or stood in clumps, smoking, talking, or staring aimlessly.

Way off through the trees I noticed the flashing of red, blue, and yellow lights, marking the location of the access route I'd failed to find. In my mind I saw the police cruisers, fire engines, rescue trucks, ambulances, and vehicles of citizen volunteers that would clog that road by tomorrow morning.

The wind shifted and the smell of smoke grew stronger. I turned and saw a thin, black plume curling upward just beyond the next ridge. My stomach tightened, for I was close enough now to detect another odor mingling with the sharp, acrid scent.

Being a forensic anthropologist, it is my job to investigate violent death. I have examined hundreds of fire victims for coroners and medical examiners, and know the smell of charred flesh. One gorge over, people were burning.

I swallowed hard and refocused on the rescue operation. Some who had been inactive were now moving across the site. I watched a sheriff's deputy bend and inspect debris at his feet. He straightened, and an object flashed in his left hand. Another deputy had begun stacking debris.

"Shit!"

I started picking my way downward, clinging to underbrush and zigzagging between trees and boulders to control my balance. The gradient was steep, and a stumble could turn into a headlong plunge.

Ten yards from the bottom I stepped on a sheet of metal that slid and sent me into the air like a snowboarder on a major wipeout. I landed hard and began to half roll, half slide down the slope, bringing with me an avalanche of pebbles, branches, leaves, and pinecones.

5

To stop my fall, I grabbed for a handhold, skinning my palms and tearing my nails before my left hand struck something solid and my fingers closed around it. My wrist jerked painfully as it took the weight of my body, breaking my downward momentum.

I hung there a moment, then rolled on to my side, pulled with both hands, and scooched myself to a sitting position. Never easing my grasp, I looked up.

The object I clutched was a long metal bar, angling skyward from a rock at my hip to a truncated tree a yard upslope. I planted my feet, tested for traction, and worked my way to a standing position. Wiping bleeding hands on my pants, I retied my jacket and continued downward to level ground.

At the bottom, I quickened my pace. Though my *terra* felt far from *firma*, at least gravity was now on my side. At the cordoned-off area, I lifted the tape and ducked under.

"Whoa, lady. Not so fast."

I stopped and turned. The man who had spoken wore a Swain County Sheriff's Department jacket.

"I'm with DMORT."

"What the hell is DMORT?" Gruff.

"Is the sheriff on site?"

"Who's asking?" The deputy's face was rigid, his mouth compressed into a hard, tight line. An orange hunting cap rested low over his eyes.

"Dr. Temperance Brennan."

"We ain't gonna need no doctor here."

"I'll be identifying the victims."

"Got proof?"

In mass disasters, each government agency has specific responsibilities. The Office of Emergency Preparedness, OEP, manages and directs the National

Disaster Medical System, NDMS, which provides medical response and victim identification and mortuary services in the event of a mass fatality incident.

To meet its mission, NDMS created the Disaster Mortuary Operational Response Team, DMORT, and Disaster Medical Assistant Team, DMAT, systems. In officially declared disasters, DMAT looks after the needs of the living, while DMORT deals with the dead.

I dug out and extended my NDMS identification.

The deputy studied the card, then tipped his head in the direction of the fuselage.

"Sheriff's with the fire chiefs." His voice cracked and he wiped a hand across his mouth. Then he dropped his eyes and walked away, embarrassed to have shown emotion.

I was not surprised at the deputy's demeanor. The toughest and most capable of cops and rescue workers, no matter how extensive their training or experience, are never psychologically prepared for their first major.

Majors. That's what the National Transportation Safety Board dubbed these crashes. I wasn't sure what was required to qualify as a major, but I'd worked several and knew one thing with certainty: Each was a horror. I was never prepared, either, and shared his anguish. I'd just learned not to show it.

Threading toward the fuselage, I passed a deputy covering a body.

"Take that off," I ordered.

"What?"

"Don't blanket them."

"Who says?"

I showed my ID again.

"But they're lying in the open." His voice sounded flat, like a computer recording.

7

"Everything must remain in place."

"We've got to do something. It's getting dark. Bears are gonna scent on these" – he stumbled for a word – "people."

I'd seen what *Ursus* could do to a corpse and sympathized with the man's concerns. Nevertheless, I had to stop him.

"Everything must be photographed and recorded before it can be touched."

He bunched the blanket with both hands, his face pinched with pain. I knew exactly what he was feeling. The need to do something, the uncertainty as to what. The sense of helplessness in the midst of overwhelming tragedy.

"Please spread the word that everything has to stay put. Then search for survivors."

"You've got to be kidding." His eyes swept the scene around us. "No one could survive this."

"If anyone *is* alive they've got more to fear from bears than these folks do." I indicated the body at his feet.

"And wolves," he added in a hollow voice.

"What's the sheriff's name?"

"Crowe."

"Which one?"

He glanced toward a group near the fuselage.

"Tall one in the green jacket."

I left him and hurried toward Crowe.

The sheriff was examining a map with a half dozen volunteer firefighters whose gear suggested they'd come from several jurisdictions. Even with head bent, Crowe was the tallest in the group. Under the jacket his shoulder looked broad and hard, suggesting regular workouts. I hoped I would not find myself at cross purposes with Sheriff Mountain Macho.

8

When I drew close the firemen stopped listening and looked in my direction.

"Sheriff Crowe?"

Crowe turned, and I realized that macho would not be an issue.

Her cheeks were high and broad, her skin cinnamon. The hair escaping her flat-brimmed hat was frizzy and carrot red. But what held my attention were her eyes. The irises were the color of glass in old Coke bottles. Highlighted by orange lashes and brows, and set against the tawny skin, the pale green was extraordinary. I guessed her age at around forty.

"And you are?" The voice was deep and gravelly, and suggested its owner wanted no nonsense.

"Dr. Temperance Brennan."

"And you have reason to be at this site?"

"I'm with DMORT."

Again the ID. She studied the card and handed it back.

"I heard a crash bulletin while driving from Charlotte to Knoxville. When I phoned Earl Bliss, who's leader of the Region Four team, he asked me to divert over, see if you need anything."

A bit more diplomatic than Earl's actual comments.

For a moment the woman did not reply. Then she turned back to the firefighters, spoke a few words, and the men dispersed. Closing the gap between us, she held out her hand. The grip could injure.

"Lucy Crowe."

"Please call me Tempe."

She spread her feet, crossed her arms, and regarded me with the Coke-bottle eyes.

"I don't believe any of these poor souls will be needing medical attention."

9

"I'm a forensic anthropologist, not a medical doctor. You've searched for survivors?"

She nodded with a single upward jerk of her head, the type of gesture I'd seen in India. "I thought something like this would be the ME's baby."

"It's everybody's baby. Is the NTSB here yet?" I knew the National Transportation Safety Board never took long to arrive.

"They're coming. I've heard from every agency on the planet. NTSB, FBI, ATF, Red Cross, FAA, Forest Service, TVA, Department of the Interior. I wouldn't be surprised if the pope himself came riding over Wolf Knob there."

"Interior and TVA?"

"The feds own most of this country; about eighty-five percent as national forest, five percent as reservation." She extended a hand at shoulder level, moved it in a clockwise circle. "We're on what's called Big Laurel. Bryson City's off to the northwest, Great Smoky Mountains National Park's beyond that. The Cherokee Indian Reservation lies to the north, the Nantahala Game Land and National Forest to the south."

I swallowed to relieve the pressure inside my ears.

"What's the elevation here?"

"We're at forty-two hundred feet."

"I don't want to tell you how to do your job, Sheriff, but there are a few folks you might want to keep out—"

"The insurance man and the snake-bellied lawyer. Lucy Crowe may live on a mountain, but she's been off it once or twice."

I didn't doubt that. I was also certain that no one gave lip to Lucy Crowe.

"Probably good to keep the press out, too."

"Probably."

"You're right about the ME, Sheriff. He'll be here. But the North Carolina emergency plan calls for DMORT involvement for a major."

I heard a muffled boom, followed by shouted orders. Crowe removed her hat and ran the back of her sleeve across her forehead.

"How many fires are still burning?"

"Four. We're getting them out, but it's dicey. The mountain's mighty dry this time of year." She tapped the hat against a thigh as muscular as her shoulders.

"I'm sure your crews are doing their best. They've secured the area and they're dealing with the fires. If there are no survivors, there's nothing else to be done."

"They're not really trained for this kind of thing."

Over Crowe's shoulder an old man in a Cherokee Volunteer PD jacket poked through a pile of debris. I decided on tact.

"I'm sure you've told your people that crash scenes must be treated like crime scenes. Nothing should be disturbed."

She gave her peculiar down-up nod.

"They're probably feeling frustrated, wanting to be useful but unsure what to do. A reminder never hurts."

I indicated the poker.

Crowe swore softly, then crossed to the volunteer, her strides powerful as an Olympic runner's. The man moved off, and in a moment the sheriff was back.

"This is never easy," I said. "When the NTSB arrives they'll assume responsibility for the whole operation."

"Yeah."

At that moment Crowe's cell phone rang. I waited as she spoke.

"Another precinct heard from," she said, hooking the

11

handset to her belt. "Charles Hanover, CEO of Air TransSouth."

Though I'd never flown it, I'd heard of the airline, a small, regional carrier connecting about a dozen cities in the Carolinas, Georgia, and Tennessee with Washington, D.C.

"This is one of theirs?"

"Flight 228 was late leaving Atlanta for Washington, D.C. Sat on the runway forty minutes, took off at twelve forty-five P.M. The plane was at about twenty-five thousand feet when it disappeared from radar at one oh seven. My office got the 911 call around two."

"How many on board?"

"The plane was a Fokker-100 carrying eighty-two passengers and six crew. But that's not the worst of it."

Her next words foretold the horror of the coming days.

2

"The UGA soccer teams?"

Crowe nodded. "Hanover said both the men and women were traveling to matches somewhere near Washington."

"Jesus." Images popped like flashbulbs. A severed leg. Teeth with braces. A young woman caught in a tree.

A sudden stab of fear.

My daughter, Katy, was a student in Virginia, but often visited her best friend in Athens, home of the University of Georgia. Lija was on athletic scholarship. Was it soccer?

Oh, God. My mind raced. Had Katy mentioned a trip? When was her semester break? I resisted the impulse to grab my cell phone.

"How many students?"

"Forty-two passengers booked through the university. Hanover thought most of those were students. Besides the athletes there would be coaches, trainers, girlfriends, boyfriends. Some fans." She ran a hand across her mouth. "The usual."

13

The usual. My heart ached at the loss of so many young lives. Then another thought.

"This will be a media nightmare."

"Hanover opened with that concern." Crowe's voice dipped with sarcasm.

"When the NTSB takes over they'll deal with the press."

And with the families, I didn't add. They, too, would be here, moaning and huddling for comfort, some watching with frightened eyes, some demanding immediate answers, belligerence masking their unbearable grief.

At that moment blades whumped, and we saw a helicopter come in low over the trees. I spotted a familiar figure beside the pilot, another silhouette in the rear. The chopper circled twice, then headed in the opposite direction from where I assumed the road to be.

"Where are they going?"

"Hell if I know. We're not oversupplied with landing pads up here." Crowe lowered her gaze and replaced her hat, tucking in frizz with a backhand gesture.

"Coffee?"

Thirty minutes later the chief medical examiner of the State of North Carolina walked into the site from the west, followed by the state's lieutenant governor. The former wore the basic deployment uniform of boots and khaki, the latter a business suit. I watched them pick their way through the debris, the pathologist looking around, assessing, the politician with head bowed, glancing neither left nor right, holding himself gathered tightly, as if contact with his surroundings might draw him in as a participant rather than an observer. At one point they stopped and the ME spoke to a deputy. The

14

man pointed in our direction, and the pair angled toward us.

"Hot damn. A superb photo op." Said with the same sarcasm she'd directed toward Charles Hanover, the Air TransSouth CEO.

Crowe crumpled her Styrofoam cup and jammed it into a thermos bag. I handed her mine, wondering at the vehemence of her disapproval. Did she disagree with the lieutenant governor's politics, or was there personal history between Lucy Crowe and Parker Davenport?

When the men drew close the ME showed ID. Crowe waved it aside.

"No need for that, Doc. I know who you are."

So did I, having worked with Larke Tyrell since his appointment at North Carolina's chief medical examiner in the mid-1980s. Larke was cynical, dictatorial, and one of the best pathologist-administrators in the country. Working with an inadequate budget and a disinterested legislature, he had taken an office in chaos and turned it into one of the most efficient death investigative systems in North America.

My forensic career was in its infancy at the time of Larke's appointment, and I had just qualified for certification by the American Board of Forensic Anthropology. We met through work I was doing for the North Carolina State Bureau of Investigation, re-assembling and identifying the corpses of two drug dealers murdered and dismembered by outlaw bikers. I was one of Larke's first hires as a consulting specialist, and had handled the skeletal, the decomposed, the mummified, the burned, and the mutilated dead of North Carolina ever since.

The lieutenant governor extended one hand, pressed

15

a hankie to his mouth with the other. His face was the color of a frog's belly. He said nothing as we shook.

"Glad you're in country, Tempe," said Larke, also crushing my fingers in his grip. I was rethinking this whole handshake business.

Larke's "in country" idiom was Vietnam-era military, his dialect pure Carolina. Born in the low country, Larke grew up in a Marine Corps family, then did two hitches of his own before heading off to medical school. He spoke and looked like a spit-and-polish version of Andy Griffith.

"When do you head north?"

"Next week is fall break," I responded.

Larke's eyes narrowed as he did another sweep of the site.

"I'm afraid Quebec may have to do without its anthropologist this autumn."

A decade back I'd participated in a faculty exchange with McGill University. While in Montreal I'd begun consulting to the Laboratoire de Sciences Judiciaires et de Médecine Légale, Quebec's central crime and medico-legal lab. At the end of my year, recognizing the need for a staff forensic anthropologist, the provincial government had funded a position, equipped a lab, and signed me up on a permanent consultant basis.

I'd been commuting between Quebec and North Carolina, teaching physical anthropology at UNC-Charlotte and consulting to the two jurisdictions, ever since. Because my cases usually involved the less-than-recent dead, this arrangement had worked well. But there was an understanding on both ends that I would be immediately available for court testimony and in crisis situations.

An aviation disaster definitely qualified as a crisis

16

situation. I assured Larke that I would cancel my October trip to Montreal.

"How did you get here so quickly?"

Again I explained my trip to Knoxville and the phone conversation with the DMORT leader.

"I've already talked to Earl. He'll deploy a team up here tomorrow morning." Larke looked at Crowe. "The NTSB boys will be rolling in tonight. Until then everything stays put."

"I've given that order," Crowe said. "This location is pretty inaccessible, but I'll post extra security. Animals will probably be the biggest problem. Especially when these bodies start to go."

The lieutenant governor made an odd sound, spun, and lurched off. I watched him brace against a mountain laurel, bend, and vomit.

Larke fixed us with a sincere Sheriff of Mayberry gaze, shifting his eyes from Crowe to me.

"You ladies are making a very difficult job infinitely easier. Words can't express how much I appreciate your professionalism."

Shift.

"Sheriff, you keep things squared away here."

Shift.

"Tempe, you go on and give your lecture in Knoxville. Then pick up whatever supplies you'll need and report back tomorrow. You're going to be here awhile, so inform the university. We'll secure a bunk for you."

Fifteen minutes later a deputy was dropping me at my car. I'd been right about a better route. A quarter mile up from where I'd parked, a dirt track cut off from the Forest Service road. Once used for hauling timber, the

17

tiny trail meandered around the mountain, allowing access to within a hundred yards of the main crash site.

Vehicles now lined both sides of the logging trail, and we'd passed newcomers on our way downhill. By sunrise both the Forest Service and county roads would be jammed.

As soon as I was behind the wheel I grabbed my cell phone. Dead.

I did a three-point turn and headed toward the county road. Once on Highway 74, I tried again. The signal was back, so I punched in Katy's number. A machine picked up after four rings.

Uneasy, I left a message, then set the tape in my head to play the "don't-be-an-idiot-mother" lecture. For the next hour I tried to focus on my upcoming presentation, pushing away thoughts of the carnage I'd left behind and the horror I'd face the following day. It was no go. Images of floating faces and severed limbs shattered my concentration.

I tried the radio. Every station carried accounts of the crash. Broadcasters reverently talked of the death of young athletes and solemnly hypothesized as to cause. Since weather did not seem to be a factor, sabotage and mechanical failure were the favored theories.

Hiking out behind Crowe's deputy, I'd spotted a line of sheared-off trees oriented opposite my point of entrance. Though I knew the damage marked the plane's final descent path, I refused to join in the speculation.

I entered I–40, switched stations for the hundredth time, and caught a journalist reporting from overhead a warehouse fire. Chopper sounds reminded me of Larke, and I realized I hadn't asked where he and the lieutenant governor had landed. I stored the question in the back of my brain.

18

At nine, I redialed Katy.

Still no answer. I rewound the mind tape.

Arriving in Knoxville, I checked in, contacted my host, then ate the Bojangles' chicken I'd picked up on the outskirts of town. I phoned my estranged husband in Charlotte to request care for Birdie. Pete agreed, saying I'd be billed for cat transport and feeling. He hadn't talked to Katy for several days. After delivering a mini-version of my own lecture, he promised to try to reach her.

Next, I phoned Pierre LaManche, my boss at the Labaratoire de Sciences Judiciaires et de Médecine Légale, to report that I would not be in Montreal the following week. He'd heard reports of the crash and was expecting my call. Last, I rang my department chair at UNC-Charlotte.

Responsibilities covered, I spent an hour selecting slides and placing them into carousel trays, then showered and tried Katy again. No go.

I glanced at the clock. Eleven-forty.

She's fine. She's gone out for pizza. Or she's at the library. Yes. The library. I'd used that one many times when I was in school.

It took a very long time to fall asleep.

By morning, Katy hadn't called and was still not picking up. I tried Lija's number in Athens. Another robotic voice requested a message.

I drove to the only anthropology department in America located in a football stadium, and gave one of the more disjointed talks of my career. The host of the guest lecture series listed my DMORT affiliation in his introduction and mentioned that I would be working the Air TransSouth recovery. Though I could supply

19

little information, follow-up queries largely ignored my presentation and focused on the crash. The question-and-answer period lasted forever.

As the crowd finally milled towards the exits, a scarecrow man in a bow tie and cardigan made straight for the podium, half-moon glasses swinging across his chest. Being in a profession with relatively few members, most anthropologists know one another, and our paths cross and recross at meetings, seminars, and conferences. I'd met Simon Midkiff on several occasions, and knew it would be a long session if I wasn't firm. Looking pointedly at my watch, I gathered my notes, stuffed my briefcase, and descended from the platform.

"How are you, Simon?"

"Excellent." His lips were cracked, his skin dry and flaky, like that of a dead fish lying in the sun. Tiny veins laced the whites of eyes overshadowed by bushy brows.

"How is the archaeology business?"

"Excellent, as well. Since one must eat, I am engaged in several projects for the cultural resources department in Raleigh. But mainly I spend my days organizing data." He gave a high-pitched laugh and tapped a hand to one cheek. "It seems I've collected an extraordinary amount of data throughout my career."

Simon Midkiff earned a doctorate at Oxford in 1955, then came to the United States to accept a position at Duke. But the archaeology superstar published nothing and was denied tenure six years later. Midkiff was given a second chance by the University of Tennessee, again failed to produce publications, and again was let go.

Unable to obtain a permanent faculty position, for thirty years Midkiff had hung around the periphery of academia, doing contract archaeology and teaching courses as replacement instructors were needed at colleges and universities in the Carolinas and Tennessee. He was notorious for excavating sites, filing the requisite reports, then failing to publish his findings.

"I'd love to hear about it, Simon, but I'm afraid I have to run."

"Yes, indeed. Such a terrible tragedy. So many young lives." His head moved sadly from side to side. "Where exactly is the crash?"

"Swain County. And I really must get back." I started to move on, but Midkiff made a subtle shift, blocking my path with a size-thirteen Hush Puppy.

"Where in Swain County?"

"South of Bryson City."

"Perhaps you could be a bit more specific?"

"I can't give you coordinates." I did not mask my irritation.

"Please forgive my beastly rudeness. I've been excavating in Swain County, and I was worried about damage to the site. How selfish of me." Again the giggle. "I apologize."

At that moment my host joined us.

"May I?" He waggled a small Nikon.

"Sure."

I assumed the Kodak smile.

"It's for the departmental newsletter. Our students seem to enjoy it."

He thanked me for the lecture and wished me well with the recovery. I thanked him for the accommodations, excused myself to both men, collected my slide carousels, and hurried from the auditorium.

Before leaving Knoxville I located a sporting goods store and purchased boots, socks, and three pairs of khakis, one of which I put on. At an adjoining pharmacy I grabbed two packages of Hanes Her Way cotton bikinis. Not my brand, but they would do. Shoving the panties and extra khakis into my overnighter, I pointed myself east.

Born in the hills of Newfoundland, the Appalachians parallel the East Coast on their plunge from north to south, splitting near Harpers Ferry, West Virginia, to form the Great Smoky and Blue Ridge chains. One of the world's oldest upland regions, the Great Smoky Mountains rise to over 6,600 feet at Clingmans Dome on the North Carolina-Tennessee border.

Less than an hour out of Knoxville, I'd traversed the Tennessee towns of Sevierville, Pigeon Forge, and Gatlinburg, and was passing east of the dome, awed, as always, by the surreal beauty of the place. Molded by aeons of wind and rain, the Great Smokies roll across the south as a series of gentle valleys and peaks. The forest cover is luxuriant, much of it preserved as national land. The Nantahala. The Pisgah. The Cherokee. The Great Smoky Mountains National Park. The soft, mohair greens and smokelike haze for which these highlands are named create an unparalleled allure. The earth at its best.

Death and destruction amid such dreamlike loveliness was a stark contrast.

Just outside Cherokee, on the North Carolina side, I managed another call to Katy. Bad idea. Again, her voice mail answered. Again I left a message: *Phone your mother*.

I kept my mind miles from the task ahead. I thought about the pandas at the Atlanta zoo, the fall lineup on NBC, luggage retrieval at the Charlotte airport. Why was it always so slow?

I thought about Simon Midkiff. What an odd duck.

What were the chances a plane would drop precisely in his dig?

Avoiding the radio, I slipped in a CD of Kiri Te Kanawa, and listened to the diva singing Irving Berlin.

It was almost two when I approached the site. A pair of cruisers now blocked the county road just below its junction with the Forest Service road. A National Guardsman directed traffic, sending some motorists up the mountain, ordering others back down. I produced ID and, the guardsman checked his clipboard.

"Yes, ma'am. You're on the list. Park on up at the holding area."

He stepped aside, and I squeezed through a gap between the cruisers.

A holding area had been created from an overlook built to accommodate a fire tower and a small field on the other side of the road. The cliff face had been stripped back to increase the size of the inside tract, and gravel had been spread as a precaution against rain. It was at this location that briefings would take place and relatives counseled until a family assistance center could be established.

Scores of people and vehicles filled both sides of the road. Red Cross trailers. Television vans with satellite dishes. SUVs. Pickups. A hazardous-materials truck. I squeezed my Mazda between a Dodge Durango and a Ford Bronco on the uphill side, grabbed my over-nighter, and wove toward the blacktop.

Emerging opposite the overlook, I could see a collapsible school table at the base of the tower, outside one of the Red Cross trailers. A convention-sized coffeemaker gleamed in the sun. Family members huddled around it, hugging and leaning on one another,

23

some crying, others stiffly silent. Many clutched Styrofoam cups, a few spoke into cell phones.

A priest circulated among the mourners, stroking shoulders and squeezing hands. I watched him bend to speak to an elderly woman. With his hunched posture, bald head, and hooked nose he resembled the carrion-eating birds I'd seen on the plains of East Africa, an unfair comparison.

I remembered another priest. Another dead watch. That man's sympathetic hovering had extinguished any hope I'd sustained that my grandmother would recover. I recalled the agony of that vigil, and my heart went out to those gathering to claim their dead.

Reporters, cameramen, and soundmen jockeyed for position along the low stone wall bordering the over-look, each team seeking the choicest backdrop for its coverage. As with the 1999 Swissair crash in Peggy's Cove, Nova Scotia, I was certain that scenic panoramas would feature prominently in every broadcast.

Shouldering my bag, I headed downhill. Another guardsman allowed me on to the logging trail, which had been converted overnight to a two-lane gravel road. An access route now led from the expanded trail into the crash site. Gravel crunched underfoot as I walked through the freshly cut tunnel of trees, the scent of pine tainted by the faint odor of early stage putrefaction.

Decontamination trailers and Porta-Johns lined barricades blocking access to the primary site, and an Incident Command Center had been set up inside the restricted area. I could see the familiar NTSB trailer, with its satellite dish and generator shed. Refrigerated trucks were parked beside it, and stacks of body bags lay on the ground. This temporary morgue would be the staging site for transfer of remains to a more permanent incident morgue.

Backhoes, cherry pickers, dump trucks, fire engines, and squad cars were scattered here and there. The solitary ambulance told me that the operation had officially changed from "search and rescue" to "search and recovery". Its vigil was now for injured workers.

Lucy Crowe stood inside the barricades talking with Larke Tyrell.

"How's it going?" I asked.

"My phone never stops." Crowe sounded exhausted. "Almost turned the damn thing off last night."

Over her shoulder I could see the debris field where searchers in masks and Tyvek jumpsuits moved in straight lines, eyes to the ground. Occasionally someone squatted, inspected an item, then marked the spot. Behind the team, red, blue, and yellow flags dotted the landscape like colored pins on a city map.

Other white-suited workers milled around the fuselage, wing tip, and engine, taking pictures, jotting notes, and speaking into tiny Dictaphones. Blue caps identified them as NTSB.

"The gang's all there," I said.

"NTSB, FBI, SBI, FAA, ATF, CBS, ABC. And, of course, the CEO. If they've got letters, they're here."

"This is nothing," said Larke. "Give it a day or two." He peeled back a latex glove and checked his watch.

"Most of the DMORTs are at a briefing at the incident morgue, Tempe, so there's no sense you suiting up now. Let's head in."

I started to object but Larke cut me off.

"We'll walk back together."

While Larke went to decontamination, Lucy gave me directions to the incident morgue. It wasn't necessary.

I'd spotted the activity while driving up the county road.

"Alarka Fire Department's about eight miles back. Used to be a school. You'll see swing sets and slides, and the engines parked in a field next door."

On our hike up to the holding area the ME filled me in on recent developments. Foremost among them, the FBI had received an anonymous tip of an on-board bomb.

"Good citizen was kind enough to share this information with CNN. The media are slathering like hounds with a brisket."

"Forty-two dead students is going to make this a Pulitzer event."

"There's the other bad news. Forty-two may be a low number. Turns out more than fifty booked through UGA."

"Have you seen the passenger list?" I could barely get the question out.

"They'll have it at the briefing."

I felt icy cold.

"Yessir," Larke went on. "We screw up on this one, the press will eat us alive."

We separated and hurried to our cars. Somewhere along the road I drove into a pocket of reception, and my phone beeped. I hit the brakes, afraid of losing the signal.

The message was barely discernible through the static.

"Dr. Brennan, this is Haley Graham, Katy's roommate. Um. I played your messages, four of them, I think. And Katy's dad. He called a couple of times. Anyway, then I heard about the crash, and" – Rattling – *"well, here's the thing. Katy left for the weekend, and I'm not sure where she is. I know Lija phoned a couple of times earlier this week, so*

26

I'm kinda worried that maybe Katy went to visit her. I'm sure that's stupid, but I thought I'd call and ask if you'd talked to her. Well" – More rattling. *"Anyway. I sound like a geek, but I'd feel better if I knew where Katy was. O.K. 'Bye."*

I punched the autodial for Pete's number. He still had not spoken to our daughter. I dialed again. Lija still did not answer her phone.

The cold fear spread through my chest and curled around my breastbone.

A pickup honked me out of the way.

I continued down the mountain, craving but dreading the upcoming meeting, certain of my first request.

3

One of DMORT's first duties in a mass disaster is the establishment of an incident morgue as close to the scene as possible. Favored sites include coroner and medical examiner offices, hospitals, mortuaries, funeral homes, hangars, warehouses, and National Guard armories.

When I arrived at the Alarka Fire Department, chosen to receive the bodies from Air TransSouth 228, the front lot was already packed, and a score of cars waited at the entrance. I got in line and crept forward, drumming my fingers and looking around.

The back lot had been set aside for the refrigerated trucks that would transport victims. I watched a pair of middle-aged women drape the fence with opaque sheeting in anticipation of photographers, both professional and amateur, who would arrive to violate the privacy of the dead. A breeze twisted and snapped the plastic as they struggled to secure it to the chain linking.

I finally reached the guard, showed ID, and was allowed to park. Inside, dozens of workers were setting up tables, portable X-ray units and developers, computers, generators, and hot water heaters. Bathrooms were being scrubbed and sanitized, and a staff break room and changing areas were being constructed. A conference room had been created in one rear corner. A computer center and the X-ray station were going up in another.

The briefing was in progress when I entered. People lined the makeshift walls and sat around portable tables pushed together in the center of the "room." Fluorescent lights hung by wires from the ceiling, casting a blue tint on tense, pale faces. I slipped to the back and took a seat.

The NTSB investigator in charge, Magnus Jackson, was finishing an Incident Command System overview. The IIC, as Jackson was called, was lean and hard as a Dobermann pinscher, with skin almost as dark. He wore oval wire-rimmed glasses; his graying hair was cropped close to his head.

Jackson was describing the NTSB "go team" systems. One by one he introduced those heading the investigative groups under his command: structures, systems, power plants, human performance, fire and explosion, meteorology, radar data, event recorders, and witness statements. Investigators, each in a cap and shirt marked *NTSB* in bold yellow letters, rose or waved as Jackson ran down the roster.

Though I knew these men and women would determine why Air TransSouth 228 fell from the sky, the hollow feeling in my chest would not go away, making it hard to concentrate on anything but the passenger list.

A question snapped me back.

"Have the CVR and FDR been located?"

"Not yet."

The cockpit voice recorder captures radio transmissions and sounds in the cockpit, including the pilots' voices and engine noise. The flight data recorder monitors flight operating conditions, such as altitude, airspeed, and heading. Each would play an important role in determining probable cause.

When Jackson finished, an NTSB family affairs specialist discussed the Federal Family Assistance Plan for Aviation Disasters. He explained that the NTSB would serve as liaison between Air TransSouth and the victims' families. A family assistance center was being established at the Sleep Inn in Bryson City to serve as the collecting point for antemortem identification information, facts that family members would provide to help identify remains as those of a son or daughter. Despite myself, I shivered.

Charles Hanover stood next. He looked strikingly ordinary, like a pharmacist and member of the Elks rather than the CEO of a regional airline. His face was ashen and his hands trembled. A tic pulled his left eye, another the corner of his mouth, and one side of his face jumped when the two fired simultaneously. There was something benign and sad about the man, and I wondered how Crowe could have found him offensive.

Hanover reported that Air TransSouth had set up a toll-free number to handle public inquiries. Phones were being installed in the family assistance center, and personnel had been appointed to meet regularly with family members who were present, and to maintain contact with those who were not. Arrangements had been made for mental health and spiritual support.

My agitation grew as the briefing dragged on. I'd heard it all before, and I wanted to see that list.

30

A representative of the Federal Emergency Management Agency discussed communications. NTSB headquarters, the command center at the crash site, and the incident morgue were now linked, and FEMA would assist the NTSB in the dissemination of public information.

Earl Bliss spoke about DMORT. He was a tall, angular man with thinning brown hair slicked back and severely parted. As a high school student, Earl had taken a part-time job picking up bodies on weekends. Within ten years, he'd purchased his own funeral home. Named Early because of his premature arrival into the world, Earl had lived his entire forty-nine years in Nashville, Tennessee. When not deployed on mass fatality incidents, he favored string ties and played banjo in a country-and-western band.

Earl reminded the representatives of the other agencies that each DMORT team was composed of private citizens with particular expertise, including pathologists, anthropologists, dentists, fingerprint specialists, funeral directors, medical records technicians and transcribers, X-ray technicians, mental health specialists, and security, administrative, and support personnel.

One of the ten regional DMORT teams was activated at the request of local officials for natural disasters, aircraft and other transportation accidents, fires, bombings, terrorist attacks, and incidents of mass murder/suicide. Earl mentioned recent deployments. The bombing of the Murrah Federal Building, Oklahoma City, 1995. The Amtrak derailment, Bourbonnais, Illinois, 1999. Commuter aircraft accidents, Quincy, Illinois, 1996, and Monroe, Michigan, 1997. Korean Air Flight 801, Guam, 1997; Egypt Air Flight 990,

31

Rhode Island, 1999; and Alaska Airlines Flight 261, California, 2000.

I listened as Earl described the modular design of the incident morgue, and explained how remains would move through it. All victims and personal effects would be tagged, coded, photographed, and X-rayed in the remains identification section. Disaster victim packets, DVPs, would be created, and human bodies, body parts, and tissue would be sent on to the post-mortem data collection section for autopsy, including anthropological, dental, and fingerprint examination.

All post-mortem findings would be computerized in the identification section. Records provided by families would also be entered there, and antemortem and post-mortem information would be compared. Following analysis, remains would be sent to a holding area to await release.

Larke Tyrell was the last to take the floor. The medical examiner thanked Earl, drew a deep breath, and surveyed the room.

"Ladies and gentlemen, we've got a lot of grieving families out there searching for peace of mind. Magnus and his boys are going to help them by figuring out what knocked this plane out of the sky. We'll contribute to that process, but our main job here will be victim identification. Having something to bury speeds the healing, and we're going to try our damnedest to send a casket home to each and every family."

I remembered my hike through the woods, and knew what many of those coffins would hold. In the coming weeks DMORT, local, and state personnel would go to extraordinary lengths to identify every scrap of tissue associated with the crash. Fingerprints, dental and medical records, DNA, tattoos, and family photos would be the main sources of information, and the team anthropologists would be intimately involved in the ID process. Despite our best efforts, little would be left to put in some caskets. A severed limb. A charred molar crown. A cranial fragment. In many cases, what went home would weigh only grams.

"Once site processing is complete, all remains will be brought here from the temporary morgue," Larke continued. "We expect transport to start in the next few hours. That's when the real work begins for us. You all know your jobs, so I've got just a few reminders, then I'll shut up."

"That'll be a first."

Mild laughter.

"Don't separate any personal effects from any set of remains until they're fully photographed and written up."

My mind slid to Raggedy Ann.

"Not every set of remains will go through every stage of processing. The folks doing intake will decide what goes where. But if a station is skipped, indicate that clearly in the disaster victim packet. I don't want to be guessing later if dental wasn't done because there weren't any teeth, or because that station got overlooked. Put something on every sheet in the packet. And be sure that information stays with the body. We want full documentation on every ID.

"One more thing. As I'm sure you've heard, the FBI received a call about an explosive device. Be alert for blast effects. Check X rays for bomb parts and shrapnel. Examine lungs and eardrums for pressure damage. Look for peppering and flash burns on the skin. You know the drill."

Larke paused and looked around the room.

"Some of you are first-timers, others have done this before. I don't have to tell any of you how hard the next few weeks are going to be. Take breaks. No one works more than twelve hours per day. If you feel over-whelmed, talk to a counselor. There's no weakness in that. These folks are here for your benefit. Use them."

Larke clipped his pen to the legal pad he was holding.

"Guess that about does it, except for thanking my staff and Earl's DMORT folks for getting here so quickly. As for the rest of you, clear out of my morgue."

As the room emptied, I crossed to Larke, determined to ask about the passenger list. Magnus Jackson arrived at the same moment and nodded a greeting. I'd met the IIC while working a commuter crash some years back, and knew he was not one for trading pleasantries.

"Howdy, Tempe," Larke said to me, then turned to Jackson.

"I see you've brought a full team."

"There's going to be a lot of pressure on this one. We'll have close to fifty on site by tomorrow."

I knew that only superficial examination of the wreckage would be done in situ. Once photographed and recorded, the plane's parts would be removed and taken to a permanent location for reassembly and analysis.

"Anything else on the bomb?" Larke asked.

"Hell, it's probably a crank, but the media already has this thing wrapped up slicker than snail spit. CNN's calling him the Blue Ridge Bomber, geography be damned. ABC floated the Soccer Bomber, but it just doesn't have the alliterative ring."

"The FBI's coming on board?" Larke asked.

"They're here, pawing at the fence, so it may not be long."

I broke in, unable to wait another moment.

"Do we have a passenger list?"

The ME slid a printout from his pad and handed it to me.

I experienced a kind of fear I'd rarely felt in my life.

Please, God.

The word receded as I raced through the names. Anderson. Beacham. Bertrand. Caccioli. Daignault. Larke spoke, but his words didn't penetrate.

A lifetime later, I unclamped my teeth from my lower lip and resumed breathing.

Neither Katy Brennan Petersons nor Lija Feldman was on the list.

I closed my eyes and inhaled deeply.

I opened them to questioning looks. Offering no explanation, I returned the printout, the profound relief already blunted by a sense of guilt. My daughter was alive, but the children of others lay dead on a mountain. I wanted to work.

"What would you like me to do?" I asked Larke.

"Earl has the morgue under control. Go work recovery. But once transport starts I'll need you here."

Back at the site, I went directly to a decontamination trailer and donned masks, gloves, and jumpsuit. Looking more like a spaceman than an anthropologist, I nodded to the guard, circled the barricade, and crossed to the temporary morgue for an update.

The exact location of every flagged item was being entered into a CAD-type program using technology called Total Station. The position of airplane parts, personal effects, and human remains would later be plotted on to virtual grids and printed out as hard copy. Since the technique was far quicker and less labor-intensive than the traditional system of mapping with strings and grids, the removal of remains had already begun. I headed out across the debris field.

The sun was arcing toward the tree line, and delicate shadows spiderwebbed the carnage. Klieg lights had been set up, and the smell of putrefaction had strengthened. Otherwise, little had changed in the time I'd been gone.

For the next three hours I assisted my colleagues in tagging, photographing, and packaging what was left of the passengers of Air TransSouth 228. Complete corpses, limbs, and torsos went into large body bags, fragments into small ones. The bags were then hauled uphill and placed on racks in refrigerated trailers.

The temperature was warm, and I perspired inside my suit and gloves. Flies swarmed, attracted by the rotting flesh. Several times I had to fight nausea as I scraped up entrails or brain tissue. Eventually, my nose and mind numbed. I didn't notice when the sky went red and the lights clicked on.

Then I came to the girl. She lay face up, legs bent backward in the middle of her shins. Her features had been gnawed, and the exposed bone glowed crimson in the sunset.

I straightened, wrapped my arms around my middle, and drew several steadying breaths. In, out. In, out.

Dear God. Wasn't a thirty-thousand-foot plunge enough? Must creatures degrade what remained?

These children had danced, played tennis, ridden the roller coaster, checked their e-mail. They represented the dreams of their parents. But no longer. Now they would be framed photos resting on closed caskets.

I felt a hand on my shoulder.

"Time for a break, Tempe."

Earl Bliss's eyes peered at me from the slit between his mask and cap.

"I'm fine."

"Take a break. That's an order."

"O.K."

"At least an hour."

Halfway to the NTSB command center I stopped, dreading the chaos I knew I'd find. I needed serenity. Life. Birds singing, squirrels chasing, and air that was free of the smell of death. I reversed direction and walked toward the woods.

Skirting the edge of the debris field, I spotted a break in the trees and remembered that Larke and the lieutenant governor had appeared at that point, coming from their helicopter. Up close, I could see the route they had probably taken. Perhaps a trail or streambed at one time, it was now a meandering, treeless passage littered with rocks and bordered by scrub. Stripping off mask and gloves, I headed into the forest.

As I moved deeper into the trees the organized hubbub around the wreckage receded, and forest sounds took over. Thirty yards in, I climbed on to a fallen sourwood, drew my feet to my bum, and gazed up at the sky. Yellow and rose now streaked the red as nightfall crawled toward the horizon. It would soon be dark. I couldn't stay long.

I let my brain cells pick their topic.

The girl with the ravaged face.

No. New category.

The cells chose living people.

Katy. My daughter was over twenty now, moving off on a life of her own. It was what I wanted, of course, but the severing of ties was hard. The child Katy had passed through my life and disappeared. I was now meeting the young woman Katy, and liking her very much.

But where is she? the cells asked.

Next.

Pete. We were better friends separated than we'd ever been married. On occasion, he actually talked to me and listened to me. Should I ask for a divorce and move on, or roll with the status quo?

The cells had no answer.

Andrew Ryan. I'd been thinking of him a lot lately. Ryan was a homicide detective with the provincial police in Montreal. Though we'd known each other for nearly a decade, it was only last year that I'd agreed to date him.

Date. I had my usual cringe reaction. There had to be a better term for singles over forty.

The cells had no suggestion.

Nomenclature aside, Ryan and I had never pulled it off. Before our first official social outing, he had gone undercover, and I hadn't seen him in months. At times like this, I missed him intensely.

I heard rustling in the underbrush and held my breath to listen. The woods were quiet. Seconds later I heard it again, this time on my other side. The movement sounded too large for a rabbit or squirrel.

The brain cells sounded a low-level alarm.

Thinking perhaps Earl had followed me, I stood up and looked around. I was alone.

For a full minute nothing moved, then the rhododendron to my right jiggled, and I heard a low growl. I whirled but saw only leaves and bushes. Eyes probing into the shrubbery, I slipped off the log and planted my feet.

Moments later there was another growl, followed by a high-pitched keening.

The cells called in the limbic guys, and adrenaline shot to every part of my body.

Slowly, I squatted and reached for a rock. Hearing movement behind me, I pivoted in that direction.

My eyes met other eyes, black and gleaming. Lips curled back over teeth pale and slick in the deepening twilight. Between the teeth, something horrifyingly familiar.

A foot.

The cells struggled for meaning.

The teeth were embedded in a human foot.

The cells linked to recently stored memories. A mangled face. A deputy's comment.

Oh, God! A wolf? I was unarmed. What to do? Threaten?

The animal stared at me, its body feral and emaciated.

Run?

No. I had to get the foot. It belonged to a person. A person with family and friends. I wouldn't abandon it to scavengers.

Then a second wolf emerged and positioned itself behind the first, teeth bared, saliva darkening the fur around its mouth. It snarled and the lips quivered. Slowly, I stood and raised the rock.

"Back!"

Both animals halted, and the first wolf dropped the foot. Sniffing the air, the ground, the air again, it lowered its head, raised its tail, took a step in my direction, then sidled away a few feet and stopped, motionless and watching. The other wolf followed. Were they uncertain or did they have a plan? I started to retreat, heard a snap, and turned to see three more animals at my back. They appeared to be slowly circling.

"Stop!"

I screamed and threw the rock, catching the closest animal near its eye. He yelped and twisted, scampering backward. The others froze for a moment, then resumed circling.

Placing my back to the fallen tree, I twisted a branch from side to side, trying to detach it.

The circle was getting smaller. I could hear their panting, smell their bodies. One of the group took a step inside the circle, then another flicking its tail up, down. It stood staring, soundless.

The branch broke, and at the sound the wolf jumped back, then stood again and stared.

Grasping my branch like a baseball bat, I screamed, "Beat it, you scavengers. Get out of here," and lunged at the lead wolf, swinging my club.

The wolf easily jumped out of the way, retreated a few feet, then resumed circling and snarling. As I was readying my lungs for the loudest yell that had ever escaped them, someone beat me to it.

"Scram, you goddamn fur balls. Yo! Haul ass!"

Then one missile followed by another landed near the lead wolf.

The wolf scented, snarled, then spun and loped off into the underbrush. The others hesitated, then moved off behind him.

Hands trembling, I dropped the branch and braced myself against the fallen sourwood.

A figure in Tyvek and mask ran toward me and heaved another rock in the direction of the disappearing wolves. Then a hand went up and removed the mask. Though barely visible in the twilight gloom, I recognized the face.

But it couldn't be. This was too improbable to be real.

40

4

"Nice swing. You looked like Sammy Sosa."

"The goddamn thing was getting ready to go for my throat!" It was almost a shriek.

"They don't attack live people. They were only trying to drive you away from their dinner."

"Did one of them explain that to you personally?"

Andrew Ryan plucked a leaf from my hair.

But Ryan was underground somewhere in Quebec.

"What in hell are you doing here?" Slightly calmer.

"Is that a thank-you, Goldilocks? Maybe Riding Hood would be more appropriate, given the circumstances."

"Thanks," I mumbled, brushing bangs off my forehead. Though I *was* grateful for the intervention, I preferred not to cast it as a rescue.

"Nice do."

He reached for my hair again, and I parried the move. As usual when our paths crossed, I was not looking my best.

"I'm scraping up quarts of brain matter, and a wolf

pack was just sizing me up as a candidate for joining the dismembered, and you find fault with my styling gel?"

"Is there a reason you're out here by yourself?"

His paternalism irritated me. "Is there a reason you're here at all?"

The lines in his face tensed. Such nice lines, each placed exactly where it ought to be.

"Bertrand was on the plane."

"Jean?"

The passenger list. Bertrand. It was a common name, so I'd never thought of Ryan's partner.

"He was escorting a prisoner." Ryan drew air through his nostrils, exhaled. "They were connecting to an Air Canada flight at Dulles."

"Oh, God. Oh, my God. I am so sorry."

We stood mute, unsure what to say, until the silence was pierced by an eerie, quavering sound, followed by a series of high-pitched yips. Were our friends challenging us to a rematch?

"We'd better get back," Ryan said.

"No argument here."

Ryan unzipped his jumpsuit, took a flashlight from his belt, flicked the switch, and raised it to shoulder level.

"After you."

"Wait. Let me have the light."

He handed it to me, and I crossed to the spot where I'd first seen the wolf.

Ryan followed.

"If you're hunting mushrooms, this is not a good time."

He stopped when he saw what lay on the ground.

The foot looked macabre in the yellow beam, its flesh ending in a crushed mass just above the ankle. Shadows danced in and out of the grooves and pits left by carnivore teeth.

Pulling fresh gloves from my pocket, I snapped one on and picked up the foot. Then I marked the spot with another glove and secured it with a rock.

"Shouldn't it be mapped?"

"We can't tell where the pack found this. Besides, if we leave the thing here it's puppy chow."

"You're the boss."

I followed Ryan out of the woods, holding the foot as far from my body as possible.

When we got back to the command center, Ryan went into the NTSB trailer and I took my find to the temporary morgue. After hearing my explanation of its provenance and why I'd collected it, the intake team assigned it a number, bagged it, and sent it to one of the refrigerated trucks. I rejoined the recovery operation.

Two hours later Earl found me and delivered a note: *Report to the morgue. 7 A.M. LT.*

He produced an address and told me I was done for the day. No amount of argument would change his mind.

I went to decontamination, showered under scalding water for as long as I could take it, and put on fresh clothes. I left the trailer with Christmas-bow skin, but at least the smell was gone.

Clomping down the steps, as exhausted as I'd ever been, I noticed Ryan leaning against a bubble-top cruiser ten feet up the access road, talking with Lucy Crowe.

"You look beat," said Crowe when I drew near.

"I'm good," I said. "Earl pulled me in."

"How's it going out there?"

"It's going."

I felt like a midget talking to them. Both Ryan and Crowe topped six feet, though she had him beat in shoulder breadth. He looked like a point guard; she was a power forward.

Not in a mood to chat, I asked Crowe for directions and excused myself.

"Hold it, Brennan."

I allowed Ryan to catch up, then gave him a "don't bring it up" look. I did not want to discuss wolves.

As we walked, I thought of Jean Bertrand with his designer jackets, matching ties, and earnest face. Bertrand always gave the impression he was trying too hard, listening too closely, afraid to miss an important clue or nuance. I could hear him, flipping from French to English in his own personal brand of Franglais, laughing at his own jokes, unaware that others weren't.

I remembered the first time I'd met Bertrand. Shortly after arriving in Montreal, I'd gone to a Christmas party hosted by the SQ homicide unit. Bertrand was there, mildly drunk, and newly partnered with Andrew Ryan. The hotshot detective was already something of a legend, and Bertrand's veneration flowed undisguised. By evening's end the hero worship had grown embarrassing for everyone. Especially Ryan.

"How old was he?" I voiced the question without thinking.

"Thirty-seven." Ryan was right there in the middle of my thoughts.

"Jesus."

We reached the county road and headed uphill.

"Whom was he escorting?"

"A guy named Rémi Petricelli, known to his friends as Pepper."

I knew the name. Petricelli was a bigwig in the Quebec Hells Angels, reputed to have ties to organized crime. The Canadian and American governments had been investigating him for years.

"What was Pepper doing in Georgia?"

"About two months ago a small-time trafficker named Jacques Fontana ended up charcoal in a Sabaru Outback. When every road led to his door, Pepper decided to sample the hospitality of his brothers in Dixie. Long story short, Pepper was spotted in a bar in Atlanta, the locals nailed him, and last week Georgia agreed to extradite. Bertrand was hauling his ass back to Quebec."

We'd arrived at my car. Across at the overlook, a spotlighted man held a mike while an assistant powdered his face.

"Which brings more players to the table," Ryan went on, his voice leaden.

"Meaning?"

"Pepper had juice. If he'd decided to deal, a lot of his friends would be in deep-dish shit."

"I'm not following."

"Some powerful people probably wanted Pepper dead."

"Enough to kill eighty-seven other people?"

"Without a hitch in their breathing."

"But that plane was full of kids."

"These guys aren't the Jesuits."

I was too shocked to respond.

Seeing my face, Ryan switched tracks. "Hungry?"

"I need to sleep."

"You need to eat."

"I'll stop for a burger," I lied.

Ryan stepped back. I unlocked my door and drove off, too tired and heartsick to say good night.

*

Since every room in the area had been grabbed by the press and NTSB, I was booked into a small B&B on the outskirts of Bryson City. It took several wrong turns and two inquiries to find it.

True to its name, High Ridge House sat atop a summit at the end of a long narrow lane. It was a two-story white farmhouse with intricate woodwork on the doors and windows, and on the beams, banisters, and railings of a wide veranda wrapping around the front and sides. In the porch light I could see wooden rockers, wicker planters, ferns. Very Victorian.

I added my car to a half dozen others in a postage-stamp lot to the left of the house, and followed a flagstone path flanked by metal lawn chairs. Bells jangled as I opened the front door. Inside, the house smelled of wood polish, Pine-Sol, and simmering lamb.

Irish stew is perhaps my favorite dish. As usual, it brought Gran to mind. Twice in two days? Maybe the old girl was looking down.

In moments a woman appeared. She was middle-aged, about five feet tall, with no makeup and thick gray hair pulled into an odd sausage roll on the top of her head. She wore a long denim skirt and a red sweatshirt with *Praise the Lord* scrolled across her chest.

Before I could speak, the woman embraced me. Surprised, I stood angled down with hands out, trying not to strike her with my overnighter or laptop.

After a decade the woman stepped back and gazed at me with the intensity of a player receiving serve at Wimbledon.

"Dr. Brennan."

"Tempe."

46

"It's the Lord's work you're doing for these poor dead children."

I nodded.

"Precious in the sight of the Lord is the death of his saints. He tells us that in the Book of Psalms."

Oh, boy.

"I'm Ruby McCready, and I'm honored to have you at High Ridge House. I intend to look after each and every one of you."

I wondered who else was quartered there, but said nothing. I would find out soon enough.

"Thank you, Ruby."

"Let me take that." She reached for my bag. "I'll show you to your room."

My hostess led me past a parlor and dining room, up a carved wooden staircase, and down a corridor with closed doors on either side, each bearing a small hand-painted plaque. We made a ninety-degree turn at the far end of the hall and stopped in front of a single door. Its nameplate said *Magnolia*.

"Since you're the only lady, I put you in Magnolia." Though we were alone, Ruby's voice had become a whisper, her tone conspiratorial. "It's the only one with its own WC. I reckoned you'd appreciate the privacy."

WC? Where in the world did they still refer to bathrooms as water closets?

Ruby followed me in, placed my satchel on the bed, and began fluffing pillows and lowering shades like a bellman at the Ritz.

The fabric and wallpaper explained the floral appellation. The window was draped, the tables skirted, and ruffles adorned every edge in the room. The maple rocker and bed were stacked with pillows, and a million figurines filled a glass-fronted cabinet. On top sat

47

ceramic renderings of Little Orphan Annie and her dog, Sandy, Shirley Temple dressed as Heidi, and a collie I assumed to be Lassie.

My taste in home furnishings tends towards the simple. Though I have never cared for the starkness of modern, give me Shaker or Hepplewhite and I am happy. Surround me with clutter and I start to get itchy.

"It's lovely," I said.

"I'll leave you to yourself now. Dinner's at six, so you missed that, but I left stew to simmerin'. Would you like a bowl?"

"No, thank you. I'm going to turn in."

"Have you eaten dinner?"

"I'm not very hungr—"

"Look at you, you're thin as the broth at a homeless shelter. You can't go with nothin' on your stomach."

Why was everyone so concerned with my diet?

"I'll bring up a tray."

"Thank you, Ruby."

"I don't need thankin'. One last thing. We've got no locks here at High Ridge House, so you come and go as you like."

Though I'd showered at the site, I unpacked my few things and took a long, hot bath. Like rape victims, those who clean up after mass fatalities often overbathe, driven by a need to purge mind and body.

I came out of the bathroom to stew, brown bread, and a mug of milk. My cell phone rang as I was poking at a turnip. Fearing the messaging service would kick in, I lunged for my purse, dumped its contents on to the bed, and fished through hair spray, wallet, passport, organizer, sunglasses, keys, and makeup. I finally found the phone and clicked on, praying the caller was Katy.

It was. My daughter's voice triggered such emotion in

48

me, I had to struggle to keep my voice steady.

Though evasive about her whereabouts, she sounded happy and healthy. I gave her the number at High Ridge house. She told me she was with a friend and would return to Charlottesville on Sunday night. I didn't request, nor did she offer, the gender specifics of her pal.

The soap and water, combined with the long-awaited call from my daughter, had done the trick. Almost giddy with relief, I was suddenly famished. I devoured Ruby's stew, set my travel alarm, and fell into bed.

Maybe the House of Chintz wouldn't be so bad.

The next morning I rose at six, put on clean khakis, brushed my teeth, dabbed on blush, and drew my hair up under a Charlotte Hornets' cap. Good enough. I headed downstairs, intending to ask Ruby about laundry arrangements.

Andrew Ryan occupied a bench at a long pine table in the dining room. I took a chair opposite, returned Ruby's cheery "Good morning," and waited while she poured coffee. When the kitchen door swung closed behind her, I spoke.

"What are you doing here?"

"Is that all you ever say to me?"

I waited.

"The sheriff recommended this place."

"Above all others."

"It's nice," he said, gesturing around the room. "Loving." He raised his mug to a message above our heads: *Jesus Is Love* had been burned into knotty pine and varnished for posterity.

"How did you know I was here?"

"Cynicism causes wrinkles."

"It doesn't. Who told you?"

"Crowe."

"What's wrong with the Comfort Inn?"

"Full."

"Who else is here?"

"There are a couple of NTSB boys upstairs and a special agent from the FBI. What makes them special?"

I ignored that.

"I'm looking forward to guy-bonding in the bathroom. Two others are on the main floor, and I hear there are some journalists squeezed into a bonus room in the basement."

"How did you get a room here?"

The Viking blues went little-boy innocent. "Must have been lucky timing. Or maybe Crowe has pull."

"Don't even think about using my bathroom."

"Cynicism."

Ruby arrived with ham, eggs, fried potatoes, and toast. Though my normal routine is cereal and coffee, I dug in like a recruit at boot camp.

Ryan and I ate in silence while I did some mental sorting. His presence annoyed me, but why? Was it his supreme self-confidence? His custodial attitude? His invasion of my turf? The fact that less than a year ago he'd prioritized the job over me and disappeared from my life? Or the fact that he'd reappeared exactly when I'd needed help?

As I reached for toast I realized he'd said nothing about his stint undercover. Fair enough. Let him bring it up.

"Jam, please."

He passed it.

Ryan *had* gotten me out of a nasty spot.

I spread blackberry preserves thicker than lava.

The wolvers weren't Ryan's fault. Nor was the crash.

50

Ruby poured refills.

And the man *has* just lost his partner, for God's sake. Compassion overrode irritation.

"Thanks for your help with the wolf thing."

"They weren't wolves."

"What?" Irritation boomeranged back.

"They weren't wolves."

"I suppose it was a pack of cocker spaniels."

"There are no wolves in North Carolina."

"Crowe's deputy talked about wolves."

"The guy probably wouldn't know a wombat from a caribou."

"Wolves have been reintroduced into North Carolina." I was sure I'd read that somewhere.

"Those are red wolves and they're on a reserve down east, not in the mountains."

"I suppose you're an expert on North Carolina wildlife."

"How did they hold their tails?"

"What?"

"Did the animals hold their tails up or down?"

I had to think.

"Down."

"A wolf holds its tail straight out. A coyote keeps its tail low, raises it to horizontal when threatening."

I pictured the animal sniffing, then raising its tail and locking me into its gaze.

"You're telling me those were coyotes?"

"Or wild dogs."

"There are coyotes in Appalachia?"

"There are coyotes all over North America."

"So what?" I made a mental vow to check.

"So nothing. I just thought you might want to know."

"It was still terrifying."

51

"Damn right. But it's not the worst thing you've ever been through."

Ryan was right. Though frightening, the coyote incident was not my worst experience. But the days that followed were contenders. I spent every waking moment up to my elbows in shattered flesh, separating commingled remains and reassociating body parts. As part of a team of pathologists, dentists, and other anthropologists, I determined age, sex, race, and height, analyzed X rays, compared antemortem and postmortem skeletal features, and interpreted injury patterns. It was a gruesome task, made even grimmer by the youth of most of those being analyzed.

For many, the stress was too much. Some hung in, running on the rim until tremors, tears, or unbearable nightmares finally won out. These were the ones who would require extensive counseling. Others simply packed up and slipped back home.

But for most, the mind adjusted and the unthinkable became the ordinary. We mentally detached and did what needed doing. Each night as I lay in bed, lonely and exhausted, I was comforted by the day's progress. I thought of the families, and assured myself that the system was working. We would grant them closure of sorts.

Then specimen number 387 arrived at my station.

5

I'd forgotten the foot until a body tracker brought it to me.

Ryan and I had rarely crossed paths since our first breakfast. I'd been up and gone each day before seven, returning to High Ridge House, long after dark to shower and collapse into bed. We'd exchanged only "Good morning" or "Have a good one," and we'd yet to discuss his time undercover or his role in the crash investigation. Because a Quebec law officer had been on the plane, the Canadian government had asked that Ryan be involved. All I knew was that the request had been granted.

Blocking thoughts of Ryan and coyotes, I emptied the body bag on to my table. In recent days I'd processed dozens of severed limbs and appendages, and the foot no longer seemed macabre. In fact, the frequency of lower leg and ankle trauma was so high it had been discussed at that morning's meeting. The pathologists and anthropologists agreed that the injury pattern was disturbing.

There is little one can say from eyeballing a foot. This

one had thickened yellow nails, a large bunion, and lateral displacement of the big toe, indicating an older adult. The size suggested female gender. Though the skin was the color of toast, I knew this meant nothing since even short-term exposure can bleach or darken flesh.

I popped the X rays on to a light box. Unlike many of the films I'd viewed, these revealed no foreign objects embedded in the foot. I noted that on a form in the disaster victim packet.

The cortical bone was thin, and I could see remodeling at many of the phalangeal joints.

O.K. The lady was old. Arthritis and bone loss fit with the bunion.

Then I got my first surprise. The X ray showed tiny white clouds floating among the toe bones, and scooped-out lesions at the margins of the first and second metatarso-phalangeal joints. I recognized the symptoms immediately.

Gout results from inadequate uric acid metabolism, leading to the deposition of urate crystals, particularly in the hands and feet. Nodules form adjacent to joints, and, in chronic cases, the underlying bone is eroded. The condition is not life-threatening, but those affected experience intermittent periods of pain and swelling. Gout is relatively common, with 90 percent of all cases occurring in men.

So why was I seeing it in a female?

I returned to the table, picked up a scalpel, and got my second surprise.

Though refrigeration can cause drying and shrinkage, the foot looked different from the remains I'd been seeing. Even in the charred bodies and body parts I'd examined, the deep tissue remained firm and red. But the flesh inside the foot was soupy and discolored, as though something had accelerated its rate of decomposition. I made a note, planning to seek other opinions.

Using my scalpel, I teased back muscle and tendon until I could position my callipers directly against the largest bone, the calcaneus. I measured its length and breadth, then the length of a metatarsal, and jotted the figures into a form in the disaster victim packet, and on to a page in a spiral pad.

Stripping off my gloves, I washed, then took the tablet to my laptop in the staff lounge. I called up a program called Fordisc 2.0, entered the data, and asked for a discriminant function analysis using the two calcaneal measurements.

The foot classified as that of a black male, though the typicality and posterior probabilities indicated the results were meaningless. I tried a male-female comparison, independent of ancestry, and the program again placed the foot in the male range.

O.K. Jockey shorts fit with gout. Maybe the guy was small. Atypical size could explain the weakness of the racial classification.

Returning for the packet, I crossed to the identification section, where a dozen computers sat on tables, and bundled wires snaked across the floor. A records specialist worked at each terminal, entering data obtained from the family assistance center and information provided by the forensic specialists, including fingerprint, X ray, anthropology, pathology, and dental details.

I spotted a familiar figure, half-moon glasses on the end of her nose, upper teeth nibbling her lower lip. Primrose Hobbs had been an ER nurse for over thirty years when she switched from defibrillators to data sets and moved to the medical records department at Presbyterian Hospital in Charlotte. But she hadn't severed herself completely from the world of traumatic injury. When I joined DMORT, Primrose was already a seasoned member of the Region Four Team. Past sixty, she was patient, efficient, and shocked by absolutely nothing.

"Can we run one?" I asked, dragging a folding chair next to hers.

"Hang on, baby." Primrose continued to type, her face illuminated by the screen's glow. Then she closed a folder and turned to me.

"What have you got?"

"A left foot. Definitely old. Probably male. Possibly black."

"Let's see who needs a foot."

DMORT relies on a software package called VIP, which tracks the progress of remains, stores all data, and facilitates the comparison of antemortem and postmortem information. The program handles more than 750 unique identifiers for each victim, and stores digital records such as photographs and radiographs. For each positive identification, VIP creates a document containing all parameters used.

Primrose worked the keys and a postmortem grid appeared. The first column showed a list of case numbers. She moved sideways through the grid to a column headed "Body Parts Not Recovered" and scrolled down. To date, four bodies had been logged without a left foot. Primrose moved through the grid, highlighting each.

Number 19 was a white male with an estimated age of thirty. Number 38 was a white female, with an estimated age of twenty. Number 41 was an African-American female with an estimated age of twenty-five. Number 52 was a male lower torso, African American, with an estimated age of forty-five.

"It could be fifty-two," I said.

Primrose scrolled to the height and weight columns. The gentleman tagged as number 52 was estimated to have stood six feet two inches and weighed two hundred and fifty pounds.

"No way," I corrected myself. "This is not a sumo tootsie."

Primrose leaned back and removed her glasses. Frizzy gray hairs spiraled out at her forehead and temples, escapees from the bun atop her head.

"This event is more dental than DNA, but I've logged quite a few isolated body parts." She let the glasses drop on to a chain around her neck. "So far we've had few matches. That will improve as more bodies flow through, but you may have to wait for DNA."

"I know. I hoped we might get lucky."

"You're sure it's male?"

I explained the discriminant function analysis.

"So the program takes your unknown and compares it to groups for whom measurements have been recorded."

"Exactly."

"And this foot fell in with the boys."

"Yes."

"Maybe the computer got it wrong."

"That's very possible since I'm not sure about the race."

"That matters?"

"Sure. Some populations are smaller than others. Look at the Mbuti."

She raised gray eyebrows.

"The pygmies of the Ituri rain forest," I explained.

"We've got no pygmies here, sugar."

"No. But there might have been Asians on board. Some Asian populations are smaller than Westerners, so they'd tend to have smaller feet."

57

"Not like my dainty size tens." She lifted a booted foot and laughed.

"What do I feel certain about is the age. This person was over fifty. Quite a bit over, I think."

"Let's check the passenger list."

She replaced the glasses, hit keys, and an antemortem grid appeared on the screen. This spread sheet was similar to the postmortem grid except that most of its cells contained information. There were columns for first name, last name, date of birth, blood type, sex, race, weight, height, and myriad other variables. Primrose clicked to the age column and asked the program to sort by that criterion.

Air TransSouth 228 had carried only six passengers over the age of fifty.

"So young for the good Lord to be callin' 'em home."

"Yeah," I said, staring at the screen.

We were silent a moment, then Primrose moved the cursor and we both leaned in.

Four males. Two females. All white.

"Let's sort by race."

The antemortem grid showed sixty-eight whites, ten African Americans, two Hispanics, and two Asians among the passengers. The entire cabin crew and both pilots were white. None of the blacks was over forty. Both Asians were in their early twenties, probably students. Masako Takaguchi had been lucky. She'd died in one piece and was already identified.

"I guess I'd better try another approach. For now you can enter an age estimate of fifty plus. And the victim had gout."

"My ex has gout. Only human thing about that man." Another laugh, straight from the belly.

"Mmm. Could I ask one other favor?"

"Sure, baby."

"Check Jean Bertrand."

She found the row and moved the cursor to the status column.

To date, Bertrand's body had not been identified.

"I'll be back when I know more on this one," I said, collecting the packet for number 387.

Returning to the foot, I removed and tagged a small plug of bone. If a reference sample could be found, an old gallstone, a Pap smear, hair or dandruff from a brush or comb, DNA might prove useful in establishing identity. If not, DNA testing could determine gender, or could link the foot to other body parts, and a tattoo or dental crown might send the victim home.

As I sealed the specimen bag and made notes in the file, something bothered me. Was the computer in error? Could I have been right in my initial impression that the foot belonged to a woman? Very possible. It happened all the time. But what about age? I was certain these were the bones of an older person, yet no one on the plane fit that profile. Could some pathology other than gout be skewing my assessment?

And what about the advanced putrefaction?

I cut a second slice of bone from the highest intact point on the tibia, tagged and sealed it. If the foot remained unidentified, I would attempt a more precise age estimate using histological features. But microscopic analysis would have to wait. Slides were being made at the ME facility in Charlotte, and the backlog was monumental.

I rebagged the foot, returned it to the body tracker in charge of the case, and moved on, continuing with a day identical to the previous four. Hour after hour I sorted bodies and body parts, probing their most intimate details. I didn't notice when others came and went, or when daylight dimmed in the windows high above our heads.

I'd lost all track of time when I glanced up to see Ryan rounding a stack of pine caskets at the far end of the fire station. He walked to my table, his face as tense as I'd ever seen it.

"How's it going?" I asked, lowering my mask.

"It'll be a bloody decade before this is sorted out."

His eyes were dark and shadowed, his face as pale as the flesh that lay between us. I was shocked by the change. Then, realization. While my grief was for strangers, Ryan's pain was personal. He and Bertrand had partnered for almost a decade.

I wanted to say something comforting, but all I could think of was "I'm so sorry about Jean."

He nodded.

"Are you all right?" I asked gently.

His jaw muscles bulged, relaxed.

I reached across the table, wanting to take his hand, and we both looked at my bloody glove.

"Whoa, Quincy, no gestures of sympathy."

The comment broke the tension.

"I was afraid you'd pocket the scalpel," I said, snatching up the implement.

"Tyrell says you're done for the day."

"But I—"

"It's eight o'clock. You've been here thirteen hours."

I looked at my watch.

"Meet me back at the temple of love and I'll update you on the investigation."

My back and neck ached, and my eyelids felt like they'd been lined with sand. I placed both hands on my hips and arched backward.

"Or I could help you" – When I returned to vertical Ryan's eyes locked into mine and his brows flicked up and down – "relax."

"I'll be asleep before I hit the pillow."

"You've got to eat."

"Jesus, Ryan, what is this concern with my nutrition? You're worse than my mother."

At that moment I spotted Larke Tyrell waving at me. He pointed to his watch then made a slicing movement across his throat. I nodded and gave him a thumbs-up.

Telling Ryan that I'd take the briefing, and only the briefing, I zipped the remains into their pouch, made notes in the disaster victim packet, and returned everything to the body tracker. Stripping down to my street clothes, I washed and headed out.

Forty minutes later Ryan and I sat with meat loaf sandwiches in the kitchen of High Ridge House. He'd just voiced his third complaint concerning the absence of beer.

"The drunkard and the glutton shall come to poverty," I replied, pounding on a ketchup bottle.

"Says who?"

"According to Ruby, the Book of Proverbs."

"I will make it felony to drink small beer." The weather had cooled and Ryan was wearing a ski sweater, the cornflower blue a perfect match for his eyes.

"Did Ruby say that?"

"Shakespeare. *Henry VI.*"

"Your point being?"

"Like the king, Ruby is being autocratic."

"Tell me about the investigation." I took a bite of my sandwich.

"What do you want to know?"

"Have the black boxes been recovered?"

"They're orange. You have ketchup on your chin."

"Have the flight recorders been found?" I blotted my face, wondering how a man could be so attractive and so annoying at the same time.

"Yes."

"And?"

"They've been sent to the NTSB lab in Washington, but I've listened to a copy of the cockpit voice recording. Worst twenty-two minutes I've ever spent."

I waited.

"The FAA has a sterile cockpit rule below ten thousand feet, so for the first eight minutes or so the pilots are all business. After that they're more relaxed, responding to air traffic controllers, chatting about their kids, their lunch, their golf games. Suddenly there's a pop, and everything changes. They're breathing hard and shouting to each other."

He swallowed.

"In the background you hear beeps then chirps then wails. A member of the recorders group identified each sound as we listened. Autopilot disconnect. Overspeed. Altitude alert. Apparently that meant they'd managed to level off for a while. You hear all this and you picture those guys struggling to save their plane. Shit."

He swallowed again.

"Then there's this chilling whooping noise. The ground proximity warning. Then a loud crunch. Then nothing."

Somewhere in the house a door slammed, then water ran through pipes.

"You know how it is when you watch nature films? You've got no doubt that the lion is going to gut that gazelle, but you hang in anyway, then feel awful when it

62

happens. It's like that. You hear these people moving from normalcy into nightmare, knowing they're going to die and there's not a damn thing you can do about it."

"What about the flight data recorder?"

"That'll take weeks, maybe even months. The fact that the voice recorder worked as long as it did says something about break-up sequence, since power is lost to the recorders once the engines and generator go. But all they're saying now is that input ceased abruptly during a seemingly normal flight. That could indicate a midair disaster."

"An explosion?"

"Possibly."

"Bomb or mechanical failure?"

"Yes."

I gave him a withering look.

"The repair records indicate there were minor problems with the plane over the past two years. Normal parts were reworked, and some sort of switch was replaced twice. But the maintenance records group is saying it looks pretty routine."

"Any progress on the tipster?"

"The calls were made from a pay phone in Atlanta. Both CNN and the FBI have tapes, and voice analysis is being done."

Ryan swigged his lemonade, made a face, set it on the table.

"What's the word from the body teams?"

"This is strictly between us, Ryan. Anything official has to come from Tyrell."

He curled his fingers in a "go on" gesture.

"We're finding penetrations and a lot of lower leg and ankle fractures. That's not typical of ground impact."

I flashed back to the gouty foot, and again felt puzzled.

Ryan must have read my face.

"What now, buttercup?"

"Can I bounce something off you?"

"Shoot."

"This is going to sound weird."

"As opposed to your normally conventional views."

More withering eye action.

"Remember the foot we rescued from the coyotes?"

He nodded.

"It doesn't match any passenger."

"What doesn't fit?"

"Mainly age, and I feel pretty confident in my estimate. There was no one that old on the plane. Could someone have boarded without being listed?"

"I can look into it. We used to hitch rides in the military, but I suspect that would be pretty tough on a commercial flight. Airline employees sometimes ride free. It's called deadheading. But they'd be listed on the manifest."

"You were in the military?"

"Crimean War."

I ignored that.

"Could someone have given a ticket away? Or sold it?"

"You're required to show a picture ID."

"What if the ticketed passenger checks in, shows ID, then passes the ticket to someone else?"

"I'll ask."

I finished my pickle.

"Or could someone have been transporting a biological specimen? This looks muckier than the stuff I've been processing."

He looked at me sceptically. "Muckier?"

"The tissue breakdown seems more advanced."

"Isn't decay rate affected by the environment?"

64

"Of course it is."

I dabbed up ketchup and popped the last of my sandwich into my mouth.

"I think biological specimens have to be reported," Ryan said.

I recalled times I'd flown with bones, boarding with them as carry-ons. In at least one instance I'd transported tissue sealed in Tupperware so I could study saw marks left by a serial killer. I wasn't convinced.

"Maybe the coyotes got the foot someplace else," I suggested.

"Such as?"

"An old cemetery."

"Air TransSouth 228 nosed into a cemetery?"

"Not directly into one." I remembered my encounter with Simon Midkiff and his worry about his dig, and realized how absurd I must sound. Nevertheless, Ryan's skepticism irked me. "You're the expert on canids. Surely you're aware that they drag things around."

"Maybe the foot took a jolt in life that makes it look older than its actual age."

I had to admit that was possible.

"And more decomposed."

"Maybe."

I gathered napkins and utensils and carried our plates to the sink.

"Look, how 'bout we stroll Coyote Canyon tomorrow, see if anyone's pushing up daisies?"

I turned to look at him.

"Really?"

"Anything to ease your troubled mind, cupcake."

That's not how it went.

6

I spent the next morning separating flesh into four individuals. Case number 432 came from a burned segment of fuselage that lay in a valley north of the main crash site. Inside the body bag I found one relatively intact corpse missing the top of the skull and the lower arms. The bag also contained a partial head and a complete right arm with a portion of mandible embedded in the triceps muscle. Everything was congealed into a single charred mass.

I determined that the corpse was that of a black female in her early twenties who stood five feet seven at the time of death. Her X rays showed healed fractures of the right humerus and scapula. I classified number 432 as fragmented human remains, recorded my observations, and sent the body on to odontology.

The partial head, a white male in his late teens, became number 432A, and was also forwarded for dental analysis. The jaw fragment belonged to someone older than number 432A, probably a female, and went on to the dentists as number 432C. The state

66

of bone development suggested that the unrelated arm came from an adult over twenty. I calculated upper and lower limits for stature, but was unable to determine gender since all hand and arm bone measurements fell into the overlap range for males and females. I sent the arm to the fingerprint section as case number 432D.

It was twelve-fifteen when I looked at my watch. I had to hurry.

I spotted Ryan through a small window in the morgue's back door. He was sitting on the steps, one long leg outstretched, the other raised to support an elbow as he spoke into a cell phone. Opening the door, I could hear that his words were English, his tone agitated, and I suspected the business was other than official.

"Well, that's the way it's going to be."

He turned a shoulder when he saw me, and his answers grew terse.

"Do what you want, Danielle."

I waited until he had disconnected, then joined him on the porch.

"Sorry I'm late."

"No problemo."

He flipped the cover and slid the phone into his pocket, his movements stiff and jerky.

"Problems on the home front?"

"What's your pleasure for lunch? Fish or fowl?"

"Nice dodge," I said, smiling. "And about as subtle as a full court press."

"The home front is not your concern. Subtle enough?"

Though my mouth opened, no words emerged.

"It's just a personal disagreement."

"Have a lover's spat with the Archbishop of Canterbury for all I care, just don't treat me to the performance." Heat flamed my cheeks.

"Since when are you curious about my love life?"

"I couldn't care less about your love life," I snapped.

"Thus the inquisition."

"What?"

"Let's forget it." Ryan reached out, but I stepped back.

"You *did* ask me to meet you here."

"Look, this investigation has us both on edge."

"But I don't take cheap shots at you."

"What I don't need is more browbeating," he said, lowering the shades from the top of his head.

"Browbeating?" I exploded.

Ryan repeated his question. "Fish or fowl?"

"Go fowl your own fish."

I whirled and lunged for the doorknob, my face burning with anger. Or was it humiliation? Or hurt?

Inside, I slammed then leaned against the door. From the lot I heard an engine, then the squeal of brakes as a truck arrived with twenty more cases. Rolling my head, I saw Ryan kick a heel at the ground, then cross to his rental car.

Why had he made me so furious? I'd spent a lot of time thinking of the man during his months undercover. But distancing myself from Ryan had become so routine, I'd never considered the possibility that someone else might enter his life. Was that now the case? While I wanted to know, I sure as hell wasn't going to ask.

I turned back to find Larke Tyrell regarding me intently.

"You need some R and R."

68

"I'm taking two hours this afternoon." I'd requested the break so Ryan and I could search the area where I'd found the foot. Now I'd have to do it alone.

"Sandwich?" Larke tilted his chin toward the staff lounge.

"Sure."

Minutes later we were seated at one of the folding tables.

"Squashed subs and pulverized chips," he said.

"My usual order."

"How's LaManche?" Larke had selected what looked like tuna on wheat.

"Back to his usual cantankerous self."

Being the director of the medico-legal unit, Pierre LaManche was Larke Tyrell's counterpart at the lab in Montreal. My two bosses had known each other for years through membership in the National Association of Medical Examiners and the American Academy of Forensic Sciences. LaManche had suffered a heart attack the previous spring but was fully recovered and back to work.

"Mighty glad to hear that."

As we peeled cellophane and popped sodas, I remembered the ME's first appearance at the site.

"Can I ask you something?"

"Sure." He watched me carefully, his eyes chestnut in the sunlight angling down from an overhead window.

"Jesus, Larke, I'm fine, so quit with the stress assessment. Lieutenant-Detective Ryan just happens to be a horse's ass."

"Noted. You sleeping O.K.?"

"Like Custer after Little Bighorn." I avoided the impulse to roll my eyes.

"What's your question?"

69

"When you and the lieutenant governor arrived last week, where did the chopper land?"

I upended my chip bag and poured fragments into my hand.

"There's a house a spit west of the crash site. The pilot liked the lay of the land so that's where he puts us down."

"There's a landing strip?"

"Hell, no, just a small clearing. I thought Davenport was gonna soil his Calvin Kleins, he was so scared." Larke chuckled. "It was like a scene out of *M*A*S*H*. Triggs kept insisting we head back out, and the pilot kept saying, 'Yes, sir, yes, sir,' then put that bird exactly where he wanted."

I palmed the chips into my mouth.

"Then we just worked our way toward the site. I'd say it was maybe a quarter mile."

"It's a house?"

"An old cabin or something. I didn't pay much attention."

"Did you see a road?"

He shook his head. "Why the questions?"

I told him about the foot.

"I didn't notice a cemetery, but there's no harm poking around out there. You sure these were coyotes?"

"No."

"Be safe; take a radio and can of Mace."

"Do coyotes hunt during the day?"

"Coyotes hunt whenever they feel like it."

Great.

North Carolina's official tree is the longleaf pine, its official flower the dogwood. The shad boat, the salt-water bass, and the Eastern box turtle have been similarly honored. The state boasts wild ponies on the Shackleford Banks and the nation's highest suspension bridge at Grandfather Mountain. The Old North State flows from the peaks of the southern Appalachians in the west, across the hills of the piedmont, to the marshlands, beaches, and barrier islands along its eastern shore. It is Mount Mitchell and the Outer Banks. Blowing Rock and Cape Fear. Linville Gorge and Bald Head Island.

North Carolina's geography splits its residents along ideological lines. The high-country crowd plays recreational roulette mountain biking, hang gliding, whitewater kayaking, rock climbing, and, in winter, downhill skiing and snowboarding. The less reckless go in for golf, antiques, bluegrass music, and the viewing of foliage.

Fans of the low country favor salt air, warm sand, ocean fishing, and Atlantic breakers. Temperatures are mild. The locals have never owned mittens or snow tires. Except for the occasional shark or renegade gator, the fauna is nonthreatening. Golf, of course, also permeates the low country.

While I am awed by the beauty of foaming rivers, cascading falls, and towering trees, my allegiance has always been to the sea. I prefer ecozones where shorts and sundresses suffice, and only one layer is needed. Give me a swimsuit catalog and forget Eddie Bauer. All things considered, I'd rather be at the beach.

These thoughts drifted through my mind as I circled the debris field. The day was clear but breezy, the smell of decay less apparent. Though victim recovery was well along, and few bodies littered the ground, the big picture looked relatively unchanged. Bio-suited figures still wandered about and crawled through the wreckage, though some now wore caps marked *FBI*.

71

I found Larke's opening and cut into the woods. Though the high-altitude sunlight was warm, the temperature dropped appreciably when I moved into shadows. I followed the trail I'd taken the week before, now and then stopping to listen. Branches tapped and scraped, and dead leaves tumbled across the ground with soft ticking sounds. Overhead, a woodpecker drummed a staccato tattoo, paused, repeated itself.

I was wearing a bright yellow jacket, wanting to surprise no one, and hoping the Tommy Hilfiger colors would suggest avoidance to the coyote mind. If not, I'd zap the furry buggers. Inside my pocket I clutched a small can of Mace.

At the fallen sourwood, I dropped to one knee and scanned the forest floor. Then I rose and looked around. Other than my Louisville Slugger branch, there was no hint of my canid adventure.

I continued along the subtle passageway. The ground was slightly concave, and I had to take care not to turn an ankle on a rock hidden beneath leaves. Though lower than the surrounding scrub, the vegetation at times rose almost to my knees.

I kept my eyes roving, watching for critters or signs of internment. Larke's house meant human settlement, and I knew that old farmsteads often included family burials. One summer I'd directed a dig at the top of Chimney Rock. Intending to excavate only the cabin, we'd uncovered a tiny graveyard, unlisted on any document. Also timber rattlers and water moccasins, I suddenly remembered.

I pressed on through cool, dark shade, thorns and twigs tugging my clothes and insects dive-bombing my face. Gusts sent shadows dancing, changing shape around me. Then, without warning, the trees gave way

72

to a small clearing. As I emerged into sunlight a white-tailed deer raised its head, stared, then disappeared.

Ahead sat a house, its back snugged to a sheer rock cliff that rose straight up for several hundred feet. The structure had a thick-walled foundation, dormer windows, and a sloping roof with wide eaves. A covered porch hid the front, and an odd stone wall peeked from behind the left side.

I waved. Waited. Called out. Waved again.

No challenging voice or bark. Nor any sound of welcome.

I shouted again, hoping a *Deliverance* redneck did not have me in his crosshairs.

Silence.

Banjos dueling in my head, I started across the meadow. Though it was blindingly bright away from the trees, I left my sunglasses in my pocket. In addition to your run-of-the-mill holler rustics, these mountains sheltered white-supremacist, paramilitary types. Strangers were not encouraged to visit.

I could see that the grounds largely had been taken back by nature. What had once been lawn or garden was now overgrown with stunted white alder, sourwood, Carolina silverbell, and numerous shrubs I didn't recognize. Beyond the bushes, big-tooth aspen, Fraser magnolia, poplar, maple, oak, beech, and Eastern white pine mixed with unfamiliar trees. Kudzu draped everything in tangled webs of green.

As I walked to the front steps, goose bumps spread along my arms and a sense of uneasiness wrapped around me like a cold, wet shawl. A feeling of menace hung over the place. Was it born of the dark, weathered wood, the blind, boarded windows, or the jungle of vegetation that kept the dwelling in perpetual gloom?

"Hello?" My heartbeat quickened.

Still no dogs or mountain men.

One look told me the house had not been thrown up quickly. Or recently. The construction was as solid as London's Newgate prison. Though I doubted George Dance drew the plans, this designer shared the prison architect's distrust of portals on to the world. There were no expanses of glass to maximize the mountain view. No skylights. No widow's walks. Constructed of rock and thick, unstained planking, the place had clearly been built for function. I couldn't tell if it had last been visited at the end of the summer or at the end of the Great Depression.

Or if someone was inside now, watching my movements through a crack or gun hole.

"Is anyone home?"

Nothing.

I climbed to the porch and knocked.

"Hello?"

No sounds of movement.

Sidestepping to a window, I brought my eyes close to the shutters. Heavy, dark material hid the interior. I twisted and turned my head, angling for a view, until the feathery brush of a spider sent me jumping backward.

I descended the steps, circled the house on an overgrown flagstone path, and stepped through an arch into a gloomy little courtyard. The enclosure was surrounded by eight-foot stone walls overhung by lilac bushes, their leaves dark against the greens and yellows of the forest beyond. Except for moss, nothing grew on the hard-packed, moist ground. The dank little quadrangle seemed completely incapable of sustaining life.

I turned my gaze back to the house. A crow circled and settled on a nearby branch, a small black silhouette against brilliant blue. The bird cawed twice, clicked its beak, then lowered its head in my direction.

"Tell the mistress I stopped by," I said with more self-assurance than I felt.

The crow regarded me briefly, then flapped into the air.

Turning, I caught a flicker, like sunlight glinting off broken glass. I froze. Had I seen movement in an upstairs window? I waited a full minute. Nothing stirred.

The yard had only one entrance, so I retraced my steps and surveyed the far side of the property. Brush filled the space between forest and house, ending in a jungle of dead hollyhocks crowding the foundation. I walked the area, but saw no evidence of burials, disturbed or intact. My only discovery was a broken metal bar.

Frustrated, I returned to the front porch, inserted the bar between the shutters, and pried gently. There was no give. I applied more pressure, curious, but not wanting to cause damage. The wood was solid and would not budge.

I looked at my watch. Two forty-five. This was useless. And stupid, if the property wasn't abandoned. If proprietors existed, they were away, or wanted it to seem so. I was tired, sweaty, and itchy from thousands of tiny scratches.

And I had to admit, the place creeped me out. Though I knew my reaction was irrational, I felt a sense of evil pervading the grounds. Deciding to make inquiries in town, I dropped the bar and headed back to the crash site.

Driving toward the morgue, I pondered the mysterious lodge. Who had built it? Why? What was it about the place that made me so uneasy?

7

Ryan was lying in wait when I arrived at High Ridge House shortly after nine. I didn't see him until he spoke.

"Looks like we've got an explosion."

I paused, one hand on the screen door handle.

"Not now, Ryan."

"Jackson's going to make a statement tomorrow."

I turned in the direction of the porch swing. Ryan had one heel on the banister and was pushing himself slowly back and forth. When he drew on his cigarette, a tiny red glow lighted his face.

"It's certain?"

"As Madonna's lost virginity."

I hesitated, wanting news of the investigation, but wary of the bearer.

"It's been a sincerely fucked-up day, Brennan. I apologize for any misbehavior."

Though I'd had little time to dwell on it, the noon-time confrontation had led me to a decision. I was ending the circle of disaster that had been my relationship with Ryan. From now on our interactions would be strictly professional.

"Tell me."

Ryan patted the swing.

I crossed to him but remained standing.

"Why an explosion?"

"Sit."

"If this is a come-on, you can—"

"There's cratering and fiber penetration."

In the half-light of the overhead bulb Ryan's face looked drained of life. He inhaled deeply, then flicked his butt into Ruby's ferns. I watched sparks comet through the dark, imagining the plunge of Air TransSouth 228.

"Do you want to hear this?"

Placing my pack between us, I dropped on to the swing.

"What's cratering?"

"Cratering is caused when a solid or liquid is suddenly converted to a gas."

"As in detonation."

"Yes. An explosion rockets the temperature thousands of degrees and sends out shock waves that create a gas wash effect on metal surfaces. That's how the explosives group experts described it. They showed slides at today's briefing. It looks kind of like an orange peel."

"They're finding cratering?"

"They've spotted it on fragments. Rolled edges, too, which is another indicator."

He gave the swing a gentle push.

"What's fiber penetration?"

"They're seeing the fibers of some materials driven through other, undamaged materials. All under high-powered microscopes, of course. They're also finding heat fractures and flash melting at the ends of some fibers."

Another oscillation, and I tasted the Greek salad I'd wolfed down after leaving the morgue.

"Don't rock the swing."

"Some of the blow-up photos are amazing."

I zipped my jacket and tucked my hands into the pockets. Though the days were still warm, the nights were growing crisp.

"So cratering and rolled edges on metal, and flash melting and penetration of fibers means an explosion. Our lower leg injuries fit with that."

"So does the fact that a large part of the fuselage landed intact."

I planted a foot to stop our forward motion.

"It all adds up to an explosion."

"Caused by?"

"Bomb. Missile. Mechanical failure. The FAA's Aviation Explosives Security Unit will conduct chromatographic analysis to determine what chemicals might be present, and radiophotography and X-ray diffraction to identify molecular species. And one other. Oh, yeah. Infrared spectrophotometry. Not sure what that one's for, but it has a nice ring. That is, if they can arm-wrestle the job away from the FBI crime lab."

"Missile?" It was the first I'd heard of that possibility.

"Not likely, but it's been suggested. Remember all the hoopla about a missile bringing down TWA 800? Pierre Salinger bet his nuts the navy was to blame."

I nodded.

"And these hills are home to a number of militia groups. Maybe Eric Rudolph's white-trash buds got into the arms racket and bought a new toy."

78

Rudolph was wanted in connection with a number of abortion clinic attacks and as a suspect in the bombing at the 1996 Olympic Games in Atlanta. Rumors persisted that he'd fled to these hills.

"Any idea where this explosion was centered?"

"It's too early to tell. The cabin-interior documentation group is compiling a seat damage charge that'll help pinpoint the blast."

Ryan pushed with his toes, but I held the swing firm.

"Our group is doing the same for wounds and fractures. Right now it looks like the worst injuries occurred in the back of the plane." The anthropologists and pathologist were diagramming the distribution of trauma by seat location. "What about the radar group?"

"Nothing unexpected. Following takeoff, the flight routed north-east from the airport towards Athens. The Atlanta air traffic control center is in charge up to Winston-Salem, where Washington takes over, so the plane never left Atlanta ATC. The radar shows an emergency call by the pilot twenty minutes and thirty seconds into the flight. Approximately ninety seconds later the target broke into two, possibly three pieces, and disappeared from the screen."

Headlights appeared far down the mountain. Ryan and I watched them climb through the dark, swing on to the drive, then cut out in the lot to the left of the house. Moments later a figure materialized on the path. When it crossed in front of us, Ryan spoke.

"Long day?"

"Who's that?" The man was barely an imprint against the black of the sky.

"Andy Ryan."

"Well, *bonsoir*, sir. I'd forgotten you were billeted here." The voice sounded like years of whiskey. All I could make of its owner was a burly man in a dozer cap.

"The lilac shower gel is mine."

"I've been respecting that, Detective Ryan."

"I'd buy you a beer but the bar just closed."

The man climbed to the porch, dragged a chair opposite the swing, placed an athletic bag beside it, and sat. The dim light revealed a fleshy nose and cheeks mottled with broken veins.

When introduced, FBI Special Agent Byron McMahon removed the hat and bowed in my direction. I saw thick white hair, centered and splayed like a cockscomb.

"This one's on me." Unzipping the bag, McMahon produced a six-pack of Coors.

"Devil liquor," said Ryan, pulling a beer from the plastic web.

"Yes," agreed McMahon. "Bless him." He waggled a can at me.

I wanted that beer as much as I'd wanted anything in a long time. I remembered the feel of booze filtering through my veins, the warmth rising inside me as the molecules of alcohol blended with my own. The sense of relief, well-being.

But I'd learned some things about myself. It had taken years, but I now understood that every double helix in me carries a pledge to Bacchus. Though craving the release, I knew the euphoria would be temporary, the anger and self-loathing would last a long time. I could not drink.

"No, thanks."

"There's plenty where this came from."

"That's the problem."

McMahon smiled, freed a can, and dropped the others into his bag.

"So what's the thinking at the FBI?" Ryan asked.

80

"Some son of a bitch blew a plane out of the sky."

"Who does the Bureau like?"

"Your biker buddies score high on a lot of dance cards. This Petricelli was a lowlife sleaze with soup for brains, but he was well connected."

"And?"

"Could be a professional hit."

A breeze swayed Ruby's baskets, and black shadows danced on the banisters and floorboards.

"Here's another script. Mrs. Martha Simington was seated in 1A. Three months ago Haskell Simington insured his wife for two million big ones."

"That's a chunk of change."

"Goes a long way toward easing hubby through his pain. Oh, and I forgot to mention. The couple have been living apart for four years."

"Is Simington enough of a mutant to cap eighty-eight people?" Ryan drained his Coors and tossed the empty into McMahon's athletic bag.

"We're getting to know Simington real well."

McMahon mimicked Ryan's performance with his empty can.

"Here's another scenario: 12F was occupied by a nineteen-year-old named Anurudha Mahendran. The kid was a foreign student from Sri Lanka and played goalie on the soccer team."

McMahon released two more beers and handed one to Ryan.

"Back home, Anurudha's uncle works for Voice of Tigers Radio."

"As in Tamil Tigers?"

"Yes, ma'am. The guy's a loudmouth, undoubtedly slots high on the government's wish list for terminal illness."

"You suspect the Sri Lankan government?" I was astounded.

"No. But there are extremists on both sides."

"If you can't persuade unc, go for the kid. Send a message."

Ryan popped the new beer.

"It may be a long shot, but we have to consider it. Not forgetting our local resources, of course."

"Local resources?" I asked.

"Two country preachers who live near here. The Reverend Isaiah Claiborne swears the Reverend Luke Bowman shot the plane down." Another pop. "They're rival snake handlers."

"Snake handlers?"

I ignored Ryan's question. "Claiborne witnessed something?"

"He insists he saw a white streak shoot from behind Bowman's house, followed by an explosion."

"Is the FBI taking him seriously?"

McMahon shrugged. "The time tallies. The location would be right with regard to the flight path."

"What snakes?" Ryan persisted.

"Any word on the voice tapes?" I segued to another subject, not wanting further commentary on the spiritual fervour of our mountain neighbors.

"The calls were made by a white American male with no distinguishable accent."

"That narrows the field to how many million?"

I caught movement in McMahon's eyes, as though he were seriously considering the question.

"A few."

McMahon drained his beer, crumpled the can, and added it to his collection. Rising, he wished us both a good evening, and headed for the door. The bell jangled, and moments later a light went on in an upstairs window.

Save for the creak of Ruby's planters, the porch was totally quiet. Ryan lit a cigarette, then, "Did you do coyote patrol?"

"Yes."

"And?"

"No coyotes. No exposed coffins."

"Did you find anything interesting?"

"A house."

"Who lives there?"

"Hansel and Gretel and the cannibal witch." I stood. "How the hell should I know?"

"Was anyone home?"

"No one rushed out to offer me tea."

"Is the place abandoned?"

I slung my pack over one shoulder and considered the question.

"I'm not sure. There were gardens once, but those have gone to hell. The house is so well built it's hard to know if it's being maintained or if it's just impervious to damage."

He waited.

"There is one peculiar thing. From the front, the place is just another unpainted mountain lodge. But around back it has a walled enclosure and a courtyard."

Ryan's face went apricot, receded into the darkness.

"Tell me about these snake handlers. You have snake handlers in North Carolina?"

I was about to decline when the bell tinkled again. I looked, expecting to see McMahon, but no one appeared.

"Another time."

Opening the outer screen, I found the heavy wooden

door ajar. Once inside, I pushed it tight and tested the handle, hoping Ryan would do the same. Then I trudged to Magnolia, intent on a shower and bed. I was barely in the room when someone tapped softly.

Thinking it was Ryan, I set my face in the hard stare and cracked the door.

Ruby stood in the hall, her features looking solemn and deeply creased. She wore a gray flannel robe, pink socks, and brown slippers shaped like paws. Her hands were clasped at chest level, fingers tightly interlaced.

"I'm about to turn in." I smiled.

She gazed at me gravely.

"I've had dinner," I added.

One hand rose, as if to pluck something from the air. It trembled slightly.

"What is it, Ruby?"

"The devil assumes many forms."

"Yes." I wanted desperately to bathe and sleep. "But I'm sure you're way ahead of him."

I reached out to touch her shoulder, but she stepped back and the hands found each other again.

"They fly with Lucifer in the face of divinity. They blaspheme."

"Who does?"

"They've grasped the keys of Hades and of death. Just like it says in Revelation."

"Ruby, please speak to me in plain English."

Her eyes were wide, the nodes in the corners pink and shiny with moisture.

"You're from foreign parts so you can't be knowing."

"Knowing what?" Irritation curled the edges of my voice. I was not in a mood for parables.

"There's evil here."

The beer?

"Detective Ryan an—"

"Wicked men scoff at the Almighty."

This was going nowhere.

"Let's talk about this tomorrow."

I grasped the doorknob, but a hand flew out and clutched my arm. Calluses scratched the sleeve of my nylon jacket.

"The Lord God has sent a sign."

She drew even closer.

"Death!"

Gently preying loose the bony fingers, I squeezed Ruby's hand and stepped back. I watched her through the gap as the door swung shut, her small body frozen, the sausage curl crawling her skull like a dull, gray serpent.

8

The next day honored someone. Christopher Columbus, I think. By midmorning it had turned into a nightmare.

I drove to the morgue through mist so thick it obliterated the mountains, and worked until ten-thirty. When I broke for coffee, Larke Tyrell was in the staff room. He waited while I filled a cup with industrial sludge and added white powder.

"There's something we need to talk about."

"Sure."

"Not here." He looked at me a long time. The look meant something, and I felt a prick of anxiety.

"What is it, Larke?"

"Come on."

Taking my arm, he propelled me out the back door.

"Tempe, I don't know how to say this." He swirled his coffee, and iridescent clouds slid across the surface.

"Just say it." I kept my voice low and level.

"There's been a complaint."

I waited.

"I feel terrible about this." He studied his cup a few

86

more seconds, then raised his eyes to mine. "It's about you."

"Me?" I was incredulous.

He nodded.

"What did I do?"

"The complaint cites unprofessional behavior of a nature sufficient to compromise the investigation."

"Such as?"

"Entering the site without authority and mishandling evidence."

I stared at him in disbelief.

"And trespass."

"*Trespass?*" A cold fist was closing around my gut.

"Did you poke around that property we talked about?"

"It wasn't trespass. I wanted to talk to the owners."

"Did you try to break in?"

"Of course not!"

I flashed on myself prying a shutter with a rusty bar.

"And I had authorization to enter the crash site last week."

"Whose?"

"Earl Bliss sent me there. You know that."

"See, here's the problem, Tempe." Larke rubbed a hand across his chin. "At that point DMORT hadn't been requested."

I was stunned.

"In what way did I mishandle evidence?"

"I hate to even ask this." The hand went back to the chin. "Tempe—"

"Just ask."

"Did you pick up remains that hadn't been logged?"

The foot.

"I told you about that." Stay calm. "I made a judgment call."

He said nothing.

"Had I left that foot, it would now be coyote dung. Talk to Andrew Ryan. He was there."

"I'll do that."

Larke reached out and squeezed my arm.

"We'll sort this out."

"You're taking this seriously?"

"I have no choice."

"Why is that?"

"You know the press are snapping at my backside. They're gonna jump on this like a hound with a one-eyed hare."

"Who made this complaint?" I blinked back tears.

"I can't tell you that."

He dropped his hand and stared off at the mist. It was lifting now, revealing the landscape in a slow, upward peel. When he turned back, there was an odd expression on his face.

"But I will tell you that powerful people are involved."

"The Dalai Lama? The Joint Chiefs of Staff?" Anger hardened my voice.

"Don't be mad at me, Tempe. This investigation is big news. If problems develop, no one's going to want to own them."

"So I'm being set up in case a scapegoat is needed."

"It's nothing like that. I just have to go through proper procedures."

I took a deep breath.

"What happens now?"

He looked straight at me and his voice softened.

"I'm going to have to ask you to leave."

"When?"

"Now."

It was my turn to stare into the mist.

High Ridge House was deserted in the middle of the day. I left a note for Ruby, thanking her and apologizing for my abrupt departure and for my coolness the night before. Then I gathered my belongings, tossed them into my Mazda, and drove off so fast the tires threw up a gravel spray.

All the way home to Charlotte I stopped and started hard, screeching from lights then weaving from lane to lane once I reached the highway. For three hours I crawled up bumpers and rode the horn. I talked to myself, trying out words. *Vile. Despicable. Vicious.* Other drivers avoided my eyes and gave me lots of space.

I was irate and depressed at the same time. The injustice of an anonymous accusation. The helplessness. For a week I'd been working under brutal conditions, seeing, smelling, and feeling death. I'd dropped everything, devoted myself to the effort, then been dismissed like a servant suspected of stealing. No hearing. No opportunity for explanation. No thank-you. Pack and go.

Besides the professional humiliation, there was the personal let-down. Though we'd been friends for years, and Larke knew I was scrupulous about professional ethics, he hadn't defended me. Larke was not a cowardly man. I had expected more of him.

The wild driving served its purpose. By the outskirts of Charlotte my cascading fury had congealed into cold resolve. I'd done nothing inappropriate and I would clear my name. I would find out what this grievance was, quash it, and finish my work. And I would confront the accuser.

My empty town house destroyed that resolve. No one to greet me. No one to hold me and tell me I'd be fine. Ryan was quibbling with a distant Danielle, whoever she was. Ryan had told me it was none of my business. Katy was with her friend, gender unspecified, and Birdie and Pete were far across town. I threw down my bags, flung myself on the sofa, and dissolved into tears.

Ten minutes later I lay quietly, chest heaving, feeling like a kid coming off a tantrum. I'd accomplished nothing and felt drained. Dragging myself to the bathroom, I blew my nose, then checked my phone messages.

Zero to brighten my mood. A student. Salesmen. My sister, Harry, calling from Texas. A query from my friend Anne: Could we get together for lunch since she and Ted were leaving for London?

Great. They were probably dining at the Savoy as I erased her words. I decided to collect Birdie. At least he would purr in my lap.

Pete still lives in the house we shared for almost twenty years. Though it is worth hundreds of thousands of dollars, the fence is mended with a wooden block, and a makeshift goal sags in the backyard, testimonial to Katy's soccer years. The house is painted, the gutters cleaned, the lawn mowed by professionals. A maid maintains the inside. But beyond normal upkeep, my estranged husband believes in laissez-faire and the quick patch. He feels no obligation to protect area real estate values. I used to worry about neighborhood protests. The separation relieved me of that.

A furry brown face watched through the fence as I swung on to the drive. When I climbed from the car, it crinkled and gave a low "rrup!"

"Is he here?" I asked, slamming the door.

The dog lowered its head, and a purple tongue dropped from its mouth.

I circled to the front and rang. No response.

I rang again. A key still hung from my chain, but I wouldn't use it. Though we'd been living apart for over two years, Pete and I were still stepping carefully in establishing the new order between us. The sharing of keys involved an intimacy I didn't want to imply.

But it was Thursday afternoon and Pete would be at the office. And I wanted my cat.

I was digging in my purse, when the door opened.

"Hello, attractive stranger. Need a place to sleep?" said Pete, surveying me from top to bottom.

I was wearing the khakis and Doc Martens I'd donned for the morgue at six that morning. Pete was perfect in a three-piece suit and Gucci loafers.

"I thought you'd be at work."

I wiped knuckles across the mascara smears on my lower lids, and took a quick peek inside the house. If I spotted a woman I'd die of humiliation.

"Why *aren't* you at work?"

He glanced left, then right, lowered his voice, and gestured me close, as if imparting secure information. "Rendezvous with the plumber."

I didn't want to contemplate what had gone so wrong that Mr. Fix It would call in an expert.

"I came for Birdie."

"I think he's free." Pete stepped back. I entered a foyer lighted by my great-aunt's chandelier.

"How about a drink?"

I drilled him a look that could slice feldspar. Pete had witnessed many of my Academy Award performances, and knew better.

"You know what I mean."

"A Diet Coke would be nice."

While Pete rattled glassware and ice cubes in the kitchen, I called up the stairs to Birdie. No cat. I tried the parlor, dining room, and den.

Once upon a time, Pete and I had lived together in these rooms, reading, talking, listening to music, making love. We'd nurtured Katy from infant to toddler to adolescent, redecorating her room and adjusting our lives with each passage. I'd watch the honeysuckle come and go through the window over the kitchen sink, welcoming every season. Those had been fairy-tale days, a time when the American dream seemed real and attainable.

Pete reappeared, transformed from attorney-chic to yuppie-casual. The jacket and vest were gone, the tie loosened, the shirtsleeves rolled to below the elbows. He looked good.

"Where's Bird?" I asked.

"He's been keeping to the upper decks since Boyd checked in."

He handed me a mug with *Uz to mums atkal jaiedzer!* scrolled around the glass. "To that we must drink again!" in Latvian.

"Boyd's the dog?"

A nod.

"Yours?"

"Interesting point. Have a seat and I'll share with you the saga of Boyd."

Pete got pretzels from the kitchen and joined me on the couch.

"Boyd belongs to one Harvey Alexander Dineen, a gentleman recently in need of pro bono defense. Completely surprised by his arrest, and lacking family, Harvey requested that I look after his dog

92

until the misunderstanding with the state was cleared up."

"And you agreed?"

"I appreciated his confidence in me."

Pete licked salt from a pretzel, bit off the large loop, and washed it down with beer.

"And?"

"Boyd's on his own for a minimum of ten and a maximum of twenty. I figured he'd get hungry."

"What is he?"

"He thinks of himself as an entrepreneur. The judge called him a con man and a career criminal."

"I meant the dog."

"Boyd's a chow. Or at least most of him is. We'd need DNA testing to clarify the rest."

He ate the other half of the pretzel.

"Been out with any good corpses lately?"

"Very funny." My face must have suggested that it was not.

"Sorry. Must be grim up there."

"We're getting through it."

We made small talk for a while, then Pete invited me for dinner. Our usual routine. He asked, I refused. Today I thought of Larke's allegations, Anne and Ted's London adventure, and my empty condo.

"What are you serving?"

His eyebrows shot up in surprise.

"Linguini con sauce vongole."

A Pete specialty. Canned clams on overcooked pasta.

"Why don't I pick up steaks while you deal with the plumber. When the pipes are flowing, we can grill the meat."

"It's an upstairs toilet."

"Whatever."

"It will be good for Bird to see that we're friends. I think he still blames himself."

Pure Pete.

Boyd joined us at dinner, sitting beside the table, eyes glued to the New York strips, now and then pawing a knee to remind us of his presence.

Pete and I talked about Katy, about old friends, and about old times. He discussed some current litigation, and I described one of my recent cases, a student found hanging in his grandmother's barn nine months after his disappearance. I was pleased that we'd reached a comfort level at which normal conversation was possible. Time flew, and Larke and his complaint receded from my thoughts.

After a dessert of strawberries on vanilla ice cream, we took coffee to the den and switched on the news. The Air TransSouth crash was the lead story.

A grim-faced woman stood at the overlook, the Great Smoky Mountains rolling behind her, and talked of a meet in which thirty-four athletes would never compete. She reported that the cause of the crash was still unclear, although a mid-air explosion was now almost certain. To date forty-seven victims had been identified, and the investigation was continuing around the clock.

"It's smart they're giving you time off," Pete said.

I didn't answer.

"Or did they send you down here on a secret mission?"

I felt a tremor in my chest and kept my eyes on my Doc Martens.

Pete slid close and raised my chin with an index finger.

"Hey, babe, I'm only kidding. Are you O.K.?"

94

I nodded, not trusting myself to speak.

"You don't look too O.K."

"I'm fine."

"Do you want to tell me about it?"

I must have, for the words poured out. I told him about the days of gore, about the coyotes and my attempts to pinpoint the foot's origin, about the anonymous complaint and my dismissal. I left out nothing but Andrew Ryan. When I finally wound down my feet were curled beneath me, and I was clutching a throw pillow to my chest. Pete was regarding me intently.

For a few moments neither of us spoke. The schoolhouse clock ticked loudly from the den wall, and I wondered idly who kept it wound.

Tick. Tick. Tick.

"Well, this has been fun," I said, unwinding my legs.

Pete took my hand, his eyes still steady on my face.

"What are you going to do about it?"

"What can I do?" I said irritably, pulling free. I was already embarrassed by my outpouring and dreaded what I knew was coming. Pete always gave the same advice when aggravated by others. "Fuck 'em."

He surprised me.

"Your DMORT commander will clear up the issue of entering the site. The foot is central to the rest. Was anyone around when you picked the thing up?"

"There was a cop nearby." I focused on the pillow.

"Local?"

I shook my head.

"Did he see the coyotes?"

"Yes."

"Do you know who he is?"

Oh yes.

I nodded.

"That should settle that. Have this cop contact Tyrell and describe the situation." He leaned back. "The trespass is going to be tougher."

"I wasn't trespassing," I said hotly.

"How strongly did you feel about this foot?"

"I don't think it fits with anyone on the passenger list. That's why I was snooping around."

"Because of the age."

"Largely. It also looked more decomposed."

"Can you prove the age?"

"What do you mean?"

"Are you absolutely certain the foot donor was that old?"

"No."

"Is there any other test that can more firmly establish your age estimate?" Pete, the lawyer.

"I'll check the histology once the samples are processed."

"When is that?"

"Slide preparation is taking forev—"

"Go there tomorrow. Get your slides bumped. Don't quit until you know the guy's collar size and the name of his bookie."

"I could try."

"Do it."

Pete was right. I was being a pansy.

"Then ID Foot Man and shove it up Tyrell's ass."

"How do I do that?"

"If your foot didn't come from the plane, it must be local."

I waited.

"Start by finding out who owns that property."

"How do I do *that*?"

"Has the FBI checked the place out?"

"They're involved in the crash investigation, but until there's proof of sabotage, the Bureau isn't officially in charge. Besides, given my current status, I doubt they're going to share their thoughts with me."

"Then find out on your own."

"How?"

"Check the title to the property and the tax rolls at the county courthouse."

"Can you walk me through that?"

I took notes as he talked. By the time he finished, my resolve was back. No more whining and self-pity. I'd probe that foot until I knew every detail of its owner's life. Then I'd find out where it came from, nail an ID, and paste it to Larke Tyrell's forehead.

"Thank you so much, Pete."

I leaned over and kissed him on the cheek. Without hesitating, he drew me in. Before I could pull back, he returned my cheek kiss, then another, then his lips slid to my neck, my ear, my mouth. I smelled the familiar mix of sweat and Aramis, and a million images burst into my brain. I felt the arms and chest I'd known for two decades, that had once held only me.

I loved making love with Pete. I always had, from that first earthquake magic in his tiny room on Clarke Avenue in Champaign, Illinois, to the later years, when it became slower, deeper, a melody I knew as well as the curves of my own body. Making love with Pete was all-encompassing. It was pure sensation and total detachment. I needed that now. I needed the familiar and comforting, the shattering of my consciousness, the stopping of time.

I thought of my silent apartment. I thought of Larke and his "powerful people," of Ryan and the unknown

Danielle, of separation and distance. Then Pete's hand slid to my breast.

"Fuck 'em," I thought.

Then I thought of nothing else.

9

I awoke to the sound of a phone. Pete had drawn the shades, and the room was so dim I needed several rings to locate it.

"Meet me at Providence Road Sundries tonight and I'll buy you a burger."

"Pete, I—"

"You drive a hard bargain. Meet me at Bijoux."

"It's not the restaurant."

"Tomorrow night?"

"I don't think so."

The lined hummed.

"Remember when I wrecked the Volkswagen and insisted we push on?"

"Georgia to Illinois with no headlights."

"You didn't speak to me for six hundred miles."

"It's not like that, Pete."

"Didn't you enjoy last night?"

I loved last night.

"It's not that."

I heard voices in the background and looked at the clock. Eight-ten.

"Are you at work?"

"Yes, ma'am."

"Why are you phoning?"

"You asked me to wake you."

"Oh." An old routine. "Thanks."

"No problem."

"And thanks for keeping Birdie."

"Has he made an appearance?"

"Briefly. He looked edgy."

"The old Bird has become set in his ways."

"Birdie never liked dogs."

"Or change."

"Or change."

"Some change is good."

"Yes."

"I have changed."

I'd heard that from Pete. He'd said it after his tryst with a court reporter three years earlier, again following a Realtor episode. I hadn't waited for the trifecta.

"That was a bad time for me," he went on.

"Yeah. Me, too."

I hung up and took a long shower, reflecting on our failings. Pete was where I'd always turned for advice, comfort, support. He'd been my safety net, the calm I'd seek after a day of tempest. The breakup had been devastating, but it had also brought out strength I'd never known I had.

Or ever used.

When I'd toweled off and wrapped my hair, I studied myself in the mirror.

Question: What was I thinking last night?

Answer: I wasn't. I was angry, hurt, vulnerable, and alone. And I hadn't had sex in a very long time.

Question: Would it happen again?

Answer: No.

Question: Why not?

Why not? I still loved Pete. I had since first laying eyes on him, barefoot and bare-chested on the steps of the law school library. I'd loved him as he lied about Judy, then Ellen. I'd loved him as I packed and left two years ago.

And I obviously still found him sexy as hell.

My sister, Harry, has a Texas expression. Flat ass stupid. Though I love Pete, and find him sexy, I am not flat ass stupid. *That's* why it would not happen again.

I wiped steam from the glass, remembering the old me looking back from that same mirror. My hair was blond when we first moved in, long and straight to my shoulders. It's short now, and I've abandoned the golden surfer look. But gray hairs are sneaking in, and I'll soon be checking out the Clairol browns. The lines have increased and deepened around my eyes, but my jawline is firm and my upper lids have stayed put.

Pete always said my butt was my best feature. That, too, has remained in place, though effort is now required. But, unlike many of my contemporaries, I own no spandex and have never hired a personal trainer. I possess no treadmill, step machine, or stationary bike. I do not enroll in aerobics or kickboxing classes, and have not run in an organized race in over five years. I go to the gym in T-shirts and FBI shorts, tied at the waist with a drawstring. I jog or swim, lift, then leave. When the weather is nice, I run outside.

I've also tried to tighten up on what I eat. Daily

vitamins. Red meat no more than three times a week. Junk food no more than five.

I was positioning my panties when my cell phone rang. Racing to the bedroom, I upended my purse, retrieved the phone, and hit the button.

"Where have you disappeared to?"

Ryan's voice was completely unexpected. I hesitated, panties in one and, phone in the other, unable to think of a thing to say.

"Hello?"

"I'm here."

"Here where?"

"I'm in Charlotte."

There was a pause. Ryan broke it.

"This whole thing is a crock of sh—"

"Have you talked to Tyrell?"

"Briefly."

"Did you describe the coyote scene?"

"Vividly."

"And he said?"

"Thank ya, sir." Ryan mimicked the ME's drawl.

"This isn't Tyrell's idea."

"There's something off center about the whole thing."

"What do you mean?"

"I'm not sure."

"What's off center?"

"Tyrell was jumpy. I've only known him a week, but jumpy is not normal demeanor for him. Something is making him squirm. He knows you didn't tamper with remains, and he knows Earl Bliss ordered you up here last week."

"So who's behind the complaint?"

"I don't know, but I sure as hell intend to find out."

102

"It's not your problem, Ryan."

"No."

"Any developments in the investigation?" I switched the subject.

I heard a match flare, then a deep inhalation.

"Simington is starting to look like a good choice."

"The guy with the heavily insured wife?"

"It's better than that. The new widower owns a company that does highway construction."

"So?"

"Easy access to plastic X."

"Plastic X?"

"Plastic explosive. The stuff was used in Vietnam, but now it's sold to private industry for construction, mining, demolition. Hell, farmers can get it to blast out tree stumps."

"Aren't explosives tightly controlled?"

"Yes and no. The regs for transport are tighter than those for storage and use. If a highway is under construction, for example, you need a special truck with escorts and a prescribed route bypassing congested areas. But once the stuff is on-site it's usually stored in a mobile vault in the middle of a field with the word *explosive* written on it in large letters.

"The company hires some old geezer as guard and pays him minimum wage, mainly to meet insurance requirements. Vaults can be burgled, misplaced, or simply disappear."

Ryan drew on his cigarette, exhaled.

"The military is supposed to account for every ounce of plastic explosive, but construction crews don't have to ledger up that precisely. Say a blaster gets ten sticks, uses three quarters of each, and pockets the rest. No one's the wiser. All the guy needs is a detonator and he's in business. Or he can sell the stuff black market. Explosives are always in demand."

"Assuming Simington filched explosives, could he have gotten them on board?"

"Apparently it's not all that hard. Terrorists used to take plastique, flatten it to the thickness of a wad of bills, and put it in their wallets. How many security guards check the bills in your wallet? And you can get an electrical detonator the size of a watchcase these days. The Libyan terrorists that blew up Pan Am 103 over Lockerbie slipped the stuff on in a cassette case. Simington could have found a way."

"Jesus."

"I've also had news from *la belle province*. Earlier this week a group of homeowners got suspicious about a Ferrari parked on their street. It seems sports cars costing over a hundred thousand dollars don't commonly overnight in that part of Montreal. Turned out to be a good call. Police found the owner, one Alain 'the Fox' Barboli, stuffed in the trunk with two bullets in his head. Barboli was a member of the Rock Machine and had ties to the Sicilian Mafia. Carcajou's got it."

Opération Carcajou was a multiagency task force devoted to the investigation of outlaw bikers in Quebec province. I'd worked with them on a number of murders.

"Does Carcajou think Barboli was revenge for Petricelli?"

"Or Barboli was involved in the Petricelli hit and the big boys are sanitizing the witness list. If there *was* a hit."

"If Simington could get his hands on explosives, the Hells Angels would have no problem."

"Like buying Cheez Whiz at the 7-Eleven. Look, why don't you get back up here and tell this Tyrell—"

104

"I want to check some bone samples to make sure I'm right on my age estimate. If that foot didn't come from the plane, the tampering charges will be irrelevant."

"I mentioned your suspicions about the foot to Tyrell."

"And?"

"And nothing. He brushed it off."

Again I felt the flush of anger.

"Have you turned up any unlisted passengers?"

"No. Hanover swears deadheading is strictly regulated. No paper, no ride. The Air TransSouth employees we've interviewed confirm their CEO's claim."

"Anyone who might have been transporting body parts?"

"No anatomists, anthropologists, podiatrists, orthopedic surgeons, or corrective footwear salesmen. And Jeffrey Dahmer isn't flying these days."

"You're a scream, Ryan."

I hesitated.

"Has Jean been identified?"

"He and Petricelli remain among the missing."

"They'll find him."

"Yeah."

"You all right?"

"Tough as nails. How 'bout you? Feeling lonely all by yourself?"

"I'm fine," I said, staring at the bed I'd just vacated.

North Carolina has a centralized medical examiner system, with headquarters in Chapel Hill and regional offices in Winston-Salem, Greenville, and Charlotte. Due to geography, and to its physical layout, the Charlotte branch, dubbed the Mecklenburg County Medical Examiner, was chosen for the processing of specimens collected at the incident morgue in Bryson City. A technician had been loaned from Chapel Hill, and a temporary histology unit had been set up.

The Mecklenburg County Medical Examiner is part of the Harold R. "Hal" Marshall County Services Center, which takes up both sides of College Street between Ninth and Tenth, just on the edge of uptown. The facility's home was once a Sears Garden Center. Though an architectural orphan, it is modern and efficient.

But Hal's tenure may be threatened. Shunned for years, the land on which the center sits, with its views of condos, shops, and bistros, has caught the interest of developers as more fitting for mixed-use commercial expansion than for use as county offices, parking lots, and a morgue. American Express gold cards, cappuccino makers, and Hornets and Panthers club seats may soon flourish where scalpels, gurneys, and autopsy tables used to hold sway.

Twenty minutes after finally donning the panties, I pulled into the MCME lot. Across College, the homeless were being served hot dogs and lemonade from folding tables. Blankets covered the moss strip between sidewalk and curb, displaying shoes, shirts, and socks for the taking. A score of indigents milled about, nowhere to go, in no hurry to get there.

Locking the car, I walked to the low-rise redbrick structure and was buzzed through the glass doors. After greeting the ladies up front, I checked in with Tim Larabee, the Mecklenburg County ME. He led me to a computer that had been set aside for crash victim processing and pulled up case number 387. It was probably violating the terms of my banishment, but I had to take the chance.

DNA testing was being done at the Charlotte-Mecklenburg crime laboratory, and those results were not yet available. But the histology was ready. The samples I'd cut from the ankle and foot bones had been shaved into slivers less than one hundred microns thick, processed, stained, and placed on slides. I got them and settled at a microscope.

Bone is a miniature universe in which birth and death occur constantly. The basic unit is the osteon, composed of concentric loops of bone, a canal, osteocytes, vessels, and nerves. In living tissue osteons are born, nourished, and eventually replaced by newer units.

When magnified and viewed under polarized light, osteons resemble tiny volcanoes, ovoid cones with central craters and flanks that spread out to flatbands of primary bone. The number of volcanoes increases with age, as does the count of abandoned calderas. By determining the density of these features one arrived at an age estimate.

First I looked for signs of abnormality. In the cross-section of a long bone, thinning of the shaft, scalloping of its inner or outer edges, or abnormal deposition of woven bone can indicate problems, including fracture healing or unusually rapid remodeling. I saw no such anomalies.

Satisfied that a realistic age estimate was possible, I increased the magnification to one hundred and inserted a rule ocular micrometer into the eyepiece. The grid contained one hundred squares, with each side measuring one millimetre at the level of the section. Moving from slide to slide, I studied the miniature landscapes, carefully counting and recording the features within each grid. When I'd finished and plugged my totals into the proper formulae, I had my answer.

The owner of the foot had been at least sixty-five, probably nearer to seventy.

I leaned back and considered that. No one on the manifest was close to that age range. What were the options?

One. An unlisted traveler was on board. A septuagenarian dead-header? A senior citizen stowaway? Unlikely.

Two. A passenger had carried the foot on board. Ryan said they'd found no one whose profile suggested an interest in body parts.

Three. The foot was unrelated to Air TransSouth 228.

Then where did it come from?

I dug a card from my purse, checked the number, and dialed.

"Swain County Sheriff's Department."

"Lucy Crowe, please."

"Who's calling."

I gave my name and waited. Moments later I heard the gravelly voice.

"I probably shouldn't be talking to you."

"You've heard."

"I've heard."

"I could try to explain, but I don't think I understand the situation myself."

"I don't know you well enough to judge."

"Why *are* you talking to me?"

"Gut instinct."

"I'm working to clear this up."

"That'd be good. You've got 'em buzzing at the top of the heap."

"What do you mean?"

"I just had a call from Parker Davenport."

"The lieutenant governor?"

"Himself. Ordered me to keep you off the crash site."

"Doesn't he have better things to worry about?"

"Apparently you're a hot topic. My deputy took a call this morning. Fellow wanted to know where you live and where you were staying up here."

"Who was he?"

"Wouldn't give a name, hung up when my deputy insisted."

"Was he press?"

"We're pretty good at spotting that."

"There's something you can do for me, Sheriff."

I heard the sound of long-distance air.

"Sheriff?"

"I'm listening."

I described the foot, and my reasons for doubting its association with the crash.

"Could you check on missing persons for Swain and the surrounding counties?"

"Got any descriptors beside age?"

"Sixty-three to sixty-six inches in height, with bad feet. When the DNA's in I'll know the gender."

"Time frame?"

Despite the soft tissue preservation, I decided on broad parameters.

"One year."

"I know we've got some here in Swain. I'll pull those up. And I suppose there's no harm in sending out a few queries."

When we'd disconnected, I sealed the slide case and returned it to the technician. As I drove toward home new questions burned in my brain, fanned by feelings of anger and humiliation.

Why wasn't Larke Tyrell defending me? He knew the

109

commitment I felt to my work, knew I'd never compromise an investigation.

Could Parker Davenport be Tyrell's "powerful people"? Larke was an appointed official. Could the lieutenant governor be putting pressure on his chief medical examiner? Why?

Could Lucy Crowe's reaction to Davenport be accurate? Was the lieutenant governor concerned with his image and planning to use me for publicity purposes?

I remembered him at the crash site, hanky to his mouth, eyes down to avoid the carnage.

Or was it me he was avoiding? An unpleasant feeling shifted inside me, and I tried to erase the image. It was no good. My mind was like a computer with no delete button.

I thought of Ryan's advice. Pete's. Both were saying the same thing.

I dialed Information, then placed a call.

Ruby answered after two rings.

I identified myself and asked if Magnolia was available.

"The room's empty, but I offered it to one of the downstairs boarders."

"I'd like to check back in."

"They told me you were gone for good. Cleared the bill."

"I'll pay you for a week in advance."

"Must be the Lord's will the other 'un hasn't moved up there yet."

"Yes," I answered, with an enthusiasm I didn't feel. "The Lord's will."

10

Charlotte is a poster child for multiple personality disorder, the Sybil of cities. It is the New South, proud of its skyscrapers, airport, university, NBA Hornets, NFL Panthers, and NASCAR racing. Headquarters to Bank of America and First Union, it is the nation's second largest financial center. It is home to the University of North Carolina at Charlotte. It yearns to be a world-class city.

Yet Charlotte remains nostalgic for the Old South. In its affluent southeast quadrant, it is stately homes and tidy bungalows garnished by azaleas, dogwoods, rhododendrons, redbuds, and magnolias. It is winding streets, front porch swings, and more trees per square mile than any burg on the planet. In spring, Charlotte is a kaleidoscope of pink, white, violet, and red. In fall it blazes with yellow and orange. It has a church on every corner and people attend them. The erosion of the genteel life is a constant topic of conversation, but the same folks lamenting its passage keep one eye on the stock market.

I live at Sharon Hall, a turn-of-the-century estate in the elegant old neighborhood of Myers Park. Once a graceful Georgian manor, the Hall had fallen into disrepair by the 1950s and was donated to a local college. In the mid-eighties the two-and-a-half-acre property was purchased by developers, upfitted, and reincarnated as a modern condominium complex.

While most of the Hall's residents occupy the main house, or one of its recently constructed wings, my condo is a tiny structure on the western edge of the property. Records indicate the building started life as an addition to the coach house, but no document describes its original function. For lack of a better term it is simply called the Annex.

Though cramped, my two stories are bright and sunny, and my small patio is perfect for geraniums, one of the few species able to survive my horticultural ministrations. The Annex has been home since my marital breakup, and it suits me perfectly.

The sky was resolutely blue as I entered the gate and circled the grounds. The petunias and marigolds smelled of autumn, their perfume mingling with the scent of drying leaves. Sunshine warmed the bricks of the Hall's buildings, walks, and perimeter wall.

Rounding the Annex, I was surprised to see Pete's Porsche parked next to my patio, Boyd's head protruding from the passenger side. Spotting me, the dog pricked his ears, pulled in his tongue, then let it dangle again.

Through the back window I could see Birdie in his travel cage. My cat did not look pleased with the transport arrangements.

As I pulled parallel to Pete's car, he rounded the building.

112

"Jesus, am I glad I caught you." His face looked anxious.

"What is it?"

"A client's knitting plant just went up in flames. The case is certain to become a matter of litigation, and I've got to get out there with some experts before would-be fire inspectors muck things up."

"Out where?"

"Indianapolis. I was hoping you'd take Boyd for a couple of days."

The tongue disappeared, dropped again.

"I'm leaving for Bryson City."

"Boyd loves the highlands. He'd be great company."

"Look at him."

Boyd's chin now rested on the window ledge, and saliva trickled down the car's outside panel.

"He'd be protection."

"That's a stretch."

"Really. Harvey didn't like unexpected visitors, so he trained Boyd to sniff out strangers."

"Especially those in uniform."

"The good, the bad, the ugly, even the beautiful. Boyd makes no distinctions."

"Isn't there a kennel where he can board?"

"It's full." He glanced at his watch, then gave me his most beguiling choirboy look. "And my flight leaves in an hour."

Pete had never refused when I'd needed help with Birdie.

"Go. I'll figure something out."

"You're sure?"

"I'll find a kennel."

Pete squeezed both my arms.

"You're my hero."

113

There are twenty-three kennels in the greater Charlotte area. It took an hour to establish that fourteen were fully booked, five did not answer, two could not accommodate a dog over fifty pounds, and two would take no dog without a personal interview.

"Now what?"

Boyd raised and cocked his head, then went back to licking my kitchen floor.

Desperate, I made another call.

Ruby was less fastidious. For three dollars a day the dog was welcome, no personal audience required.

My neighbour took Birdie, and the chow and I hit the road.

Halloween has its roots in the pagan festival of Samhain. Held at the onset of winter and the beginning of the Celtic New Year, Samhain was the time when the veil between living and dead was thinnest, and spirits roamed the land of mortals. Fires were extinguished and rekindled, and people dressed up to frighten away the unfriendly departed.

Though the holiday was still two weeks off, the residents of Bryson City were into the concept in a big way. Ghouls, bats, and spiders were everywhere. Scarecrows and tombstones had been erected in front yards, and skeletons, black cats, witches, and ghosts dangled from trees and porch lights. Jack-o'-lanterns leered from every window in town. A couple of cars had rather realistic replicas of human feet protruding from their trunks. Good time to actually dispose of a body, I thought.

By five I'd settled Boyd into a run behind High Ridge House, and myself into Magnolia. Then I drove to the sheriff's headquarters.

Lucy Crowe was on the phone when I appeared in her doorway. She waved me into her office, and I took one of two chairs. Her desk filled most of the small space, looking like something at which a Confederate general might have penned military orders. Her chair was also ancient, brown leather and studded, with stuffing oozing from the left arm.

"Nice desk," I said when she'd hung up.

"I think it's ash." The sea-foam eyes were just as startling as on our first meeting. "It was made by my predecessor's grandfather."

She leaned back, and the chair squeaked musically.

"Tell me what I've missed."

"They say you've damaged the investigation."

"Sometimes you get bad press."

Her head did a j-stroke. "What have you got?"

"That foot was walking the earth at least sixty-five years. No one on the plane had that privilege. I need to establish that this was not crash evidence."

The sheriff opened a folder and spread its contents on her blotter.

"I've got three missing persons. Had four, but one turned up."

"Shoot."

"Jeremiah Mitchell, black male, age seventy-two. Disappeared from Waynesville eight months ago. According to patrons at the Mighty High Tap, Mitchell left the bar around midnight to buy hooch. That was February fifteenth. Mitchell's neighbor reported him missing ten days later. He hasn't been seen since."

"No family?"

"None listed. Mitchell was a loner."

"Why the neighbor's concern?"

"Mitchell had his ax and the guy wanted it back.

115

Visited the house several times, finally got tired of waiting, went to see if Mitchell was in the drunk tank. He wasn't, so the neighbor filed an MP report, thinking a police search might flush him."

"And his ax."

"A man's nothing without his tools."

"Height?"

She ran a finger down one of the papers.

"Five foot six."

"That fits. Was he driving?"

"Mitchell was a heavy drinker, traveled by foot. Folks figure he got himself lost and died of exposure."

"Who else?"

"George Adair." She read from another form. "White male, age sixty-seven. Lived over to Unahala, disappeared two weeks ago. Wife said he went fishing with a buddy and never came back."

"What was the buddy's story?"

"Woke one morning and Adair wasn't in the tent. Waited a day, then packed up and went home."

"Where was the fatal fishing trip?"

"The Little Tennessee." She swiveled and stabbed at a spot on a wall map behind her. "Up the Nantahala Mountains."

"Where's Unahala?"

Her finger moved a fraction toward the northeast.

"And where's the crash site?"

Her finger barely moved.

"Who's contestant number three?"

When she turned back, the chair sang another verse.

"Daniel Wahnetah, age sixty-nine. Cherokee from the reservation. Failed to show up for his grandson's birthday on July twenty-seventh. Family reported him missing on August twenty-sixth when he pulled a no-show for his own party." Her eyes moved down the paper. "No height reported."

"The family waited a month?"

"Except in winter, Daniel spends most of his time out in the woods. He has a string of camps, works a circuit hunting and fishing."

She leaned back, and the chair squeaked a tune I didn't know.

"Looks like Jesse Jackson's Rainbow Coalition. If it's one of these guys, nail the race and you've got your man."

"That's it?"

"Folks pretty much stay put up here. Like the idea of dying in their beds."

"See if any of these guys had foot problems. Or if they left shoes at home. Sole imprints could be useful. And start thinking about DNA. Head hair. Extracted teeth. Even a toothbrush might be a source if it hasn't been cleaned or reused. If there's nothing left from the victim we could work with a comparison sample from a blood relative."

She jotted a note.

"And be discreet. If the rest of the body is out there and someone's responsible, we don't want to tip them into finishing what the coyotes began."

"I hadn't thought of that," she said, her voice chalky.

"Sorry."

Again the head movement.

"Sheriff, do you know who owns property about a quarter mile west of the crash site? A house with a walled garden?"

She gazed at me, the eyes like pale green marbles.

"I was born in those mountains, been sheriffing here almost seven years. Until you came along I had no idea

117

there was anything up that hollow but pine."

"I don't suppose we could get a warrant, have a look inside."

"Don't suppose."

"Isn't it odd that no one knows about the place?"

"Folks keep to themselves up here."

"And die in their beds."

Back at High Ridge House, I took Boyd for a long walk. Or he took me. The chow was psyched, sniffing and baptizing every plant and rock along the road. I enjoyed myself on the downhill lap, awed by soft-focus mountains rolling to the horizon like a Monet landscape. The air was cool and moist, smelling of pine, and loam, and traces of smoke. The trees were alive with the twitter of birds settling in for the night.

The uphill run was another story. Still enthused, Boyd continued to pull on the leash like White Fang mushing across the Arctic. By the time we reached his pen my right arm was dead and my calves ached.

I was closing the gate when I heard Ryan's voice.

"Who's your friend?"

"Boyd. And he's seriously vicious." I was still out of breath, and the words came out chopped and ragged.

"In training for extreme dog walking?"

"Have a good night, boy," I said to the dog.

Boyd concentrated on crunching small brown pellets that looked like petrified jerky.

"You talk to dogs, but not to your old partner?"

I turned and looked at him.

"How ya doing, little fella?"

"Don't even think of scratching my ears. I'm doing well. And yourself?"

"Splendid. We were never partners."

"Did you do your age thing?"

"I was right on."

I checked the lock, then turned to face him.

"Sheriff Crowe's got three elderly MPs. Any scoop on the Bates Motel?"

"Nada. No one knows the place exists. If anyone's using it, they must beam themselves in and out. Either that or no one's talking."

"I'm going to check the tax rolls as soon as the courthouse opens tomorrow. Crowe's following up on the MPs."

"Tomorrow's Saturday."

"Damn." I avoided the impulse to slap my forehead.

Preoccupied with Larke's dismissal of me, I'd lost all track of the days. Government buildings are closed on weekends.

"Damn," I repeated for emphasis, and turned back toward the house. Ryan fell into step beside me.

"Interesting briefing today."

"Oh?"

"The NTSB has compiled preliminary damage diagrams. Come to headquarters tomorrow and I'll pull them up for you."

"Will my presence cause you problems?"

"Call me crazy."

The investigation had taken over much of the Bryson City area. Up on Big Laurel, work continued at the NTSB command center and temporary morgue established at the crash site. Victim identification was progressing at the incident morgue housed in the Alarka Fire Department, and a family assistance center had been set up at the Sleep Inn on Veterans' Boulevard.

In addition, the federal government had rented space

in the Bryson City Fire Department and allotted portions to the FBI, NTSB, ATF, and other organizations. At ten the next morning Ryan and I were seated at a desktop computer in one of the tiny cubicles honeycombing the building's upper floor. Between us were Jeff Lowrey, of the NTSB's cabin-interior documentation group, and Susan Katzenberg of the structures group.

As Katzenberg explained her group's preliminary ground-wreckage diagram, I kept a wary eye out for Larke Tyrell. Though I was with the feds, and not really in violation of Larke's banishment, I didn't want a confrontation.

"Here's the wreckage triangle. The apex is at the crash site, then the trail extends back along the flight path for almost four miles. That's consistent with a parabolic descent from twenty-four thousand feet at approximately four miles per minute climbing to pure vertically down."

"I processed bodies recovered more than a mile from the primary wreckage field," I said.

"The pressure hull was breached in midair, permitting the bodies to fall out in flight."

"Where were the flight recorders?" I asked.

"They were found with pieces of the aft fuselage, about halfway along the wreckage trail." She pointed at the screen. "In the F-100 the recorders are located in the unpressurized fuselage aft of the rear pressure bulkhead. They went early when something blew out aft and up."

"So the wreckage pattern is consistent with a midair disintegration sequence?"

"Yes. Anything without wings, that is, without aerodynamic lift generation, falls in a ballistic trajectory, with the heavier stuff going farther horizontally."

120

She indicated a large cluster of items, then moved her finger along the trail.

"The initial wreckage on the ground would be the small, light stuff."

She pushed back from the computer and turned to Ryan and me.

"I hope that helps. Gotta run."

Lowery took over when she'd gone. The monitor's glow deepened the lines in his face as he bent over the keyboard. He entered commands, and a new pattern filled the screen, looking like a Seurat in primary colors.

"First we established a set of general guidelines to describe the condition of the recovered seats and seat units."

He pointed out colors in the pattern.

"Seats with minimal damage are indicated by light blue, those with moderate damage by dark blue, those with severe damage by green. Seats classified as 'destroyed' are shown in yellow, those classified as 'fragmented' in red."

"What do the categories mean?" I asked.

"Light blue means the seat legs, back, pan, and armrest are intact, as is the safety belt restraint system. Dark blue means there's minor deformation to one or more of those components. Green means both fractures and deformation are present. Yellow indicates a seat with at least two of the five components fractured or missing, and red indicates damage to three or more components."

The diagram showed a plane interior with lavatory, galleys, and closets behind the cockpit, eight seats in first class and eighteen rows in coach, double on port, triple on starboard. Behind the last row, which was double on both sides, was another set of galleys and lavatories.

A child could have interpreted the pattern. The colors flowed from cool blue to flaming red as they spread from forward to aft, indicating that seats closest to the cockpit were largely intact, those in mid-cabin more damaged, those behind the wings largely demolished. The highest concentration of red was at the rear left of the plane.

Lowery hit the keys and a new chart came up.

"This shows passenger seat assignments, though the aircraft wasn't full and people might have moved around. The cockpit voice recorder indicates that the captain had not turned off the 'Fasten Seat Belt' sign, so most passengers should have been seated with their belts fastened. The voice recorder also indicates that the captain had released the flight attendants to begin cabin service, so they could have been anywhere.

"Will you ever be able to tell who was seated and who wasn't?"

"Recovered seats will be examined for evidence of belt restraint, things like belt loading, belt cuts, occupant-related deformation. With data from the medical/anthropology group we'll try to correlate seat damage with body fragmentation."

I listened, knowing the bodies would be coded, just as the seats had been. Green: body intact. Yellow: crushed head or loss of one extremity. Blue: loss of two extremities with or without crushed head. Red: loss of three or more extremities or complete transection of body.

"The autopsy reports will also show where passengers with penetrating materials, thermal burns, or chemical burns were seated within the cabin," Lowery went on. "We'll also try to correlate right-versus-left-side injury patterns with right-versus-left-seat deformation."

"What does that tell you?" Ryan asked.

"A high degree of correlation would suggest that passengers remained seated through most of the crash sequence. A poor correlation would mean either they were not in their assigned seats, or they became separated from their seats fairly early in the sequence."

I felt a chill thinking of the terror-filled final moments of those passengers.

"The docs will also give us data on anterior-versus-posterior injuries, which we'll correlate to fore-versus-aft seat deformation."

"Why?" Ryan.

"It's assumed that the forward position of the plane combined with the protective effect of the seat at the occupant's back result in predominantly anterior injuries."

"Unless the passenger is separated from the seat."

"Exactly. Also, in crashes with forward velocity, forward-facing seats are deformed in the forward direction. In midair breakups, that pattern may not occur, since portions of the plane may have tumbled prior to impact."

"And?"

"Of the seats recovered so far, over seventy percent show detectable deformation in the fore-aft plane. Of those, less than forty percent were deformed in the forward direction."

"Meaning in-flight destruction."

"No doubt about it. Susan's group is still studying the mode of breakup. They'll try to reconstruct the exact sequence of failure, but it's pretty clear there was a sudden, catastrophic midair event. That means that parts of the fuselage tumbled prior to ground impact. I'm a little surprised there isn't more variation among the various sections, but these things never follow the book. What is clear is that the seats in each section show nearly identical impact loading."

He worked the keys, and the original diagram filled the screen.

"And there's little doubt where the blast occurred." He pointed to the splotch of fiery red at the left rear of the cabin.

"An explosion doesn't necessarily mean a bomb."

We swiveled to see Magnus Jackson standing at the cubicle entrance. He looked at me a long time but said nothing. The screen glowed rainbow bright behind us.

"The rocket scenario has been given some new credibility," Jackson said.

We all waited.

"There are now three witnesses claiming to have seen an object shoot into the sky."

Ryan crooked an arm over the back of his chair. "I've talked to the Right Reverends Mr. Claiborne and Mr. Bowman, and I'd estimate a combined IQ in the woolly worm range."

I wondered how Ryan knew about woolly worms but didn't ask.

"All three witnesses give times and descriptions that are virtually identical."

"Like their genetic codes," Ryan quipped.

"Will these witnesses take lie detector tests?" I asked.

"They probably think a microwave will fry their genitals," Ryan said.

Jackson almost smiled, but Ryan's jokes were beginning to annoy me.

"You're right," Jackson said. "There's a healthy suspicion of authority and science in the rural areas up here. The witnesses refuse to submit to polygraphs on the grounds that the government could use the technology to alter their brains."

"Give them upgrades?"

Jackson did smile briefly. Then the investigator in charge studied me again, and left without another word.

"Can we go back to the seating chart? I asked.

Lowery entered a sequence of keystrokes and the diagram filled the screen.

"Can you superimpose the seat damage over that?"

Another few keys and the Seurat was in place.

"Where was Martha Simington seated?"

Lowery pointed to the first row in first class: "1A."

Pale blue.

"And the Sri Lankan exchange student?"

"Anurudha Mahendran – 12F, just forward of the right wing."

Dark blue.

"Where were Jean Bertrand and Rémi Petricelli?"

Lowery's finger moved to the last row on the left.

"Twenty-three A and B."

Fiery red.

Ground zero.

11

Following the briefing, Ryan and I bought lunch at Hot Dog Heaven and watched tourists at the Great Smoky Mountains Railroad Depot as we ate. The weather had warmed, and at one-thirty in the afternoon the temperature was in the low eighties. The sun was bright, the wind barely a whisper. Indian summer in Cherokee country.

Ryan promised to ask about progress in victim identification, and I promised to dine with him that night. As he drove off I felt like a housewife whose children had just started full-day school: a long afternoon of yawning until the troops reappeared.

Returning to High Ridge House, I took Boyd for another walk. Though the dog was delighted, the outing was really for me. I was restless and edgy and needed physical exertion. Crowe hadn't called, and I couldn't get into the courthouse until Monday. As I was barred from the morgue and persona non grata with my colleagues, further research into the foot was at a standstill.

I then tried reading but by three-thirty could take it

no longer. Grabbing purse and keys, I set out, going somewhere.

I'd hardly left Bryson City when I passed a mile marker for Cherokee.

Daniel Wahnetah was Cherokee. Was he living on the reservation at the time of his disappearance? I couldn't remember.

In fifteen minutes I was there.

The Cherokee Nation once ruled 135,000 square miles of North America, including parts of what are now eight states. Unlike the Plains Indians, so popular with producers of Western movies, the Cherokee lived in log cabins, wore turbans, and adopted the European style of dress. With Sequoyah's alphabet, their language became transcribable in the 1820s.

In 1838, in one of the more infamous betrayals in modern history, the Cherokee were forced from their homes and driven 1,200 miles west to Oklahoma on a death march christened the Trail of Tears. The survivors came to be known as the Western Band of Cherokee. The Eastern Band is composed of the descendants of those who hid out and remained in the Smoky Mountains.

As I drove past signs for the Oconaluftee Indian Village, the Museum of the Cherokee Indian, and the outdoor drama *Unto These Hills*, I experienced my usual anger at the arrogance and cruelty of manifest destiny. Though geared toward the dollar, these contemporary enterprises were also attempts at heritage preservation, and demonstrated the tenacity of another people screwed over by noble pioneer ancestors.

Billboards plugged Harrah's Casino and the Cherokee Hilton, living proof that Sequoyah's descendants shared his aptitude for cultural borrowing.

So did downtown Cherokee, where T-shirt, leather, knife, and moccasin stores elbowed for space with gift and souvenir emporiums, fudge shops, ice cream parlors, and fast-food joints. The Indian Store. The Spotted Pony. The Tomahawk Mini-Mall. The Buck and Squaw. Teepees sprouted from roofs and painted totem poles flanked entrances. Aboriginal kitsch extraordinaire.

After several unsuccessful passes up and down Highway 19, I parked in a small lot several blocks off the main drag. For the next hour I joined the tourist mass swarming walkways and businesses. I appraised genuine Cherokee ashtrays, key chains, back stretchers, and tom-toms. I inspected authentic wooden tomahawks, ceramic buffalo, acrylic blankets, and plastic arrows, and marveled at the ringing of the cash registers. Had there ever been buffalo in North Carolina?

Now who's screwing whom? I thought, watching a young boy hand over seven dollars for a neon-feathered headdress.

Despite the culture of commercialism, I enjoyed stepping back from my normal world: Women with bite marks on their breasts. Toddlers with vaginal abrasions. Drifters with bellies full of antifreeze. A severed foot. Goosefeather headdresses are preferable to violence and death.

It was also a relief to step out of the emotional quagmire of puzzling relationships. I bought postcards. Peanut butter fudge. A caramel apple. My problems with Larke Tyrell and my confusion about Pete and Ryan receded to another galaxy.

Walking past the Boot Hill Leather Shop, I had a sudden impulse. Beside Pete's bed I'd noticed the slippers that Katy had given him when she was six years old. I'd buy him moccasins as a thank-you for boosting my spirits.

Or whatever it was that he had boosted.

As I was poking through the bins, another thought struck me: Perhaps genuine imitation Native-American footwear would cheer Ryan's spirits over the loss of his partner. O.K. Two for one.

Pete was easy. Eleven D translates to "large" in moccasin. What the hell did Ryan wear?

I was comparing sizes, debating whether an extra large would fit a six-foot-three Irish-Canadian from Nova Scotia, when a series of synapses fired in my brain.

Foot bones. Soldiers in Southeast Asia. Formulae for distinguishing Asian remains from those of American blacks and whites.

Could it work?

Had I taken the necessary measurements?

Grabbing one large and one extra large, I paid and raced for the parking lot, anxious to return to Magnolia to check my spiral notebook.

I was approaching my car when I heard an engine, glanced up, and saw a black Volvo moving in my direction. At first my mind didn't register danger, but the car kept coming. Fast. Too fast for a parking lot.

My mental computer. Velocity. Trajectory.

The car was speeding directly toward me!

Move!

I didn't know which way to throw myself. I guessed left and hit the ground. In seconds the Volvo flashed by, showering me with dirt and gravel. I felt a blast of wind, gears shifted close to my head, and the smell of exhaust filled my lungs.

The engine sounds receded.

I lay flat on the ground, listening to my pounding heart.

My mind connected. Look up!

When I turned my head the Volvo was rounding a corner. The sun was low and straight in my eyes, so I caught only a glimpse of the driver. He was hunched forward, and a cap hid most of his face.

I rolled and pushed myself to a sitting position, brushed dirt from my clothes, and glanced around. I was alone in the lot.

Rising on shaky legs, I threw my purse and package into the backseat, slid behind the wheel, and hit the locks. Then I sat a moment massaging my throbbing shoulder.

What the hell had just happened?

All the way to High Ridge House I replayed the scene. Was I becoming paranoid, or had someone tried to run me down? Was the driver drunk? Blind? Stupid?

Should I report the incident? To Crowe? To McMahon?

Had the silhouette seemed familiar? I'd automatically thought "he," but was it a man?

I decided to ask Ryan's opinion at dinner.

Back in Ruby's kitchen, I made tea and drank it slowly. By the time I'd climbed to Magnolia, my nerves had calmed and my hands were steady. I made a call to the university in Charlotte, not really expecting an answer. My assistant picked up on the first ring.

"What are you doing at the lab on Saturday?"

"Grading."

"Right. I appreciate your dedication, Alex."

"Grading exercises is part of my job. Where are you?"

"Bryson City."

130

"I thought you were finished there. I mean, your job was finished. I mean . . ." She trailed off, unsure what to say.

Her embarrassment told me that news of my dismissal had reached the university.

"I'll explain when I get back."

"You go, girl." Lamely.

"Listen, can you grab the lab copy of my book?"

"Eighty-six or ninety-eight?"

I'd been the editor of a book on forensic techniques that had become a leading text in its field, largely due to the excellent work of the contributing authors I had managed to assemble, but including a couple of my own chapters as well. After twelve years it had been updated with a second, entirely new edition.

"The first one."

"Hold on."

In seconds she was back.

"What do you need?"

"There's a chapter on population differences in the calcaneus. Flip to that."

"Got it."

"What's the percentage of correct classification when comparing Mongoloid, black, and white foot bones?"

There was a long pause. I could picture her scanning the text, forehead creasing, glasses creeping down her nose.

"Just below eighty percent."

"Not great."

"But wait." Another pause. "That's because the whites and blacks don't separate well. The Mongoloids could be distinguished with eighty-three to ninety-nine percent accuracy. That's not too bad."

"O.K. Give me the list of measurements."

I had a sinking feeling as I wrote them down.

"Now see if there's a table that gives the unstandardized canonical discriminant function coefficients for American Indians, blacks, and whites." I would need these figures for comparison to coefficients I would derive from the unknown foot.

Pause.

"Table Four."

"Will you fax that chapter to me?"

"Sure."

I gave her Primrose Hobbs's name and fax number at the incident morgue in Bryson City. Hanging up, I dug out the notes I'd taken on case number 387.

When I punched another number and asked for Primrose Hobbs a voice told me she was not there, but asked if I would like her number at the Riverbank Inn.

Primrose also answered on the first ring. This was my lucky day.

"Hey, sweetie pie, how you doin'?"

"I'm good, Primrose."

"Don't you let these slanders get you down. God will do what God will do, and he knows it's all bunk."

"I'm not."

"One day we're going to sit down, play us some more bid whit, and laugh at all this."

"I know."

"Though I must say, for a smart woman, Tempe Brennan, you are the sorriest bid whit player I've ever sat at a table with." She laughed her deep, throaty laugh.

"I'm not very good at card games."

"You sure got that right."

Again the laugh.

"Primrose, I need a favour."

"Just ask, sugar."

I gave a condensed version of the history of the foot, and Primrose agreed to go to the morgue early Sunday morning. She would read the fax, call me, and I would walk her through the missing measurements. She commented again on the charges against me, and suggested anatomical locations in which Larke Tyrell could store them.

I thanked her for her loyalty and disconnected.

Ryan chose Injun Joe's Chili Joint for dinner. I chose The Misty Mountain Café, featuring nouvelle cuisine and spectacular views of Balsam Mountain and Maggie Valley. When reasonable discussion failed to resolve the impasse, we flipped a coin.

The Misty Mountain looked more like a ski lodge than a café, built of logs, with high ceilings, fireplaces, and lots of glass. Upon our arrival we were informed that a table would be available in ninety minutes, but wine could be served on the patio immediately.

Joe seated us without delay. Even when I win, I lose.

One look told me *le joint* catered to a different market than *le café*. A half dozen TVs broadcast a college football game, and men in dozer caps lined the bar. Couples and groups occupied tables and booths, denimed and booted, most looking like a haircut or shave had not played a part in their recent past. Mixed into the crowd were tourists in brightly colored wind-breakers, and a few faces I recognized from the investigation.

Two men worked the bar, pulling taps, scooping ice, and pouring liquour from bottles in front of a dingy mirror. Each had pasty skin and lank brown hair tied in a ponytail and secured with a bandana. Neither looked Injun, and neither shopped at Armani. One wore a

T-shirt plugging Johnson's Brown Ale, the other a group called Bitchin' Tits.

On a platform in back, across from a pool table and pinball machines, members of a band adjusted equipment, directed by a woman in black leather pants and Cruella makeup. Every few seconds we'd hear the amplified tap of her finger, then a count from one to four. Her sound tests barely overrode the TV play-by-play and the clicks and dings of the pinball machines.

Nevertheless, the band looked like it had enough acoustic power to reach Buenos Aires. I suggested we order.

Ryan scanned the room and made a hand gesture. A woman, maybe forty or so, with overmoussed hair and an out-of-season tan, appeared at our table. A plastic badge gave her name as Tammi. With an *i*.

"Whatillitbe?" Tammi poised pencil over pad.

"May I have a menu?" I asked.

Tammi sighed, retrieved two menus from the bar, and slapped them on the table. Then she looked at me with forbidding patience.

Click. Click. Click. Ding. Ding. Ding. Ding.

My decision did not take long. Injun Joe offered nine types of chili, four burgers, a hot dog, and mountain meat loaf.

I requested the Climbingbear Burger and a Diet Coke.

"I've heard you make killer chili here." Ryan showed Tammi a lot of teeth.

"Best in the west." Tammi showed Ryan even more.

Tap. Tap. Tap. Tap. One. Two. Three. Four.

"It must be hard to wait on so many people at the same time. I don't know how you do it."

"Personal charm." Tammi tilted her chin and threw out one hip.

"How's the Walkingstick Chili?"

"Hot. Like me."

I fought a gag impulse.

"I'll go for it. And a bottle of Carolina Pale."

"Coming atcha, cowboy."

Click. Click. Click. Click. Ding. Ding. Ding. Ding. Tap. Tap. One. Two. Three. Four.

I waited until Tammi was out of earshot, which, given the din, was about two steps.

"Nice choice."

"One should mingle with the locals."

"You were pretty critical of the locals this morning."

"One must keep a finger on the pulse of the common man."

"And woman." *Tap. Tap.* "Cowboy."

Tammi returned with a beer, a Diet Coke, and a million miles of teeth. I smiled her back to the kitchen.

"Anything new since this morning?" I asked when she'd gone.

"Seems Haskell Simington may not be such a hot pick. Turns out he's worth zillions, so a two mill policy on his wife isn't that unusual. Besides being worth megabucks, the guy named their kids as beneficiaries."

"That's it?"

Ryan waited out another sound check.

"The structures group reported that three quarters of the plane has been trucked down the mountain. They're reassembling in a hangar near Ashville.

Tap. Tap. Tap. One. Screeeeeeeech. Two. Three. Four.

Ryan's eyes drifted to a TV behind my head.

"That's it?"

"That's it. Why the orange paw prints?"

"It's a Clemson home game."

He looked a question at me.

"Never mind."

Tammi was back after three downs.

"I gave you extra cheese," she purred, bending low to give Ryan a spectacular view of cleavage.

"I love cheese." Ryan gave her another blinding smile, and Tammi held position.

Tap. Tap. One. Two. Three. Four.

I glared at Tammi's breasts, and she removed them from my line of vision.

"Will that be all?"

"Ketchup." I picked up a French fry.

"Any talk about my visit to headquarters this morning?"

When I lifted my burger a cheese umbilicus clung to the plate.

"Special Agent McMahon said you looked good in jeans."

"I didn't see McMahon there." The bun was raining soggy clumps on to the cheese connector.

"He saw *you*. At least from the back."

"What's the FBI position on my dismissal?"

"I can't speak for the entire Bureau, but I know McMahon isn't fond of your state's second in command."

"I don't know for certain that Davenport is behind the complaint."

"Whether he is or not, McMahon has no time for him. He called Davenport a brainless buttwipe." Ryan spooned chili into his mouth, followed it with beer. "We Irish are poets at heart."

"That brainless buttwipe can probably have you invited back to Canada."

"How was your afternoon?"

"I went to the reservation."

"Did you see Tonto?"

136

"How did I know you would ask that?"

I reached into my bag and produced the moccasins.

"I wanted you to have something from my native land."

"To atone for the way you've been treating me lately?"

"I've been treating you as a colleague."

"A colleague who'd like to suck your toes."

My stomach did that little flippy thing.

"Open the package."

He did.

"These are kickin'."

Resting an ankle on one knee, Ryan replaced a deck shoe with a moccasin. A big-haired deb at the bar stopped peeling the label from her Coors to watch him.

"Made by Sitting Bull himself?"

"Sitting Bull was Sioux. These were probably made by Wang Chou Lee."

He reversed, and did the other foot. The deb jabbed an elbow at her companion.

"You may not want to wear them here."

"Certainly I do. They were a gift from a colleague."

He wrapped the deck shoes in the moccasin bag and went back to his chili.

"Meet any interesting aboriginals?"

I wanted to say no. "Actually, I did."

He looked up with eyes blue enough to blend in with a village full of Finns.

"Or, I might have."

I told him about the Volvo incident.

"Jesus, Brennan. How do—"

"I know. How do I get myself into these situations. Do you think I should worry about it?" I was hoping he would say no.

137

Ding. Ding. Ding. Ding.

Tap. Tap. One. Two. Three. Four.

Chili.

Beer.

Fragments of conversation.

"The deconstructionists tell us that nothing is real, but I've discovered one or two truisms in life. The first is, when attacked by a Volvo, take it seriously."

"I'm not sure the guy meant to run me down. Maybe he didn't see me."

"Did you think so at the time?"

"That's how it felt."

"Second truism: Volvo first impressions are generally correct."

We'd finished eating and Ryan was in the men's room when I noticed Lucy Crowe enter and make her way toward the door. She was in uniform and looked armed and deadly.

I waved but Crowe didn't notice. I stood and waved again, and a voice bellowed, "You're blocking the game. Park it or haul it."

Ignoring the suggestion, I flapped both arms. Crowe saw me, nodded, and held up an index finger. As I sat, the bartender handed her a glass, then leaned forward to whisper something.

"Hey, sweet cheeks!"

A redneck scorned is never pretty. I continued to ignore, he continued to taunt.

"Hey, you with the windmill act."

The redneck was ratcheting up when he spotted the sheriff moving in my direction. Realizing his error, he swigged his beer and reengaged with the game.

Ryan and Crowe reached the booth simultaneously. Noticing Ryan's feet, the sheriff looked at me.

138

"He's Canadian."

Ryan let it pass and resumed his seat.

Crowe set her 7UP on the table and joined us.

"Dr. Brennan has a story she wants to share," said Ryan, pulling out his cigarettes.

I looked icicles at him. I would have preferred a lifetime of tax audits to telling Crowe of the Volvo incident.

She listened without interrupting.

"Did you get the license number?"

"No."

"Can you describe the driver?"

"Wearing a cap."

"What kind of cap?"

"I couldn't tell." I could feel my cheeks flush with humiliation.

"Was anyone else present?"

"No. I checked. Look, the whole thing may have been an accident. Maybe it was a kid peeling out in Daddy's Volvo."

"Is that what you think?" The celery eyes were locked on mine.

"No. I don't know."

I placed my hands on the tabletop, pulled them back, and wiped spilled beer on to my jeans.

"While I was on the reservation I thought of something that might be helpful," I said, changing the subject.

"Oh?"

I described the foot bone research and explained how the measurements could be used to determine racial background.

"So I may be able to sort out your rainbow coalition."

"I'll talk with Daniel Wahnetah's kin tomorrow."

139

She swirled the ice in her 7UP.

"But I unearthed some interesting facts about George Adair."

"The missing angler?"

A Crowe nod.

"Adair saw his doctor twelve times during the past year. Seven of those visits were for throat problems. The other five were for pain in his feet."

"Hot dog."

"It gets better. Adair's only gone one week, his grieving widow takes a trip to Las Vegas with the next-door neighbor."

I waited while she drained her 7UP.

"The neighbor is George Adair's best friend."

"And fishing buddy?"

"You've got it."

12

The next morning I slept until eight, fed Boyd, and overdosed on one of Ruby's mountain breakfasts. My hostess had bonded with the dog, and that day's Scripture lauded the fish of the sea, the fowl of the air, and things that creepeth upon the earth. I wondered if Boyd qualified as a creeper but didn't ask.

Ryan hadn't appeared by the time I left the dining room. Either he was out early, sacking in, or passing up the hotcakes, bacon, and grits. We'd returned from Injun Joe's around eleven the previous night, and he'd proffered his usual invitation. I'd left him on the front porch, swinging without me.

I was climbing to Magnolia when my cell phone rang. It was Primrose, calling from the incident morgue.

"You must have risen with the birds."

"Have you been outside?" she asked.

"Not yet."

"It's a great gettin'-up morning out there."

"Did you get the fax?"

"I surely did. Studied the descriptions and diagrams and took every measurement."

"You're amazing, Primrose."

I double-stepped the last few stairs, raced to my room, and opened the file on case number 387. After jotting down the new figures, we compared Primrose's data with that which I'd already collected.

"Each of your measurements is within one millimeter of mine," I said. "You're good."

"You got that right."

Confident that inter-observer error would not be a problem, I thanked her, and asked when I could get the chapter. She suggested I meet her at the parking lot gate in twenty minutes. In her opinion, entry into the morgue was not yet an option for me.

Primrose must have been watching, for as soon as I left the highway she emerged through the morgue's back door and began picking her way across the lot, cane in one hand, plastic grocery bag in the other.

Meanwhile, the guard came forward, read my license plate, and checked a clipboard. Then he shook his head, held one hand in a halt gesture, and signaled, and signaled me to reverse direction with the other. Primrose approached him and said a few words.

The guard continued to signal and shake his head. Primrose leaned close and spoke again, old black woman to young black man. The guard rolled his eyes, then folded his hands across his chest and watched her continue toward my car, a five-star general in boots, fatigues, and granny bun.

Leaning on her cane, she handed the bag through the driver's-side window. Her face was serious a moment, then a smile lighted her eyes, and she patted me on the shoulder.

"Don't you pay this trouble no mind, Tempe. You

haven't done any of those things and they'll see that soon."

"Thanks, Primrose, You're right, but it's hard."

"Course it is. But I'm keeping you in my prayers."

Her voice was as soothing as a Brandenburg Concerto.

"In the meantime, you just take one day at a time. One damn day at a time."

With that she turned and set off toward the morgue.

I'd rarely heard Primrose Hobbs curse.

Back in my room, I pulled out the chapter, flipped to Table IV, plugged in the measurements, and did the math.

The foot classified as American Indian.

I calculated again, using a second function.

Though closer to the cluster for African Americans, the foot still fell with the Native Americans.

George Adair was white, Jeremiah Mitchell was black. So much for the missing fisherman and the man who'd borrowed his neighbor's ax.

Unless he'd wandered back to the reservation, Daniel Wahnetah was looking like a match.

I checked my watch. Ten forty-five. Late enough.

The sheriff was not in. No. They would not phone her at home. No. They would not give out her pager number. Was this an emergency? They would relay the message that I had called.

Damn. Why hadn't I gotten Crowe's pager number?

For the next two hours I engaged in irrelevant activity, directed by the brain for tension relief rather than goal attainment. Behaviorists call it displacement.

Following a laundry session involving panties in the bathroom sink, I sorted and organized the contents of my briefcase, deleted temporary files from my laptop, balanced my checkbook, and rearranged Ruby's glass animal collection. I then phoned my daughter, sister, and estranged husband.

Pete did not answer, and I assumed he was still in Indiana. Katy did not answer, and I made no assumptions. Harry kept me on the phone for forty minutes. She was quitting her job, having trouble with her teeth, and dating a man named Alvin from Denton. Or was it Denton from Alvin?

I was testing the ring options on my phone when a strange baying arose from the yard, like a hound in a Bela Lugosi movie. Peering through the screen, I saw Boyd seated in the middle of his run, head thrown back, a wail rising from his throat.

"Boyd."

He stopped howling and looked around. Far down the mountain I heard a siren.

"I'm up here."

The dog stood and cocked his head, then the purple tongue slid out.

"Look up, boy."

Reverse cock.

"Up!" I clapped my hands.

The chow spun, ran to the end of the pen, sat, and resumed his love song to the ambulance.

The first thing one notices on meeting Boyd is his disproportionately large head. It was becoming clear that the dog's cranial capacity was in no way related to the size of his intellect.

Grabbing jacket and leash, I headed out.

The temperature was still warm, but the sky was slowly filling with dark-centered clouds. Wind flapped my jacket and gusted leaves and pine needles across the gravel yard.

144

This time we did the uphill lap first, Boyd charging ahead, huffing and coughing as the collar tightened across his larynx. He raced from tree to tree, sniffing and squirting, while I gazed into the valley below, each of us enjoying the mountain in our own way.

We'd gone perhaps a half mile when Boyd froze and his head shot up. The fur went stiff along his spine, his mouth half opened, and a growl rose from the back of his throat, a sound quite different from the siren display.

"What is it, boy?"

Ignoring my question, the dog lunged, ripping the leash from my grip, and charged into the woods.

"Boyd!"

I stamped my foot and rubbed my palm.

"Damn!"

I could hear him through the trees, barking like he was on scrap yard sentry duty.

"Boyd, come back here!"

The barking continued.

Cursing at least one creature that creepeth, I left the road and followed the noise. I found him ten yards in, dashing back and forth, yapping at the base of a white oak.

"Boyd!"

He continued running, barking, and snapping at the oak.

"*BOYD!*"

He skidded to a stop and looked in my direction.

Dogs have fixed facial musculature, making them incapable of expression. They cannot smile, frown, grimace, or sneer. Nevertheless, Boyd's eyebrows made a movement that clearly communicated his disbelief.

Are you crazy?

"Boyd, sit!" I pointed a finger and held it on him.

He looked at the oak, back at me, then sat. Never lowering the finger, I picked my way to him and regained the leash.

"Come on, dog breath," I said, patting his head, then tugging him toward the road.

Boyd twisted and yipped at the oak, then turned back and did the eyebrow thing.

"What *is* it?"

Rrrrup. Rup. Rup.

"O.K. Show me."

I gave him some leash, and he dragged me towards the tree. Two feet from it, he barked and whipped around, eyes shining with excitement. I parted the vegetation with a boot.

A dead squirrel lay among the sow thistle, orbits empty, brown tissue sheathing its bones like a dark, leathery shroud.

I looked at the dog.

"Is this what's got your fur in a twist?"

He dropped on front paws, rump in the air, then rose and took two hops backward.

"It's dead, Boyd."

The head cocked, and the eyebrow hairs rotated.

"Let's go, mighty tracker."

The rest of the walk was uneventful. Boyd found no more corpses, and we clocked a much better time on the downhill run. Rounding the last curve I was surprised to see a cruiser parked under the trees at High Ridge House, a Swain County Sheriff's Department shield on its side.

Lucy Crowe stood on the front steps, a Dr Pepper in one hand, Smokey hat in the other. Boyd went right to her, tail wagging, tongue drooping like a purple eel. The sheriff set her hat on the railing and ruffled the dog's fur.

He nuzzled and licked her hand, then curled on the porch, chin on forepaws, and closed his eyes. Boyd the Deadly.

"Nice dog," said Crowe, wiping a hand on the seat of her pants.

"I'm minding him for a few days."

"Dogs are good company."

"Um."

Obviously, she'd never spent time with Boyd.

"I had a talk with the Wahnetah family. Daniel still hasn't returned."

I waited while she sipped her soda.

"They say he stood about five-seven."

"Did he complain about his feet?"

"Apparently he never complained about anything. Didn't talk much at all, liked to be alone. But here's an interesting sidebar. One of Daniel's campsites was out at Running Goat Branch."

"Where's Running Goat Branch?"

"Spit and a half from your walled enclosure."

"No shit."

"No shit."

"Was he there when he went missing?"

"The family wasn't sure, but that was the first place they checked."

"I've got another sidebar," I said, my excitement growing.

I told her about the discriminant function classification placing the foot bones closest to those of Native Americans.

"Now can you get a warrant?" I asked.

"Based on what?"

I ticked off points by raising fingers.

"An elderly Native American went missing in your

147

county. I have a body part fitting that profile. This body part was recovered in proximity to a location frequented by your missing person."

She cocked an eyebrow, then did her own ticking.

"A body part that might or might not be related to an aviation disaster. An old man who might or might not be dead. A property that might or might nor be implicated in either situation."

The hunch of an anthropologist who might or might not be the spawn of Satan. I didn't say it.

"Let's at least go to his camp and look around," I pushed.

She thought a moment, then looked at her watch.

"That I can do."

"Give me five minutes." I gestured at Boyd.

She nodded.

"Come on, boy."

The head came up and the eyebrows puckered.

A ping in my mind. The dead squirrel. My line of work makes me unusually sensitive to the smell of putrefaction, yet I hadn't detected a trace. Boyd went ballistic at ten yards.

"Could the dog ride along?" I asked. "He's not cadaver-trained, but he's pretty good at sniffing out carrion."

"He sits in back."

Eleven days had passed since the Air TransSouth crash. All remains had been taken to the morgue, and the last of the wreckage was being hauled down the mountain. The recovery operation was winding down, and the change was evident.

The county road was now open, though a sheriff's deputy protected the entrance to the Forest Service

148

road. The families and press were gone, and only a handful of vehicles occupied the overlook holding area.

Crowe cut the engine where the road ended, about a half mile beyond the cutoff to the crash site. A large granite outcropping lay to the right. Clipping a radio to her belt, she crossed the gravel track and walked the uphill side, carefully studying the tree line.

I leashed Boyd and followed, keeping him as close to me as I could. After a full five minutes the sheriff cut left and disappeared up the embankment into the trees. I gave Boyd his head, and was dragged along in her wake.

The land climbed steeply, leveled off, then shot downward into a valley. As we moved farther from the road, the trees closed around us, and everything started to look the same. But the landmarks given by the Wahnetah family made sense to the sheriff. She found the path they'd described, and from it a small dirt road. I couldn't tell if it was the same logging trail that passed by the wreckage field or another similar to it.

It took Crowe forty minutes to locate Daniel's cabin, set among beech and pine at the edge of a small creek. I probably would have walked right past it.

The camp looked as though it had been thrown up in an afternoon. The shack was wood, the floor dirt, the roof corrugated tin, extended in front to provide shelter for a makeshift bench beside the door. A wooden table and another bench sat to the left front of the shanty, a tree stump to the right. Out back I could see a pile of bottles, cans, tires, and other refuse.

"How do you suppose the tires got there?" I asked.

Crowe shrugged.

Gingerly, I cracked the door and stuck my head inside. In the gloom I could make out a cot, an aluminum lawn chair, and a collapsible table holding a rusty camp stove and a collection of plastic dishes and cups. Fishing gear, a bucket, a shovel, and a lantern hung from nails. Kerosene cans lined the floor. That was it.

"Would the old man leave his fishing gear if he planned to move on?"

Another shrug.

Lacking a real plan, Crowe and I decided to split up. She searched the creek bank while I walked the surrounding woods. My canine companion sniffed and peed contentedly.

Returning to the shack, I secured Boyd to a table leg, swung the door wide, and propped it with a rock. Inside, the air smelled of mildew, kerosene, and muscatel. Millipedes skittered as I shifted objects, and at one point a daddy longlegs high-stepped up my arm. I found nothing to indicate where Daniel Wahnetah had gone or when he'd left. Or why.

Crowe reappeared as I was poking through the refuse heap. After toeing over dozens of wine bottles, cracker tins, and Dinty Moore beef stew cans, I gave up and picked my way out to join her.

Trees whispered in the wind. Leaves sailed across the ground in a colorful regatta, and a corner of the corrugated tin rose and fell with a scraping sound. Though the air felt dense and heavy, there was movement all around us.

Crowe knew what I was thinking. Without a word she pulled a small spiral-bound atlas from her jacket and flipped through the pages.

"Show me," she said, handing me the book.

The map she'd chosen was a close-up of the piece of Swain County in which we stood. Using elevation lines, the county road, and the logging trails, I located the crash site. Then I estimated the position of the courtyard house and pointed to it.

"Here."

Crowe studied the topography around my finger.

"You're sure there's a structure back in there?" I heard doubt in her voice.

"Yes."

"It's less than a mile."

"By foot?"

She nodded, a slower motion than usual.

"There's no road I know of, so we might as well go overland."

"Can you find it?"

"I can find it."

We spent an hour threading our way through trees and brush, up one ridge and down another, following a track that was clear to Crowe but invisible to me. Then, at an ancient pine, its trunk knotted and worn, we emerged on to a path that even I could recognize.

We came to a high wall, vaguely familiar from my previous visit. Every sense sharpened as we moved along the mossy stone. A jay cawed, shrill and strident, and my skin seemed to tighten on my body. There was something here. I knew it.

Boyd continued to amble and snuffle, oblivious to my tension. I wrapped the leash around my palm, tightened my grasp.

Within yards, the wall made a ninety-degree turn. Crowe rounded the corner and I followed, my grip so tight I felt my nails dig into my palm.

The trees ended three quarters of the distance up the wall. Crowe stopped at the verge of the woods and Boyd and I caught up.

Ahead and to the left I spotted another walled

enclosure, the rock face rising in the distance beyond. I had my bearings. We'd approached from the rear of the property; the house lay ahead of us, its back to the escarpment. The wall we'd been skirting surrounded a larger area I hadn't noted on my first visit. The courtyard was within the larger enclosure.

"I'll be damned." Crowe reached down and released the safety on her gun.

She called out as I had done. Called again.

Eyes and ears alert, we proceeded to the house and climbed the steps. The shutters were still closed, the windows still draped. I was gripped by the same sense of foreboding as on my first visit.

Crowe stepped to the side of the door and gestured with an arm. When Boyd and I had moved behind her, she knocked. Still no answer.

She knocked again, identified herself. Silence.

Crowe raised her eyes and looked around.

"No phone lines. No power lines."

"Cell phone and generator."

"Could be. Or the place could be deserted."

"Do you want to see the courtyard?"

"Not without a warrant I don't."

"But, Sheriff—"

"No warrant, no entry." She looked at me, her eyes unblinking. "Let's go. I'll buy you a Dr Pepper."

At that moment, a light rain began to fall. I listened to drops tick softly on the porch roof, frustration seething in me. She was right. It was nothing but a hunch. But every cell in my being was telling me that something important lay close at hand. Something evil.

"Could I run Boyd around the property to see if he has any thoughts?"

"Keep him outside the walls, I've got no objection.

152

I'll check for vehicular access. If folks are coming here, they must be driving."

For fifteen minutes Boyd and I crisscrossed the brush to the west of the house, much as I had on my first trip. The dog showed no reaction. Though I was beginning to suspect the squirrel hit had been a fluke, I decided to make one last sweep, skirting the edge of the forest up to its terminus at the second enclosure. This would be virgin territory.

We were twenty feet from the wall when Boyd's head snapped up. His body tensed, and the hair prickled along his back. He rotated his snout, testing the air, then growled in a way I'd heard only once, deep and feral and vicious. Then he lunged, choking and barking as though possessed.

I staggered, barely able to hold him.

"Boyd! Stop!"

Spreading my feet, I grabbed the leash with both hands. The dog continued to pull, muscles straining, forefeet scrabbling inches above the ground.

"What is it, boy?"

We both knew.

I hesitated, heart pounding. Then I unwrapped the leash and let it fall.

Boyd flew to the wall and exploded in a frenzy of barking, approximately six feet south of the back corner. I could see that the mortar was crumbling at that point, and that a dozen stones had tumbled free, leaving a gap between the ground and the wall's foundation.

I ran to the dog, crouched at his shoulder, and inspected the gap. The soil was moist and discolored. Overturning a fallen stone, I saw a dozen tiny brown objects.

Instantly, I knew what Boyd had found.

13

I did not go to the Swain County Courthouse on Monday. Instead, I recrossed the mountains west to Tennessee, and by mid-morning was approximately thirty miles northwest of Knoxville, approaching the entrance to the Oak Ridge National Laboratory. The day was wet and gloomy, and my wipers slapped a steady cadence back and forth, clearing two fans on the misty windshield.

Through the side window I could see an old woman and toddler feeding swans on the bank of a small lagoon. At the age of ten I'd had a run-in with an ugly duckling that could have taken out a commando force. I questioned the wisdom of their outing.

After showing ID at a guardhouse, I drove across a vast parking area to the reception center. My host was waiting, signed me in, and we returned to the car. Another hundred yards, and my new ORNL badge and license plates were verified at a third checkpoint before I was allowed to pass through a chain-link fence surrounding the compound.

154

"Pretty tight security. I thought this was Department of Energy."

"It is. Most of the work involves energy conservation, computers and robotics, biomedical and environmental conservation, medical radioisotope development, that sort of thing. We maintain security to protect DOE intellectual property and physical equipment. There's also a high-flux isotope reactor on-site."

Laslo Sparkes was in his thirties but already nurturing a stout paunch. He had short, slightly bowed limbs and a round face, pock-marked on the cheeks.

Oak Ridge began as a World War II wonder baby, constructed in just three short months in 1943. Thousands were dying in Europe and Asia, and Enrico Fermi and his colleagues had just achieved nuclear fission in a squash court under the stands of the football stadium at the University of Chicago. Oak Ridge's mission had been simple: build the atomic bomb.

Laslo directed me through a labyrinth of narrow streets. Turn right here. Left. Left. Right. Except for its vast size, the complex looked like an apartment project in the Bronx.

Laslo indicated a dark brick building identical to a score of other dark brick buildings.

"Park here," he said.

I pulled over and cut the engine.

"I really appreciate your doing this on such short notice."

"You were there when I asked for help."

Years earlier, Laslo had needed bone for his master's research in anthropology, and I'd provided samples. We'd kept in touch throughout his doctoral work and during the decade he'd been a research scientist at Oak Ridge.

Laslo waited while I retrieved a small cooler from the trunk, then led me into the building and up the stairs to his lab. The room was small and windowless, every millimeter crammed with battered steel desks, computers, printers, refrigerators, and a million machines that glowed and hummed. Glass vials, water containers, stainless-steel instruments, and boxes of latex gloves lined the countertops, and cardboard cartons and plastic buckets were stacked below.

Laslo led me to a work space in back and reached for the cooler. When I handed it to him, he removed a plastic bag, peeled off the tape, and peeked inside.

"Give this to me again," he said, sniffing the bag's contents.

As I explained my trek with Lucy Crowe, Laslo poured dirt from the bag into a glass container. Then he began entering information on to a blank form.

"Where did you sample?"

"I collected where the dog indicated, under the wall and under the stones that had fallen out. I figured that soil would be most protected."

"Good thinking. Normally the corpse acts as a shield for the soil, but stones would have had the same effect."

"Does rain create problems?"

"In a protected environment the heavy, mucoidlike secretions produced from anaerobic fermentation bind the soil together, making dilutional factors from rainfall insignificant."

He sounded like he was reading from one of his articles in the *Journal of Forensic Sciences*.

"Keep it simple, please. This is way off my field."

"You spotted the decomp stain."

"Actually, my dog did." I indicated a plastic vial. "The pupae are what tipped me."

Laslo withdrew the jar, twisted off the lid, and shook a number of casings into the palm of his hand. Each looked like a miniature football.

"So maggot migration had taken place."

"*If* the stain is from a decomp episode." I'd had all night to worry over Boyd's discovery. Though I was sure his nose and my instincts were correct, I wanted proof.

"Maggot pupae definitely suggest the presence of a corpse." He replaced the casings. "I think your dog was right on."

"Can you determine if it was an animal?"

"The amount of volatile fatty acids will tell us if the body was over one hundred pounds. Very few mammals get that big."

"What about hunting? A deer or bear could get that big."

"Did you find any hairs?"

I shook my head.

"Decaying animals leave behind tons of hair. And bones, of course."

When an organism dies, scavengers, insects, and microbes take an immediate interest, some munching from the outside, others from within, until the body is reduced to bone. This is known as decomposition.

Ruby would talk in terms of dust to dust, but the process is much more complicated than that.

Muscle, comprising 40 to 50 percent of the weight of a human body, is formed of protein, which is composed of amino acids. At death, the fermentation of fat and protein yields volatile fatty acids, or VFAs, through bacterial action. Inside the gut, other microbes do their part. As putrefaction advances, liquids ooze from the body, carrying with them the VFAs. Death investigators call the mixture soup.

Laslo's research focused at the microbial level, analyzing organic components contained in the dirt under and around a body. Years of work had demonstrated a correlation between the decay process and VFA production.

I watched him filter soil through a stainless-steel sieve.

"Exactly what do you look for in the dirt?"

"I don't use soil, I use soil solution."

I must have looked blank.

"The liquid component between soil particles. But first I have to clean it."

He weighed the sample.

"As body fluids flow through, the organic matter becomes bound to the soil. I can't use chemical extractants for separation, because that would partially dissolve the volatile fatty acids from the decomposing body."

"And alter their measurements."

"Exactly."

He placed the soil in a centrifuge tube and added water.

"I used deionized water in a ratio of two to one."

The tube went on to a vortex for one minute to mix the solution. Then he transferred it to a centrifuge and closed the lid.

"The temperature inside is held at five degrees. I'll centrifuge for forty minutes, then filter the sample to remove any remaining microorganisms. After that it's simple. I'll check the pH, acidify with a formic acid solution, and pop the thing into the gas chromatograph."

"How about a crash course."

Laslo finished adjusting settings, then gestured to a desk and we both sat.

158

"O.K. As you know, I'm looking at the products of muscle and fat breakdown called volatile fatty acids. Are you familiar with the four stages of decomposition?"

Anthropologists and death investigators think of corpses as being in one of four broad stages: fresh, bloated, decayed, or skeletal.

I nodded.

"There's little change in VFAs in a fresh corpse. In the second stage, a body bloats due to anaerobic fermentation, primarily in the gut. This causes skin breakage and the leakage of fermentation by-products rich in butyric acids."

"Butyric acids?"

"Volatile fatty acids include forty-one different organic compounds, of which butyric acid is one. Butyric, formic, acetic, propionic, valeric, carproic, and heptanoic are detectable in soil solution because they're soluble in water. Two of them, formic and acetic, are too abundant in nature to be of much use."

"Formic is the one that causes pain from any bites, right?"

"That's the one. Caproic and heptanoic are only found in significant amounts during the colder winter months. Propionic, butyric, and valeric are my boys. They're released from a decomposing corpse and deposited in soil solutions in specific ratios."

I felt like I was back in Biochem 101.

"Since butyric and propionic acids are formed by anaerobic bacteria in the gut, the levels are high during the bloat stage."

I nodded.

"Later, during decay, aerobic bacteria join the act."

"So at stage three there's a surge in all VFA formation."

"Yes. Then there's a rapid fall-off at the onset of stage four."

"No flesh, no bacteria."

"The soup kitchen closes."

Behind us the centrifuge hummed softly.

"I've also found that all fatty acids values are highest just after maggot migration."

"When larvae abandon the corpse to pupate."

"Yes. Until that point the presence of the insects tends to restrict the flow of body fluids into the soil."

"Doesn't pupation occur at approximately four hundred ADD?" ADD stands for "accumulated degree days," a figure calculated by summing average daily temperatures.

"With some variation. Which brings up a good point. VFA production is temperature dependent. That's why it can be used to determine time since death."

"Because a corpse will produce the same ratios of propionic, butyric, and valeric acids for any given accumulated degree days."

"Exactly. So the volatile fatty acid profile can provide an estimate of TSD." TSD is the investigator's short-hand for "time since death."

"Did you get the National Weather Service data?"

He went to a set of shelves and returned with a printout.

"It was amazingly fast. Normally it takes much longer. But we do have a slight problem. For a really accurate TSD estimate I need three things. First, the specific fatty acid ratios."

He pointed at a computer screen linked to the gas chromatograph.

"We'll have those shortly. Second, the National

160

Weather Service data at the location where the corpse was found."

He held up the printout.

"Third, information on the weight and condition of the corpse. And you ain't got no body." He sang the last.

"Everyone's a comedian."

"Two variables are important: the amount of moisture in the soil, and the weight of the body prior to decomposition. Because everyone has a different ratio of fat and muscle tissue, if I don't have a body, I use a standard of one hundred fifty pounds, then apply a correction factor. I think we're safe in assuming your deceased weighed between one hundred and three hundred pounds?"

"Yes. But in doing this, our range broadens, right?"

"Unfortunately. Did you try a rule-of-thumb estimate?"

Since volatile fatty acid liberation ceases at accumulated degree days 1,285 plus or minus 110, it is possible to obtain a rough estimate of time since death by dividing the average daily temperature on the day a corpse is found into 1,285. I'd done this for Lucy Crowe. Yesterday's average temperature in Bryson City was 18°C (64°F), yielding a maximum time since death of seventy-one days.

"That would be the date on which full skeletonization had taken place, and no more VFAs would be detectable."

Laslo looked at the wall clock.

"Let's see how accurate you were."

He rose, filtered and vortexed the soil solution sample, tested its acidity, then placed the tube into the gas chromatograph. After closing and sealing the chamber, and adjusting the settings, he turned back to me.

161

"Let's give this a few minutes. Coffee?"

When we returned the screen showed a series of peaks in varying colors, and a list of components and their concentrations.

"Each curve shows the concentration of a volatile fatty acid per gram of dry weight of soil. First I'll correct for dilution and soil moisture."

He hit a few keys.

"Now I can calculate an ADD for each VFA."

He started with butyric acid.

"Seven hundred accumulated degree days."

He performed more calculations, using each acid. With one exception the ADDs fell within the 675 to 775 range.

"Now I'll use the National Weather Service data to determine the number of days needed to obtain 675 to 775 accumulated degree days. We may have to adjust later if the readings at your body site differ from the officially recorded temperatures. Normally, I like to know that in advance, but it's not a major problem."

A few more keystrokes. I held my breath.

"Forty-one to forty-eight days. That's your range. According to your calculation, full skeletonization would have taken place in seventy-one days."

"So death occurred six to seven weeks ago."

He nodded. "But keep in mind that this time frame is based on an estimated, not an actual, predeath weight."

"And at the time the stain was produced, the body was fleshed and actively decomposing."

He nodded.

"But I ain't got no body."

"And nobody cares for me."

★

162

I drove straight to Lucy Crowe's office. The rain had stopped, but dark clouds shouldered each other low over the mountains, jockeying for position with their heavy loads.

I found the sheriff eating a corn dog behind the Civil War desk. Seeing me, she wiped crumbs from her mouth, then arced the stick and wrapper into a trash can across the room.

"Two points," I said.

"All net. No rim."

I laid hard copy in front of her and took a chair. She studied the VFA profile a full minute, elbows splayed on the desktop, fingers on her temples. Then she looked up.

"I know you're going to explain this."

"Volatile fatty acids."

"Meaning?"

"A body decomposed inside that wall."

"Whose?"

"The VFA ratios suggest a time since death of six to seven weeks. Daniel Wahnetah was last seen in late July, reported missing in August. It's now October. Do the math."

"Assuming I accept that premise, which I don't necessarily, how did Wahnetah's foot get to the crash scene?"

"If Boyd smelled decomposition, so could coyotes. They probably dragged the foot from under the wall. There's room where the foundation has crumbled."

"And left the rest of him?"

"They probably couldn't detach anything else."

"And how did Wahnetah get inside the courtyard?"

I shrugged.

"And how did he die?"

"That's sheriffing. I do the science."

Down the hall Hank Williams crooned the "Long-Gone Lonesome Blues." Static made the music sound like it was coming from another era.

"Is that enough for a warrant?" I asked.

The sheriff studied the paper for another full minute. Finally she looked up, the eyes to die for hard on mine. Then she reached for the phone.

By the time I left the sheriff's office a light rain was falling. Headlights, stoplights, and neon signs twinkled and shimmered in the dusk of early evening. The air was heavy with the smell of skunk.

Outside at High Ridge House, Boyd lay in his dog-house, chin on paws, gazing at the raindrops. He raised his head when I called and gave me a look to indicate I should do something. Seeing that I wasn't, he sighed noisily and settled back down. I filled his dish and left him to ponder his sodden world.

Inside, the house was still. I climbed the stairs to the slow *tick-tick-tick* of Ruby's hall clock. No sound came from any bedroom.

Rounding the corner at my end of the hall, I was surprised to see the door to Magnolia slightly ajar. I pushed it inward. And froze.

The drawers in my room had been rifled, the bed stripped. My briefcase had been emptied, and papers and manila folders lay scattered across the floor.

My mind locked on one word.

No! No! No!

I tossed my purse on the bed, flew to the wardrobe, and threw open the doors.

My laptop sat tucked in back, exactly as I'd left it. I pulled it out and clicked it on, my mind still racing.

164

What was in the room? What was in the room? What was in the room?

Quick mental inventory. Car keys. Credit cards. Driver's license. Passport. All had been with me.

Why? Why? Why?

A quick ransack for valuables, or was someone after something specific? What was there that anyone would want?

What? What? What?

When the computer booted I checked a few files. Everything seemed fine.

I went to the bathroom and splashed cold water on my face. Then I closed my eyes and played a childhood game I knew would calm me. Silently, I ran through the lyrics of the first song to come to mind. "Honky Tonk Women."

The time-out with Mick and the Stones worked. Steadier, I returned and began gathering papers.

I was still filing when I heard a knock, and opened the door to Andrew Ryan. He held two DoveBars in his right hand.

Ryan's eyes swept over the mess.

"What the fuck went on in here?"

I just looked at him, not trusting my voice.

"Is anything missing?"

I swallowed.

"The only thing of value was the computer, and they left that."

"Pretty much rules out robbery."

"Unless the intruder was interrupted."

"Looks like they tossed the place looking for something."

"Or just to be ornery."

Why?

"Ice cream?" Ryan offered.

We ate our DoveBars and considered possible explanations. None was persuasive. The two most likely were someone looking for money or someone letting me know he or she didn't care for me.

When Ryan had gone, I stacked the remaining folders and went to run a bath. Throwing back the shower curtain, I got my next shock.

Ruby's ceramic figurine of Orphan Annie lay at the bottom of the tub, her face smashed, her limbs shattered. Sandy dangled from the showerhead, a makeshift noose tight around his neck.

Again, my mind flew, my hands trembled. This message had nothing to do with money. Someone clearly didn't care for me.

Suddenly, I remembered the Volvo. Was that episode a threat? Was this intrusion another? I fought the impulse to run down the hall to Ryan's room.

I considered the lockless doors and thought about bringing Boyd inside. Then who would be threatened?

An hour later, lying in bed and somewhat more logical, I reflected on the strength of my reaction to the invasion of my space. Had it been anger or fear that had sent me over the edge? At whom should I be angry? What should I fear?

Sleep did not come easily.

14

When I came downstairs the next morning, Ryan was questioning Ruby about my intruder. Byron McMahon sat across from him, dividing his attention between the interrogation and a trio of fried eggs.

Ruby had one comment.

"Satan's minions are among us."

I was annoyed by her nonchalance toward the rifling of my possessions, but let it go.

"Was anything taken?" asked McMahon. Good. The FBI was on my case.

"I don't think so."

"Been irritating someone?"

"I suspect my dog has. Dogs bark." I described what had been done to Annie and Sandy.

Ryan looked at me oddly but said nothing.

"This place isn't exactly Los Alamos. Anyone could walk in and out of here." McMahon forked up fried potatoes. "What else have you been up to lately? I haven't seen you around."

I told him about the foot and the courtyard house,

ending with the VFA profile I'd gotten the day before. I did not tell him about my current status in the crash investigation, but left that gap for him to fill. As I spoke, his grin slowly dissolved.

"So Crowe is going for a warrant?" he asked, cop cool.

I was about to answer him when my cell phone sounded the *William Tell* Overture. The men looked at each other as I clicked it on.

The call was from Laslo Sparkes at Oak Ridge. I listened, thanked him, and rang off.

"Rossini calling?" Ryan asked.

"I was testing the ring options and forgot to change it back." I jabbed my egg and yolk spurted on to the table. "I wouldn't have pegged *you* as an opera buff."

"Zinger." McMahon reached for a slice of toast.

"It was the anthropologist at Oak Ridge."

"Let me guess. He's profiled the soup, and the missing body is D. B. Cooper."

Ryan was on a roll. Ignoring him, I directed my response to McMahon.

"He found something while filtering the remaining soil."

"What's that?"

"He didn't say. Just that the item might be useful. He's going to stop by Bryson City sometime later in the week on his way to Asheville."

Ruby returned, cleared plates, left.

"So you're off to the courthouse?" Ryan.

"Yes." Terse.

"Sounds like detecting."

"Somebody's got to do it."

"It can't hurt to know who owns that property." McMahon drained his cup. "After today's briefing I have to shoot down to Charlotte to interview some asswipe claiming to have information about a militia group up here in Swain. Otherwise, I'd tag along."

He drew a card from his wallet and placed it in front of me.

"If they're uncooperative at the courthouse, wave this. Sometimes the acronym induces a mood swing."

"Thanks." I pocketed the card.

McMahon excused himself, leaving Ryan and me and three empty mugs.

"Who do you think tossed your room?"

"I don't know."

"Why?"

"They were looking for your shower gel."

"I wouldn't belittle this. How about I poke around, ask a few questions?"

"You know that'd be a journey into pointlessness. These things are never solved."

"It would let folks know that someone is curious."

"I'll talk with Crowe."

I rose to leave and he took my arm.

"Do you want backup at the courthouse?"

"In case of an armed attack by the recorder of deeds?"

He looked away, back at me.

"Would you like *company* at the courthouse?"

"Aren't you going to the NTSB briefing?"

"McMahon can fill me in. But there's one condition."

I waited.

"Change your phone."

"Hi-Ho, Silver," I said.

The Swain County Administration Building and Courthouse replaced its predecessor in 1982. It is a rectangular concrete building, with a low-angled roof of red galvanized metal, that sits on the bank of the Tuckasegee River. Though lacking the charm of the old domed courthouse at Everett and Main, the structure is bright, clean, and efficient.

The tax office is located on the ground floor, immediately off a tiled octagonal lobby. When Ryan and I entered, four women looked up from computers, two behind a counter directly ahead, two behind a counter to our left.

I explained what we wanted. Woman number three pointed to a door at the back of the room.

"Land Records Department," she said.

Eight eyes traveled with us across the floor.

"Must be where they archive the classified stuff," Ryan whispered as I opened the door.

We entered to find another counter, this one guarded by a tall, thin woman with an angular face. It brought to mind my father's old picture of Stan Musial.

"May I help you?"

"We'd like to look at the county tax index map."

The woman put a hand to her mouth, as though the question startled her.

"The tax map?"

I began to suspect my request was a first. Taking Byron McMahon's card from my pocket, I walked to the counter and handed it to her.

Madam Musial eyeballed the card. "Is this, like, the actual FBI?"

When she looked up, I nodded.

"Byron?"

"It's a family name." I smiled winningly.

"Do you have a gun?"

170

"Not here." Not anywhere, but that would tarnish the image.

"Does this have to do with the airplane crash?"

I leaned close. She smelled of mint and overperfumed shampoo. "What we're looking for would be critical to the investigation."

Behind me, I heard Ryan's feet shift.

"My name is Dorothy." She handed back the card. "I'll get it."

Dorothy went to a map case, pulled out a drawer approximately two inches high, withdrew a large sheet, and spread it on the counter.

Ryan and I bent over the map. Using township boundaries, roads, and other markers, we pinpointed the section containing the courtyard house. Dorothy observed from her side of the divide, vigilant as an Egyptologist displaying a papyrus.

"Now we'd like section map six-two-one, please."

Dorothy smiled to indicate she was part of the sting, went to another case, and returned with the document.

Earlier in my career as an anthropologist, when I had done some archaeology, I'd spent hours with U.S. Geological Survey maps and knew how to interpret symbols and features. The experience came in handy. Using elevations, creeks, and roads, Ryan and I were able to zero in on the house.

"Section map six twenty-one, parcel four."

Keeping my finger on the spot, I looked up. Dorothy's face was inches from mine.

"How long will it take to pull up the tax records for this property?"

"About a minute."

I must have looked surprised.

"Swain County is not a pumpkin patch. We *are* computerized."

Dorothy went to a rear corner in her "secure" area and lifted a plastic cover from a monitor and keyboard. Ryan and I waited as she fastidiously folded the plastic, placed it on an overhead shelf, and booted the computer. When the program was up and running she keyed in a number of commands. Seconds passed. Finally, she entered the tax number and the screen filled with information.

"Do you want hard copy?"

"Please."

She unveiled a Hewlett-Packard bubble-jet printer similar to the first one I'd ever owned. Again we waited while she folded and stored the plastic cover, took one sheet of paper from a drawer, and placed it in the feeder tray.

Finally, she hit a key, the printer whirred, and the paper disappeared then oozed out.

"I hope this helps," she said, handing it to me.

The printout gave a vague description of the property and its buildings, its assessed value, the owner's name and mailing address, and the address to which the tax bills were being sent.

I passed it to Ryan, feeling deflated.

"H&F Investment Group, LLP," he read aloud. "The mailing address is a PO box in New York."

He looked at me.

"Who the hell is the H&F Investment Group?"

I shrugged.

"What's LLP?"

"Limited liability partnership," I said.

"You could try the deed room."

We both turned to Dorothy. A touch of pink had sprouted on each cheek.

"You could look up the date that H&F bought the property, and the name of the previous owner."

"They'd have that?"

She nodded.

We found the register of deeds around the corner from the tax office. The records room was situated behind the obligatory counter, through a set of slatted swinging doors. Shelves lining the walls and filling free-standing cases held deed books spanning hundreds of years. Recent ones were square and red, their numbers stated in plain gold lettering. Older volumes were ornately decorated, like leather-bound volumes of first editions.

It was like a treasure hunt, with each deed sending us backward in time. We learned the following:

The H&F Investment Group was an LLP registered in Delaware. Ownership of tax parcel number four transferred to the partnership in 1949 from one Edward E. Arthur. The description of the property was charming, but a bit loose by modern standards. I read it aloud to Ryan.

"The property begins at a Spanish oak on a knob, the corner of state grant 11807, and runs north ninety poles to the Bellingford line, then up the ridge as it meanders with Bellingford's line to a chestnut in the line of the S. Q. Barker tract—"

"Where did Arthur get it?"

I skipped the rest of the survey and read on.

"Do you want to hear the 'party of the first part' bits?"

"No."

". . . having the same land conveyed by deed from Victor T. Livingstone and wife J. E. Clampett, dated March 26, 1933, and recorded in Deed Book number

52, page 315, Records of Swain County, North Carolina."

I went to the shelf and pulled the older volume.

Arthur had obtained the property from one Victor T. Livingstone in 1933. Livingstone must have purchased it from God, since there were no records before that time.

"At least we know how the happy homeowners got in and out."

The Livingstone and Arthur deeds both described an entrance road.

"Or *get* in and out." I was still not convinced the property was abandoned. "While we were there Crowe found a track leading from the house to a logging trail. The turnoff at the trail is obscured by a makeshift gate completely overgrown with kudzu. When she showed me the entrance I couldn't believe it. You could walk or drive past it a million times without ever seeing it."

Ryan said nothing.

"Now what?"

"Now we wait for Crowe's warrant."

"And in the meantime?"

Ryan grinned, and his eyes crinkled at the corners.

"In the meantime we talk to the attorney general of the great state of Delaware, find out what we can about the H&F Investment Group."

Boyd and I were sharing a club sandwich and fries at the porch at High Ridge House when Lucy Crowe's squad car appeared on the road below. I watched her wind upward toward the driveway. Boyd continued to watch the sandwich.

"Spending quality time?" Crowe asked when she'd reached the stairs.

174

"He says I've been neglecting him."

I held out a slice of ham. Boyd tipped his head and took it gently with his front teeth. Then he lowered his snout, dropped the ham on the porch, licked it twice, and wolfed it down. In seconds his chin was back on my knee.

"They're just like kids."

"Mmm. Did you get the warrant?"

Boyd's eyes moved as my hand moved, alert for lunch meat or fries.

"I had a real heart-to-heart with the magistrate."

"And?"

She sighed and removed her hat.

"He says it's not enough."

"Evidence of a body?" I was shocked. "Daniel Wahnetah could be decomposing in that courtyard even as we speak."

"Are you familiar with the term junk science? I am. It was thrown at me at least a dozen times this morning. I think old Frank is going to start his own support group. Junk Science Victims Anonymous."

"Is the guy an idiot?"

"He's never going to Sweden to collect a prize, but he's usually reasonable."

Boyd raised his head and blew air through his nose. I put my hand down and he sniffed, then gave it a lick.

"You're neglecting him, again."

I offered a slice of egg. Boyd dropped it, licked it, sniffed, licked again, then left it on the porch.

"I don't care for egg in club sandwiches, either," Crowe said to Boyd. The dog moved his ear slightly, to indicate that he'd heard, but kept his eyes on my plate.

"It gets worse," Crowe went on.

Why not?

175

"There have been additional complaints."

"About me?"

She nodded.

"By whom?"

"The magistrate wouldn't share that information. But if you go anywhere near the site, the morgue, or any crash-related record, item, or family member, I am to arrest you for obstruction of justice. That includes this courtyard property."

"What the hell is going on?" My stomach tightened in anger.

Crowe shrugged. "I'm not sure. But you're out of that investigation."

"Am I allowed to go to the public library?" I spat.

The sheriff rubbed the back of her neck and rested a boot on the bottom step. Beneath her jacket I could see the bulge of a gun.

"There's something very wrong here, Sheriff."

"I'm listening."

"My room was ransacked yesterday."

"Theories?"

I told her about the figurines in the bathtub.

"Not exactly a Hallmark greeting."

"It's probably that Boyd's annoying someone." I said it hopefully, but didn't really believe my own words.

Boyd's ears shot forward at the sound of his name. I gave him a slice of bacon.

"Is he a barker?"

"Not really. I asked Ruby if he makes noise when I'm away. She said he howls a bit, but nothing extraordinary."

"What does Ruby say about it?"

"Satan's minions."

"Maybe you have something that someone wants."

176

"Nothing was taken, though all my files were thrown around. The whole room was trashed."

"Did you keep notes on this foot?"

"I'd taken them with me to Oak Ridge."

She looked at me a full five seconds, then nodded her nod.

"Makes that Volvo episode a little more suspect. You watch yourself."

Oh yes.

Crowe leaned over and brushed off the toe of her boot, then looked at her watch.

"I'll see if I can get the DA to push harder."

At that moment Ryan's rental car appeared in the valley. The driver's-side window was open and his silhouette looked dark against the car's interior. We watched him climb the mountain and turn into the drive. Moments later he strode up the path, his face looking drawn and tense.

"What is it?"

I heard Crowe's hat brush the top of her thigh.

Ryan hesitated a beat, then, "There's still no sign of Jean's body."

I could read naked misery in his demeanor. And more. Self-imposed guilt. The conviction that his absence from the partnership had caused Bertrand to be on that plane. Detectives without partners are limited in what they can investigate. That makes them available for courier duty.

"They'll find him," I said softly.

Ryan let his eyes rove the horizon, his back rigid, his neck muscles tight as twisted ropes. After a full minute, he shook out and lit a cigarette, cupping the flame in both hands.

"How did your afternoon go?" He flicked the match.

I told him about Crowe's meeting with the magistrate.

"Your foot may be a dead issue."

"What do you mean?"

He blew smoke through his nostrils, then pulled something from his jacket pocket.

"They also found this."

He unfolded a paper and handed it to me.

15

I stared, first in confusion, then in dawning comprehension.

Ryan had given me a composite produced on a color printer. There were three images, each showing a fragment of plastic. In the first I could make out the letters *b-i-o-h-a-z*. In the second, a truncated phrase: *-aboratory servic-*. A red symbol practically leaped from the third picture. I'd seen dozens at the lab, and recognized it instantly.

I looked at Ryan.

"It's a biohazard container."

He nodded.

"Which wasn't on the manifest."

"No."

"And everyone thinks it held a foot."

"Opinion is running in that direction."

Boyd nudged my hand, and I absently held out the rest of the sandwich. He looked at me, as though assuring himself there was no mistake, then took the booty and moved off, opting for distance in case it was a misunderstanding, after all.

"So they're admitting that the foot does not belong to any passenger."

"Not exactly. But they're opening up to the possibility."

"What does this do to the warrant?" I asked Crowe.

"It won't help."

She pushed back from the step, stood with feet apart, and replaced her hat.

"But something's reeking under that wall, and I intend to find out what."

She gave her Sheriff Crowe head dip, turned, and walked up the path. Moments later we saw her bubble top wending down the mountain.

I felt Ryan's stare and brought my gaze back to him.

"Why did the magistrate nix the warrant?"

"Apparently the guy's a candidate for the Flat Earth Society. On top of that, he'll issue a warrant for obstruction if I so much as shed a skin cell." My cheeks burned with anger.

Boyd crossed the porch, snout down, head moving from side to side. Reaching the swing, he sniffed up my leg, then sat and stared at me with his tongue out.

Ryan drew on his cigarette, flicked it on to the lawn. Boyd's eyes shifted sideways, then back to me.

"Did you find out about H&F?"

Ryan had gone to his "office" to phone Delaware.

"I thought the request might be processed more expeditiously if it came from the FBI, so I asked McMahon to make the call. I'll be at the reassembly site all afternoon but I can ask him tonight."

Reassembly. The piecing together of the airplane as it had been before the event. Total reassembly is a tremendous drain on time, money, and manpower, of which the NTSB had precious little. They do not attempt it in every major, do so reluctantly when public clamor demands. They undertook it with TWA 800 because the Brits had done it with Pan Am 103, and they didn't want to be out-performed.

With fifty dead students, reassembly was a given.

For the past two weeks trucks had been carrying the wreckage from Air TransSouth 228 across the mountains to a rented hangar at the Asheville airport. Parts were being laid out on grids corresponding to their positions on the Fokker-100. Parts that could not be associated with specific sections of the plane were being sorted according to structure type. Unidentifiable parts were being sorted according to position of recovery at the crash site.

Eventually, every scrap would be catalogued and subjected to a range of tests, then reassembled around a wood-and-wire frame. Over time an aircraft would take shape, like a slow-motion reverse, with a million fragments drawing together to form a recognizable object.

I'd visited reassembly sites on other crashes, and could picture the tedious scene. In this case the process would move more quickly since Air TransSouth 228 had not been driven into the ground. The plane had come apart in midair and plummeted to earth in large pieces.

But I would not see it. I was exiled. My face must have registered my despondency.

"I can put off the meeting." Ryan laid a hand on my shoulder.

"I'm O.K."

"What are you going to do this afternoon?"

"I'm going to sit here and finish my lunch with Boyd. Then I'm going to drive into town and buy dog food, razors, and shampoo."

"Will you be all right?"

"I may have trouble finding the ones with double blades. But I'll persevere."

"You can be a pain in the ass, Brennan."

"See. I'm fine."

I managed a weak smile.

"Go to your meeting."

When he'd gone, I gave Boyd the last of the fries.

"Any preferred brands?" I asked.

He didn't answer.

I suspected Boyd would eat just about anything but boiled eggs.

I was stuffing wrappers into the carry-out bag when Ruby shot out the front door and grabbed my arm.

"Quick! Come quick!"

"What is—"

She dragged me off the swing and into the house. Boyd danced along, nipping at my jeans. I wasn't sure if it was Ruby's urgency that excited him or his entry on to forbidden turf.

Ruby pulled me straight to the kitchen, where an ironing board stood with a pair of Levi's draped across it. A wicker basket rested below, heaped to the rim with crumpled laundry. Neatly pressed garments hung from cabinet knobs around the room.

Ruby pointed to a twelve-inch black-and-white TV on a counter opposite the board. A ribbon at the bottom of the screen announced fast-breaking news. A newscaster spoke about the graphic, his face grim, his voice serene. Though reception was poor, I had no trouble identifying the figure over his left shoulder.

The room receded around me. I was aware of nothing but the voice and the snowy picture.

". . . an inside source revealed that the anthropologist has been dismissed, and that an investigation is under way. Charges have not yet been filed, and it is unclear if the crash investigation has been compromised, or if victim identifications have been affected. When contacted, Dr. Larke Tyrell, North Carolina's chief medical examiner, had no comment. In other news . . ."

"That's you, isn't it?"

Ruby brought me back.

"Yes," I said.

Boyd had stopped racing around the kitchen and was sniffing the floor below the sink. His head came up when I spoke.

"What's he saying?" Ruby's eyes were the size of Frisbees.

Something snapped, and I rolled over her like a tsunami.

"It's a mistake! A goddamn mistake!" It was my voice, shrill and harsh, though I hadn't consciously formed the words.

The room felt hot, the smell of steam and fabric softener cloying. I spun and rushed for the door.

Boyd flew after me, paws jumbling the carpet runner as we raced down the hall. I burst out the door and across the lawn, the bell jangling in my wake. Ruby must have thought I was possessed by the Archfiend himself.

When I opened the car Boyd bounded in and centered himself in back. His head protruding through the gap between the seats. I hadn't the will to stop him.

Sliding behind the wheel, I did some deep breathing, hoping to turn a page in my mind. My heartbeat normalized. I began to feel guilty about my outburst, but couldn't force myself to return to the kitchen to apologize.

Boyd chose that moment to lick my ear.

At least the chow doesn't question my integrity, I thought.

"Let's go."

During the ride into Bryson City, I answered call after call on my cell phone, each a reporter. After seven "no comments," I turned it off.

Boyd shifted between his center spot and the left rear window, reacting with the same low growl to cars, pedestrians, and other animals. After a time he ceased serving notice on everyone of just who he was, and stared placidly as the sights and sounds of the mountains flashed by.

I found everything I needed at an Ingles supermarket on the southern edge of town. Herbal Essence and Gillette Good News for me, Kibbles 'n Bits for Boyd. I even sprang for a box of Milk-Bone jumbos.

Buoyed by finding the razors, I decided on an outing.

Approximately three miles beyond the Bryson City line, Everett Street becomes a scenic roadway that snakes through the Great Smoky Mountains National Park above the north shore of Lake Fontana. Officially the highway is called Lakeview Drive. To locals it is known as the Road to Nowhere.

In the 1940s, a two-lane backtop led from Bryson City along the Tuckasegee and Little Tennessee Rivers to Deal's Gap near the Tennessee state line. Realizing the creation of Lake Fontana would flood the highway, the TVA promised a new north-shore road. Construction began in 1943, and a 1,200-foot tunnel was eventually built. Then everything stopped, leaving Swain County with a road and tunnel to nowhere, and with wounded feelings as to its low rank in the universal order of things.

"Want to take a ride, boy?"

Boyd showed enthusiasm by placing his chin on my right shoulder and running his tongue up the side of my face. One thing I admired about him was his agreeable nature.

The drive was beautiful, the tunnel a perfect monument to federal folly. Boyd enjoyed racing from end to end while I stood in the middle and watched.

Though the outing cheered me, the improvement in my mood was short-lived. Just after leaving the park, my engine gave an odd ping. Two miles before the town line it pinged gain, chunked repeatedly, then segued into a loud, ratchety, persistent noise.

Veering on to the shoulder, I cut the motor, draped my arms around the steering wheel, and rested my forehead on them, my temporary lift in spirits replaced by a sense of despondency and anxiety.

Was this ordinary car trouble, or had someone tampered with my engine?

Boyd laid his chin on my shoulder, indicating that he, too, found it a disturbing question, and not entirely paranoid.

We'd been like that a few minutes when Boyd growled without raising his head. I ignored this, assuming he'd spotted a squirrel or a Chevy. Then he shot to his feet and gave three sharp woofs, an impressive sound inside a Mazda.

I looked up to see a man approaching my car from the

highway side. He was small, maybe five foot three, with dark hair combed straight back. He wore a black suit, perfectly fitted, but probably new in the early sixties.

Drawing close, the man raised knuckles to tap the glass, but pulled back as Boyd erupted again.

"Easy, boy."

I could see an old pickup angled on to the shoulder across the road, the driver's door open. The truck looked empty.

"Let's see what the gentleman has to say."

I cracked my window.

"Are you ill, ma'am?" The voice was rich and resonant, seeming to come from deeper inside than the small stature allowed. The man had a hooked nose and intense dark eyes, and reminded me of someone, though I couldn't recall whom. From his tone I could tell Boyd was thinking Caligula.

"I may have thrown a rod." I had no idea what that meant, but it seemed like an engine noise sort of thing to say.

"May I offer assistance?"

Boyd growled suspiciously.

"I'm on my way into town. It would be no trouble to drop you at a repair shop, ma'am."

Sudden synapse. The man looked and sounded like a miniature Johnny Cash.

"If there's a garage you can recommend, I'll call ahead and ask for a tow."

"Yes, of course. There's one right up the road. I have the number in my glove compartment.

Boyd was having none of it.

"Shh." I reached back and stroked his head.

The man crossed to his truck, rummaged, then returned with a slip of thin yellow paper. Holding my cell phone in clear view, I lowered the window another few inches and accepted it.

The form looked like the carbon copy of a repair bill. The writing was almost illegible, but a header identified the garage as P & T Auto Repair, and gave an address and phone number in Bryson City. I tried to make out the customer signature, but the ink was too smeary.

When I turned on my cell, the screen told me I had missed eleven calls. Scrolling through, I recognized none of the numbers. I dialed the auto repair shop.

When the phone was answered I explained my situation and asked for towing.

How would I be paying?

Visa.

Where are you?

I gave the location.

Can you find transportation?

Yes.

Come on in and leave the car. They'd send a truck within the hour.

I told the voice at the other end that P & T had been recommended by a passerby, and that I would be riding to the garage with this man. Then I read off the bill number, hoping that P or T was writing it down.

With the call completed, I lowered the window, smiled at Johnny Cash, and dialed again. Speaking loudly, I left Lieutenant-Detective Ryan a message, detailing my intended whereabouts. Then I looked at Boyd. He was looking at the man in the dark suit.

Closing the window, I grabbed my purse and the grocery bag.

"How could things possibly get worse?"

Boyd did the eyebrow thing but said nothing.

*

Dropping the bag behind the seat, I took the middle position and gave Boyd the window. When our Samaritan slammed the door, the dog stuck his head out and tracked his movement to the driver's side. Then a pickup truck whizzed by with a pair of weimaraners in the bed, and Boyd's interest shifted. When he tried to rise, I pushed him on his haunches.

"That's a fine dog, ma'am."

"Yes."

"No one's going to bother you with that big fella around."

"He can be vicious when he's being protective."

We drove in silence. The phone rang. I checked the number, ignored the call. After a while, my rescuer spoke.

"I saw you on TV, didn't I?"

"Did you?"

"I've got trouble with stillness, turn the set on when I'm home alone. I don't pay it much mind, just look up now and again. It's kind of like having company."

He grinned, acknowledging his own foolishness.

"But I do have a knack for faces. It's mighty useful in my line of work."

He pointed in my direction. I noticed that the hand was gray and unnaturally smooth, as though the flesh had ballooned, then contracted with only a vague memory of its original form.

"I'm sure I saw you today." The hand returned to the steering wheel. The hawk eyes shifted from the road to me and back again. "You're with the air crash investigation."

I smiled. Either he hadn't listened to the story, or he was being polite.

The hand came toward me.

"Name's Bowman."

We shook. His grip was steel.

"Temperance Brennan."

"That's a powerful name, young lady."

"Thank you."

"Are you anti-saloon?"

"I'm sorry?"

"I am among those who see intoxicating liquor as the main cause of crime, poverty, and violence in this great nation. Fermented liquor is the greatest threat to the nuclear family ever spawned by Lucifer." He pronounced it *nucular*.

The name Bowman suddenly clicked.

"Are you Luke Bowman?"

"I am."

"The Reverend Luke Bowman?"

"You've heard of me?"

"I'm staying with Ruby McCready at High Ridge House." It was irrelevant but seemed safe.

"Sister McCready is not one of my flock, but she's a good woman. Keeps a fine Christian house."

"Is there a Mr. McCready?" I'd been curious for some time but had never asked.

Now the eyes remained on the road. Seconds passed. I thought he wasn't going to answer.

"I'm gonna leave that question alone, ma'am. Best to let Sister McCready tell the tale as she sees fit."

Ruby had a tale?

"What's the name of your church?"

"The Eternal Light Holiness-Pentecostal House of God."

The Southern Appalachians are home to a fundamentalist Christian sect known as the Church of God with Signs Following, or the Holiness Church. Inspired by biblical passages, adherents seek the power of the Holy Ghost by repenting their sins and leading godly lives. Only thus is one anointed, and thereby able to follow the signs. These signs include speaking in tongues, casting out demons, healing the sick, handling serpents, and ingesting toxic substances.

In more populated areas preachers establish permanent congregations. Elsewhere, they work a circuit. Services last hours, the centerpiece sometimes being the drinking of strychnine and the handling of poisonous snakes. Preachers accumulate fame and followers based on their oratorical skills and immunity to venom. Each year someone dies.

The distorted hand now made sense. Bowman had been bitten more than once.

Bowman turned left a few blocks past the supermarket where I'd made my purchases, then right on to a rutted side street. P & T Auto Repair was situated between businesses offering glass replacement and small-appliance repair. The reverend pulled in and cut the engine.

The garage was a blue aluminum-sided rectangle with an office at one end. Through the open door I made out a cash register, counter, and trio of heads in dozer caps.

The other end of the building held a work bay in which a battered Chevy station wagon was pedestaled on a hydraulic lift, its doors flung wide. The car looked as though it were taking flight.

An old Pinto and two pickups were parked outside the office. I did not see a tow truck.

As Bowman got out, Boyd began what I knew was not a Pinto growl. Following his line of vision I spotted a black-and-brown dog lying inside the office door. It looked pure pit bull.

The flesh on Boyd's snout compressed against his gums. His body tensed. The growl deepened.

Damn. Why hadn't I brought a leash?

Wrapping my fingers around Boyd's collar, I opened the door and we both jumped down. Bowman met us with a length of rope.

"Had this in back," he said. "Flush can be peevish."

I thanked him and tied the rope to Boyd's collar. Boyd remained focused on the other dog.

"I'd be glad to hold him while you talk with the mechanic."

I looked at Boyd. He was staring fixedly at Flush, thinking flank steak.

"Thanks. That might be wise."

Crossing the lot, I stepped through the door and circled Flush. An ear twitched, but he didn't look up. Maybe pit bulls are calm because they are secure in the belief that they can kill anyone or anything that provokes them. I hoped Boyd would keep quiet and keep his distance.

The office had the usual tasteful garage appointments. A calendar with a photo of the Grand Canyon and tear-off sheets for each month. A cigarette machine. A glass case containing flashlights, maps, and an assortment of automotive paraphernalia. Three kitchen chairs. A pit bull.

A pair of geezers occupied two of the chairs. In the third sat a middle-aged man in an oil-stained work shirt and pants. The men stopped talking when I entered, but no one rose.

Assuming the younger man was either P or T, I introduced myself and asked about the tow.

He answered that the wrecker was on its way, should be back in twenty minutes. He'd look at my car as soon as he finished the Chevy.

How long would that be?

He couldn't say, but offered me the chair if I wanted to wait.

The air inside was packed tight with smells. Gas, oil, cigarette smoke, geezers, dog. I elected to wait outside.

Returning to Luke Bowman, I thanked him for his kindness and reclaimed my dog. Boyd was straining at his collar, every fiber focused on the pit bull. Flush was either sleeping or playing possum, waiting for the chow to approach.

"You'll be all right by yourself?"

"My car will be here any minute. And there's a detective on his way over. If it's going to take long he can give me a lift back to High Ridge House. But thank you again. You've been a lifesaver."

My phone rang again. I checked the number, ignored the call. Bowman watched. He seemed reluctant to leave.

"Sister McCready is housing quite a few crash investigation folks up there, i'n't she?"

"Some are there."

"That air crash is nasty business." He pinched his nostrils then shook his head.

I said nothing.

"Do they have any idea what brought that plane down?"

He must have seen something in my face.

"You didn't hear my name from Ruby McCready, did you, Miss Temperance?"

"It came up in a briefing."

"Lord God Almighty."

The dark eyes seemed to grow darker for an instant. Then he dropped his chin, reached up, and massaged his temples.

"I've sinned, and my Savior wants confession."

Oh boy.

When Bowman looked back up his eyes were moist. His voice cracked as he spoke the next sentence.

"And the Lord God sent you to bear witness."

16

Back in the truck, it took Luke Bowman a full half hour to unburden his soul. During that time I had four calls from the media. I finally turned the unit off.

As Bowman talked, the phrase "obstruction of justice" floated through my mind. The rain started again. I watched fat drops wriggle through the windshield film and pockmark puddles in the lot. Boyd lay curled at my feet, persuaded at last that leaving Flush undisturbed was a better plan.

My car arrived, rolling behind the wrecker like sea salvage. Bowman continued his strange narrative.

The station wagon was lowered and moved to join the Pinto and pickups. The man in the oil-stained clothing opened a door and steer-pushed my Mazda into the bay. Then he raised the hood and peered under.

Bowman talked on, seeking absolution.

Finally the reverend stopped, his tale finished, a place near his god reestablished. It was then that Ryan swung into the lot.

When Ryan got out of his car, I lowered my window

and called out. Crossing to the truck, he leaned down and spread his forearms on my window ledge.

I introduced Bowman.

"We've met." Moisture glistened like a halo around the perimeter of Ryan's hair.

"The reverend has just relayed an interesting story."

"Has he?" The iceberg eyes studied Bowman.

"It may translate into something helpful to you, Detective. It may not. But it's God's honest truth."

"Feeling the devil's riding crop, brother?"

Bowman looked at his watch.

"I'll let this fine lady tell it to you."

He turned the key and Boyd raised his head. When Ryan stepped back and opened my door, the chow stretched and hopped out, looking slightly annoyed.

"Thank you, again."

"It was my pleasure." He looked at Ryan. "You know where to find me."

I watched the pickup lurch across the lot, its tires shooting spray from the water-filled ruts.

I'd never known Bowman's brand of faith. Why had he told me what he had? Fear? Guilt? A desire to cover his ass? Where were his thoughts now? On eternity? On repentance? On the pork chops he'd defrosted for tonight's dinner?

"What's the status of your car?" Ryan's question brought me back.

"Hold on to Boyd while I go check."

I ran to the work bay, where P/T was still under my hood. He thought the problem might be a water pump, would know tomorrow. I gave him my cell phone number and told him I was staying with Ruby McCready.

When I returned to the car, Ryan and Boyd were

already inside. I joined them, brushing rain from my hair.

"Would a broken water pump make a loud noise?" I asked.

Ryan shrugged.

"How come you're back from Asheville so early?"

"Something else came up. Listen, I'm meeting McMahon for dinner. You can entertain us both with Bowman's parable."

"Let's drop Rinty off first."

I hoped we weren't going to Injun Joe's.

We didn't.

After settling Boyd at High Ridge House, we drove to the Bryson City Diner. The place was long and narrow like a railroad car. Chrome booths jutted from one side, each with its own condiment tray, napkin holder, and miniature jukebox. A chrome counter ran the length of the other, faced by stools bolted to the floor at precise intervals. Red vinyl upholstery. Plastic-domed cake bins. Coat rack at the door. Rest rooms in back.

I liked the place. No promise of a mountain view or ethnic experience. No confusing acronym. No misspelling for alliterative cuteness. It was a diner and the name said that.

We were early for the dinner crowd, even in the mountains. A few customers sat at the counter, grumbling over the weather or talking about their problems at work. When we entered, most glanced up.

Or were they talking about me? As we moved to the corner booth I felt eyes on my back, sensed nudges directing attention toward me. Was it my imagination?

We'd no sooner sat than a middle-aged woman in a white apron and pink dress approached and issued handwritten menus sheathed in plastic. The name "Cynthia" was embroidered over her left breast.

I chose pot roast. Ryan and McMahon went for meat loaf.

"Drinks?"

"Ice tea, please. Unsweetened."

"Same here." McMahon.

"Lemonade." Ryan stayed deadpan, but I knew what he was thinking.

Cynthia looked at me a long time after jotting our order, then tucked the pencil above her ear. Circling the counter, she tore off the sheet and pinned it to a wire above the service window.

"Two sixes and a four," she bellowed, then turned to look at me again.

The paranoia flared anew.

Ryan waited until Cynthia brought drinks, then told McMahon I had a statement from Luke Bowman.

"What the hell were you doing with Bowman?" There was concern in his voice. I wondered if it was there out of worry for my safety, or out of knowledge that meddling in the investigation could get me arrested.

"My car broke down. Bowman gave me a lift. Don't ask me why that inspired the baring of his soul."

I unsheathed a straw and jammed it into my tea.

"Do you want to hear this?"

"Go ahead."

"It seems the reverends Bowman and Claiborne have been slugging it out over ministerial boundaries for some time. The Holiness movement isn't what it once was, and the parsons are forced to compete for followers from a dwindling pool. This takes showmanship."

"Could we back up? We're talking snakes here, right?" Ryan asked.

I nodded.

"What do snakes have to do with holiness?"

This time I did not ignore Ryan's question.

"Holiness followers interpret the Bible literally, and cite specific passages that mandate the handling of snakes."

"What passages?" Ryan's voice dripped with scorn.

"'In my name shall they cast out devils; they shall speak with new tongues. They shall take up serpents; and if they drink any deadly thing, it shall not hurt them.' The Gospel of Mark, chapter sixteen, verses sixteen and eighteen."

Ryan and I stared at McMahon.

"'Behold I give unto you the power to tread on serpents and scorpions, and over all the power of the enemy; and nothing by any means shall hurt you.' Luke, chapter ten, verse nineteen," McMahon continued.

"How do you know that?" Ryan said.

"We all carry baggage."

"I thought you trained in engineering."

"I did."

Ryan circled back to the reptiles.

"Are the snakes tamed in some way? Are they accustomed to being handled, or have their fangs been pulled, or their venom milked?"

"Apparently not," McMahon said. "They use diamondbacks and water moccasins caught in the hills. Quite a few handlers have died."

"Isn't it illegal?"

"Yes," said McMahon. "But in North Carolina snake handling is merely a misdemeanor, and rarely enforced."

Cynthia arrived with our meals, left. Ryan and I shook salt and pepper. McMahon covered everything on his plate with gravy.

"Go on, Tempe," he said.

"I'll try to reconstruct this as best I can."

I tested a green bean. It was perfect, sweet and greasy after hours of cooking with sugar and bacon fat. God bless Dixie. I had several more.

"Though he denied it in his interview with the NTSB, Bowman *was* outside his house that day. And he *was* launching things into the sky."

I halted for a bite of pot roast. It was equal to the beans.

"But not rockets."

The men waited while I forked another piece of meat, swallowed. Chewing was hardly necessary.

"This is really good."

"What was he launching?"

"Doves."

Ryan's fork stopped in midair.

"As in birds?"

I nodded. "It seems the reverend relies on special effects to keep the faithful interested."

"Sleight of hand?"

"He prefers to think of it as theater for the Lord. Anyway, he says he was experimenting the afternoon Air TransSouth 228 went down."

Ryan urged me on with a gesture of his fork.

"Bowman was working up a sermon on the Ten Commandments. He planned to wave a clay model of the tablets, and finish with a replay of Moses destroying the originals in anger over the Hebrew people's abandonment of their faith. As a finale, he'd dash the mockups to the ground, and admonish the congregation to repent. When they begged forgiveness, he'd hit a couple of levers and a flock of doves would rise up in a cloud of smoke. He thought it would be effective."

199

"Mind-blowing," said Ryan.

"So that's his tell-all tabloid confession? He was in the backyard playing with pigeons and smoke?" said McMahon.

"That's his story."

"Does he do this type of thing regularly?"

"He likes spectacle."

"And he lied when questioned because he couldn't risk his parishioners finding out they were being duped?"

"So he says. But then the Almighty tapped him on the shoulder, and he began to fear the loss of his soul."

"Or fear a bump in federal prison." Ryan's scorn had increased.

I finished my green beans.

"It actually makes sense," McMahon said. "The other witnesses, including Claiborne, stated they saw something shoot into the sky. Knowing the reliably unreliable nature of eyewitnesses, pigeons and smoke would tally."

"Doves," I corrected. "They're more papal."

"The NTSB has pretty much ruled out the rocket theory, anyway," McMahon went on.

"Oh?"

"For a number of reasons."

"Give me one."

"There's not been a single trace of a missile found anywhere within a five-mile radius of the wreckage field."

McMahon spread mashed potatoes on a forkful of meat loaf.

"And there's no twinning."

"What's twinning?"

"Basically, it involves cracking in the crystalline structure of metals such as copper, iron, or steel. Twinning requires forces greater than eight thousand meters per second. Typically, that means a military explosive. Things like RDC or C4."

"And twinning is absent?"

"So far."

"Meaning?"

"The usual components of pipe bombs, things like gunpowder, gelignites, and low-strength dynamite, aren't powerful enough. They only reach forces of one thousand meters per second. That doesn't create enough shock to produce twinning, but it's plenty of force to cause havoc on an aircraft. So lack of twinning doesn't rule out a detonation." He emptied the fork. "And there's plenty of evidence of an explosion."

At that moment Ryan's cell phone rang. He listened, and replied in clipped French. Though I understood his words, they made little sense without the benefit of the Quebec end of the conversation.

"So the NTSB isn't much further ahead than it was last week. Something blew inside the rear of the plane, but they have no idea what or why."

"That's about it," McMahon agreed. "Though the rich husband has been ruled out as a suspect. Turns out the guy was a candidate for priesthood. Made a quarter-million-dollar donation to the Humane Society last year when they found his lost cat."

"And the Sri Lankan kid?"

"The uncle is still broadcasting in Sri Lanka, and there have been no threats, notes, public statements, nothing from anyone over there. That angle looked like a dead end, but we're still checking."

"Has the investigation been handed over to the FBI?"

"Not officially. But until terrorism is ruled out, we're not going away."

Ryan ended his phone conversation and fumbled for a cigarette. His face was fixed in an expression I couldn't read. Remembering my Danielle blunder, I didn't ask.

McMahon had no such compunction.

"What's happened?"

After a pause, "Pepper Petricelli's wife is missing."

"She took off?"

"Maybe."

Ryan lit up, then scanned the table for an ashtray. Finding none, he jammed the match into his sweet potato pudding. There was an awkward silence before he continued.

"A crackhead named André Metraux was busted for possession yesterday in Montreal. Being unenthused about a long separation from his pharmaceuticals, Metraux offered to flip for consideration."

Ryan drew deeply, then blew smoke through both nostrils.

"Metraux swears he saw Pepper Petricelli at a steak house in Plattsburgh, New York, last Saturday night."

"That's impossible," I burst out. "Petricelli is dead. . . ." My voice trailed off on the last word.

Ryan's eyes did a long sweep of the diner, then came back to rest on mine. In them I saw pure agony.

"Four passengers remain unidentified, including Bertrand and Petricelli."

"They don't think – Oh, my God, what *do* they think?"

Ryan and McMahon exchanged glances. My heartbeat quickened.

"What is it you're not telling me?"

202

"Don't go schizoid. We're not keeping things from you. You've had a rough day, and we thought it could wait until tomorrow."

I felt anger coalesce like fog inside my chest.

"Tell me," I said evenly.

"Tyrell attended the briefing today to present an updated trauma chart."

I felt miserable at being excluded, and lashed out. "*There's* a news story."

"He says he has remains that don't fit anyone on the manifest."

I stared at him, too surprised to speak.

"Only four passengers remain missing. All were in the left rear of the plane. Their seats were pretty much pulverized, so it's to be expected the occupants did not fare well."

Ryan drew on his cigarette again, exhaled.

"Twenty-two A and B were occupied by male students. Bertrand and Petricelli were behind them in row twenty-three. Tyrell claims to have tissue fitting none of the eighty-four passengers already identified, and none of these four."

"Such as?"

"A shoulder fragment with a large tattoo."

"Someone could have gotten a tattoo before the flight."

"A portion of jaw with elaborate bridgework."

"Fingerprints," McMahon added.

I took a moment to digest this.

"What does it mean?"

"It could mean a lot of things."

McMahon caught Cynthia's eye and signaled for the check.

"Maybe the biker boys got a stand-in and Petricelli

really was enjoying a porterhouse in New York last weekend." Ryan's voice was tempered steel.

"What are you implying?"

"If Petricelli wasn't on that plane it means one of two things. Either Bertrand was persuaded by greed or force to make a career change . . ."

Ryan took one last pull and added his butt to the sweet potatoes.

". . . or Bertrand was murdered."

Back in my room, I treated myself to a long hot bubble bath, followed by a talcum powder chaser. Only slightly relaxed, but smelling of honeysuckle and lilac, I propped myself in bed, raised my knees to my chest, pulled up the blankets, and turned on my phone. I'd missed seventeen calls. Finding no familiar numbers, I dumped the messages and made a call I'd been putting off.

Though fall break had ended and university classes had resumed the day before, I'd requested continued leave after finding the decomp stain at the courtyard house. I hadn't actually said it, but neither had I corrected my chair's assumption that I was still involved in victim processing. In a sense, I was.

But today's media delirium had made me apprehensive. Taking a deep breath, I scrolled to Mike Perrigio's number and hit "dial." I was about to click off after seven rings, when a woman picked up. I asked for Mike. There was a long pause. I could hear a lot of racket in the background, a child crying.

When Mike came on, he was brusque, almost cold. My classes were covered. Keep checking in. Dial tone.

I was still staring at the phone when it rang again.

The voice was totally unexpected.

Larke Tyrell asked how I was. He'd heard I was back in Bryson City. Could I meet with him the next day? Zero-nine-hundred at the family assistance center? Good, good. Take care.

Again, I sat staring at the little black handset, not knowing whether to feel crushed or buoyed. My boss at the university obviously knew of the news coverage. That had to be bad. But Larke Tyrell wanted to talk. Had the chief ME come around to my position? Had this other errant tissue persuaded him that the great foot controversy did not involve crash remains?

I reached for the chain on the bedside lamp. Lying in a silence filled with crickets, I felt that my issues were at last being resolved. I was confident of vindication, and never questioned the venue or purpose of the morning's meeting.

That was a mistake.

17

The first thing I noticed on opening my eyes was a sheet of paper wedged against the braided rug.

The clock said seven-twenty.

Throwing back the covers, I retrieved the paper and scanned the contents. It was a fax containing six names.

Shivering in panties and T-shirt, I checked the header information: *Sender: Office of the Attorney General, State of Delaware. Recipient: Special Agent Byron McMahon. Subject: H&F, LLP.*

It was the list of H&F officers. McMahon must have forgotten to mention it the night before and had slipped it under my door. I read the names. Nothing clicked.

Chilled through, I tucked the fax into the outer pocket of my computer case, ran on tiptoes into the bathroom, and hopped into the shower. Reaching for the shampoo, I suffered my first defeat of the day.

Damn! I'd left my groceries in Luke Bowman's truck.

Filling the empty shampoo container with water, I

gave my hair a low-lather scrub. After blowing it dry and applying makeup, I slipped on khakis and a white cotton blouse, then checked my image.

The woman in the mirror looked appropriately prim, but a bit too casual. I added a cardigan, buttoned at the top as Katy had instructed. Wouldn't want to look like a dork.

I checked again. Stylish but professional. I hurried downstairs.

Too tense for breakfast, I threw down coffee, fed Boyd the dregs from the Alpo bag, had a nervous tinkle, and collected my purse. I'd just crossed the front door threshold when I stopped short.

I had no wheels.

I was standing on the porch, looking good but feeling panicky, when the door flew open and a boy of about seventeen emerged. His hair was dyed blue and shaved to a single strip running from his forehead to the nape of his neck. His nose, eyebrows, and earlobes displayed more metal than a Harley shop.

Ignoring me, the young man clumped down the stairs and disappeared around the house.

Seconds later, Ryan appeared, blowing steam across the top of a mug.

"What's up, buttercup?"

"Who the hell was that kid?"

"The studded Smurf?" He took an experimental sip. "Ruby's nephew, Eli."

"Nice look. Ryan, I hate to ask, but I have a meeting with Tyrell in twenty minutes and just realized I have no car."

He dug into a pocket and tossed me his keys.

"Take mine. I'll ride with McMahon."

"Are you sure?"

"You're not on the rental contract. Don't get arrested."

In the past, family assistance centers were established near accident sites in order to facilitate transfer of records. This practice was abandoned once psychologists began to recognize the emotional impact on relatives of being in such proximity to the death scene.

The FAC for Air TransSouth 228 was at a Sleep Inn in Bryson City. Ten rooms had been converted into offices by replacing beds and armoires with desks, chairs, telephones, and laptops. It was here that antemortem records had been collected, briefings had been held, and families had been informed of identifications.

All that was finished now. With the exception of a single pair, the rooms that had once swarmed with grieving relatives, NTSB personnel, medical examiner interviewers, and Red Cross representatives had reverted to their original function.

Security was also not what it had been. Pulling into the lot, I was surprised to see journalists chatting and drinking from Styrofoam cups, obviously awaiting a breaking story.

So intent was I on a timely arrival, it never crossed my mind that the story was me.

Then, a cameraman shouldered his minicam.

"There she is."

Other cameras went up. Microphones shot out, and shutters clicked like gravel in a power mower.

"Why did you move remains?"

"Did you tamper with disaster victim packets?"

"Dr. Brennan . . ."

"Is it true that evidence is missing from cases you processed?"

"Doctor . . ."

Strobes flashed in my face. Microphones nudged my chin, my forehead, my chest. Bodies pressed against me, moved with me, like a tangle of seaweed clinging to my limbs.

I kept my eyes straight, acknowledging no one. My heart hammered as I pushed forward, a swimmer struggling toward shore. The distance to the motel seemed oceanic, insurmountable.

Then, I felt a strong hand on my arm, and I was in the lobby. A state trooper was locking the glass doors, glaring at the mob outside.

"You all right, ma'am?"

I didn't trust my voice to reply.

"This way, please."

I followed to a bank of elevators. The trooper waited with hands clasped, feet spread as we ascended. I stood on rubbery legs, trying to recompose my thoughts.

"How did the press find out about this?" I asked.

"I wouldn't know that, ma'am."

On the second floor, the trooper walked to Room 201, squared his shoulders to the wall beside the door.

"It's not locked." He fixed his eyes on something that was not me.

Drawing two steadying breaths, I turned the knob and entered.

Seated behind a desk on the far side of the room was North Carolina's second in command. Of a zillion thoughts winging through my mind at that moment, this is the one I remember: Parker Davenport's color had improved since I'd seen him on the day of the crash.

To the lieutenant governor's left sat Dr. Larke Tyrell, to his right, Earl Bliss. The ME looked at me and nodded. The DMORT commander's eyes wouldn't meet mine.

"Dr. Brennan, please have a seat." The lieutenant governor gestured to an armchair directly in front of the desk.

As I sat, Davenport leaned back and laced his fingers on his vest. The view behind him was spectacular, a Smoky Mountain postcard in explosive fall color. Squinting into the glare, I recognized my disadvantage. Had Tyrell been in charge, I'd have known the seating arrangement was strategy. I wasn't sure Davenport was that smart.

"Would you like coffee?" Davenport asked.

"No, thank you."

Looking at Davenport, I had difficulty imagining how he had lasted so long in public office. He was neither tall nor short, dark nor fair, smooth nor craggy. His hair and eyes were nondescript brown, his speech flat and without inflection. In a system that elects its leaders based on looks and eloquence, Davenport was clearly a noncontender. In a word, the man was unmemorable. But perhaps this was his greatest asset. People voted for Davenport, then forgot him.

The lieutenant governor unlaced his fingers, examined his palms, then looked at me.

"Dr. Brennan, some very disturbing allegations have been brought to my attention."

"I'm glad we're meeting to clear this up."

"Yes." Davenport leaned into the desk and opened a folder. To its left lay a videocassette. No one spoke as he selected and perused a document.

"Let's get right to the meat of this."

"Let's."

"Did you enter the site of the Air TransSouth crash

210

on October fourth prior to the arrival of NTSB or medical examiner officials?"

"Since I was in the area, Earl Bliss asked me to stop by." I looked at the DMORT commander. His eyes remained on the hands in his lap.

"Did you have official orders to go there?"

"No, sir, but—"

"Did you falsely identify yourself as an official representative of the NDMS?"

"No, I did not."

Davenport checked another paper.

"Did you interfere with local authorities in their search-and-recovery efforts?"

"Absolutely not!" I felt heat rise up my neck and into my face.

"Did you order Deputy Anthony Skinner to remove protective covering from a crash victim, knowing there was risk of animal predation?"

"That's standard protocol."

I turned to Earl and Larke. Neither man was looking at me. Stay calm, I told myself.

"It is alleged that you broke *protocol*," Davenport emphasized my word, "by removing remains prior to documentation."

"That was a unique situation requiring immediate action. It was a judgment call, which I explained to Dr. Tyrell."

Davenport leaned farther forward, and his tone grew hard.

"Was stealing those remains also a judgment call?"

"What?"

"The case to which we refer is no longer at the morgue."

"I know nothing about that."

The insipid brown eyes narrowed.

"Really."

Davenport picked up the cassette, crossed to a TV/VCR unit, and inserted it. When he hit "play," a ghostly, gray scene filled the screen, and I knew instantly I was viewing a surveillance tape. I recognized the highway and the entrance to the morgue parking lot.

Within seconds my car entered the frame. A guard waved me away. Primrose appeared, spoke to the guard, tapped her way to the car, and handed me a bag. We exchanged a few words, then she patted my shoulder, and I drove off.

Davenport hit "stop" and rewound the tape. As he returned to his chair, I looked at the other two men. Both were studying me, their faces unreadable.

"Let me summarize," said Davenport. "Following a highly irregular sequence of events, the specimen in question, the specimen that you claim to have wrested from coyotes, is now missing."

"What does that have to do with me?"

Davenport picked up another paper.

"Early Sunday morning, a data-entry technician named Primrose Hobbs removed fragmented human tissue bearing morgue number 387 from a refrigerated trailer containing cases in process. She then proceeded to the admitting section and withdrew the disaster victim packet associated with those remains. Later that morning, Miss Hobbs was seen transferring a package to you in the morgue parking lot. That transaction was recorded, and we have just observed it."

Davenport drilled me with a look.

"Those remains and that packet are now gone, Dr. Brennan, and we believe you have them."

"I would strongly suggest you speak with Miss Hobbs." My voice dripped icicles.

"That was, of course, our first endeavor. Unfortunately, Miss Hobbs has not reported to work this week."

"Where is she?"

"That is unclear."

"Has she checked out of her motel?"

"Dr. Brennan, I realize that you are a board-certified forensic anthropologist of international stature. I am aware that you have consulted to Dr. Tyrell in the past, as well as to coroners worldwide. I am told that your credentials are unimpeachable. That makes your behavior in this matter all the more puzzling."

Davenport turned to his companions, as if enlisting support.

"We don't know why you've developed an obsession with this case, but it is clear that your interest has gone far beyond what is professional or ethical."

"I've done nothing wrong."

For the first time, Earl spoke.

"Your intentions may be honorable, Tempe, but unauthorized removal of a victim shows very poor judgment."

He dropped his eyes and flicked a nonexistent particle from his pants.

"And this is a felony," Davenport chimed in.

I spoke to the DMORT commander.

"Earl, you know me. You know I would never do that."

Before Earl could reply, Davenport exchanged the paper in his hand for a brown envelope, and shook two photos from it. He glanced at the larger, laid it on the desk, then pushed it toward me with one finger.

For a moment I thought it was a joke.

213

"That is you, Dr. Brennan, is it not?"

Ryan and I were eating hot dogs across from the Great Smoky Mountains Railroad Depot.

"And Lieutenant-Detective Andrew Ryan from Quebec." He pronounced it Qwee-bec.

"What is the relevance of this, Mr. Davenport?" Though my face was burning, I kept my voice frigid.

"Exactly what is your relationship with this man?"

"Detective Ryan and I have worked together for years."

"But I am correct in assuming that your relationship extends beyond the professional, am I not?"

"I have no intention of answering questions about my private life."

"I see."

Davenport pushed the second photo across the desk. I was too stunned to speak.

"I surmise from your reaction that you know the gentleman pictured with Detective Ryan?"

"Jean Bertrand was Ryan's partner." Shock waves were passing through every cell in my body.

"Are you aware that this Bertrand is being investigated in conjunction with the Air TransSouth crash?"

"Where is this going?"

"Dr. Brennan, I shouldn't have to spell it out. Your" – he feigned indecision over word selection – "colleague has ties to a principal suspect. You yourself have acted" – again the careful search – "erratically."

"I have done nothing wrong," I repeated.

Davenport tilted his head and twisted his mouth, neither smiling nor grimacing. Then he sighed, indicating what a burden this was for all.

"Perhaps, as Mr. Bliss has suggested, your only offense has been one of misjudgment. But in tragedies

214

of this nature, with so much media attention, and so many grieving families, it is of utmost importance that those involved avoid even the appearance of impropriety."

I waited. Davenport began gathering papers.

"Reports of suspected misconduct are being lodged with the National Disaster Medical System, the American Board of Forensic Anthropology, and the Ethics Committee of the American Academy of Forensic Sciences. The chancellor of your university will also be informed."

Cold fear shot through me.

"Am I suspected of committing a crime?"

"We must consider every possibility, painstakingly and impartially."

Something snapped. I shot to my feet, fingers tightening into fists.

"There's nothing impartial about this meeting, Mr. Davenport, and you have no intention of treating me fairly. Or Detective Ryan. Something's wrong, very wrong, and I've been set up as some sort of scapegoat."

Tears burned the backs of my lids. It's the glare, I told myself. Don't you dare cry!

"Who turned this meeting into a publicity circus?"

Red splotches appeared in Davenport's cheeks, looking oddly out of place in the bland complexion.

"I have no idea how the press found out about this meeting. The leak did not come from my office."

"And the surveillance photo? Where did that order originate?"

Davenport did not answer. The room was deathly quiet.

I uncurled my fingers and drew a deep breath. Then I impaled Davenport with a look.

"I perform my duties scrupulously, ethically, and out of concern for both the living and the dead, Lieutenant Governor Davenport." I kept my voice level. "I do not deviate from protocol. Dr. Tyrell knows that and Mr. Bliss knows that."

My eyes moved to Larke, but he looked away. Earl's attention remained focused on his pants. I turned back to Davenport.

"I don't know what's going on, or why it's going on, but I will find out."

I pointed a finger to emphasize every word.

"I. Will. Find. Out."

With that, I turned and walked from the room, quietly closing the door behind me. The trooper trailed me down the corridor, into the elevator, and across the motel lobby.

The parking lot was an encore of my arrival. Though my escort defended one flank, I was accosted on all others. Cameras rolled, microphones jabbed, and strobes flashed. Questions were shouted in the round. Pushing forward, head down, arms clasped to my chest, I felt more trapped than I had by the coyote pack.

At Ryan's car, the trooper restrained the onslaught with both arms while I unlocked and opened the door. Then he bullied the crowd back, and I broke free and shot on to the highway.

As I drove, my face cooled and my pulse normalized, but a million questions swirled in my brain. How long had I been under surveillance? Could this explain the ransacking of my room? How far would they go? Why?

Would they be back?

Who were "they"?

My eyes flew to the rearview mirror.

216

Where in God's name was that foot? Had someone actually taken it? If so, for what purpose?

How did they know it was gone? Who had wanted that foot on Monday? Why?

Where was Primrose Hobbs?

The lieutenant governor's office was not typically included in the disaster inquiry loop. Why was Davenport taking such an interest?

Could I actually be facing criminal charges? Should I obtain counsel?

I was completely absorbed in these questions, driving robotically, seeing and responding to my surroundings, but registering nothing on a conscious level. I don't know how far I'd driven when a loud whoop sent my eyes back to the rearview mirror.

A police cruiser rode my bumper, headlights flashing like a strobotron.

18

I slowed and pulled on to the shoulder. The cruiser followed.

Traffic whizzed by, normal people on their way to normal places.

I was staring in the rearview mirror when the cruiser's door opened and Lucy Crowe climbed out. My first reaction was relief. Then she put on her hat, squared it carefully, suggesting this was not a social call. I wondered if I should get out too, decided to stay put.

Crowe walked to my car, looking tall and powerful in her sheriff's livery. I opened the door.

"Mornin'," she said, giving her inverted nod.

I nodded back.

"New car?" She spread her feet and placed hands on her hips.

"Borrowed. Mine took an unscheduled sabbatical."

Crowe was not asking for a license or posing the usual questions, so I assumed this was not a traffic stop. I wondered if I was about to be arrested.

"Got something you're probably not going to want to hear."

The radio on her belt sputtered, and she adjusted a knob.

"Daniel Wahnetah turned up last night."

I almost couldn't ask.

"Alive?"

"Very. Knocked on his daughter's door around seven, had dinner with the family, then went home to bed. Daughter called me this morning." She spoke loudly over the rush of traffic.

"Where was he for three months?"

"West Virginia."

"Doing what?"

"She didn't offer that."

Daniel Wahnetah was not dead. I couldn't believe it.

"Any developments on George Adair or Jeremiah Mitchell?"

"Not a word."

"Neither really fits the profile." My voice was tight.

"Guess this doesn't help you much."

"No."

Though I'd never allowed myself to say it, I'd been counting on the foot belonging to Wahnetah. Now I was back to zero.

"But I am happy for the Wahnetah family."

"They're good people."

She watched my fingers worrying the steering wheel.

"I heard about the news report."

"My phone's ringing so much it's now off. I just left a meeting with Parker Davenport, and there was a crazy media scene outside the Sleep Inn."

"Davenport." She hooked an elbow over the top of the car door. "There's a real peckerwood."

219

"What do you mean?"

She looked up the road, then back at me. Sunlight glinted off her aviator shades.

"Did you know that Parker Davenport was born not far from here?"

"No, I didn't."

She was quiet a moment, lost in memories that were hers alone.

"I take it you don't like the man."

"Let's just say his poster's never going to hang above my bed."

"Davenport told me that the foot is now missing and accused me of taking it." I had to pause to keep the tremor from my voice. "He also said that a data technician who helped me take measurements has also disappeared."

"Who's that?"

"An elderly black lady named Primrose Hobbs."

"I'll ask around."

"You know this is all bullshit," I said. "What I can't figure out is why Davenport is gunning for me."

"Parker Davenport has his own mind about things."

A truck rumbled by, blasting us with a wave of hot air. Crowe straightened.

"I'm going to talk with our DA, see if I can't inspire a push for that warrant."

Something suddenly struck me. Though Larke Tyrell had cited trespass when he'd banished me from the investigation, the issue of the courtyard house hadn't been raised today.

"I tracked down the owners."

"I'm listening."

"The property has belonged to an investment group called H&F since 1949. Before that it was owned by

Edward E. Arthur, before that Victor T. Livingstone."

She shook her head.

"You're talking way before my time."

"I've got a list of the H&F officers in my room. I could bring it by your office after I check on my car."

"I need to swing by Fontana when I'm done with the DA. We've got Fox Friggin' Mulder over there thinks he's found an alien." She looked at her watch. "I should be back by four."

I drove back to High Ridge House, feeling feverish with anxiety. To work off the tension I offered Boyd a jog. I also felt I should make up for breakfast. Not one for grudges, he accepted with enthusiasm.

The road was damp from yesterday's rain, and our feet made soft popping sounds on the muddy gravel. Boyd panted and his tags jingled. Jays and sparrows were the only other creatures breaking the stillness.

The view was another Impressionist tableau, an endless expanse of valleys and hills polished and buffed by a brilliant morning sun. But the wind had shifted overnight and now carried an edge. Each time we moved into shadow, I sensed winter and shortening days.

The exercise calmed me, but not much. As I climbed the stairs to Magnolia, my chest tightened at the memory of Monday's intrusion. Today my door was closed, my belongings intact.

I showered and put on fresh clothes. As I turned on the phone it rang in my hand. I answered with rigid fingers. Another journalist. I hung up and dialed Pete.

As usual, a machine took the call. Though I was anxious for an opinion on my legal situation, I knew it was useless to try his other numbers. Pete had both car and cell phones, but rarely recharged either. If he did progress that far, he'd forget to turn the unit on, or he'd leave it on a dashboard or bedroom dresser.

Frustrated, I dug out McMahon's fax, stuffed it in my purse, and headed downstairs.

I was making an egg salad sandwich when Ruby backed through the swinging door into the kitchen, a blue plastic laundry basket in her arms. She wore a white blouse, fake pearls, sweatpants, socks, and slippers, and her hair roll looked freshly lacquered. Her appearance suggested a morning outing, followed by a change from the waist down.

"Can I do that for you?" she asked.

"I'm fine."

She set down the basket and walked to the sink, slippers flapping against her heels.

"I'm real sorry about your room."

"I had nothing of value up there."

"Someone must have come in while I was to market." She picked up a dish towel, sniffed it. "Sometimes I wonder what the world's coming to. The Lord—"

"These things happen."

"We've never had stealing in this house." She turned to me, the towel twisted between her hands. "I don't blame you for being angry."

"I'm not angry at you."

She took a quick breath, opened her mouth, closed it. I had the impression she was about to say something, changed her mind, wary of how the telling might impact her life. Good. I was too strung out for sympathetic listening.

"Can I get you a drink?"

"Do you have lemonade?"

She tossed the towel into her basket and crossed to

222

the refrigerator. Withdrawing a plastic pitcher, she filled a glass and set it next to my sandwich.

"And that television business and all."

"All through school, I was never once voted most popular."

I smiled, not wanting Ruby to see how agitated I was. The gesture must have looked as strained as it felt.

"It isn't funny. You shouldn't let them do this."

"I can't control the press, Ruby."

She got a paper plate, placed my sandwich on it.

"Cookies?"

"Sure."

She added three sugar cookies, then looked straight into my eyes.

"'Blessed are ye when men shall revile you, and persecute you, and shall say all manner of evil against you falsely."

"The people who matter know these accusations are false." Keep cool.

"Then maybe you need to be controlling someone else."

She hoisted the basket on to her hip and left without a backward glance.

Hoping for more rational conversation, I went outside to lunch with Boyd. I was disappointed. The chow inhaled the cookies, then watched without comment as I ate the sandwich and considered my options.

Arriving at the garage, I learned that the problem with my car was minor, but a pump was required. The absent letter, either P or T, was in Asheville, and would try to obtain the part. Assuming that mission went well, repairs could be finished the next afternoon.

Could be. I noticed that the Chevy, Pinto, and pickups remained exactly where they'd been the day before.

I checked the time. Two-thirty. Crowe wouldn't be back yet.

Now what?

I requested a phone directory and was handed a 1996 edition, dog-eared and reeking of petroleum products. Two hands were required to part the pages.

While there was no entry for the Eternal Light Holiness-Pentecostal House of God, I did find a listing for L. Bowman on Swayney Creek Road. P/T knew the intersection but could provide nothing more. I thanked him and returned to Ryan's car.

Following P/T's instructions, I headed out of town. As he'd predicted, Swayney Creek dead-ended into Highway 19 between Ela and Bryson City. I stopped at a filling station to ask directions to Bowman's house.

The attendant was a kid of about sixteen with greasy black hair, separated down the crown and tucked behind the ears. White flecks littered his part like snowflakes along a muddy creek.

The kid put down his comic and glanced at me, his eyes scrunched as though sensitive to light. Picking a cigarette from a scalloped metal dish, he drew deeply, then jerked his chin in the direction of Swayney Creek.

"It's about two miles north." Smoke billowed out with his answer.

"Which side?"

"Look out for a green mailbox."

Walking out, I felt squinty eyes on my back.

Swayney Creek was a thin black tongue that dropped sharply after leaving the highway. The road descended for the next half-mile, then leveled off and passed

224

through a long stretch of mixed-conifer forest. A creek ran along one side, the water so clear I could see individual pebbles littering the bottom.

Driving north, I passed few signs of habitation. Then the road curved east, climbed slightly, and I spotted an opening in the trees, a rusty green mailbox to its right. Drawing close, I saw the name "Bowman" carved on a plaque hung below the box with two short segments of chain.

I turned on to the dirt lane and crept forward, hoping I had the right Bowman. Pine, spruce, and hemlock towered above, choking off all but a few shoots of sunlight. Fifty yards up, Luke Bowman's house squatted like a solitary sentinel guarding the forest road.

The reverend lived in a weathered frame bungalow, with a porch at one end and a shed at the other. Together they were stacked with enough firewood to heat a medieval castle. Bright turquoise awnings angled over windows to either side of the front door, looking as out of place in the gloom as the Golden Arches on a synagogue.

The "front yard" was black with shade and carpeted with a thick mat of leaves and pine needles. A gravel path crossed it, leading from the door to a rectangle of gravel at the road's end.

I pulled next to Bowman's pickup, cut the engine, and turned on my phone. Before I could get out, the front door opened and the reverend appeared on the stoop. Again, he was dressed in black, as though wanting to remind even himself of the soberness of his calling.

Bowman didn't smile, but his face relaxed when he recognized me. I climbed out of the car and walked up the path. Small brown mushrooms bordered each side.

"I'm sorry to disturb you, Reverend Mr. Bowman. I left a shopping bag in your truck."

"You surely did. It's in the kitchen." He stepped back. "Please, come inside."

I brushed past him into a dim interior heavy with the odor of burned bacon.

"Would you like something to drink?"

"No, thank you. I can't stay."

"Please, have a seat."

He gestured into a small living room crammed with furniture. The pieces looked as though they'd been purchased by the roomful, then placed exactly as on the showroom floor. Only closer together.

"Thanks."

I sat on a brown velour sectional, the centerpiece of a three-piece grouping still covered in plastic. Though the weather was cool the windows were open, and the perfectly matched brown plaid curtains billowed inward with the breeze.

"I'll get your things."

He disappeared and a door opened, allowing muted voices, bongs, and applause of a television game show to drift out. I looked around.

The room was devoid of personal items. There were no wedding or graduation pictures. Not one snapshot of the kids at the beach or the dog in a party hat. The only images were of haloed persons. I recognized Jesus, and a chap I thought might be John the Baptist.

After several minutes, Bowman returned. The plastic slipcover crackled as I rose.

"Thank you."

"It was a pleasure, Miss Temperance."

"And thank you again for yesterday."

"I was glad to help. Peter and Timothy are the best

226

mechanics in the county. I've taken my trucks to them for years."

"Reverend Mr. Bowman, you've lived here a long time, haven't you?"

"All my life."

"Do you know anything about a lodge house with a courtyard near the spot where the plane went down?"

"I remember my daddy talking about a camp out that way near Running Goat Branch, but never a lodge."

I had a sudden thought. Shifting the bag on to my left hip, I dug out McMahon's fax and handed it to Bowman.

"Are any of these names familiar to you?"

He unfolded and read the paper. I watched closely, but saw no change in his expression.

"Sorry."

He handed back the fax, and I returned it to my purse.

"Have you ever heard of a man named Victor Livingstone?"

Bowman shook his head.

"Edward Arthur?"

"I know an Edward Arthur lives over near Sylva. Used to be Holiness, but left the movement years ago. Brother Arthur used to claim he was led to the Holy Ghost by George Hensley himself."

"George Hensley?"

"The first man to take up serpents. Brother Arthur said they made acquaintance during Reverend Hensley's time in Grasshopper Valley."

"I see."

"Brother Arthur's got to be close to ninety by now."

"He's still alive?"

"As God's holy word."

227

"He was a member of your church?"

"He was one of my father's flock, as devoted a man as ever breathed God's air. Army changed him. Kept the faith for a few years after the war, then just stopped following the signs."

"When was that?"

"Around forty-seven or forty-eight. No. That's not right." He pointed a gnarled finger. "The last service Brother Arthur attended was for Sister Edna Farrell's passing. I recall that because Papa had been praying for the renewal of the man's faith. About a week after the funeral Papa paid Brother Arthur a visit, and found himself preaching down the barrel of a gun. After that, he give up."

"When did Edna Farrell die?"

"Nineteen forty-nine."

Edward Arthur had sold his land to the H&F Investment Group on April 10, 1949.

19

I found Edward Arthur in a vegetable patch behind his log cabin. He wore a wool plaid shirt over denim coveralls, rubber boots, and a ragged straw hat that might once have belonged to a gondolier. He paused when he saw me, then went back to turning dirt.

"Mr. Arthur?" I asked.

The old man continued jabbing a pitchfork at the ground, then pushing on it with a shaky foot. He had so little strength the prongs barely penetrated, but he repeated the movement again and again.

"Edward Arthur?" I spoke more loudly.

He didn't answer. The fork made a soft thud each time he thrust it at the soil.

"Mr. Arthur, I can see that you're busy, but I'd like to ask you a few questions."

I set my face in what I hoped was an encouraging smile.

Arthur straightened as best he could and walked to a wheelbarrow loaded with rocks and dead vegetation. When he removed his shirt I saw scrawny arms and hands covered with liver spots the size of lima beans. Exchanging the pitchfork for a hoe, he tottered back to the row where he'd been working.

"I'd like to ask you about a piece of property near Running Goat Branch."

For the first time Arthur looked at me. His eyes were rheumy, the rims red, the irises so pale they were almost colorless.

"I believe you used to own acreage in that vicinity?"

"Why you coming to me?" His breathing sounded wheezy, like air being sucked through a filter.

"I'm curious about who bought your land."

"Are you FBI?"

"No."

"You one of them crash people?"

"I was with the investigation, but I'm not any longer."

"Who sent you here?"

"No one sent me, Mr. Arthur. I found you through Luke Bowman."

"Whyn't you put your questions to Luke Bowman?"

"Reverend Bowman didn't know anything about your land, except that it might have been a campground at one time."

"That's what he said, was it?"

"Yes, sir."

Arthur pulled a parrot-green kerchief from a pocket and ran it across his face. Then he dropped the hoe and hobbled toward me, his back as rounded as a turkey vulture's. When he drew close I could see coarse white hair sprouting from his nostrils, neck, and ears.

"Can't say much about the son, but Thaddeus Bowman was as pesky a man as ever drew air. Ran a hallelujah house for forty years."

"You were one of Thaddeus Bowman's followers?"

"Till I learnt all that casting out o' demons and speaking in tongues was a heap of horseshit."

Arthur hawked up phlegm and spat into the dirt.

"I see. You sold your land after the war?"

He went on as if I hadn't spoken.

"Thaddeus Bowman kept hounding me to repent, but I was on to other things. The damned fool wouldn't accept my leavin' until I put it to him from the business end of a squirrel rifle."

"Mr. Arthur, I'm here to ask about the property you bought from Victor Livingstone."

"Didn't buy no property from Victor Livingstone."

"Records indicate Livingstone transferred title to you in 1933."

"I was nineteen in 1933. Got myself married."

This seemed to be going nowhere.

"Did you know Victor Livingstone?"

"Sarah Masham. She died in birthing."

His answers were so disjointed I wondered if he was senile.

"The seventeen acres was our weddin' present. They got a word for that."

The creases around his eyes deepened with concentration.

"Mr. Arthur, I'm sorry for taking you away from your garden, bu—"

"Dowry. That's the word. It was her dowry."

"What was her dowry?"

"Ain't you asking 'bout that land t' Running Goat?"

"Yes, sir."

"Sarah's daddy gave it to us. Then she died."

"Victor Livingstone was your wife's father?"

"Sarah Masham Livingstone. That was my first wife.

231

We was married three years when she passed. Wasn't but eighteen. Her daddy was so tore up, he went and died, too."

"I'm so sorry, Mr. Arthur."

"That's when I lit outta here and threw in with George Hensley over t' Tennessee. He's the one got me to taking up serpents."

"What happened with the Running Goat property?"

"City fella asked if he could rent it, run a little camp. I wanted nothing to do with the place, so I said hell, yes. Seemed like easy money."

Again he cleared his throat and spat.

"It was a campground?"

"They came up for huntin' and fishin', but you ask me, it was mostly to hide from their womenfolk."

"Was there a house?"

"They stayed with tents and campfires and all, till I built the lodge." He stayed his head. "Beats me what some fools consider fun."

"When did you build the lodge?"

"Before the war."

"Did it have a walled courtyard?"

"What the hell kinda question is that?"

"Did you build a stone wall and make a courtyard?"

"I wasn't puttin' up no friggin' Camelot."

"You sold the land in 1949?"

"Sounds right."

"The year you broke with Thaddeus Bowman."

"Eyeh."

"Luke Bowman remembered that you left his father's congregation right after Edna Farrell died."

Again the eyes creased.

"You implyin' something, young lady?"

"No, sir."

"Edna Farrell was a fine Christian lady. They should have done better by her."

"Would you mind telling me who bought the camp?"

"Would you mind tellin' me why you're wantin' to know my business?"

I was quickly revising my estimate of Edward Arthur. Because he was old and taciturn I had presumed his faculties might be dulled. The man in front of me was as cagey as Kasparov. I decided to play it straight.

"I'm no longer involved in the crash investigation because I've been accused of acting improperly. The charges are false."

"Eyeh."

"I believe there's something wrong in that lodge, and I want to know what. The information may help clear my name, but I think my efforts are being blocked."

"You been there?"

"Not inside."

He started to speak, but a gust of wind grabbed his hat and sent it reeling across the garden. Purple lips drew back against toothless gums, and a scarecrow arm shot out.

Bolting, I overtook the hat and pinned it with a foot. Then I brushed it clean and carried it back to Arthur.

The old man shivered as he took the boater and pressed it to his chest.

"Would you like your shirt, sir?"

"Turnin' cold," he said

When he'd finished buttoning, I helped him gather his tools and store them with the wheelbarrow in a shed behind the cabin. As he closed the door, I re-posed my question.

"Who bought your land, Mr. Arthur?"

He clicked the padlock, tugged it twice, and turned to face me.

"You'd best stay clear of that place, young lady."

"I promise you, sir, I won't go there alone."

Arthur regarded me for so long, I thought he wasn't going to answer. Then he stepped close and raised his face to mine.

"Prentice Dashwood."

He spat "Prentice" with such force that saliva misted my chin.

"Prentice Dashwood bought your land?"

He nodded, and the watery old eyes darkened.

"The devil hisself," he hissed.

When I phoned Crowe's office, a deputy informed me that the sheriff was still in Fontana. I sat a moment, clicking my keys on the steering wheel and staring at Arthur's cabin.

Then I started the car and pulled out.

Though fat, black-green clouds were rapidly gathering, I drove with the windows down, the air buffeting my face. I knew wind would soon whip the trees, and rain would wash across the pavement and down the mountain face, but for the moment the air felt good.

Taking Highway 19, I headed back toward Bryson City. Two miles south of town I spotted a small wooden sign and turned off on to a gravel road.

The Riverbank Inn lay a quarter mile down the road, on the banks of the Tuckasegee River. It was a one-story, yellow stucco affair built in a 1950s ranch design. Its sixteen rooms stretched to the left and right of a central office, each with its own front entrance and porch in back. A plastic jack-o'-lantern grinned from every stoop, and an electrified skeleton hung from a tree outside the main entrance.

Clearly, the inn's appeal lay in setting and not in decorating or architectural style.

Pulling up outside the office, I saw only two other vehicles, a red Pontiac Grand Am with Alabama plates, and a blue Ford Taurus with North Carolina plates. The cars were parked in front of units two and seven.

As I passed the skeleton, it gave a warbly moan, followed by a high-pitched mechanical laugh. I wondered how often Primrose had to endure the display.

The motel lobby had the same feel as High Ridge House. A strand of bells hanging on the door, chintz curtains, knotty pine. A plaque welcomed me, and introduced the owners as Ralph and Brenda Stover. Another jack-o'-lantern smiled from the counter.

A man in a Redskins jersey sat beside Jack, leafing through a copy of *PC World*. He looked up when I jingled in, and smiled at me across the lobby. I assumed this was Ralph.

"May I help you?" Ralph had thinning blond hair, and his skin was pink and Simonize shiny.

"I'm Dr. Tempe Brennan," I said, extending a hand.

"Ralph Stover."

As we shook, his medical ID bracelet jangled like the bells on the door.

"I'm a friend of Primrose Hobbs," I said.

"Yes?"

"Mrs. Hobbs has been staying here for the past two weeks?"

"She has."

"She's working with the crash investigation."

"I know Mrs. Hobbs." Ralph's smile never wavered.

"Is she in?"

235

"I can ring her room if you'd like."

"Please."

He dialed, listened, replaced the receiver.

"Mrs. Hobbs is not answering. Would you like to leave a message?"

"I take it she has not checked out."

"Mrs. Hobbs is still registered."

"Have you seen her today?"

"No."

"When did you last see her?"

"I can't possibly keep track of all our guests."

"Mrs. Hobbs hasn't been to work since Sunday, and I'm concerned about her. Could you please tell me what room she's in?"

"I'm sorry, but I can't do that." The smile widened. "Policy."

"She could be ill."

"The maid would report a sick guest."

Ralph was as polite as a policeman on a traffic stop. O.K. I can do polite.

"This is really important." I placed a palm lightly on his wrist and looked into his eyes. "Can you tell me what Mrs. Hobbs drives so I can see if her car is in your lot?"

"No, I cannot."

"Can we go together to check her room?"

"No."

"Will you go while I wait here?"

"No, ma'am."

Pulling back my hand, I tried another tack.

"Would Mrs. Stover remember when she last saw Mrs. Hobbs?"

Ralph laced his fingers and laid his hands on the magazine. The hair on his forearms looked pale and wiry against the calamine-pink skin.

"You are asking the same questions the others asked, and my wife and I will give you the same answers we gave to them. Unless served with an official warrant we will open no room, and divulge no information about any guest." His voice was buttery smooth.

"What others?"

Ralph drew a long, patient breath.

"Is there anything else I can help you with?"

I honed my voice to scalpel sharp.

"If Primrose Hobbs comes to any harm because of your *policy*, you'll wish you'd never sent away for that hotel-motel management course."

Ralph Stover's eyes narrowed but the smile held firm.

I pulled a business card from my purse and jotted down my cell phone number.

"If you have a change of heart, give me a call."

I turned and strode toward the door.

"You have a nice day, ma'am."

I heard the flip of a magazine page, the jangle of a bracelet.

Gunning the engine, I raced from the lot, sped up the highway, and pulled on to the shoulder fifty yards north. If I knew human nature, curiosity would drive Stover to Primrose's room. And he would go there immediately.

Hurriedly locking the car, I sprinted back to the Riverbank turn-off and cut into the woods. Then I picked my way forward, paralleling the gravel road, until I had a clear view of the motel.

My intuition was right on. Ralph was just arriving at unit four. He checked to his left, then his right, unlocked the door, and slipped inside.

Minutes passed. Five. Ten. My breathing slowed to normal. The sky darkened and the wind picked up.

237

Overhead, pines arched and dipped, like ballerinas doing arm positions *sur les pointes*.

I thought about Primrose. Though we'd known each other for years, I knew very little about the woman. She had married, divorced, had a son somewhere. Beyond that, her life was a blank. Why was that? Had she been unwilling to share, or had I never bothered to ask? Had I treated Primrose like one of the many who pass time with us, delivering our mail, typing our reports, cleaning our houses, while we pursue our own interests, oblivious to theirs?

Perhaps. But I knew Primrose Hobbs well enough to be certain of one thing: She would never willingly leave a job unfinished.

I waited. Lightning streaked from an eggplant cloud, illuminating its interior like a million-watt artery. Thunder rumbled. The storm was not far off.

Finally, Stover emerged, pulled the door shut and jiggled the knob, then hurried up the sidewalk. When he was safely inside the office, I began circling, keeping my distance and using the trees for cover. The back of the inn stretched ahead of me on one side, the river on the other, trees between them. I moved through the trees to a point I estimated was opposite unit four, then paused to listen.

Water boiling over rocks. Boughs swishing in the wind. A train whistle. Valves slamming inside my chest. Thunder, louder now. Quicker.

I crept to the edge of the tree line and peeked out.

A row of wooden porches projected from the back of the motel, each with a black wrought-iron numeral nailed to its railing. My instincts had been good again. Only five yards of grass separated me from unit four.

I took a deep breath, darted across the gap, and

double-stepped the four risers. Dashing across the porch, I reached out and yanked the screen door. It opened with a grating squeak. The wind had suddenly calmed, and the sound seemed to shatter the heavy air. I froze.

Stillness.

Sliding between the screen and inner door, I leaned close and peered through the glass. Green-and-white gingham blocked my view. I tried the knob. No go.

I eased the screen door closed, moved to the window, and tried again. More gingham.

Noticing a gap where the lower border met the sill, I placed my palms on the window frame and pushed up. Tiny white flakes fluttered down around my fingers.

I pushed again, and the window jogged upward an inch. Again I froze. In my mind I heard an alarm, saw Ralph burst from the office with a Smith & Wesson.

Turning palms up, I wriggled my fingers into the gap.

What I was doing was illegal. I knew that. Breaking into Primrose's room was precisely the wrong move given my present situation. But I needed to assure myself that she was all right. Later, if it turned out that she wasn't, I needed to know that I had done what I could to help her.

And, to be honest, I needed to do this for myself. I had to find out what had happened to that foot. I had to track Primrose down and show that panel of men that they were wrong.

I spread my feet and pushed. The window opened another inch.

I heard the first *patta-patta-pat* as fat drops slapped the floorboards. Dime-sized blotches multiplied and merged around my boots.

I manipulated the window another two inches.

It was then that the storm broke. Lightning streaked, thunder cracked, and rain fell in torrents, turning the porch into a shimmering rink.

I abandoned the window and pressed my body to the wall, hoping for protection from the overhang. Within seconds water soaked my hair and dripped from my ears and nose. My clothes molded to me like papier-mâché on a wire frame.

Millions of drops cascaded off the roof and the porch. They bit into the lawn, met up, and coursed in channels between the blades of grass. They formed a river in the gutter above my head. Wind slapped leaves against the wall and my legs, sent others twirling across the ground. It carried the scent of wet earth and wood, of numberless creatures hunkered into burrows and nests.

Shivering, I waited it out, my back against the stucco, hands under armpits. I watched drops bead a spider-web, build, then bow the fibers. Its maker watched too, a small brown bundle on an outer filament.

Islands were born. Continental plates shifted. A score of species disappeared from the planet forever.

Suddenly my cell phone shrilled, the sound so unexpected I almost jumped from the porch.

I clicked on.

"No comment!" I shrieked, expecting another reporter.

Lightning shot straight to the treetops. Thunder snapped.

"Where the hell are you?" said Lucy Crowe.

"The storm came up quickly."

"You're outside?"

"Are you back in Bryson City?"

"I'm still out at Fontana Lake. Do you want to ring me when you've gotten inside?"

"That could be a while." I had no intention of telling her why.

Crowe spoke to someone else, came back on the line.

"Afraid I've got more bad news for you."

I heard voices in the background, then the crackle of a police radio.

"Looks like we've found Primrose Hobbs."

20

While I was meeting with our esteemed lieutenant governor and friends, the owners of a marina were finding a body.

As was their custom, Glenn and Irene Boynton rose at dawn and dealt with the morning rush, renting equipment, selling bait, filling coolers with ice, sandwiches, and canned drinks. When Irene went to check on a bass boat returned late the previous day, an odd rippling drew her to the end of the dock. Peering into the water, the woman was terrified to see two lidless eyes staring back.

Following Crowe's directions, I found Fontana Lake, then the narrow dirt track leading to the marina. The rain had tapered off, though the leaves overhead were still dripping. I wound through puddles toward the lake, my tires throwing up a spray of mud and water.

As the marina came into view, I saw a wrecker, an ambulance, and a pair of police cruisers bathing a parking area in oscillating red, blue, and yellow light. The marina stretched along the shore on the lot's far side. It consisted of a dilapidated rental office–gas station–general store, with narrow wooden piers jutting into the water at both ends. A wind sock fluttered from a corner of the building, its bright colors jauntily snapping in the breeze, jarringly at odds with the grim scene on the ground below.

A deputy was interviewing a couple in jean shorts and windbreakers on the southernmost pier. Their bodies were tense, their faces the color of pale putty.

Crowe stood on the office steps talking to Tommy Albright, a hospital pathologist who occasionally did autopsies for the medical examiner. Albright was wrinkled and scrawny, with sparse white hair combed straight across his crown. He'd been making Y-incisions since the Precambrian, but I'd never worked with him.

Albright watched me approach then held out a hand. We shook. I nodded to Crowe.

"I understand you knew the victim."

Albright tipped his head in the direction of the ambulance. The doors stood open, revealing a shiny white pouch lying on a collapsible gurney. Bulges told me the body bag was already occupied.

"We pulled her out just before the storm broke. Are you willing to try a quick visual?"

"Yes."

No! I didn't want to do this. Didn't want to be here. Didn't want to identify Primrose Hobbs's lifeless body.

We walked to the ambulance and climbed in back. Even with the doors open the smell was noticeable. I swallowed hard.

Albright unzipped the bag and the odor rolled over us, a nauseating cocktail of stagnant mud, seaweed, lake creatures, and putrefying tissue.

"I'd guess she was in the water two or three days. She's not scavenged too badly."

Holding my breath, I looked into the bag.

It was Primrose Hobbs, but it wasn't. Her face was bloated, her lips swollen like those of a tropical fish in an aquarium. The dark skin had sloughed in patches, revealing the pale underside of her epidermis, and giving her body a mottled appearance. Fish or eels had devoured her eyelids, and nibbled her forehead, cheeks, and nose.

"Won't be too much problem with cause," said Albright. "Course, Tyrell will want a full autopsy."

Primrose's wrists were wrapped with electrical tape, and I could see a thin wire embedded in her neck.

I tasted bile, swallowed hard.

"Garroted?"

He nodded. "Bastard wrapped the line around her throat, then tightened it in back with some kind of tool. Very effective in cutting off the windpipe."

I placed a hand over my nose and mouth and leaned in. Jagged lines scored the flesh on one side of Primrose's neck, scratched by her nails as she clawed for life with her bound hands.

"It's her," I said, lunging from the ambulance. I needed air. Miles and oceans of fresh air.

Hurrying to the far end of the unoccupied pier, I stood a moment, arms wrapped around my middle. A boat whined in the distance, grew loud, receded. Waves lapped below my feet. Frogs croaked from the weeds lining the shore. Life continued, oblivious to the death of one of its creatures.

I thought about Primrose, pictured her hobbling out to our final meeting in the morgue parking lot. A sixty-two-year-old black woman with a nursing degree, a weight problem, proficiency at cards, and a fondness for rhubarb crumble. There. I did know something about my friend.

My chest gave a series of heaves.

Steady.

I pulled a ragged breath.

Think.

What could Primrose have done, known, or seen that could have brought such violence down on her? Was she killed because of her involvement with me?

Another tremor. I gulped air.

Or was I magnifying my own role? Was her death random? We Americans are the world's leading producers of homicide. Was Primrose Hobbs bound and strangled for nothing more than her car? That made no sense. Not the garroting and the duct tape. This was a planned murder and she was the intended victim. But why?

Hearing doors slam, I turned. The attendants were climbing into the front of the ambulance. Seconds later, the engine revved, and the vehicle crawled up the dirt road.

Good-bye, old friend. If I brought you to this, please, please, forgive me. My lower lip trembled, and I bit down hard.

You will not cry. But why not? Why hold back tears of mourning for a good and gentle person?

I looked out across the lake. The sky was clearing, and the pines on the far shore stood out blue-black against the first pink rays of dusk. I recalled something else.

Primrose Hobbs loved sunsets. I gazed at the sunset and wept until I felt angry. Beyond angry. I felt a hot, red rage burning inside me.

245

Bridle it, Brennan. Use it.

Vowing to find answers, I drew a deep breath and walked up the pier to rejoin Crowe and Albright.

"What did she drive?" I asked.

Crowe consulted a spiral pad.

"Blue Honda Civic. Ninety-four. North Carolina plates."

"It's not parked at the Riverbank Inn."

Crowe looked at me strangely.

"Car could be on its way to Saudi Arabia by now," said Albright.

"I told you that the victim was helping me with my investigation."

"I'll want to talk to you about that." Crowe.

"Find anything here?" I asked.

"We're still looking."

"Tire tracks? Footprints?" I knew it was stupid as soon as I said it. The rain would have obliterated such impressions.

Crowe shook her head.

I scanned the pickups and SUVs left behind by fishermen and pleasure boaters. Two sixteen-foot aluminum outboards bobbed in their slips.

"Any permanent tie-ups at the marina?"

"It's strictly a rental business."

"That means a lot of people coming and going every day. Pretty busy spot for a body dump."

"Rentals are due back by eight P.M. Apparently things quiet down after that."

I indicated the couple with the putty faces. They were alone on the dock now, hands in their pockets, unsure what they were supposed to do next.

"Are those the owners?"

"Glenn and Irene Boynton. They say they're here

246

every night until eleven, return around six in the morning. They live up the road."

Crowe indicated the dirt track.

"They claim to notice cars at night. Worry about kids messing with their boats. Neither one heard or saw a thing over the past three days. For what it's worth. A perp wouldn't exactly advertise that he was using your dock to off-load a corpse."

The celery eyes appraised the scene, came back to me.

"But you're right. This would be an odd choice. There's a small road kisses the shore about a half mile up from here. We're thinking that was the toss-in point."

"Two, three days seems a little long for the currents to carry her here," added Albright. "Body may have been deadheaded awhile."

"Deadheaded?" I snapped, furious at his callousness.

"Sorry. Old logging term. Refers to snagged timber."

I was almost afraid to ask the next question.

"Was she sexually assaulted?"

"Clothing's on, underwear's in place. I'll test for semen, but I doubt it."

We stood silent in the gathering dusk. Behind us, the docks creaked and settled against the waves. A cold breeze blew off the water, carrying the scent of fish and gasoline.

"Why would someone garrote an old lady?" Though I spoke aloud, the question was really for me, not my companions.

"Why do these sick bastards do any of the things they do?" Albright replied.

I left them and walked toward Ryan's car. The ambulance and wrecker were gone, but the cruisers remained, pulsing blue light across the muddy lot. I sat a moment, staring at the hundreds of prints left by the feet of ambulance attendants, wrecker operators, police, the pathologist, and myself. Primrose's last disaster scene.

I turned the key and headed back toward Bryson City, tears coursing down my cheeks.

When I checked my messages later that evening, I found one from Lucy Crowe. I returned her call and told her everything I knew about Primrose Hobbs, ending with our Sunday-morning rendezvous at the morgue.

"And that foot and all its paperwork are now missing?"

"So I was told. Primrose was probably the last person to see the stuff."

"Parker Davenport told you she signed it out. Did she sign it back in?"

"Good question."

"Tell me about security."

"All DMORT and ME personnel have IDs, as do the people from your department and the Bryson City PD who work security. A guard checks IDs at the perimeter fence, and there's a sign in/sign out sheet inside the morgue. A color-coded dot goes on your badge each day."

"Why?"

"In case someone manages to duplicate the ID, they'd have no way of knowing that day's color."

"What about after hours?"

"By now there's probably a smaller crew left at the morgue, mostly records and computer staff, some medical personnel. There'd be no one there at night except your deputy or a Bryson City cop."

I pictured the lieutenant governor with his video-cassette.

"There is a surveillance camera on the gate."

"What about the computers?"

"Every VIP user has a password, and only a limited number of people can enter or delete data."

"Assuming Hobbs returned it, where would that foot have been?"

"At the end of the day everything goes into reefer trucks marked 'unprocessed,' 'in process,' or 'identified.' Cases are located with a computer tracking system."

"How hard would it be to break in?"

"High school kids have hacked the Pentagon."

I heard distant conversation, like voices drifting through a wormhole in space.

"Sheriff, I think Primrose Hobbs was murdered because of that foot."

"Or the thing could be a biological specimen."

"A woman examines an object which is the subject of controversy, that object disappears, and the woman turns up dead three days later. If there's no link it's one hell of a coincidence."

"We're looking at every angle."

"Have you learned why no one reported her missing?"

"Apparently, parts of the operation are shifting to Charlotte. When Hobbs failed to show at the morgue on Monday, her coworkers figured she had gone there. Folks in Charlotte assumed she was still in Bryson City. She was in the habit of phoning her son on Saturdays, so he had no clue that anything was amiss."

I wondered about Primrose's son. Was he married? A father? In the army? Gay? Were mother and child close?

Occasionally my work casts me as the bearer of life's most terrible news. In one visit, families are shattered, lives forever altered. Pete had said that most marine officers in Vietnam days would rather engage the enemy than visit a home in middle America to deliver a message of death. I wholeheartedly shared those sentiments.

I imagined the son's face, blank at first, confused. Then, with comprehension, agony, grief, the pain of an open wound. I closed my eyes, sharing at that moment his crushing despair.

"I dropped in at the Riverbank Inn."

Crowe's voice brought me back.

"After the marina, I swung by for a chat with Ralph and Brenda," she said. "They admitted they hadn't seen Hobbs since Saturday, but didn't consider it odd. She'd left without explanation twice during her stay, so they assumed she'd gone off again."

"Gone off where?"

"They figured she was visiting family."

"And?"

"Her room suggested otherwise. All her toiletries were there, toothbrush, dental floss, face cream, the things a woman takes when she travels. Her clothes were still in the dresser, suitcase empty under the bed. Her arthritis medication was sitting on the nightstand."

"Purse? Car keys?"

"Negative. Looks like she may have left the room on her own, but she wasn't planning to be away overnight."

Crowe listened while I described my own visit to the inn, leaving out nothing but my larcenous intentions.

"Why do you suppose Ralph went into her room?"

"Your intuition may have been right. Curiosity. Or maybe he knows more than he's letting on. Maybe he

250

wanted to get something out. I don't have that yet, but we *will* be watching Mr. Stover. We'll also talk to anyone acquainted with the victim, look for witnesses who might have seen her during the time she was missing. You know the drill."

"Round up the usual suspects."

"In Swain County, that ain't many."

"Was there nothing in that room to suggest where she might have gone? An address? A map? A toll ticket?"

The line hummed.

"We found two numbers next to the phone."

As she read the digits, my stomach tightened.

The first rang at High Ridge House. The second rang the cellular on my belt.

An hour later I lay in bed, trying to sort and evaluate what I knew.

Fact: My mysterious foot did not belong to Daniel Wahnetah. Possibility: The foot came from a corpse at the courtyard house. The ground stain contained volatile fatty acids. Something had decomposed there. Possibility: The foot came from Air TransSouth 228. Biohazard containers and other problem body parts had been recovered near the wreckage.

Fact: The foot and its dossier were now missing. Possibility: Primrose Hobbs had kept the material. Possibility: Primrose Hobbs had returned the material, which was then taken by someone else.

Fact: The remains of Jean Bertrand and Pepper Petricelli had not been identified. Possibility: Neither man was on the plane. Possibility: Both the detective and his prisoner were on board, their bodies pulverized by the explosion.

Fact: Jean Bertrand was now a suspect.

251

Fact: A witness claimed to have seen Piper Petricelli in upstate New York. Possibility: Bertrand had been turned. Possibility: Bertrand had been burned.

Fact: I had been accused of stealing evidence. Possibility: I was no longer trusted because of my relationship with Andrew Ryan, Bertrand's SQ partner. Possibility: I was being set up as a scapegoat to prevent me from participating in the investigation. But which investigation, the plane crash or the courtyard house? Possibility: I was at risk. Somebody had tried to run me down and had trashed my room.

A tickle of fear. I held my breath, listening. Silence.

Fact: Primrose Hobbs had been murdered. Possibility: Her death was a random act of violence. More likely: Her death was related to the missing foot.

Fact: Edward Arthur obtained the property at Running Goat Branch in 1933 through his marriage to Sarah Livingstone. He rented it as a campground, then built a lodge, then sold the land in 1949 to a man named Prentice Dashwood, but title was taken in the name of H&F Investment Group, LLP. Arthur had not erected any stone walls or a courtyard. Who was Prentice Dashwood?

I turned on the lamp, retrieved McMahon's Delaware fax, and scurried back to bed, my lips chattering. Huddled under the covers, I reread the names.

W. G. Davis, F. M. Payne, C. A. Birkby, F. L. Warren, P. H. Rollins, M. P. Veckhoff.

The only name that was remotely familiar was that of Veckhoff. A Charlottean named Pat Veckhoff had served in the North Carolina senate for sixteen years. He had died suddenly the previous winter. I wondered if there was a link to the M. P. Veckhoff on the list.

Returning the room to darkness, I lay back and searched for connections among the things I knew. It was hopeless. Images of Primrose kept disrupting my concentration.

Primrose at her computer, glasses on the end of her nose. Primrose in the parking lot. Primrose at the scene of a commuter plane crash, 1997, Kinston, North Carolina. Primrose across a card table, playing bid whit, Primrose in Charlotte. The Presbyterian Hospital cafeteria. I was eating vegetarian pizza made with canned peas and asparagus. I remembered hating the pizza, but not why I had met Primrose there.

Primrose lying in a body bag.

Why, dear God?

Was she carefully chosen, researched, stalked, then overpowered as part of an elaborate plan? Or was she selected by chance? Some psycho's sick impulse. The first blue Honda. The fourth woman to exit the mall. The next black. Was death part of the plan, or did things go badly wrong, spinning out of control to one irreversible moment?

Violence against women is not a recent phenomenon. The bones of my sisters litter history and prehistory. The mass grave at Cahokia. The sacred cenote at Chichén Itzá. The Iron Age girl in the bog, hair shorn, blindfolded and leashed.

Women are conditioned to be wary. Walk faster at the sound of footsteps. Peek through the hole before opening the door. Stand by the controls in the empty elevator. Fear the dark. Was Primrose simply another marcher in a random parade of female victims?

Who was I kidding? I knew the reason. Had no doubt.

Primrose Hobbs had been killed because she fulfilled

a request. My request. She had accepted a fax, taken measurements, and provided data. She had helped me, and in doing that she had threatened someone.

I'd gotten her involved, and that someone had butchered her for it. The guilt and sorrow formed a physical weight pressing on my chest.

But how had Primrose posed a threat? Had she uncovered something that I did not know? Had she realized the significance of that discovery, or had she been unaware of its importance? Had she been silenced for what she knew, or for what someone feared she would figure out?

And what about me? Was I also a threat to some homicidal madman?

My thoughts were interrupted by a soft wailing from below. Throwing back the covers, I pulled on jeans and a sweatshirt and slipped into my deck shoes. Then I tiptoed through the silent house and out the back door.

Boyd was sitting beside his doghouse, nose pointed at the night sky. On seeing me, he sprang to his feet and waggled the entire back half of his body. Then he dashed to the fence and went bipedal. Leaning on forepaws, he stretched his neck and gave a series of yips.

I reached over and scratched his ears. Boyd lapped my hand, giddy with excitement.

When I entered the pen and leashed him, the dog went hyperactive, spinning and kicking up dirt.

"Be cool." I pointed a finger at his snout. "This is against the rules."

He looked at me, tongue dangling, eyebrows dancing. I led him across the yard and into the house.

Moments later we lay in the dark, Boyd on the carpet beside my bed. I heard him sigh as he settled chin on forepaws.

I fell asleep with my hand on his head.

21

The next morning I woke early, feeling cold and empty but unsure why. It came to me in a thick, dreadful wave.

Primrose was gone.

The combined agonies of loss and guilt were almost paralyzing, and I lay still a long time, wanting nothing to do with the world.

Then Boyd nuzzled my hip. I rolled over and scratched his ear.

"You're right, boy. Self-pity does no one any good."

I rose, threw on clothes, and sneaked Boyd out to his run. During my absence a note appeared on the door to Magnolia. Ryan would be spending another day with McMahon and wouldn't need his car. The keys I'd left on his bureau were now on mine.

When I turned on my phone, I had five messages. Four journalists and P & T. I called the repair shop, dumped the rest.

The job was taking longer than anticipated. The car should be ready by tomorrow.

We'd gone from "could" to "should." I was encouraged.

But what now?

An idea rose from deep in my past. The favorite refuge of a worried or restless little girl. It couldn't hurt, and I might uncover something useful.

And for a few hours, at least I would be anonymous and inaccessible.

Following toast and Frosted Flakes, I drove to the Marianna Black Public Library, a one-story redbrick box at the corner of Everett and Academy. Cardboard skeletons flanked the entrance, each with a book held in its hands.

A tall, spindly black man displaying several gold teeth occupied a counter at the main entrance. An older woman worked beside him, securing a chain of orange pumpkins above their heads. Both turned when I entered.

"Good morning," I said.

"Good morning." The man showed a mile of precious metal. His lilac-haired companion eyed me suspiciously.

"I'd like to look at back issues of the local paper." I smiled disarmingly.

"The *Smoky Mountain Times*?" asked Mrs. Librarian, laying down her staple gun.

"Yes."

"How far back?"

"Do you have material from the thirties and forties?"

Her frown deepened. "The collection begins in 1895. It was *Bryson City Times* back then. A weekly. The older publications are on microfilm, of course. You can't view the originals."

"Microfilm will be fine."

257

Mr. Librarian began opening and stacking books. I noticed that his nails were buffed, his clothes immaculate.

"The viewer is in the overflow room, beside the genealogy section. You may only have one box at a time."

"Thank you."

Mrs. Librarian opened one of two metal cabinets behind the counter and withdrew a small gray box. "I'd better explain the machine."

"Please, you mustn't bother. I'll be fine. I'm familiar with microfilm viewers."

I read her expression as she handed me the microfilm. A civilian loose in the stacks. It was her worst nightmare.

Settling at the machine, I checked the box's label: *1931–1937.*

An image of Primrose flashed into my mind, and tears blurred my vision.

Stop. No grieving.

But why was I here? What was my objective? Did I have one, or was I merely hiding out?

No. I had a goal.

I was still convinced that the courtyard property lay at the center of my problems, and wanted to learn more about who had been associated with it. Arthur had told me he'd sold his land to one Prentice Dashwood. But beyond that, and the names on McMahon's fax, I was unsure what I was looking for.

In truth, I held little hope of finding anything helpful but had run out of ideas. And I had to do something about the charges against me. I couldn't return to Charlotte until my car was repaired, and I was barred from any other form of inquiry. What the hell. History should teach something.

A poster had decorated Pete's office during his stint in uniform, guiding words embraced by JAG attorneys uncommitted to the military system: *Indecision Is the Key to Flexibility*.

If the maxim was good enough for officer-lawyers of the United States Marine Corps, it seemed good enough for me. I'd look for everything.

I inserted the film and wound it through the viewer. The machine was a hand-crank model, probably manufactured before the Wright brothers went flying at Kitty Hawk. Text and pictures swam in and out of focus. Within minutes I felt a headache begin to organize.

I flicked through spool after spool, making trip after trip to the front desk. By the late 1940s, Mrs. Librarian relented and allowed me a half dozen boxes at a time.

I skimmed over charity events, car washes, church socials, and local dramas. The crime was mostly petty, involving traffic offenses, drunk and disorderly, missing property, and vandalism. Births, deaths, and weddings were announced, garage and barn sales advertised.

The war had claimed a large number from Swain County. From '42 to '45 the pages were filled with their names and photos. Each death was a feature story.

Some citizens did manage to die in their beds. In December of 1943, the passing of Henry Arlen Preston was front-page news. Preston had been a lifelong resident of Swain County, an attorney, a judge, and part-time journalist. His career was recounted in radiant detail, the highlights being a term in Raleigh as a state senator, and the publication of a two-volume work on the birds of western North Carolina. Preston died at the age of eighty-nine, leaving behind a widow, four children, fourteen grandchildren, and twenty-three great-grandchildren.

The week following Preston's death, the *Times* reported the disappearance of Tucker Adams. Two column inches on page six. No photo.

The obscure little notice touched something in me. Had Adams enlisted secretly, then died overseas as one of our many unknowns? Had he returned, surprised his neighbors with tales of Italy or France, then gone on to live his life? Had he fallen from a cliff? Run off to Hollywood? Though I searched for a follow-up, nothing more on Adams's disappearance was reported.

The rugged terrain had also claimed its victims. In 1939 a woman named Hilda Miner left home to deliver a strawberry pie to her granddaughter. She never arrived, and the pie tin was discovered beside the swollen Tuckasegee River. Hilda was presumed drowned, though her body was not located. A decade later the same waters took Dr. Sheldon Brodie, a biologist at Appalachian State University. A day after the professor's body washed up, Edna Farrell was thought to have fallen into the river. Like Miner, Farrell's remains were never found.

I leaned back and rubbed my eyes. What had the old man said about Farrell? They should have done better by her. Who were "they"? Done better in what way? Was he referring to the fact that Farrell's body wasn't recovered? Or was he unhappy with the quality of Thaddeus Bowman's memorial service?

In 1959 the fauna claimed a seventy-four-year-old Cherokee named Charlie Wayne Tramper. Two weeks after his disappearance, Charlie Wayne's rifle turned up in a remote valley on the reservation. Bear tracks and spoor suggested the cause of death. The old man was buried with full tribal ceremony.

I'd worked on victims of bear attacks, and knew what had remained of Charlie Wayne. I shook the image from my mind.

The list of environmental hazards courtesy of Mother Nature went on. In 1972 a four-year-old girl wandered from a campground in Maggie Valley. The little body was dragged from a lake the following day. The next winter two cross-country skiers froze to death when caught in a sudden blizzard. In 1986 an apple farmer named Albert Odell went searching for morels and never returned.

I found no reference to Prentice Dashwood, to the Arthur property, or to the officers of the H&F Investment Group. The closest I came was a May 1959 spread on a fiery crash on Highway 19. Six hurt, four killed. Pictures showed tangled wreckage. Dr. Anthony Allen Birkby, sixty-eight, from Cullowhee, died three days later of multiple injuries. I took note. Though the name was not uncommon, one C. A. Birkby was listed on McMahon's fax.

By noon, my head pulsed and my blood sugar had dropped to a level incapable of sustaining life. I slipped a granola bar from my purse, did a stealthy peel, and munched quietly as I cranked my zillionth spool through the viewer.

Issues from recent years were not yet on microfilm, and by midafternoon I was able to switch to hard copy. But the headache had already escalated from a minor disturbance to major pains that swirled across my frontal, temporal, and occipital lobes and pulsed at an epicenter behind my right eye.

Final stretch. The tough get going. Bring it home. Remember the Gipper.

Shit.

I was flipping through papers from the current year, scanning headlines and photographs, when a name caught my eye. George Adair. The missing fisherman.

The coverage of Adair's disappearance was detailed, giving the exact time and place of the fatal fishing trip, a description of the victim, and an itemized account of what he was wearing, right down to his high school ring and St. Blaise medal.

Another childhood flashback. The parish priest. The blessing of throats on St. Blaise Day. What was the story? Blaise was reputed to have saved a child from choking on a fish bone. The medal made sense. Crowe said Adair complained of throat problems.

Adair's companion was interviewed, as were his wife, friends, former employer, and priest. A grainy picture was printed beside the story, the pendant clearly visible around his neck.

Who was Crowe's other missing person? I searched my pounding brain. Jeremiah Mitchell. February. I moved back almost eight months and began a more careful perusal. Small things began to connect.

Jeremiah Mitchell's disappearance was reported in one short paragraph. On February 15 a seventy-two-year-old black male left the Mighty High Tap and walked into oblivion. Anyone having information blah, blah, blah.

Old ways die hard, I thought, feeling a prickle of anger. White man goes missing: feature story. Black man goes missing: blurb on page seventeen. Or maybe it was station in life. George Adair had a job, friends, family. Jeremiah Mitchell was an unemployed alcoholic who lived alone.

But Mitchell had once had kin. A follow-up appeared

262

in early March, again a single paragraph, seeking information and citing the name of his maternal grandmother, Martha Rose Gist. I stared. How far back had I seen that name?

I returned to the boxes, jumping the microfilm weeks at a turn. The obituary appeared on May 16, 1952, along with six inches in the arts column. Martha Rose Gist had been a potter of local fame. The article included a picture of a beautifully decorated ceramic bowl, but none of the artist.

Damn!

Checking to be sure the overflow room was empty, I clicked on my cell. Six messages. Ignoring them, I dialed Crowe's number, muffling the beeps with my jacket.

"Sheriff Crowe."

I didn't bother announcing myself.

"Are you familiar with Sequoyah?" I asked in a loud whisper.

"Are you in church?"

"The Bryson City library."

"Iris catches you, she'll rip off your lips and feed them to her shredder."

I assumed Iris was the lilac-haired dragon I'd met at the entrance.

"*Sequoyah?*"

"Sequoyah invented an alphabet for the Cherokee language. Hang around long enough and someone will buy you an ashtray decorated with the symbols," she said.

"What was Sequoyah's family name?"

"You want my final answer?"

"I'm serious."

"Guess."

263

"This is important," I hissed.

"His name was Guess. Or Gist, depending on the transliteration. Why?"

"Jeremiah Mitchell's maternal grandmother was Martha Rose Gist."

"The potter?"

"Yes."

"I'll be damned."

"You know what that means?"

I didn't wait for her answer.

"Mitchell was part Cherokee."

"This is a library!"

Iris's words scorched the side of my face.

I held up a finger.

"Hang up instantly!" She spoke as loud as a human can without using the vocal cords.

"Is there a newspaper printed on the reservation?"

"The *Cherokee One Feather*. And I think there's a tribal photo archive at the museum."

"Gotta go." I disconnected and shut off the power.

"I'm going to have to ask you to leave." Iris stood with hands on hips, the gestapo protectress of the printed word.

"Shall I return the boxes?"

"That will not be necessary."

It took three stops to find what I needed. A trip to the offices of the *Cherokee One Feather*, located in the Tribal Council Center, revealed that the paper had only been in print since 1966. While there had been a predecessor publication years before, *The Cherokee Phoenix*, the current staff had no photos or back issues in their possession.

The Cherokee Historical Association had pictures,

but most had been taken as promotional shots for the outdoor theatrical production *Unto These Hills*.

I hit pay dirt at the Museum of the Cherokee Indian, directly across the street. When I repeated my request, I was taken to a second-floor office, issued cotton gloves, and allowed to graze through their photo and newspaper archives.

Within an hour I had confirmation.

Martha Rose Standingdeer was born in 1889 on the Qualla Boundary. She wed John Patrick Gist in 1908 and gave birth to a daughter, Willow Lynette, the following year.

At the age of seventeen, Willow married Jonas Mitchell at the AME Zion Church in Greenville, South Carolina. Their wedding portrait shows a delicate girl in a cloche veil and Empire gown, a bouquet of daisies in her hands. At her side stands a man with skin much darker than that of his bride.

I studied the picture. Though rawboned and homely, Jonas Mitchell was appealing in a strange sort of way. Today, he might have modeled for Benetton ads.

Willow Mitchell gave birth to Jeremiah in 1929, died of tuberculosis the following winter. I found no mention of Jonas or his son after that date.

I sat back, processing what I'd learned.

Jeremiah Mitchell was at least one half Native American. He was seventy-two years old when he disappeared. The foot must surely be his.

My deductive centers logged in immediately. The dates didn't correlate.

Mitchell went missing in February. The VFA profile gives a post-mortem interval of six to seven weeks, placing the death in late August or early September.

Maybe Mitchell survived the night of the Mighty High Tap. Maybe he ventured off, then returned and died of exposure six months later.

Ventured off?

On a trip.

A seventy-two-year-old alcoholic with no car or money?

It happens.

Uh-huh. Died of exposure in summer?

I sat, stumped and frustrated by a million facts I couldn't integrate.

Hoping pictures would be more headache friendly, I switched to the photo archives.

Again, small things caught my attention.

I'd gone through fifty or sixty folders when an eight-by-ten black-and-white aroused my interest. Flower-draped casket. Mourners, some in broad-shouldered baggy suits, others in traditional Cherokee dress. I flipped to the back. A yellowed label identified the event in faded ink: *Charlie Wayne Tramper Funeral. May 17, 1959*. The old man who had gone missing and been killed by a bear.

My gaze roved over the faces, then froze on one of two young men standing apart from the crowd. I was so surprised I gasped.

Though forty years younger, there was no mistaking that face. He would have been in his late twenties in 1959, newly arrived from England. A professor of archaeology at Duke. An academic superstar about to fade.

Why was Simon Midkiff at Charlie Wayne Tramper's funeral?

My eyes slid right, and this time the gasp was audible. Simon Midkiff was standing shoulder to shoulder with a man who would later rise to the office of lieutenant governor.

Parker Davenport.

Or was it? I stared at the features. Yes. No. This man was much younger, thinner.

I hesitated, looked around. No one had poked through this file for half a century. It wasn't stealing. I would return the print in a few days, no damage done.

I slipped the photo into my purse, returned the folder to its drawer, and bolted.

Outside, I dialed Raleigh Information, requested a number for the Department of Cultural Resources, then waited while the connection was made. When a voice answered I asked for Carol Burke. She came on in less than ten seconds.

"Carol Burke."

"Carol, this is Tempe Brennan."

"Good timing. I was just about to close it up for the day. Are you planning to dig up another graveyard?"

Among its many duties, the North Carolina Department of Cultural Resources is responsible for heritage preservation. When development involving state or federal moneys, permits, licenses, or lands is proposed, Carol and her colleagues order surveys and excavations to determine if prehistoric or historic sites will be threatened. Highway projects, airport work, sewer lines – without their clearance, no ground is broken.

Carol and I met in the days when archaeology was my main focus. Twice Charlotte developers had retained me to help relocate historic cemeteries. Carol had overseen both projects.

"Not this time. I'd like information."

"I'll do my best."

"I'm curious about the site Simon Midkiff is digging for you."

"Currently?"

"Yes."

"He's not doing anything for us at the moment. At least nothing of which I'm aware."

"Isn't he excavating in Swain County?"

"I don't think so. Hold on."

By the time she returned, I'd walked to Ryan's car and opened the door.

"Nope. Midkiff hasn't worked for us in over two years and isn't likely to any time soon because he still owes us a site report from his last contract."

"Thanks."

"I wish all my requests were this simple."

I'd barely put down the phone when it rang again. A journalist from the *Charlotte Observer*. A reminder of my continuing notoriety. I clicked off without comment.

A thousand cranial vessels pulsed in my skull. Nothing made sense. Why had Midkiff lied? Why had he and Davenport attended the Tramper funeral? Did they know each other back then?

I needed aspirin. I needed lunch. I needed an objective listener.

Boyd.

After popping two Bayers, I collected the chow, and we set forth. Boyd rode with his head out the passenger window, nose to the air, twisting and turning to suck in every discernible odor. Watching him at the Burger King drive-through, I thought of the squirrel, then the wall at the courtyard house. Just *what* had his former owner trained him to find?

Suddenly, I had an idea. A place to picnic and check out names.

The Bryson City Cemetery is located on Schoolhouse Hill, overlooking Veterans Boulevard on one side, a mountain valley on the other. The drive took seven minutes. Boyd did not understand the delay and kept prodding and licking the food bag. By the time I pulled into the cemetery, the cardboard tray was so soggy I had to carry it with two hands.

Boyd dragged me from stone to stone, peeing on several, then kicking back divots with his hind feet. Finally, he stopped at a pink granite column, turned, and yipped.

Sylvia Hotchkins
Entered this world January 12, 1945.
Left this world April 20, 1968.
Taken too early in the spring of her life.

Sixty-eight was a rough year for all of us, Sylvia.

Certain she would enjoy the company, I settled at the base of a large oak shading Sylvia's grave and ordered Boyd to sit beside me. He complied, his eyes fixed on the tray in my hand.

When I withdrew a burger, Boyd sprang to his feet.

"Sit."

He sat. I peeled off the paper and gave him the burger. He rose, separated it into components, then ate the meat, bun, and lettuce-tomato garnish sequentially. Finished, he focused on my Whopper, muzzle spotted with ketchup.

"Sit."

He sat. I spread fries on the grass and he began

picking them delicately off the surface so they wouldn't sink between the blades. I unwrapped my Whopper and slipped a straw into my drink.

"Now here's the deal."

Boyd glanced up, went back to the fries.

"Why would Simon Midkiff have gone to the funeral of a seventy-four-year-old Cherokee killed by a bear in 1959?"

We both ate and thought about that.

"Midkiff is an archaeologist. He might have been researching the Eastern Band Cherokee. Maybe Tramper was his guide and historian."

Boyd's attention shifted to my burger. I replenished his potatoes.

"O.K. I'll buy that."

I took a bite, chewed, swallowed.

"Why was Parker Davenport there?"

Boyd looked at me without raising his head from the fries.

"Davenport grew up near here. He probably knew Tramper."

Boyd's ears flicked forward, back again. He finished the last of his fries and stared at mine. I flipped him a few.

"Perhaps Tramper and Davenport had mutual friends on the reservation. Or maybe Davenport was already building a political base in those days."

I threw out another half dozen fries. Boyd reengaged.

"How about this? Did Davenport and Midkiff know each other back then?"

Boyd's head came up. His eyebrows spun and his tongue dropped.

"If so, how?"

He cocked his head and watched as I finished my

burger. I tossed him the rest of my fries, and he ate them as I sipped my Diet Coke.

"Here's the big one, Boyd."

I gathered wrappers and bunched them with the remains of the tray. Seeing no more food, Boyd flopped on to his side, sighed loudly, and closed his eyes.

"Midkiff lied to me. Davenport wants my head on a spike. Is there a link?"

Boyd had no answer.

I sat with my back to the oak, absorbing warmth and light. The grass smelled freshly mown, the leaves dry and sun-baked. At one point Boyd rose, turned four times, then resettled at my side.

A short time later a man came over the crest of the hill, leading a collie on a length of rope. Boyd sat up and barked at the dog but didn't make an aggressive move. The late-afternoon sunshine was mellowing woman and beast. Reeling him in, I got to my feet.

As dusk gathered, we strolled among the gravestones. Though I spotted no one from the H&F list, and no Dashwoods, I did find markers with familiar names. Thaddeus Bowman. Victor Livingstone and his daughter, Sarah Masham Livingstone. Enoch McCready.

I remembered Luke Bowman's words, and wondered what had caused the death of Ruby's husband in 1986. Instead of answers, I was finding more questions.

But one mystery was solved. One missing person found. Turning to go, I stumbled across an unadorned slab in the cemetery's southernmost corner. Its face was inscribed with a simple message.

Tucker Adams
1871–1943
R.I.P.

22

Leaving the cemetery, I drove to High Ridge House, settled Boyd for the night, and returned to my room, unaware that it would be my busiest telephone evening since junior high.

I'd hardly hit the power switch when Pete called.

"How's Big B?"

"Enjoying the mountain food and fauna. Are you back in Charlotte?"

"Hung up in the Hoosier state. Is he straining your patience?"

"Boyd has a unique take on life."

"What's new?"

I told him about Primrose.

"Oh, babe, I'm really sorry. Are you O.K.?"

"I'll be fine," I lied. "There's more."

I summarized the interrogation with Davenport, and listed the complaints the lieutenant governor planned to file.

"Sounds like a mainline mind fuck."

"Don't try to impress me with legal jargon."

"This has to be politically motivated. Any conjectures as to why?"

"He doesn't like my hair."

"I do. Did you establish anything more about the foot?"

I told him about the histological age estimate, about the racial classification, and about the formerly and currently missing Daniel Wahnetah and Jeremiah Mitchell.

"Mitchell sounds like a winning candidate for the foot."

I described the photo of Charlie Wayne Tramper's funeral and my phone call to Raleigh.

"Why would Midkiff lie to you about doing a dig?"

"He doesn't like my hair. Should I get an attorney?"

"You have one."

"Thanks, Pete."

Next, it was Ryan. He and McMahon had finished late and would be returning to the assembly site at dawn, so they were overnighting in Asheville.

"Problems with your phone?"

"The media are scenting blood in the water, so I've had it turned off. Besides, I spent a lot of the day in the library."

"Learn anything?"

"Mountain life is hard on old folks."

"What do you mean?"

"I don't know. Seems like a lot of seniors drown, freeze to death, or end up in the food chain around here. I'll take the flatlands, thanks. What goes with the investigation?"

"The chemical guys are picking up weird traces."

"Explosives?"

"Not necessarily. I'll fill you in tomorrow."

"Have Bertrand and Petricelli been found?"

"No."

Lucy Crowe beeped in at that point, and I clicked over. She had little to report and no warrant.

"The DA doesn't want to second-guess the magistrate without something more solid."

"What the hell do these people want? Miss Scarlet in the library, candlestick in hand?"

"She finds your argument contradictory."

"Contradictory?"

"The VFA profile says something died during the summer. Mitchell disappeared in February. Madam Prosecutor is convinced the stain is from an animal. Says you can't bust in on a citizen for aging meat in his backyard."

"And the foot?"

"Crash victim."

"Anything on Primrose's murder?"

"Turns out Ralph Stover is no hayseed. The gentleman owned a company in Ohio, holds patents on a number of microchips. In eighty-six Ralph underwent a metamorphosis following a cardiac event. He sold out for megabucks and bought the Riverbank. Been a country motel owner ever since."

"Any police record?"

"Two DWIs back in the seventies, otherwise the guy's clean."

"Does it make sense to you?"

"Maybe he watched too many *Newhart* reruns, dreamt of being an innkeeper."

The next to ring was my friend at Oak Ridge. Laslo Sparkes asked if I'd be available in the morning. We made a date for nine o'clock. Good. Maybe he had some more results from the soil samples.

The final call came from my department chair. He opened by apologizing for his abruptness Tuesday night.

"My three-year-old put our kitten in the Kenmore to dry it after a fall into the toilet. My wife had just rescued the poor thing, and everyone was hysterical. Kids crying. Wife crying, trying to get the cat to breathe."

"How awful. Is it all right?"

"The little guy pulled through, but I don't think he's seeing too well."

"He'll come around."

There was a pause. I could hear his breath against the receiver.

"Well, Tempe, there's no easy way, so I'm just going to say it. The chancellor asked me to meet with him today. He's received a complaint about your behavior during the crash investigation and has decided to suspend you pending a full inquiry."

I remained silent. Nothing I was doing in Bryson City was under the auspices of the university, though I was on its payroll.

"With pay, of course. He says he doesn't believe a word of it but has no choice in the matter."

"Why not?" I already knew the answer.

"He's afraid of the negative publicity, feels he has to protect the university. And apparently the lieutenant governor is on his case directly and being a real hard-ass about this."

"And, as everyone knows, the university is funded by the legislature." My hand was clenched on the phone.

"I tried every argument I could think of. He wouldn't budge."

"Thanks, Mike."

"You're welcome back in the department anytime. You could file a grievance."

"No. I'm going to sort this out first."

I went through my bedtime ritual with toothpaste, soap, Oil of Olay, hand cream. Cleansed and lubricated, I turned off the lights, crawled under the blankets, and screamed as loud as I could. Then I hugged knees to chest and for the second time in two days began to cry.

It was time to give up. I'm not a quitter, but I had to face reality. I was getting nowhere. I'd uncovered nothing persuasive enough to obtain a warrant, discovered little at the courthouse, struck out with the newspapers. I'd stolen from a library and had almost committed breaking and entering.

It wasn't worth it. I could apologize to the lieutenant governor, resign from DMORT, and return to my normal life.

My normal life.

What *was* my normal life? Autopsies. Exhumations. Mass fatalities.

I am constantly asked why I've chosen such a morbid vocation. Why I work with the mutilated and decomposed.

Through time and introspection, I have come to understand my choices. I want to serve both the living and the dead. The dead have a right to be identified. To have their stories drawn to a close and to take their place in our memories. If they died at the hands of another, they also have a right to have those hands brought to account.

The living as well deserve our support when the death of another alters their lives: The parent desperate for news of a missing child. The family hopeful of remains from Iwo Jima or Chosin or Hué. The villagers bereft at a mass grave in Guatemala or Kurdistan. The mothers and husbands and lovers and friends dazed at an overlook in the Smoky Mountains. They have a right to information, explanations, and also a right to have murderous hands brought to account.

It is for these victims and the mourners that I tease posthumous tales from bones. The dead will remain dead, whatever my efforts, but there have to be answers and accountability. We cannot live in a world that accepts the destruction of life with no explanations and no consequences.

Of course, an ethics violation would end my career in forensics. If the lieutenant governor had his way, I would effectively be barred from pursuing my profession. An expert witness under an ethical cloud is roadkill on cross-examination. Who would have confidence in any opinion of mine?

Anger replaced self-pity. I would not be driven out of forensics by unfounded accusations and innuendo. I couldn't give in. I had to prove that I was right. I owed it to myself. Even more, I owed it to Primrose Hobbs and her mourning son.

But how?

What to do?

I tossed and turned, feeling like that spider in the rain. My world was under attack by forces stronger than me, and I lacked the power to keep it together.

Sleep finally came, but there was no relief.

When agitated, my brain weaves thoughts into psychedelic collages. All night disjointed images floated in and out of focus.

I was in the incident morgue, sorting body parts. Ryan ran past. I called out, asking what had happened to the foot. He didn't stop. I tried to chase him, but my feet wouldn't move. I kept shouting, reached out, but he drew farther and farther away.

Boyd raced around a cemetery, a dead squirrel hanging from his mouth.

Willow Lynette Gist and Jonas Mitchell posed for a wedding picture. In her hand the Cherokee bride clutched the foot I'd taken from coyotes.

Judge Henry Arlen Preston held a book out to an old man. The man started to walk away, but Preston followed, insisting he take the offering. The old man turned and Preston dropped the book. Boyd snatched it up and ran down a long gravel road. When I caught up and took the object from him, it was no longer a book but a stone tablet, the name "Tucker Adams" carved on its face, and 1943, the year they both died, one a prominent citizen, the other obscure.

Simon Midkiff sat on a chair in the P & T garage office. Next to him was a man with long gray braids and a Cherokee headband.

"Why are you here?" Midkiff asked me.

"I can't drive," I replied. "There was a crash. People were killed."

"Is Birkby dead?" asked gray braids.

"Yes."

"Did they find Edna?"

"No."

"They won't find me either."

Gray braid's face morphed into that of Ruby McCready, then into the bloated features of Primrose Hobbs.

I screamed and my head jerked from the pillow. My eyes flew to the clock. Five-thirty.

Though the room was chilly, my back was slick with perspiration, my hair plastered to my head. I threw back the covers and ran on tiptoes for a drink of water. Gazing into the mirror, I rolled the glass across my forehead.

I returned to the bedroom and flicked on a light. The window was opaque with predawn blackness. Frost spiderwebbed the corners of the glass.

I pulled on sweats and socks, took out a tablet, and settled at the table. After dividing several sheets into thirds, I began writing down images from my dream.

Henry Arlen Preston. The coyote foot. The braided old man in Cherokee headgear. Had that been Charlie Wayne Tramper? I wrote the name, followed by a question mark. Edna Farrell. Tucker Adams. Birkby, Jonas and Willow Mitchell. Ruby McCready. Simon Midkiff.

Next, I added what I knew about each character.

Henry Arlen Preston: Died 1943. Age eighty-nine. Attorney, judge, writer. Birds. Family man.

Coyote foot: Elderly male. Native-American ancestry. Height approximately five foot six. Dead last summer. Found near Arthur/H&F property. TransSouth passenger?

Charlie Wayne Tramper: Cherokee. Died 1959. Age seventy-four. Bear attack. Midkiff and Davenport attended the funeral.

Edna Farrell: Died 1949. Holiness follower. Drowned. Remains not recovered.

Tucker Adams: Born 1871. Disappeared then died, 1943.

Anthony Allen Birkby: Died 1959. Car crash. C. A. Birkby on list of H&F officers.

Jonas Mitchell: African American. Married Willow Lynette Gist. Father of Jeremiah Mitchell.

Willow Lynette Gist: Daughter of Martha Rose Gist,

279

Cherokee potter. Mother of Jeremiah Mitchell. Died of TB, 1930.

Though he wasn't in the dream, I made out a slip for Jeremiah Mitchell. African American–Cherokee. Born 1929. Loner. Disappeared last February.

Ruby McCready: Alive and well. Husband Enoch dead, 1986.

Simon Midkiff: Doctorate from Oxford, 1955. Duke, 1955 to 1961. University of Tennessee, 1961 to 1968. Attended Tramper funeral in 1959. Knew Davenport (or was at least at the same funeral). Lied about working for Department of Cultural Resources.

When I'd finished I spread the slips on the table and studied them. Then I began arranging them according to different criteria, starting with gender. The piles were very lopsided, the smaller containing only Edna Farrell, Willow Lynette Gist, and Ruby McCready. I created a slip for Martha Rose Gist. Nothing seemed to connect the women.

Next I tried race. Charlie Wayne Tramper and the Gist-Mitchell lineage went into one pile, along with the coyote foot. I began a chart and drew a line between Jeremiah Mitchell and the foot.

Age. Again I was struck by the number of old people. Though Henry Arlen Preston had managed to die in bed, appropriate, perhaps, for a distinguished judge, few others on the list had had that luxury. Tucker Adams, seventy-two. Charlie Wayne Tramper, seventy-four. Jeremiah Mitchell, seventy-two. I made out a slip for the missing fisherman, George Adair, sixty-seven. All were old.

The window was moving from black to pewter. I decided to sort by birth dates. Nothing. I tried death dates.

Judge Henry Arlen Preston passed away in 1943. According to his tombstone, Tucker Adams also died in 1943. I remembered the feature article on Preston, the brief inside report on Adams's disappearance less than a week later. I placed their slips together.

A. A. Birkby died in 1959. Charlie Wayne Tramper died in 1959. When was the wreck in which Birkby died? May. The same month Charlie Wayne went missing.

Oh?

I paired the slips.

Edna Farrell died in 1949. Hadn't someone drowned just the day before?

Sheldon Brodie, professor of biology at Appalachian State University. Brodie's body was found. Farrell's wasn't.

I made a slip for Brodie and set it with the one for Edna Farrell.

I stared at the three sets of paired slips. Was it a pattern? Someone is killed or dies, within days another death occurs? Were people dying in pairs?

I started a list of questions.

Edna Farrell's age?

Earlier drowning. Strawberry pie. Age? Date?

Tucker Adams's cause of death?

Jeremiah Mitchell, February. George Adair, September. Others?

The room was the color of the rising sun, and I could hear bird sounds through the closed window. A rectangle of light fell across the table, illuminating my questions and scribbled notes.

I stared at the paired slips, feeling there was something else. Something important. Something my subconscious had not had time to place in the collage.

*

281

Laslo was devouring biscuits and gravy when I arrived at the Everett Street Diner. I ordered pecan pancakes, juice, and coffee. While we ate, he told me about the conference he was going to attend at UNC-Asheville. I told him about Crowe's inability to obtain a search warrant.

"So the good old boys are skeptical," he said, nodding to the waitress that he had finished.

"And girls. The DA is a woman."

"Then this may not help."

He pulled a paper from his briefcase and handed it to me. As I read, the waitress refilled our cups. I looked up when I'd finished.

"Basically the report agrees with what you told me on Monday at your lab."

"Yes. Except for the part about the caproic and heptanoic acid concentrations."

"The conclusion that they look unusually high."

"Yes."

"What does that mean?"

"Elevated levels of the longer-chained VFAs usually mean the corpse has been exposed to cold, or that it underwent a period of decreased insect and bacterial activity."

"Does that alter your estimate of time since death?"

"I still think decomposition began in late summer."

"Then what's the significance?"

"I'm not sure."

"Is this a common finding?"

"Not really."

"Great. That will convert the disbelievers."

"Maybe this will be more helpful."

This time he took a small plastic vial from his briefcase.

"I found this when filtering the rest of your soil sample."

The container held a tiny white chip, no larger than a grain of rice. I unscrewed the cap, slid the object on to my palm, and studied it closely.

"It's a fragment of tooth root," I said.

"That's what I thought, so I didn't treat it with anything, just brushed off the dirt."

"Holy shit."

"That's what I thought."

"Did you take a peek under the scope?"

"Yep."

"How does the pulp chamber look?"

"Chock-full."

Laslo and I signed evidence transfer forms and I packed the vial and report into my briefcase.

"Could I ask you one last favor?"

"Absolutely."

"If my car is ready, could you help me return the one I'm driving, then take me to the shop where mine is being fixed?"

"No problem."

When I called P & T an automotive miracle had occurred: The repairs were complete. Laslo followed me to High Ridge House, delivered me to P & T, then went on to his conference. After a brief discussion of pumps and hoses with one of the letters, I paid the bill and slid behind the wheel.

Before leaving P & T, I turned on my phone, scrolled through my programmed numbers, and hit "dial."

"Charlotte-Mecklenburg Police Department Crime Laboratory."

"Ron Gillman, please?"

"Who's calling?"

"Tempe Brennan."

He came on in seconds.

"The infamous Dr. Brennan."

"You've heard."

"Oh yes. Will we be printing and booking you here?"

"Very funny."

"I suppose it's not. I won't even ask if there's anything to it. Are you getting things cleared up?"

"I'm trying. I may need a favor."

"Shoot."

"I have a tooth fragment I want profiled for DNA. Then I want that profile compared to one you've done on a bone sample from the Air TransSouth crash. Can you do that?"

"I don't see why not."

"How soon?"

"Is this urgent?"

"Very."

"I'll put it on a fast track. When can you get the new sample to me?"

I looked at my watch.

"Two o'clock."

"I'll call over to the DNA section right now, smooth the way. See you at two."

I turned the key and swung into traffic. There were a couple more things I needed to do before leaving Bryson City.

23

This time the lilac dragon was by herself.

"Just need to check a couple of details on microfilm," I said, beaming my most winning smile.

Her face did a ménage à trois of emotions. Surprised. Suspicious. Stern.

"It would be very, very helpful if I could take several reels at a time. You were so kind about that yesterday."

Her face softened somewhat. Sighing loudly, she went to the cabinet, removed six boxes, and placed them on the counter.

"Thank you so much," I purred.

Crossing toward the overflow room, I heard a stool squeak, and knew she was craning in my direction.

"Cellular phones are strictly prohibited in the library!" she hissed to my retreating back.

Unlike my prior visit, I whipped through the spools, taking notes on specific items.

In less than an hour I had what I needed.

Tommy Albright was not in, but a drawly female voice

promised to deliver my message. The pathologist rang back before I'd hit the outskirts of Bryson City.

"In 1959 a Cherokee named Charlie Wayne Tramper died in a bear attack. Would a file that old still exist?"

"Maybe, maybe not. That was before we centralized. What do you need to know?"

"You remember the case?" I couldn't believe it.

"Hell, yes. I poked through what was left of that ole boy."

"Which was?"

"I've seen my share of bear bait, but Tramper was the worst. Those little bastards tore the bejeezus out of him. Carried his head clean off."

"The skull was not recovered?"

"No."

"How did you ID him?"

"Wife recognized the rifle and clothing."

I found the Reverend Luke Bowman gathering fallen branches in his shadowy front yard. Save for the substitution of a black windbreaker, he was dressed exactly as on our previous meetings.

Bowman watched me pull next to his pickup, added his armful to a pile beside the drive, and approached my car. We spoke through the open window.

"Good morning, Miss Temperance."

"Good morning. Beautiful day for yard work."

"Yes, ma'am, it is." Fragments of bark and dry leaves clung to his jacket.

"Could I ask you something, Reverend Mr. Bowman?"

"Of course."

"How old was Edna Farrell when she died?"

"I believe Sister Farrell was just shy of eighty."

286

"Do you remember a man named Tucker Adams?"

His eyes narrowed, and the tip of his tongue slid across his upper lip.

"Adams was elderly, died in 1943," I prompted.

The tongue disappeared and a gnarled finger sighted on me. "I surely do. I was ten years old when that old fellow wandered off from his farm. I helped search for him. Brother Adams was blind and half deaf, so the whole community pitched in."

"How did Adams die?"

"Everyone assumed he just died in the woods. We never found him."

"But his grave is in the cemetery on Schoolhouse Hill."

"No one's buried there. Sister Adams put the headstone up a couple of years after her husband went missing."

"Thank you. You've been very helpful."

"I see the boys got your car to running."

"Yes."

"Hope they didn't charge too much."

"No, sir. It seemed fair."

I pulled into the sheriff's department lot directly behind Lucy Crowe. She parked her cruiser, then waited with hands on hips as I turned off the engine and retrieved my briefcase. Her face looked drawn and cheerless.

"Rough morning?"

"Some morons stole a golf cart from the country club, left it a mile up Conleys Creek Road. Two seven-year-olds found the thing and ran it into a tree. One's got a broken collarbone, the other a concussion."

"Teenagers?"

"Probably."

We spoke as we walked.

"Anything new on the Hobbs murder?"

"One of my deputies was working security Sunday morning. He remembers seeing Hobbs enter the morgue around eight, remembers you. The computer shows she checked the foot out at nine-fifteen, back in at two."

"She kept it that long after talking to me?"

"Apparently."

We climbed the steps and were buzzed through the outside door, then again through a barred prison gate. I followed Crowe down a corridor and across an outer workroom to her office.

"Hobbs signed out of the morgue at three-ten. A guy from Bryson City PD was working the afternoon shift. He doesn't recall seeing her leave."

"What about the surveillance camera?"

"This is beautiful."

Crowe unclipped a radio from her belt, placed it on a cabinet, and dropped into her chair. I took one of those opposite the desk.

"The thing went out around two Sunday afternoon, stayed down until eleven Monday morning."

"Did anyone see Primrose after she left the morgue?"

"Nope."

"Did you discover anything in her room?"

"The lady was fond of Post-its. Phone numbers. Times. Names. Lots of notes, mostly work-related."

"Primrose was always losing her glasses, wore them on a cord around her neck. She worried about being forgetful." I felt a cold spot in my chest. "Any clue about her destination Sunday afternoon?"

"Not a word."

A deputy entered and placed a paper on the sheriff's desk. She glanced at it briefly, back to me.

"I see your wheels are running again."

My Mazda was the talk of Swain County.

"I'm heading down to Charlotte, but I want to show you a couple of things before I go."

I handed her the purloined photo of the Tramper funeral.

"Recognize anyone?"

"I'll be goddamned. Parker Davenport, our venerable lieutenant governor. The little twerp looks like he's fifteen." She returned the print. "What's the significance?"

"I'm not sure."

Next, I handed her Laslo's report, waited while she read.

"So the DA was right."

"Or I was right."

"Oh?"

"How about this scenario? Jeremiah Mitchell died after leaving the Mighty High Tap last February. His body was stored in a freezer or refrigerator, removed, then placed outside later."

"Why?" She tried to keep the skepticism out of her voice.

I withdrew the notes I'd taken at the library, took a deep breath, and began.

"Henry Arlen Preston died here in 1943. Three days later a farmer named Tucker Adams disappeared. He was seventy-two. Adams's body was never found."

"What does that have to d—"

I held up a hand.

"In 1949 a biology professor named Sheldon Brodie drowned in the Tuckasegee River. A day later Edna

Farrell disappeared. She was around eighty. Her body was never found."

Crowe picked up a pen, placed the tip on the blotter, and slid it end over end through her fingers.

"In 1959 Allen Birkby was killed in an automobile accident on Highway 19. Two days after the wreck Charlie Wayne Tramper disappeared. Tramper was seventy-four. His body was recovered, but it was badly mangled, the head missing. The ID was strictly circumstantial."

I looked up at her.

"That's it?"

"What day did Jeremiah Mitchell disappear?"

Crowe dropped the pen, opened the drawer, and withdrew a file.

"February fifteenth."

"Martin Patrick Veckhoff died in Charlotte on February twelfth."

"Lots of people die in February. It's a lousy month."

"The name 'Veckhoff' is on the list of H&F officers."

"The investment group that owns that weird property near Running Goat Branch?"

I nodded.

"So is 'Birkby.'"

She leaned back and rubbed the corner of one eye. I pulled out Laslo's find and set it in front of her.

"Laslo Sparkes found this in the dirt we collected near the wall at the Running Goat house."

She studied but did not reach for the vial.

"It's a tooth fragment. I'm taking it to Charlotte for DNA testing to establish whether it goes with the foot."

Her phone rang. She ignored it.

"You need to get a reference sample for Mitchell."

She hesitated a moment. Then, "I can look into it."

"Sheriff."

The kiwi eyes met mine.

"This may be bigger than Jeremiah Mitchell."

Three hours later Boyd and I were crossing Little Rock Road, heading north on I-85. The Charlotte skyline rose in the distance, like a stand of saguaro in the Sonoran Desert.

I pointed the highlights out to Boyd. The giant phallus of the Bank of America Corporate Center. The syringelike office building on The Square housing the Charlotte City Club, with its circular green cap of a roof and antenna sticking straight up from the center. The jukebox contour of One First Union Center.

"Look at that, boy. Sex, drugs, and rock and roll."

Boyd raised his ears but said nothing.

While Charlotte's neighborhoods may be small-town cozy, its downtown is a city of polished stone and tinted glass, and its attitude toward crime is au courant. The Charlotte-Mecklenburg Police Department is housed in the Law Enforcement Center, an enormous concrete structure at Fourth and McDowell. The CMPD employs approximately 1,900 officers and 400 unsworn support personnel, and maintains its own crime laboratory, second only to that of the SBI. Not bad for a populace of less than 600,000.

Exiting the expressway, I cut across downtown and pulled into the visitors' lot at the LEC.

Officers entered and left the building, each uniformed in deep blue. Boyd growled softly as one crossed close to the car.

"See that emblem on the shoulder patch? It's a hornet's nest."

Boyd made a yodel-like noise but kept his nose at the window.

"During the Revolutionary War, General Cornwallis encountered such pockets of intense resistance in Charlotte that he branded the area a hornet's nest."

No comment.

"I have to go inside, Boyd. You can't."

Disagreeing, Boyd stood.

I promised to be gone less than an hour, gave him my last emergency granola bar, cracked the windows, and left him.

I found Ron Gillman in his corner office on the fourth floor.

Ron was a tall, silver-haired man with a body that suggested basketball or tennis. The only blemish was a Lauren Hutton gap in his upper dentition.

He listened without interrupting as I told him my theory about Mitchell and the foot. When I'd finished, he held out a hand.

"Let's see it."

He slipped on horn-rimmed glasses and studied the fragment, rolling the vial from side to side. Then he picked up the phone and spoke to someone in the DNA section.

"Things move faster if the request comes from here," he said, replacing the receiver.

"Fast would be good," I said.

"I've already checked on your bone sample. That's done, and the profile's gone into the database we set up for the crash victims. If we get results on this" – he indicated the vial – "we'll feed them in and search for a hit."

"I can't tell you how much I appreciate this."

He leaned back and placed his hands behind his head.

"You really put your finger in someone's eye, Dr. Brennan."

"Guess I did."

"Any thoughts as to whose?"

"Parker Davenport."

"The lieutenant governor?"

"That's the one."

"How did you rile Davenport?"

I turned palms up and shrugged.

"It's hard to help if you're not forthcoming."

I stared at him, torn. I'd shared my theory with Lucy Crowe. But that was Swain County. This was home. Ron Gillman directed the second largest crime lab in the state. While the force was funded locally, money came to it via federal grants administered in Raleigh.

Like the ME. Like the university.

What the hell.

I gave him a condensed version of what I'd told Lucy Crowe.

"So you think the M. P. Veckhoff on your list is state senator Pat Veckhoff from Charlotte?"

I nodded.

"And that Pat Veckhoff and Parker Davenport are tied together in some way?"

Another nod.

"Davenport and Veckhoff. The lieutenant governor and a state senator. That's heavy."

"Henry Preston was a judge."

"What's the link?"

Before I could answer, a man appeared in the doorway, the name "Krueger" embroidered above the pocket of his lab coat. Gillman introduced Krueger as the technical leader of the DNA section. He, along with

293

another analyst, examined all DNA evidence at the lab. I rose and we shook hands.

Gillman handed Krueger the vial and explained what I wanted.

"If there's something there, we'll get it," he said, giving a thumbs-up gesture.

"How long?"

"We'll have to purify, amplify, document all along the way. I might be able to give you a verbal in four or five days."

"That would be great." Forty-eight hours would be great, I thought.

Krueger and I signed evidence transfer forms, and he disappeared with the specimen. I waited as Gillman took a call. When he hung up, I asked a question.

"Did you know Pat Veckhoff?"

"No."

"Parker Davenport?"

"I've met him."

"And?"

"He's popular. People vote for him."

"And?"

"He's a royal pain in the ass."

I produced the Tramper funeral photo.

"That's him. But it was a long time ago."

"Yes."

He handed back the picture.

"So what's your explanation for all this?"

"I don't have one."

"But you will."

"But I will."

"Can I help?"

"There is something you can do for me."

★

I found Boyd curled in granola crumbs, sound asleep. At the sound of the key, he shot to his feet and barked. Realizing this was not a sneak attack, he placed one forepaw on each front seat and wagged his hips. I slid behind the wheel, and he began removing makeup from the side of my face.

Forty minutes later I pulled up at the address Gillman had found for me. Though the residence was only ten minutes from downtown, and five minutes from my condo at Sharon Hall, it had taken that long to work through my usual Queens Road confusion.

Charlotte's street names reflect its schizoid personality. On the one hand the street-naming approach was simple: They found a winner and stuck with it. The city has Queens Road, Queens Road West, and Queens Road East. Sharon Road, Sharon Lane, Sharon Amity, Sharon View, and Sharon Avenue. I've sat at the intersection of Rea Road and Rea Road, Park Road and Park Road. There was also a biblical influence: Providence Road, Carmel Road, Sardis Road.

On the other hand, no appellation seemed adequate for more than a few miles. Streets change names with whimsy. Tyvola becomes Fairview, then Sardis. At one point Providence Road reaches an intersection at which a hard right keeps one on Providence; going straight places one on Queens Road, which immediately becomes Morehead; and going left puts one on Queens Road, which immediately becomes Selwyn. The Billy Graham Parkway begets Woodlawn, then Runnymede. Wendover gives rise to Eastway.

The Queens sisters are the most evil by far. I give visitors and newcomers one driving rule of thumb: If you get on to anything named Queens, get off. The policy has always worked for me.

Marion Veckhoff lived in a large stone Tudor on Queens Road East. The stucco was cream, the woodwork dark, and each downstairs window was a latticework of lead and glass. A neatly trimmed hedge bordered the property, and brightly colored flowers crowded beds along the front and sides of the house. A pair of enormous magnolias all but filled the front yard.

A lady in pearls, pumps, and a turquoise pantsuit was watering pansies along a walk bisecting the front lawn. Her skin was pale, her hair the color of ginger ale.

With a warning to Boyd, I got out and locked the door. I shouted, but the woman seemed oblivious to my presence.

"Mrs. Veckhoff?" I repeated as I drew close.

She spun, spraying my feet with her hose. Her hand jerked, and the water was redirected on to the grass.

"Oh, dear. Oh, my. I'm so sorry."

"It's no problem at all." I stepped back from the water puddling the flagstone. "Are you Mrs. Veckhoff?"

"Yes, dear. You're Carla's niece?"

"No, ma'am. I'm Dr. Brennan."

Her eyes went slightly out of focus, as if consulting a calendar somewhere over my shoulder.

"Did I forget an appointment?"

"No, Mrs. Veckhoff. I wondered if I might ask you a few questions about your husband."

She recentered on me.

"Pat was a state senator for sixteen years. Are you a reporter?"

"No, I'm not. Four terms is quite an achievement."

"Being in public office took him away from home too much, but he loved it."

"Where did he travel?"

"Raleigh, mostly."

"Did he ever visit Bryson City?"

"Where's that, dear?"

"It's in the mountains."

"Oh, Pat loved the mountains, went there whenever he could."

"Did you travel with your husband?"

"Oh no, no. I have arthritis, and . . ." Her voice trailed off, as though uncertain where to go with the thought.

"Arthritis can be very painful."

"Yes, it surely is. And those trips were really Pat's time with the boys. Do you mind if I finish my watering?"

"Please."

I walked beside her as she moved along the pansy beds.

"Mr. Veckhoff went to the mountains with your sons?"

"Oh, no. Pat and I have a daughter. She's married now. He went with his chums." She laughed, a sound halfway between a choke and a hiccup. "He said it was to get away from his women, to put the fire back into his belly."

"He went to the mountains with other men?"

"Those boys were very close, been friends since their school days. They miss Pat terribly. Kendall, too. Yes, we're getting old. . . ." Again her voice tapered into silence.

"Kendall?"

"Kendall Rollins. He was the first to go. Kendall was a poet. Do you know his work?"

I shook my head, outwardly calm. Inside my heart was thumping. The name "Rollins" was on the H&F list.

"Kendall died of leukemia when he was fifty-five."

"That's very young. When was that, ma'am?"

"Nineteen eighty-six."

"Where did your husband and his friends stay in the mountains?"

Her face tensed, and the comma of skin under her left eye jumped.

"They had some kind of lodge. Why are you asking about all this?"

"A plane crashed recently near Bryson City, and I'm trying to learn what I can about a nearby property. Your husband might have been one of the owners."

"That terrible affair with all those students?"

"Yes."

"Why do young people have to die? A young man was killed flying to my husband's funeral. Forty-three years old." Her head wagged.

"Who was that, ma'am?"

She looked away.

"He was the son of one of Pat's friends, lived in Alabama, so I'd never met him. Still, it broke my heart."

"Do you know his name?"

"No."

Her eyes would not meet mine.

"Do you know the names of the others who went to the lodge?"

She began fidgeting with the nozzle.

"Mrs. Veckhoff?"

"Pat never talked about those trips. I left him to it. He needed privacy, being in the public eye so much."

"Have you ever heard of the H&F Investment Group?"

"No." She remained focused on the hose, her back to me, but I could see tension in her shoulders.

"Mrs. Veck—"

"It's late. I have to go inside now."

"I'd like to find out if your husband had an interest in that property."

Twisting off the spray, she dropped the hose and hurried up the walk.

"Thanks for your time, ma'am. I'm sorry to have kept you so long."

She turned with the door half open, one veiny hand on the knob. From inside the house came the soft bong of Westminster chimes.

"Pat always said I talk too much. I denied it, told him I was just the friendly type. Now I think he was probably right. But it gets lonely being by yourself."

The door closed, and I heard a bolt slide into place.

It's O.K., Mrs. Veckhoff. Your answers were bullshit, but they were charming bullshit. And very informative.

I dug a card from my purse, wrote my home address and number on it, and stuck it into the doorjamb.

24

It was past eight when my first visitor arrived.

After leaving Mrs. Veckhoff, I'd bought a rotisserie chicken at the Roasting Company, then collected Birdie from my neighbor. The three of us had shared the fowl, Bird's tail fluffing like a feather duster each time Boyd moved in his direction. I was scraping plates at the sink when I heard the knock.

Pete stood on the back stoop, a bouquet of daisies in one hand. As I opened the door, he bowed at the waist and proffered the flowers.

"On behalf of my canine associate."

"Not necessary, but appreciated." I held open the door, and he went past me into the kitchen.

Boyd bounded over at the sound of Pete's voice, dropped snout on to front paws, rump in the air, then began cavorting around the kitchen. Pete clapped and called his name. Boyd went berserk, barking and racing in circles. Birdie bolted.

"Stop. He'll scratch the floor."

Pete took a chair at the table and Boyd moved beside him.

"Sit."

Boyd stared at Pete, eyebrows dancing. Pete tapped the dog's rump, and Boyd sat, chin upon his master's knee. Pete began a two-handed ear scratch.

"Got any beer?"

"Root beer."

"Right. How'd you two get along?"

"Fine."

I opened and placed a Hire's in front of him.

"When did you get back?" Pete lowered and tipped the bottle so Boyd could drink.

"Today. How did things go in Indiana?"

"The local arson investigators were about as sophisticated as the Bobbsey twins. But the real problem was the liability insurance adjuster representing the roofer. His client was working on a roof patch with an acetylene torch in the exact area where the fire started."

He wiped the mouth of the bottle with his hand and drank.

"This asshole knew the cause and origin. We knew the cause and origin. He knew we knew it. We knew he knew we knew, but his official position was that they needed additional investigation."

"Will it go to court?"

"Depends on what they offer." He lowered the root beer again, and Boyd slurped. "But it was good to have a break from chow breath, here."

"You love that dog."

"Not as much as I love you." He gave me his "Goofy Pete" grin.

"Hmm."

"Any progress on your DMORT problems?"

301

"Maybe."

Pete looked at his watch.

"I want to hear all about it, but right now I'm bushed."

He drained the bottle and stood. Boyd shot to his feet.

"I think I will mosey with my dog."

I watched them leave, Boyd dancing around Pete's legs. When I turned, Birdie was peering in from the hall doorway, feet positioned for a quick retreat.

"Good riddance" is what I said. Miffed is what I felt. The damn dog hadn't looked back once.

Birdie and I were watching *The Big Sleep* when the second knock sounded. I was in a T-shirt, panties, and my old flannel robe. He was in my lap.

Ryan stood on the doorstep, face ashen in the porch light. I avoided repeating my usual opener. He'd tell me soon enough why he was in Charlotte.

"How did you know I'd be here?"

He ignored my question.

"Spending the evening by yourself?"

I tipped my head. "Bacall and Bogart are in the study."

I opened the door, as I had for Pete, and he brushed past me into the kitchen. I smelled cigarette smoke and perspiration, and assumed he'd driven straight from Swain County.

"Will they mind if I make it a foursome?" Though his words were light, his face told me his heart was not.

"They're flexible."

He followed me to the den, and we settled at opposite ends of the couch. I clicked off the TV.

"Bertrand's been ID'ed."

I waited.

"Mostly dental. And some other" – his Adam's apple rose and fell – "fragments."

"Petricelli?"

He shook his head, a short, tight gesture.

"They were seated at ground zero, so Petricelli may be vapor. What they found of Bertrand was two valleys over from the main site." His voice was tight and shaky. "Embedded in a tree."

"Has Tyrell released the body?"

"This morning. I'm escorting it to Montreal on Sunday."

I wanted to wrap my arms around his neck, to press my cheek to his chest and stroke his hair. I didn't move.

"The family wants a civil ceremony, so the SQ's organizing a funeral for Wednesday."

I didn't hesitate.

"I'm going with you."

"That's not necessary." He kept opening and closing one hand around the other. His knuckles looked hard and white as a row of pebbles.

"Jean was my friend, too."

"It's a long trip."

His eyes glistened. He blinked, leaned back, and ran both hands up and down his face.

"Would you like me to go?"

"What about this pissing match with Tyrell?"

I told him about the tooth fragment, held back the rest.

"How long will the profiling take?"

"Four or five days. So there's no reason I have to stay here. Would you like me to go?"

He looked at me, and a wrinkle formed at the corner of his mouth.

"I have a feeling you will, anyway."

Knowing he would spend the next two days arranging transport for Bertrand's casket and meeting with McMahon at FBI headquarters, Ryan had booked a room at the Adams Mark Hotel near uptown. Or perhaps he had other reasons. I didn't ask.

The next day I researched names on the H&F list, and learned only one thing. Once outside my own lab my investigative skills are limited.

Encouraged by my success in Bryson City, I spent a library morning with back issues of the *Charlotte Observer*. Though a mediocre public official, State Senator Pat Veckhoff had been a model citizen. Otherwise, I discovered zilch.

The Internet produced a few references to the poetry of Kendall Rollins, the poet Mrs. Veckhoff had mentioned. That was it. Davis. Payne. Birkby. Warren. They were common names, leading into labyrinths of useless information. The Charlotte White Pages listed dozens of each.

That evening, I took Ryan to dinner at the Selwyn Pub. He seemed withdrawn and preoccupied. I didn't push.

Sunday afternoon Birdie went to Pete, and Ryan and I flew to Montreal. What remained of Jean Bertrand traveled below in a glossy metal casket.

We were met at Dorval Airport by a funeral director, two hearse attendants, and four uniformed officers of the Sûreté du Québec. Together we escorted the body into town.

October can be glorious in Montreal, with church spires and skyscrapers piercing a crisp, blue sky, the mountain burning brightly in the background. Or it can be gray and cheerless, with rain, sleet, or even snow.

This Sunday the temperature flirted with freezing, and dark, heavy clouds hung over the city. Trees looked stark and black, lawns and parkways frosted white. Burlap-wrapped shrubs stood guard outside homes and businesses, floral mummies bundled against the cold.

It was past seven by the time we delivered Bertrand to an Urgel Bourgie in St-Lambert. Ryan and I parted ways, he being taken to his condo at Habitat, I to mine in Centre-ville.

Arriving, I threw my overnighter on the bed, turned on the heat, checked my answering machine, and then the refrigerator. The former was full, flashing like a blue light at a Kmart special. The latter was empty, stark white walls and smeared glass shelves.

LaManche. Isabelle. Four telemarketers. A McGill graduate student. LaManche.

Digging a jacket and gloves from the hall closet, I walked to Le Faubourg for provisions.

By the time I returned, the condo had warmed. I built a fire anyway, needing its comfort more than its heat. I was feeling as down as I had at Sharon Hall, haunted by the specter of Ryan's mysterious Danielle, saddened by the prospect of Bertrand's funeral.

As I stir-fried scallops and green beans, sleet began ticking against the windows. I ate at the hearth, thinking of the man I'd come to bury.

The detective and I had worked together over the years, when murder victims caused our paths to cross, and I'd come to understand certain things about him. Incapable of deviousness, he'd seen the world in black and white, with cops on one side of a moral line, criminals on the other. He'd had faith in the system, never doubting it would sort the good guys from the bad.

Bertrand had visited me here the previous spring, devastated by an incomprehensible break with Ryan. I pictured him sitting on my couch that night, wretched with anger and disbelief, not knowing what to say or do, the same feelings now overpowering Andrew Ryan.

After dinner, I loaded the dishwasher, stoked the fire, then took the handset to the sofa. Mentally switching to French, I dialed LaManche's home number.

My boss said he was glad I'd come to Montreal, even though the circumstances were so sad. There were two anthropology cases at the lab.

"Last week a woman was found, nude and decomposed, wrapped in a blanket in Parc Nicholas-Veil."

"Where is that?"

"The far northern edge of the city."

"CUM?"

The Communauté Urbaine de Montréal Police, or Montreal Urban Community Police, have jurisdiction over everything on the island of Montreal.

"*Oui*. Sergent-détective Luc Claudel."

Claudel. The highly regarded bulldog of a detective who would grudgingly work with me, but remained unconvinced that female forensic anthropologists were helpful to law enforcement. Just what I needed.

"Has she been ID'ed?"

"There is a presumptive identification, and a man has been arrested. The suspect is claiming she fell, but Monsieur Claudel is suspicious. I would like you to examine the cranial trauma." LaManche's French, always so proper.

"I'll do it tomorrow."

The second case was less urgent. A small plane had crashed two years earlier near Chicoutimi, the copilot

306

never found. A segment of diaphysis had recently washed up in that vicinity. Could I determine if the bone was human? I assured him I could.

LaManche thanked me, asked about the Air TransSouth recovery, and expressed sorrow over Bertrand's death. He did not inquire about my problems with the authorities. Surely the news would have reached him, but he was too discreet to raise a painful subject.

The telemarketers I ignored.

The graduate student had long since obtained the needed reference.

My friend Isabelle had hosted one of her soirees the previous Saturday. I apologized for missing her call, and her dinner party. She assured me there would be another soon.

I had just replaced the handset when my cell phone rang. I sprinted across the room and dug it out, once again vowing to find a better storage location than my purse. It took a moment for the voice to register.

"Anne?"

"What are you doing?" she asked.

"Finalizing world peace. I just got off the phone with Kofi Annan."

"Where are you?"

"Montreal."

"Why the hell are you back in Canada?"

I told her about Bertrand.

"Is that why you sound so bummed?"

"Partly. Are you in Charlotte? How was London?"

"What does that mean? Partly?"

"You don't want to know."

"Of course I do. What's wrong?"

I unloaded. My friend listened. Twenty minutes later I took a breath, not weeping but close.

307

"So the Arthur property and unidentified foot issue are separate from the crash complaint issue?"

"Sort of. I don't think the foot came from anyone on the flight. I have to prove that."

"You think it's this Mitchell character who's been missing since February?"

"Yes."

"And the NTSB still doesn't know what took that plane out?"

"No."

"And all you know about this property is that some guy named Livingstone gave it as a wedding gift to some guy named Arthur who sold it to some guy named Dashwood."

"Uh-huh."

"But the deed is in the name of an investment group, not Dashwood."

"H&F. In Delaware."

"And some of the officers' names match up to the names of people who died right before local seniors went missing."

"You're good."

"I took notes."

"Sounds ridiculous."

"Yes. And you have no idea why Davenport is on a tear for you?"

"No."

Silence hummed across two countries.

"We heard about some lord in England named Dashwood. A friend of Benjamin Franklin's, I think."

"That should crack this wide open. How *was* London?"

"Great. But too much the ABC tour."

"ABC tour?"

"'Another bloody cathedral.' Ted likes history. He even dragged me through a bunch of caves. When will you be back in Charlotte?"

"Thursday."

"Where are we going for Thanksgiving?"

Anne and I met when we were young and pregnant, I with Katy, she with her son, Brad. That first summer we'd all packed up and taken the babies to the ocean for a week. We'd been going to one beach or another every summer and Thanksgiving ever since.

"The kids like Myrtle. I like Holden."

"I want to try Pawleys Island. Let's have lunch. We'll discuss it and I'll tell you all about my trip. Tempe, things will get back to normal. You'll see."

I fell asleep listening to sleet, thinking of sand and palmetto, and wondering if I had any chance at all of having a normal life again.

The Laboratoire de Sciences Judiciaires et de Médecine Légale is the central medico-legal and crime laboratory for the province of Quebec. It is located on the top two floors of the Édifice Wilfrid-Derome, known to locals as the Sûreté du Québec, or SQ building.

By nine-thirty Monday morning I was in the anthropology-odontology lab, having already attended the morning staff meeting, and collected my *Demande d'Expertise en Anthropologie* request form from the pathologist assigned to each case. After determining that the copilot long-bone shaft actually came from the lower leg of a mule deer, I wrote a brief report and turned to Claudel's lady.

I arranged the bones in anatomical order on my worktable, did a skeletal inventory, then checked indicators of age, sex, race, and height for consistency

309

with the presumed ID. This could be important, since the victim had been toothless, and dental records did not exist.

I broke at one-thirty and ate my bagel with cream cheese, banana, and Chips Ahoy! cookies while watching boats sailing under cars driving over the Jacques Cartier Bridge far below my office window. By two I was back with the bones, and by four-thirty I had finished my analysis.

The victim *could* have shattered her jaw, orbit, and cheekbone and smashed the depressed fractures into her forehead by falling. From a hot air balloon or high-rise building.

I called Claudel and left a verbal opinion of homicide, locked up, and went home.

I spent another night by myself, cooking and eating a chicken breast, watching a rerun of *Northern Exposure*, reading a few chapters of a novel by James Lee Burke. It was as though Ryan had dropped from the planet. I was asleep by eleven.

The next day was spent documenting the battered lady: photographing my findings with regard to biological profile and photographing, diagramming, describing, and explaining the injury patterns on her skull and face. By late afternoon I'd compiled a report and left it in the secretarial office. I was removing my lab coat when Ryan appeared at my office door.

"Need a lift to the funeral?"

"Rough couple of days?" I asked, taking my purse from the bottom desk drawer.

"There's not a lot of sunshine in the squad."

"No," I said, meeting his gaze.

"I'm completely jammed up with this Petricelli thing."

"Yes." My eyes never left his.

"Turns out Metraux isn't quite so sure about eyeballing Pepper."

"Because of Bertrand?"

He shrugged.

"These bastards will dime their own mothers for an afternoon out."

"Risky."

"As tap water in Tijuana. Do you want the ride?"

"If it's not too much trouble."

"I'll pick you up at eight-fifteen."

Since Sergeant-détective Jean Bertrand had died while on duty, he was given full state honors. La Direction des Communications of the Sûreté du Qué had informed every police force in North America, using the CPIC system in Canada and the NCIC system in the United States. An honor guard flanked the casket at the funeral parlor. The body was escorted from there to the church, from the church to the cemetery.

While I had expected a large turnout, I was astounded by the mass of people who showed up. In addition to Bertrand's family and friends, his fellow SQ officers, members of the CUM, and many from the medico-legal lab, it looked like every police department in Canada, and many in the United States, had sent representatives. French and English media sent reporters and TV crews.

By noon, the bits of Bertrand that passed for his corpse lay in the ground at the Notre-Dame-des-Neiges Cemetery, and Ryan and I were winding our way down the mountain toward Centre-ville.

"When do you fly out?" he asked, splitting off Côte-des-Neiges on to rue St-Mathieu.

"Eleven-fifty tomorrow morning."

"I'll pick you up at ten-thirty."

"If you're aspiring to a position as my chauffeur, the pay is lousy."

The joke plunged to its death before I'd finished saying it.

"I'm on the same flight."

"Why?"

"Last night the Charlotte PD busted an Atlanta lowlife named Pecan Billie Holmes."

He dug a pack of du Maurier's from his pocket, tapped one out on the steering wheel, and placed it between his lips. After lighting up with one hand, he inhaled, then blew smoke through both nostrils. I lowered my window.

"Seems the Pecan had a lot to say about a certain telephone tip to the FBI."

25

The next few days felt like a plunge on the Mind Eraser at Six Flags. After weeks of the slow climb, suddenly everything broke. But there was nothing amusing about the ride.

It was late afternoon when Ryan and I touched down in Charlotte. In our absence, fall had caught on, and a strong breeze flapped our jackets as we walked to the parking garage.

We drove directly downtown to the FBI office at Second and Tryon. McMahon had just returned from interviewing Pecan Billie Holmes at the jail.

"Holmes was coked to the eyeballs when they hauled his butt to the bag last night, yelling and screaming, offering to roll over on everything back to a Little League game his team threw in the fourth grade."

"Who is this guy?" Ryan.

"A thirty-eight-year-old three-time loser. Hangs on the fringes of the Atlanta biker scene."

"Hells Angels?"

McMahon nodded.

"He's not a full patcher, doesn't have the brains of a banana Popsicle. The club tolerates him as long as he's useful."

"What was Holmes doing in Charlotte?"

"Probably here for a Rotary luncheon," McMahon said.

"Does Holmes really know who phoned in the bomb tip?" I asked.

"At four A.M. he had an inside track. That's why the arresting officers phoned us. By the time I got there, a night's sleep had dulled the Pecan's enthusiasm for sharing."

McMahon lifted a mug from his desk, swirled and examined the contents as one might a stool sample.

"Fortunately, at the time of his arrest the scumbag was on probation for bouncing rubber all over Atlanta. We were able to persuade him that full disclosure was in his own best interest."

"And?"

"Holmes swears he was present when the scheme was hatched."

"Where?"

"The Claremont Lounge in midtown Atlanta. That's about six blocks from the pay phone where the call was made."

McMahon set down the mug.

"Holmes says he was drinking and snorting blow with a couple of Angels named Harvey Poteet and Neal Tannahill. The boys were talking about Pepper Petricelli and the crash when Poteet decided it would be cool to diddle the FBI with a false lead."

"Why?"

"Barstool brilliance. If Petricelli was alive, it would scare him into silence. If he'd gone down with the plane,

314

a message would go out. Talk and the brothers erase you from the planet. A freebie."

"Why would these assholes talk business in front of an outsider?"

"Poteet and Tannahill were doing lines in Holmes's car. Our hero was out cold in the backseat. Or so they thought."

"So the whole thing was a hoax," I said.

"Appears so." McMahon moved the mug beyond the edge of the blotter.

"Metraux's backing off on his Petricelli sighting," Ryan added.

"There's a surprise."

Down the hall a phone rang. A voice called out. Heels clicked down the corridor.

"Looks like your partner and his prisoner just got on the wrong flight."

"So the Sri Lankans are clean, Simington is up for Humanitarian of the Year, and the Angels are nothing but merry pranksters. We're back to square one with a blown plane and no explanation." Ryan.

"I got a call from Magnus Jackson as I was leaving Bryson City. He claims his investigators are picking up evidence of slow burning."

"What kind of evidence?" I asked.

"Geometric burn patterns on debris."

"Which means?"

"Fire prior to the explosion."

"A mechanical problem?"

McMahon shrugged.

"They can separate precrash from postcrash burning?" I pushed.

"Sounds like crap to me."

McMahon grabbed the mug and got out of his chair.

315

"So the Pecan may be a hero."

Ryan and I stood.

"And Metraux's not finding a seller's market," said Ryan.

"Ain't life grand."

I hadn't told Ryan about Parker Davenport's insinuations concerning himself and Bertrand. I did so now, outside the Adams Mark Hotel. Ryan listened, hands tight on his knees, eyes straight ahead.

"That rat-brained little prick." Headlights moved across his face, distorting lines and planes rigid with anger.

"This should dampen that line of reasoning."

"Yes."

"I'm sure Davenport's reaming me has nothing to do with you or Bertrand. That was a sidebar to his real agenda."

"Which is?"

"I have every intention of finding out."

Ryan's jaw muscles bunched, relaxed.

"Who the fuck does he think he is?"

"Powerful people."

His palms rubbed up then down his jeans, then he reached over and took my hand.

"Sure I can't buy you dinner?"

"I need to collect my car."

Ryan dropped my hand, flipped the handle, and got out of the car.

"I'll call you in the morning," I said.

He slammed the door and was gone.

Back at the Annex, my answering machine flashed four messages.

Anne.

Ron Gillman.

Two hang-ups.

I dialed Gillman's pager. He phoned back before I'd filled Birdie's bowls.

"Krueger says you've got a match on the DNA."

My stomach and tonsils changed places.

"He's sure?"

"One chance in seventy godzillion of error. Or whatever figures those guys throw around."

"The tooth and foot come from the same person?" I still couldn't believe it.

"Yes. Go get your warrant."

I dialed Lucy Crowe. The sheriff was out, but a deputy promised to find her.

There was no answer in Ryan's room.

Anne picked up on the first ring.

"Figure out who your bomber is?"

"We figured out who it isn't."

"That's progress. How about dinner?"

"Where's Ted?"

"At a sales meeting in Orlando."

My cupboard would have made Mother Hubbard proud. And I was so agitated I knew sitting at home would be sheer torture.

"Foster's in thirty minutes?"

"I'll be there."

Foster's Tavern is a subterranean hideaway with somber wood paneling and tufted black leather rising to midwall. A carved bar wraps around one end, battered tables fill the other. Blood cousin to the Selwyn Avenue Pub, the tavern is small, dark, and flawlessly Irish.

Anne had the Guinness stew and Chardonnay. Were

317

I in the game, I'd have gone for a black and tan, but Anne always had Chardonnay. I ordered corned beef and cabbage, a Perrier with lime. Normally I ask for lemon, but the green seemed more fitting.

"So who's been ruled out?" Anne asked, finger-tipping a speck from her wine.

"I can't really discuss that, but there's other progress I can tell you about."

"You've figured out the early temperature history of the solar system."

She flicked the particle. Her hair looked blonder than I remembered.

"That was last week. Did you lighten your hair?"

"A mistake. What's this progress?"

I told her about the DNA hit.

"So your foot belongs to whoever went soupy inside the wall."

"And it wasn't any jive deer."

"Who was it?"

"I'll bet the farm it was Jeremiah Mitchell."

"The black Cherokee."

"Yes."

"Now what?"

"I'm waiting for a call from the Swain County sheriff. With the DNA match, a warrant should be a piece of cake. Even from that medieval moron of a magistrate."

"Nice alliteration."

"Thanks."

Over dinner, we decided on Wild Dunes at Thanksgiving. The rest of the time Anne described her trip to England. I listened.

"Did you see *anything* besides cathedrals and monuments?" I asked when she paused for breath.

"Caves."

318

"Caves?"

"Totally bizarre. This guy named Francis Dashwood had them dug sometime in the eighteenth century. He wanted a Gothic atmosphere, so he had this corny three-sided stone structure built around the entrance. Cathedral windows, doors, and arches, a stone-bordered portal in the center, and a black wrought-iron fence at each side. Creates a sort of courtyard. Gothic chic, complete with souvenir shop, café, and white plastic tables and chairs for the thirsty medieval tourist."

She took a sip of wine.

"You enter the caves through a long white tunnel with a low, rounded ceiling."

"Why white?"

"It's all fake. The caves were chiseled out of chalk."

"Where are they?"

"West Wycombe in Buckinghamshire. It's about an hour's drive northwest of London. Someone told Ted about the place so we had to stop off on our way to Oxford." She rolled her eyes. "Tempe, these caves are mondo bizarro. Passages meander all over the place, with little rooms and crannies and side branches. And they're filled with all sorts of creepy carvings."

"Creepy?"

"Most of the engravings look like the work of kids, but they're way too grotesque."

"Like what?"

"A face with a cross gouged into its forehead, another wearing a sorcerer's hat, the mouth and eyes perfect O's."

She gave what she must have considered a ghostly grimace.

"Tunnels split, then rejoin, then change direction for no reason. There's a Banqueting Hall, and a River Styx, complete with fake stalactites, that you have to cross to enter a chamber called the Inner Temple. My personal favorite was a winding passage to nowhere stuffed with tacky mannequins of Dashwood and his cronies."

"Why did Dashwood dig the caves?"

"Maybe he had more money than brains. The guy's mausoleum is there, too. Looks like the Coliseum."

She drained her wine, swallowed quickly as another idea struck her.

"Or maybe Frank was an eighteenth-century Walt Disney. Planned to make millions opening the place as a tourist attraction."

"Didn't they provide an explanation?"

"Yeah. Outside the cave there's a long brick corridor with wall hangings that give the history. I was taking pictures, so I didn't read them. Ted did."

She rechecked her glass, found it still empty.

"Just down the road, there's an elaborate English manor called Medmenham Abbey. The place was built by twelfth-century Cistercian monks, but Dashwood bought and renovated it to use as a country getaway. Gothic walls, crumbling entrance with engraved motto arching above."

She said this in a breathy voice, moving her hand in a semicircle above her head. Anne is a real estate agent and sometimes describes things in Realtorese.

"What did the motto say?"

"Damned if I know."

Coffee arrived. We added cream, stirred.

"After our phone conversation the other day, I kept thinking about this guy Dashwood."

"The name Dashwood is not uncommon."

"How common is it?"

"I can't quote numbers."

"Do you know anyone named Dashwood?"

"No."

"Uncommon enough."

It was hard to maneuver around that.

"Francis Dashwood lived two hundred and fifty years ago."

She was in midshrug when my cell phone rang. I clicked on quickly, apologizing with a grimace to the other patrons. While I find cell phones in restaurants the height of rudeness, I hadn't wanted to chance missing Lucy Crowe's call.

It was the sheriff. I talked as I hurried outside. She listened without interrupting.

"That's good enough for a warrant."

"What if this asshole still won't issue?"

"I'm going to drop by Battle's house right now. If he stonewalls, I'll think of something."

When I returned to the table, Anne had ordered another glass of Chardonnay and a stack of photos had appeared. I spent the next twenty minutes admiring shots of Westminster, Buckingham Palace, the Tower, the Bridge, and every museum in greater London.

It was almost eleven when I pulled in at Sharon Hall. As I swung around the Annex, the headlights picked up a large brown envelope on my front stoop. I parked in back, cut the engine, and cracked a window.

Only crickets and traffic noises on Queens Road.

I sprinted to the back door and slipped inside. Again, I listened, wishing Boyd were with me.

Nothing cut the silence but the whir of the refrigerator, the hammering of Gran's mantel clock.

I was about to call Birdie when he appeared in the doorway, stretching first one hind leg, then the other.

"Was someone here, Bird?"

He sat and gazed at me with round yellow eyes. Then he licked a forepaw, dragged it across his right ear, repeated the maneuver.

"Obviously you're not worried about intruders."

I crossed to the living room, put my ear to the door, then stepped back and turned the knob. Birdie observed from the hall. No sign of any person. I took the package inside and locked the door behind me.

Birdie watched politely.

My name was written on the envelope in a swirly, feminine hand. There was no return address.

"It's for me, Bird."

No reply.

"Did you see who left it?"

I shook the package.

"Probably not the way the bomb squad would do it."

I tore a corner and peeked inside. A book.

Ripping open the envelope, I withdrew a large, leather-bound journal. A note was taped to the front cover, penned on delicate peach stationery by the same hand that had placed my name on the outer packaging.

My eyes raced to the signature.

Marion Louise Willoughby Veckhoff.

26

Dr. Brennan,

I am a useless old woman. I have never had a job or held office. I have not written a book or designed a garden. I have no gift for poetry, painting, or music. But I was a loyal and obedient wife all the years of my marriage. I loved my husband, supported him un-questioningly. It was the role to which my upbringing led me.

Martin Patrick Veckhoff was a good provider, a loving father, an honest businessman. But, as I sit, deafened by the silence of another sleepless night, questions burn inside my heart. Was there another side to the man I lived with for almost six decades? Were there things that weren't right?

I am sending you a diary that my husband kept under lock and key. Wives have a way, Dr. Brennan, wives alone with time on their hands. I found the diary years ago, returned to it again and again, listened, followed the news. Kept silent.

The man killed on the way to Pat's funeral was

323

Roger Lee Fairley. His obituary gives the date. Read the journal. Read the clippings.

I'm not sure what it all means, but your visit frightened me. These past few days I have peered deep into my soul. Enough. I cannot endure one more night alone with the dread.

I am old, soon to die. But I ask one thing. If my suspicions prove correct, do not disgrace our daughter.

I apologize for my rudeness on Friday last.

> *Regretfully,*
> *Marion Louise Willoughby Veckhoff*

Burning with curiosity, I double-checked the security system, made myself a cup of tea, and took everything to my study. After collecting notebook and pen, I opened the journal, removed and upended an envelope I found stuck between the pages.

Neatly trimmed clippings fluttered to my desk, some without identification, others from the *Charlotte Observer*, the *Raleigh News & Observer*, the *Winston-Salem Journal*, the *Asheville Citizen-Times*, also known as "the Voice of the Mountains," and the *Charleston Post and Courier*. Most were obituaries. A few were feature stories. Each reported the death of a prominent man.

The poet Kendall Rollins succumbed to leukemia on May 12, 1986. Among those surviving Rollins was his son, Paul Hardin Rollins.

The small hairs on my neck reached for the ceiling. P. H. Rollins was on the list of H&F officers. I made note.

Roger Lee Fairley died when his small plane went down in Alabama eight months back. O.K., that's what Mrs. Veckhoff said. I jotted the name and date. February 13.

The oldest item described the 1959 highway accident that killed Anthony Allen Birkby.

The other names meant nothing. I added them to my list, along with their dates of death, laid the clippings aside, and turned to the diary.

The first entry was made on June 17, 1935, the last in November 2000. Flipping through the pages, I could see that the handwriting changed several times, suggesting multiple authors. The final three decades were chronicled in a taut, cramped script almost too small to read.

Martin Patrick Veckhoff was tightly wrapped, indeed, I thought, returning to the first page. For the next two hours I plowed through faded script, now and then glancing at my watch, distracted by thoughts of Lucy Crowe.

The journal contained not a single proper name. Codes or nicknames were used throughout. Omega. Ilus. Khaffre. Chac. Itzmana.

I recognized an Egyptian pharaoh here, a Greek letter there. Some handles sounded vaguely familiar, others not at all.

There were financial accounts: money in, money out. Repairs. Purchases. Awards. Demerits. There were descriptions of events. A dinner. A business meeting. A literary discussion.

Beginning in the forties another type of entry began to appear. Lists of code names, followed by sets of strange symbols. I flipped through several. The same players reappeared year after year, then disappeared, never to be seen again. When one went out, a new one came in.

I counted. There were never more than eighteen names on any of these rosters.

325

When I finally leaned back, my tea was cold, and my neck felt as though it had been hung from a line and allowed to dry in the wind. Birdie was asleep on the love seat.

"All right. Let's go at it the other way round."

The cat stretched but didn't open an eye.

Using the dates I'd taken from Mrs. Veckhoff's clippings, I fast-forwarded through the journal. A list of code names was entered four days after Birkby's car crash. Sinuhe appeared for the first time, but Omega was missing. I scanned subsequent lists. Omega was never mentioned again.

Had Anthony Birkby been Omega?

Using this hypothesis, I flashed ahead to 1986.

Within days of Kendall Rollins's death, a list appeared. Mani replaced Piankhy.

Heart beating slightly faster, I continued with the clipping dates.

John Morgan died in 1972. Three days later, a list. Arrigatore checked in. Itzmana vanished.

William Glenn Sherman died in 1979. Five days later Veckhoff recorded a list. Ometeotl debuted. Rho was history.

Every death notice clipped by Mrs. Veckhoff was followed within days by a code name list. In each instance, a regular disappeared, and a newcomer joined the roster. Matching clippings with journal entries, I correlated code names with real names for everyone dead since 1959.

A. A. Birkby: Omega; John Morgan: Itzmana; William Glenn Sherman: Rho; Kendall Rollins: Piankhy.

"But what about the early years?"

Bird had no idea.

326

"O.K., back the other way."

I flipped to a clean page in my notebook. Every time an entry showed the replacement of one code name with another, I noted the date. It didn't take long.

In 1943, Ilus was replaced by Omega. Could that have been the year Birkby joined H&F?

In 1949, Narmer took over for Khaffre.

Pharaoh in, pharaoh out. Was it some sort of Masonic group?

I moved forward, added the year for each list.

Nineteen fifty-nine, 1972, 1979, 1986.

I stared at the years. Then I flew to my briefcase, pulled out other notes, and checked.

"Sonofabitch!"

I looked at my watch: 3.20 A.M. Where the hell was Lucy Crowe?

To say I rested poorly would be like saying Quasimodo had a bad back. I tossed and turned, hovering on the edge but never moving into real sleep.

When the phone rang I was already up, sorting laundry, sweeping the patio, snipping dead leaves, drinking cup after cup of coffee.

"Did you get it?" I almost shrieked.

"Repeat the punch line."

"I can't tie up the line, Pete."

"You have call waiting."

"Why are you phoning at seven in the morning?"

"I have to return to Indiana to reinterview Itchy and Scratchy."

It took me a moment to connect.

"The Bobbsey twins?"

"I've downgraded them. I'm calling to tell you that Boyd will be furloughed to the Granbar Kennel."

"What? The towels were too rough here?"

"He didn't want to impose."

"Isn't Granbar awfully expensive?"

"Knowing I'm in Big Law, Boyd has come to expect a certain lifestyle."

"I could work him in."

"You like that dog," he wheedled.

"That dog is a moron. But there's no reason to lay out bucks when I'm still stuck with five pounds of Alpo."

"The Granbar staff will be crushed."

"They'll work through it."

"I'll bring him by in an hour."

I was spray-cleaning the inside of the trash can when the phone rang again. Lucy Crowe's voice was taut with frustration.

"It's still no go with the magistrate. I don't get it. Frank's usually reasonable, but he got so angry this morning I thought he was going to have a heart attack. I backed off because I was afraid I'd kill the weasel."

I told her what I'd found in the Veckhoff diary.

"Can you check on MPs from seventy-two and seventy-nine?"

"Yeah."

A long silence rolled down from the highlands. Finally, "I noticed a metal bar when we were out at that place, lying in the dirt by the front porch."

"Oh?" My burglary tool.

Another pause.

"If wreckage is discovered on property within reasonable proximity of an airplane crash, my office has jurisdiction during the period of active recovery."

"I see."

"Only for matters relating directly to the crash. To

328

check for survivors who might have crawled off, for example. Maybe died under the house."

"Or inside the courtyard."

"Anything suspicious found while inside, I'd need a regular warrant."

"Of course."

"There are still two passengers unaccounted for."

"Yes."

"Did that bar look like wreckage to you?"

"Could have been a piece from the cabin floor."

"That was my impression. Guess I'd better take a look."

"I can be there by two."

"I'll wait."

By three, Boyd and I were in the backseat of a Jeep, Crowe at the wheel, a deputy riding shotgun. Two others were behind us in a second vehicle.

The chow was as pumped as I was, though for different reasons. He rode with his head out the window, nose twisting like a weather vane in a tropical storm. Now and then I'd push down on his haunches. He'd sit, rise immediately.

The radio sputtered as we raced along the county road. Passing the Alarka Fire Department, I noted that only one reefer truck and a few cars were parked in the lot. A Bryson City cruiser guarded the entrance, its driver bent over a magazine spread across the steering wheel.

Crowe took the blacktop to its end, then the Forest Service road, where I'd left my car three weeks earlier. Ignoring the cutoff to the crash site, she proceeded another three quarters of a mile and turned on to a different logging trail. After crawling upward for what seemed like miles, she stopped, studied the forest to either side, advanced, repeated the process, then took us off road. Our backup followed closely.

The Jeep bounced and pitched, branches scraping its top and sides. Boyd pulled in like a box turtle, and I yanked my arm from the window ledge. The dog whipped his head from right to left, spraying saliva on everyone. The deputy pulled a hanky from his pocket and wiped his neck but said nothing. I tried to remember his name. Was it Craig? Gregg?

Then the trees stepped back, yielding to a narrow dirt track. Ten minutes later, Crowe braked, alighted, and swung back what looked like an entire thicket. When we proceeded, I could see that what she'd moved was a gate, entirely overgrown with kudzu and ivy. Moments later the Arthur house came into view.

"I'll be goddamned," said the deputy. "This place in the 911 book?"

"Listed as abandoned," said Crowe. "I never knew it was here."

Crowe pulled to the front of the house and honked twice. No one appeared.

"There's a courtyard around to the side." Crowe nodded in that direction. "Tell George and Bobby to cover that entrance. We'll enter in front."

They got out, simultaneously releasing the safety clips on their guns. As the deputy walked back to the second Jeep, Crowe turned to me.

"You stay here."

I wanted to argue, but her look told me no way.

"In the Jeep. Until I call you."

I rolled my eyes but said nothing. My heart was hammering, and I shifted about more than Boyd.

Crowe sounded another long blast on the horn while

scanning the upper windows of the house. The deputy rejoined her, a Winchester pump held diagonally across his chest. They crossed to the house and climbed the steps.

"Swain County Sheriff's Department." Her call sounded tinny in the thin air. "Police. Please respond."

She banged on the door.

No one came forth.

Crowe said something. The deputy spread his feet and raised the shotgun, and the sheriff began hammering the door with her boot. There was no give.

Crowe spoke again. The deputy replied, keeping the barrel of his weapon trained on the door.

The sheriff walked back to the Jeep, sweat dampening the carrot frizz escaping her hat. She rummaged in back, returned to the porch with a crowbar.

Wiggling the tip between two shutters, she applied the full force of her body weight. A more earnest rendition of my own jimmying act.

Crowe repeated the movement, adding a Monica Seles grunt. A panel yielded slightly. Sliding the bar farther into the crack, she heaved again, and the shutter flew back, hitting the wall with a loud crash.

Crowe laid down the bar, braced herself, then smashed a foot through the window. Glass shattered, sparkled in the sun as it showered the porch with jagged shards. Crowe kicked again and again, enlarging the opening. Boyd urged her on with excited barks.

Crowe stood back and listened. Hearing no movement, she poked her head inside and called out again. Then the sheriff unholstered her gun and disappeared into darkness. The deputy followed.

Centuries later the front door opened, and Crowe

stepped on to the porch. She waved a "come on" gesture.

I leashed Boyd with clumsy hands and wrapped the loop around my wrist. Then I dug a Maglite from my pack. Blood pounded hard below my throat.

"Easy!" I aimed a finger at his nose.

He practically dragged me out of the Jeep and up the steps.

"The place is empty."

I tried to read Crowe's face, but it was registering nothing. No surprise, disgust, uneasiness. It was impossible to guess her reaction or emotion.

"Better leave the dog here."

I tied Boyd to the porch railing. Clicking on the flashlight, I followed her inside.

The air that hit me was not as musty as I expected. It smelled of smoke and mildew and something sweet.

My olfactory lobe scanned its database. Church.

Church?

The lobe separated into components. Flowers. Incense.

The front door opened directly into a parlor that spanned the entire width of the house. Slowly, I swept my light from right to left. I could make out sofas, armchairs, and occasional tables, grouped in clusters and draped with sheets. Floor-to-ceiling bookshelves covered two sides.

A stone fireplace filled the room's northern wall, an ornate mirror decorated its southern. In the dim glass I could see my beam slide among the shrouded shapes, our own two images creeping with it.

We progressed slowly, taking the house a room at a time. Dust motes swirled in the pale yellow shaft, and an occasional moth fluttered across like a startled animal in headlights on a two-lane black-top. Behind us, the deputy held his shotgun raised. Crowe clutched her gun double-handed, close to her cheek.

The parlor opened on to a narrow hallway. Staircase on the right, dining room on the left, kitchen straight ahead.

The dining room was furnished with nothing but a highly polished rectangular table and matching chairs. I counted. Eight at each side, one at each end. Eighteen.

The kitchen was in back, its door standing wide open.

Porcelain sink. Pump. Stove and refrigerator that had seen more birthdays than I had. I pointed to the appliances.

"Must be a generator."

"Probably downstairs."

I heard the sound of voices below, and knew her deputies were in the basement.

Upstairs, a hallway led straight down the middle of the house. Four small bedrooms radiated from the central artery, each with two sets of homemade bunks. A small spiral staircase led from the end of the hall to a third-floor attic. Tucked under the eaves were two more cots.

"Jesus," said Crowe. "Looks like Spin and Marty at the Triple R."

It reminded me of the Heaven's Gate cult in San Diego. I held my tongue.

We were circling back down when either George or Bobby appeared on the main staircase at the far end of the hall. The man was flushed and perspiring heavily.

"Sheriff, you gotta see the basement."

"What is it, Bobby?"

A bead of sweat broke from his hairline and rolled down the side of his face. He backhanded it with a jerky gesture.

"I'll be goddamned if I know."

27

A set of wooden stairs shot straight from the kitchen down to an underground cellar. The sheriff ordered Deputy Nameless to remain topside while the rest of us went down.

Bobby led, I followed, Crowe brought up the rear. George waited at the bottom, flashlight darting like a klieg on opening night.

As we descended, the air went from cool to refrigerator cold, and murky dimness gave way to pitch-black. I heard a click behind me, saw Crowe's beam at my feet.

We gathered at the bottom, listening.

No scurrying feet. No whirring wings. I aimed my light into the darkness.

We were in a large windowless room with a plank ceiling and cement floor. Three sides were plaster, the fourth formed by the escarpment at the back of the house. Centered in the cliff-side wall was a heavy wooden door.

When I stepped backward, my arm brushed fabric. I

spun and my beam swung down a row of pegs, each holding an identical red garment. Handing my flashlight to George, I unhooked and held one up. It was a hooded robe, the type worn by monks.

"Holy mother of Jesus." I heard Bobby wipe his face. Or cross himself.

I retrieved my flash, and Crowe and I probed the room, spotlighted by George and Bobby.

A full sweep produced nothing indigenous to a basement. No worktable. No Peg-Board hung with tools. No gardening equipment. No laundry tub. No cobwebs, mouse droppings, or dead crickets.

"Pretty damn clean down here." My voice echoed off cement and stone.

"Look at this." George angled his beam to where plaster met ceiling.

A bearlike monster leered from the darkness, its body covered with gaping, bloody mouths. Below the animal was one word: *Baxbakualanuxsiwae*.

"Francis Bacon?" I asked, more to myself than to my companions.

"Bacon painted people and snarling dogs, but never anything like this." Crowe's voice was hushed.

George moved his light to the next wall, and another monster stared down. Lion mane, bulging eyes, mouth wide to devour a headless infant gripped between its hands.

"That's a bad copy of one of Goya's Black Paintings," Crowe said. "I've seen it in the Prado in Madrid."

The more I got to know the Swain County sheriff, the more she impressed me.

"Who is the creep?" George asked.

"One of the Greek gods."

A third mural depicted a raft with billowed sail. Dead and dying men littered the deck and dangled overboard into the sea.

"Enchanting," said George.

Crowe had no comment as we crossed to the rock wall.

The door was held in place by black wrought-iron hinges, drilled into stone and cemented in place. A segment of chain connected a circular wrought-iron handle to a vertical steel bar adjacent to the frame. The padlock looked shiny and new, and I could see fresh scars in the granite.

"This was added recently."

"Step back," Crowe ordered.

As we withdrew, our beams widened, illuminating words carved above the lintel. I played my light over them.

Fay ce que voudras

"French?" Crowe asked, sliding her flashlight into her belt.

"Old French, I think. . . ."

"Recognize the gargoyles?"

A figure decorated each corner of the lintel. The male was labeled "Harpocrates," the female "Angerona."

"Sounds Egyptian."

Crowe's gun exploded twice, and the smell of cordite filled the air. She stepped forward, yanked, and the chain slithered loose. There was no resistance when she lifted the latch.

She pulled on the handle and the door opened outward. Cold air rolled over us, smelling of dark hollows, sightless creatures, and epochs of time underground.

337

"Maybe it's time to bring him down," said Crowe.

I nodded, and double-stepped up the stairs.

Boyd showed his usual exuberance at being included, prancing and snapping the air. He lapped my hand, then danced beside me into the house. Nothing on the ground floor dampened his delight.

Starting down the basement steps, I felt his body tense beside my leg.

I added an extra coil to the wrap around my hand, and allowed him to pull me down the steps and across toward Crowe.

Three feet short of the door he exploded, lunging and barking as he had at the wall. Cold prickled up my spine and across my scalp.

"All right, keep him over there," said Crowe.

Grabbing his collar with both hands, I dragged Boyd back and gave Bobby the leash. Boyd continued to growl loudly and attempted to pull Bobby forward. I rejoined Crowe.

My flash revealed a cavelike tunnel with a series of alcoves to either side. The floor was dirt, the ceiling and walls solid rock. Height to the tunnel's arched top was approximately six feet, width was about four feet. Length was impossible to tell. Beyond five yards, it was a black hole.

My pulse had now slowed since I'd entered the house. It now went for a personal best.

Slowly we crept forward, our beams probing the floor, the ceiling, the walls, the recesses. Some were nothing more than shallow indentations. Others were good-sized caves with vertical metal bars and central gates at their mouths.

"Wine cellars?" Crowe's question sounded muffled in the narrow space.

338

"Wouldn't there be shelving?"

"Check this out."

Crowe illuminated a name, then another, and another, chiseled the length of the tunnel. She read them aloud as we progressed.

"Sawney Beane. Innocent III. Dionysus. Moctezuma. . . . Weird bedfellows. A pope, an Aztec emperor, and the party meister himself."

"Who's Sawney Beane?" I asked.

"Hell if I kno—"

Her beam left the wall and shot straight into nothing. She threw out an arm, catching me across the chest. I froze.

Our lights leapt to the dirt at our feet. No drop-off.

We rounded the corner and inched forward, sweeping our beams from side to side. I could tell from the sound of the air that we had entered a large chamber of some sort. We were circling its perimeter wall.

The names continued. Thyestes. Polyphemus. Christie o' the Cleek. Cronus. I recognized no one from Veckhoff's diary.

Like the tunnel, the chamber gave on to a number of alcoves, some with bars, others ungated. Directly opposite our entrance point we found a wooden door, similar to that at the head of the tunnel, and secured with the same chain-and-padlock arrangement. Crowe dealt with it in the same way.

As the door swung inward, cold, foul air slithered out. Behind me I could hear Boyd barking as if possessed.

The odor of putrefaction can be altered by the mode of death, sweetened by some poisons, tinted with pear or almond or garlic by others. It can be retarded by chemicals, augmented by insect activity. But the essence

339

is unmistakable, a heavy, fetid mix that heralds the presence of rotting flesh.

Something dead lay in that alcove.

We entered and circled left, keeping to the wall as we had in the outer chamber. Five feet in, my beam caught an irregularity on the floor. Crowe saw it at the same time.

We focused our lights on a patch of coarse, dark soil.

Wordlessly, I handed my Maglite to Crowe and pulled a collapsible spade from my backpack. Keeping my left hand on the stone wall, I squatted and scraped at the ground with the side of the blade.

Crowe holstered her gun, hooked her hat to her belt, and trained twin beams on the ground before me.

The stain gave way easily, revealing a boundary between freshly turned earth and hard-packed floor. The smell of decay increased as I lifted soil and laid it to the side.

Within minutes I hit something soft and pale blue.

"Looks like denim." Crowe's eyes glistened, and her skin gleamed amber in the pale yellow light.

I followed the faded fabric, lengthening the opening.

Levi's, contoured around a scarecrow leg. I worked my way down to a shriveled brown foot, angled ninety degrees at the ankle.

"That's it." Crowe's voice caused my hand to jump.

"What?"

"This is no airplane passenger."

"No."

"I don't want a bad crime scene. We're shut down until I have a warrant."

I didn't argue. The victim in that pit deserved to have his or her story told in court. I would do nothing to compromise a potential prosecution.

340

I rose and tapped my spade against the wall, carefully removing adhering soil. Then I folded the blade, stuck it in my pack, and reached for my light.

On the hand off, the beam shot across the alcove and glinted off something in the farthest recess.

"What the hell's that?" I asked, squinting into the dark.

"Let's go."

"We should hit your magistrate with everything we can."

I picked my way toward the point where I'd seen the flash. Crowe hesitated a moment, followed.

A long bundle lay tucked against the base of the wall. The bundle was wrapped in shower curtains, one transparent, one translucent blue, and tied with several lengths of rope. I approached and ran my light over the surface.

Though blurred by layers of plastic, I could make out details in the clear upper half. Matted hair, a red plaid shirt, ghostly white hands bound at the wrists. I pulled gloves from my pack, snapped them on, and gently rolled the bundle.

Crowe's hand flew to her mouth.

A face, purple and bloated, eyes milky and half closed. Cracked lips, a bulging tongue pressed to the plastic like a giant leech.

Noticing an oval object at the base of the throat, I brought my light close. A pendant. I pulled out my knife and slit the plastic. The hiss of escaping gas was followed by an overpowering stench of putrefaction. My stomach recoiled, but I didn't pull back.

Holding my breath, I teased back the plastic with the tip of the knife.

A male silhouette was clearly visible on a small silver

341

medal, arms crossed piously at the throat. Engraved letters formed a halo around the head. I held the light obliquely to bring out the name.

Saint Blaise.

We had found the missing fisherman with the ailing throat. George Adair.

This time I suggested a different route. Crowe agreed. Leaving Bobby and George to secure the site, the sheriff and I drove to Bryson City and pulled Byron McMahon from a football game he was watching on the parlor TV at High Ridge House. Together we prepared an affidavit, which the special agent took directly to a federal magistrate judge in Asheville.

In less than two hours McMahon called Crowe. Based on the probability of a hate crime, and on the possible involvement of federal lands, due to the proximity of a reservation and national parks, a search warrant had been issued.

It fell to me to phone Larke Tyrell.

I found the ME at home, and, from background noise, guessed he was involved with the same football game.

Though Larke's words were cordial, I could tell my call unnerved him. I did not take time to assuage his anxiety, or to apologize for the lateness of the hour.

The ME listened while I explained the situation. Finally, I stopped. Silence stretched so long I thought we'd been disconnected.

"Larke?"

When he spoke again, his tone had changed.

"I want you to handle this. What do you need?"

I told him.

"Can you pick it up at the incident morgue?"

342

"Yes."

"Do you want personnel?"

"Who's still there?"

"Maggie and Stan."

Maggie Burroughs and Stan Fryeburg were death investigators with the Office of the Chief Medical Examiner in Chapel Hill, deployed to Bryson City for the processing of Air TransSouth 228. Both were graduates of my body recovery workshop at the university, and both were excellent.

"Tell them to be ready at seven."

"Roger."

"This has nothing to do with the plane crash, Larke."

"I know that. But these are dead bodies in my state."

There was another long pause. I heard an overwrought announcer, a cheering crowd.

"Tempe, I—"

I did not help him out.

"This has gone too goddamned far."

I listened to a dial tone.

What the hell did that mean?

I had other things to worry about.

The next day I was up at dawn, at the Arthur house by seven-thirty. The scene had been transformed overnight. A sheriff's deputy now stood guard at the kudzu gate, others at the front and back doors. A generator had been activated, and every light in the house was on.

When I arrived, George was helping McMahon load books and papers into cardboard boxes. Bobby was covering the mantel with white powder. As I passed on my way to the kitchen, McMahon winked and wished me good luck.

I spent the next four days like a miner, descending to

the basement at dawn, surfacing at noon for a sandwich and coffee, then descending again until after dark. Another generator and lights were brought in to illuminate my underground world, so day and night became indistinguishable.

Tommy Albright arrived on the morning of day one. After examining and photographing the bundle I was certain contained George Adair, he released the body for transport to the Harris Regional Hospital in Sylva.

While Maggie worked the decomp stain inside the courtyard wall, Stan helped me photograph the cellar floor. Then we exhumed the alcove burial, slowly exposing the corpse, recording body position and grave outline, and screening every particle of dirt.

The victim lay facedown on a gray wool blanket, one arm twisted beneath the chest, the other curled around the head. Decomposition was advanced, the organs soup, the head and hands largely skeletonized.

When the remains were fully uncovered and documented, we began removal. Transferring the cadaver to a body bag, I noted that the left pants leg was badly torn, the leg missing below the knee.

I also noticed concentric fractures in the right temporo-parietal region of the skull. Linear cracks radiated up the sides of the central depression, turning the whole into a spiderweb of fragmented bone.

"Somebody really blasted this guy." Stan had stopped screening to look at the skull.

"Yes."

My outrage was building as it always did. The victim had been dealt a skull-shattering blow, then dumped in a hole like last year's mulch. What kind of monster did such things?

Another thought pierced through my anger.

344

This corpse was buried only inches below the ground surface. Though putrefied, considerable soft tissue remained, indicating a relatively recent death. Did earlier victims lie beneath? In other alcoves? I kept my eyes and mind open.

Maggie joined us in the basement on day two, having excavated a ten-foot square to a depth of twelve inches around and below the courtyard stain. Though the job was tedious, her efforts paid off. Two isolated teeth turned up in the screen.

While Stan finished sifting dirt from the alcove burial, Maggie and I probed every inch of the cellar floor, testing for the presence of buried objects and for differences in soil density. We found eight suspicious locations, two in the original alcove, two in the main chamber, and four in a dead-end tunnel off the chamber's west side.

By late afternoon we'd dug a test trench at each location. The suspect spots in the main room yielded only sterile soil. The other six sites produced human bone.

I explained to Stan and Maggie how we would proceed. I would request help from the sheriff's department with photography and screening. Stan would continue in the alcove. Maggie and I would begin with the tunnel sites.

I directed my crew with professional detachment, the calm of my voice and the composure of my face wildly out of sync with my pounding heart. It was my worst nightmare. But what *was* that nightmare? How many more bodies would we unearth, and why were they there?

Maggie and I were excavating the first two tunnel disturbances when a figure appeared at the entrance, caught between our spots and a light in the main chamber. I couldn't make out the silhouette, and wondered if a member of the transport team was coming to ask a question.

One step and I knew.

Larke Tyrell walked toward me, gait precise, back ramrod straight. I rose but did not greet him.

"I've been trying your portable."

"The press have me on autodial."

He did not pursue it.

"What's the count?"

"At this point, two decomposed bodies and two skeletons. There's bone in at least four other locations."

His eyes moved from my face to the pits where Maggie and I were uncovering skeletons, each with tightly flexed limbs.

"They look like prehistoric bundle burials."

"Yes, but they're not."

His gaze swung back to me.

"You would know that."

"Yes."

"Tommy sent the two decomps to Harris Regional, but they're not going to want their autopsy room tied up. I'll order everything transferred to the incident morgue and keep the place operational for as long as you need."

I did not reply.

"You will do this?"

"Of course."

"Everything is under control?"

"Here it is."

"I'm looking forward to your report."

"I have excellent penmanship."

"I thought you'd like to know that the last of the Air

TransSouth passengers has been identified."

"Petricelli and the students in 22A and B?"

"Petricelli, yes. And one of the students."

"Only one?"

"Two days ago the young man assigned to seat 22B phoned his father from Costa Rica."

"He wasn't on the plane?"

"While in the waiting area, a man offered him a thousand bucks for his boarding pass."

"Why didn't he come forward earlier?"

"He was in the rain forest and completely cut off, never heard about the crash until he returned to San José. Then he hesitated a few days before calling home, knowing the jig was up for torpedoing the semester."

"Who is the substitute passenger?"

"The unluckiest bastard in the universe."

I waited.

"A tax accountant from Buckhead. We found him through a thumbprint."

He looked at me a very long moment. I stared back. The tension between us was palpable.

"This is not the place, Tempe, but we do need to talk. I am a fair man, but I have acted unfairly. There have been pressures."

"Complaints."

Though Maggie kept her eyes down, the rhythm of her trowel changed. I knew she was listening.

"Even wise people make unwise choices."

With that, he was gone.

Again, I wondered what he meant. Whose unwise choices? Mine? His? Someone else's?

The next forty-eight hours were spent with trowels and brushes and human bones. My team dug and documented while Crowe's deputies hauled and sifted dirt. Ryan brought me coffee and doughnuts and news of the crash. McMahon brought me reports on the operation upstairs. I gave him Mr. Veckhoff's diary, and explained my notes and theories during lunch breaks.

I forgot the names engraved in stone. I forgot the strange caricatures watching silently from walls and ceilings. I forgot the bizarre underground chambers and caves in which I worked.

We recovered eight people in all, the last on Halloween.

The following day we learned who blew up Air TransSouth 228.

28

"A pipe. The kind that you put in your mouth and smoke."

McMahon nodded.

"In a checked bag." My voice registered my incredulity.

"An airline employee remembers telling this guy arriving at the last moment that his duffel was too large for the overhead bin and he would have to check it. The guy was sweaty and distracted, and pulled off his sports jacket and stuffed it into the duffel before giving it to a baggage handler. They're saying he left a hot pipe in the pocket of the jacket."

"What about smoke detectors? Fire detectors?"

"Baggage compartments don't have them."

Ryan, McMahon, and I were seated in folding chairs in a briefing room at NTSB central. I could see Larke Tyrell at the end of our row. The front of the room was filled with personnel of the response and investigative teams, the back crammed with journalists.

Magnus Jackson was making a statement, projecting visuals on to a screen behind him.

"Air TransSouth 228 was brought down by an unpredictable confluence of events resulting in fire, explosion, depressurization, and in-flight breakup. In that order. I'll take it step by step, take questions when I'm done."

Jackson worked the keys of a laptop, bringing up a diagram of the passenger cabin.

"On October fourth, at approximately eleven forty-five A.M. passenger Walter Lindenbaum presented himself to Air TransSouth agent James Sartore for boarding of Flight 228. Agent Sartore had just announced last call for boarding and stated that Mr. Lindenbaum was extremely agitated, concerned that his late arrival had caused the forfeiture of his seat.

"Mr. Lindenbaum had two bags, a small one and a larger canvas duffel. Agent Sartore informed Mr. Lindenbaum that there was no overhead space left for the duffel and that it was too large to fit under the seat. He tagged the bag and told Lindenbaum to leave it on the jetway and the baggage handler would take care of it. Mr. Lindenbaum then removed a knitted fabric sport jacket, put it in the duffel, and boarded the aircraft."

Jackson brought up a credit card receipt.

"Mr. Lindenbaum's credit card records reflect the purchase of a one-liter bottle of 151-proof Demerara rum on the evening prior to flight."

More keystrokes, and the receipt was replaced by several views of a charred canvas bag.

"The Lindenbaum bag and its contents, *and these objects alone, of all the artifacts recovered from the crash*" – the phrase emphasized by a hard look to the audience – "manifest geometric burn patterns showing symmetry and more combustion inside than outside."

He traced the patterns with his laser pointer.

"Interviews with family members have disclosed that Walter Lindenbaum was a pipe smoker. He was of the habit when entering a no-smoking area of slipping his pipe into his pocket and relighting it later. All evidence points to the presence of a smoldering pipe in the pocket of the Lindenbaum jacket when that jacket went into the cargo bay."

A murmur spread through the back of the room. Hands shot up and questions were shouted. Jackson ignored them as he projected additional pictures of burned clothing, unfolded then folded.

"Inside the baggage compartment, fragments of smoldering tobacco and ash spilled from the pipe bowl and communicated incandescent combustion to surrounding fabrics in the bag, generating what we call a hot spot."

More shots of burned canvas and clothing.

"Let me repeat. Geometric burn patterns have been found on no other items recovered from the wreckage. I'm not going to go into it here, but the press release explains how evidence of slow burning of folded clothes inside the bag cannot be explained by anything that occurred *after* a midair explosion."

The next visual showed smoke-blackened fragments of glass.

"Mr. Lindenbaum's rum bottle. Inside the loosely packed duffel, smoke spread at a temperature consistent with that of the localized combustion, a temperature warmer than the bottle and its contents, which were not involved in the combustion process. The bottle remained intact, and smoke was deposited on it. These deposits, seen in this view, have been analyzed by our lab. The products of decomposition present in the smoke are consistent with the point of origin as I am describing it. Traces of tobacco smoke were positively identified on the bottle, among other traces, especially since forensic analysis also disposed of unburned tobacco strands in the pipe bowl as reference."

Jackson switched to a diagram of the plane.

"In the Fokker-100, fuel lines run under the cabin floor, above the baggage compartments, from wing tanks to aft-mounted engines."

He traced the route with his pointer, clicked to a close-up of a fuel line, then zoomed in on a fitting.

"Our structures team has found evidence of a fatigue crack in a fuel line fitting where it passes through the bulkhead at the rear of the baggage compartment. In all likelihood, this crack was generated by a flawed through-fitting acting as a stress riser."

A magnified image of a hairline fracture filled the screen.

"Heat from the incandescent combustion in Mr. Lindenbaum's duffel aggravated the crack, allowing minute quantities of vaporized fuel to dissipate from the line into the hold."

He brought up a dirty and discolored chunk of metal casing.

"Localized heat degradation, manifested in localized discoloration, is clearly recognizable on the fuel line at the point of failure due to heat exposure. I'll go to simulation now."

Keys clicked, the screen went blank, then filled with an animation of an F-100 in flight. Time ticked in one-second increments at the top of the screen.

The Lindenbaum duffel could be seen high in the left rear of the baggage compartment, immediately below seats 23A and B. I watched it ooze from pink, to salmon, to red, a cold lump in the pit of my stomach.

"Incandescent combustion in the duffel," Jackson narrated. "A first ignition sequence."

Pale blue specks began to seep from the bag.

"Smoke."

The particles formed a fine, transparent mist.

"The baggage compartment is pressurized the same as the passenger cabin, meaning it is supplied with air containing an adequate proportion of oxygen. The significance is that there is a lot of warm air moving around down there."

The mist slowly dispersed. Red colored the ends of the Lindenbaum suitcase.

"Though it was contained at first, the smoke eventually spread from the duffel. The heat eventually pierced, and then there was a development to laminar flaming combustion outside the duffel, igniting the suitcases on each side and giving off dense smoke."

Tiny black dots appeared at a fuel line running along the inner wall of the baggage compartment. I stared, mesmerized, as the dots multiplied and slowly descended, or were entrained in the ambient air movement.

"Then began the second ignition sequence. When fuel began to dissipate out of the pressurized line, the quantity was so minute it vaporized and mixed with the air. As the fuel expanded in a vapor state it sank, since fuel fumes are heavier than ambient air. At that point an odor would have been present and easily detected."

Traces of blue appeared in the passenger cabin.

"Smoke seeped into the cabin through the ventilation, heating, and air-conditioning system, and eventually to the exterior via the pressurization outflow valve."

I thought of Jean Bertrand. Had he noticed the odor? Seen the smoke?

There was a flash, red spread outward from the Lindenbaum suitcase, and a jagged hole appeared in the rear of the baggage compartment.

"Twenty minutes and twenty-one seconds into the flight, vaporized fuel crossed a wire bundle, which apparently contained some arcing wires, and ignited in a deafening detonation. This explosion can be heard on the cockpit voice recorder."

I remembered Ryan's account of the pilot's last words, felt the same helplessness he had described.

"The circuit failed."

I thought of the passengers. Had they felt the shock? Heard the explosion? Did they realize they were going to die?

"The initial explosion blew from the pressurized baggage compartment into the unpressurized fuselage behind, and air loads began tearing parts from the plane. At that point, more fuel escaped from the line and flaming fire ensued in the hold."

Jackson identified items as they separated and fell to the ground.

"Skin from the aft fuselage. Speed brakes."

The room was deathly quiet.

"Air loads then blew up through the vertical tail and dislodged the horizontal stabilizer and elevators."

The plane in the animation pitched nose down and plunged toward the ground, the passenger cabin still intact. Jackson hit a key and the screen went blank.

No one seemed to breathe or move. Seconds passed. I heard a sob, or perhaps only a deep breath. A cough. Then the room exploded.

"Mr. Jackson—"

"Why weren't smoke detect—"

"Mr. Jack—"

"How long—"

"I'll take questions one at a time."

Jackson pointed to a woman with Buddy Holly frames.

"How long would it have taken to raise the temperature in the duffel to the point of fire?"

"Let me clarify one thing. We're talking about incandescence, a glowing type of combustion generated when the little oxygen available comes in direct contact with a solid, like coals or embers. This is not flaming combustion. In a small volume like the bag's interior, incandescence could be quickly established and maintained at around five hundred to six hundred degrees Fahrenheit."

His finger found another journalist.

"How could the rum bottle survive the fire in the bag?"

"Easy. On the other end of the temperature spectrum, incandescence can reach eleven hundred to twelve hundred degrees Fahrenheit, the temperature of a lit pipe or cigarette. That's hardly enough to alter a glass bottle containing liquid."

"And the smoke deposits would remain on the bottle?"

"Yes. Unless it was subjected to a very intense and sustained fire, which was not the case, as it occurred inside the suitcase."

The finger moved.

"The metal fatigue marks survived as well?"

"To melt steel you need temperatures of twenty-five hundred degrees Fahrenheit or more. Beach marks, your typical evidence of fatigue, generally survive fires of the intensity I'm describing."

355

He pointed to a reporter from the *Charlotte Observer*.

"Did the passengers know what was happening?"

"Those seated close to the flash point would have felt the shock. Everyone would have heard the explosion."

"What about smoke?"

"Smoke would have seeped into the passenger cabin via the heating and air-conditioning system."

"Were the passengers conscious the whole time?

"The type of combustion I've described can give off noxious gases which may affect people very quickly."

"How quickly?"

"The old, the young, perhaps as fast as ninety seconds."

"Could these gases have gotten into the passenger compartment?"

"Yes."

"Have traces of smoke or noxious gases been found in the victims?"

"Yes. Dr. Tyrell is going to make a statement shortly."

"With so much smoke, how can you be sure about the source of the deposits on the rum bottle?" The questioner looked about sixteen.

"Fragments of the Lindenbaum pipe were recovered, and reference studies were conducted using unburned strands of tobacco adhering to the inside of the bowl. The deposits on the bottle were the by-products of the combustion of that tobacco."

"How could there have been a fuel leak?" Shouted from the back.

"When fire broke out in the hold, flame impingement affected only a segment of the fuel line. This pulled the wall of the line, or induced a stress that opened very slightly the seed failure."

Jackson called on a reporter who looked and sounded like Dick Cavett.

"Are you telling us that the initial fire did not directly cause the explosion?"

"Yes."

"What caused the explosion?" he persisted.

"An electrical failure. That's the second ignition sequence."

"How sure can you be?"

"Reasonably certain. When electricity sparks an explosion, the electrical energy is not lost, it must ground. Damage due to electrical grounding has been identified on the same segment of fuel line. Such damage is normally seen on copper items and rather seldom on steel parts."

"I can't believe that the fire in the suitcase didn't cause the explosion." Cavett made little attempt to hide his skepticism. "Wouldn't that be more normal?"

"Your question makes sense. It's really what we thought at first, but you see, the fumes are not yet mixed enough with air at such short distance from the source of emission. The fumes must mix before ignition can occur, but when it does, the blast is deafening."

Another hand.

"Was the analysis done by certified fire and explosion specialists?"

"Yes. Outside experts were brought in."

Another questioner stood.

Eighty-eight people were dead because one man was preoccupied about losing his seat. The whole thing was a tragic mistake.

I looked at my watch. Crowe would be waiting.

Feeling numb, I slipped from the room. I had victims waiting whose deaths were not due to simple carelessness.

The reefer trucks were gone from the grounds of the Alarka Fire Department. The lot held only the company's displaced engines and the vehicles of those assisting me. A single deputy guarded the entrance.

Crowe was there when I arrived. Seeing me, she climbed from her cruiser, collected a small leather case, and waited. The sky was pewter, and a cold wind was tearing through the gorge. Gusts teased her hat brim, subtly reshaping it around her face.

I joined her, and we entered what was now a different type of incident morgue. Stan and Maggie worked at autopsy tables, arranging bones where crash victims recently had lain. Four tables held unopened cardboard boxes.

I greeted my team and hurried to the cubicle I was using as an office. As I exchanged my jacket for a lab coat, Crowe took the chair opposite my desk, zipped open the case, and withdrew several folders.

"Nineteen seventy-nine came up zilch. All MPs accounted for. There were two from 1972."

She opened the first folder.

"Mary Francis Rafferty, white female, age eighty-one. Lived alone over in Dillsboro. Her daughter checked on her every Saturday. One week Rafferty wasn't in her home. Never seen again. It was presumed she wandered off and died of exposure."

"How often have we heard that?"

She went to the next folder.

"Sarah Ellen Deaver, white female, age nineteen. Left home to go to her job at a convenience store on Highway 74. Never got there."

"I doubt we've got Deaver out there. Anything from Tommy Albright?"

"George Adair's positive," Crowe confirmed.

"Dental?" I asked.

"Yes." Pause. "You know that first alcove burial was missing its left foot?"

"Albright phoned me."

"Jeremiah Mitchell's daughter thought she recognized some of the clothing. We're getting blood from a sister."

"Albright asked me to cut bone samples. Tyrell's promised to rush them through. Did you check the other dates?"

"Albert Odell's family provided the name of his dentist."

"He's the apple farmer?" I asked.

"Odell's the only MP still out from eighty-six."

"Many dentists don't keep records past ten years."

"Dr. Welch didn't sound like the brightest bulb in the marquee. I'm driving over to Lauada this afternoon to see what he has."

"What about the others?" I knew what her answer would be even as I asked the question.

"The others will be tough. It's been over fifty years for Adams and Farrell, over forty for Tramper."

She withdrew three more folders and laid everything on my desk.

"Here's what I've managed to dig up." She stood. "I'll let you know what I get from the dentist."

When she'd gone I spent a few moments perusing the folder. The one for Tucker Adams contained only the press items I'd already seen.

Edna Farrell's record was a little better, and included handwritten notes taken at the time of her disappearance. There was a statement by Sandra Jane Farrell, giving an account of Edna's last days and a detailed physical description. Edna had fallen from a horse as a young woman, and Sandra described her mother's face as "lopsided."

I snatched up a black-and-white snapshot with scalloped edges. Though the image was blurry, the facial asymmetry was obvious.

"Way to go, Edna."

There were photos of Charlie Wayne Tramper, and his disappearance and death were reported in several newspaper articles. Otherwise, there was little in the way of written information.

The following days were like the first I'd spent at the Alarka Fire Department, living with the dead from dawn until dusk. Hour after hour I sorted and arranged bones, determined sex and race, estimated age and height. I searched for indicators of old injury, past illness, congenital peculiarity, or repetitive movement. For each skeleton I built as complete a profile as was possible working from remains devoid of living tissue.

In a way, it was like processing a crash, where names are known from the passenger roster. Based on Veckhoff's diary, I was convinced I had a limited population because the dates entered in his lists matched precisely the disappearance dates of seniors from Swain and adjoining counties: 1943, Tucker Adams; 1949, Edna Farrell; 1959, Charlie Wayne Tramper; 1986, Albert Odell.

Believing them to be the earliest in time, we started with the four tunnel burials. While Stan and Maggie cleaned, sorted, numbered, photographed, and X-rayed, I studied bones.

I found Edna Farrell early. Skeleton number four was

that of an elderly female whose right cheekbone and jawbone deviated sharply from the midline due to fractures that had healed without proper intervention.

Skeleton number five was incomplete, lacking portions of the rib cage, arms, and lower legs. Animal damage was extensive. Pelvic features told me the individual was male and old. A globular skull, flaring cheekbones, and shoveling on the front teeth suggested Native-American ancestry. Statistical analysis placed the skull squarely in the Mongoloid camp. Charlie Wayne Tramper?

Number six, the most deteriorated of the skeletons, was that of an elderly Caucasoid male who had been toothless at the time of his death. Save for a height estimate of over six feet, I found no unique markers on the bones. Tucker Adams?

Skeleton number three was that of an elderly male with healed fractures of the nose, maxilla, third, fourth, and fifth ribs, and right fibula. A long, narrow skull, Quonset hut nasal bridge, smooth nasal border, and anterior projection of the lower face suggested the man was black. So did the Fordisc 2.0 program. I suspected he was the 1979 victim.

Next, I examined the skeletons found in the alcove with Mitchell and Adair.

Skeleton number two was that of an elderly white male. Arthritic changes in the right shoulder and arm bones suggested repeated extension of the hand above the head. Apple picking? Based on the state of preservation, I guessed this individual had died more recently than those buried in the tunnel graves. The apple farmer, Albert Odell?

Skeleton number one was that of an elderly white female with advanced arthritis and only seven teeth.

Mary Francis Rafferty, the woman from Dillsboro whose daughter had found her mother's house empty in 1972?

By late afternoon Saturday, I felt confident I had matched the bones with their proper names. Lucy Crowe helped by finding Albert Odell's dental records, the Reverend Luke Bowman by remembering Tucker Adams's height. Six foot three.

And I had a pretty good idea as to manner of death.

The hyoid is a small, horseshoe-shaped bone embedded in the soft tissue of the neck, high up behind the lower jaw. In the elderly, whose bones are often brittle, the hyoid fractures when its wings are compressed. The most common source of compressive force is strangulation.

Tommy Albright phoned as I was preparing to close up.

"Find any more hyoid fractures?"

"Five out of the six."

"Mitchell, too. He must have put up a helluva fight. When they couldn't strangle him, they smashed his head in."

"Adair?"

"No. But there's petechial hemorrhage."

Petechiae are minute blood clots that appear as dots in the eyes and throat, and are strong indicators of asphyxiation.

"Who the hell would want to strangle old people?"

I did not answer. I'd seen other trauma on the skeletons. Trauma I found puzzling. Trauma I would not mention until I understood more.

When he hung up, I went to burial four, picked up the thighbones, and brought them to the magnifier light.

Yes. It was there. It was real.

362

I collected the femora from every skeleton, and took the bones to a dissecting scope.

Tiny grooves circled each right proximal shaft and ran the length of each line aspera, the roughened ridge for muscle attachment on the back side of the bone. Other gashes ran horizontally, above and below the joint surfaces. Though the number of marks varied, their distribution was consistent from victim to victim.

I cranked the magnification as high as it would go.

When I focused, the grooves crystallized into sharp-edged crevices, V-shaped in cross section.

Cut marks. But how could that be? I'd seen cut marks on bone, but only in cases of dismemberment. Except for Charlie Wayne Tramper and Jeremiah Mitchell, these individuals had been buried whole.

Then why? And why only the right femora? *Was* it only the right femora?

I was about to begin a reexamination of every bone when Andrew Ryan burst through the door.

Maggie, Stan, and I looked up, startled.

"Have you been listening to the news?" Ryan asked, flushed and perspiring despite the coolness.

We shook our heads.

"Parker Davenport was found dead about three hours ago."

29

"Dead?"

Emotions snapped inside me. Shock. Pity. Anger. Wariness.

"How?"

"A single bullet to the brain. An aide found him at his home."

"A suicide?"

"Or a setup."

"Is Tyrell doing the post?"

"Yeah."

"Has it hit the media?"

"Oh, yeah. They're pissing their pants for information."

Relief. The pressure would lift from me. Guilt. A man is dead and you think first of yourself.

"But the thing's wrapped tighter than the U.S. war plan."

"Did Davenport leave a note?"

"None found. What's up here?" He gestured toward the autopsy tables.

"Got some time?"

"The crash was due to carelessness and mechanical failure." He spread his arms. "I'm a free man."

The wall clock said seven forty-five. I told Stan and Maggie to call it a day, then led Ryan to my cubicle and explained the Veckhoff diary.

"You're suggesting that random elderly persons were murdered following the deaths of prominent citizens?" He tried but failed to keep the skepticism from his voice.

"Yes."

"And no one noticed."

"The disappearances weren't frequent enough to suggest a pattern, and the selection of aged victims created less of a ripple."

"And this granny-napping has been going on for half a century?"

"Longer."

It did sound preposterous, and this made me edgy. When edgy, I get mouthy.

"And gramps was fair game, too."

"And the perps used the Arthur house to dispose of the bodies."

"Yes, but for more than just disposing."

"And this was some sort of group in which everyone had a code name."

"Has," I snapped.

Silence.

"Are you talking cult?"

"No. Yes. I don't know. I don't think so. But I do think the victims were used in some sort of ritual."

"Why is that?"

"Come with me."

I walked him from table to table, making introductions and pointing out details. Finally, I took him to the dissecting scope and focused the lens on Edna Farrell's right femur. When he'd studied it, I inserted one of Tucker Adams's thighbones. Rafferty. Odell.

The pattern was unmistakable. Same nicks. Same distribution.

"What are they?"

"Cut marks."

"As in knife?"

"Something with a sharp blade."

"What do they mean?"

"I don't know."

Each bone made a soft thunk as I replaced it on the stainless steel. Ryan watched me, his face unreadable.

My heels clicked loudly as I crossed to the sink, then walked to my cubicle to remove my lab coat and put on my jacket. When I returned, Ryan was standing over the skeleton I believed to be the apple farmer, Albert Odell.

"So you know who they are."

"Except for that gentleman." I indicated the elderly black male.

"And you think they were strangled."

"Yes."

"What the hell for?"

"Talk to McMahon. That's police work."

Ryan followed me out to the parking lot. As I was sliding behind the wheel, he shot off one more question.

"What kind of twisted mutant would snatch old people, choke them to death, and play with their bodies?"

The answer would come from an unexpected source.

Back at High Ridge House, I made myself a ham salad sandwich, grabbed a bag of Sunchips and a handful of sugar cookies, and headed out to dine with Boyd.

Though I apologized profusely for my negligence over the past week, his eyebrows barely moved, and his tongue remained firmly out of sight. The dog was annoyed.

More guilt. More self-censure.

After giving Boyd the sandwich, chips, and cookies, I filled his bowls with water and chow, and promised him a long walk the following day. He was sniffing the Alpo as I slipped away.

I reprovisioned myself and took the snack to my room. A note lay on the floor. Based on the mode of delivery, I suspected it had come from McMahon.

It had. He asked that I stop by FBI headquarters the next day.

I wolfed down my dinner, took a hot bath, and phoned a colleague at UNC-Chapel Hill. Though it was past eleven, I knew Jim's routine. No morning classes. Home around six. After dinner, a five-mile run, then back to his archaeology lab until 2 A.M. Except when excavating, Jim was nocturnal.

After greeting and a brief catch-up, I asked for his help.

"Doing some archaeology?"

"It's more fun than my usual work," I said noncommittally.

I described the strange nicks and striations without revealing the nature of the victims.

"How old is this stuff?"

"Not that old."

"It's odd that the marks are restricted to a single bone, but the pattern you're describing sounds suspicious. I'm going to fax you three recent articles and a number of my own photos."

I thanked him and gave him the morgue number.

367

"Where is that?"

"Swain County."

"You working with Midkiff?"

"No."

"Someone told me he was digging up there."

Next, I phoned Katy. We talked about her classes, about Boyd, about a skirt she'd seen in the Victoria's Secret catalog. We made plans for the beach at Thanksgiving. I never mentioned the murders or my growing trepidation.

After the phone call, I climbed into bed and lay in the dark, visualizing the skeletons we'd recovered from the cellar. Though I'd never seen an actual case, I knew in my heart what the strange marks meant.

But why?

I felt horror. I felt disbelief. Then I felt nothing until the sun warmed my face at 7 A.M.

Jim's photos and articles lay on the fax machine when I arrived at the morgue. *Nature*, *Science*, and *American Antiquity*. I read each and studied his pictures. Then I reexamined every skull and long bone, taking Polaroids of anything that looked suspicious.

Still, I could not believe it. Ancient times, ancient peoples, yes. These things didn't happen in modern America.

A sudden synapse.

One more phone call. Colorado. Twenty minutes later, another fax.

I stared at it, the paper trembling slightly in my hand.

Dear God. It was undeniable.

I found McMahon at his temporary headquarters in the Bryson City Fire Department. As with the incident morgue, the function of the FBI office had changed.

McMahon and his colleagues had shifted their focus from crash to crime scene investigation, their paradigm from terrorism to homicide.

Space formerly occupied by the NTSB was now empty, and several cubicles had been merged to create what looked like a task force squad room. Bulletin boards that had once featured the names of terrorist groups and militant radicals now held those of eight murder victims. In one cluster, the positive IDs: Edna Farrell. Albert Odell. Jeremiah Mitchell. George Adair. In another, the unknown and those still in question: John Doe. Tucker Adams. Charlie Wayne Tramper. Mary Francis Rafferty.

Though every name was accompanied by a date of disappearance, the amount and type of information varied considerably from board to board.

On the opposite end of the room, more boards displayed photos of the Arthur house. I recognized the attic cots, the dining room table, the great room fireplace. I was examining shots of the basement murals when McMahon joined me.

"Cheerful stuff."

"Sheriff Crowe thought that was a copy of a Goya."

"She's right. It's *Saturn Devouring His Children*."

He tapped a photo of the raft scene.

"This one's by Théodore Géricault. Know him?"

I shook my head.

"It's called *The Raft of Medusa*."

"What's the story?"

"We're checking."

"Who's the bear?"

"Same answer. We ran the name but came up with zip. Can't be that many Baxbakualanuxsiwaes out there."

He removed a thumbtack with his nail and handed me a list.

"Familiar with anyone on the playbill?"

"The names from the tunnel walls?"

"Yeah. Special Agent Rayner's working them."

Three folding tables lined the back of the room. One held a computer, the others cardboard boxes, each marked with date and provenance: *Kitchen drawer L3. Living room, north wall bookcase.* Other boxes were stacked on the floor.

A young man in shirtsleeves and tie worked at the computer. I'd seen him at the Arthur house, but we hadn't met. McMahon gestured from the agent to me.

"Roger Rayner, Tempe Brennan."

Rayner looked up and smiled, then went back to his monitor.

"We've nailed a few of the more obvious players. The Greek and Roman gods, for example."

I noted comments following some names. Cronus. Dionysus. The Daughters of Mineus. The Daughters of Pelias. Polyphemus.

"And the pope and the Aztec emperor popped right up. But who the hell is Dasakumaracarita? Or Abd al-Latif? Or Hamatsa?" He pronounced the names syllable by syllable. "At least I can say 'Sawney Beane' or 'John Gregg.'"

He ran a hand through his hair and it did its rooster thing.

"I figured an anthropologist might recognize some obscure goddess or something."

I was staring at one name, my nerve cells tingling. Hamatsa.

Moctezuma. The Aztecs.

Saturn devouring his children.

"Is there somewhere we can talk in private?" My voice sounded high and shaky.

McMahon gave me an odd look, then led me into an adjacent cubicle.

I took a moment to collect my thoughts.

"What I'm about to say is going to sound ludicrous, but I'd like you to hear me out."

He leaned back and laced his fingers across his paunch.

"Among the Kwakiutl of the Pacific Northwest, the Hamatsa were a society of tribal elite. Young men who hoped to become Hamatsa went through a lengthy period of isolation."

"Like fraternity pledges."

"Yes. During their time in the forest the initiates would periodically appear on the outskirts of the village, demented and screaming, charge in, bite flesh from the arms and chests of those unfortunate enough to be present, then disappear into the woods."

McMahon's eyes were on his hands.

"Shortly before the end of his exile, each initiate was brought a mummy that had been soaked in salt water, cleaned, and split open. The initiate was expected to smoke-cure the corpse for the final ritual."

I swallowed.

"During that ritual the aspirant and senior members of the brotherhood devoured portions of the corpse."

McMahon did not look at me.

"Are you familiar with the Aztecs?"

"Yes."

"They appeased their gods through the ritual eating of human beings."

"Cannibalism?"

McMahon's eyes finally met mine.

"On a grand scale. When Cortés and his men entered Moctezuma's capital, Tenochtitlán, they found mounds of human skulls in the city square, others impaled on spikes. Their estimate was over one hundred thousand."

Silence. Then, "Saturn ate his children."

"Polyphemus captured Ulysses and dined on his crew."

"Why the pope?"

"I'm not sure."

McMahon disappeared, returned in moment.

"Rayner's looking him up."

He looked at a note, scratched a clump of hair.

"Rayner found the Géricault painting. It's based on the 1816 wreck of a French frigate, *La Méduse*. According to the story, survivors ate the dead while stranded at sea."

I was about to show McMahon my own findings when Rayner appeared in the doorway. We listened as he read from scribbled notes.

"I don't think you want the old boy's entire résumé, so I'll give you the highlights. Pope Innocent III is best known for organizing the Fourth Lateran Council in twelve fifteen A.D. Anyone who was anyone in Christendom was told to get his butt to this meeting."

He looked up.

"I'm paraphrasing. With all the honchos convened, Innocent decreed that henceforth the words *hoc est corpus meum* were to be taken literally, and the faithful were required to believe in transubstantiation. That's the idea that, at Mass, the bread and wine are changed into the body and blood of Christ."

He looked up again to see if we were with him.

"Innocent decreed that the act isn't symbolic, it's real. Apparently this question had been debated for about a thousand years, so Innocent decided to settle the issue. From then on, if you doubted transubstantiation, you were guilty of heresy."

"Thanks, Roger."

"No problem." He withdrew.

"So what's the link?" McMahon asked.

"Innocent defined the most sacred ceremonial act of Christianity as true God-eating. It's what anthropologists call ritual anthropophagy."

A childhood memory. A nun in traditional habit, crucifix on her breast, chalk on her hands.

"Do you know the origin of the word *host*?"

McMahon shook his head.

"*Hostia*. It means 'sacrificial victim' in Latin."

"You think we're dealing with some fringe group that gets high on cannibalism."

I took a steadying breath.

"I think it's much worse than that."

"Worse than what?"

We both turned. Ryan stood in the spot recently occupied by Rayner. McMahon gestured at a chair.

"Worse than drooling over myths and allegorical paintings. I'm glad you're here, Ryan. You can verify what I'm about to describe."

I pulled Jim's photos from my briefcase and handed the first to McMahon.

"That is the reconstructed leg bone of a red deer. The gashes were made with a sharp instrument, probably a stone knife. Notice how they cluster around the tendon and ligament attachment points, and at the joints."

McMahon passed the photo to Ryan, and I handed him several more.

"Those are also animal bones. Notice the small distribution of cut marks and striations."

Next picture.

"Those are fragments of human bone. They were recovered from the same cave in southeastern France where the animal bones were found."

"Looks like the same pattern."

"It is."

"Meaning?"

"Butchery. The bones were stripped of flesh and cut or twisted apart at the joints."

"How old is this stuff?"

"One hundred thousand to one hundred and twenty thousand years. The site was occupied by Neanderthals."

"Is this relevant?"

I gave him several more prints.

"Those are also human bones. They were recovered at a site near Mesa Verde, in southwestern Colorado."

"Anasazi?" Ryan asked, reaching for a photo.

"Yes."

"Who are the Anasazi?" McMahon.

"Ancestors of groups like the Hopi and Zuni. This site was occupied by a small group around 1130 to 1150 A.D., during a period of extreme drought. A colleague from Chapel Hill did the digging. These are his photos. At least thirty-five adults and kids were butchered. Notice that the pattern is identical."

I fed them another photo.

"Those are stone tools found in association with the human bones. Tests confirmed the presence of human blood."

Another.

"That ceramic cooking pot held the residue of human tissues."

"How can they be sure these marks aren't caused by

abrasion? Or by animals? Or by some sort of burial ritual? Maybe they cut up the dead to prepare them for the afterlife. That could explain the bloody tools and pot."

"That was exactly the argument until this was discovered."

I passed them another photo.

"What the hell is that?" McMahon gave it to Ryan.

"After seven people were killed, cooked, and eaten in a small underground room at this site, one of the diners squatted over the cold hearth and defecated."

"Holy shit."

"Exactly. Archaeologists call preserved feces coprolites. Bio-chemical tests showed traces of digested human muscle protein in this particular beauty."

"Could the protein have gotten there by some other route?"

"Not myoglobin. Tests also showed this guy had eaten almost nothing but meat for eighteen hours prior to his grand gesture."

"That is great stuff, Tempe, but I've got eight stiffs and a pack of reporters breathing down my neck. Other than perps with a morbid taste in art and literature, how is this relevant? You're showing me people who have been dead for centuries."

I placed three more photos on his desk.

"Ever heard of Alfred G. Packer?"

He glanced at his watch, then at the pictures.

"No."

"Alfie Packer is reputed to have killed and eaten five people in Colorado during the winter of 1874. He was tried and convicted of murder. The victims were recently exhumed and analyzed."

"What the hell for?"

"Historic accuracy."

Ryan circled behind McMahon. As the two men studied the bones of the Packer victims, I got up and spread my Polaroids across the desk.

"I took these at the morgue this morning."

Like spectators at a tennis match, their eyes shifted among the Neanderthals, the Anasazi, the Packer victims, and my Polaroids. For a very long time no one spoke.

McMahon broke the silence.

"Jesus, Mary, and Joseph in a bloody pear tree."

30

No one had anything to add to that.

"Who the hell are these lunatics?" Ryan's question broke the silence.

McMahon responded.

"The H&F Investment Group is buried under more layers than Olduvai Gorge. Veckhoff's dead, so he's not talking. Following up on your suggestion, Tempe, we tracked down Rollins and Birkby through their fathers. Rollins lives in Greenville, teaches English at a community college. Birkby owns a chain of discount furniture stores, has homes in Rock Hill and Hilton Head. Each gentleman tells the same story: inherited his interest in H&F, knows nothing about the property, never visited there."

I heard a door open, voices in the corridor.

"W. G. Davis is a retired investment banker living in Banner Elk. F. M. Payne is a philosophy professor at Wake Forest. Warren's an attorney in Fayetteville. We found the counselor on his way to the airport, had to spoil his little getaway to Antigua."

"Do they admit to knowing one another?"

"Everyone tells the same story. H&F is strictly business, they never met. Never set foot on the property."

"What about prints inside the house?"

"The recovery team lifted zillions. We're running them but it will take time."

"Any police records?"

"Payne, the professor, was busted for pot in seventy-four. Otherwise, nothing came up. But we're checking every cell these guys have ever shed. If one of them peed on a tree at Woodstock, we'll get a sample. These assholes are dirty as hell, and they're going down for murder."

Larke Tyrell appeared in the doorway. Deep lines creased his forehead. McMahon greeted him, went in search of additional seating. Tyrell spoke to me.

"I'm glad you're here."

I said nothing.

McMahon returned with a folding metal chair. Tyrell sat, his spine so erect it made no contact with the backrest.

"What can I do for you, Doc?" McMahon.

Tyrell removed a handkerchief, wiped his forehead, then refolded the linen in a perfect square.

"I have information that is highly sensitive."

The Andy Griffith eyes shifted from face to face, but he did not say the obvious.

"I'm sure you are all aware that Parker Davenport died of a gunshot wound yesterday. The wound appears to be self-inflicted, but there are disturbing elements, including an extremely high level of trifluoperazine in his blood."

We all looked blank.

"The common name is Stelazine. The drug is used in the treatment of psychotic anxiety and agitated depressions. Davenport had no prescription for Stelazine, and his doctor knows of no reason he would be taking it."

"A man in his position wouldn't have trouble getting what he wanted." McMahon.

"That's true, sir."

Tyrell cleared his throat.

"Minute traces of trifluoperazine were also detected in the body of Primrose Hobbs, but immersion and decomposition had complicated the picture, so a definitive finding was not possible."

"Does Sheriff Crowe know this?" I asked.

"She knows about Hobbs. I'll tell her about Davenport when I leave here."

"Stelazine wasn't found among Hobbs's belongings."

"Nor did she have a prescription."

My stomach tightened. I had never seen Primrose take so much as an aspirin.

"Equally disturbing are phone calls made by Davenport on the evening of his death," Larke went on.

Tyrell handed McMahon a list.

"You may recognize some of the numbers."

McMahon scanned the printout, then looked up.

"Sonofabitch. The lieutenant governor phoned the H&F officers just hours before blowing his brains out?"

"What?" I blurted.

"Or had them blown out." Ryan.

McMahon passed me the list. Six numbers, five names. W. G. Davis, F. M. Payne, F. L. Warren, C. A. Birkby, P. H. Rollins.

"What was the sixth call?"

"The number traces to a rented cabin in Cherokee. Sheriff Crowe is checking it out."

"Tempe, show Dr. Tyrell what you just showed me."
McMahon reached for his phone.

"It's time to run these bastards to ground."

Larke wanted to examine the marks firsthand, so we
went straight to the morgue. Though I'd had nothing
since coffee at seven, and it was after one, I had no
appetite. I kept seeing Primrose, wondering what she'd
discovered. What threat she'd posed. And a new
question: Was her murder linked to the death of the
lieutenant governor?

Larke and I spent an hour going over the bones, the
ME looking and listening closely, now and then asking
a question. We'd just finished when my cell phone rang.

Lucy Crowe was in Waynesville but had something
she needed to discuss. Could we meet around nine at
High Ridge House? I agreed.

As we were disconnecting she asked a question.

"Do you know an archaeologist named Simon
Midkiff?"

"Yes."

"He may be involved with this H&F bunch."

"Midkiff?"

"His was the sixth number Davenport dialed before
his death. If he tries to contact you, agree to nothing."

As we talked, Larke photocopied the pictures and
articles. When he was done, I told him what Crowe had
said. He posed a single question.

"Why?"

"Because they're crazy," I answered, still distracted
by Crowe's comment about Midkiff.

"And Parker Davenport was one of them."

He slid the photocopies into his briefcase, impaled
me with exhausted eyes.

"He tried professional sabotage to keep you from that house." Larke swept an arm in the direction of the tables. "To divert you from this."

I did not reply.

"And I was suckered in."

Still, I remained silent.

"Is there anything I can say to you?"

"There are things you can say to my colleagues."

"Letters will go to the AAFS, the ABFA, and the NDMS immediately." He grabbed my wrist. "And I will phone the head of each organization first thing Monday to explain personally."

"And the press?" Though I knew he was suffering, I could force no warmth into my voice. His disloyalty had hurt me, professionally and personally.

"That will come. I must determine how best to handle it."

Best for whom? I wondered.

"If it's any consolation, Earl Bliss acted on my orders. He never believed anything against you."

"Most who know me did not."

He released my arm but his eyes held firm. Overnight he'd come to look like a tired old man.

"Tempe, I was trained as a military man. I believe in respecting the chain of command and carrying out the lawful orders of my superiors. That predisposition led me not to question things I should have questioned. The abuse of power is a terrible thing. Failure to resist corrupting pressure is equally contemptible. It's time for this old dog to rouse and get off the porch."

I felt a deep sadness as I watched him leave. Larke and I had been friends for many years. I wondered if we could ever be friends again.

As I made coffee, my thoughts shifted to Simon

381

Midkiff. Of course. It all made sense. His intense interest in the crash site. The lies about excavating in Swain County. The photo with Parker Davenport at Charlie Wayne Tramper's funeral. He was one of them.

A sudden flashback. The black Volvo that had almost run me down. The man at the wheel had looked vaguely familiar. Could it have been Simon Midkiff?

I was completing my report on Edna Farrell when my cell phone rang a second time.

"Sir Francis Dashwood was a prolific guy."

The statement came from a different galaxy than the one in which my mind was orbiting.

"I'm sorry?"

"It's Anne. I was organizing stuff from our London trip and came across a pamphlet Ted bought at the West Wycombe caves."

"Anne, this is not—"

"There are gobs of Dashwoods still around."

"Gobs?"

"Descendants of Sir Francis, later known as Lord le Despencer, of course. Just for fun I popped the name Prentice Dashwood into a genealogical site where I'm registered. I couldn't believe how many hits I got. One was particularly interesting."

I waited.

Nothing.

I cracked.

"Do we do this with twenty questions?"

"Prentice Elmore Dashwood, one of Sir Frank's many descendants, left England in 1921. He opened a haberdashery in Albany, New York, made bundles of money, and eventually retired."

"That's it?"

"During his years in America, Dashwood wrote and self-published dozens of pamphlets, one of which recounted tales of his great-great-great-something, Sir Francis Davenport the Second."

"And the other pamphlets?" If I didn't ask, this would take forever.

"You name it. The song lines of the Australian Aboriginals. The oral traditions of the Cherokee. Camping. Fly-fishing. Greek mythology. A brief ethnography of the Carib Indians. Prentice was quite the Renaissance man. He penned three booklets and several articles that focused exclusively on the Appalachian Trail. Apparently Big P was a real mover in getting the trail started back in the twenties."

Oh? A mecca for hikers and trekkers, the AT starts at Mount Katahdin in Maine and runs along the Appalachian ridgeline to Springer Mountain in Georgia. Much of the trail lies in the Great Smoky Mountains. Including Swain County.

"Are you still there?"

"I'm here. Did Dashwood spend time here in North Carolina?"

"He wrote five pamphlets on the Great Smokies." I heard paper rustle. "Trees. Flowers. Fauna. Folklore. Geology."

I remembered Anne's tale of her visit to West Wycombe, pictured the caves under the H&F house. *Could* this guy Anne was talking about be the Prentice Dashwood of Swain County, North Carolina? It was a striking name. Could there be a connection to the British Dashwoods?

"What else did you find out about Prentice Dashwood?"

"Not a thing. But I can tell you that old Uncle Francis

383

hung with a wild crowd back in the eighteenth century. Called themselves the Monks of Medmenham. Listen to the list. Lord Sandwich, who at one point commanded the Royal Navy, John Wilkes—"

"The politician?"

"Yep. William Hogarth, the painter, and poets Paul Whitehead, Charles Churchill, and Robert Lloyd."

"Impressive roster."

"Very. Everyone was a member of Parliament or the House of Lords. Or a poet or whatever. Our own Ben Franklin dropped in now and then, though he was never an official member."

"What did these guys do?"

"Some accounts claim they engaged in satanic rites. According to the current Sir Francis, author of the booklet we picked up on our trip, the monks were just jolly fellows who got together to celebrate Venus and Bacchus. I take that to mean women and wine."

"They held wild parties in the caves?"

"And at Medmenham Abbey. The current Sir Francis admits to his ancestor's sexual frolics but denies the devil worship. He suggests the satanism rumor came from the boys' somewhat irreverent attitude toward Christianity. They also referred to themselves as the Knights of Saint Francis, for example."

I could hear her biting an apple, then chewing.

"Everyone else called them the Hell Fire Club."

The name hit me like a sledgehammer.

"What did you say?"

"The Hell Fire Club. Big in Ireland in the 1730s and 1740s. Same deal. Overprivileged devos mocking religion and getting drunk and laid."

Anne had a way of cutting to the quick.

"There were attempts to suppress the clubs, but they

weren't effective. When Dashwood gathered his little group of philanderers, the label Hell Fire naturally transferred."

Hell Fire. H&F.

I swallowed.

"How long is this booklet?"

"Thirty-four pages?"

"Can you fax me a copy?"

"Sure. I can get two pages on one sheet."

I gave her the number and went back to my report, forcing myself to concentrate. Within minutes the fax rang, screeched, and bonged, then began to spit out pages. I stayed with my description of Edna Farrell's facial trauma. Some time later the machine reengaged. Again, I resisted the impulse to rush to it and gather Anne's pages.

When I'd completed the Farrell report, I began another, a million thoughts screaming for ascendancy. Though I tried to focus, images broke through again and again.

Primrose Hobbs. Parker Davenport. Prentice Dashwood. Sir Francis. The Hell Fire Club. H&F. Was anything connected? The evidence was growing. There must be a connection.

Had Prentice Dashwood rekindled his ancestor's idea of an elitist boys' club here in the Carolina mountains? Had the members been more than hedonistic dilettantes? How much more? I pictured the cut marks, suppressed a shudder.

At four the guard came in to say that a deputy had fallen sick, another was stranded with a malfunctioning cruiser. Crowe sent her apologies but needed him to control a domestic situation. I assured him I'd be fine.

I worked on, the silence of the empty morgue

wrapping around me like a living thing except for the hum of a refrigerator. My breath, my heartbeat, my fingers clicking the keyboard. Outside, branches scraped windowpanes high overhead. A train whistle. A dog. Crickets. Frogs.

No car horns. No traffic noises. No living person for miles.

My sympathetic nervous system kept the adrenaline in front row, center. I made frequent errors, jumped at every squeak and tap. More than once I wished for Boyd's company.

By seven I'd finished with Farrell, Odell, Tramper, and Adams. My eyes burned, my back ached, and a dull headache told me that my blood sugar was in the cellar.

I copied my files to floppy, closed down my laptop, and went to collect Anne's fax.

Though I was anxious to read about the eighteenth-century Sir Francis, I was too tired, too hungry, and too edgy to be objective. I decided to return to High Ridge House, walk Boyd, talk with Crowe, then read the pamphlet in the comfort and safety of my bed.

I was gathering pages when I heard what sounded like gravel crunching.

I froze, listening.

Tires? Footsteps?

Fifteen seconds. Thirty.

Nothing.

"Time to boogie," I said aloud.

Tension made my movements jerky, and I dropped several papers from the basket. Gathering them from the floor, I noticed that one differed. The type was larger, the text arranged in columns.

I flipped through the other pages. Anne's cover sheet. The front of the pamphlet. The rest were brochure text, two pages to a sheet, each numbered sequentially.

I remembered the machine's pause. Could the odd page have arrived as a separate transmission? I looked but found no return fax number.

Taking everything to my office, I placed Anne's material in my briefcase and lay the mismatched sheet on my desk. As I read the contents, my adrenaline rocketed even higher.

The left column contained code names, the middle one real names. Dates appeared after some individuals, forming an incomplete third column.

Ilus	Henry Arlen Preston	1943
Khaffre	Sheldon Brodie	1949
Omega	A. A. Birkby	1959
Narmer	Martin Patrick Veckhoff	
Sinuhe	C. A. Birkby	
Itzmana	John Morgan	1972
Arrigatore	F. L. Warren	
Rho	William Glenn Sherman	1979
Chac	John Franklin Battle	
Ometeotl	Parker Davenport	

Only one name was unfamiliar. John Franklin Battle.
Or was it? Where had I heard that name?
Think, Brennan. Think.
John Battle.
No. That's not right.
Franklin Battle.
Blank.
Frank Battle.
The magistrate who'd stonewalled the search warrant!
Would a mere magistrate qualify for membership?

387

Had Battle been protecting the H&F property? Had he sent me the fax? Why?

And why was the most recent date more than twenty years old? Was the list incomplete? Why?

Then a terrifying thought.

Who knew I was here?

Alone.

Again I froze, listening for the faintest indicator of another presence. Picking up a scalpel, I slipped from my office to the main autopsy room.

Six skeletons stared upward, fingers and toes splayed, jaws silent beside their heads. I checked the computer and X-ray sections, the staff kitchenette, the makeshift conference room. My heart beat so loudly it seemed to overpower the stillness.

I was poking my head into the men's toilet when my cell phone sounded for the third time. I nearly screamed from the tension.

A voice, smooth as a double latte.

"You're dead."

Then empty air.

31

I called McMahon. No answer. Crowe. Ditto. I left messages: Seven thirty-eight. Leaving Alarka for High Ridge House. Call me.

Picturing the empty lot, the deserted county road, I punched Ryan's number.

Another image. Ryan, facedown on an icy drive. I'd asked for his help that other time in Quebec. It had gotten him shot.

Ryan has no jurisdiction, Brennan. And no personal responsibility.

Instead of "send," I hit the delete button.

My thoughts ricocheted like the metal sphere in a pinball game.

Someone should be told of my whereabouts. Someone I would not be placing in danger.

Sunday night. I dialed my old number.

"Hello." A woman's voice, mellow as a purring cat.

"Is Pete there?"

"He's in the shower."

I heard a wind chime tinkle. A wind chime I'd hung years ago outside my bedroom window.

"Is there a message?"

I clicked off.

"Fuck it," I muttered. "I'll take care of myself."

Slinging purse and laptop over one shoulder, I rewrapped my fingers around the scalpel and readied my keys in the other hand. Then I cracked the door and peered out.

My Mazda was alone with the exiled hook-and-ladder trucks. In the deepening twilight, it looked like a warthog facing off with a herd of hippos.

Deep breath.

I bolted.

Reaching the car, I threw myself behind the wheel, slammed down the locks, revved the motor, and raced from the lot.

When I'd gone a mile, I began to calm, and an ill-focused anger seeped over the fear. I turned it on myself.

Jesus, you're like the heroine in a B-grade movie. One crank call and you scream for the help of a big strong man.

Seeing deer on the shoulder, I checked my speed. Eighty. I slowed, returned to chiding myself.

No one leaped from behind the building, or grabbed your ankle from under the car.

True enough. But the fax was not a crank. Whoever sent that list knew I'd be the one to receive it. Knew I was alone at the morgue.

As I drove through Bryson City, I checked the rearview mirror repeatedly. The Halloween decorations now looked menacing rather than festive, the skeletons and tombstones macabre reminders of the hideous events that had unfolded nearby. I gripped the wheel, wondering if the souls of my skeletal dead wandered the world in search of justice.

Wondering if their killers wandered the world in search of me.

At High Ridge House, I cut the engine and peered down the road I'd just climbed. No headlights wound their way up the mountain.

I wrapped the scalpel in a Wendy's napkin and zipped it into my jacket pocket for return to the morgue. Then I gathered my belongings and dashed to the porch.

The house was quiet as a church on Thursday. The parlor and kitchen were empty, and I passed no one on my way to the second floor. I heard no rustling or snoring from behind Ryan's or McMahon's doors.

I'd barely removed my jacket when a soft knock made me jump.

"Yes?"

"It's Ruby."

Her face was tense and pale, her hair glossier than a page from *Vogue*.

When I opened the door she handed me an envelope.

"This come for you today."

I glanced at the return address. Department of Anthropology, University of Tennessee.

"Thank you."

I started to close the door but she held up a hand.

"There's something you need to know. Something I need to tell you."

"I'm very tired, Ruby."

"It wasn't an intruder that wrecked your room. It was Eli."

"Your nephew?"

"He's not my nephew."

She halted.

"The Gospel of Matthew tells us that whoever shall put away his wife—"

"Why would Eli trash my things?" I was not in the mood for religious discourse.

"My husband left me for another woman. She and Enoch had a child."

"Eli?"

She nodded.

"I wished terrible things for them. I wished them to burn in hell. I thought, if thine eye offend thee, pluck it out. I plucked them from my life."

I heard the muffled sound of Boyd's barking.

"When Enoch passed, God touched my heart. Judge not and ye shall not be judged; condemn not and ye shall not be condemned; forgive and ye shall be forgiven."

She sighed deeply.

"Eli's mother died six years ago. The boy had no one, so I took him in."

Her eyes dropped, returned to mine.

"A man's foes shall be they of his own household. Eli hates me. Takes joy in tormenting me. He knows I take pride in this house. He knows I like you. He was just getting at me."

"Perhaps he just wants attention."

Look at the kid, I thought, but didn't say it.

"Perhaps."

"I'm sure he'll come around in time. And don't worry about my things. Nothing was taken." I changed the subject. "Is anyone else here?"

She shook her head.

"I believe McMahon's gone off to Charlotte. Haven't seen Mr. Ryan all day. Everyone else has checked out."

Again, I heard barking.

"Has Boyd been a nuisance?"

"Dog's been ornery today. Needs exercising." She brushed her skirt. "I'm off to church. Shall I bring dinner before I leave?"

"Please."

Ruby's roast pork and yam pudding had a calming effect. As I ate, the panic that had sent me racing through the twilight gave way to a dismal loneliness.

I remembered the woman on Pete's phone, wondered why hearing her voice felt like a kick in the gut. I know postcoital somnolence when I hear it, but so what? Pete and I were both adults. I'd left him. He was free to see whomever he pleased.

Condemn not and ye shall rock.

I wondered how I really felt about Ryan. I knew he was a bastard, but at least he was a winsome bastard, though I could do without his smoking. He was smart. He was funny. He was dizzyingly handsome, but completely unaware of his effect on women. And he cared about people.

Lots of people.

Like Danielle.

So why had Ryan's number been one of the first I'd started to dial? Was it just that he was nearby, or was he more than a colleague, a person I would think of for protection or comfort?

I remembered Primrose and was again flattened with remorse. I'd involved my friend and now she was dead. I'd gotten her killed. The guilt was crushing, and I was sure it would follow me the rest of my life.

Enough. Read the letter Ruby brought. It will thank you for the lecture and say it was splendid.

It did. The envelope also contained a copy of the

student newsletter with its photo of me and Simon Midkiff. To say I looked tense would be like saying Olive Oyl was on the thin side.

But Simon Midkiff took best of show. I studied his face, wondering what had been in his mind that day. Had he been sent to pump me for information? Had he come on his own? My scientific colleagues often attend one another's lectures. Was it he who had faxed me the code name list? If so, why would he divulge his complicity?

My musings were interrupted by a sharp yip, followed by another.

Poor Boyd. He was the only being on the planet whose loyalty never wavered, and I ignored him. I checked my watch. Eight-twenty. Time for a quick run before Crowe arrived at nine.

I locked my computer and briefcase in the wardrobe in case Eli decided on a return engagement. Then I threw on my jacket, grabbed flashlight and leash, and headed downstairs.

Night had taken full control, ushering in a zillion stars but no moon. The porch lights did little to dispel the darkness. As I crossed the lawn, my limbic system began firing questions.

What if someone is watching?

Like Eli the Avenging Adolescent?

What if the call was not a prank?

Don't be melodramatic, I reasoned. It's the weekend after Halloween, and kids are kicking up their heels. You left messages with McMahon and Crowe.

What if they don't check?

The sheriff will be here in forty minutes.

A stalker might be out there right now.

What could happen in the company of a seventy-pound chow?

That seventy-pound chow yipped again, and I sprinted the last few yards to his pen. Hearing footsteps, he placed forepaws on the chain-linking and raised himself to a bipedal stance.

When he recognized me, Boyd went ballistic, pushing back, bounding forward, jumping up, and pushing off the fence again. He repeated the cycle several times, like a hamster on a wheel, then stood again on hind feet, threw back his head, and barked steadily.

Saying doggy things, I ruffled his ears and clipped on the leash. He nearly dragged me chowside in his lunge toward the gate.

"We're only going to the end of the property," I warned, leveling a finger at his nose.

He cocked his head, twirled the brows, and yipped once. When I lifted the latch, he bounded out and raced in circles, nearly toppling me.

"I envy your energy, Boyd."

He lapped my face as I disentangled the leash from between his legs, then we started up the road. Light from the porch barely reached the edge of the lawn, and within ten yards I clicked on my flash. Boyd stopped and growled.

"It's a flashlight, boy."

I reached down and patted his shoulder. He rotated his head and licked my hand, then doubled back, did a little dance, and pressed his body against my legs.

I was about to move on when I felt him tense. His head dropped, his breathing changed, and a low rumble rose from his throat. He did not respond to my touch.

"What is it, boy?"

More rumbling.

"Not another dead squirrel."

I reached out to stroke him and felt hackles. Not good. I tugged the leash.

"Come on, boy, we're turning back."

He would not move.

"Boyd."

The growl grew deeper, more savage.

I aimed my light where Boyd was staring. The beam crawled over tree trunks and was sucked into dead zones of blackness between.

I yanked the leash harder. Boyd whipped left and barked. I swept my light in that direction.

"This isn't funny, dog."

Then my eyes made out a form. Or had it been a trick of shadow? In the moment I glanced down at Boyd, what I thought I'd seen vanished. Or had it been there at all?"

"Who's there?" Fear crimped my voice.

Nothing but crickets and frogs. A fallen tree lodged against one still standing groaned and creaked in the air.

Suddenly I heard movement behind me. Footfalls. The rustling of leaves.

Boyd turned and snapped, lunging as far as the leash would allow.

"Who's there?" I repeated.

A silhouette emerged from the trees, denser than the surrounding night. Boyd snarled and tore at the leash. The dark shape moved toward us.

"Who is it?"

No answer.

I thrust the flashlight and leash into one hand and reached for my cell phone with the other. Before I could autodial, it slipped from my shaking fingers.

"Stay back!" It was almost a shriek.

I raised the light to shoulder level. As I was

readjusting the leash for better control, about to reach for the phone, my grip loosened. Boyd broke free and charged, teeth gleaming, a fierce growl rumbling from his throat.

In an instant the silhouette altered shape. An arm uncurled.

Boyd leaped.

A flash. A deafening crack.

The dog bounced off the silhouette, dropped to the ground, whimpered, and lay still.

"Boyd!"

Tears ran down my cheeks. I wanted to tell him I'd take care of him. Tell him he'd be all right, but my body was paralyzed with fear, and no words came from my mouth.

The form moved swiftly toward me now. I turned to run. Hands grabbed me. I twisted, wrenched free. The shadow coalesced into a man.

He hit me with his full weight, his shoulder beneath my armpit. The shock of the impact sent me falling sideways.

The last thing I remembered was breath on my face, sprawling. Then the crack of my skull against igneous rock.

The dream was frightening. An airless place. I couldn't move. I couldn't see. Then something stroked my cheek.

I opened my eyes to a reality more hellish than any nightmare.

My mouth was stuffed and wrapped with tape. I was blindfolded.

My heart shrank in my chest.

I can't breathe!

397

I tried raising a hand to my face. My wrists were tied over my chest.

The rag filled my mouth with an acrid taste. A tremor began below my tongue.

I'm going to vomit! I'm going to choke!

I felt panic, began to shake.

Move!

I tried shifting, and a cocoon of fabric moved with me. I smelled dust and mildew and spoiled vegetation.

I kicked out, thrust with my head.

The movement shot arrows through my brain. I lay still, waiting for the pain to subside.

Breathe through your nose. In. Out. In. Out.

The throbbing lessened slightly.

Think!

I was imprisoned in some sort of bag. My hands and feet were bound. But where was I? How had I gotten here?

Disjointed memories. The morgue. The empty county road. Ruby's troubled face. Primrose Hobbs.

Boyd!

Oh, dear God. Not Boyd! Had I killed the dog, too?

In. Out.

I rolled my head and felt a lump the size of a plum. Another wave of nausea.

In. Out.

More synapses.

The attack. The faceless form.

Simon Midkiff? Frank Battle? Could my captor be the moron magistrate?

I twisted my wrists, trying to loosen the tape. More nausea.

Clamping my teeth, I rolled on to my side. If I did vomit, I didn't want to aspirate the contents.

The movement made my stomach heave. I filled my lungs and the contractions receded.

I lay rigid, listening. I had no idea how long I'd been unconscious, or how I'd arrived at my present location. Was I still in the woods at High Ridge House? Had I been taken elsewhere? Was my attacker just feet away?

My heart rate slowed by a nanosecond, and cogent thought began to creep back.

It was then the thing crawled across my cheek. I heard dry insect sounds, felt movement in my hair, then the tickle of an antennae on my skin.

A scream formed in my throat. I rolled back and forth, batting at my face, my hair. Blinding pain seared my brain, and my innards jammed up against the back of my throat.

Quiet! One functioning brain cell commanded.

Cockroaches! The others shrieked.

I tugged at my jacket, tried to pull it up over my head. It wouldn't go.

Lie still!

My heart hammered the order against my ribs.

Be still. Be still. Be still.

Slowly, I calmed, and reason returned.

Get out.

Run.

But not into another trap.

Think.

Listen.

Bare branches hissing in the wind. A chirp. Leaves skittering across the ground.

Forest sounds.

I peeled back a layer of sound.

Water swirling around rocks.

River sounds.

Another layer.

Far away and barely there, a loonlike wail followed by a strange giggle.

Gooseflesh spread across my arms and up my throat. I knew where I was.

32

I strained, barely breathing. Had I really heard what I thought I had? Minutes crept by. Doubt crept in. Then it sounded again, faint and surreal.

An undulating moan, a high-pitched laugh.

The electric skeleton!

I was not far from the Riverbank Inn. Where Primrose had stayed. Where she had never been seen again.

I pictured Primrose's bloated face, saw the gouges left by underwater feeders.

I lay bound, gagged, and blindfolded in a sack beside the Tuckasegee River!

I had to break free!

My skull pounded from its encounter with the rock. The rag cut off my air, and tasted of garbage and filth. The duct tape burned my cheeks and lips, and fired splinters of light up my optic nerve.

And I could hear the swish of roaches on my nylon jacket, feel their movement in my hair and on my jeans.

My thoughts flew in a thousand directions.

Again, I listened. Hearing no indicators of a human presence, I began manipulating my bindings, breathing steadily through my nose.

My stomach swirled, my mouth grew dry.

Millennia passed. The tape loosened a millimeter.

Tears of frustration welled behind my mashed lids.

No weeping!

I kept at my ankles and wrists, yanking, twisting, tugging, stopping periodically to monitor for sound outside my bag.

Roaches scuttled across my face, their feet feathery on my skin.

Go away! I screamed in my mind. *Get the fuck off!*

I struggled on. Sweat dampened my hair.

My mind soared like a nocturnal bird, and I looked down on myself, a helpless larva on the forest floor. I pictured the blackness around me and wished for the safety of a familiar night haven.

A twenty-four-hour coffee shop. A tollbooth. A precinct house. A nurses' station in a sleeping ward. An ER.

Then I remembered.

The scalpel!

Could I reach it?

I drew my knees to my chest, scrunching the hem of my jacket as far up as possible. Then I jerked my elbows across the nylon, raising my hips each time. Blindly I inched the pocket forward, gauging its progress by touch.

Reading my clothing like a Braille map, I located the nylon loop attached to the pull tab and grasped it between the fingertips of both hands.

I held my breath, applied downward pressure.

My fingers slid down the nylon and off the end.

Damn!

I tried again, with the same result.

Over and over I repeated the maneuver, fishing, squeezing, pulling, until my hand cramped and I wanted to scream.

New plan.

Pressing the zipper tab to my thigh with the back of my left hand, I bent my right wrist and tried to hook a finger through the loop. The angle was too shallow.

I bent my hand farther. No go.

Using the fingers of my left hand, I placed pressure on my right, increasing the backward angle. Pain screamed up the tendons of my forearm.

As I thought my bones would snap, my index finger found the loop and slipped through. I tugged gently. The tab gave, and my bound wrists followed it down. With the zipper open, it was easy to slide the fingers of one hand into the pocket and withdraw the scalpel.

Carefully cradling my prize, I rolled on to my back and wedged the instrument against my stomach. Then I peeled off the napkin by rolling the scalpel between my hands. Rotating the blade toward my body, I began sawing the tape that bound my wrists. The scalpel was razor sharp.

Easy. Careful. Don't carve your wrist.

In less than a minute my hands were free. I reached up and tore the bindings from my lips. Flames raced across my face.

Don't scream!

I yanked the rag from my mouth, alternately gulped air and spat. Gagging on my own foul saliva, I sliced through the blindfold circling my head and ripped it from my eyes.

Another burst of fire as skin and some eyebrows went with the tape. With shaking hands, I reached down and freed my ankles.

I was slashing at the bag when a sound paralyzed my arm.

The chunk of a car door!

How far away? What to do? Play dead?

My arm flew, a piston driven by a will of its own.

Feet rustled through leaves. My mind calibrated.

Fifty yards.

I jabbed at the canvas. Up, down. Up, down.

The rustling grew louder.

Thirty yards.

I thrust my boots into the opening, thrashed out with all my strength. The tearing sounded like a shriek in the stillness.

The rustling paused, resumed, faster, more reckless.

Twenty yards.

Fifteen.

"Hold it right there."

I pictured the gun, felt bullets slam into my flesh. It didn't matter. I'd either be dead now or dead later. Better to make a fight of it while there was still the chance to resist.

"Don't move."

I flipped around, grabbed the edges I'd torn, and pulled with both hands. Then I lunged headfirst through the opening, tumbled facedown, rolled on to my feet, and stood on rubber legs, trying to focus.

"Madam, you are dead."

I bolted away from the sound of the voice.

Keeping the gurgling of the river to my left, I ran through darkness dense as an endless tunnel, one arm in front of my face. Obstacles leaped at me without warning, forcing my feet on a zigzag path.

Again and again I stumbled on some form of planetary rubble. A rock older than life itself. A fallen

404

trunk. A dead branch. I kept my balance. Burning fear gave rise to strength and speed.

The things of the night seemed to go silent. I heard no buzzing, no chirping, no padding of feet, just my own rasping breath. Behind me, footfalls, thrashing like some giant woodland beast.

Sweat soaked my clothing. Blood pounded in my ears.

My pursuer stayed with me, neither closing in nor falling back. Was he working a home court advantage? Was he the cat, I his mouse? Was he biding his time, confident the prey would be his?

My lungs burned, unable to take in enough air. A stabbing pain ripped my left side. Still, the blind urge to run.

One minute. Three. An eternity.

Then the muscles of my right thigh cramped. I slowed to a limping lope.

The cat slowed, too.

I tried to push on. It was no good. My legs and arms were going dead.

My pace dropped to a trot. Sweat trickled from my forehead and burned my eyes.

I saw the outline of a dark shape in front of my face. My outstretched hand slammed something solid. My elbow folded, and my cheek hit hard. Pain shot through my wrist. Blood moistened my palm and cheek.

With my good hand, I reached out and explored. Solid rock.

I probed farther.

More rock.

My heart shriveled.

I'd run up against a cliff wall. Water to my left. Dense trees to my right.

The cat knew. I had nowhere to go.

Don't panic!

I pulled out the scalpel and held it behind me. Then I turned, back to the wall, and faced my attacker.

He spoke before I saw him.

"Bad routing."

He was breathing hard, and I could smell the rancid odor of sweat and rage.

"Stay away from me!" I yelled with more bravado than I felt.

"Why should I do that?" Taunting.

I knew that voice. The caller at the morgue. But I'd also heard it in person. Where?

Crunching, then a black cutout appeared in the darkness.

"Don't take one step closer," I hissed.

"You're in an odd position to give orders."

"Come near me and I'll kill you." I grasped the scalpel like a lifeline.

"The proverbial rock and hard place, I'd call it."

More crunching. The cutout resolved itself into a man, arm extended in my direction. Broad shoulders, thick arms.

It was not Simon Midkiff.

"Who are you?"

"Surely you know that by now."

I heard the click of a safety uncatching.

"You killed Primrose Hobbs. Why?"

"Because I could."

"And you plan to kill me."

"With the greatest of pleasure."

"Why?"

"Your meddling destroyed a holy thing."

"Who are you?"

406

"Kulkulcan."

Kulkulcan. It was one I knew.

"The Mayan deity."

"Why settle for a pharaoh or some faggot Greek?"

"Where is the rest of your society of sickos?"

"If it wasn't for that miserable crash you'd never have stumbled on to us. Your busybody intrusiveness uncovered things you had no right to know. It has fallen to Kulkulcan to exact vengeance."

The melodious voice was now tinged with fury.

"It's over for your Hell Fire Club."

"It will never be over. Since the dawn of time the mediocre masses have tried to suppress the intellectually superior. It never works. Conditions can make us dormant, but we reemerge when the climate changes."

To what egomaniacal delusion was I listening?

"It was my time to enter the ranks of the holy," he continued, oblivious to the fact that I hadn't replied. Or indifferent. "I found my offering. I made my sacrifice. I honored the ritual that you have profaned."

"Jeremiah Mitchell or George Adair?"

"Irrelevant. Their names don't matter. I was chosen. I was ready. I followed the way."

Keep him talking, my mind reasoned. Someone knows where you are. Someone is doing something.

"Kulkulcan is a creator god. You destroy life."

"Mortals are transient. Wisdom endures."

"Whose?"

"The wisdom of the ages, shown to those worthy to receive it."

"And you ensure its survival through ritual slaughter?"

"The body is a material envelope, of no lasting value. We discard it in the end. But wisdom, strength, the essence of the soul, these are the forces that prevail."

407

I let him rant on.

"The brightest of the species must be nurtured. Those passing from this earth must yield their mana to those who remain, add to the strength and wisdom of the chosen."

"How?"

"Through blood, heart, muscle, and bone."

Dear God, it was true.

"You think you can increase your IQ by consuming the flesh of others?"

"As flesh wastes away, so does strength. But mind, spirit, intellect, those elements are transferable through the very cells of our bodies."

I clutched the scalpel so tightly my knuckles ached.

"Herodotus told of the eating of kinsmen among the Issedones of Central Asia, who grew strong and ruled. Strabo found it among the Irish clans. Many conquering peoples gained strength through eating the flesh of their enemies. Eat the weak and grow stronger. It's as old as man himself."

I thought of the Neanderthal bones, the victims in the kiva near Mesa Verde. The skeletons in my morgue.

"Why the elderly?"

"The aged hold the greatest reservoirs of wisdom."

"Or do old people simply make easier targets?"

"My dear Miss Brennan. Would you rather that your flesh contribute to the advancement of chosen beings or be consumed by maggots?"

Anger welled, overrode fear.

"You egotistical, demented prick."

"Fee-fi-fo-fum, I smell the blood of an Englishman. Be he alive or be he dead, I'll grind his bones to make my bread."

At a distance, the skeleton moaned, cackled.

I was confronted by madness! Who was this man? How did I know him?

I began inching along the wall, holding the scalpel behind me with my right hand, feeling with my left. I'd taken a half dozen steps when a powerful beam shot out of the dark, blinding me like a possum on a backyard fence. I threw up an arm.

"Going somewhere, Miss Brennan?"

In the backglow I could see his lower face, lips drawn back in murderous rage.

Stay away from him!

I pivoted to run, tripped, and fell. As I scrabbled to right myself, the shadow sprang, closed the gap, and a hand reached out and grabbed my ankle. My feet went out from under me again, and my knees cracked against alluvium. The scalpel flew into darkness.

"You goddamn treacherous cow!"

The golden voice was now sizzling with fury.

I kicked out but couldn't break his grip. His fingers were like steel clamping through my jeans.

Never more afraid in my life, I gouged my elbows into the earth, trying to hitch myself forward, kicking out with my free leg. Suddenly, his full weight was on me. A knee pinned my back, and a hand pressed my face into the ground. Dirt and debris filled my nose, my mouth.

I thrashed wildly, kicking and clawing to get out from under him. He'd dropped his flash and it lay on the ground, lighting us like some writhing, two-headed beast. As long as I could move, he would not get that garrote wire around my throat.

My hand touched something jagged and hard, and my fingers closed around it. I twisted my torso and struck out blindly.

I heard the soft thunk of rock against bone, then the metallic clink of steel on granite.

"Bitch!"

He slammed his fist into my right ear. Lightning exploded in my head.

He released his grasp, fumbled to retrieve the gun. I jerked an elbow backward and caught him along the border of his jaw. His teeth cracked and his head flew back.

A shriek like that of a wounded animal.

I pushed with all my strength and his knee slipped off my back. In less than a second I scrambled to my knees and crawled toward the flashlight. He regained his balance and we dived at the same time. I got it.

I swung as hard as I could and connected with his temple. A thump, a grunt, and he fell backward. Clicking off the beam, I lunged toward the trees and crouched behind a pine.

I didn't move. I didn't blink. I tried to reason.

Don't thrash into the trees. Don't turn your back on him. Maybe as he moves you can slip past him, run back toward the inn, scream for help.

Dead calm, broken only by his panting. Seconds passed. Or maybe it was hours. I felt dizzy from the blow to my head, couldn't track time or space or distance.

Where was he?

A voice from near the ground. "I have found the gun, Miss Brennan."

A single shot exploded in the stillness.

"But we both know I don't need it now that that cur of yours is out of the way."

His voice came to me as though under water.

"I'm going to make you pay for this. Really pay."

I heard him rise.

"I have a necklace I want to show you."

I inhaled deeply, trying to clear my head. He was coming at me with the garrote.

Out of the corner of my eye, a glimmer. I turned. Three slivers of light were bobbing toward me. Or was I hallucinating?

"Freeze!" A gravelly female voice.

"Drop it!" Male.

"Stop!" A different male voice.

A muzzle flashed in the darkness in front of me. Two shots rang out.

Return fire from the direction of the voices. The ping of a bullet ricocheting off rock.

A thud, an expulsion of air. The sound of a body sliding down the rock wall.

Running feet.

Hands on my throat, my wrist.

"—pulse is strong."

Faces above me, swimming like a mirage on a summer sidewalk. Ryan. Crowe. Deputy Nameless.

"—ambulance. It's O.K. We didn't hit her."

Static.

I struggled to sit.

"Lie back." Gentle pressure on my shoulders.

"I have to see him."

One circle of light slid to the cliff where my assailant sat motionless, legs stretched in front, back against rock. Slowly, the light illuminated feet, legs, torso, face. I knew who he was.

Ralph Stover, the not-so-happy owner of the Riverbank Inn, the man who would not let me into Primrose's room. He stared sightlessly into the night, chin forward, brain slowly oozing on to a stain on the rock behind his head.

33

I left Charlotte at dawn on Friday and drove west through heavy fog. The shifting vapors lightened as I climbed toward the Eastern Continental Divide, vanished outside Asheville.

Leaving Highway 74 at Bryson City, I drove up Veterans' Boulevard, past the cutoff to the Fryemont Inn, turned right on Main, and parked opposite the old courthouse, now a senior citizens' center. I sat a moment watching sunlight glisten on its little gold dome, and thought of those seniors whose bones I'd unearthed.

I pictured a tall, gangling man, blind and nearly deaf; a fragile old woman with a crooked face. I imagined them on these same streets all those years ago. I wanted to put my arms around them, to tell each of them that things were being put right.

And I thought about those who had perished on Air TransSouth 228. So many stories had only begun. Graduations not attended. Birthdays not celebrated. Voyages not taken. Lives obliterated because of one fatal voyage.

I took my time walking to the fire station. I'd spent a month in Bryson City, had come to know it well. I was leaving now, my work completed, but a few questions remained.

When I arrived McMahon was packing the contents of his cubicle into cardboard boxes.

"Breaking camp?" I asked from the doorway.

"Hey, girl, you're back in town." He cleared a chair, gestured me into it. "How are you feeling?"

"Bruised and scraped but fully functional."

Amazingly, I'd sustained no serious injury during my romp in the woods with Ralph Stover. A slight concussion had sent me to the hospital for a couple of days, then Ryan had driven me to Charlotte. Assured I was fine, he'd flown back to Montreal, and I'd spent the rest of the week on the couch with Birdie.

"Coffee?"

"No thanks."

"Mind if I keep working?"

"Please."

"Has someone regaled you with the whole strange tale?"

"There are still gaps. Take it from the top."

"H&F was some kind of hybrid between Mensa and the Billionaire Boys Club. It didn't start out that way, was originally just a bunch of businessmen, doctors, and professors coming to the mountains to hunt and fish.

"Back in the thirties."

"Right. They'd camp on Edward Arthur's land, hunt during the day, drink and party all night. Applaud themselves on their extraordinary intelligence. The group got to be very close over the years, eventually formed a secret society which they called H&F."

"The founding father being Prentice Dashwood."

413

"Dashwood was the first prior, whatever the hell that means."

"H&F stands for Hell Fire," I said. "Hell Fire Clubs flourished in eighteenth-century England and Ireland, the most famous being the brainchild of Sir Francis Dashwood. Prentice Dashwood of Albany, New York, was a descendant of Sir Francis. Mama was an unnamed Hell Fire lady." I'd done a lot of reading during my time on the couch. "Sir Francis had four sons named Francis."

"Sounds like George Foreman."

"The man was proud of his name."

"Or the least creative progenitor in history."

"Anyway, the original Hell Fires had a healthy skepticism for religion and loved lampooning the church. They referred to themselves as the Knights of Saint Francis, to their parties as 'devotions,' to their steward as 'prior.'"

"Who were these assholes?"

"The rich and powerful of Merry Old England. Ever hear of the Bohemian Club?"

McMahon shook his head.

"It's a highly select, all-male club whose members have included every Republican president since Calvin Coolidge. They gather for two weeks every year at a secluded campground in Sonoma County, California, called the Bohemian Grove."

McMahon paused, a folder in each hand.

"That does ring a bell. The few journalists that have gotten in over the years have been thrown out and their stories killed."

"Yep."

"You're not suggesting our political and industrial bigwigs plot murder at these rendezvous?"

"Of course not. But the concept is similar: powerful

414

men camping in seclusion. Bohemian Club members are even reported to use mock-druidic rituals."

McMahon taped a carton, slid it across the floor, and placed another on his desk.

"We've netted all but one of the H&F members, and we're accumulating the story bit by bit, but it's slow. Needless to say, no one's enthused about talking to us, and everyone is lawyered to the gills. Each of the six officers will be charged with multiple counts of homicide, but it's unclear what the culpability is for the rest of the pack. Midkiff claims only the leaders participated in murder and cannibalism."

"Has Midkiff been given immunity?" I asked.

He nodded. "Most of our info is coming from him."

"He sent the code name fax?"

"Yes. He'd reconstructed what he remembered. Midkiff left the group in the early seventies, claims he was never involved in any killing. Didn't know about Stover. He says he reached a point last week where he couldn't live with himself anymore."

McMahon began transferring papers from a file cabinet to the box.

"And he was afraid for you."

"Me?"

"You, darlin'."

I took a moment to absorb that.

"Where is he now?"

"The judge didn't think he was a flight risk or in personal danger, so he's out. He's still living in a rental cabin in Cherokee."

"Why did Parker Davenport call Midkiff before shooting himself?"

"To warn him that the lid was about to blow. Apparently the two remained friends after Midkiff withdrew from H&F. It was largely because of the lieutenant governor that Midkiff remained unmolested all these years. Davenport kept the club convinced that Midkiff posed no threat; in return, Midkiff kept his mouth shut."

"Until now."

"Until now."

"What has he told you?"

"H&F had eighteen members at any given time. Of those, six lucky boys made up the inner circle. Very exclusive. Only when a member of that inner circle died was a replacement chosen from the group at large. The initiation banquet was black tie; red, hooded robe; dessert provided by the inductee."

"Human flesh."

"Yes. Remember the Hamatsa you told me about?"

I nodded, too revolted to reply.

"Same deal. Only our gentlemen cannibals restricted themselves to sharing the flesh of one thigh from each victim. It was like a blood brotherhood pact. Though the whole club met regularly at the Arthur house, Midkiff swears that only members of the inner circle knew what really went on at these initiations."

I thought of Ralph Stover's words to me. "I found my offering."

"Tucker Adams was killed in 1943 when inner-circle member Henry Arlen Preston died, and Anthony Allen Birkby joined the elite. When Sheldon Brodie drowned in 1949, Martin Patrick Veckhoff was the new inner-circle choice and Edna Farrell was his victim. Anthony Allen Birkby perished in a car wreck a decade later, his son was given the inner-circle nod, and Charlie Wayne Tramper ended up on the Communion table."

"Wasn't Tramper killed by a bear?"

"Young Birkby may have cheated a bit. The Tramper funeral was where Parker Davenport met Simon Midkiff, by the way. Midkiff knew Tramper through his research on the Cherokee."

"Did Midkiff know what had happened to Tramper?"

"Claims he had no clue."

"How did Midkiff get hooked up with H&F?"

"In 1955 the young professor was newly arrived from England, and had been told to look up Prentice Dashwood, an old family friend. Dashwood recruited Midkiff into H&F."

"He never made it to the inner circle."

"No."

"But Davenport did."

"Following the Tramper funeral, Midkiff gradually introduced Davenport to the brothers. The idea of an intellectual elite appealed to Davenport, and he joined up."

"Even though he was from Swain County, Davenport had never known about the lodge?"

"Not before he joined. Apparently no one did. These guys were amazing at keeping themselves hidden. They'd sneak in and out after dark. Over the years, everyone forgot the place was there."

"Everyone except old Edward Arthur and Luke Bowman's father."

"Right." McMahon perused the contents of a drawer as if unsure whether to pack or discard them.

"And the club put nothing on paper."

"Very little."

He emptied another drawer into the box, reinserted it in the desk, opened another.

"What is all this shit?" He straightened and looked at me. "Continuing with the chronology, John Morgan died in 1972, Mary Francis Rafferty was killed, and F. L. Warren moved up. By this time, Midkiff was getting disenchanted. He quit shortly after that."

"So he may not have been a party to any murders."

"It looks that way. But Davenport's dirty. In 1979 he was chosen to replace William Glenn Sherman in the inner circle. Davenport's canapé was the unidentified black male."

"Was it significant that the victims were drawn from different races and both sexes?"

"The idea was to maximize the breadth of spiritual intake."

"Jesus."

"Kendall Rollins succumbed to leukemia in 1986 and his son Paul took his place."

"Albert Odell was the victim?"

"Correct."

McMahon dumped the second drawer.

"What happened with Jeremiah Mitchell and George Adair?"

"Major fuck-up. When Martin Patrick Veckhoff checked out last February, Roger Lee Fairley was slated for coronation. He was informed of the requirements, and Mitchell was grabbed and killed. Fairley's sudden death on the way to the Veckhoff funeral created a problem, and Mitchell was put on ice while the succession issue was resolved."

"By whom?"

"Ralph Stover was told that it would soon be his turn to move from the outer to the inner circle, was advised of the conditions, and was asked to perform a few extra duties. He stored Mitchell's body in a freezer at the Riverbank Inn."

I suppressed a shudder.

"That's why the volatile fatty acid readings were off."

"Exactly. In early September Stover was officially proposed to succeed Veckhoff, and Mitchell's body was taken back and placed in the courtyard in preparation for an induction ceremony. That's when things began to unravel. Some within the inner circle opposed Stover's promotion, seeing him as too zealous, too unstable. The dispute dragged on, decomposition began, meaning the body couldn't be used for the ritual and the corpse had to be buried in the cave."

"But not before a coyote visitation."

"Bless them."

"Stover did the dirty work again."

"He's our man."

McMahon upended another drawer, taped the box, and labeled it with a felt-tip pen.

"Anyway, after weeks of wrangling, the Stover faction prevailed. George Adair was abducted on October first. The crash occurred on October fourth."

"I retrieved the foot on October fifth."

He stacked the box with the earlier ones and opened a file drawer.

"As you know, Stover also killed Primrose Hobbs. Lucy Crowe found Stelazine in his apartment at the Riverbank Inn. The prescription was written by a Mexican doctor for none other than Parker Davenport. Stover had four capsules in his pocket Sunday night. The same drug he used on Primrose."

He looked at me.

"She also found a length of wire that matches the garrote from Hobbs's neck."

The cold fist. It still didn't seem possible that Primrose was dead.

"He told me he did it because he could."

"An order may have come from the inner circle, or he may have been acting on his own. Perhaps he feared she'd discovered something. He probably stole her key and password to remove the foot from the morgue and alter the file."

"Has the foot been found?"

"Never will be, I suspect. Hang on."

McMahon disappeared into the hall, returned with two more empty boxes.

"How can so much crap accumulate in one month?"

"Don't forget the rubber snake."

I pointed to an artifact on his desk.

"I'm curious how Crowe found me."

"She and Ryan hit High Ridge House minutes apart Sunday night, well past the time you should have arrived. Finding your car in the lot but no sign of you in the house, they went looking. When they found the dog—"

He glanced up, quickly back to the box. I kept my face neutral.

"Apparently your chow got hold of Stover's wrist before he was shot. Ryan found a medical bracelet with Stover's name on it lying next to the dog's snout. Crowe made the connection based on something Midkiff had told her."

"The rest is history."

"The rest is history."

He threw the snake into the box, changed his mind and took it out.

"Ryan headed back to Quebec?"

"Yes."

Again, I kept my face neutral.

"I don't know the monsieur that well, but his partner's death really turfed him."

"Yes."

420

"Throw in the niece, and I'm amazed the guy held it together."

"Yes." The niece?

"'Danielle the Demon,' he called her."

McMahon crossed to his jacket and tucked the snake into a pocket.

"Said we'd probably read about the kid in the papers one day."

The niece?

I felt a smile tug the corners of my mouth.

At times neutrality is difficult.

I found Simon Midkiff bundled in overcoat, gloves, and muffler, dozing in a rocker on his front stoop. A brimmed cap hid most of his face, and I suddenly thought of another question.

"Simon?"

His head snapped up and the watery eyes blinked in confusion.

"Yes?"

He wiped a hand across his mouth, and a filament of saliva glistened on wool. Removing the glove, he dug under layers of clothing, withdrew glasses, and slid them on to his nose.

Recognition.

"I'm glad to see you are all right." Chains looped to either side of his head, throwing delicate shadows across his cheeks. The skin looked pale and paper-thin.

"Can we talk?"

"Of course. Perhaps we should go inside."

We entered a combination kitchenette–living area with one interior door, which I presumed led to a bedroom and bath. The furnishings were lacquered pine, and looked like they'd come from a home workshop.

Books lined the baseboards, and notebooks and papers covered a table and desk. A dozen boxes were stacked at one end of the room, each marked with a series of archaeological grid numbers.

"Tea?"

"That would be nice."

I watched as he filled a kettle, took Tetley's bags from their paper holders, placed cups on saucers. He seemed frailer than I remembered, more stooped.

"I don't get many visitors."

"This is lovely. Thank you."

He led me to an afghan-draped sofa, placed both cups on a coffee table made from a slice of tree trunk, and dragged a chair opposite.

We both drank. Outside, I heard the whiney buzz of an outboard motor on the Oconaluftee River. I waited until he was ready.

"I'm not sure how well I can talk about it."

"I know what happened, Simon. What I don't understand is why."

"I wasn't there in the beginning. What I know comes from others."

"You knew Prentice Dashwood."

He leaned back, and his eyes shifted to another time.

"Prentice was an insatiable reader with a staggering array of knowledge. There was nothing that didn't interest him. Darwin. Lyell. Newton. Mendelyev. And the philosophers. Hobbs. Aenesidemus. Baumgarten. Wittgenstein. Lao-tzu. He read everything. Archaeology. Ethnology. Physics. Biology. History."

He interrupted to sip his tea.

"And he was wonderful at spinning yarns. That's how it began. Prentice told stories of his ancestor's Hell Fire Club, describing the members as rakish good fellows

422

who banded together for riotous profanity and intellectual conversation. The idea seemed benign enough. And for a while it was."

His cup trembled in its saucer as he set it down.

"But Prentice had a darker side. He believed that certain human beings were more valuable than others." His voice trailed off.

"The intellectually superior," I prodded.

"Yes. As Prentice aged, his worldview was strongly influenced by his cross-cultural reading on cosmology and cannibalism. His grasp on reality diminished."

He paused, sorting through things he could say.

"It started out as frivolous blasphemy. No one really believed it."

"Believed what?"

"That eating the dead negated the finality of death. That partaking of the flesh of another human being allowed the assimilation of soul, personality, and wisdom."

"Is that what Dashwood believed?"

One bony shoulder shrugged.

"Perhaps he did. Perhaps he simply used the idea, and for the inner circle the actual act, as a way to keep the club intact. Collective indulgence in the forbidden. The in-group, out-group mindset. Prentice understood that cultural rituals exist to reinforce the unity of those performing them."

"How did it start?"

"An accident."

He sniffed.

"A bloody accident. A young man showed up at the lodge one summer. God knows what he was doing way out there. There was a lot of drinking, a fight, the boy was killed. Prentice proposed that everyone—"

He withdrew a hanky and ran it over his eyes.

"This took place before the war. I learned about it years later when I overheard a conversation that was not for my ears."

"Yes."

"Prentice cut slivers of muscle from the boy's thigh and required everyone to partake. They had no inner-outer-circle distinction back then. It was a pact. Each was a participant and equally guilty. No one would talk about the boy's death. They buried the body in the woods, the following year the inner circle was formed, and Tucker Adams was killed."

"Intelligent men accepted this insanity? Educated men with wives, and families, and responsible jobs?"

"Prentice Dashwood was an extraordinarily charismatic man. When he spoke, everything made sense."

"Cannibalism?" I kept my voice calm.

"Do you have any idea how pervasive the theme of humans eating humans is in Western culture? Human sacrifice is mentioned in the Old Testament, the Rig-Veda. Anthropophagy is central to the plot of many Greek and Roman myths; it's the centerpiece of the Catholic Mass. Look at literature. Jonathan Swift's 'Modest Proposal' and Tom Prest's tale of Sweeney Todd. Movies *Soylent Green*; *Fried Green Tomatoes*; *The Cook, the Thief, His Wife, Her Lover*; Jean-Luc Godard's *Weekend*. And let's not forget the children: Hansel and Gretel, the Gingerbread Man, and various versions of Snow White, Cinderella, and Red Riding Hood. Grandma, what big teeth you have!"

He drew a tremulous breath.

"And, of course, there are the participants of necessity. The Donner party; the rugby team stranded in the Andes; the crew of the yacht *Mignonette*; Marten

424

Hartwell, the bush pilot marooned in the Arctic. We are fascinated by their tales. And we embrace our famous-for-fifteen-minutes serial killer cannibals with even greater curiosity."

Another deep breath, exhaled slowly.

"I can't explain it, don't condone it. Prentice made everything sound exotic. We were naughty boys sharing an interest in a wicked topic."

"*Fay ce que voudras.*"

I recited the words carved above the entrance to the basement tunnel. During my convalescence, I'd learned that the Rabelais quote in sixteenth-century French also graced the archway and fireplaces at Medmenham Abbey.

"'Do what you like,'" Midkiff translated, then laughed mirthlessly. "It's ironic. The Hell Fires used the quote to sanction their licentious indulgence, but Rabelais actually credits the words to Saint Augustine. 'Love God and do what you like. For if with the spirit of wisdom a man loves God, then, always striving to fulfil the divine will, what he wishes should be the right thing.'"

"When did Prentice Dashwood die?"

"Nineteen sixty-nine."

"Was someone killed?" We had found only eight victims.

"There could be no replacement for Prentice. Following his death no one was elevated to the inner circle. The number dropped to six and remained there."

"Why wasn't Dashwood on the fax you sent me?"

"I wrote down what I could recollect. The list was far from complete. I know almost nothing about those who joined after I left. As for Prentice, I just couldn't—" He glanced away. "It was so long ago."

For a long moment, neither of us spoke.

"You really didn't know what was going on?"

"I put it together after Mary Francis Rafferty died in 1972. That's when I withdrew."

"But said nothing."

"No. I give no excuse."

"Why did you tip Sheriff Crowe about Ralph Stover?"

"Stover joined the club after I dropped out. That's why he moved to Swain County. I've always known he was unstable."

I remembered my most recent question.

"Was it Stover who tried to run me down in Cherokee?"

"I heard it was a black Volvo. Stover has a black Volvo. That incident convinced me that he really was dangerous."

I gestured at the boxes.

"You're digging here, aren't you, Simon?"

"Yes."

"Without permission from Raleigh."

"The site is crucial to the lithic assemblage sequence I'm constructing."

"That's why you lied to me about working for the Department of Cultural Resources."

He nodded.

I set down my cup and stood.

"I'm sorry things haven't turned out as you'd hoped." I was sorry, but couldn't forgive what he had known and not reported.

"When the book is published people will recognize the value of my work."

Outside, the day was still clear and cool, with no haze in the valleys or along the ridges.

Twelve-thirty. I had to hurry.

34

The turnout for Edna Farrell's funeral was larger than I expected, given that she'd been dead for more than half a century. In addition to members of her family, much of Bryson City, and many from the police and sheriff's departments had gathered to lay the old woman to rest. Lucy Crowe came, and so did Byron McMahon.

Stories of the Hell Fire Club now eclipsed accounts of the Air TransSouth crash, and reporters were there from across the South-east. Eight seniors butchered and buried in the basement of a mountain lodge, the lieutenant governor discredited, and more than a dozen prominent citizens jailed. The media were calling them the Cannibal Murders, and I was forgotten like last year's sex scandal. While I was sorry that I could not shield Mrs. Veckhoff and her daughter from the publicity and public humiliation, I was relieved to be out of the spotlight.

I hung back during the graveside service, thinking of the many exits our departing lives can take. Edna Farrell didn't die in her bed but departed through a much more melancholy door. So did Tucker Adams, at rest under the weathered plaque at my feet. I felt great sadness for these people, so long dead. But I felt comfort in the knowledge that I had helped bring their bodies to this hill. And satisfaction that the killings were at last at an end.

When the mourners dispersed, I approached and laid a small bouquet on Edna's grave. Hearing footsteps behind me, I turned. Lucy Crowe was walking in my direction.

"Surprised to see you back so soon."

"It's my hard Irish head. Impossible to crack."

She smiled.

"It's so beautiful up here." My gaze swept over the trees, the tombstones, the hills and valleys spreading to the horizon like orange velveteen.

"It's why I love the highlands. There is a Cherokee creation myth that tells how the world was created from mud. A vulture flew over, and where his wings beat down, there were valleys. Where his wings rose, there grew mountains."

"You are Cherokee?"

A Crowe nod.

Another question answered.

"How's your situation with Larke Tyrell?"

I laughed.

"Two days ago I received a letter of commendation from the Office of the Chief Medical Examiner assuming full responsibility for the misunderstanding, exonerating me of any wrongdoing, and thanking me for my invaluable contribution to the Air TransSouth recovery. Copies were sent to everyone but the Duchess of York."

428

We left the cemetery and walked up the blacktop to our cars. I was inserting my key when she asked another question.

"Did you identify the gargoyles on the tunnel entrance?"

"Harpocrates and Angerona were the Egyptian gods of silence, a reminder to the brothers of their oath of secrecy. Another gimmick borrowed from Sir Francis."

"The names?"

"Literary and historic references to cannibalism. Some are pretty obscure. Sawney Beane was a fourteenth-century cave-dwelling Scot. The Beane family was supposed to have slaughtered travelers and taken them home for supper. Same thing with Christie o' the Cleek. He and his family lived in a cave in Angus and dined on passing travelers. John Gregg kept the tradition alive in eighteenth-century Devon."

"Mr. B?"

"Baxbakualanuxsiwae."

"Very good."

"A Kwakiutl tribal spirit, a bearlike monster whose body was covered with bloody, snarling mouths."

"Patron saint of the Hamatsa."

"That's him."

"And the code names?"

"Pharaohs, gods, archaeological discoveries, characters in ancient tales. Henry Preston was Ilus, the founder of Troy. Kendall Rollins was Piankhy, an ancient Nubian king. Listen to this. Parker Davenport chose the Aztec god Ometeotl, the lord of duality. Do you suppose he was aware of the irony?"

"Ever take a close look at the seal of the State of North Carolina?"

I admitted that I hadn't.

"The motto is from Cicero's 'Essay on Friendship' – 'Esse Quam Videri.'"

The Coke-bottle eyes held mine.

"'To be rather than to seem.'"

Winding down Schoolhouse Hill, I couldn't help but notice a bumper sticker on the car ahead.

Where will you spend eternity?

Though placed in a broader time frame than I'd been considering, the decal posed the same question that was on my mind. Where would I spend the time ahead? More pointedly, with whom?

During my convalescence, Pete had been caring and helpful, bringing flowers, feeding Birdie, heating soup in the microwave. We'd watched old movies, engaged in long conversations. When he was away, I spent hours recalling our life together. I remembered the good times. I remembered the fights, the minor irritations that simmered, then eventually escalated into full-scale battle.

I had resolved one thing: I loved my estranged husband, and we would always be bound in our hearts. But we could no longer be bound in our beds. While handsome, and loving, and funny, and smart, Pete shared something with Sir Francis and his Hell Fire mates: His hat would always be off to Venus.

Pete was a wall I could beat myself against forever. We made much better friends than spouses, and henceforth, I would keep us that way.

I turned on to Main at the bottom of the hill.

I'd also considered Andrew Ryan.

Ryan the colleague. Ryan the cop. Ryan the uncle.

Danielle was not a paramour. She was a niece. That was good.

I considered Ryan the man.

The man who wanted to suck my toes.

That was very good.

Because of the wound Pete had inflicted, I'd been hovering on the edge of a relationship with Ryan, wanting to get close but keeping my distance, like a moth drawn to a flame. Attracted but afraid.

Did I need a man in my life?

No.

Did I want one?

Yes.

What were the words of the song? I'd rather be sorry for something I did, than for something that I didn't do.

I'd decided to give Ryan a try and see how it went.

I had one more stop in Bryson City. A stop I couldn't wait to make.

I parked outside a redbrick building at the corner of Slope and the Bryson Walk. When I entered the glass door, a woman in surgical scrubs looked up and smiled.

"Is he ready?"

"Very. Have a seat."

She disappeared, and I settled into a plastic chair in the waiting area.

Five minutes later she led Boyd out. His chest was taped, and one foreleg had been shaved. Seeing me, he gave a little hop, then limped over and placed his head on my lap.

"Is he in pain?" I asked the vet.

"Only when he laughs."

Boyd rolled his eyes upward at me, and the purple tongue dropped out.

"How are you doing, big guy?" I nuzzled his ears and

touched my forehead to his.

Boyd sighed.

I straightened and looked at him.

"Are you ready to go home?"

He yipped and his eyebrows danced.

"Let's do it."

I could hear a laugh in his bark.

Afterword

When I sat down to create *Fatal Voyage*, I could not have imagined the horror that struck on September 11th. That reality outstripped anything I might have conceived as fiction.

Like Tempe, I am familiar with the aftermath of death. I work for coroners in two jurisdictions. I have testified before the United Nations Tribunal on Genocide in Rwanda, and I have spent time in a mass grave in the Guatemalan highlands. I have dealt with the physical casualties that were the victims and the emotional casualties that are the survivors.

Like Tempe, I serve on DMORT, a governmental disaster response team. In that capacity, I travelled to New York City to help with the World Trade Center recovery effort. Even as a professional familiar with bereavement and loss, I was unprepared for the emotional impact of that experience. At times I felt crushed by the scale of devastation. At times, overwhelmed by sadness. Rejuvenation came from a schoolgirl's card, a prayer penned by a Sunday school class, a scout troop's carefully painted banner.

I draw strength from the strength of my countrymen.

Above all, I felt proud to be one small part of the incredible team of men and women working to bring assistance, comfort, and a measure of closure to families, a city, a nation.

Kathy Reichs, October 2001

**Read on for an exclusive extract from the new
Temperance Brennan thriller**
Grave Secrets
coming in July 2002 from William Heinemann

1

"I am dead. They killed me, as well."

The old woman's words cut straight to my heart.

"Please tell me what happened that day." Maria spoke so softly I had to strain to catch the Spanish.

"I kissed the little ones and left for market." Eyes down, voice toneless. "I did not know that I would never see them again."

K'akchiquel to Spanish, then reversing the linguistic loop, reversing again as answers followed questions. The translation did nothing to blunt the horror of the recitation.

"When did you return home, Mrs. Ch'i'p?"

A que hora regreso usted a su casa, Senora Ch'i'p?

Chike ramaj xatzalij pa awachoch, Ixoq Ch'i'p?

"Late afternoon. I'd sold my beans."

"The house was burning?"

"Yes."

"Your family was inside?"

A nod.

I watched the speakers. An ancient Mayan woman,

her middle-aged son, the young cultural anthropologist, Maria Paiz, calling up a memory too terrible for words. I felt anger and sorrow clash inside me like the thunderheads building on the horizon.

"What did you do?"

"We buried them in the well. Quickly, before the soldiers came back."

I studied the old woman. Her face was brown corduroy. Her hands were calloused, her long braid more gray than black. Fabric lay folded atop her head, bright reds, pinks, yellows, and blues, woven into patterns older than the mountains around us. One corner rose and fell with the wind.

The woman did not smile. She did not frown. Her eyes met no one's, to my relief. I knew if they lingered on mine even briefly, the transfer of pain would be brutal. Maybe she understood that and averted her gaze to avoid drawing others into the hell those eyes concealed.

Or perhaps it was distrust. Perhaps the things she had seen made her unwilling to look frankly into unknown faces.

Feeling dizzy, I upended a bucket, sat, and took in my surroundings.

I was six thousand feet up in the western highlands of Guatemala, at the bottom of a steep-sided gorge. The village of Chupan Ya. Between the Mountains. About one hundred and twenty-five kilometers northwest of Guatemala City.

Around me flowed a wide river of green, lush forest interspersed with small fields and garden plots, like islands. Here and there rows of man-made terraces burst through the giant checkerboard, cascading downward like playful waterfalls. Mist clung to the highest peaks, blurring their contours into Monet softness.

I'd rarely seen surroundings so beautiful. The Great Smoky Mountains. The Gatineau, Quebec under northern lights. The barrier islands off the Carolina coast. Haleakula volcano at dawn. The loveliness of the backdrop made the task at hand even more heartbreaking.

As a forensic anthropologist, it is my job to unearth and study the dead. I identify the burned, the mummified, the decomposed, and the skeletonized who might otherwise go to anonymous graves. Sometimes the identifications are generic, Caucasoid female, mid-twenties. Other times I can confirm a suspected I.D. In some cases, I figure out how these people died. Or how their corpses were mutilated.

I am used to the aftermath of death. I am familiar with the smell of it, the sight of it, the idea of it. I have learned to steel myself emotionally in order to practice my profession.

But the old woman was breaking through my determined detachment.

Another wave of vertigo. The altitude, I told myself, lowering my head and breathing deeply.

Though my home bases are North Carolina and Quebec, where I serve as forensic anthropologist to both jurisdictions, I'd volunteered to come to Guatemala for one month as temporary consultant to the *Fundación de Antropología Forense de Guatemala*. The Guatemalan Forensic Anthropology Foundation, FAFG, was working to locate and identify the remains of those who vanished during the 1962 to 1996 civil war, one of the bloodiest conflicts in Latin American history.

I'd learned a lot since my arrival one week before. Estimates of the missing ranged from one to two hundred thousand. The bulk of the slaughter was carried out by the Guatemalan Army and by paramilitary organizations affiliated with the army. Most of those killed were rural peasants. Many were women and children.

Typically, victims were shot or slashed with machetes. Villages were not always as fortunate as Chupan Ya. There they'd had time to hide their dead. More often, bodies were buried in unmarked mass graves, dumped in rivers, left under the ruins of huts or houses. Families were given no explanations, no lists of those missing, no records. A UN Clarification Commission referred to these massacres as a genocide of the Mayan people.

Families and neighbors referred to their missing members as the "*desaparecidos*". The disappeared. The FAFG was trying to find them, or, more accurately, their remains, and I had come to help.

Here in Chupan Ya, soldiers and civil patrollers had entered on an August morning in 1982. Fearing they'd be accused of collaborating with the local guerilla movement and punished, the men fled. The women were told to gather with their children in groups. Trusting, or perhaps fearing the military, they obeyed. When the soldiers located the women at the designated farms, they were raped for hours, then killed. Every house in the valley was burned to the ground.

Survivors spoke of five mass graves. Twenty-three women and children were said to lie at the bottom of the well behind Mrs. Ch'i'p.

The old woman continued her story. Over her shoulder I could see the structure we'd erected three days earlier to protect the well site from rain and sun. Backpacks and camera cases hung from metal uprights, and tarps covered the opening of the pit beneath. Boxes, buckets, shovels, picks, brushes, and storage containers lay as we'd left them early that morning.

Rope had been strung from pole to pole around the excavation to create a boundary between spectators and workers. Inside the restraint sat three idle members of the FAFG team. Outside it stood the villagers who came each day to observe in silence.

And the police guards who'd been told to shut us down.

We'd been close to uncovering evidence when we received the order to halt. The soil had begun yielding ash and cinders. Its color had changed from mahogany to graveyard black. We'd found a child's hairclip in the sifting screen. Fragments of cloth. A tiny sneaker.

Dear God. Did the old woman's family really lie only inches below the point at which we'd stopped?

Five daughters and nine grandchildren. Shot, macheted, and burned in their home together with neighboring women and children. How does one endure such loss? What could life offer her but endless pain?

Shifting my gaze back to the surrounding country-side, I noted half a dozen farmsteads carved out of the foilage. Adobe walls, tile roofs, smoke curling from cooking fires. Each had a dirt yard, outdoor privy, and an emaciated brown dog or two. The wealthier had chickens, a scrawny hog, a bicycle.

Two of Mrs. Ch'i'p's daughters had lived in the cluster of huts half-way up the eastern escarpment. Another had lived on top, where we'd parked the FAFG vehicles. These women were married, she didn't remember their ages. Their babies were three days, ten months, two, four, and five years old.

Her youngest daughters were still at home. They'd been eleven and thirteen.

440

Families, connected by a network of footpaths, and by a network of genes. Their world was this valley.

I imagined Mrs. Ch'i'p returning that day, perhaps descending the same dirt trail our team struggled down each morning and up each evening. She had sold her beans. She was probably happy.

Then horror.

Two decades is not long enough to forget. A lifetime is not long enough.

I wondered how often she thought of them. Did their phantoms walk with her as she trudged to market, following the same course she'd taken that fatal day? Did they slip past the tattered rag covering her window when darkness claimed the valley each night? Did they people her dreams? Did they come to her smiling and laughing as they'd been in life? Or bloodied and charred as she'd found them in death?

My vision blurred, and I dropped my head again, stared at the dirt. How was it possible for human beings to do that to other human beings? To helpless and unresisting women and children? In the distance, I heard the rumble of thunder.

Seconds, maybe years later, the interview stopped, an untranslated question left dangling in space. When I looked up, Maria and her interpreter had shifted their attention to the hill behind me. Mrs. Ch'i'p remained focused on her sandals, hand to cheek, fingers curled like a newborn.

"Mateo's back," said Elena Norvillo, an FAFG member from the El Petén region. I turned as she pushed to her feet. The rest of the team observed from under the tent.

Two men were working their way down one of the many footpaths that meandered through the gorge, the

441

leader in blue windbreaker, faded jeans, brown cap. Though I couldn't read them from where I sat, I knew the letters above his brim said FAFG. The six of us waiting wore identical caps. The man following was suited and tied, and carried a collapsible chair.

We watched the pair pick their way through scraggly corn surrounded by a half-dozen subsidiary crops, careful to damage nothing. A bean seedling. A potato plant. Minor to us, but critical food or income to the family that owned it.

When they drew within twenty yards, Elena shouted. "Did you get it?"

Mateo gave a thumbs-up.

The injunction to suspend excavation had come from a local magistrate. According to his interpretation of the exhumation order, no work was to proceed outside the presence of a judge, the Guatemalan equivalent of a district attorney. Visiting early this morning and finding no judge on site, the magistrate had ordered digging halted. Mateo had gone to Guatemala City to have this ruling overturned.

Mateo led his companion directly to the two uniformed guards, members of the National Civil Police, and produced a document. The older cop shifted the strap of his semi-automatic, took the paper and read, head down, shiny black bill reflecting the dimming afternoon light. His partner stood with foot thrust forward, a bored expression on his face.

After a brief exchange with the suited visitor, the senior cop returned the order to Mateo, and nodded.

The villagers watched, silent but curious, as Juan, Luis, and Rosa stood and exchanged high-fives. Mateo and his companion joined them at the well. Elena followed.

Crossing to the tent, I glanced again at Mrs. Ch'i'p and her adult son. The man was scowling, hatred seeping from every pore. Hatred for whom, I wondered? For those who had butchered his family? For those who had come from a different world to disturb their bones? For distant authorities who would block even that small effort? For himself for having survived that day? His mother stood woodenly, face impassive.

Mateo introduced the suited man as Roberto Amado, a representative from the district attorney's office. The Guatemala City judge had ruled that Amado's presence would satisfy the requirements of the exhumation order. Amado would be with us for the duration, observing and recording in order to validate quality of work for the court.

Amado shook hands with each of us, moved to a corner of the covered area, unfolded his chair, and sat. Mateo began issuing orders.

"Luis, Rosa, please sift. Tempe and I will dig. Juan, haul dirt. We'll rotate as needed."

Mateo had a small, V-shaped scar on his upper lip that broadened into a U whenever he smiled. Today, the V remained narrow as a spike.

"Elena, document and photograph. Skeletal inventory, artifact inventory, photo log. Every molecule goes on record."

"Where are Carlos and Molly?" asked Elena.

Carlos Menzes was a member of an Argentine human rights organization who'd been advising the FAFG since its formation in 1992. Molly Carraway was an archaeologist newly arrived from Minnesota.

"They're driving the other truck out here for transport. We'll need another vehicle when we're ready to leave with all the equipment and artifacts."

443

He glanced at the sky.

"The storm is two hours off, maybe three if we're lucky. Let's find these people before there's more legal bullshit."

As I collected trowels and placed them in a bucket tied to a length of rope, Mateo zipped the court order into his pack and hung it over a cross bar. His eyes and hair were black, his body a fire hydrant, short and thick. Tubes of muscle bulged in his neck and arms as he and Luis flung back the tarps covering the mouth of the excavation.

Mateo placed a boot on the first of the dirt steps we'd terraced into a pit wall. Edges crumbled, sending dirt two meters to the floor below. The dropping particles made soft ticking sounds as Mateo slowly climbed down.

When he reached bottom, I lowered the bucket, then zipped my windbreaker. Three days had taught me well. May was pleasant in the highlands, but underground the clammy cold knifed straight to your marrow. I'd left Chupan Ya each evening chilled through, my digits numb.

I descended as Mateo had done, placing my feet sideways, testing each makeshift tread. My pulse accelerated as the gloom closed around me.

Mateo held up a hand and I took it. Stepping off the last riser, I stood in a hole no more than six feet square. The walls and floor were slick, the air dank and rotten.

My heart thumped below my sternum. A bead of sweat raced down the furrow overlying my spine.

Always in narrow, dark places.

I turned from Mateo, pretended to clean my trowel. My hands trembled.

Closing my eyes, I fought past the claustrophobia. I

thought of my daughter. Katy as a toddler. Katy at the University of Virginia. Katy at the beach. I pictured my cat, Birdie. My townhouse in Charlotte. My condo in Montreal.

I played the game. First song to pop into my mind. Neil Young. "Harvest Moon". I ran through the lyrics.

My breathing eased. My heart slowed.

I opened my eyes and checked my watch. Fifty-seven seconds. Not as good as yesterday. Better than Tuesday. Much better than Monday.

Mateo was already on his knees, scraping the damp earth. I moved to the opposite corner of the pit, and for the next twenty minutes we worked in silence, troweling, inspecting the ground, scooping dirt into buckets.

Objects emerged with increasing frequency. A shard of glass. A chunk of metal. Charred wood. Elena bagged and recorded each item.

Noise reached us from the world above. Banter. A request. The bark of a dog. Now and then I'd glance up, unconsciously reassuring my id.

Faces peered down. Men in gaucho hats, women in traditional Mayan weaves, toddlers clinging to their skirts. Babies stared with round, black eyes, secured to their mothers by rainbow textiles. I saw a hundred variations on high cheek bones, black hair, sienna skin.

On one upward glance I noticed a little girl, arms above her head, fingers curled around the restraining rope. Typical kid. Chubby cheeks, dirty feet, pony tails.

A stab of pain.

The child was the same age as one of Mrs. Ch'i'p's granddaughters. Her hair was bound with barrettes identical to the one we'd found in the screen.

I smiled. She turned her face and pressed it to her

445

mother's legs. A brown hand reached down and stroked her head.

According to witnesses, the hole in which we worked had been intended as a cistern. Begun but never completed, it was hastily transformed into an unmarked grave on the night of the massacre.

A grave for people identical to those keeping vigil above.

Fury swirled in me as I resumed digging.

What twisted psyches could perpetrate such atrocities?

Focus, Brennan. Channel your outrage to uncover evidence. Do that which you are able to do.

Ten minutes later my trowel touched something hard. Laying the implement aside, I cleared mud with my fingers.

The object was slender, like a pencil, with an angled neck ending in a corrugated upper surface. Above the neck, a tiny cap. Surrounding neck and cap, a circular cup.

I sat back on my heels and studied my find. A femur and pelvis. The hip of a child no older than two.

I looked up, and my gaze met that of the little girl. Again she whipped away. But this time she turned back, peeked through the folds of her mother's skirt, smiled shyly.

Sweet Jesus in heaven.

Tears burned the back of my lids.

"Mateo."

I pointed at the little bones. Mateo crawled to my corner.

Along most of its length, the femur was mottled gray and black from exposure to fire and smoke. The distal end was crumbly white, suggesting more intense burning.

446

For a moment neither of us spoke. Then Mateo crossed himself, and said in a low voice,

"We've got them."

When Mateo stood and repeated the phrase, the entire team gathered at the edge of the well.

A fleeting thought. We've got whom, Mateo? We've got the victims, not the assassins. What chance is there that any of these government-sanctioned butchers will ever face charges, let alone be punished?

Elena tossed down a camera, then a plastic marker stamped with the numeral "1". I positioned the case number and took several shots.

Mateo and I went back to troweling, the others to sifting and hauling. After an hour I took my turn at the screen. Another hour, and I climbed back down into the well.

The storm held off, and the cistern told its story.

The child had been one of the last lowered into the clandestine grave. Under and around it lay the remains of others. Some badly burned, others barely singed.

By late afternoon seven case numbers had been assigned, and five skulls stared out from a tangle of bones. Three of the victims were adults, at least two were adolescents. Number one was a child. For the others, age estimation was impossible.

At dusk, I made a discovery that will stay with me the rest of my life. For over an hour I'd been working on skeleton number five. I'd exposed the skull and lower jaw, and cleared dirt from the vertebrae, ribs, pelvis, and limbs. I'd traced the legs, found the foot bones mingled with those of the person beside.

Skeleton five was female. The orbits lacked heavy ridges, the cheek bones were smooth and slender, the mastoids small. The lower half of the body was enveloped in remnants of a rotted skirt identical to a dozen above my head. A coroded wedding band circled one fragile phalange.

Though the colors were faded and stained, I could make out a pattern in material adhering to the upper torso. Between the arm bones, atop the collapsed rib cage, lay a bundle with a different design. Cautiously, I separated a corner, eased my fingertips underneath, and teased back the outer layer of fabric.

Once, at my Montreal lab, I was asked to examine the contents of a burlap bag found on the shore of an inland lake. From the bag I withdrew several rocks, and bones so fragile at first I thought they were those of a bird. I was wrong. The sack held the remains of three kittens, weighted down and heaved into the water to drown. My disgust was so powerful I had to flee the lab and walk several miles before resuming work.

Inside the bundle clutched by skeleton five, I found an arch of tiny vertebral disks with a miniature rib cage curving around it. Arm and leg bones the size of matches. A minute jaw.

Mrs. Ch'i'p's infant grandchild.

Among the paper thin cranial fragments, a 556 projectile, the type fired by an assault rifle.

I remembered how I'd felt at the slaughter of kittens, but this time I felt rage. There were no streets to walk here at the gravesite, no way to work off my anger. I stared at the little bones, trying to picture the man who had pulled the trigger. How could he sleep at night? How could he face people in the day?

At six Mateo gave the order to quit. Up top the air smelled of rain, and veins of lightning pulsated inside heavy, black clouds. The locals had gone.

Moving quickly, we covered the well, stored the

equipment we would leave behind, and loaded up that which we would carry. As the team worked, rain began plinking in large, cold drops on the temporary roof above our heads. Amado, the D.A.'s representative, waited with lawn chair folded, face unreadable.

Mateo signed the chain of custody book over to the police guards, then we set off through the corn, winding one behind another like ants on a scent trail. We'd just begun our long, steep climb when the storm broke. Hard, driving rain stung my face and drenched my hair and clothes. Lightning flashed. Thunder boomed. Trees and cornstalks bent in the wind.

Within minutes, water sluiced down the hillside, turning the path into a slick, brown stream of mud. Again and again I lost my footing, hitting hard on one knee, then the other. I crawled upward, right hand clawing at vegetation, left hand dragging a bag of trowels, feet scrambling for traction. Though rain and darkness obscured my vision, I could hear others above and below me. Their hunched forms whitened each time lightning leapt across the sky. My legs trembled, my chest burned.

An eon later I crested the ridge and dragged myself onto the patch of earth where we'd left the vehicles eleven hours earlier. I was placing shovels in the bed of a pick-up when Mateo's satellite phone sounded, the ring barely audible above the wind and rain.

"Can someone get that?" Mateo shouted.

Slipping and sliding toward the cab, I grabbed his pack, dug out the handset, and clicked on.

"Tempe Brennan." I shouted.

"Are you still at the site?" English. It was Molly Carraway, my colleague from Minnesota.

"We're just about to pull out. It's raining like hell," I shouted, backhanding water from my eyes.

"It's dry here."

"Where are you?"

"Just outside Sololá. We were late leaving. Listen, we think we're being followed."

"Followed?"

"A black sedan's been on our ass since Guatemala City. Carlos tried a couple of maneuvers to lose it, but the guy's hanging on like a bad cold."

"Can you tell who's driving?"

"Not really. The glass is tinted an—"

I heard a loud thump, a scream, then static, as though the phone had been dropped and was rolling around.

"Jesus Christ!" Carlos's voice was muted by distance. "Molly?"

I heard agitated words that I couldn't make out.

"Molly, what is it?"

Shouts. Another thump. Scraping. A car horn. A loud crunch. Male voices.

"What's happening?" Alarm raised my voice an octave.

No response.

A shouted command.

"Fuck you!" Carlos.

"Molly! Tell me what's going on!" I was almost screaming. The others had stopped loading to stare at me.

"No!" Molly Carraway spoke from a distant galaxy, her voice small and tinny and filled with panic. "Please. No!"

Two muted pops.

Another scream.

Two more pops.

Dead air.